A King Production presents…

Bitch

CHRONICLES *Bitch Series 1-5*

Special Collector's Edition

JOY DEJA KING

ISBN 13: 978-1942217350
ISBN 10: 1-942217-35-8

Cover concept by Joy Deja King
Cover model: Joy Deja King

Cover layout & graphic design by: www.anitaart79.wixsite.com/bookdesign
Typesetting: Anita J.
Editor: Linda Williams and Dolly Lopez

Library of Congress Cataloging-in-Publication Data;
King, Deja Joy
Bitch Complete: a novel by Joy Deja King

For complete Library of Congress Copyright info visit;
www.joydejaking.com Twitter: @joydejaking

A King Production
P.O. Box 912, Collierville, TN 38027

A King Production and the above portrayal logo are trademarks of A King Production LLC.

This Book is Dedicated To My:

Family, Readers, and Supporters.
I LOVE you guys so much. Please believe that!!

A KING PRODUCTION

Bitch

The Beginning...

JOY DEJA KING

Can't Knock the Hustle

Coming from nothing and having nothing are two dif ferent things. Yeah, I came from nothing, but I was determined to have it all. And how couldn't I?

I exploded into this world when "Hood Rich" wasn't an after-thought, but the only thought. You turn on the televi sion and every nigga is iced out with an exotic whip sit ting on 24inch rims, surround-ed by a bitch in a gstring, a weave down to her ass, poppin' that booty. So the chicks on the videos were dropping it like it's hot for the rap-pers and singers while the bitches around my way were dropping it for our own superstars. Dealing with a street nigga on say the Alpo status a legendary drug kingpin was like being Beyoncé herself on Jig-ga Man's arm.

A bitch like me was thirsty for that. I'd been on some type of hustle since I was in Pampers.

I grew up in the grimiest Brooklyn projects during the '90s. It was worse than being in prison because you knew there was some-thing better out there; you just didn't know how to get it. You never saw green grass or flowers blooming. Instead of looking up to teach-ers, lawyers or doctors, you worshipped the local drug dealers who hustled to survive and escape their ex istence. Even as a little girl, I knew I wanted more out of life. Somehow hustling was in my blood.

First, I hustled for my moms' attention because she was too busy turning tricks to pay me any mind. I never knew who my daddy was, so while my moms was fucking in her bedroom, I would wait outside the door with my legs crossed, holding my favorite teddy bear in one arm as I sucked my thumb. When the tricks would come out, I would look at them with puppy dog eyes and ask, "Are you my daddy?" The question would freak them out so badly they'd toss me a few dollars so I would shut the fuck up.

One day when I was five, my mother was looking for something in my drawers, she came across a bunch of fives and tens and some twenties. The total was five hundred and some change. Of course, she wanted to know where all the money came from. When I told her that the money came from her business clients (that's what my moms called them), she lit up. She tossed me up in the air and said, "Baby, you my good luck charm. I knew one day you'd make me some money."

On that rare occasion she showed me mad love. As young as I was, I equated my mother's newfound interest in me with love. From that moment on, I learned how to hustle for my moms' attention – that is, by providing her with money.

Where I grew up, everyone hated "The Man," so they wouldn't report shit, even child abuse or neglect. When I was really young, my neighbors helped look out for me, when neces sary. One neighbor, Mr. Duncan, used to babysit me while my mother "Worked." In the projects, we all minded our own business and had the same code of silence that the police have among themselves – we didn't snitch on each other.

Somehow, my moms' customers never messed with or even fondled me. I think it's because people say I got these funny looking eyes. Even when I was little I had an attitude that said, "Don't fuck wit' me."

By the time I was fifteen with all the tricks my moms pulled, we were still dead ass broke, living in the Brooklyn projects. She couldn't save a dime because with hooking comes drugging and my moms stayed high. I guess that's all you can do to escape the nightmare of having all types of nasty, greasy fat motherfuckers pounding your back out every damn day. The characters that I saw coming in and out of our apartment were enough to make me want to sew up my pussy so nobody could get between my legs.

One day when I came home from school, I found my moms sprawled out on the couch with a half empty bottle of whiskey in one hand, as she tried to toke her last pull off a roach in the other hand. Her once long, wavy sandy hair was now thin and straggly. The curves that once made every hood chick roll their eyes in envy were just a bag of bones. You wouldn't even recognize the one time ghetto queen unless you looked into the green eyes she inherited from her mulatto father.

Without a word, I gave the living room a lick and a promise. I emptied several full ashtrays, picked up the dirty glasses scattered about the floor and wiped off the cocktail table. Out of the corner of my eye, I watched my moms sit up and stare at me for a long five minutes. She had the strangest look on her face.

Finally she spoke up. "Precious, you sure are growing up to be a pretty girl." Although we were in each other's face on an everyday basis, it was as if this were the first time my mother had seen me in many years. I didn't know how to respond so I kept cleaning up. "Didn't you hear what yo' mama said?"

"Yes, I heard you."

"Well you betta say thank you."

"Thank you, Mama."

"You welcome, baby."

As I continued to clean I couldn't help but feel uncomfortable with the glare my moms was giving me. It was the same look she'd get when she was about to get her hands on some prime dope.

"Baby, you know that your mother is getting up there in age. I can't put it down like I used to."

I looked my moms directly in the eye, but I said nothing. I was thinking to myself, *What the fuck that got to do wit' me"*

"So, baby, I was thinking maybe you need to start helping me out a little more."

"Help out more how, I basically give you my whole paycheck?" I didn't understand what the fuck she was talking about. I barely went to school because I had what was supposed to be a part time job at a car detailing shop.

Damn near every cent I made, I used to pay bills and maintain my appearance. I couldn't afford to rock all the brand name hot shit, but because I had style, I was able to throw a few cheap pieces together to make it look real official. Luckily I inherited my moms' beauty and body so I could just about make a potato sack look sexy.

"Baby, that little job you got ain't bringing home no money. It's just enough to maintain. I'm talking about getting a real job."

"Mama, I'm only fifteen. It's only so many jobs I can get and so much money I can make. Boogie not even suppose to give me all the hours he have me doing at the shop. That's why he pays me under the table."

"Precious, as pretty as you are you can be making thou sands of dollars."

"Doing what? What job you know is going to pay a fif teenyearold high school student thousands of dollars?"

"The oldest profession in the booksex," my moms said as if she was asking me to do something as innocent as bak ing cookies for a living.

"You 'un lost your damn mind. What you tryn' to be nowmy pimp?"

"You betta watch yo' mouth, little girl. I'm yo' mama. Don't forget that."

"Don't you forget it. You must have if you asking me to sell my ass so I can take care of you."

"Not me - us. Shit, I took care of yo' ass for the last fif teen years. Breaking my back and wearing out my pussy to provide us with a good life."

"This is what you call a good life?" I said as I looked around the small, broke down, two bedroom apartment. The hardwood floors were cracking, the walls had holes and the windows didn't even lock. It was nothing to catch a few roaches holding court in the kitchen and living room, or a couple of rats making a dash across the floor.

My moms stood up and started fixing her unruly hair, pat ting down her multicolored flannel pajamas and twisting her mouth in that 'how dare you' position as if she were an up standing citizen who was being disrespected in her own home. "You listen here," she began as she pointed her bony finger with its gnawed down nail. "A lot of these children around here don't even have a place to stay. It might not be much but it's mine."

That, too, was a lie. My moms didn't even own this raggedy-ass apartment; she rented it. But I didn't feel like reminding her of that because I wanted this going-nowhere conversation to be over.

"I hear you, Ma, but I don't know what to tell you. I'm not following in your footsteps by selling my pussy to some low down niggas for money."

"Well then you betta start looking for some place to live, 'cause I can't take care of the both of us."

"You tryna tell me you would put me out on the streets?"

"You ain't leaving me a choice, Precious. If you can't bring home some extra money, then I'll have to rent out your bedroom to pay the bills."

"Who is gon' pay you for that piece of shit of a room?"

"Listen, I ain't 'bout to sit up here and argue wit' you. Either you start bringing home some more money or find another place to live. It's up to you. But if you don't give me a thousand dollars by the first of the month, I need you out by the second."

With that my moms' skeletal body disappeared into her dungeon of a bedroom. She was practically sentencing me to the homeless shelter. There was no way I could give her a thousand dollars a month unless I worked twentyfour hours a day, seven days a week at the detail shop. But what made this so fucked up was that my moms basically wanted me to pay for her out-of-control drug habit. This wasn't even about the bills because our Section 8 rent and other bills totaled no more than four hundred dollars a month. Because the street life had beaten down my moms, she was beating me over the head with bullshit.

With my moms giving me no way out, I began my own hustle. I decided to get the money by selling my ass, but I was going to pick and choose who was able to play between my legs. My job at the car detailing shop came in handy. Nothing but top oftheline hustlers parlayed through, but before, I never gave them the time of day. They were always trying to holla at a sistah, but the shade I gave them was thick.

Boogie, my boss, appreciated that. He was an older dude who took his illegal drug money and opened up his shop. He was in his forties, donned a baldhead and wore two basketball sized diamond studs in each ear. He wore sweat suits and a new fresh pair of sneakers everyday. He could afford any type of car he wanted, but he remained loyal to Cadillac Devilles. He had three: one in red, white and black.

"Boogie, who that nigga in the droptop Beamer?" I asked when some dude I'd never seen before pulled up.

"Oh that's Azar. He moved here from Philly, why you ask?"

"I ain't neva seen him 'round here before, and I wanted to know who he was."

"Is that all, Precious?" Boogie asked, knowing it was more than that.

"Actually, to keep it real wit' you Boogie I'm looking for a man."

"What?" Boogie stopped dead in his tracks. "Looking for a man? One of the reasons I digged you so much, Precious, was because you wasn't fucking with none of these hustlers that came through here. Why the sudden change?"

"I'm not gonna get into all that Boogie, but I will tell you I really don't have a choice. I need money and fucking wit' a fosho nigga seems to be the only way to get it."

"Precious, you are much too young to have those types of worries. I could always give you a raise."

"Boogie, unless that raise is a few thousand dollars then it ain't gonna do me no good." Shit, I figured if I had to give my moms a thousand dollars a month, I might as well make a few for me. If I had to sell my ass, then I might as well get top dollar.

"I don't know what you need all that money for, Precious, but if you looking to fuck with a baller, then let me school you on a few things. For one, get your fuck game right."

"What you mean by that?"

"I mean if you want one of these niggas out here to spend some serious paper on you, you gotta learn to sex them real good. You know you're a beautiful girl, so attracting a big timer's attention is the easy part. But to have a nigga willing to spend the way you want, your head and pussy game have to be on point. Just giving you something to think about."

I watched as Boogie went outside to talk to a few guys that just pulled up in G5's. I was still thinking about the advice he gave me. Boogie was right, if I wanted to really land a hustler and keep him, I had to get my fuck game in order. The funny thing was from watching my moms selling her ass all my life, it turned me off from sex. I was probably the last virgin in my hood. I definitely needed a lot of work, and I needed to find someone that I could practice on before I actually went out there and tried to find my baller.

After work I came home and my moms was lying in her regular spot on the dingy couch. She was so bad off that she would've had to pay a nigga to fuck her. I hated to see my moms so broken down. One thing I promised myself was that no matter what, I would never let myself go out like that. I would play niggas; they would never play me.

Sex You Up

Since time wasn't on my side, I only had a week to scope out all the dudes that were coming in and out the detailing shop. I was carefully seeking out my victim. He had to be cute, paid and, hopefully, willing to spend his money freely. In two more weeks it was going to be the first and my moms was still threatening to throw me the fuck out.

I had narrowed down my search to three dudes. The nigga Azar, was actually my first choice, because not only did he have the droptop beamer, but he also came through in a Range and a big body Benz. He was a fine ma'fuckah, too. He put me in the mind of Allen Iverson, with the corn rows and all. But Boogie forewarned me that the nigga was gangsta. You couldn't halfass him. He wasn't just giving his money to any ol' random bitch. Yo' shit had to be tight.

Since I still hadn't learned how to fuck, I was a little skeptical about trying my hand with him. The other two dudes were some come up type niggas. They were always trying to kick it with me. They would hit me off with a hun dred dollar tip when they paid. I knew them dudes would lace me with some real paper if I gave them some.

Plus they were only aight' in the looks department. They would pay me just so they could sport a dime piece. They were the easy marks, but I wanted Azar. Something about him made my pussy wet.

On a rare day of going to school I peeped my cornyass neighbor Jamal. He was a real straightlaced type dude. He was a rare guy in the neighborhood who had a mother and father in his home. They were a hard working couple, but due to their lack of education, they were barely getting by.

Jamal was supposed to be their savior. See, Jamal was a certified genius. He was only in ninth grade but taking twelfth grade classes. There was no doubt he would get a full scholarship to any college of his choosing. All the top prep schools around the country wanted him to attend their school, but Jamal's parents refused to let him leave home.

They felt he was too young and would get brainwashed in the white man's world. So he just took all advanced classes in preparation for his college departure.

"What's up, Jamal?" I walked up beside him. His eyes damn near popped out of his thickrimmed bifocals. Which didn't surprise me, because we had been living next to one another our entire lives and I never spoke more than two words to him besides, "Nigga move"?

"Precious." He paused for a minute, looking at me, not sure if he heard me correctly.

"Yeah, what's up, Jamal?" I asked in a sweet voice. "How you doing?"

"I'm doing okay. Just on my way home to study for an exam I have in a couple of days." I couldn't front, the dedi cation that dude had for his books was crazy. I had to admit I somewhat admired the ghetto nerd.

"That's cool. I was wondering if maybe we could study together. I've been working so hard at my parttime job that I fell behind on a lot of work. I was hoping you could help me catch up. I know how smart you are."

By this time Jamal and I had stopped at the top of the stairs of our high school. He was the first to notice some students stopping and staring at our odd pairing. But I didn't give a damn. I needed this nigga so fuck what they thought.

"Precious, you want to study with me? But you don't even like me."

"Jamal, that's not true. I just always got so much to deal with." Everybody in the building and surrounding parts knew my moms was a crack whore. His parents would even come over sometimes complaining about hearing the bed banging up against their wall when my moms was servicing her clients. By the way Jamal was looking at me, I could tell he felt sorry for me. I don't normally like pity but what ever would accomplish what I needed to get done.

"OK. When do you want to study?" I knew Jamal was looking forward to helping me out, especially since he had a crush on me since he was eight years old.

"How about today?" I knew that seemed sudden, but time wasn't on my side.

"I don't know, Precious. I really need to study for my exam, how about Wednesday? By then I would've taken the test."

"Jamal, you know you'll ace that exam with your eyes closed. I really need you today." I could see that he was de bating it in his mind so to warm him up I stroked his hand and said, "Please, Jamal, you do want me to pass." With that we headed home.

I knew Jamal's parents both worked two jobs and didn't get home until after nine. For the first hour we worked on English and Math. I was trying to pay attention and seem interested in what Jamal was teaching, but my mind was on something else. Finally I had to get down to the nitty gritty of what I needed him for. "Jamal, have you ever had sex before?"

"Excuse me?" Jamal belted out, looking obviously shocked by my question.

"You heard me. Has your little thing ever gotten wet off some pussy juices?" I knew my line of questions was mak ing Jamal uncomfortable, but I had to get right to it.

"Precious, we're supposed to be studying, not talking about sex."

"I know, Jamal, but there's a reason for this. See, I'm a virgin." I could see Jamal eyeing me sideways as if I was lying. With my mother being a known whore and all, I'm sure I was the last person he expected to be a virgin.

I continued, "I'm interested in dating this guy, but see he is used to experienced women. If I tried to get with him and he knew I was a virgin, he would laugh at me like I was some little girl. I need to be able to hold my own when we get down to it."

"That's interesting, Precious, but how do I fit in with any of that?"

"I want to practice learning how to fuck on you." As soon as the words left my lips, Jamal's skinny ass fell off his chair and hit the hardwood floor. He patted his hands on the floor looking for the bifocals that flew off his face. It was obvious he was damn near blind without them so I went to assist him with his search. I knelt down and handed him his glasses and for the first time got a good look at Jamal. He wasn't bad look ing; almost cute. He had full, thick eyebrows that highlighted his light reddish skin. His profound jaw line gave him an almost model look.

"Here you go, Jamal," I said as I put his glasses back on.

"Thanks, Precious," Jamal said as he brushed himself off and stood up extra straight, trying to pretend he wasn't embarrassed by his fall. "Where were we?" Jamal grabbed my English book, diverting his attention from the proposi tion I just made him.

"We were talking about us, Jamal. Why won't you let me sex you up? I'm pretty sure you'll enjoy it."

"Sex me up? Why me? Precious, you're the prettiest girl in our school, probably the prettiest girl I've ever seen. Any guy would love to be your first," he said in a way that echoed his confusion as to why I was interested in having sex with him.

"Listen, Jamal. Honestly, for some reason I feel I can trust you. I don't believe you'll run around telling everybody we fucked. You know how these clownass niggas out here are. They'd have a field day letting the whole hood know they popped my cherry. It's also very convenient because we live right next door to one another. Come on, Jamal. It'll be fun."

I tapped my foot as Jamal stood there thinking about who knows whatI had no idea. Any other boy in his posi tion would give their right arm to have sex with me but he probably felt some kinda way. He probably figured he would remain a virgin until he was at least twentyone and his first time would be with his wife. But if he was as smart with the ladies as he was with the books, he would jump at the once in a life time opportunity. How many boys were actually able to have sex with their first crush?

"OK, I'll do it." Jamal was quiet for a moment. "When do you want to get started?" Jamal questioned, probably hoping I would say in about a week. That would then give him time to watch some porno's that I'm sure his father had stashed somewhere, and practice his own moves. I know he secretly hoped that maybe this would turn into more than an experiment for me, and he could become my boyfriend.

"Today," I said as I began unbuttoning my jeans and pulling off my sweater. Before Jamal knew it, I was standing in front of him with just my bra and panties on. It was obvious the only woman he had seen in person with her bra and pant ies on was his mother and she definitely didn't look like me. Jamal's dick instantly perked up as he studied my smooth, un blemished skin. I grabbed the condom that was in my jean pocket and handed it to Jamal.

"We definitely not tryn' to make no babies up in here." By being so aggressive, I knew Jamal doubted my virginity story.

"Where do you want to do the deed at?"

"A bed would be nice," I said, wanting to get started. See, to me this was a job, a potential well-paying one. Ja mal led me to his cramped bedroom full of scientific posters and what looked to be chemistry projects. He had to knock a pile of books off the center of his bed so we could get busy.

After Jamal just stood staring at me for five minutes, I realized I would have to lead the way. He was totally petrified, but it didn't matter because I planned on doing all the work anyway. After stripping him down to his underwear, I could see his dick trying to escape his boxer shorts. I was surprised that he was working with a nicesized tool. I be gan reaching for his boxers, but he lightly pushed my hand away like he was scared.

"Come on, Jamal. We almost there. Ain't no reason for you to be afraid." He finally lay down on the bed, after he took off his underwear. I stepped out of my bra and panties and decided to ride him like a horse jockey.

I heard that if you want to have control over a man you need to ride him. I definitely wanted to control Azar, so my pony game had to be tight. I ripped open the condom pack age and slid it on Jamal's dick. I could feel his body shaking due his nervousness. It was a damn shame that the blind was leading the blind, but I had no doubt we would both be pros before long.

I lifted my ass on top and took the tip of Jamal's dick and slowly let it play with the lips of my pussy. Then as I started getting wet, I led it to the center of my clit. Jamal was now making low moans as I let the head go in a little deeper. I wanted to take my time because, shit, I was a virgin and I wanted to minimize the pain as much as possible. I then let another three inches slide inside of me and I let out a slight scream as he hit that spot.

Once I got over that hump, the next couple of inches weren't as bad and it started feeling good. It was feeling good to Jamal too, because his once low moans were reach ing a much louder pitch. After about five minutes my wide hips began rocking in a seductive pace. I seemed like a natural. Before long I found myself turning around on his manhood and riding him from the back. Right when I was really getting into the groove, Jamal let out a loud "Ahhhh hhh," as he bust a nut.

When I got up, Jamal took off his condom and noticed the slight traces of blood. He looked at me with a big grin and said, "You really were a virgin."

For the next week, everyday after school Jamal and I got our sex on. As I predicted, we became pros. We even performed oral sex on one another and he told me just how to suck it so I would have him cumming within minutes.

    With only a week left before the first of the month, it was time to see if all my practice had paid off. With some money I had saved, I went and purchased a sexy Baby Phat outfit to wear to work. Although a bitch needed to hold on to her last dollar, I thought of this as an investment. Tomorrow I planned on landing Azar. I knew he had scheduled an afternoon full service detailing job, and I planned to look so damn good he would have no choice but to holla!

Irresistible Chick

I woke up early the next morning to put in extra time for my appearance. The Baby Phat onepiece jean jumpsuit I was rockin' was hot. I purchased some Steve Madden heels to set it off. I usually wore my hair in a long braid, but the night before, I put in a deep conditioner so my natural waves would hang smooth and free. I dapped on some clear lip gloss to give that justgaveablowjob look.

When I stepped out my bedroom, to my disappointment, my moms was up earlier than usually. Her eyes bulged when she got a whiff of me. "Precious Cummings, where you go ing looking like dat?" she barked, holding on to her glass of whiskey. My moms couldn't get over how beautiful I looked. I was always pretty, but this was something else.

"Work."

"Work, looking like dat? Um, well, that outfit you got on looks awfully expensive. I hope you ain't playing wit' my paper."

"Ma, you'll have your money by the first. Now excuse me, I have a job to go to unlike some people." I slammed the door and headed for work before I fucked around and slapped the shit out of my moms.

When I got to work I only saw Boogie's car parked out front. I did come a little early because I didn't want to be stuck in the house with my drunken mother. Boogie was behind the cash register getting things in order before business officially started. "What's up, Boogie," I said as he counted some mon ey. He nodded his head, acknowledging me but keeping his eyes on the money, not wanting to lose his count.

As I sat my belongings down the next thing I heard was, "Oh shit, what the fuck happened to you?"

"What you mean?" I asked, fully aware that he was speaking about my transformation. I usually came to work in jeans or sweats. So with my hair out and the formfitting attire, I knew Boogie was in shock.

"Damn, baby, you is fine. I'm not trying to hit on you, because you are much too young for my blood, but baby, you are going to make somebody a lucky man."

"Why, thank you, Boogie. That is my hope." I tried to sound all proper.

"Who knew you had all that going on?" he added, shak ing his head in disbelief.

For the next three hours all I did was turn down dudes offering me they number.

All they kept asking was, "Who's the new girl?" No one could believe that I was the same person.

They always thought I was pretty in a young girl way, but now I was looking like a woman. That shit was blow ing their minds. Honestly, though, I didn't care what all the other dudes thought about me. I was only interested in impressing one person and that was Azar.

I was chewing my gum and blowing bubbles, dying for him to pull up. When the clock hit two o'clock, Azar pulled up in his brand new 2002 white CL600. I visualized myself flossing in the passenger seat next to him. We would be the King and Queen of the streets.

Keeping to his normal routine, he sat outside and kicked it with the other fellas until his car was done. When he came in side, the first thing he asked was, "Where's the usual girl at?" In the few times he had been in here, I'd never heard his voice. He would hand me two bills and head out. The first couple of times when I tried to give him back his change, he would sim ply put his hand up, letting me know to keep it. He had a slick, sexy voice that complimented his look.

"It's me, I'm the same girl."

He studied me hard; trying to see what was different about me.

"I decided to let my hair down - that's all."

"My fault. I need to start paying better attention to what's right in front of my eyes."

"Don't worry about it," I said with a slight smile. *This nigga even lick his lips in the same sexy way Allen Iverson do after he completes a sentence*, I thought.

"Nah, I'd rather worry. To think all this time a pretty piece like you was right in front of me. That's a problem. We have to play catch up, "'cause you a real beauty."

"Thank you." Azar was making me blush. Mad niggas had told me I was beautiful before but not a dude on Azar's level. It was like if I were walking down the street and Bob by Valentino stepped to me and asked me to Slow Down.

"What's your name anyway?"

"Precious."

"That's sexy, just like you. How 'bout we go and catch a movie and dinner, Precious? Say tonight, if you not busy."

"I'd like that."

"Cool. What time you get off work."

"Seven."

"Alright. I'll be here then." When Azar exited, I wanted to jump up and down. I couldn't believe that, just like that, this dude was checking for me. Half of the work was done, now I needed to get him to give up some paper. Exactly how to get him to do that was something I felt needed to be discussed with Boogie. He was a playa. He would know what a playa does.

It was a quarter to seven when the last customer left and I finally had some alone time with Boogie. "Boogie, can I speak to you for a minute?"

"Yeah, what's up?"

"Boogie, Azar asked me out and he's picking me up from work today. He'll be here in fifteen minutes, so I don't have long to get your advice about something."

"I knew you had your eyes on that boy. So what you need my advice about?"

"How can I get Azar to spend his money on me?" I asked straight up. I knew I could be honest with Boogie like that. He believed women should come off, especially if she was fucking.

"I'm glad you asked me that, little lady. With this new look you have going on; men are going to be coming at you from all directions. It's important that if you want to get in this game, you play it correctly so you can get all you're worth. I personally think you're worth a lot. You're what I would call the top of the line, Precious. Hell, if you were ten years older I would make you mine. With that said, when you dealing with these hustlers on the street, you have to ask for what you want."

"Ask? Isn't that a little rude?"

"It's not what you ask; it's how you ask it. The same way a man is going to ask to get between your legs, the same way you ask him for whatever you want. Understand some thing, Precious. You're prime pussy. You can deal with any of these niggas out here. Starting with

Azar is a good look. He's big time and low key with his shit. But after whatever you have going on with him is over, you can only fuck with niggas that are equal or above him. That's how you keep your stock up. That's how a lot of women pull themselves down. They start letting any ole type of piece of shit run up in them. No one is going to want to invest in that."

After Boogie said his last sentence, I saw Azar pull up. He arrived at seven o'clock on the dot. I grabbed my purse and said, "Thanks, Boogie," as I kissed him goodbye.

When I sat in Azar's car, I was in awe. I had never sat in a Benz before. Even though I worked in a detailing shop and flashy cars were coming in all the time, Boogie never let me leave from behind the cashier desk. He stressed he needed my presence up front at all times. My ass melted in the seat. It was the softest leather I had ever felt in my life. Azar's Benz was a custom white-on-white and his copper-toned complexion just glistened behind the wheel. Azar headed over the Brooklyn Bridge to the city. I rarely ever went to the city. It was like another world to me.

That night was crazy for me. Azar was the first date I had ever been on, and he came correct. After the movie he took me to some fancy restaurant, and I even had a drink. Nobody even bother to card me. I didn't want the night to end. When Azar pulled up to my apartment building I was surprised that he hadn't tried to make a move on me. When I was about to get out the car, he grabbed my arm. "I want to see you tomorrow."

"I'd like that."

"Good. What would you like to do?" I thought about what he asked for a second and decided to try my hand.

"I would love if you took me shopping. I want to look good for you." There was complete silence, and I wasn't sure if Azar was going to push me out his whip and speed off, offended by my suggestion. To my surprise he wasn't.

"I want you to look good for me, too. What time do you get off work tomorrow? I'll pick you up?"

"Actually, I have to go to school," I said wondering if he would start questioning my age."

"No problem, I'll pick you up from there."

"I'm in high school, Azar," I admitted, knowing he would eventually find out anyway.

"I figured that. Give me the time and address. I'll be there." After giving Azar the information he kissed me on the cheek and drove off. I was stunned at how cool he was. Although I knew Azar was only nineteen, I wasn't sure how he was going to take dealing with a fifteen year old.

When I opened the door to the apartment, some funky looking nigga was stumbling out. I looked him up and down and my moms said from the couch, "Oh, he was just look ing at your bedroom. He's a potential tenant."

"That won't be necessary, you'll get your damn money," I said, slamming the door on the bum. I then walked to my room and slammed the door again.

The next day after school I rushed to get outside to meet Azar. I was looking forward to going shopping. When I reached the entrance to the school I was startled when Jamal approached me. I hadn't seen him in a couple of days.

"Where have you been, Precious? You haven't come over to study lately."

"I know, Jamal. Our studying is over. I learned every thing I need-ed to."

"So just like that it's over?"

"Jamal, it never started. I told you from jump that I needed your help to prepare me for this boy I was interested in. Well, now he's interested so we done."

"Precious, wait," Jamal said as he grabbed my arm.

"Nigga, you betta get the fuck off me. Who you think you grabbing on?" I was burning a hole through Jamal. He was out of line putting his hands on me.

"Precious, I'm sorry. I didn't mean to grab your arm. I guess I miss you."

"Miss me? Jamal, we ain't in no relationship. It is what it is. We both got something out of it; now it's time to let it go. I'll see you around."

When I walked off, I knew Jamal was watching my every step. He must of felt some kinda way when he saw me get in the car with Azar. But that wasn't my problem. He knew there were no strings attached. It wasn't my fault if he caught feelings.

Once again Azar headed towards the bridge when I got in the car with him. "You really love the city don't you?"

"You said you wanted to go shopping. I'm taking you to the official stores so I can lace you right." I looked at Azar in shock. Never did I think we would go shopping in the city. I figured he would take me to Macy's at Kings Plaza, and I was excited about that. So when we pulled up to Saks 5th Avenue, my jaw dropped. Me and my girlfriend Inga used to talk about what it would be like to shop in a store like this. Never did I believe the day would actually come that it could.

"Damn, Azar, I ain't neva been in Saks before."

"That's why I'm glad you made the suggestion I take you shopping. If you gonna hang wit' me, yo' shit need to be tight. Your style is a reflection of me. The chick in my passenger seat gotta be on point."

That was hot. That must have meant Azar was planning on keeping me around for a minute. I smiled at the thought.

For the next week, Azar and I spent all our free time together. He would pick me up from school or from my job. Then we would either go out to eat, to the movies or just kick it at his crib. We still hadn't fucked, but Azar didn't seem to be stress ing it. Before I knew it the first of the month had rolled around and I didn't have a dollar to my name. When Azar took me shopping, I swear he dropped three G's on me like it was noth ing. But he still hadn't put cash money in my hands. It was true I hadn't asked for any, but still he never offered. After spend ing the day together, I knew I couldn't roll up in my moms' crib without her money. My hands were sweaty as I built up the nerve to ask Azar for the grand. I had to admit that we both seemed to be feeling each other, but I still didn't know just how cool we were. I kept thinking about what Boogie said. It's not what you ask, it's how you ask.

"Azar, I need you to do me a huge favor."

"What is it, Ma?"

"I know you took me on that fly-ass shopping spree, but I'm in a bit of a bind. My moms is stressing me to help her with her bills. I'm deadass broke and I was wonder ing if you could help me out." I held my head down the whole time I asked because I didn't want to see the look in his eyes. For all I knew, he could say to himself that this straight gold-diggin' bitch ain't getting a dime from me.

"How much you need?" he asked calmly.

"A thousand," I said, still looking down.

He pulled out a wad of cash and started counting out hundreds. He handed me the money and said, "Don't ever be afraid to ask me for nothing. As long as you're dealing wit' me, we cool. I got you."

Walking up the stairs to my apartment building, I count ed the money Azar gave me and realized he gave me an extra fifteen hundred dollars. This dude had me straight tripping. I couldn't believe he was treating me so good and I hadn't even fucked him. I knew he was paid and the money he hit me off with was nothing to him, but still he didn't have to give it to me. The moment I walked through the door my moms was waiting with drool basically coming down her mouth. She was so thirsty for her money. I decided to fuck with her just to see how thirsty she was.

"You got my money?" she asked all common like.

"I need more time. I couldn't get it."

"I figured yo' silly ass wouldn't be able to come through. You been spending all that time wit' that boy and you can't even get no money outta him. I went in yo' closet and saw all those designer clothes he bought you. You betta take that shit back and get my money."

"I can't do that, I don't have the receipts."

"Well then go pack yo' shit up and get the fuck out my house. Go stay wit' that nigga you been fucking."

"You would really put your own daughter out on the street."

"You damn right."

"You really are a no good whore," I said as I tossed the ten hundred dollar bills to the floor. "Pick that shit up like the thirsty bitch you are." I went in my room, locked the door and blasted my music. My moms was truly a simple-ass trick. For the first time, I had to admit to myself that I was ashamed to be her daughter.

For the next few weeks, Azar and I grew closer and closer. One night when we were chilling at his crib, I decided that since he was never making a move on me, I'd have to do so. "Azar, do I look good to you?"

"Why you gonna ask me a silly-ass question like that. Do you think I would have you all up in my face if you didn't look good to me?"

"So why haven't you tried to have sex with me?"

"Because I can get sex from anybody, I'm not stressing it like that. I figured when you're ready you'd let me know."

"Well, I'm ready."

"You sure, Ma? I ain't in no rush."

"I know. But you've been so good to me. I want to be good to you." I did want to be good to Azar, but I also want ed to put all the moves on him that I learned from fucking Jamal. Shit, I didn't want to feel like I put all that work in with Jamal for nothing.

That night I put it on Azar. First, I gave him the best blowjob this side of Brooklyn. His eyes rolled back and his body jerked as I deep throated him. "Oh, Precious, just like that baby. Yeah, oh damn, baby," he said, moving the back of my head in a constant rhythm. I really fucked his mind up because not only did I let him come in my mouth, but I also swallowed. Then I rode his dick and when he screamed my name, I knew I had blown his mind.

Gangsta Lovin'

After putting it on Azar we officially became a couple. One day when he was dropping me off at work, he said, "Precious, tell Boogie this is your last day."

"Excuse me?"

"You heard me. I don't want you working here no more."

"Why not?"

"I really shouldn't have to explain myself to you, but since you're young, and this is new to you, I will. I don't want you at this shop no more. Too many niggas come through and I know they be tryna holla. One, because you fine as shit, and also because they know you my girl, they may try to get fly wit' they shit.

"I keep a low profile. The last thing I want to do is get extra 'cause one of these clown niggas steps out of line, or because you do. Enough said, so tell Boogie, 'peace,' and I'll pick you up at six."

I gave Azar a kiss goodbye, and that was it. He was right, though because I did begin scheming on getting two more just like him. With all the money Azar was now hitting me off with, if I had two other dudes to do the same, I would be sitting as pretty as a pussy cat. I already paid my moms up for four months in advance, but I was ready to get the hell out that dump. It didn't make sense to me to be giving her a thousand a month for some bullshit apartment, when for that amount I could be in my own crib.

Because of my age, of course, that would be a problem, but Azar had a hook up with a super, and he was working on getting me my own place. He suggested that I move in with him, but I told him my moms would probably try to have him locked up if I did that. My Moms stayed so high that she really didn't give a fuck if I was coming or going, but she would flip her wig if the steady money I was hitting her off with came to a halt. Soon I would be turning sixteen and it wouldn't matter no way.

One night after coming from Junior's for some bangingass cheesecake, Azar said he needed to make a stop. He pulled up to the Marcus Garvey housing complexes. "Baby, you stay right here. I'll be back in a minute."

Although I lived in the projects myself and had been walking through them all my life, for some reason, I was feeling some type of way waiting in Azar's car in the dead of night. My stomach felt weary as I watched the typical corner boys walking behind the buildings with a crack head following to make the exchange, money for crack, hand to hand. There were other groups of dudes blasting they music, smoking blunts and guzzling down liquor, hitting on the local chicken heads, roaming the blocks. I was so caught up in checking out the scene that I almost didn't hear the gunshots that were ringing in the smoke filled air.

"Oh shit," I screamed when I zeroed in on Azar hauling ass out the building he went in less than ten minutes ago. From the one good light coming from the entrance of the project building, I had a clear view of Azar running with a big bag and aiming a 9mm at who I couldn't see. Before I could even think, Azar was coming around to the driver's side and all I heard was what sounded like an explosion as the glass from the back seat windows shattered.

"Open the fucking door," Azar roared as he pulled the door latch back and forth. He left the keys in the ignition when he ran inside, and I forgot I locked the doors the min ute he was out of sight. I fidgeted with the unlock button because my nerves were shot. As soon as I heard the click of the door unlocking, I noticed the dude who blasted out the window getting closer to the car. He was just blasting out bullets like he was the terminator. I kept my head down as Azar put the petal to the metal and sped off, but not be fore he did, the dude blasted off one last bullet shattering the entire back window.

"Azar, what the fuck happened? Why that nigga bust off on you like that?"

I looked down at my hands, and they were shaking. I was trying to remain calm as possible in a situation like this, but inside I was freaking out. All it took was one bullet to end your life and that nigga who was chasing Azar had let out enough to kill a whole army.

Although my head was still down, I was giving Azar the third degree. But he wasn't saying shit. He was just hauling ass. Even with my head down, I was still able to look to the side and see Azar was sweating puddles. I stayed down for what seemed like another fifteen minutes until Azar came to a stop.

"I have to run up in my crib and get some shit. If you see anybody suspicious pull off and we'll meet up at your crib. But just drive far enough to get out of sight, then ditch the car and jump in a cab to take you home."

"Azar, I can't drive. I don't even have my license." I couldn't believe this nigga was trying to make me drive his car with no license and the back windows all busted out.

My hands were shaking, so I slid them under my thighs because I didn't want Azar to know how badly I was stressing.

"You'll fucking learn to drive tonight if need be."

"Why can't you just drop me off at home? This is some oh-other shit."

Then Azar lifted my chin and looked in my eyes real se rious. "You my girl, I take care of you. You telling me you not riding this out wit' me?" he asked in the most serious voice I'd ever heard him speak in.

"Baby, I got you. Go handle what you have to do and if no one shows up, then I'll be right here waiting. If not, I'll see you at my moms' crib."

When Azar got out the car, I just shook my head in dis gust. I didn't know what type of bullshit Azar was caught up in, but won't no nigga worth dying for. I was tempted to drive right out his life, but I knew Azar would find me and he might bust off on me for ditching his ass. It didn't mat ter now because in the blink of an eye Azar was back with three big ass bags he put in his trunk.

There was dead silence as Azar drove to his garage and pulled out his Range and left the Benz. I told him I wanted to go home but he begged for me to stay with him at the hotel room he got. Without him saying it, it was clear he could never go back to his apartment and needed to stay at the hotel until he came up with a better plan. That was cool for him but I didn't want to be on the run from some street niggas.

Hell, I still didn't know what had jumped off in that building. But after Azar handed me 5 G's for what he called "Trooping it" I decided staying with him at least for the night, might not be all that bad.

I hardly slept that whole night. Then my stomach was growling 'cause a bitch was hungry. I wanted to order some room service, but Azar paranoid ass didn't want nobody delivering us food. That shit sounded crazy, but I was like whatever. He went out and brought back every breakfast item from McDonald's and I ate that shit up like it was my last meal. Finally after my belly was full, I bit the bullet and questioned Azar again.

"Baby, what happened last night?" Azar closed his eyes and put his head back. I figured that once again there would be a long period of silence. Then he began to speak.

"The moment I knocked on the door I knew the vibe was off. But I couldn't walk away," he said with frustration in his voice.

"Walk away from what?" I asked, feeling like I was pulling teeth trying to get an explanation from him.

"Man, I'm slipping. I thought them niggas shoot straight from the hip, but they shady. When the cat opened the door, and I stepped in the apartment, shit just went haywire."

"Damn, what happened?" I asked, now leaning closer, dying to know how shit ended in a blaze of bullets.

"So I step in, homeboy close the door and my new buy er start beefing about my product, saying the heroin I gave him was garbage. I was like, "Yeah, OK. Give me my shit back, 'cause I know this nigga lying."

"How you know he lying?" I inquired. This was the first time I ever heard a first hand account of a drug transaction going bad, my ears were plugged.

"Yo', I fuck wit' these Columbians. They got the best dope on the streets, hands down. So it's three of us in the room, and I'm eying these two niggas tryna get a feel as to what they next move gonna be. So then the nigga that's the farthest away from me start pacing back and forth saying he ain't got the product no more.

"So I'm like a'ight, give me my bread. At this point, I already peeped this black duffel bag on the side of the wall. My instincts were telling me my paper was in there, and I wasn't leaving without it. So I told the niggas you got two options: either give me my product or my bread, but I'm leaving wit' one."

"What did the dude say?"

"The two niggas looked at each other, speaking wit' they eyes, and that was my sign to pull out my heat. Them nig gas had three hundred and fifty thousand of mine. Some body was gonna be lullaby off that shit. I asked them one more time for my bread or my drugs.

When I caught the nigga standing closest to me wink his eye, "I put a bullet right through it."

"Oh, shit, then what happened?"

"Yo, I blasted off on the other nigga, but instead of the cat I just shot falling back on the wall, his body fell to ward me and he knocked my arm causing me to miss my aim. It gave the other nigga time to gain his momentum and he started busting off. I used his partner's body as a shield while I grabbed the duffel bag and fled. You know what happened next, the nigga left standing came at me wit' death on his mind. I know for a fact he and his people's gonna be looking for me."

I didn't even know what to say to Azar. I understood why he had to go hard on those dudes because they were trying to rob him, but unfortunately he didn't finish the job. There is nothing worse than for your enemy to be walking the streets looking to get you. You got to spend the rest of your life watching your back unless you catch his back first. "So what you gon' do now, Azar?" I asked, doubting he even knew.

"Get the fuck outta Brooklyn for a minute. That apart ment I was checking up on for you in Harlem should be ready in a week. I already paid the nigga. We supposed to pick up the keys tomorrow. But we can't move in until the end of next week."

All I heard was we, and I had already told Azar that my moms would shit bricks if she found out we was living to gether.

"Azar, you know my moms ain't going for us living to gether," I said feeling stressed about the whole situation.

"I know, but you'll be sixteen in a couple of months. We just won't let her know just yet. You can still stay there with her for the time being. Them niggas won't think to look for me in Harlem. I'll keep a low profile and see what the streets are talking 'bout."

The next day Azar and I drove to Harlem and picked up the keys to the new apartment. It was in a renovated eleva tor building on 142nd and Riverside Drive. Azar introduced me to the super as his girlfriend who would also be living there with him. Azar also gave me a bag and told me to hide it somewhere safe at my moms crib. He ex plained it was emergency money just in case anything went down. He also stressed the importance of learning how to drive and getting my license when I turned sixteen. So for the next couple of days, we drove out to this big empty parking lot in Long Island, and I practiced. Later on that day I stopped at home to hide the bag Azar gave me.

Luckily, in my closest, one of the floor panels was slightly lifting so I hid the bag under there and covered it with my shoes and boxes.

I hadn't been home in about three days but my moms wasn't tripping, especially after I hit her off with an extra few hundred dollars and told her to buy herself something nice. I grabbed a few things and headed right back out. Azar was outside waiting for me, so I didn't want to take too long. He was still worried about coming through the Brooklyn projects. When I got back in the car, Azar was looking scared as shit. "Baby, is everything al right? You didn't see nobody did you?"

"Naw, I just don't like being nowhere around here," he said, driving off.

"Well, you the one who wanted me to drop off that bag at my moms' crib."

"I know it ain't yo' fault. You've been a soldier through all this." Azar held my hand and gazed at me for a minute, then he continued, "Honestly, Precious, I don't know what I would do without you. I really came off by having you as my girl. I can feel that you're loyal. That means everything to me, especially with the business that I'm in. Baby, you got me open."

Azar continued his speech until we pulled up to the Marriot on Adams Street. I felt he was molding me to be Bonnie to his Clyde, which wasn't cool with me at all. This was about getting money to pay off my greedy-ass moms and take care of myself, but now Azar had me caught up in some gangsta shit. I was mad about it.

When we got out the car and headed up to our room, I wasn't feeling right. It was like all eyes were on me, but they really weren't. Azar's paranoia was rubbing off on me, and that feeling wasn't good. Right when Azar was opening the door, he paused. "Oh shit. I left the bag in the car."

"We can get it later," I said, anxious to get inside and lie down.

"No, it's the bag with all the money I took from them boys. Baby, I gotta shit bad as a ma'fuckah. Will you run down to the truck and get it?"

Last thing I felt like doing was going back to the car, but I grabbed his car and room keys and walked away. I heard Azar scream, "Thanks, Baby," as I made my way to the elevator.

When I finally got to the ground level, the garage was deserted. It was quiet to the point that it was spooky. I hur ried and ran to the car, grabbed the bag and sprinted back towards the elevator. As I waited for the doors to open, I felt the cold tip of steel on the back of my head. "Ain't this some shit," I blurted out. You know how you so scared you can't even be scared; that's how I felt. I knew that was a gun ready to blow the back of my brains out, but as bad as I wanted to cry, scream or run, I was numb. I just thought to myself, *Is this it?Is this how I'm going to leave this world, brains splattered in the Marriot garage?*

"I don't want to kill you," I heard the baritone voice fi nally speak. "If you do what I ask, then you can walk away alive. The choice is yours."

"What's the choice?" I spit, sounding more confident than what I was.

"All I want is my money and your boyfriend's life. If I don't get both, then I'm takin' yours."

"My boyfriend? Who my boyfriend?" I asked, wanting to see if he really knew who I was. I knew by asking the question I was trying his patience, but there was that slight chance this was a case of mistaken identity, although that was highly unlikely.

"Bitch, don't play wit' me. I saw you and yo' man, Azar, leave them projects a half hour ago. If I put my money on it, you was the same girl that was in the car wit' him a week ago when I blasted out his windows. I would hate to blast you now since technically you don't have nuttin' to do with this, but I will."

"So you saying if I give you what you want you'll leave me the fuck alone? I won't ever have to be bothered wit' you again?"

"I give you my word."

"Why you gotta kill Azar, though?" I asked, making a last ditch effort to save Azar's life. "Isn't the money enough?"

"That was my brother he put a bullet in. He gotta die. Enough talking. What's it gonna be?"

That decision was easy. I handed over the bag I just re trieved from the trunk of the car. Then I handed him the room key, "Room 716." All this took place with my back turned away from him.

When he walked off, I made a quick turn to get a look at him. I only caught the side of his face, but it was one I would never forget. He had a thick, long, razor edge scar going from the top to the bottom of his chin. The elevator doors closed behind him, and I jumped in the Range and headed home.

On UPN's ten o'clock news they said that an unidentified man had been found shot once in the head sitting on the toilet inside his hotel room. I knew it was Azar and I actually felt bad for him. But what could I do? It was his life or mine. Like I said before; ain't no man worth dying for.

The next day I packed up my shit and moved to the apartment in Harlem. The money in the bag Azar asked me to hold was $50,000.I was going to use some of that to buy furniture for the place. I told my moms I was moving out but would still hit her off every month. That way she wouldn't try to cause no problems for me.

After I left my moms, I went to see Boogie at the detail ing shop and told him how one day I was at Azar's crib, and he said he had to step out for a few but never came back. I explained that I believed some sort of foul play happened, and he was never coming back. I told him that Azar left me the keys to his Range, and he had two other cars at a garage.

Next, I made Boogie a business proposition attached with a favor. "Boogie, you can have all three cars. Take them to your friends at the chop shop and sell off the parts. That's easy money for you." Boogie had a lot of money, but he always liked to make more. It didn't matter how little or how much.

"Yeah, I can do that. Azar have some nice rides."

"Just so you know, a couple of the windows in the Benz got blasted out."

"What the fuck happened...don't even tell me. I don't want to know. So what do you get out of this, Precious?"

"All I want is a car of my own."

"You not even sixteen, nor do you have a license."

"Boogie, I'll be sixteen next month, and I'll be getting my drivers license."

"With a car you have to pay insurance, and you definitely can't park it in them projects you live at."

"Boogie, I got all that covered. Just get me the car."

"Alright. What you want?"

"A baby Benz."

"Don't you think you need to start off with a nice Honda or Toyota to keep your insurance down? Yo' boy, Azar, dis appeared, so you don't have him to help you out. I could al ways give you your old job back, but it will probably cover the insurance and nothing else."

"I appreciate you looking out, Boogie, but I'm good. I won't have a note, so I'll be able to maintain the insurance. You also don't have to worry about the car being parked in the projects - I actually moved."

"Where?" he asked, curiosity written all over his face.

"I'll call you with the address when I get settled in. How long do you think it'll take to get me my car?"

"I need at least a month."

"Good. By that time I'll have everything straight on my end." I handed Boogie the keys and wrote down the address to the garage. There was no doubt he would come through.

As promised, Boogie hooked me up with a silver C240. It took a few months, but it worked out perfectly. It gave me enough time to pass my driving test and get my new crib in order. I also transferred high schools. I continued to hit my moms off, and she never questioned my whereabouts.

For the next two years, I managed to graduate high school and keep up my rent and all other bills. The super was mad cool. He questioned me a couple of times about Azar, but I would always say he was out of town. Then one day I pretended to be distraught and was crying right outside the hallway where I knew the super could hear me.

When he asked me what was wrong, I told him Azar broke up with me, and that I was devastated. By this time I was eighteen, so I was able to convince him to let me still stay and put the apartment in my name without a credit check. When I hugged him to show my appreciation I rubbed my ample breast against his chest and let him rub his hands down my ass. He was so grateful that he took an additional two hundred dollars off my rent every month.

It didn't really matter, though, because after Azar got killed, all I fucked with was hustlers. They threw money at me like it wasn't nothing. I worked my shit out so good that I still had a large chunk of the $50,000 that I was supposed to hold for Azar - that is, before he died. It seemed that every nigga I fucked with, I just got them open.

Just Me & My Bitch

It had been a little over two years since Azar's murder, but I knew this year was my time to shine. It seemed like overnight I went from living with my dope junky mom to flexing in my own fly ass crib with a Benz to match. I could come and go as I pleased, answering to nobody.

As I strolled down 125th and Lenox relishing in my ghetto dreams, I noticed a guy staring me down. I was used to niggas' mouths watering as they imagined how the in sides of my pussy felt. When I reached the corner I stood in that 'I know I'm the shit' position. With my low waist jeans perfectly accentuating the gap between my slightly curved legs and five-foot-five-inch hourglass figure, the dude was in complete awe.

The closer the dude got to me, the more appealing I became. My butterscotch complexion glistened under the afternoon sun. The wind slightly blew through my wavy golden brown hair, which stopped around midback. My glossy lips added to my sensual looks. I'm sure the nigga felt he was supposed to have spotted me lounging on a Mi ami Beach instead of walking the grimy streets of Harlem.

"Excuse me, Ma, but can I speak to you for a moment please?" he asked in his most sincere voice.

I paused for a moment and ogled the stranger up and down. I then folded my arms and smacked my lips before speaking. "Nigga, I'm not yo' Ma. Save that shit for the next bitch."

"Hold up a minute," he said as he reached to grab my arm. I instantly pulled away with my eyes speaking for me. He knew they read, back the fuck off. "I'm sorry, I didn't mean to grab on you like that, but I didn't want you to walk away."

"Hum huh," I said, rolling my eyes to let the stranger know he was getting on my last nerves.

"No disrespect, but you are far too gorgeous to be speaking with so much venom."

"Excuse me. Who the fuck is you? The Preacher's son?"

"Nah, my pops is dead, but when he was alive, he definitely wasn't a Preacher," he said with a devious chuckle.

"So why how I speak matter to you, since you ain't no savior?" I asked, hoping the nigga would keep walking.

"I said my pops wasn't a Preacher; I didn't say I wasn't a savior."

"How you know I need saving?" I asked, becoming more drawn into this slick talking dude's conversation.

"I don't see a ring on your finger," he said as he gently massaged my left hand.

"Maybe I don't want a ring on my finger," I snapped, pulling my hand away.

"All queens deserve to be blessed with the finest rings, and you are definitely a queen. If you don't mind will you tell me your name?"

"Precious," I answered in a silky tone, which was in contrast to my once gritty voice.

"Damn, your mother knew what time it was when you were born, 'cause you damn sure precious."

"Cute, but I've heard all these lines before."

"I don't care about all those other cats that fed you lines. I'm a real 'G' so my line is the only line that matters."

Damn, this nigga feeling himself, I thought to myself. After getting over my initial attitude, for the first time I actually swallowed the whole essence of the man standing before me. His flawless mahogany skin was highlighted by a low cut, full of jetblack curls. He was sixfoottwo and a solid oneninety. His full lips were decorated with perfect white teeth. I had to admit he was fine. "So what's your name?" I said, warming up to him.

"Nico. Nico Carter."

"It's nice to meet you, Nico. So what you want from me?"

"Your company or maybe your hand in marriage, or maybe a pretty baby."

"Nigga, I ain't making no baby for you."

"You say that now, but just give me a month. You'll be begging to have my seed."

"You real confident with yours. What you pushing?" I asked, trying to get down to business. He was fine, but if he was broke, it didn't make a damn bit of difference.

"What you mean what I'm pushing?" Nico asked with confusion in his voice.

"You know what I mean. What type of whip you got?"

"Precious, that's not the type of question you ask a man when you just meet him," he said, sounding like a con cerned father lecturing his daughter.

"He might get the wrong impression and assume you're a paper chaser," he added.

"Sweetheart, you got me confused with the next bitch. I don't give a fuck what impression I give off. I don't fuck wit' broke niggas. A broke nigga make for a dry pussy. You feel me? So are you gonna tell me what you pushing, or do I need to keep strolling and go about my business?"

I knew every instinct in Nico's body was telling him to walk away and never look back at the danger standing be fore him, but being a typical nigga with a hard-on, his lust prevailed. "I tell you what, let me take you on a date, and I promise you won't be disappointed."

"I guess that means you not gonna tell me what type of wheels you got. I hope you not walking, because if you are, you'll be on that date solo." Nico laughed. "What's so funny?"

"You. Just give me your digits. You definitely gonna be my per-manent piece."

I figured that instead of turning Nico off with my slick with-the-mouth antics, I was pulling him further in. He probably wasn't used to my type, a woman so blatant with it. He had to respect the fact that I let it be known that you either come correct or don't come at all.

"What's up, Maria?" I said, walking in the Dominican spot for my weekly wash and blow out. Maria responded with her standard nod and smile, which was fine with me since my beautician could barely speak English. After the deep conditioning and roller set I was under the dryer, dreading the hour process. Luckily, I came prepared with the latest magazines to pass time. I was enthralled in read hottest MC's when the rattle of someone pounding on my dryer jarred me from my concentration.

"What's up, homegirl?" Inga grinned as our eyes met. Inga and I had been cool since sixth grade, but in the last year or so we became real close. When I moved out my moms' crib and changed schools I would get lonely for female company sometimes. All the girls at my new school had established their cliques and looked at me as an outsider. Plus, they couldn't take that all they boyfriends was sweating my ass. Inga would come over and stay with me just about every weekend. We would just kick it together or go out on double dates since we both liked hustlers.

"Bitch, you was about to catch it," I said, giving her a pound. "I didn't know who the fuck was banging on my dryer like a crazy person. I should've known it was yo' wild ass."

"What you reading?" Inga asked as she sat down in the seat next to me.

"Just some rap bullshit. I'm starting to believe all this socalled beef just be a publicity stunt. These niggas will do anything for air- time."

"You got that right, and we be right there reading that bullshit like its gospel," Inga said as we nodded our heads in agreement. "So what's up wit' you tonight, you going to the club?"

"Actually, I'm supposed to be going on a date."

"A date? Who you fucking wit', Precious?"

"I ain't fucking wit' nobody. I just met this dude on my way over here, and we supposed to be hanging out tonight."

"He got money?" Inga asked, while rubbing her fingers together.

"If he don't pull up to the crib in some official shit, I won't have no problem telling him to forget my name and number."

"You got that right. It's too many niggas out here do ing it to be wasting your time with a thirsty cat. But if he is rolling in the dough, hook me up with one of his friends. Truth be told, you know niggas making paper usually roll in crews."

"I got you. If he's official I'll turn you on. I haven't forgotten about that Jamaican cat you hooked me up with. I didn't even have to fuck that nigga; all he wanted to do was eat my pussy and take me shopping. A bitch was hurt when he got locked up, he was lacing me lovely."

"Yeah, he was real big on you. I speak to his cousin, and he told me that nigga still be checking for you. He even asked me if I could talk to you about going to visit him in prison. I didn't have the heart to tell him it would never happen. So I just said you went to visit your peoples down south for a minute."

"OK. What the fuck can he do for me behind bars, ex cept tell me where he hid his stash?" I said, viewing my watch, seeing how much time I had left under this hotass dryer. I then looked back up at Inga, inspecting the shaky hairstyle she was rocking. "You came to let Maria do your hair?"

"Nah, I still have this weave. I'm tryn' to rock this until I get all my money's worth. I was on my way to the beauty supply store and peeped you in here and wanted to holla."

I couldn't help but think that Inga had got all her mon ey's worth and then some off the tired looking tracks that were barely hanging on to her scalp. But I knew Inga's dol lars were tight and she couldn't afford the necessary four to six week redo that was required to keep your weave fresh.

"Oh, that's cool. I was planning on hitting you later anyway. If my date is a bust, let's go shake our asses at the club tonight. If it's all good, I'll hit you tomorrow so we can set up a double date.

"That'll work," Inga said as she strutted out of the beau ty shop.

That night I got dressed for my date to the sounds of "The Emancipa-tion of Mimi." Although I loathed that diz zy acting bimbo, Mariah Car-ey, I had to admit her CD was kinda hot. Nico already called and said he was on his way so I was just giving myself the finishing touches.

I put on my hot pink Juicy Couture terry cloth dress with match-ing shoes. I still didn't know if this date was go ing to even happen, so I wasn't stressing it too much. Since my apartment wasn't facing the street I couldn't even look out my window to see what type of whip he was pushing before wasting my time and going downstairs. When my cell phone rang again, I figured it was Nico telling me he was down-stairs. No way was I giving him my home num ber 'cause he still was on my suspect list.

When I got to the front door entrance I tried to peep around to catch a glimpse of Nico's ride. All I saw was an old Chevy parked out front with the hazardous lights flash ing. If that was that nigga's car, I was going to cuss him the fuck out for wasting my time. He had to know by just look ing at me that it wasn't that kind of party. Then I heard my right out front. I was so pissed I bit my bottom lip.

When I walked further out, someone beeped their horn and I noticed the hottest 2005 red SL65 AMG with banging rims. My face lit up like a Christmas tree. When I sat down in the car, the first thing Nico said was, "I bet you thought that banged up Chevy was mine," we both burst out laughing.

"You know I did, ma'fuckah."

"Seriously, Precious, you are way too beautiful to talk like that. Plus my name isn't ma'fuckah."

"I apologize. You know what I meant to say, Nico." I didn't mind giving him a little life cause his wheels were crazy and the nigga was even finer out his street clothes. He had on some top line Sean John shit. Not the sweat suit gear, but the slacks and button up shirt. His wrist was heavy with the Jay-Z limited edition platinum version Audemars Piguet watch. I was feeling his style.

"So where do you want to go tonight?" he asked, doing a U-turn in the middle of my street.

"Maybe dinner."

"You got a place in mind?"

"You pick the spot," I wanted to see what his restaurant game was looking like anyway. He jumped on the Westside Highway. We eventually ended up on Lafayette Street at a spot called Butter. The place was sexy. I was surprised because it was a white joint with a bunch of model type looking motherfuckers. It was cool though and the food was a'ight to be a white establishment. After dinner it was still early and Nico suggested we go to the movies. But I declined. I wanted to find out everything I could about him. So we drove to the park across from St. Nicholas Ave. and just talked.

"So, Nico, tell me about yourself."

"What do you want to know?"

"Everything." So Nico started from when he was a kid.

"My father got murdered when I was thirteen. Of course he was a street nigga. He used to hustle with my best friend Ritchie's dad.

"I've known Ritchie since I was three years old. He's like my brother. We grew up in the same projects and our mother's were best friends. After my dad got killed, shortly after, Ritchie's dad got locked up on some Federal charges and got life. With both of them gone I had to step up as the man of the house.

"I was determined to pick up where my dad left off, which meant getting my drug hustle on. One of my dad's captains took me under his wings and molded me into the perfect solider. But hustling was embedded in my blood, so I conquered the game with rapid speed. I have that deadly combination of intellect and street smarts. I can run circles around anyone that crosses my path.

"As I got higher up in the ranks, I tried to bring Ritchie in the mix, but he became withdrawn when his father got locked up. To make matters worse his mother got strung out on crack. Eventually it got so bad that he moved in with me and my mother, because his moms couldn't take care of him anymore. It took a few years, but Ritchie came out of his shell and we made a pact to never leave one another's side until death do us part." Nico paused and looked at me for a moment." "I can't believe I just told you all that. I don't even usually open myself up like this. But that's OK, because you are going to be my girl, I know it."

"Why you stressin' for me to be your girl?" I was curious to know. It was obvious that Nico was large and in charge. He probably had bitches throwing pussy at him from every direction. So I had to know what his fascination with me was.

"Besides the fact that you are unbelievably gorgeous, something about you is dark."

"Dark? What the fuck?"

Nico gave me that look. "I meant to say, 'What you mean.'" *This cussing situation was definitely gonna be a problem, I thought to myself.*

"That same look I got in my eyes, you got it in yours. I've never met a woman or man besides my father with that look."

"What look is that?"

"It's a combination of many things. The average nigga wouldn't be able to handle you, but I know I can and will. We are going to do big things together."

With the majority of niggas I fucked with, I wouldn't give them no ass until they had tricked a few G's on me first, but not with Nico. I willingly gave up the pussy that first night. It was crazy because no matter how hard I tried, he wouldn't let me get on top. That let me know he was de termined to maintain control over me and our relationship. The way he put it on me, though I didn't have a problem with it. From that day on it was like that Biggie record, *"Just Me And My Bitch"*.

Hollyhood

Being Nico's girl was like being the First Lady. The streets bowed down to me as if I was their queen. I had to take it back to Brooklyn on a regular basis and represent my hood. See, Harlem wasn't my hood, I rep'd for BK. The first time I drove up to Boogie's spot in Nico's SL65, the place paused. They knew it was Nico's shit, and I had to be his girl to be pushing it. For everyone else who didn't know, there was no doubt in their mind I was some powerful ma'fucka's wifey.

I loved the stares and glares I received from dealing with a kingpin. Even for the people who hated on me, they didn't have the balls to say anything to my face. Nico's reputation preceded him, and no one crossed him, and since I seemed to be the closest thing to him, they didn't dare cross me.

Everything between me and Nico happened so fast. The next morning after we twisted each other out, he said I was moving in with him. He didn't ask, he demanded. He was so damn cocky, confident, and controlling with his shit, but it turned me on like crazy. I was open for it anyway. I agreed to move in with him, but I also kept my spot. As much as I digged Nico, I knew that any bitch that was about her business maintained her own crib. Nico had a couple of Brooklyn Heights.

Anybody that is familiar with Brooklyn knows that is prime property. I'm talking million-dollars-and up cribs. I didn't understand how Nico maneuvered that, but that just showed how official his shit was. At first I didn't even feel comfortable being in the same neighborhood with all those rich pricks, and Nico could see how frustrated I was be coming.

One day he sat me down and schooled me. "Precious, understand something. The only way you become rich is surrounding yourself with rich people. I know this might seem like a bit much to you, but pretty soon instead of you worrying about who all these rich people are around you, they'll be trying to figure out who you are."

Nico was right. After a while a couple of ladies in the neighborhood would see me pulling up in my 6Series con vertible and would try to make conversation with me. They was curious about who I was. They swore down I was in the Entertainment Industry. When they got to asking me a million questions, I would slightly tilt down my Jackie O shades and say, "Sorry can't chat. I must be going," real Hollywood like.

I said to myself, *let it stay a mystery*. If I have anything to do with it, they will die trying to figure that shit out. It was bananas because in Brooklyn Heights, Nico and I were looked upon as a respectable couple who was just doing it, but the ghetto ran through our bloods. We both lived for the streets.

I didn't normally go with Nico when he was handling business, but this particular day on our way to do some shop ping in the city we made a stop at one of the many blocks Nico had on lock for a spontaneous spot check. It was his way of making sure his workers were doing their part and holding it down. Nico was the man, and when he pulled up in the hood with rims spinning all shenanigans came to a halt, and everyone stood in attention.

Although his best friend Ritchie was his right hand man, he didn't garner the same level of respect as Nico. The whole borough knew that Nico basically handed large portions of the business over to his best friend out of loy alty, not because Ritchie earned it, although Nico didn't see it that way. As far as he was concerned he and Ritchie were brothers. "How's it looking, my man?" Nico asked his field lieutenant, Tommy.

"It's all good. It's Friday, so you know the clientele is steady and the money is right," the stocky worker bragged.

"That's what I like to hear. I was checking up on you. You seem to have everything under control, so I'm out," Nico said giving Tommy a pound. "Hit me later with those numbers."

"I got you boss." Right when we were pulling off, Ritchie pulled up.

"What's up, my nigga?" Ritchie said as he knelt down on Nico's side of the car door. He then noticed I was in the car, "What's up, Precious?"

"The same thing, Ritchie."

"When you gon' hook me up wit' one of your girls?"

"I told you I don't fuck wit' bitches like that. The only chick I fucks wit' is Inga."

"Well hook it up."

"Ritchie, every time you tell me to do that shit you al ways cancel at the last minute."

"I tell you what. You and Nico come, we can do it fo' sho' tonight."

"Why we gotta come?" I smacked. I knew Inga would want it that way, but I wanted to make Ritchie feel like I was doing his ass a favor.

"Com' on. Stop trippin'. It'll be fun, right?" He play fully punched Nico's shoulder, trying to get him to cosign on the outing.

"Yeah, it'll be cool."

"A'ight', I'll call her. We can go to the Harlem Grill. I heard they have some good food."

If I had to be bothered with Ritchie's silly ass at least I could get a good meal out the deal. "Put her number in your phone so you can make the arrangements to pick her up." After Ritchie plugged Inga's number in his phone, he noticed Tommy and told him to come here.

"Tommy, make sure you don't leave until all business is dried up. We don't need nobody slacking off," Ritchie said, trying to execute some authority. Tommy nodded his head as if agreeing with what Ritchie said, but I knew he gave it no merit.

From the few occasions I observed Ritchie, he had a way of making unnecessary comments in an attempt to make his presence known. I wondered if Nico ever picked up on that, but since he never mentioned it maybe he didn't. He had a blind eye when it came to Ritchie, anyway. Because I knew for a fact that Ritchie was straight jealous of Nico; it was written in his eyes.

"Man, you too lax with these niggas. They be coming at you like ya friends instead of your workers," Ritchie said with agitation.

"Nah, it's not like that. They know who's boss, but I prefer for them to feel comfortable around me."

"Comfortable. Fuck that, you better make them goofy niggas fear you. They need to know if they step out of line it can happen."

"Man my temper is legendary so they all know it can happen. But fear brings about lies. Our crew is the eyes and ears of the streets. They gottta believe they can tell me any thing, whether good or bad.

Without the information from the streets I'm powerless. If that means making my crew feel at ease then so be it."

"I hear you, but I still say you need to put your foot in they ass every now and then," Ritchie stressed.

As I listened to them exchange words, I knew that Ritchie didn't understand that Nico had a different style of dictatorship. Ritchie's browbeating style actually worked well for many bosses in Nico's position, but Nico vehe mently opted against it. See, Nico wasn't big on bluffing. If he had to instill fear in you, that meant your time was up, and your life was over. He maintained a calm, cool and collected persona that made even his worse enemies respect him. When the dark side of Nico appeared everyone knew to stay away.

"I'll think about what you said," Nico answered, trying to get off the subject. "What time do you want to meet up at Harlem Grill?"

"Nine is good."

"So we'll see you there, and don't have us waiting on you neither," Nico added with a smile, knowing how it was nothing for Ritchie to be late or not show up at all.

After Nico and I went shopping, he dropped me off at home so he could handle some business before we went out. The moment my bags hit the floor, I called Inga. "What up?"

"What's going on, Precious?"

"Not too much. Did Ritchie call you?"

"Not yet, why is he supposed to?" I looked at my watch and saw it was quarter to five. "That nigga so simple. Yeah, he was supposed to call. The four of us is going to the Har lem Grill for dinner."

"Word...wait hold on a minute. My phone beeping." As I waited for Inga to click back over from the other line, I twisted my mouth up, thinking how slack Ritchie was. We saw that nigga at twelve in the afternoon, and it damn near five and he still hadn't called Inga. That's why he couldn't keep no girlfriend 'cause he was one of those simpleass dudes. I could never comprehend why Nico had so much love for him. "I'm back. That was Ritchie on the other line."

"Oh he finally decided to call," I said sarcastically.

"Girl, yeah, he said he'll pick me up at eight-thirty. What you wearing?"

"Probably something I got today when Nico and I went shopping."

"Yah stay shopping. I hope Ritchie generous like Nico so I can start flossin'."

"I doubt it. I ain't neva seen Ritchie wit' no official bitch. 'Cause an official bitch wouldn't be able to deal wit' his clown ass on no long term basis."

"Well, maybe they ain't neva fucked him right. 'Cause he's a cutie."

"Whateva. Let me get myself together 'cause I been running round all day. I'll see you tonight."

When I hung up with Inga, I just rolled my eyes. Inga was my girl, but she always got so caught up in nigga's way before they started feeling her. I could tell by the sound of her voice that she was already feeling Ritchie, and knowing him, he was just looking for a big butt to bust a nut in.

Of course Nico and I arrived first and on time for our reserva tion at the Harlem Grill. The hostess led us to a table in the back. After our second drink, Ritchie and Inga came walking in the spot like they were on time. I knew it wasn't Inga's fault, but because she had a big Kool-Aid smile on her face from be ing so happy to be with Ritchie, she was guilty by association.

"What took ya so long?" I asked just to fuck with Ritchie.

"The traffic on the bridge was backed up." Inga said, already trying to come to the defense of her clown-ass date.

"Oh, it was moving fine when we were coming across."

"What ya want to drink?" Nico said, trying to keep the peace. For the rest of the dinner Nico and Ritchie talked, and me and Inga engaged in our own conversation. After finishing up there Nico took us to this DL spot called Zip Code.

Nico had to do a special knock just to gain entrance. He said it was an exclusive lounge for the topnotch hustlers. We stayed for a couple of hours poppin' bottles and listening to music. I stepped away for a few minutes to use the bathroom, and when I came back, Ritchie's hand was damn near inside Inga's coochie. She was giggling, and he was whispering in her ear. Right when I was about to tell them to get a room, Ritchie said they was breaking out. I gave Inga a hug goodbye and told her to call me.

"I had a good time tonight," Nico said as he drove us home. "We should all hang out more often."

"Baby, do you really think we should be making long term dinner dates with those two? I mean how long can their relationship actually last?"

"Ritchie seemed like he was really feeling her."

"Yeah, feeling up her ass."

"Stop it. I'm just saying they seem to enjoy one another. It's cool. Inga's your best friend and Ritchie's mine. We have a nice little family thing going on."

I secretly hoped that Ritchie was so bad in bed Inga would kick him to the curb before anything started. As far as I was concerned, Ritchie was bad news, and I didn't want him in no family of mine.

"Let me ask you something, Nico."

"Go right ahead."

"You don't ever feel like Ritchie just riding yo' dick and not bringing nothing to the table? He always got some shit to pop about how you need to do this and how you need to handle your business like that, but it's all dead noise. That shit don't bother you, 'cause it sure as hell gets on my nerve."

"Precious, you too hard on Ritchie. Sometimes a cat has to throw his weight around a little bit in order to feel like a man, but it's harmless. Ritchie might have his shortcom ings, but the reason why I keep him by my side is because he's loyal. With the game I'm in, that's a character flaw. These niggas out here ain't got no loyalty to nobody, but Ritchie got my front and my back." Then Nico turned and looked at me with a smirk on his face and said, "Listen here. I'm like a dog, I don't speak, but I understand every thing. Ritchie is good people, trust me."

I sat there in the passenger seat, just nodding my head. The conversation was a lost cause. Nico was dead set on his opinion of Ritchie, which was disappointing to me. I always viewed Nico as a dude that was beyond reproach when it came to his street savvy. But if he honestly believed that Ritchie was a loyal dude, then he had the game all fucked up.

The following afternoon Inga called me, sounding like she was on her honeymoon. "Girl, that nigga Ritchie can fuck. He just left here like an hour ago."

"Where was yo' moms at when all that fucking was jumping off?"

"She went to Philly this weekend to visit her sister, so I had the place to myself. He's coming to get me later on this evening so we can go to the movies. Girl, I'm in love wit' that nigga."

"Whateva, Inga. You say that about every dude that beats that coochie good."

"Precious, this time was different. He was so gentle with me and before he left, he gave me five hundred dol lars and told me to get my hair and nails done. You know it don't cost no five hundred dollars to get that shit done. He's feeling me, and I'm feeling him too."

I had to admit that I was surprised by what Inga was tell ing me. I always thought of Ritchie as being a fiveminute fucker. I definitely didn't think he would lay up with a bitch or leave her money. Five hundred was a drop in the bucket for him, but the point was he gave it to her and told her to get her nails and hair done. Not only that, they were going on a second date already. Maybe Ritchie wasn't as bad as I thought. And if Inga was happy, then so be it. She deserved for a nigga to lace her. Now maybe she would keep her weave a little bit tighter.

"Inga, I'm happy for you. But don't get too caught up in Ritchie. I would hate for him to get you open, then break your heart."

When I got off the phone with Inga, I called Nico. I want ed to see if he had heard from Ritchie and got any feedback. Inga was my girl, and I would feel some kinda way if Ritchie played her out. Nico's cell went straight to voice mail. His phone was doing that a lot lately. For a second I wondered if the nigga was creeping on me with the next bitch but decided I was being paranoid. Not saying that Nico wasn't capable of cheating like any other man, but Nico knew he would have to be extra discreet with his shit. I do not play that. When and if Nico fucked around on me, it better be when he's going in and out of town.

Later on that day, I had an appointment at Boogie's detailing shop so I decided to stop by my moms' crib. I hadn't seen her in a few months, and even though I didn't fuck with her like that, I wanted to make sure she hadn't died of a drug overdose. I used my key, and when I opened the door, my moms was lying on the couch, butt ass naked with some dude on top of her. Empty bottles of liquor were around the couch and some needles and pipes were sitting on the table next to them.

For a moment I thought they were dead because their bod ies were motionless, but then they both started moaning as they changed positions on the couch. I walked over to the ste reo and blasted the music to wake the two junkies up.

"What the fuck?" the two of them said in unison as they jumped up off the couch. When I had their full attention I turned the stereo back off.

"Who the hell is you?" the bony Chris Rock lookalike screamed. He didn't look like new money Chris Rock, but 'Pookie' "*New Jack City*" Chris Rock.

"I'm her daughter, you nasty-looking crack head."

"Who the fuck you talking to?" the Pookie lookalike asked as he wiped the crust from his eyes and mouth. He motioned his arms towards me like it was about to be on.

"Nigga, I'm talking to you, and you betta watch how you speak to me. I know you heard of Nico Carter. Well, that's my man, and it wouldn't take nothing but a phone call to have your life ended, so back the fuck up." I had to put some sort of fear in the dude because junkies can be some of the stupidest, overly confident ma'fuckahs out here.

"Both of ya calm down. It's too early in the morning for this shit."

My moms was straight trippin'.

"It's two o'clock in the afternoon; the morning been ended. Now, my man," I said, pointing my finger at the clothes lying on the floor. "You need to get yo' shit and get the fuck up outta here 'cause I want to speak to my moms."

He looked over at my moms like she was supposed to say something, but I was still hitting her off with paper so she just turned her face away like her name was Bennet and she ain't in it.

I stood with my arms folded as the dude moved in slow motion getting dressed. He even tried to cover himself. "Nigga, ain't nobody checking for that little dick you got over there. Hurry the fuck up."

When he picked up his keys, he tried to grab the small amount of drugs they had left and my moms smacked his hand. "I paid for this shit. Get yo' hands off my drugs."

"Listen, we ain't 'bout to have no crack head fight up in here. Take that shit, Pookie, and get the fuck up outta here."

"My name ain't Pookie. It's Leroy."

"Whateva, nigga, just go." When I turned my head for a minute making sure Leroy was gone and then locked the door, my moms tried to disappear into the bathroom. I went back there and started banging on the door. "Yo, I want to speak to you."

"Precious, damn. I'm shittin'. Give me a minute." Fifteen minutes later, my moms came strolling out of the bathroom like nothing happened.

"You a grown woman and can do whateva you like, but not on my dime. You're bringing any ole type of dirty nig gas in here fucking them wit' no condom or nothin'. Are you tryna die of AIDS?"

"Just because you give me money, I'm still yo' mother, and you don't tell me what to do," she said, opening up the refrigerator and pulling out a beer.

"I tell you what then, how 'bout I don't give you no mo' money, and you do whateva the fuck you like."

"Precious, you know I need that money. You my only source of income."

"Then act like it. I would prefer if you'd check yourself in some sort of rehab, which I would gladly pay for, but if not, keep them dirty niggas outta here. You neva know. They might flip out on you one day and kill yo' ass. I know one day I'm gonna have to bury you, but I would hate for it to be over some shit like that."

"You neva know, Precious. I might have to bury you first." Something about the way my moms said that sent chills up my spine.

"Just do what I ask. Here, take this." I pulled out a wad of cash and counted out fifteen hundred dollars. I knew she would probably smoke it up in less than a week, but some where inside of me I wished my mother would get straight.

Every time I looked into her beautiful green eyes, I saw hope.

When I got in the car, I called Nico again, and this time he picked up the phone. "What's up, baby? Where you at?"

"Just in these streets handling business."

"Oh, I called you earlier and your phone went straight to voice mail."

"I don't know what that was about. Where you at?" He tried to change the subject.

"I just left my moms' crib. She was in there wit' some grimy nigga. I so wish she'd get off those damn drugs and get her life together."

"Baby girl, once a junkie always a junkie."

I knew the odds of what Nico was saying was true, but the fact that he said it bothered me. I was looking for a sym pathetic ear, not a self righteous point of view.

"Have you talked to Ritchie?" I said, now wanting to change the subject.

"For a minute-why?"

"Inga said they supposed to go on another date tonight. Maybe you was right about them feeling each other."

"Oh, that's alright. I'ma see him in a few, and I'll ask him."

"Don't make it seem like you spying for me, so I can go back and tell Inga."

"I'm not. I know how to handle my man."

"So what time are you gon' be home tonight?"

"Probably late. I got mad shit to do. But I'll call you later."

My stomach was getting that queasy feeling which wasn't a good sign. The little bitch that's your conscience, who taps you on the shoulder when something is up, was doing a motherfucking tap dance on my shit. The message was clear: Nico was definitely creeping.

Although my instincts were screaming that at me, I needed some confirmation. I also wanted to find out the best way to handle it. The only person I trusted to discuss my suspicions with and who could give me sound advice was my main man, Boogie. I put my car in drive and head ed to the detailing shop.

When I arrived, Boogie was in front checking out a cus tomer's new Lamborghini, but he would have to continue that another time.

"Excuse me. I need to borrow Boogie for a minute," I said to the oldass man who had no business pushing a sports car with all that speed. One wrong move on his stick shift and he would die of a heart attack. "Boogie, sorry for interrupting you, but this is an emergency. I'm sure the look of stress is written all over my face."

"Nah, I don't see stress. You looking like a Ghetto Queen to me," Boogie said, checking out my gear and bling.

"I appear that way on the outside, but on the inside I'm just tryna to maintain."

"From what I hear you're more than maintaining. I hear Nico is taking real good care of you. The streets say ya live like rap superstars."

"Oh, that's what the streets say? They saying anything else?"

"Anything like what?"

"You know, about what bitch is fucking my man."

"Precious, I know you ain't getting caught up in all the silly shit. That's the main problem when these men fuck with you young girls. You all get upset about irrelevant shit."

"What's irrelevant about wanting to know if my man is fucking around on me?"

"Because as long as he is taking care of home who really gives a fuck? You driving around here in the most expensive cars, designer clothes, dripping in diamonds and living in nice asscribs, but that still ain't enough. You gotta have a nigga's balls on a platter. I don't know what Nico is doing with his dick. All I know is that you are looking and living better than ever. Count your blessings and be done with it. If you start looking for shit on Nico you'll find it. Then you're going to cause a whole bunch of trouble for nothing."

"I hear you, Boogie. You know I always appreciate your advice."

"Good. Make sure you use it."

On my way home I replayed the conversation I had with Boogie over and over again. What he said made a lot of sense. I decided to give it a rest. Unless some shit about Nico and another bitch slapped me in the face, I would chill.

For the next few weeks I continued with my normal activi ties, except for hanging with Inga. She and Ritchie were kick ing it hard. I was on my way to meet her at the Dominican spot to get our hair done, since we hadn't hung out in a minute. Inga was already there when I arrived. I was surprised about how good she looked. She had on a fitted white jersey jumpsuit that emphasized her small waist and bodacious ass. She took out her weave and her hair was cut in one of those classic Chinese bobs. It was hot because Inga's hair was jet black and it com plimented her coffeebrown complexion. By no means was Inga on my level lookswise, but she was holding her own. "Look at you, girl," I said, giving Inga a hug.

"I'm spending Ritchie's money right, huh?"

"Damn right. That outfit is slammin,' and I'm loving your hair."

"Yeah, Ritchie said he was tired of getting his fingers caught in my tracks when we be fucking. So I decided to rock my own hair."

"It look good. You looking real official, Inga. A bitch is impressed." After getting our hair and nails done, we stopped by Amy Ruth's for some banging soul food. Inga went on and on about how happy she was with Ritchie and how pleased she was to have a man that was taking care of her. I was glad for her too, although I still felt Ritchie was a snake.

"So how are things going with you and Nico?" Inga fi nally asked, after going on about her and Ritchie since the moment I met up with her.

"Everything's cool, I guess."

"What you mean you guess" Ya the Ghetto King and Queen. You should be on top of the world."

"I suppose, but between you and me, I think Nico cheating on me. I know all niggas get they shit off, but I don't think it's no wham-bam, thank you, ma'am shit."

"Why you say that?"

"Just a feeling, but I could be wrong." I could see Inga fidgeting and playing with her nails like she was nervous. "Inga, do you have something to say, 'cause you my girl? If you know something, spit it out."

"Precious, I didn't want to say nothin' because I thought it was just some hating shit by jealous bitches. But a week ago when I was at that beauty supply store, I ran into Tani sha and Vonda. We were just kicking it, and then they asked me about you. I told them you was cool and kept the con versation moving, but they kept going back to you. They told me that they heard Nico was fucking wit' this chick named

Porscha from Queens. I honestly didn't believe them. I thought they were just throwing salt in the game."

"I'm sorry, Precious. Honestly though, they could still be lying, it may not be true."

"How did they hear about it?"

"Tanisha said her cousin is good friends with the girl Porscha, and she was bragging about how she was fuck ing wit' Nico Carter. She said she knew he had a girl, but she didn't care 'cause he had some good dick and kept her pockets heavy."

My stomach was now doing somersaults. I knew every thing Inga said was true because I'd been feeling like Nico was creeping on me anyway. To have my suspicions con firmed had me nauseated. This meant the whole hood knew Nico was screwing this bitch behind my back. I didn't know how I was going to play this shit out.

"Inga, don't tell Ritchie we had this conversation. I don't want Nico to know anything about this until I figure out what I'm gonna do."

"No doubt, but honestly, Precious, this shouldn't even matter. Ritchie always talking about how strung out Nico is over you and how he never been like this over any other girl he fucked wit'. Forget about those other bitches. You know they just dying to walk in your shoes."

I listened to every word Inga said, but it didn't make a difference. My instincts had been right all along. Nico was twisting the next bitch back out and right under my nose. What had me really vexed was that the nigga was shitting so close to where he lay. I was probably the topic of con versation in every hood's hair and nail salon in the five bor oughs. Nico had disrespected me to the fullest, and I had no choice but to teach him a lesson.

The Set Up

For the next couple of week's, everyday and every night I thought about the information Inga gave me. As bad as I wanted to put a knife through Nico's heart, I re mained silent. I was spending every moment trying to figure out how to cause him the type of pain where he would wish he was dead, but he was very much alive. It was difficult though, because I couldn't just dump him and be with the next nigga; the code of the streets wouldn't allow that. The only dude I would want was someone on Nico's level, and all kingpin's wifey and exwifey were off limits. I also wanted to make sure my paper was intact before I bounced. There were so many things to think about. But the one thing I was sure ofa nigga was not gonna play me. That meant Nico had to go.

Friday night, Inga and I decided to go to Cherry Lounge because my girl, Medina did the party there. I was looking forward to drinking some bubbly and dancing to some hip hop. Nico and Ritchie were out of town, so Inga and I both thought this would be the perfect time to have some fun. The line was around the building when we walked up, but Medina was at the door and let us right in. Since we wanted to pop bottles, the lady that handled the tables led us back to the VIP section.

We were the only women with our own table in the VIP section. We were surrounded by some recognizable street hustlers and music industry dudes. Before long, the place was packed and the crowd was jumping to 50 Cent and The Game. As I guzzled down my third glass of champagne, I noticed Tanisha and two other chicks I didn't recognize walking towards us.

"What's up, Precious? What's up Inga?"

We both nodded our heads, acknowledging Tanisha.

"This is my cousin Michelle and her friend Porscha."

I know the color from my face had to disappear. I was in shock that Tanisha had the nerves to bring the bitch that was fucking my man to our table. She deserved a good old fashion beat down over that shit. I couldn't help but stare down who I somewhat considered my competition.

Technically, she wasn't competition because I was the one that represented as wifey, but because I was competi tive by nature I had to look at her that way. I couldn't lie the girl was pretty and had a nice body too. We kinda had the same sort of look, except she was more hardcore looking in the face. I didn't know if it was due to age or just living a hard knock life.

"Tanisha, since yo' silly ass wanted to bring your people over here let's cut right to it. Porscha, are you fucking my man Nico?" I asked, looking her straight in the eyes.

"Excuse me?"

"Bitch, you heard me. You fucking my man, Nico, or what?"

"As a matter of fact I am, bitch," she responded adding a twist to her neck. Inga, Tanisha and her cousin, Michelle stood all frozen. They didn't know what was going to happen next, so when I jumped over the table and swung my champagne bottle at Porscha, I knew Tanisha instantly regretted trying to be fly and bringing her fat ass over to my table.

Right when the bottle was about to collide with Pors cha's head, her cousin snapped out of her daze and knocked it out my hand. It didn't matter because I had two good fists that would finish the job for me. I threw my whole body on top of Porscha. She was petite so she went down like a thin piece of paper. I just kept swinging on the bitch. A right and a left then another right and another left.

The bitch was helpless. Right when her cousin was about to jump on my back, Inga stepped up and let her know to back the fuck up. Everybody knew Inga could fight. But the funny thing was, because of how I looked, the whole hood slept on me, but I was bout it.

Inga was probably the only person that knew I could fight my butt off, and that's only because I whipped her ass one time. I kept throwing the punches, then I took my shoe off and clobbered the bitch with my heel. Right when I started seeing blood the bouncers ran up and lifted me off the bruised and bloody hussy. The chick was in shock. Before the bouncers got me completely off her, I spit at the hoe and said, "Now go tell Nico I whipped yo' ass, bitch."

Luckily Medina was my girl, so they didn't try to get extra with it. They simply asked us to leave and told me I would be more than welcome to come back next week. Management was actually looking out for me because they weren't sure when Porscha finally got up off the floor if she would call the police and press charges.

Honestly, I didn't give a fuck because I would turn around and whip that bitch's ass again.

"Girl, are you OK?" Inga asked when we were walking to my car.

"I'm fine, but can you drive?" My adrenaline was pumping and the last thing I wanted to do was get in a car accident. About ten minutes into our ride home, Inga burst out laughing.

"Precious, you jumped over that table like you was part of the WWF. You put a beating on that bitch. I know they regretting they ever stepped to our table."

"I know, right?" I said, laughing too. I couldn't help but think about the scared expression on Porscha's face when I was pounding on that ass.

"Do you think she called Nico yet?"

"I hope she did, that's one less thing I gotta discuss wit' his ass. How is he gonna explain this bullshit away. That bitch sure had it coming, though. I wish I could've had five more minutes wit' her simple ass."

I slept until the middle of the afternoon the next day. I couldn't stop the dreams of beating the shit out of Porscha. Right when I was about to take my knife and slit her throat, I felt someone patting my arm and saying my name. When I opened my eyes, it was Nico.

"Baby, are you OK?" I shrugged my arm wanting him to get out my face and mad that he interrupted me right before I was about to end Porscha's life. "I came home as soon as I heard what happened."

"I'm fine. You need to go check on yo' bitch."

"Precious, what are you talking about?"

"Don't play wit' me, Nico. I know all about you and Porscha. That's why yo' phone always be going to voice mail 'cause you laying up wit' that bitch. Nigga, fuck you." I pulled the blankets over my head so I could go back to sleep.

Nico grabbed the covers and threw them on the floor.

"I told you about that slick-ass mouth of yours," he said, pointing his finger at me like he was scolding me. Now Nico had totally disrupted my sleep and I was wide awake, ready for war.

"I don't give a fuck whether you like what is coming out my mouth or not. You running round here fucking that cunt, and then the dumb bitch wanna step to me at the club. You lucky I didn't kill the bitch."

"Precious, I'm not fucking that girl. I barely know the chick. Whatever she told you was a lie."

"Nico, you must think you dealing wit' a straight fool. Who's the one that called you about the fight I was in?"

Nico paused for a minute because my question caught him off guard.

"Inga called Ritchie and told him, and then he told me."

I just nodded my head as I walked to my purse to get my cell phone.

"Who you calling?"

"Inga. I'ma ask her if she called Ritchie and told him what happened."

Nico grabbed the phone out my hand, so I went and picked up the cordless and he grabbed that too.

"What the fuck you need to call Inga for? There is no reason to get her in the middle of our shit."

"Bitch, you put her in the middle. You know damn well you didn't find out from Ritchie. That trifling Porscha called you crying the blues, and that's how yo' lyin' ass found out what happened. I'm done wit' yo' punkass. Go be wit' her, 'cause I won't have no problem replacing yo' bitch ass."

Nico grabbed me by my throat and slammed me against the wall. His eyes were blood shot red and beads of sweat was gathered on his forehead. He was trying to instill fear in me, but the shit wasn't working. I could really give a fuck. This nigga was a clown as far as I was concerned.

"Precious, first of all get all that leaving and being with the next man out of your head. We family now. It's 'til death do us part."

I'm sorry I had to grab on you like this, but you was flying off the handle, and I need your full attention. Precious, I'm sorry. I did fuck around with that girl, Porscha, but it was only a couple of times, nothing serious. She was out of line for even crossing your path, let alone saying a word to you, and she will be dealt with accordingly. But, baby, you can't let these scandalous hoes come in and ruin our happy home. They just jealous and sitting around waiting and plotting to take your place. You smarter than that. You can't let that happen.

I'm going to let go of your neck, but you have to promise me that you'll calm down and be mature about this shit."

I nodded my head yes to let Nico know I wouldn't black out on his ass when he let me go.

"So what you want me to do, Nico? Act like didn't noth ing happen between you and that bitch?"

"Precious, I know that's easier said then done, but I'm begging you to be the bigger person and let it go. I promise I won't fuck with her ever again. I made a mistake. I'm a man. I can admit that. I'm asking for your forgiveness. I promise I'll make it up to you."

Nico's words sounded sincere but the damage was done. He would've been better off denying the shit to the bitter end. Now I knew for a fact that he played me out with the crumb snatcher, and he had to be punished. I already smacked Porscha upside her head, and I had no doubt that Nico would rough her up pretty good too, so she was taken care of. But if Nico thought he was just gonna slide through this like the snake that he was, he was in for a rude awak ing. I would play along like it was all good in our hood, but a bitch was about to make a move, one that Nico would never forget.

For the next month, Nico bent over backwards, trying to make up for the Porscha fiasco. First, he bought me the new CLS500 that I was dying to have. Then he bought me a diamond-face Chopard watch during our trip to LA for a shopping spree on Rodeo Drive. I had never even heard of that street before.

I spotted all sorts of celebrities that I'd seen on televi sion and in magazines. I felt like I was in Wonderland. Fi nally, we went to Antigua for a week, and while sitting on the terrace at our hotel suite, Nico got down on one knee and proposed with a rock that even Lil' Kim would have to respect. Even with all that, nothing had changed as far as I was concerned. Yeah, I accepted Nico's proposal, and as far as he knew, all was forgiven. But, I was secretly planning the demise of Nico Carter.

The day after we got back from Antigua, I got dressed and headed out that evening to a lounge called Rain. I had a seat at the end of the bar so I could get a clear view of my target. From what Inga told me, I knew that every Tuesday night around ten o'clock, Ritchie came here for a couple of me that as far as she knew, Nico never came with him.

About twenty minutes after I arrived, because I purposely got there early, Ritchie came sauntering in solo. I knew he hadn't noticed me, so I walked around the back in the direction of the ladies room. When I saw where he positioned himself at the bar, I walked in a path that he would have to see me. As I made my way closer to him, I pretended to be looking in my purse for something. When I got right in front of his chair, Ritchie grabbed my arm.

"Precious, what you doing in here?"

I put my head up as if in shock to see him.

"Oh, what up, Ritchie? I was supposed to meet my girl, Tina here for a drink, but she just called and said she wasn't gonna make it. So I just went to the ladies room, and now I'm heading out."

"Since you already here, why don't you have a drink with me? Unless you in a hurry."

I looked at my watch as if I might have some place else to be. "I guess I have time for one drink." Four drinks later, Ritchie was spilling his guts and had his hand on my thigh. I knew that fake-ass nigga always wanted to fuck me, so his behavior wasn't surprising.

"Precious, you know the only reason I fucked wit' Inga was to get under your skin."

"For real? Why was you tryna get under my skin?" I questioned as if I didn't know what was up.

"You always acted so damn uppity like a nigga was trash. I knew fucking wit' yo' best friend would drive you crazy. 'Cause in all honesty, I wanted you. Inga is cool, but I settled since I couldn't have what I really wanted. If you was mine, I would treat you so good, Precious." I would neva play you out wit' a tired hoe like Porscha. I told Nico what a dumb ass he was for doing that shit to you," Ritchie added, thinking that shit would impress me. Ritchie was a man, just like Nico, and he would put his dick in the next bitch too. I always knew Ritchie was jealous of Nico, and before I cared out of concern for Nico, but now I cared for other reasons. I was going to use it to play right into what I needed him for.

"I appreciate you looking out for me, Ritchie. I'll admit I was a little hard on you, but I think it was because I was attracted to you too. I did feel some kinda way when you started dating Inga."

"I knew it, I knew it," he belted as he slammed his fist on the bar. "Baby, I knew you wanted me just as much as I wanted you."

Ritchie was a bigger clown than I thought. Even though in my mind the relationship between Nico and I was over, he was still a way better man than Ritchie could ever be.

"Ritchie, why don't we leave here so we can have some privacy. I would hate for one of Nico's people to spot us."

"Fuck Nico. He don't run me."

"Baby, I know, but he is still my man. I don't want there to be no problems."

"If I have my way he won't be your man for long."

With that Ritchie and I exited the lounge. I followed him in my car as we headed over to his place. I didn't waste no time putting it on Ritchie. I planned on riding his dick real hard for a good ten minutes so he would cum fast, and then break the fuck out. But Ritchie wanted to try and se duce a bitch. He laid me on his bed and ate my pussy for about fifteen minutes, trying to make me have an orgasm.

I guess he thought it would get me open on him. But, un fortunately, he couldn't even eat coochie better than Nico. Trying to speed the process up, I started faking having an orgasm so he would get his head out my pussy. I had to be home in an hour, 'cause I didn't want Nico to start getting suspicious and asking me a million questions. Finally, we got down to it and I had that nigga screaming my name. Inga was right. Ritchie was working with a nicesized tool, but he still disgusted me, so I couldn't enjoy it.

It didn't matter because this was work, so I treated it accordingly. He lasted five minutes longer than I expected, but once he came he was out like a light. After fixing my self up, I jumped in my car and went home.

When I got there Nico was still out so I took a shower and went to bed. The next morning I heard Nico on the phone yelling at somebody. He slammed his cell shut and threw it on the bed. "Baby, what's wrong?"

"Ritchie stupid ass. He was supposed to handle some shit for me last night, but he said he fell asleep. Ritchie's my right hand man. How the fuck is he gonna slack off when it comes to making money?"

"Don't get yourself so worked up. It'll be alright." Nico was sitting on the edge of the bed and I crawled over and began giving him a massage. "Relax."

"Precious, that feels so good," he moaned. "Yeah right there."

"Good. I wanna take your mind off everything," I said as I stopped massaging his shoulders and massaged his manhood with my mouth. He was moaning and pulling my hair tightly because it was feeling so good to him. I couldn't help but wonder if he moaned the same way when Porscha was deep throatin' his dick.

I couldn't front that shit was eating me up. I saw the bitch, and no, she didn't look better than me, and no, she didn't have a better body than me. But I had to question if she could fuck better than me. Only Nico knew the answer to that, and of course, he wasn't going to give it.

This was all the more reason I had to bring him to his knees, because this nigga had me questioning myself as a woman. And if the next bitch pussy was better than mine. That was too many things. But I would never share all these insecurities with Nico. This was pain I would bear alone.

My plan was to convince him that all was forgiven and forgotten. He would believe that all this drama only made our bond tighter, and no matter what, I would ride for him. That way, Nico will never be prepared when it all fell down.

Somebody's Gotta Die

Ritchie and I began having secret sexual tryst three times a week. If he had his way, it would've been everyday. He kept demanding that I stop dealing with Nico and be his girl. Ritchie had lost his mind. His ego and being pussy whipped was getting the best of him.

I was not about to let that fuck up my plans, so I had to constantly stroke his ego and tell him that I needed more time. He didn't even care that his friendship with Nico would be over, because he was never Nico's friend any way. I explained to him how Inga would be devastated, and although he didn't give a fuck about Nico, I didn't want to hurt Inga. Which was true. Inga was just an innocent casu alty in all this. When shit did blow up, I hoped she would understand and not take it personal.

"Where you going?" Nico asked as I grabbed the keys to my car.

"I'm picking up Inga so we can have a girls' day to gether."

"Oh cool. Call me later on."

"I will. Maybe you and Ritchie can hook up wit' us later and we can all have dinner or something," I suggested so I could get further insight into how their friendship was go ing, although I pretty much had an idea.

"Nah, that's not gonna work. Ritchie ain't been himself lately. We having major problems on a business level, so I definitely don't want to deal with him right now on a per sonal one."

"OK. I hope ya work things out soon," I said, leaving the room with a smile on my face. When I got in the car, I blasted The Game's CD and turned to track 17 *"Don't Worry"*, with Mary J. Blige. That was my shit. It's about a girl who holds it down while her nigga is locked up. That's the strongest kind of hood love. I thought Nico and I shared that, but he fucked it all up.

Inga was already outside, standing with a frown on her face when I pulled up. "What's wrong wit' you?" I asked right after she shut the door.

"Ritchie dumb ass. He been so anal lately. Every time I ask him for something, he bite my head off. He didn't even want to give me no money to go shopping. He only budged when I told him I was going wit' you. You know he didn't want to feel embarrassed and you run and tell Nico he's a cheap fuck. But still, I shouldn't have to go through all them type of changes. He don't hardly even fuck me no more. I believe that nigga might be open on some other bitch, 'cause his attitude is stank as shit. But whoever she is gonna be mad about it, cause I'm pregnant."

I damn near crashed into the dollar bus when Inga said that shit. "Pregnant? You sure?"

"Girl, yes, two months. I took the home test and went to the clinic yesterday to be sure."

"Did you tell Ritchie yet?"

"Nope."

"Inga, do you really wanna have that nigga's baby? You just said ya having problems and you think he's open off some other chick."

"I know, but the baby might make him get his act to gether. Shit, we eighteen now. Most bitches 'round here 'un had their first seed by the time their fourteen.Ritchie and Nico are both like ten years older than us. It's time for them to start a family. I know Nico gotta be tryna make you have his baby."

"Yeah, but I'm not ready for all that."

"What you waiting for? Nico Carter is the biggest hus tler in Brooklyn, if not New York. Not only that, he tryna marry you and you got that big ass rock sittin' on your en gagement finger. You betta go 'head and have that nigga's seed. When I become Ritchie's baby mama, he ain't gon' have no choice but to take care of me and his child. I'm sick of living in these projects anyway."

"Damn Inga, I don't have a good feeling about this though. I don't know if tryna lock this nigga down wit' a baby is the right move. You might end up only fucking your self. A nigga ain't gotta walk around wit' his belly poked out for all those months. Then when the load drops, you the one that gotta change them shitty pampers and stay up all times of the night until you get the baby back to sleep. All while Ritchie will still be running the streets and fucking mad other bitches, who ain't got no baby to watch. So while you think you trapping him, you only trapping yourself. And if you think that paper gonna be right, don't forget, at the end of the day, Ritchie is a street nigga. His money is illegal. It ain't like you got his Social Security number and you can take his black ass to court and ball out on a whole bunch of child support."

"I hear you, Precious, but as you know, I ain't gotta whole pile of options. I have a better chance of Ritchie staying with me if I have his baby. A nigga be having a soft spot for they first born, especially if it's a boy. Plus, girl, the baby will be cute 'cause Ritchie got that pretty hair. You'll see. Once the baby is born, he'll always have a reason to come back to me."

"Yeah, well, that's the same thing that every other baby mama living in these projects thought. But once little Ray Ray got about three and his daddy ain't nowhere to be seen, the only thing they be waiting on is that government check and food stamps. I would hate for you to be one of them, Inga."

"It'll be different for me. Trust me. Ritchie will come around."

The news that Inga just dropped on me could've easily put a monkey wrench in my plans, but I refused to let it. I told Inga from day one not to get caught up in Ritchie, let alone have a baby with him. Her stupidity wasn't going to interfere with my scheme.

After I dropped Inga back at her apartment, I stopped by my moms' crib to leave her some money and make sure won't no bum nigga residing with her. When I got to my car, another car pulled up beside me, and Ritchie was on the passenger side. The guy driving was on his cell phone. "What's up, baby? What you doing over here?"

"I was just buying some weed." I didn't want Ritchie to know that my moms lived over here just in case things didn't work out the way I planned. His silly ass might have come over, trying to shake my mom's down.

"Oh, I could've gave you some," he said smirking. "Am I gonna see you later on?"

"I'm not sure. Nico been trippin' about why I be gone so much lately." When I was about to say something else, I noticed the guy in the driver's seat flip his phone close. I didn't want no strangers hearing shit I had to say.

For some reason though, the dude seemed familiar to me, but I couldn't put my finger on where I knew him from. I figured he worked for Nico, and I might have seen him talking to Nico on the block. That was, until he turned his head to retrieve something from the backseat of the car. Suddenly I recognized the unforgettable scar engraved on the left side of his cheek. The dude probably didn't know who I was, because when he put the gun to the back of my head, my hair was pulled back in a tight bun. Right now, my hair was hanging loose and curly. I did my best not to let the shock of seeing Azar's killer show on my face.

"So you gon' try to see me, or what?"

"I'll definitely try," I said, absorbing all the crazy thoughts that were going through my mind.

"Yo, man, you seen that little bag of weed I had in the car?" Azar's killer asked Ritchie. Hearing his voice brought back my close encounter with death.

"Yeah, I put it in the glove compartment, but Butch, you don't need to be smoking 'round here. Them boys in the uniforms is out. Hold up a minute." *Butch, that's Azar's killer name*, I thought to myself.

"Ritchie, I gotta go, I'll call you later. I promise."

"You better," he yelled as Butch drove off.

I couldn't believe Ritchie was hanging with Butch. They had to be doing business together, but I doubted Nico knew anything about it. But whatever it was, it had to be no good. Butch was sheisty. The reason all that shit went down between him and Azar was because they fronted on his money and they stole his drugs. I needed to further investigate, and I knew exactly who to see. I went straight to the detailing shop to have a conversation with Boogie. I parked on the side until the last couple of cars were pulling off. When I went inside, as always, Boogie was happy to see me.

"How's my ghetto Queen?" he asked giving me a hug.

"I'm good," I said, not wasting no time. "I need to speak to you about something."

"Should've known. Follow me." Boogie escorted me to the back where his private office was. I didn't want to speak to him in front of the girl working behind the cashier desk. She could be the hood snitch for all I knew. "What you need, Precious?"

"Do you know a dude by the name of Butch?"

"Butch with the scar on his face?"

"Yeah, him."

"Yeah, I know him. I know you ain't fucking with that nigga. I heard you and Nico was engaged to get married."

"We are," I said, flashing my finger with the five-carat rock. "Just tell me what you know about him, Boogie."

"Bad news. He started off as a two-bit stickup kid, then graduated to robbing niggas for large amount of drugs. Some how, even with his ruthless ways, he stayed in the game with out getting killed and managed to come up as a major playa now. But real official hustlers don't fuck with him. He deals with a lot of these young boys that's coming up. Between me and you, some say he's the one that killed Azar."

That last bit of information I knew as a fact, and the rest just confirmed my suspicions. Ritchie was definitely up to something, and I had a feeling it meant bad news for Nico.

For the next couple of days, I tried to eavesdrop on as many of Nico's conversations as possible. Since he rarely dis cussed business with me, on my own, I had to see if Ritchie had brought Butch into the fold, or if he was still playing it close to the chest. He knew I wouldn't ask Nico about Butch, because then I would have tell Nico I saw Butch with Ritchie, and that would open up a whole other can of worms.

I considered getting the information out of Ritchie, but al though he was a snake he wasn't stupid. I ask one too many questions, and the red flags would start going up.

Getting the inside scoop on what he had planned wasn't to protect Nico. It was to make sure it didn't fuck up my own plans. Whatever Ritchie was scheming on definitely meant danger for Nico, because in this business there could only be one king. As I stood by the double doors to the den where Nico conducted the majority of his business calls, the home phone rang. I knew it had to be for me since ev erybody called Nico on his cell.

"Hello," I said, irritated that my spying was interrupted.

"Precious," I heard what sounded like Inga's voice. She was crying and yelling at the same time. Instantly I thought that Ritchie sold me out and confessed everything to her.

"Inga, are you alright?"

"No, would you please come get me? I finally told Ritchie about the baby and he flipped the fuck out."

"Don't say no more. I'm on my way." I was relieved Ritchie hadn't blown up my spot, but I was also concerned about Inga. I didn't want to disturb Nico, so I wrote him a quick note tell ing him that I had to step out and would call him.

Inga was hysterical when I picked her up. "Precious, I can't believe Ritchie's foul ass. When I told him I was pregnant he smacked the shit outta me. Do you see this bruise on the side of my face," she said, pointing to a big red mark on her cheek. "He said he ain't gon' be trapped by a baby wit' a bitch he don't even want. Then he told me that if I didn't have an abortion, he would cut the baby out of me himself. Can you believe that monster?"

"Inga, I'm sorry. So what you gon' do?"

"I don't know. I really want to have my baby, Precious. Not just because of Ritchie, but I ain't got nothing else go ing on wit' my life. Having a baby will change all that."

"On the real, Inga. A baby ain't nothing but another mouth to feed. Do you really want that type of responsibil ity, especially since Ritchie don't want no parts of it?"

"Fuck Ritchie. I don't want nothing but his money to take care of the baby anyway. You were right about him, Precious. He's a snake." From there, Inga had nothing but diarrhea of the mouth. "I don't know if you've noticed, but lately Ritchie and Nico ain't been hanging. Ritchie been kicking it wit' some new kid named Butch." Before Inga had my attention, but after she mentioned Butch's name, she had my undivid-ed attention.

"Who's Butch?" I probed to see if Inga could divulge any new information to me.

"Exactly," Inga said, looking at me to let me know we were on the same page. "I asked Ritchie the same thing, and he told me to mind my business. That made me even more curious. Last night when Ritchie thought I was sleep, I heard a knock at the door. At first I thought it was a bitch because Ritchie don't like nobody to know where he lives. I went to the top of the stairs being nosey, and I caught sight of a nigga with the most horrific scar on the side of his face.

When I heard Ritchie call him Butch, I realized that was the nig-ga he been on the phone wit' all the time. Precious, I swear them nig-gas was talking about fucking Nico over on some serious paper. I'm talking a million dollars. Ritchie tried to say that was a drop in the bucket for Nico, but it would start an all out war between him and some other nig gas, because Nico don't take nobody getting over on him and his money."

It was all making sense now.

"Ritchie was trying to take Nico out without getting any blood on his own hands. Butch was his partner in all this. They probably had big plans to run every block Nico had on lockdown together."

"When was all this supposed to be going down?"

"I'm not sure, and after the fight we got into this morn ing, I have no way of finding out. But you betta warn Nico that Ritchie's slimy ass is out to get him."

"I will," I said, knowing I had no intentions of alerting Nico to the information. "With the dime you just dropped on me, I need to get home and talk to Nico. Here's some money so you can stay at a hotel for a couple of days and get some other things you might need."

"Thanks, Precious," Inga said as I handed her eight hundred dollars.

"Inga, keep a low profile for the next few days, and if you speak to Ritchie, don't lose your cool and tell him any of the shit you just told me."

"I got you."

Right after I dropped Inga off at the hotel, my cell start ed ringing and it was Ritchie.

"Hello."

"Baby, what up?"

"You tell me."

"You, me. I want to take you on a vacation this weekend."

"Ritchie, I would love to, but you know Nico ain't having it." Today was Sunday, which meant Ritchie planned on having Nico out the way by the end of the week if he was planning a vacation with me.

"Baby, do you love me?"

"Ritchie, you know I do."

"Then let me handle Nico. Just be ready to leave Friday."

"Well, can I see you tonight? I miss you."

"I'ma be tied up for the next couple of days, but defi nitely Friday. But I'll call you."

I began wondering exactly when Ritchie started plan ning the murder of his best friend. Was it before or after he fell in love with the pussy? Right now it didn't matter. I had to come up with something fast. I had been waiting to drop the bomb on Nico when I had a hundred thousand dollars stashed, but now I had an opportunity to walk away with a cool million. With that type of money, I could leave Brook lyn and start my life over.

I was relieved when I saw Nico's car parked outside. I needed to pick his brain to see if he had any idea that Ritchie was plotting to set him up. Nico didn't hear me when I came inside, so I walked quietly where I could hear him clearly on the phone from the den. The door was open, so I stood on the side of the wall.

He was saying something about this new diesel connection Ritchie hooked him up with, and they had the potential to make a shit load of money together. He went on to say that the first go round, he was starting small with just a million worth to see how good their product sells on the streets. Then he told whoever he was talking to that he had a lot of moves to make tonight so could he stop by the warehouse and bring him the million over and he would keep it at his crib since he and Ritchie were hooking up early tomorrow to meet with the new connect and make the exchange.

I knew exactly where Nico kept his money stashed. He usually had no more than fifty thousand dollars in the house, but I guess he figured that the million would only be here overnight so it didn't matter. This was working out better than I'd hoped. As Nico finished up his call, I tiptoed upstairs so he wouldn't think I heard anything.

When Nico finally came upstairs, I was just getting out the shower and he was obviously surprised to see me.

"Baby, I didn't even know you were home," he said as I saw his dick rise up from looking at my naked wet body.

"Oh. When I got home I didn't see you so I just came up here to take a shower and go to bed. I'm a little tired."

"I hope not too tired to let me get inside of you." Nico picked me up and led me to the bed. I decided to put it on him extra good since it would be the last time he'd ever feel the inside of my pussy. After we finished, I had to admit that nobody could fuck me like Nico, but oh well, sex isn't everything.

Right when I stood up to go to the bathroom, I heard the door bell ring. "Baby, you want me to get the door."

"Nah, that's just Tommy dropping off some paperwork. I'll be back."

Yea, some paperwork in the form of a million dollars, I thought to myself. It didn't take long for Nico to come back upstairs. "That was fast."

"I told you Tommy just had to drop off some paperwork."

"Oh. You wanna go to the movies tonight?" I asked, knowing he already had plans but wanting to see what they were.

"Baby, I can't tonight but maybe tomorrow."

"Oh, you hanging out wit' Ritchie?"

"Nah, I have some business to handle."

"How are things between ya anyway, is there still tension?"

"Everything is cool. We worked it out. Ritchie snapped out of whatever funk he was in. You know we brothers; it's 'til death do us part."

When Nico finally headed out, I immediately started getting my shit together because I was working on borrowed time. I wasn't sure if I was going to be able to come back for the rest of my belongings so I gathered up as much of my stuff as I could in order of importance, starting with all my jewelry (including Nico's), furs, designer bags, shoes and then clothes. Once I got all that in the car, I went in the basement where Nico kept his money. He had no idea I knew where he stashed it since I never came down here. I actually found it by accident when Nico was out of town and there was a power outage. At that time, when I went in the basement with the flashlight, I tripped and found the box switch, and the money and a gun. There wasn't much paper so I left it there. Plus, I didn't want Nico to know I knew just in case I had to take it for whatever reason in the future.

Well, that reason had presented itself. The money was wrapped in bundles stashed inside a duffel bag. I grabbed it and the gun just in case I needed protection. After do ing one more house search to make sure I wasn't forgetting anything, I headed out.

When I got in the car, I called Inga to see if she heard from Ritchie and she told me no, so then I called him. When he answered he sounded like he was in the middle of some thing. "Ritchie, I need to see you."

"Precious, I'm busy right now. You gonna have to wait."

"I can't. It's important. It's about Nico."

"Oh shit. Did you tell him about us?"

"Listen, I need to see you," I said, not giving anymore information so he would bring his ass on.

"Alright, meet me at my crib in a half."

I knew he was shittin' bricks, hoping I didn't blow his spot to Nico and mess up the bloodshed he was plotting to start on his own. Luckily, it was dark outside so I parked my car across the street waiting for Ritchie to come home. When he pulled up I immediately called Nico.

"What's up, Baby?" Nico said, when he answered the phone.

"I was calling to tell you bye."

"What you mean, 'bye'? Where you going?"

"I can't do this no more, Nico."

"Do What? Stop talking in riddles, Precious."

"After we got back from Antigua I tried to put the whole Porscha situation behind me, but I couldn't. The only per son that was able to console me was Ritchie."

"What the fuck did you say?"

"Nico, I've been seeing Ritchie for a few months now, and we're in love. I'm pregnant and the baby is his," I said with a slight sniffle in my voice as if holding back tears.

"Precious, don't fucking play with me. This shit ain't funny."

"It's not meant to be. I've packed my stuff. I'm leaving you."

"Where the fuck are you right now?"

"On my way to Ritchie's."

"I'm going to give you one more chance to take all this bullshit back before I lose it."

"I can't take it back, Nico, 'cause it's the truth. Why do you think Ritchie was showing you so much shade? He couldn't stand the fact that I refused to leave you. But once I found out I was pregnant, I decided it was time to let you go."

"That might be my seed. How you know I'm not the father?"

"I just know," I said, sounding confident.

"Then you a dead bitch," Nico said and hung up the phone.

I pulled my car in front of Ritchie's house in plain view for Nico to see. I then walked across the street and hid be side a house under construction.

Within fifteen minutes, Nico flew down the street and jumped out his truck with gun in hand. He paused for a quick second at the side of my car and kicked it before running up Ritchie's front stairs. He banged on the door with gun drawn, and when Ritchie opened it probably thinking it was me, all I heard was Nico screaming, "Where the fuck is Precious at?" before the door slammed shut.

I was waiting to hear the first gunshot before I placed my next phone call, when I noticed a familiar looking car coming down the street. When I realized it was Butch, I had to act fast. There was no way I could let him interfere with what was going on in Ritchie's crib. I snuck around the back of the house under construction and ducked behind another car before sneaking across the street. I waited until Butch got under the darkness of Ritchie's walkway before I stopped him.

"Excuse me, Butch, but where do you think you going?"

He turned around slowly and from the streetlight he tried to get a look at my face. "Who are you?"

"I'm sure you don't remember me, but I'll neva forget your face." I had my hands behind my back, holding the gun I took from Nico.

Butch's intuition start kicking in and he knew by the expression on my face I wasn't happy to see him. He in stinctively put his hand in the back of his pants, feeling for his own gun.

"Looking for something? Outta all the times to forget your girl, you picked the wrong occasion. This is for Azar, bitch," I said as I raised my gun and let off three shots to the chest.

As the bullets exploded leaving golfball sized holes in his body, Butch finally fell backwards, landing on the bot tom step. I walked up to him and put one more bullet in his face for good measure.

Right then I heard the shots I had been waiting for ring ing out of

Ritchie's house. I left Butch leakin' on the side of the curb, ran to my car and dialed 911 from a burner I purchased as I drove off. "Yes, I heard several gunshots coming from 218 Adelphi Street. I think somebody might have been murdered."

My heart was beating so fast. It wasn't because I had just killed somebody; it was just the excitement of seeing my plan come together. I prayed that the gunshots I heard coming from Ritchie's house were that of Nico murdering him. If they weren't, everything would be ruined. I wanted Ritchie dead and Nico alive to suffer being locked up.

Patiently Waiting

Before I was two blocks away from Ritchie's house, I saw police cars speeding down the street. I knew within minutes the street would be blocked off, and at least one murder investigation would be underway, hopefully two. Although I liked having the gun I took from Nico for protection, I had to get rid of it now since Butch's body was on it and probably a few more.

I drove across the bridge to the city and tossed the gun in the Hudson River. I then drove back to Brooklyn and went to the hotel where Inga was staying. By this time it was midnight, but I knew Inga stayed up late. When I knocked on her room door, she was up watching a movie and munching on snacks.

"Girl, I was surprised when you called saying you were on your way over. Nico gon' start trippin' if you don't go home soon."

"I know, so I'm not gonna stay that long. I just wanted to bring you something."

"What?"

"Take this," I said, handing her an envelope I had in my Louis Vuitton backpack. Her mouth dropped when she opened the envelope and saw all the money. "That's fifty thousand dollars to maintain yourself for a minute. Here are the keys to my apartment on Riverside Drive. I already paid the rent up for a year so you don't have to put no mon ey towards that. Honestly, Inga, I don't want you to have Ritchie's baby for a lot of reasons, but if you decide to, this will give you a start."

"Damn, Precious, you some type of friend," Inga said, giving me a hug.

"Well, I better be going. You know how Nico can get."

I walked out of that hotel room not knowing when I would see Inga again. I didn't give Inga that money be cause I felt guilty about fucking with Ritchie. I just wanted her seed to be OK. I knew Inga would have that baby be cause she didn't understand the survival of the streets. Just because you come from the projects and see how hard it is to have something, it doesn't mean you comprehend the struggle. Inga never understood, but I hoped with the mon ey I gave her and the crib, she would try to give her baby a better life than the one we had growing up.

I needed to get out of Brooklyn fast, so I took it over to Jersey. I'd only been there a couple of times, but I did remember it was nothing like New York. I checked in at the Hyatt Regency in Jersey City. When I got in my room, it had a banging view of the Hudson River, and I thought about Butch's murder weapon being somewhere in that big body of water.

I then got undressed, and since it was too late to watch the news, I took a hot shower and fell into a deep sleep. I didn't wake up until late in the afternoon, and the first thing I checked was my cell phone. I had no missed calls or mes sages. I opened my door to get the paper, but it was just the local Star Ledger. They definitely wouldn't have Brooklyn news in there. Nothing was on television but soaps, "Judge Mathis" and talk shows. Waiting to see what happened was driving me crazy. I ordered room service thinking that eating some food would minimize my anxiety. Two more hours passed, and I decided I needed some fresh air. I also needed to find a storage place and meet up with a guy I knew to get another gun. With all the drama I had going on, it was imperative for me to keep protection on me.

Finding a place to put all my stuff until I figured out my next move was first on my list. I located a Storage USA and went in to fill out the application. Once I got the spot, I pur chased a lock and put the majority of my belongings in there, including my money. Last thing I wanted was to be caught with a million dollars, plus that shit felt like a ton of bricks.

Then I headed over to Harlem to meet up with this dude named Smokey. I used to fuck with one of his homeboys, but after he got locked up we still remained cool. Any weapon you needed, he could hook you up. I purchased another 9mm since I felt comfortable handling it, said my piece and broke out.

By the time I got back to my room, still no calls. I turned on the television to catch the six o'clock news not feeling optimistic I would find out anything, but then my patients paid off:

"This is Steve Douglass reporting live from Fort Greene. The house behind me," he turned, pointing his finger at what looked to be Ritchie's house, "Is the crime scene of a double homicide that occurred late last night in this upscale section of Brooklyn."

I held my breath, waiting to see who was the second person killed.

"The two male victims have yet to be identified, but the cops do have a suspect in custody. His name is Nico Carter, a purported notorious drug kingpin."

Not caring to hear anything else I switched off the tele vision and flopped down on the bed. "Hallelujah," I echoed as I spread my entire body across the bed. I finally felt some sort of justice. Even so, I wouldn't be completely satisfied until Nico was doing life behind bars. In one night I was able to get rid of the three people I hated most in this world. But the punishment Nico would soon endure was the sweet est. If the system prevailed, he would spend the rest of his life locked up, knowing his fiancée was fucking his best friend behind his back, and believing that I was actually pregnant by Ritchie. That was enough to make any man want to get a hold of a bed sheet and hang himself inside his jail cell. Nico had too much pride to ever commit sui cide, so he would have no choice but to spend his days and nights in confinement visualizing Ritchie twisting my back out and wondering if I screamed his name and called him daddy the way I did with him. Good for that motherfucker.

I was surprised that still nobody called me about Nico. I knew the streets had to be buzzing. The only person I really expected to call me was Inga. Boogie would never discuss that shit with me over the phone, so I decided to go see him first thing in the morning. He always got to work an hour before business officially opened. That night I went to bed early because tomorrow was going to be a long day.

When I arrived at Boogie's shop early in the morning, the door was locked. I knew he was the there because his red Deville was parked out front. I knocked for five min utes before he came to the door.

"What you doing here?" he questioned with a surprised look on his face. "I'd think you be at home waiting on a collect call from Nico."

"I haven't been staying there. I don't know exactly what went down, so I've been keeping on the low. That's why I came to see you, Boogie," I said, squeezing past him since he was blocking the door entrance.

"Sorry 'bout that," Boogie said, realizing I damn near had to knock him over to get inside. "From what I hear, it's not looking good for Nico. Supposedly the cops caught him at the scene of the crime with the murder weapon."

"On the news I saw that the murders took place at Ritchie's house, but they didn't say who the victims were."

"You haven't spoken to Nico?"

"No, I told you I haven't been home. The night it hap pened, Nico and I got in an argument, so I stayed at a hotel. I just heard about the murders yesterday."

"One of the men was Butch and the other one was Ritchie."

"Ritchie," I shrieked as if in shock. "Are the streets saying why?" In my mind I was finding it difficult to act as if this was all new to me. I hoped that Boogie didn't pick up on it.

"Word has it that Ritchie was working with Butch to cross Nico on some underhanded shit. Nico got word of it and finished them both off. What's puzzling is how Nico was so sloppy with it. He got many niggas on his payroll that murder for him like this," Boogie said, snapping his two fingers together. "Why he did the shit himself I have no idea. One thing I do know, it's not looking good for Nico Carter."

"Has he had a bail hearing?"

"I doubt it, but even so, they not setting no bail for that man. The local, state and Federal government has had a hardon for Nico for so many years. Never did they think they would get him for murdering his best friend. If they have their way, Nico Carter won't ever see the light of day."

"Thanks for the insight, Boogie, but I gotta be going. I need to stop by the house and pick up some things."

"You're taking this pretty well, Precious. You have to be worried about how you're going to maintain with Nico behind bars."

"Not really. Financially I'll be straight, especially if you help me out."

"What, you want your old job back?"

"That's funny, Boogie. You know I'm way past that."

"I thought so too, but how else can I help you?"

"I have some money stashed away, but I need to make it legiti-mate."

"Legitimate how?"

"You know, like a bank account. Maybe buy a house."

"A house? How much money we talking about?"

"A million dollars."

"How in the hell did you get hold of a million dollars? I don't want to know. The less I know the better. I'll help you, Precious, but it's gonna cost you."

"I know Boogie, this is business and you always want your cut."

"No doubt. I'll place a few phone calls. I should know something by tomorrow so stop back through in the eve ning around closing."

"Don't let anyone know you've seen me, Boogie, or about the million dollars."

"Who you trying to school? I know how to handle busi ness."

I gave Boogie a slight smile because he was the original playa in all this.

"By the way, how did the cops catch Nico at Ritchie's house?"

"An anonymous tip. I guess somebody had it in for Nico."

"I guess so," I said, walking out the door.

I was relieved to know that Nico hadn't leaked to the streets why he really killed Ritchie. Or maybe he hadn't spoken to anybody to inform them. But Nico was so pri vate, he rarely confided in anybody. Besides me, the closest person to him was Ritchie. He had no family. Right before I met him, his mother passed away. The only family he prob ably had right now was his attorney.

I decided that I would drive past our brownstone to see if the cops had blocked it off. I slowed down at the far end of the corner. There was no indication that the cops had shut it down, so I proceeded with caution moving forward.

Right then I noticed Tommy coming out the house, emptyhanded. I wondered if he'd spoken to Nico and came to retrieve the million dollars, or did he take it upon himself to get his hands on the money because Nico was locked up. I debated whether or not to pop up on him, but if he did speak to Nico, there was no telling what he was told to do to me.

When Tommy got in his truck and drove off, I left my car on the corner and crossed the street to do my own in vestigating. As I got closer to the front stairs, I immediately noticed the basement window was busted open. I wondered why our stateoftheart alarm system didn't go off when it happened, but I quickly remembered that when I bolted out the house that night, I forgot to turn it on. That moth erfucker Tommy didn't come on Nico's orders, he came to rob him. The reason I knew this was because if Nico had spoken to Tommy directly, he would've let him know where he kept the spare key hidden so he didn't come in this neighborhood busting windows out and possibly draw ing unnecessary attention to himself.

Without a second thought, I turned right back around and got in my car. Before I could finish my thoughts, my cell phone started ringing and it was Inga. "What's up, Inga?" I said calmly. I wasn't in the mood to speak to her, but I needed to hear as much street gossip as possible.

"Precious, did you hear about Ritchie?" Inga bawled. By the tears that were obviously flowing, she sounded as if she just heard about the murders.

"Yeah, you just hearing about it?"

"Hmm hun. That night when I saw you, the next morn ing I had to go to the hospital. I was having real bad cramps in my stomach and there was a little bit of blood. I just got out today."

"Did you lose the baby?" I prayed the answer would be yes.

"No, the baby is fine. The doctor told me I'ma have to take it easy throughout my pregnancy."

"With Ritchie being dead you still want to have his baby?" I asked while saying to myself, this is a dumb bitch.

"Yeah. I know Ritchie was foul, but I loved him. I guess you told Nico that Ritchie was tryna to set him up. That's why he killed him."

"Inga, I neva even had a chance. When I got home that night, Nico was already gone. I didn't even know what happened until I heard it on the news."

"Well, he must of found out some other way. Ritchie's stupid ass should've neva crossed Nico. But I can't believe Nico's in jail, you must be devastated, Precious. I know how much you love him."

"So much is going on I really haven't had time to take it all in."

"Have you spoken to Nico?"

"No, I haven't been staying at home. I wasn't sure if the cops was gonna run up in there or something."

"That's true. I heard Nico's supposed to have a bail hearing to-morrow morning. From what I hear, they doubt he gonna get bail."

"Where you hear that from?"

"This girl named Vanika."

"Who that?"

"She Corey's sister. Corey's a little nigga. He works for one of Nico's street lieutenants."

"What else she say?"

"Not too much. Just that everybody stressed 'cause wit' Nico locked up and Ritchie dead; they don't have nobody to lead the way. Them two was the only ones that dealt one on one wit' the connect. Ain't nobody heard from Nico. They don't know if the police ain't let-ting him make no phone calls or what. That's why I was wondering if you spoke to him."

"Not yet."

"So are you gonna go to court for his bail hearing tomorrow?"

"I don't know. Nico might want me to keep a low profile."

"That's true. Wit' Nico locked up I'llunderstand if you'll need your apartment back."

"Nah, don't worry about it. I'll make some other ar rangements."

"I know you ain't going back to your moms' crib."

"Nope." Inga had me feeling she was the police with all these simpleass questions she was spitting at me.

"So what do..."

"Yo, I gotta go. I'll be in touch," I said, abruptly ending the call. There was nothing left to discuss with Inga because she gave me all the pertinent information she had. The rest of the conversation would've consisted of her picking my brain, which was out of the question.

The first thing I did when I got back to the hotel room was turn to the news. I knew they probably wouldn't have any new information about the case, but I had to do something to calm my nerves. I was pacing the floor back and forth, wondering if I should go to court in the morning. I prayed they wouldn't set bail for Nico, and I needed to hear firsthand.

I arrived at the downtown Brooklyn courthouse early that morning. Once I found the courtroom where Nico's hearing would be held, I took a seat in the back. It was hot as shit in the building. It was the middle of winter and cold as hell outside, but they had it blasting to the point I was getting dizzy. I took off my coat and wanted to take off my hat, but I didn't want to be seen, especially by Nico.

More and more people started coming in filling up the wooden benches, then one particular person caught my eye. She strutted to the front of the courtroom and took a seat behind the defense table. Even to court, that chicken head bitch Porscha didn't know how to represent. She had on some lowcut red dress that was made so cheaply that if you pulled one piece of thread, the whole ensemble would fall apart. I so badly wanted to jump across these benches and finish where I left off, but I had to remind myself I was keeping a low profile. Seeing Porscha confirmed that Nico was getting exactly what he deserved. He was still seeing that bitch after he swore he was done with her. Nig gas weren't shit.

Finally at a quarter to ten they brought Nico out. When they called his name, Porscha sat up extra straight and smiled at him like she was his wife. Yeah bitch, you can do that bid wit' him too like you his wife, I thought to myself.

When the Judge called his name, Nico stood next to his high profile Jewish attorney, looking prouder than ever, even in his orange jumpsuit.

The prosecutor argued that bail shouldn't be set for Nico, not only because of the heinous nature of the crime, but because it was also a double homicide. He also stated that Nico was a flight risk, and due to his illegal drug activ ity, was a menace to society.

Nico's attorney argued that Nico was an upstanding busi nessman in the community and that he acted in self defense.

They went back and forth, and finally the judge sided with the prosecution and denied bail.

Nico's attorney immediately demanded that his client wanted a speedy trial.

Once the judge gave his ruling, I quietly got up to leave when I heard someone say, "Precious, is that you?" I tried to step up my speed, but then they got louder. "Precious Cummings, is that you?" I turned to see who had blown my cover, and instantly Nico and I made eye con tact. If looks could kill I would've died that morning in the downtown Brooklyn courthouse. Nico stared at me until the bailiff took him away.

"Don't you remember me, Precious? I used to keep you sometimes when your mother had to work."

"Yes," I said, nodding my head and wanting to punch the older lady in her mouth. "Hi, Ms. Duncan. How are you?"

"I'm good. I haven't seen you since you were a little girl. You have grown up to be so beautiful."

"Thank you," I said, trying to edge myself out the door.

"I hope you not in no trouble, being down here in the courthouse and all."

I wanted to be like, "I can ask you the same question," but I didn't want to start a scene. "No, I was just checking up on a friend of mine. I really have to be going. I'll tell my mother I saw you."

"You do that now."

Breathing a sigh of relief to finally be leaving the in ferno, Porscha scandalous ass stopped me.

"What do you want?"

"I want to know why you came down here. You know Nico don't want to see you."

"Why is that?" I asked, wondering if he confided in her about my involvement with Ritchie.

"You know why."

Yeah, I did, but she obviously didn't or she would have been humming like the bird she was. "Listen, I'm not gonna discuss my relationship wit' my fiancée with you." I held up my engagement finger that still had the massive rock that Nico laced me with. "Whateva you got going on wit' him is cool 'cause you ain't nothing but a broke down, hag gard, bootleg version of what I'll neva be. So keep it moving in that ten dollar, which includes the cost of those patent leather shoes you rockin' ensemble, and step the fuck off before I wax that ass one more time."

"Ain't nobody stuttin' you, Precious. You a dead bitch. You a dead bitch," she repeated.

My natural reflex kicked in and I balled up my fist ready to Mike Tyson her ass, when a security guard who had been watching our argument unfold, stepped in and grabbed my arm mid-air." Miss, calm-down," the officer said, now holding both my arms gently.

"Nah, let her go. I wish you would put yo' hands on me, Precious!" Porscha raged, trying to egg me on.

"I'm going to ask you to leave this area now, before I cite you for disruption," he said as Porscha rolled her eyes and walked away.

I was breathing so hard. I felt like that bitch was threat ening my life. I was consumed with anger.

"Listen, you seem like a nice young lady so please calm down and leave without having another altercation with that woman. She's not worth it. Next time I might not be there to stop you, and it could be you in front of that judge.

I nodded my head, knowing what the security guard said was true. I got my bearings together and left.

Since I was in Brooklyn, I took a ride over to my moms' apartment to see how she was doing. When I unlocked the door, I immediately closed it and looked at the apartment number to make sure I was at the right place. I opened the door back up and was bugging at how clean the place was.

The walls were newly painted, the hardwood floors were in perfect condition and the whole apartment had new furniture. It didn't even look like the same place. I opened the refrigerator and not a bottle of liquor was in sight. Noth ing but juice, water, fruit and other healthy foods, which made me wonder if my moms had died and someone else took over her apartment.

"Precious, I wasn't expecting to see you today, but I'm glad you're here," I heard my moms say.

When I turned towards the door to answer her, my heart almost stopped. I stood speechless.

"Precious, are you OK?" my moms said repeatedly as she stroked my hair.

"What happened to you?"

"I took your advice and got myself together. The last time you were here, I decided to quit using cold turkey. I truly felt ashamed that day, Precious."

I couldn't get over how beautiful my moms looked. She picked up weight and her hourglass shape was still in tact. Her skin was glowing and her sandy brown hair was cut short and streaked with blonde highlights. It made her green eyes stand out even more. All the beauty that was hidden because of the drugs was now coming through. It was amazing. I just hugged her and wouldn't let go. For the first time in my life I had a mother.

For the rest of the day we sat down and talked to each other like human beings for the first time. Every word I said was brand new to my moms because she was hearing it with a clear mind, not one that was consumed with drugs. The six hours I spent with my mother were the happiest moments of my life.

"Momma, I have to meet with a friend of mine, but I'ma come back over when I'm done. You really look incredible. I'm so proud of you."

"Thank you. You be careful. I love you, Precious."

"I love you too."

My life finally had meaning. I decided that when I bought my house, I was bringing my mother with me. We could both leave Brooklyn and start over together. Maybe even open up a beauty salon or a nail shop together. We would be the flyest mother and daughter team ever.

Getting caught up in the future I was now planning, I looked at my watch and realized I only had an hour before I was supposed to meet up with Boogie. I needed to go all the way back to my storage spot in Jersey to get the cash I had to hit him off with. There was no way I was going to make it there and back in an hour, so I called Boogie and told him I would be an hour late. Luckily traffic wasn't that bad and I was making good time.

As I was coming back over the bridge, Inga's named popped up on my cell. I figured Porscha must've told Tani sha's cousin about our episode at the courthouse this morn ing and Inga was calling to get the dirt from me. "Hello."

"What up, Precious?"

"Nothing. Just handling some things. I'm kinda busy. What's up?"

"Oh, nothing. Where you at?"

"In the streets."

"Oh, you in Brooklyn?"

"Nah, that's not what I said. I'm in the streets," I re plied, feeling funny about how Inga was coming at me.

"So when you coming back over to Brooklyn, 'cause I wanted to see you?"

"I'm not sure. You haven't been staying at my place in Harlem."

"No. Wit' the pregnancy and all, my moms wanted me to be close by family."

"That's cool."

"Do you want to stop by and pick up your apartment keys since I won't be staying there?"

"I'm good. I have an extra set. Inga, I hate to cut this short, but like I said, I'm in the middle of handling some things. We'll get up later." That nauseated feeling was coming over me but I tried to shake it off as just being overwhelmed by seeing Nico and my encounter with Porscha.

When I pulled up to Boogie's shop it was almost eight o'clock. I parked around the back so nobody could see my car from the main road.

"What up, ghetto queen?" Boogie smiled and said when I walked in the door. I knew it was because of the 100 grand I agreed to pay him for having his people set all my shit up so my money would be clean.

"I know I'm late, but I hope yo' people still coming," I said, feeling anxious.

"No doubt. I got you covered. You got that money for me?"

"Of course. It's in the car. After we finish up I'll give it to you."

"Look at you, Precious, being all business-minded. You've come a long way."

I was looking out the window blinds, patiently wait ing for Boo gie's people to show up. "Who the peoples you dealing wit' on this anyway?"

"Oh, these my folks. They fuck with a cat who deal with a lot of major hustlers out here, getting they shit in order. When I told them it was a female looking to clean up a million dollars, they damn near had a heart attack."

"You told them my name?"

"Yeah, but they family. They know old school rules. They just wanted to make sure you weren't the police or nothing. It's not every day a woman comes through with that type of money to wash."

"So, what's the dude's name?"

"Who? My nephews'?"

"No, the dude yo' nephews fuck wit."

"Oh, I think they said his name is Tommy?"

Before I could vomit, I saw Tommy's truck pulling up in front of the shop. "Oh shit, Boogie."

"What's wrong, Precious."

"Boogie, this is a trap. Shit, fuck!"

"Stop tripping. I told you them my nephews."

"Boogie, Tommy used to work for Nico. I saw him leav ing our crib yesterday. He came there looking for the money." My hands were shaking as I ran to the door to lock it.

"Precious, you sure it's the same Tommy?"

"Yes, that's his truck outside right now. Come on, Boogie, let's go out the back. I parked my car out there. We can duck these mother-fuckers before they get inside."

But before we could take another step, the front door glass flew everywhere from the bullets that Tommy sprayed. Boo gie and I both threw our bodies down on the floor.

"Get the fuck up!" Tommy yelled as he and two other guys en-tered the shop.

"Where the fuck is the million dollars, Precious?"

Boogie stood up before I did and recognized the two other men as his nephews. "Lamont, Andre, what ya doing? You got yo' friend fucking up my shop. What is this all about?"

"Listen, Boogie," the taller, darker nephew said. "We ain't got no beef wit' you, but this a million dollars we talking 'bout. The three of us gonna split that shit."

"Lamont Johnson, I know you ain't telling me you sold me out."

"Boogie, chill. You already chipped. Just have shorty hand over that money and we can all walk away from this wit' no problem."

"You sonofabitch!" Boogie yelled, leaping towards his nephews.

"Pops, you betta chill," Tommy warned as he raised his gun to Boogie's chest. Through all this I was still on the floor trying to figure out a way out of this bullshit.

"Precious, get the fuck up."

I slowly stood, locking eyes with Tommy.

"I know you didn't think I was gonna let you keep that money. Soon as I heard Nico was locked up and Ritchie was dead, I started thinking about getting hold of that money. I had to find out certain facts before I knew that the deal neva went down so the money had to still be in the house where I dropped it off. But yo' slick ass had already swooped it up by the time I got there. You taking it neva crossed my mind. I figured once the streets got word that Nico Carter was locked up, some gutsy nigga broke in his crib trying to clean him out and came across all that loot. It wasn't until my boy, Lamont here told me about a friend his uncle was helping out who had a million dollars, did it all start coming together."

"How you gonna steal from Nico? He was good to you, Tommy."

"Fuck Nico. He didn't give a damn about nobody but himself. He was living the high life while the rest of us out there busting our asses. Nico can fucking rot in that jail cell for all I care. Enough talk about that shit. Where's the money before I start dropping bodies up in here?"

"You ain't dropping shit, you punkass nigga. Now get the fuck out my shop before ya start something that you won't be able to finish."

"Old man, shut the fuck up," Tommy barked.

"Yeah, Boogie, shut the fuck up before we have to show you what's up," the once silent nephew, Andre echoed.

"Boy, I'ma whip yo' ass," Boogie trilled, raising his hand to back smack his nephew as a reminder to respect your elders. But that lesson would not be learned. Without warning, Andre blasted off his gun, shooting Boogie twice, once in the chest and last in the face. Boogie's brains splat tered on the wall and a few drops of blood even landed on my cheek. I put my hands over my mouth, horrified by what I witnessed. I knew that I would be next. They would never let me leave alive. I was an eyewitness to a murder.

"Why you do that?" Lamont said to Andre.

"It was reflex. He was about to slap me like I was a bitch."

"Fuck all that. We need to hurry up. Precious, where the money at?"

"In my car."

"A'ight, move. Let's go get it," Tommy directed. "Yah go pull the truck around to the back while I go get this money."

"We gon' clean out the register first," Lamont said.

"Nigga, we about to split a million dollars and you talking about cleaning out the cash register. What is you smoking? We need to get the fuck up outta here. Somebody could've heard the gunshots and called the police."

"You right. We gon' pull the car around." Tommy tossed moved slowly trying to buy myself time to come up with a plan. I looked straight ahead as Tommy kept his Berretta pointed to my back. I could feel him sizing me up as he smacked his lips and whistled in his attempt to taunt me.

"Damn, Precious, it's too bad shit had to end this way. You a bad bitch. I wish I could make you my girl. But if Nico ever heard about that, he would put a hit out on me from his jail cell," Tommy said with a chuckle.

"What do you think he's gonna do when he finds out you robbed me to get his money?"

"How is he gonna ever know?" That was a clear indica tion that he had no plans to let me live. "I wish I had more time. I would love to get up in that pussy," Tommy added, furthering the insult.

When we got to my car I popped the trunk. Tommy lift ed it and saw a bunch of bags stacked on top of each other. "Which bag has the money?"

"The black one."

"All these bags are black. You dig through this shit. Them goofy niggas still ain't pulled the truck around, and I'm damn sure not about to let you make a run for it while I'm rummag ing through these bags. So hurry up and get my money."

Tommy eyed me like a hawk as I pretended to look for the mon-ey. The million dollars wasn't even in the car. The only money I had was the $100,000 I brought for Boogie, and that was in the front seat. I was fidgeting around in the trunk for my savior, and when I found it I cocked my 9mm right before I tossed one of the black bags in Tommy's face. He lost his balance and the gun he was holding fell out of his hand. I used the opportunity to blast Tommy three times in the head before he even knew what hit him. I slammed the trunk and jumped in my car.

The treacherous nephews pulled up right when I was taking off. They saw Tommy splashed out on the cement and rolled right over him in their quest to get to me. Lamont was driving and Andre was busting off as we flew down Flatbush Avenue. They were gaining on me, so I pressed down on the accelerator, swerving trying not to hit any body. Two more bullets hit my car and Lamont was pulling up so Andre would be directly on my side.

The light ahead was about to turn red and I noticed a truck about to pull out from the right side of the street. When the light turned green and the truck started pulling off, I jammed my foot on the gas and swiftly cut across the car Lamont was driving and cut in front of the truck, barely sliding through. By the time Lamont realized what I was doing, he couldn't hit his brakes fast enough and he collided into the side of the truck. The entire car exploded into flames instantly.

I drove off once again beating death.

Friend or Foe

Watching Lamont and Andre die in the car explosion had me shook up. I pulled over to side of the street, as everyone watched from a distance the horrific scene that was straight out a movie flick. I was in no condition to drive to Jersey, so I headed to my mother's crib. I kept switching the radio off and on in an attempt to get my mind off every thing that happened in the last couple of hours. I couldn't believe Boogie was dead and his own nephew killed him.

The street life had no loyalty to no one, not even fam ily. Being up close as Boogie's brains were splashed every where was making my body weak. The dried up blood was still resting on my face. I had no tissue, so I tried to use my hands to scrub the blood off, but it only made my face red and bruised. This was a nightmare, and I couldn't imagine it getting any worse.

When I drove up to the projects, I sat in my car for a few minutes, getting my thoughts together. I knew my mother would immediately sense something was terribly wrong, but I wasn't ready to tell her all the grimy details of what had taken place in my life. She'd finally gotten her life together and I didn't want her stressing over my problems. Before I got out the car I fixed my hair and spit on my hands to wipe off the dried blood on my face. I was determined to appear as if everything was straight when my mother saw me.

I took a deep breath when I opened the apartment door. It was pitch black, which was unusual. My mother never went to bed before one o'clock and she always fell asleep on the living room couch with the television on.

I finally located the light switch and to my despair the entire place had been ransacked. The brand new couch my mother purchased was cut up. The kitchen cabinets were open with broken dishes everywhere. The plants that were in the window were now knocked on the floor with dirt all over. I slowly walked towards the hallway and saw the words "*You're A Dead Bitch*," written on the walls.

My whole body became flooded with the most agonizing twinge I ever experienced. At that moment, I knew my life would never be the same.

I didn't even want to walk in my mother's room because reality would truly set in. Her door was slightly ajar. When I pushed it completely open, I saw my beautiful mother's body lying there on the bed with her head completely sev ered. My knees completely buckled and I fell to the floor. For the first time, since I was a little girl, I cried. The tears flowed, and they wouldn't stop.

It was as if all the heartache and pain from so many years roared out begging to be released. I not only cried for myself, but I cried for my mother, the mother that I just found only earlier today. Now she'd been taken away from me, before I could enjoy all the moments that I dreamed of all my life. Dreams that I never believed could be possible and now they wouldn't be. The shimmer of hope my mother gave me when I looked into her beautiful green eyes today had died with her.

On my way back to Jersey, I contemplated ending my life, by driving off the side of the road. The only thing that stopped me was that I didn't have the guts. With all the bullshit I'd seen and done, I was scared to end it all. I was riddled with guilt. My revenge on Nico caused the death of Boogie and my mother. I would never be able to live that down.

When I made it back to the hotel room, I raided the mini bar and guzzled down every ounce of alcohol available. All I wanted was to sleep without enduring the pain.

"Oh goodness," I mumbled out loud when the ringing of my cell phone wouldn't stop. "What?"

"Precious, wake up," I heard Inga yelling through the phone.

"I'm up. What is it?"

"Precious, I have something to tell you." There was silence on the phone for a few seconds. "Precious are you there?"

"Yeah, what do you have to tell me?"

"It's about your mother and Boogie."

"What about them?" I asked, not wanting Inga to have a clue I already knew.

"They're dead, Precious. Both of them were murdered sometime last night."

"Damn, do they have any idea who did it or why?"

"Well, Boogie was found dead inside his shop and Tommy, that kid that worked for Nico, was found killed right outside the shop. The cops tryn' to piece all the shit together."

"What about my mother?"

"They don't know. Because of the profession she was in, they thinking it could've been anybody."

"My mother had cleaned her life up. She wasn't in that profession no more, so tell them bitchass cops and any body else that's running they mouth to shut the fuck up. They don't know nothing about my mother. She better than all of them!" I screamed, as I tried to defend my mother in death, since she was never defended in life.

"Precious, I'm sorry. I had no idea yo' moms turned her life around."

"How would you know?" I responded sarcastically.

"So when you coming back to Brooklyn?"

"Inga, I don't fucking know. Maybe neva. Coming through BK seems like a death sentence to me. Five moth erfuckers I know have died in the last week. I don't want no parts of Brooklyn right now."

"So where you gon' go?"

"Why the fuck you keep asking me so many damn questions? You been coming at me like you the feds since you called me about Nico's arrest."

"Damn, Precious, you my best friend I'm just worried about you. Excuse me."

"You got enough to worry about. You need to concentrate on that seed you got growing inside you instead of wondering when the next time I'm stopping through Brooklyn."

"You know what, Precious? I know emotionally you fucked up in the game right now. First, Nico get locked up and now both your mom and Boogie get killed. That's a lot to swallow, so I'm not gonna take none of the shit you say ing personally. Just know I'm here for you."

"Yeah, I hear you, Inga. I'll speak to you later."

My head was killing me and the conversation I had with Inga didn't help. I had to get my mind off all the bullshit. I dragged myself out of bed, took a shower and headed to Short Hills Mall. Shopping would at least numb my mind momentarily.

After racking up clothes from Fendi, Gucci, Versace and just about every other store in the mall, I went to the nail sa lon for a pedicure. I was reading my XXL magazine when I heard the girl sitting next to me complaining about how her roommate bolted on her without notice, and she didn't know how she would be able to maintain her rent. I instantly thought about how it was time for me to get the hell out of that hotel and this might be the perfect opportunity.

Before getting too excited, on the sly I sized the girl up. She reminded me of one of those college prep girl types, all goody-goody and shit. Which was cool since I needed a major break from my normal 'boutit, 'boutit chicks. When the girl got off the phone I decided to put on my best All American girl voice and inquire about her apartment.

"Hi, I didn't mean to eavesdrop on your conversation, but I heard you say something about needing a roommate." I then peeped the girl doing her own sizing up of me. She first eyed my snakeskin Gucci purse and scanned down to my matching boots. Her eyes finally landed on the few pieces of ice I was rockin'.

"Yeah, my girlfriend just broke out on me without any notice. She got some new boyfriend and moved in with him. There is no way I can afford the rent on my own. Are you looking for a place to live?"

"Actually, I am. I just moved here from Philly and I'm staying at a hotel. I was going to start looking for my own place, but it would be great to have a roommate, especially since I don't know anybody here."

"What hotel are you staying at?"

"The Hyatt Regency in Jersey City."

"Oh, I know where that is. It's nice."

"Yeah, but you can't stay in a hotel forever."

"True. Well I live in Edgewater. My rent is a little ex pensive be-cause I live on River Roadthey actually call it Rappers Row."

"Why's that?"

"Because a lot of Rappers and industry people live in the condos and high rises on that street."

"Oh that's cool. So how much is the rent?"

"Three thousand a month, so if you took the place your part would be fifteen hundred plus half for utilities. Is that within your budget?"

"Definitely. I could even pay you six months upfront so you don't have to be worried about me leaving you in a bad predicament like your other roommate did." The girls eyes lit up and I knew it would work out. Money had a way of doing that to people.

"Cool. You'll love the place. The building is fabulous and every-one is really friendly. Your room is a nice size and you have your own bathroom."

"Are you saying the place is mine?"

"I guess so, if you want it. You can come take a look to day, and if you like it you can move in immediately. Oh my goodness I'm about to have a new roommate and I don't even know your name." We both laughed.

"I'm Precious." I extended my hand. "It's nice to meet you."

"Rhonda, and it's nice to meet you, too."

After finishing up our pedicures and letting the polish dry, I followed Rhonda to her apartment. She lived in a beautiful complex called Independence Harbor. The small city was dif ferent than any place I had ever been. It seemed so bright and cheerful, nothing like the projects in Brooklyn. The apartment was spacious, and the huge windows had beautiful views of New York City and the Hudson River.

"I want it."

"Great. I'll write up an agreement between us, for your protection and mine."

"That's fine."

"You're also welcome to use the furniture that my friend left behind."

"Thanks for the offer, but I'll get my own."

"Okay, so when are you going to move in?" Rhonda asked, sound-ing extremely excited.

"Is tomorrow too soon?"

"No, that's fine."

"I'm going to get my stuff from the hotel and then start doing some furniture shopping for my bedroom."

"Precious, I have a great feeling about this."

"Me, too, Rhonda."

When I left my new roommate I did have a great feeling. Al-though only a tunnel and a bridge separated us, I felt like Brook-lyn was thousands of miles away. Before I went back to the hotel, I stopped by my storage unit to pick up all my clothes, shoes and other belongings. The only thing I left was my money. The next morning I checked out my hotel room and headed to my new apartment.

When I arrived Rhonda had our agreement already pre pared. I handed her the $9000 in cash and the biggest smile crossed her face.

"Precious, I hope you don't mind me asking, but what do you do? All your belongings are like top designer stuff. You're driving a new Benz, and your jewelry is really nice. Then you give me $9000 upfront. Money obviously isn't an issue for you."

In my mind I debated for a second if I wanted to tell Rhonda the truth. I was getting tired of talking all proper and tying to pretend to be so happy-go-lucky.

"My ex-man was a kingpin. He's the one that bought me all this stuff. Before he got locked up, he left me a nice lump of money. I'm what you call a hustler's girl."

"Wow. He must have been some hustler."

"No doubt."

"So what is he locked up for?"

"Murder."

"Who did he kill?"

"His best friend." Rhonda stood there, shaking her head. Her expression was that of surprise. She definitely didn't know anything about the streets.

"My life is awfully boring compared to the one you've seemed to live."

She had no idea, I said to myself.

"Enough about me, what do you do?"

"I work at Atomic Records in the marketing department."

"That's dope. So you must know mad celebrities?"

"Yeah, but after awhile they become just regular people who are a lot more demanding and anal."

"That's believable. They probably so used to motherfuckers kissing they ass, they start acting real simple."

"Basically," Rhonda said in agreement. "So are you go ing to look for a job? But then you probably don't need the money."

"I just graduated from high school a year ago. I was actu ally thinking about maybe going to college or some type of school. I think I do need to be more productive with my time."

"Speaking of time, I need to get to work. Make your self at home. Here's your key to the apartment and I wrote down my cell phone number and left it on the refrigerator. If you need anything, don't hes itate to call me."

"Thanks, Rhonda. You mad cool."

For the next few weeks, I got settled in my new place. I got rid of all the garbage that was in my bedroom and hooked it up with some flyass furniture I got from this place called Moda Furniture. Between decorating my new room and hanging out with Rhonda I watched the news and read the newspaper.

Because Nico's attorney requested a speedy trial, he would be going to court in the next couple of weeks. The high profile case was drawing all sorts of different opinions from legal experts. Some said he would be found guilty and many others said the Prosecution's case was weak and Nico would walk. All I thought was *Say It Ain't So*. There was no way Nico could beat the case. If he did, there would be no place on this earth I could hide. He would hunt me down like an animal.

I was already scared as it was; so scared that I didn't even want to attend my mother's funeral. I tracked down the lady, Ms. Duncan, that I ran into at the courthouse that day, and called her. She had heard about my mother's death and was actually devastated. She was one of the few people that remembered how beautiful and special my mother was at one time in her life.

I told her I was going through some things, but wanted my mother to have a beautiful funeral and tombstone. I met up with her in the city and gave her thirty thousand dollars to handle all the arrangements and to keep something for all her help. The day of the funeral I watched from a distance, not knowing if my enemies were tracking me. To my sur prise, a lot of people showed up to pay their last respects to my mother. I couldn't help but think that it was a shame how people would celebrate you in death instead of when you are still alive to see it.

"How much?" I asked the cashier, while putting my gro ceries in the cart. I seemed to live at Pathmark. In Brooklyn I ate out just about every day and night. I was constantly running the streets, so I never had time for a homecooked meal. But since I didn't know nobody in Jersey, I was al ways in the crib and whipping up meals was becoming a hobby. As I handed the cashier the money, I faintly heard the sounds of my cell ringing. My purse was lodged be tween the bags and I barely caught the call. "Hello," I said, sounding frazzled.

"Precious, I need to see you."

"Inga?" The number came up private and the voice sounded serious, so I wasn't positive if it was her or not.

"Yeah, it's me. We need to talk."

"About what?" I hadn't spoken to Inga in almost three months so her funky tone was rubbing me the wrong way.

"We can discuss that when I see you."

"No, we can discuss it right now, or you won't be seeing me."

"I don't want to do this over the phone, Precious. I need to see you face to face."

"On the real, Inga, I'm not feeling your funky attitude. I'm also not feeling meeting you somewhere 'cause how you coming at me make me think this might be some sort of set up. And if that's the case, you need to step the fuck back 'cause I would hate to have to bust off on yo' sneaky ass."

"Ain't nobody tryna set you up, Precious. No matter what, we still peoples. But I do need to speak to you, but I would prefer to do it in person."

"When?"

"Today, if possible."

"A'ight, meet me in the city in an hour. I'll call and let you know the exact location when I get there. And, Inga, don't try no slick shit."

I rushed home, put my groceries away and hopped in the shower. I got dressed quickly and then headed over to my storage spot to pick up my gun. As far as I was concerned, me and Inga were no longer peoples, and I didn't trust her. When I met up with her, if I got so much as a hint she was up to no good, I was gonna waste her ass, pregnant or not.

When I got to the city, I called Inga on her cell and told her to meet me in Union Square in twenty minutes. I was already parked on the corner, but it would give me an op portunity to observe and see if I saw anybody that looked suspicious.

Inga finally showed up, with belly poked out before her. I watched her for ten more minutes, seeing if she got on the phone with anybody or if she was making any eye contact with the people in the crowds. Once I felt safe, I grabbed my purse with the gun safely inside and walked up behind her.

"What's up, Inga?"

"Oh shit, you scared the fuck outta me, Precious."

"That was the point," I said, walking towards the bench. "Come on let's have a seat over here. So what's up?"

Inga took a deep breath before beginning.

"Precious, I want you to be honest wit' me about something."

"OK."

"Precious, were you seeing Ritchie behind my back?"

"Who told you that?"

"That don't matter."

"If you want me to answer your question it do."

"Porscha said that Nico told her that you were a snake bitch because you were fucking his best friend behind his back. He also said you was pregnant by Ritchie and was planning on leaving him so ya could be together."

"Oh, so you talk to Porscha now? Ya'll friends."

"That's not even the point, Precious. I want to know if what Nico said is true."

"No, it is the point if you fucking wit' my enemy."

"Are you gonna answer me or not?"

"I'll tell you the truth. Yeah, I was fucking Ritchie, but no, I wasn't pregnant by him, although I told Nico I was."

"But, Precious, why?" Inga asked with pain in her voice.

"Because after I found out about Porscha, I wanted Nico to pay, and I knew fucking his best friend would do the trick."

"But, you knew Ritchie was my boyfriend, and we cared about each other."

"Inga, wake up! Ritchie didn't give a fuck about you. He used you to make me jealous. He begged me to leave Nico.

"I told you not to get caught up in that nigga, but you swore he was the one. I did you a favor by getting him out yo' life, but then you wanna fuck around and have a baby for this dude."

I sat shaking my head. Inga was stunned by what I said, but she asked for the truth. "Inga, I didn't mean for you to get hurt, but Nico had to pay. Ritchie won't no good. He didn't think twice about crossing Nico. You shouldn't take any of this so personally. Ritchie didn't mean nothing to me. He was a means to an end."

"Nico didn't kill Ritchie because he found out he was setting him up. He killed him because you told him that you were fucking Ritchie," Inga said as if all the pieces were coming together. "That's what happened isn't it?"

"Why don't you ask Porscha, since she's your new yellow pages."

"I don't need to. You planned all of this. You knew Nico would kill Ritchie once he found out, and you made sure he did. You knew I was pregnant, Precious. How could you have my baby's daddy set up to be killed?"

"Inga, Ritchie didn't even want that baby. You told me yourself he said he would cut the baby out of you if you didn't have an abortion. Bitch, I'm the one that hit you off wit' 50 G's so yo' broke ass could give yo' baby a start in life. That's more than Ritchie ever did for you, or would've done. So don't sit up here, tryna blame me for getting knocked up by a man that didn't want you or his seed."

"Things might've been different if you would've stayed out of our relationship. He didn't start changing until he started fucking you. Now Ritchie is dead, and my child will neva know his father."

"Well, bitch, join the motherfucking club 'cause I don't know my daddy neither, and what." Inga turned her face away.

I didn't know if it was because of what I said or because of the afternoon sun glaring in our path. The wind was blowing the trees in all directions as adults and children relishing in the beautiful spring day strolled past us. By the idyllic picture, the strangers going by would've never expected that two former best friends were having a life changing conversation.

"Was it all worth it, just so you could punish Nico for cheating on you wit' some trick?"

"Believe it or not, I've asked myself the same question and the answer is yes. He disrespected me to the fullest, knowing that the streets be watching. If I had done the same thing to him, he would've sent me home in a body bag."

"Have you ever thought that he still might?"

"Not behind bars, he won't."

"Well, for your sake you betta pray that's where he stays. Because if Nico gets out, he won't rest until you six feet under." Inga wasn't telling me nothing that I didn't al ready know. Nico getting out could never be. It was no lon ger safe for both of us to walk the same streets.

Baller Bitch

The headline on the front cover of the "New York Post" read 'Notorious Kingpin Found Guilty of Murder'. Underneath there was a big picture of Nico hand cuffed being escorted out the courtroom. Unlike the first time I saw him in court, his ensemble didn't consist of an orange jumpsuit. He was in one of his custommade design er suits, looking more like a Wall Street business man than a coldblooded killer. I was finally able to exhale, knowing that Nico would be spending the rest of his life behind bars. After reading the inside story, I went to celebrate by cooking a big breakfast.

"Good morning, Precious," Rhonda said when I entered the kitchen.

"Good morning," I said sounding unusually chipper for this early in the morning.

"Anything good in the paper?" Rhonda asked as she picked up the paper I just put down on the counter.

"What's this?" she said, reading the headlines about Nico. "Look at him he's a hottie. Who would think someone that fine could be a murderer? Now I know where all the good looking men are locked up."

I refused to put my two cents in the conversation be the one on the cover of the Post were one in the same. "Do you have any plans tonight?" she asked, finally putting the paper down.

"No, I'm chilling."

"Well, I don't know if you feel like it, but we're having an album release party for Supreme. You're welcome to come."

"Supreme the rapper?"

"Yeah. He's a cutie right?"

"I didn't know Supreme is on the same label you work for. His music is slick. But, nah, I'm not going out tonight. But you can bring me back his new CD."

"Why don't you want to come? It'll be fun."

"I just wanna stay at home tonight, stuff my face and watch my favorite DVD, *"Paid in Full."*

"Alright. Well, don't wait up for me. I won't be home until late."

"Cool, don't shake yo' ass too hard," I said smiling. Part of me did want to go to the party, but the other part of me wanted to just chill.

I'd been feeling especially uneasy after my conversation with Inga in Union Square. Hearing her say Nico would hunt me down and kill me if he beat his case made my blood run cold. For the last few weeks I'd been on pins and needles, waiting for the trial to end and the verdict to be announced. But even hearing guilty, I wasn't completely stress free. For the rest of the day I pretty much moped around, doing en tirely too much thinking, until my cell phone rang. I hated answering private calls, but I was happy to do anything to get my mind off Nico. "Hello."

"Precious, what's up? You got a minute?" I immediately recognized Inga's voice and everything inside of me wanted to hang up the phone on her. We hadn't spoken to each other since our meeting in the city, and I had no interest in speaking to her. When she revealed that her and Porscha were now talking, which in my mind meant trading infor mation, I didn't want nothing to do with Inga.

"Yeah, I got a minute, and that's about it."

"Well, then let me get right to it. I need some money." I had to step back from my phone to make sure I heard Inga correctly.

"Excuse me. Did I hear you correctly?"

"Yes. You were the only person I knew to call for help."

"Before I even respond, what happened to the fifty G's I gave you less than six months ago?"

"It's gone. I had to buy a car and to get some things for me and the baby."

"Inga, the baby ain't even here yet and you spent all the money. What type of car did you buy?"

"That don't matter, Precious, the point is, I don't have no more, and the baby will be here in a couple of months. So I was hoping you could hit me off wit' a hundred thousand."

"I don't have a hundred thousand, and even if I did, I wouldn't give it to yo' simple ass."

"You ain't gotta call me no names, neither. I just figured since you stole that million from Nico, the least you could do was put a hundred thousand in my pocket, since you are re sponsible for making my unborn child fatherless." With that said I was tempted to break the promise I made to myself of staying out of Brooklyn so I could go whip Inga's ass.

"I don't know what kind of slick shit you tryna pop, but I didn't steal no million dollars from Nico. I'm tryna main tain out in these streets just like you. So whateva you heard or you think you know is all bullshit. As for your bastard child being fatherless, you gonna have to take the charge on that for being a stupid bitch."

"Precious, you always thought you were hot shit and you still do. You walk these streets not thinking about nobody but yourself. But bitch, you can't hide forever.

"You think you can break outta Brooklyn and leave everybody be-hind and forget about all the havoc you caused. You the reason Ritchie is dead, you the reason that Nico is locked up and my instincts tell me you responsible for Boogie and your moms, death too. But all your scheming is going to come back on you and you gon' take it in blood."

"Fuck you, Inga!" I bellowed before throwing my cell across the room where it shattered against the wall. I was getting closer to going over the edge. I immediately threw on my clothes, grabbed my purse and headed out the door.

As I hurried through the Mall toward the T-Mobile store to re-place my cell phone, a cherry red halter dress hanging in a window caught my eye. It had a wood oring and asym metric lattice hem. At that moment, I decided to go to the album release party tonight and shake my ass with Rhonda.

Never one to be on time, I arrived when the party was about to end. I had called Rhonda and told her I was on my way, and now two hours later, I was just getting to the front door of the club. There were a few people on the same time schedule as me who were also just arriving.

As I was walking in, a group of people rushed pass me to a waiting Suburban. I glanced to see who it was since there was a chaotic buzz surrounding them. In an intense second my eyes locked with a sexy looking dude.

"You need to come in, Miss. there are people waiting behind you," the humongous bouncer demanded and snapped me out of the love connection I had just made.

When I turned back around, the Suburban had driven off. *I guess it wasn't meant to be* I thought to myself.

"There you are," Rhonda said as she greeted me at the door. "That sure was a long I'm on my way, Precious."

"Sorry, girl, but time is neva on my side."

"It was time well spent," Rhonda said as she glanced over my outfit." "That dress is fierce."

"I know right, it was actually my motivation for coming out tonight. I saw it and had to rock it. I wish I would've gotten here earlier 'cause it seem like it was cute."

"Yeah, it was. All the A-list celebrities we invited showed up."

"Where's the guest of honor."

"You just missed him." *Damn, could the sexy ma'fuckah I made eye contact wit' been Supreme. There was something familiar about him. Nah, that couldn't of been that nigga*, I thought to myself. "Come over to my table and have a couple of drinks before the party is officially over."

Although Rhonda had invited me to a few industry parties, this was the first one I ever came to. It definitely wasn't like the clubs in Brooklyn. The people in here gave off this aura of being on some real phony Hollywood type shit. For the hour I was there, Rhonda spent half that time giving fake-ass hugs and kisses to a few motherfuckers that she obviously didn't like.

Everybody's favorite departing line was "I'll call you, let's do lunch." With all that said, the music was off the hook, the club was hot and, for the most part, the people were fly.

For the next few weeks, Rhonda and I lived on the party scene. After that one night I'd become addicted. There was this raw energy that engulfed you running in those circles. Since I had money to blow, I kept bottles of Cristal flowing at every club we went to. Rhonda would constantly joke with me and say, "Who was your ex-man? Was he on some New Jack City, Nino Brown type shit?"

I would just laugh and pop the next bottle. Something about Rhonda was really cool, though. I digged her so much that I even paid for her to get a complete makeover, which included hair, makeup and a new wardrobe. Rhonda was a semi-cute girl, she reminded me of a book smart version of Brandy. After we finished her makeover, she turned into the R&B version. Rhonda was overwhelmed by my generosity and her appreciation numbed all the different emotions that were swimming through my body.

"Precious, Funk Master Flex's annual car show is com ing up," Rhonda informed me while we were having dinner at Houston's. The Hawaiian steak I was devouring tasted so good that it took me a moment to even listen to what Rhonda was saying.

"Car show," I finally said, right before taking another bite.

"Yeah, he has it every year. This year it's going to be at the Convention Center in Atlantic City on June 25 and 26. I think we should go."

"That's next weekend. I'm down."

I'd never been to a car show before, and back when I worked at Boogie's car detailing shop, the niggas would come through to get they rides extra fly to show up at Flex's shit. Now I would be attending so I had to be on point. I had plenty of ice, but I went and purchased a few new pieces of bling to rock.

By accident, I found this Dominican spot called Hair Guild and the beautician blew out my hair so it was bone straight but with just the right amount of bounce. I had a closet full of clothes that I hadn't worn yet, but I still had to get a couple of new outfits just in case I didn't like anything I had at home.

Truth be told, I was hoping to find me a dude at the car show. Not to be my man but to fuck. The last time I had some dick was when I fucked Nico the night he killed Ritchie. That was months ago, and I was horny as shit. Rhonda didn't have the same problem as me because she had a boyfriend named Amir. He was a corny nigga, but he seemed like he was putting it down.

I can remember a couple of occasions when I was shaken from my sleep by the sounds of Rhonda screaming his name. Sometimes that shit would get me so turned on, I would have to finger myself until I had an orgasm and then fall back to sleep. I was tired of pleasing myself. I needed some good dick.

I was the epitome of a straight baller bitch when we pulled up on the scene in my spankin' clean Benz. Instead of putting on one of my many overthetop outfits, I kept it simple and let my body and accessories speak for me. I had on some fitting just right Apple Bottom jeans with a crisp white tank top and some opentoe stilettos. With my ears, neck and wrist dripping in diamonds it was enough said. All I heard was loud whispers of people trying to figure out who I was. I put an extra strut in my walk as I parlayed through the crowd. All eyes were on me and the bitches were all hating. I couldn't blame them, because if I wasn't me I would be hating, too.

"Precious, this place packed. Everybody up in here."

"Tell me about it, there are so many cuties I don't know where to start."

"I do," Rhonda said all bold.

"Girl, shut up. You got a man."

"So what? You think I'm letting all this go to waste on one man. Oh, please."

"Ain't this some shit. You get a makeover and you 'un turned into a hotass bitch. It was something in your eyes that always told me there was a hoe underneath there."

"You got that right. And I will forever be grateful to you, Precious, for helping me discover it." I looked at Rhonda sideways, not sure if I wanted to take credit for that. I knew what type of trouble you could get in by being a hot tamale. I hoped that Rhonda wouldn't make the mistake of biting off more than she could chew. "Stay right here, Precious, I see this guy that I've been dying to meet. I'll be back."

In that quick second, Rhonda left me standing alone, while she went and chased some dick. I couldn't be mad at her because technically I was on the same mission; she just beat me to the punch.

Dudes kept pimping past me and the closer they got, they would slow down and make eye contact to try to get a vibe if I was interested or not. I would smack my lips and roll my eyes so they would keep it moving. Then a pair of eyes met mine and a sense of familiarity came over me.

"Didn't I see you outside a club about a month ago?" the sexy ma'fuckah asked me as a few of his homeboys and a couple of bodyguards lingered beside him.

"Aren't you the rapper, Supreme?"

"Yeah, that's me," the mellow-toned MC replied. "Aren't you the young lady that was going into the club as I was leaving?"

"Yeah, that was me. You remember that." I said, surprised that he did.

"Of course, I'd never forget a face as beautiful as yours."

Now I never considered myself to be no groupie bitch. Even with all the hustler's I fucked with, I just wrote that off as me liking niggas with heavy pockets. I've watched videos and flipped through magazines seeing all these rap stars and other celebrities, and yes, the curiosity of how they lived was always there. But it wasn't that deep for me because where I came from, I was the hood superstar. I represented for my borough the same way these so-called celebrities represented for they clique.

Their fan base just so happened to reach millions of people where mine only reached thousands. But the feeling of being on top was still the same. So when Supreme was standing in front of me saying how beautiful I was, I wasn't sure if my pussy was getting extra wet because he was a rap superstar or because he was a sexy ma'fuckah. Or maybe it was a combination of both.

"Why you tryna make me blush in front of all these people out here?"

"That wasn't my intention. What I wanted was for you to walk with me, talk with me and then, hopefully exchange numbers with me. But that might be asking too much. What do you think?"

"Truthfully, I want to leave with you, be with you and hopefully chill with you for a long time." Before I could hear his response Rhonda was back.

"What's up, Supreme?" she said giving him a hug.

"Just so you know, I work with her…that's it," he said not wanting me to feel uncomfortable.

"Supreme, that's my roommate. You don't have to explain yourself."

"Word. You guys live together? Damn, Rhonda you never told me you had this at home," Supreme pointed to me with his hands in a display position as if he was a game show host."

"She came to your album release party, but I think you had already left."

"Yeah, we made eye contact on my way out. Then I was blessed to see her once again today. Damn, baby, I didn't even get your name yet."

"Precious."

"That name fits you perfectly. So are you going to walk with me or what?"

"That depends. Are you going to leave with me, be with me and chill with me?"

"You didn't even have to ask me that twice. I heard you the first time and the answer is no doubt."

With that I took Supreme's hand and spent the entire du ration of the car show as his date. Instead of staying in the hotel room with Rhonda I stayed with him in his suite at the Borgata. The first night, after all of us, including Rhonda, went out for dinner and drinks, I was ready to catch up for the sex drought I had been on.

After taking a shower I laid in the bed next to Supreme ready to do all sorts of tricks with my tongue, but he stopped me before I even made it to the nipples on his chest. "Precious, I just want you to fall asleep in my arms."

"I can do that right after we fuck."

"Baby, I don't want to fuck you?"

"What you mean you don't want to fuck me? What is something wrong wit' me or something?" I asked, feeling embarrassed that the nigga was turning me down.

"Precious, look at me," he said grabbing my face.

"Physically, you're perfect. And I want you in every way. When we become intimate, I don't want us to fuck. I want us to make love. There is a big difference. Precious, I'm truly feeling you. I was connected to you in just that brief moment we locked eyes in front of the club.

"You're special and I want our relationship to be special. That means taking our time and getting to know one another. That means getting past the lust and learning to appreciate what's on the inside. Will you do that with me, Precious? Take our time so we can build something real?"

I stared into Supreme's dark mysterious eyes in total confusion. No man had ever asked to get to know me as a person before. When I was ready to get twisted out, so were they. Here was this rap star, that probably had more pussy tossed his way than the law deemed legal, telling me that he wanted us to wait and get to know each other better first. His request seemed so pure that it was frightening to me. I didn't know how to respond, so I snuggled my warm body underneath his arms and fell asleep.

One Love

When Rhonda and I got back from Atlantic City, I couldn't get Supreme off my mind. That nigga had me straight tripping. He didn't want no ass, just conversa tion. The funny thing was in those two days I spent with him, I never felt closer to any man in my life. With all the talking we did, I got past the initial physical attraction and took time out to know the man.

Supreme was successful in getting me to do that. But I also had to admit to myself that the thought of having genuine feel ings for him was scaring me. It was too late for that, though. I'd spent the last hour lying in my bed, staring at a picture we took at the car show, just missing him.

That was a clear indication to me that the tables might've turned, and he might have me open. As I smiled at the thought, I heard my cell phone ringing, which made my smile even brighter. I knew it had to be Supreme because after my last conversation with Inga, I had that phone cut off and got a new number. The only person that had it so far was Supreme. "Hi, baby," I said with that bubbly feeling in my stomach I heard you get when you catching feelings for somebody.

"Hi, baby to you, Precious, you been on my mind every second since I got up this morning. I need to see you."

"Tell me when 'cause I need to see you too."

"How 'bout I come get you after I finish up at the studio and we catch a bite to eat."

"What time do you think that'll be?"

"Eight or nine, is that cool?

"Definitely, I can't wait to see you." As much as I was looking forward to spending time with Supreme, I wanted him to put it down on me so freakin' bad. All this datin' and waitin' was about to make me go postal. I decided I would once again make the suggestion to him that we needed to cut all the foreplay, which in this case was all this dating and talking, and go straight to the dessert.

As it started getting closer to eight, I looked through my closet, wanting to pick out the right outfit. I didn't want it to scream "Please fuck me tonight," but the underlying meaning definitely had to be in effect.

"Precious are you home?" I heard Rhonda screaming while in the middle of trying on my eighth outfit.

"Yes," I answered walking towards the living room to get her opinion about my attire. I knew Supreme had me feeling some kinda way when I took to asking Rhonda for fashion advice. "How does this look on me?" I said, lacing up my corset top.

"Pretty damn good."

I looked up to see what the hell was going on with Rhonda's voice since the sound I heard was five octaves too low.

"Oh I'm sorry, Precious. This is Robert. I was seeing if you were home to let you know I had company. But he's right. The outfit is definitely hot," Rhonda said as she play fully punched her friend on the arm for lusting after me in her face.

"Thanks, I guess I'll wear this."

"You must have a date with Supreme by the looks of you."

"Yes, as a matter of fact, I do."

"Well, have fun tonight, because I know I am." With that Rhonda grabbed Robert's hand and headed to her bed room. This was the third guy Rhonda had over here in less than a week. She was going overboard. Not one to knock any woman for getting her shit off, but she was playing a dangerous game.

As far as her boyfriend Amir went, he assumed they were still a couple. But Rhonda seemed to have other ideas. I guess all those years of niggas not paying her no mind had caused her to lose her mind. She seemed to be on a mission to fuck every dude she ever had a crush on, which obviously was a lot. Never mind her though; she was getting enough dick for the both of us. It was time for me to get my own.

Admiring the view of the city from the deck of the Charter House restaurant, I said, "Supreme, I'm glad you took me here, this is crazy romantic."

"I knew you'd like it. I want to always keep things fresh and sexy with you."

"Yeah, that's what's up."

The nighttime breeze was making a tantalizing evening even more erotic. The gaze coming from Supreme's eyes made me hopeful that he had the same desire to get our fuck on tonight as me. "Precious, you are so beautiful. Who do you resemble, your mother or your father?" he asked, fucking up my whole sex fantasy that was just playing in my mind.

"I would have to say my mother," I quickly answered.

"I can't wait to meet her. The woman that gave birth to a daughter so gorgeous has to be special." Supreme wanting to meet my mother blew me away. No man had ever shown any sort of interest in wanting to meet a parent of mine. It was a damn shame that when one finally did, my mother was dead and gone.

"Unfortunately, Supreme, that'll neva happen."

"Why? are the two of you not on good terms?"

"We ain't on no terms. My mother is dead."

"What? Damn, baby, I'm sorry. How long has she been dead?"

"About six months."

"Wow, that's so recent." Supreme sat there for a minute shaking his head. "How did she die?"

I can't believe this nigga was making me relieve this shit all over again, I said to myself.

"My mother was murdered, Supreme, and before you come asking me 'bout my daddy, 'cause I know that's next, I don't know who he is," I shrieked. "I ain't neva met my daddy. My mother was a whore; she probably didn't know who my daddy was."

"Precious, I didn't mean to get you all upset. I shouldn't have came at you with all those questions."

"It's not your fault Supreme. How were you supposed to know that I came from nothing?"

"Precious, don't ever say that about yourself. You did come from something. You don't realize how special you are. But if you let me, I'll show you."

"I'd like that." For the next couple of hours Supreme and I just talked. True to form when he took me home, he gave me a kiss goodnight and kept it moving.

"How was your date with Supreme?" Rhonda asked, still up watching television.

"It was great, up to the point he dropped me off with a kiss and goodbye. Leaving me to once again go to bed fin ger fucking myself."

"You still haven't fucked him?"

"Hell no."

"Damn, Precious, I don't know how you're able to be around a guy as fine as Supreme and not get none."

"Who you telling? All this let's get to know each other first is so '*Leave it to Cleaver.*' It also doesn't help that I have to hear you climbing walls in the middle of the night."

"Don't get mad 'cause I'm getting some and you not."

"Where is your latest fuck toy anyway?"

"In the bed knocked out. Girl, I wore his ass out. We been fucking up a storm ever since you left."

Right before Rhonda was about to go into detail about her fuck fest, there was a knock at the door. "Who could that be this late?"

"Girl, that's probably Supreme. On his way home he had to turn around because he said fuck that. I need to get inside of Precious."

"You so crazy, you better go get the door before he changes his mind."

"You don't have to tell me twice, I said opening the door. Hi baby," Instead of Supreme, I was surprised to see Amir. "Amir, hi, I was ex-pecting somebody else." I turned and looked over at Rhonda, knowing it was about to be some drama.

"That's alright. Is Rhonda here?" Amir asked, brushing past me before I could answer his question.

"Amir what you doing here?"

"I've been calling you all fucking night, but you turned your cell off and you haven't been answering your home phone. Where the fuck you been?"

"My battery on my cell died, and I just got back from going out to eat with Precious."

"Then why is Precious fully dressed and you got on your bath-robe?" *Amir appeared to be on the corny side but that nigga didn't miss a beat* I thought to myself as he imme diately questioned Rhonda's sto-ry. Before she could come back with a lame ass excuse, Robert, wear-ing just his boxer shorts came walking out her bedroom, rubbing his eyes.

"Damn, Rhonda you fucked me so good, you almost put a nig-ga out for the night," Robert said before looking up and seeing Amir standing with the look of terror on his face. I put my head down, pray-ing that Amir would be the bigger per son and walk out the door. We all remained silent, waiting for Amir's reaction. No one in the room wanted to move first. Without warning, Amir balled up his fist and punched Rhonda in her face like she was a straightup dude.

"Amir, stop!" she screamed between whacks.

"Robert, do something!" I shouted, but that punkass nigga stood there like a straight bitch. "Nigga, you not gon na help her?"

"This ain't none of my business. This between her and her man."

"You a straight bitch!" I yelled while he ran in the bed room putting on his clothes so he could bolt before Amir could whip his ass. I kept screaming for Amir to get off Rhonda, but he was in a zone. He had Rhonda in a head lock, giving one punch after another.

I had no choice but to run up on him and jump on his back. "Leave her the fuck alone, you gon kill her." But Amir was paying me no mind. He was full of rage, and I was no match for his strength.

"Bitch, get the fuck off me." One minute I had my arm around his neck, holding on to his back, the next thing I was flying across the room, knocking over the dining room chair. The fall was so hard that as I was getting up, I stum bled back down. Rhonda's cry for help were getting weak er and weaker as Amir's beating was getting tougher and tougher. I ran into my bedroom desperate to help Rhonda. I knew with the ass whipping she was enduring she was about to be on death's door.

"Nigga, don't make me use this," I said, cocking my 9mm. "Fuckin' let her go or I guarantee I will blow you away." Amir had the nerves to try and call my bluff by punching Rhonda again. I pulled that trigger so fast and put a bullet in a glass vase that was no more than three feet away from him. "Next bullet is hitting you right between the eyes."

Amir released Rhonda so quickly she almost bumped her head on the coffee table. "If I ever catch you over here or any place in the vicinity I'm shooting first and asking questions later. Now get the fuck out!"

I kept my gun aimed ready for fire as I showed Amir the door. I made sure all the locks were in place, then ran over to Rhonda to make sure she was OK. "Thank you, Precious," Rhonda managed to say with a busted lip and two black eyes.

"Girl, that nigga did a number on you. Do you wanna call the police on him?"

"Nah, I don't feel like explaining what happened. Plus, I would hate for Amir punk ass to tell them about the gun you pulled out on him. Especially since I doubt it's registered."

"Good point. But speaking of punks, can you believe that nigga Robert? He ran outta here, not even giving a fuck that Amir was going upside your head. That's a simple ass nigga right there."

"You got that right. But damn, Precious, how you learn to handle a gun like that?"

"I tried to tell you, Rhonda, I'm a street bitch. Where I'm from, we keep it poppin'. If this shit would've went down in my hood, instead of us sitting here putting this ice on your face, we would be trying to decide where we were going to dump the body."

"Damn, I guess I'm pretty lucky to have you as a friend. I've never met a girl that looks this great in a dress and can handle a gun like a professional hit woman."

"What can I say? I'm pretty skilled."

I sat up with Rhonda until she fell asleep on the couch. Amir had fucked her face up, but I wasn't surprised. I didn't take him for the Ike Turner type, but you never know how a man is going to react when he catch his bitch out there fucking around.

Amir's pride was hurt, but that didn't give him the right to beat Rhonda down like a dog. I would have let him slide with one bitch slap to get his woman in line, but he took it over the top. I was just relieved that I didn't have to commit my third murder, which could've easily turned into four. If I killed Amir, then more than likely I would've had to kill Rhonda. I couldn't take the chance of her slipping and confiding to someone what I did, and then I go to jail because I tried to protect her ass.

Thank goodness I didn't have to think about that because I liked Rhonda, she was cool with me.

It took damn near six weeks for Rhonda's face to get back to normal. Amir crazy ass had the audacity to call Rhonda apologizing and begging for them to try again. And Rhonda had the nerves to actually consider it, until I told her I would kick her ass if I ever saw his face up in this place. I could never understand, how women could stay with a man, knowing that at any moment you got out of line he would kick yo' ass. I guess that's what they call blinded by love, I called it stupidity.

"So, Rhonda, are you coming with me to Supreme's show to-night?"

"No, I have the worse cramps ever. You have to count me out."

"I guess I'm rolling solo."

"That's probably for the best. Maybe you'll finally get some."

"Okay. Can you believe I've been seeing this dude for two months and we still haven't fucked? But you know what's really bothering me, Rhonda?"

"What?"

"I know he's fucking somebody." "Why you say that?"

"Sweetheart, ain't no nigga beating his beef for no two months. Nigga's need pussy like humans need food and water. I haven't figured out whether I should be flattered or offended that he's not fucking me."

Of course, after running my mouth off to Rhonda, I was late. I rushed to Madison Square Garden, hoping to catch Supreme's performance since he was closing the show, but, of course, by the time I arrived, it was over. I knew his manager was giving him an afterparty at a suite in the W Hotel so I headed over there.

When I got to the penthouse floor, there were a crowd of people in the hallway mingling and drinking champagne creating their own party. The room door was open and when I entered I understood why so many people were in the hallway, it was like the disco inferno up in the bitch. It was wall-to-wall motherfuckers. I didn't see Supreme, so I weaved through the crowd hoping to spot him. I ended up in the back where there was a private sitting area. To my disgust, Supreme was sitting on the couch, talking up a storm with some bad J.Lo knockoff.

"Oh, so I guess you found someone to keep you company, huh, Supreme?"

"Precious, I'm glad you made it. I waited for you back stage, but you never came."

"So what, you scooped up the first piece of ass you could to replace me?"

"Excuse me?"

"Bitch, you heard what the fuck I said. Why don't you sit there like the good mutt you are and mind yo' business. This here is between me and Supreme."

"Listen, I don't know who you think you are, but" before she could continue, Supreme tried to defuse the situation.

"I apologize. Precious is a very close friend of mine, and she is misreading what's going on between us, which, for the record, is nothing," he added, turning to look at me to make sure I understood.

"Fuck you, Supreme. I knew you were full of shit. Is that why you don't fuck me, 'cause you like putting your dick in bitches like her? You stay here and entertain your little friend. I'm out."

I bolted through the crowd, furious with myself. I knew I shouldn't have let myself get open off Supreme. That nigga had me playing myself in front of other bitches like I was a two-cent chick. Finally, getting through the jungle of people, I caught my breath when I reached the hallway. Numerous guys were grabbing at me as I made my way through the party, but when I laid eyes on a Mekhi Pfifer look-alike leaning against the wall, I responded to the lust in his eyes. Without as much as a hello, we locked lips and our tongues explored each other.

For that moment I wanted to forget that Supreme made me feel like a sucker and this was my way of saying fuck you.

"What the fuck are you doing?" Supreme barked as he yanked my arms from the stranger's embrace and pushed me against the wall.

"Supreme, yo' this your girl?" The Mekhi Pfifer look alike questioned sounding like a fan.

"No, I'm just his close friend?"

"Yeah, this my girl."

"That's not what you called me when you were getting all cozy wit' miss Jenny from the block."

"Yo, shut the fuck up."

"Man, I'm sorry. I didn't know that was your girl." Somebody must've told Supreme's bodyguards there was some sort of altercation going on, because all of a sudden two big dudes came out ready to take down the Mehki Pfifer look-alike.

"Everything's cool." The boy was relieved that Supreme didn't sic his hired goons on him. "But, you can go now," Supreme said, brushing the guy off. Supreme grabbed my arm until we got to a door at the end of the hall. He took out a key, opened the door and pulled me into another suite. "What the fuck is wrong with you, Precious?" he said after he slammed the door.

"What the fuck is wrong wit' me? What about you. Carrying on wit' that bitch."

"We were talking, that's it. If you had got to the show on time and met me backstage like you were supposed to, then I wouldn't have to talk to nobody else."

"Oh, so now it's my fault you kicking it wit' the next bitch. I guess it's my fault, too that you don't want to have sex wit' me."

"Is that with this is about? You want me to fuck you, is that what you want, Precious? Hum, answer me." Supreme was now grabbing at me roughly, pulling on my dress. He put his hands around my waist and forcefully pushed my hips against him. "Oh, now you don't have nothing to say. Either you want me to fuck you or you don't, Precious. Which one is it?"

I remained silent because the nigga was turning me on. He then put his hands up my dress and ripped off my thong.

"How do you want me to fuck you, Precious, from the front or the back?" The next thing I knew, Supreme had me bent over a chair pounding my pussy out. My ass jiggled against his dick with each thrust.

"Oh, Supreme, baby you feel so good," I moaned.

"You was going to give all this ass to some nigga you didn't even know."

"No, baby, I was just tryna make you jealous."

"Don't lie to me."

"I swear, I only want you."

"You better 'cause this pussy is mine now. If you ever try some trifling shit like that again, I will fuck you up. You understand me?"

"Yes."

"You sure?"

"Yes, it won't neva happen again." That night I got the best dick down of my life. Now I understood why Supreme wanted to wait, because he knew once he put it on me, I would be officially sprung.

Face Off

Some good dick can do wonders for a bitch. Now that Supreme was slaying me on a regular basis, I didn't have a care in the world. I was acting all giddy for the nigga and it was bugging me out.

Rhonda instantly knew when I got some because she said my face kept a glow. Butterflies in your stomach, every time the phone ring hoping it's him, restless nights when you go to sleep without him by your side, scared that a bitch with a prettier face, bigger tits and ass will catch his eye and steal him away were the telltale signs that I heard so many girls speak of but never thought it would happen to me. I guess I was in love or deeply infatuated, one of the other. Whatever it was, I let myself enjoy the feeling and temporarily buried my insecurities of being hurt.

"Six dollars, please," the lady in the toll both screamed, interrupting my thoughts of love.

I searched for the twenty dollars I put to the side and the lady belted, "Hurry up."

"Hold on a minute," I looked out my rear view mirror and no other cars were behind me, so I didn't know why she was rushing me.

"Here you go," I said, handing her the twenty that fell on the floor by side of the door. The rude bitch snatched the money from me like she owned the George Washington Bridge. After she damn near tossed my change at me, I said, "Bitch, don't get mad at me 'cause you working at a toll booth. If you don't like it, get another job."

"Watch yo' mouth, you stank hoe."

I couldn't let that Jheri-curl having bitch get away with that. I stuck my head out the window and spit dead in her face. She reached her hand out and tried to grab my neck. I pressed down so hard on the gas and sped off before she tried to flag down the cop. But that's what she got for popping all that shit.

After crossing the bridge, I turned onto the Henry Hudson Parkway downtown on my way to meet Supreme at the studio. I looked at the clock and saw that I was running mad early, so I decided to stop by my old apartment on 142nd and Riverside. The tollbooth lady still had me riled up and I needed to cool down, plus, I hadn't been there in months and wanted to check on the spot. I thought about subleasing it, since Inga wasn't staying there,, but I didn't need the money, and I liked knowing that I always had a place to crash, if need be.

When I finally found a parking spot, I walked up to the building and noticed that it had been painted recently. The super was maintaining the building well, and I knew that must of meant he would be raising the rent again soon. I took the elevator to the seventh floor, and although this place didn't have all the amenities of the spot I lived in Jersey, I somewhat missed living here. It was my very first apartment, so it held a lot of sentimental value.

I heard loud music as soon as I stepped off the elevator. When I lived here, I remembered it being so quiet, so I was surprised. Everyone on my floor was either old or married with young children. When I got closer to my door, I realized the music was coming from my apartment. I put the key in and when I tried to open it, the chain blocked any further entrance. I heard a female voice scream over the music, "Is that you, Inga?"

"Hun, humm," I grumbled loudly. *I know Inga's trifling ass is not staying here. That bitch told me she was keeping her ass in Brooklyn at her mom's crib. But who the fuck is in there, Inga ain't got no sister, I thought to myself.*

I was heated at the idea of somebody chilling in my crib. I reached in my purse and pulled out the knife I al ways kept on me. I stepped away from the door so who ever opened it couldn't see me if they looked through the peep hole. The moment I heard the girl take off the chain, I grabbed the knob and pushed the door open. The door knocked the girl in the head, and she let out a yelp and covered her face. Without missing a beat, I slammed the door shut and jumped on top of the girl, pinned her arms down with my knees and put the knife to her throat. When I saw who it was, my first instinct was to slit her throat, but I needed to get some answers first.

"Porscha, what the fuck are you doing in my apartment?" She was still in pain from the door smashing her face that there was a long, pregnant pause before she fo cused on answering my question.

"I knew I should've had those locks changed," were the first words out the bitch's mouth.

"Bitch, you got bigger problems than that right now. How long has Inga been letting you stay in my crib?" Porscha dumb-ass rolled her eyes as if she had no intentions on answering my question. I put the tip of my knife to her throat and nipped it just deep enough to draw blood. She let out an involuntary scream, and I covered her mouth with my hand. "Listen to me, you two-dollar whore. I have no problem ending your life right now. So you can either answer my fucking questions or say your last prayer."

"What do you want to know," Porscha managed to say under sniffles.

"Start by telling me how long Inga been letting you stay here."

"About three months ago she gave me the key. She said you gave her the apartment."

"Now why the fuck would yo' dumbass want to lie up in my spot when you know I can't stand your motherfucking ass."

"At first, Nico told me to stop through because he want ed to see if you stashed his million dollars here. Inga and I came to look, but we didn't find it. Then she called asking you about the money, and you told her you didn't know what she was talking about. I told Nico, but he said you were lying. He told me to ask Inga if I could chill here for awhile, just in case you came through."

"Well, bitch, I'm here now, what you supposed to do?"

"For the first few weeks Nico had a couple of his boys stationed out front, watching everyday and night for you to show up, ready to do whatever to get his money back. After awhile we decided you was ghost and wasn't coming back, so Nico told his boys to forget about it. But I like having my own place, so I decided to stay."

"When you say Nico told his boys to do whatever in order to get his money, you mean kill me?"

"No, that was one thing he instructed them not to do. He said killing you was the one pleasure he would save for himself."

"Nico locked up for damn near the rest of his life. How the fuck is he ever gonna get that pleasure?"

"How the fuck I know? That nigga so crazy he's determined that somehow he will get out of jail."

"Why does Nico believe I have his money?"

"One of Nico's street informants told him that word had it that Tommy tried to cross him and went to his crib to steal the million. It wasn't there but Tommy got some information from Boogie's nephews that they were supposed to meet up wit' this chick, which was you, to make the paper clean. Something went wrong because Boogie, Tommy and the nephews all ended up dead but the money was neva found. So Nico said you still had it. When he got locked up, the streets turned on him and stole all his money. That mil lion was the only paper he had left, and he wanted it back."

"Answer me this, Porscha. Did Nico have my mother killed?"

I always thought Tommy and Boogie's nephews killed my mother, but I could never explain how they got in her apartment. The door wasn't broken, so whoever did it, my mother let them in. That didn't make sense to me because of the lifestyle my mother lived. She wouldn't open the door for nobody unless she knew you and was expecting you. So if Tommy and his boys showed up unexpectedly, they would've had to kick in the door to get to her.

"I don't know if you ready for this, Precious."

"Porscha, don't talk to me in riddles. If I'm asking the questions, then I want the answers."

"You can't say I didn't try to warn you. Nico's street informant was Inga. Her and Tommy was cool, and he told her that the nephews told him that Boogie told them that you had the million dollars.

"Inga tried to find out where you were so she could tell Tommy, but you wouldn't give her no information. So then Inga told Tommy that you might've stashed the money at your mom's crib. Inga also knew how your mom's didn't answer the door for nobody, and Tommy didn't want to cause no loud raucous kicking in the door 'cause he figured somebody might call the police. He told Inga that if she would knock on the door, acting like she was looking for you, then he would hit her off with seventyfive thousand."

"Did Inga know that Tommy and them were going to kill my mom's?"

"She figured they would, but she said yo' mom's was a crackhead anyway, and them killing her would put her out of her misery." I couldn't believe what Porscha was telling me, although it all made sense. I knew Inga felt betrayed about that sorry-ass nigga Ritchie, but to let Tommy and them kill my mother was the lowest you could go. Inga knew that as much hell as my mother put me through, she was all I had my entire life. To take her away from me was stealing my last breath.

"How could Inga do that to my mother?" I asked myself out loud.

"Precious, you know Inga blames you for her fucked up life. She believes you fucked up her relationship with Ritchie and is responsible for Nico killing him, leaving her without a father for her son. She's barely making ends meet and her mother the one that have to watch the baby while she at work."

"What happened to the fifty thousand I gave her?"

"Didn't she tell you she bought a car, clothes, jewelry and shit."

"Why don't she sell her fucking car, so she can have some damn money for the baby?"

"She totaled it in a car accident and her dumb ass let the car insurance lapse."

"Where is Inga at right now?"

"She was supposed to be on her way over here, but I'm not sure."

"Call her now and find out exactly where she at. Also find out if the baby wit' her."

"I need my cell phone."

"Where is it?"

"Right over there on that nightstand."

"Porscha, I'ma let you up so you can get your phone, but I'm keeping this knife right under your throat. If I even think you gonna try some slick shit, I'm slitting side to side. Do you understand?"

She nodded her head. I hoped the fear was instilled in her to the point that she would do as I said. It's not like I cared whether the bitch lived or died, but I did need her to get to Inga. Porscha dialed Inga's number and did exactly as I asked. When she hung up she informed me that Inga was still in Brooklyn at her mom's crib. "Let's go."

"Where we going?"

"To Brooklyn to pay a visit to my dear old friend Inga."

"Precious, I don't want no part of that. You crazy and there ain't no telling what you gonna do."

"You right. So you want to take me to Inga or should I kill you right now?"

Porscha grabbed her shoes and phone, and we went to the car. We stopped at my trunk so I could get my 9mm, then I made Porscha get on the driver's side. I kept my gun pointed at her the whole time. On our drive to Brooklyn, I kept imagining how my mother must've felt when she realized Inga had set her up. Your daughter's so-called best friend being an accessory in your death.

When Porscha pulled up to the projects Inga lived in, I scanned the area looking for the best spot to have our show down. "Drive around to that back parking lot." That parking lot was always isolated, because the hustler's needed to be where the action was, and the dope fiends needed to be near the dealers, so nobody ever came back there.

"Now what?" an exasperated Porscha questioned.

"Call Inga. Tell her that I unexpectedly showed up at the crib with the money, we got into it, and you stabbed me to death. Say you left my body at the apartment and took my car and the money. Then tell her you need her help and to come outside because you're in the back parking lot."

"What's going to happen after that?"

"If you promise not to mention a word to anyone about everything you told me and what I'm about to do to Inga, then I'll let you walk away from this whole situation alive. But you have to promise me that first."

"I promise, Precious. I won't say a word. I'll pretend like today neva even happened."

"You can't even tell Nico."

"I won't. I don't even fuck wit' Nico like that. He so obsessed wit' you that he only uses me to keep tabs on what I hear on the streets. I don't even like taking his collect calls no more because the first question he ask me is if I heard what nigga you supposed to be fucking wit.

"That shit was getting on my nerves. I was the one going to court to support him and brought him clothes so he wouldn't sit through trial in that nasty ass orange jumpsuit, spending my money on car rentals so I could go visit his ass in jail. I was writing him letters and having to suck dick to get the money to pay for the highass phone bills, I had for accepting his collect calls. I did all that shit for that nigga and he want to sit on the phone and vent about the chick that caused him to get locked up in the first place. So, no, you definitely don't have to worry about me telling Nico. I don't need to give him another reason to go on and on about you."

"Good. Now call Inga."

Porscha kicked the speech that we rehearsed and Inga fell for it hook, line and sinker. I heard her devious ass screaming with glee when Porscha told her she had the money. Not at one point did she show any remorse or sym pathy for me when Porsha said I was dead. She actually laughed and exclaimed, "Good. That bitch had it coming."

"Her mom was walking in when we were about to get off the phone. She said she had to throw on some clothes and she would be out in five minutes." Porscha explained after hanging up with Inga.

"OK, let's go."

"Where we going now?"

"I don't want her to see me in the car. Let's go stand over there underneath the stairwell opening."

"I thought you said after I called Inga, I was done and could leave."

"When we see her coming, all I want you to do is call her name and show your face, then you can bounce. Is that too much to ask?"

"Nah, I can handle that." We got out the car, and I kept the gun on Porscha as we walked towards our destination. "You can put the gun away now, Precious. I ain't gonna try to run off. I'll stay wit' you until Inga come outside. You gon kill her, not me."

"True, but you can never be too careful."

Porscha and I turned our heads simultaneously in the same direction at the sound of someone's footsteps. We both assumed it was Inga, and I nodded my head giving Porscha the sign to call out her name.

"Inga, is that you?"

"Yeah, where you at?"

"Right over here by the stairs," Porscha replied. I stepped out of sight, waiting for Inga to come closer.

"Girl, I'm so excited I can't believe you got all that paper. I can finally quit that damn job at the nursing home," Inga said as the sound of her voice became louder as she got closer to Porscha.

I stepped from behind the brick wall that was shielding me, and would've done anything to have forever captured the look on Inga's face when she saw me. "Aren't you happy to see your best friend, Inga?"

"Porscha, you set me up!"

"I ain't have no choice. She was gonna kill me if I didn't get you out here."

"Both of you stand over here," I said, pointing my gun in the direction I wanted them to move.

"Precious, I don't know what Porscha told you but its all lies."

"Save it, Inga. I heard wit' my own ears how excited you were at the news that I was dead. But I could even let that go. What I can't let go is that you set my mother up to die at the hands of Tommy and his boys."

Inga turned and glared at Porscha with hate.

"Don't look at me," Porscha said, crossing her arms and rolling her head.

"Precious, I didn't know Tommy was gonna kill your moms. I thought he was going in there to just try and find the money."

"You lying bitch. Porscha, repeat what you said Inga told you about my mother."

"She said yo' mom's was a crack head anyway and them killing her would put her out of her misery. That's what the fuck you said, Inga."

"You know what's so foul about that, Inga. When my mother opened that door you could look at her and tell she wasn't using drugs no more. I saw her earlier that day and she was more beautiful than ever.

"But you didn't care. All you wanted was yo' funky seventy-five thousand dollars. But I'll tell you what I'll do for you. I'll give that money to your mother to take care of your son. Think of it as her cashing in your life insurance policy."

"Precious, I'm so sorry. Please don't kill me. I was just hurt over the whole Ritchie situation. I fucked up, but we can get pass all this." The tears were swelling in Inga's eyes as she begged for her life.

"I think it's time for me to go head and leave now and let ya handle your business. But like we discussed, Precious, didn't none of this happen. All this stay between me and you."

"Sorry, Porscha. I had a change of heart. All of this stays with me, not you." I aimed the gun right and center where her mouth dropped when she heard the news. It all happened so fast, she couldn't even close it before I pulled the trigger. Her whole head damn near came off. "You know I neva liked that bitch."

By this time Inga was on her hands and knees as if I would show any mercy for her.

"Precious, please, it's not too late. We can start all over; get the fuck out of Brooklyn, you, me and little Ritchie."

"Tell me you didn't name your son after a nigga who didn't give a fuck about you or his seed. Bitch, I'ma kill you just for that."

With that, I put two bullets in Inga. One for the death of my mother, the other for being a stupid cunt for naming her son after his trifling father. I left the two dead snakes lying beside one another. Neither one of them bitches would be having an open casket at their funeral.

He'll Be Back

Supreme had been furious with me since the day I killed Porscha and Inga. I was supposed to have met him at the studio, and he blew my phone up and left a ton of messages when I never came. Then he kept calling Rhonda because he started getting scared, thinking something ter rible had happened to me.

When I finally called him, my brain was so fried I couldn't come up with a reasonable explanation for disappearing for all those hours. He kept saying be honest and just tell him the truth. But I couldn't seem to come up with a way to say I was out committing two murders. That's when he told me he didn't want to speak to me until I told him exactly where I had been. I was actually relieved. I had killed before, but I couldn't get murdering Inga out of my head.

A week after Inga' funeral, I kept my word and made sure her mother got hundred thousand dollars for the care of little Ritchie. I gave an extra twentyfive thousand for my guilt because, however justified I felt, I was responsible for him growing up not ever knowing his mother or father. The least I could do was give some money to hopefully help the boy have a chance at a future. Inga's mom was always a hard worker and good woman. She wouldn't go blow all the cash on material shit. She would make sure the baby was provided for.

With everything that happened and Supreme not speak ing to me, I was becoming restless. My days were getting longer and my nights shorter. I wasn't doing nothing with myself. "Girl, get out the bed," Rhonda said as she dis turbed what had now become the norm for me, sleeping my time away.

"What is it, Rhonda?"

"Wake up and do something. I'm starting to think you're a vampire. You sleep all day and watch television all night. Let's go out and have some drinks or something."

"I'm not up to it."

"You better start. Do you think Supreme laying around in his bed mourning over you?"

"I'm not mourning over Supreme. I'm just in a funk. I have a lot of shit on my mind."

"Well snap out of it. Get dressed. Let's go to the city." Rhonda was right. I'd been dragging my body around here in a daze. Being on the outs with Supreme was bothering me more than I wanted to admit.

The few times I tried to call him, he said unless I was going to come clean with him, then he had nothing to say to me. He was so not checking for me the last couple of times I called, he let it go to voice-mail. I didn't understand why he was tripping so hard. I swore to him I wasn't with another dude or anything, but that day I had an unexpected emergency that needed to be handled. His problem was that I didn't have family and I didn't have a job so what type of emergency could keep me away from him where I couldn't at least call? As bad as I wanted to believe that Supreme would get over this, he was so fucking stubborn; the reality that he might not be back was setting in.

That night Rhonda took me to some lounge called Duvet. There were beds scattered throughout the place with a bar designed to look like a block of ice. It was the typi cal crowd, mixed with models, actors, industry heads and beautiful people. The hostess sat us at a bed in the corner next to Cam'ron and his crew. Rhonda was mingling at their bed because she was real cool with his manager.

I sat there sipping on my drink, wishing I could crawl back in my own real bed. I was in no mood to be out and about, but to my devastation, Supreme was. I couldn't help but notice when he walked in the spot with a girl on his arm. She looked like some chick I'd seen in a music video or something. They sat on a bed on the other side of the room but still within my viewing area. His two bodyguards parked themselves on the bed beside them.

Seeing Supreme with that girl felt like someone stabbed me in the heart, twisted it and then left the shit on automatic rotate. The pain was so continuous it seemed it would never stop. "Precious, are you OK? You have this expression on your face like you're stuck in a nightmare."

"That sounds about right. I guess you didn't see Supreme walk in."

"No, where is he?"

"Right over there." I pointed at the bed across from us. He was in such deep conversation with his date that he hadn't even looked in my direction yet.

"I told you not to be sitting around mourning over his ass. Maybe you'll finally snap out of that coma you've been in for the last few weeks."

I looked up at Rhonda and then looked back at myself.

I had to make sure I was hearing what I thought I heard. Rhonda was actually giving me a pep talk. When that sunk in, the fire that used to burn inside of me suddenly reig nited. My eyes zoomed in on the dude poppin' bottles who had been sizing me up since I sat down.

"Do you know who that is?" I asked pointing towards the dude on the low.

"Hell yeah, that's pretty boy Mike. He owns Pristine Records."

There was no need for Rhonda to explain why they called him "Pretty Boy"; the nigga was fine. But what set him off was that even though he was pretty, you could also tell that he was a straightup thug. Trying to be discreet didn't work because after Rhonda said her piece, pretty boy Mike approached our bed.

"You mind if I sit on your bed?"

"Nah, have a seat."

"I know you seen me watching you since you stepped in the place. I didn't think you were interested until I noticed you point me out to your friend."

"Damn, you saw that? I was tryna be tactful. I guess it didn't work. But how you know I wasn't clowning you to my friend?"

"I didn't, but the fact you acknowledged my presence gave me the confidence to introduce myself to you. I'm Mike and your name is," he said, extending his hand out to me.

"Nice to meet you, Mike. My name is Precious."

"It's a pleasure to meet you. Do you live here in the city?"

"No, I rep Brooklyn, but I live in Jersey now."

"Brooklyn girl. What part of Brooklyn is you from?"

"I used to live over there in Riverdale Towers."

"Damn, that's hard knock. You look more Brooklyn Heights than Riverdale Towers."

"Don't let the face, clothes and jewelry fool you. I'm BK to the fullest."

"You know what, Precious? I believe you."

"Why's that?"

"You so damn gorgeous, I didn't even pay attention to the darkness in your eyes. That's deadly. A man has to be on top of his game to deal with you. You know I live in Jersey, but I, too, come from the school of hard knocks. I've been around these Hollywood acting cats for so long that I'm slipping. I couldn't even recognize one of my own."

"Yeah, you are slipping because when my girlfriend told me they called you pretty boy Mike, I said to myself, Yeah he might be pretty, but he's a straight up thug. These simpleass niggas around here don't see that in you but I do."

Mike put his hand on my cheek and gently rubbed the side of my face.

"You my type of girl, Precious, beautiful on the outside but tough as nails on the inside."

"Precious, I need to speak to you." It took me a minute to focus 'cause pretty boy Mike's game was kinda tight. Eventually, I came too and Supreme was standing in front of me.

"What up, Supreme?" Mike said, extending his hand but quickly putting it back down when Supreme made it clear he was showing no love.

"What do you want?" I snapped.

"To speak to you."

"Whateva you have to say, you can say it right here."

"You wanna act cute, that's cool. What the fuck are you doing over here with this nigga."

"Yo, man, there is no need for you to get all excited. Chill out."

"Pretty boy Mike, this ain't none of your business, I'm having a conversation with my girl."

"Your girl? That's hard to tell when you came in here wit' some chick."

"So is that why you letting this nigga touch all on your face 'cause you seen me with a female? That's not accept able. Get yo' shit, and let's go."

"I'm not going anywhere with you, Supreme. You not answering my calls, you been lounging on the bed ever since you swaggered in here with some other bitch and now you tryna dictate what the fuck I'm supposed to do. Kiss my ass. I'm staying right where the fuck I'm at."

Supreme reached down and grabbed my arm, trying to pull me off the bed. That's when Mike stepped in and pushed Supreme out the way, and all hell broke lose. Supreme's body guards swarmed in and attacked Mike. Then the three guys that came with Mike ran over and started busting bottles over the bodyguards heads. With all the commotion going on, Su preme grabbed my arm and practically dragged me out the club. We hopped in the Suburban that was waiting out front with him cussing at me the whole time.

"What happened to your little arm piece that you came in here with?"

"When I spotted you getting all up close and personal with that nigga Mike, I knew it was about to be some trouble so I gave her some money to take a cab home."

"So what is she supposed to be your new girlfriend?"

"No, just someone who was keeping me company while my girlfriend was supposed to be getting her mind right. But instead you was up in Duvet, getting cozy with some industry cat. I was about to bust yo' ass in there."

"I don't know why. You the one that's been giving me straight shade for the last few weeks. Do you know how sick at the stomach I was when I saw you come in the club with that girl? I thought I lost you for good."

"Honestly, Precious, when you wouldn't tell me what was going on with you I was leaning towards cutting you off. But when I saw you with that nigga I lost it. The thought of some other man in my pussy was about to make me go ballistic. We gotta find a way to work this out 'cause I can't give you up."

When we got back to my place, the first thing I did after locking the door was unzipped Supreme's jeans and put his dick in my mouth. I wanted to taste him so bad, and I also wanted him to remember what my lips felt like wrapped around his manhood. I was in love with Supreme, and I didn't ever want to worry again if he would leave me and never come back.

Death Do Us Part

Once again I was feeling alive after the thug lovin' Supreme put on me. The love I felt for Supreme was becoming so strong, that I considered him to be the man I wanted to spend the rest of my life with. Because of that, I debated whether or not I should come clean with him about my past.

Of course, not tell him everything, but enough for him to get a general idea about who I am. Or maybe who I was. Falling in love was beginning to soften my heart and make me want to change my ways. All my life, the only person I could depend on was me. Nobody had my back or gave a fuck about me. Everybody was out for self, including me. It was different now; everything had changed. I knew that Supreme was in love with me like I was in love with him. For the first time somebody valued my life and genuinely cared what happened to me.

I woke up famished and went to the kitchen. "Rhonda, what you doing here, why aren't you at work?"

"By the time I got home after escaping from all the drama you caused, I was too tired to go to work."

"Escape, how long did that shit last after we left?"

"They had to shut the club down. The fight between over to some other niggas. Pretty soon the whole club was basically fighting. The police had to come in and break that shit up. Thank goodness I had your car keys because when I looked around your ass was nowhere to be found."

"As soon as the fight broke out, Supreme got me outta there."

"Yeah, when I got home early this morning I saw his driver sitting in the car, waiting for him. I guess that means ya kissed and made up."

"Something like that." My face was beaming as I smiled from ear to ear. "So what happened to that dude Mike? Was he a'ight?"

"Yeah, he escaped out of there around the same time as me. His face was still intact. Supreme's bodyguards got pretty fucked up 'cause them dudes were busting bottles. That was some crazy shit."

"What exactly do you know about Mike?"

"Damn, Precious I thought you just said that you and Supreme were back together. You want to fuck it up and start seeing Mike too."

"No, it's nothing like that. I'm in love wit' Supreme I'm not doing nothing to fuck that up."

"Then why the interest in Mike?"

"Something about the conversation we had last night bothered me. It wasn't anything specific. A few things he said seemed odd."

"What things?"

"I can't really pinpoint it. The conversation in general. So what do you know about him?"

"Not much. He came on the scene a couple of years ago, making big moves. The first couple of artist he put out just went straight to the top of the chart, selling millions of albums. He quickly solidified himself as bigwig in the music business. People respect him. He don't cause no trouble."

"Interesting, sounds like an overnight success story."

"You can say that, and oh, yeah, he's also from Brook lyn," Rhonda added before going to her bedroom. Maybe that's what it was; certain Brooklyn niggas got this way about them. Dudes from other boroughs don't exude it. I couldn't put my finger on it, but something about pretty boy Mike I couldn't shake.

Later on that day, I got dressed because I was going to the city to meet Supreme. He was having a session at Sony Music Studio and I was determined to be on time. We were finally back on track and I wasn't going to do anything to jeopardize that. I was also looking forward to going because I had never been inside a studio before.

When I turned on 54th street, there was a Bentley in front and a couple of Benz's, Beamers and Range Rovers lined on the side of the street. It looked more like a car show than a place of business. I parked my car in the lot because I wasn't taking chances getting my shit towed.

"Hi, I'm here for Supreme's session."

"Your name?"

"Precious."

"Hold on one moment." The guy got on the phone and I assumed he was calling the studio to make sure it was OK for me to go in the session. "Sign in and go right through those doors, he's in studio A."

I followed the guy's directions and came to the door that had the letter A. When I opened the heavy wood door, I en tered into lounge. There were a few black leather couches and a television with a play station hooked up. A whole bunch of junk food was sitting on a table off to the side and mini-refrigerator was next to it.

I stayed on course and followed the loud music, which led me to the actual studio. The lights were dim, but I could see somebody in the vocal booth messing with his head phones. The guy didn't look like Supreme, though. Then a couple of guys that were hauled up in the corner smoking weed noticed me.

"Who you looking for, Mami?"

"Supreme. Is this his session?"

"Nah, this the wrong studio."

"Is this studio A?"

"Yeah, but I believe Supreme in Studio B. It's right across the hall."

"Thanks. Sorry about that."

"No problem. You more than welcome to stay," the weed smoker said in attempt to flirt with me.

"Maybe another time." As I turned to walk away, pretty boy Mike was standing in my way.

"Precious Cummings, I was hoping to run into you again. I wasn't counting on seeing you so soon though." I didn't recall telling Mike my last name, 'cause honestly I'm not really deep on conversation to do all that.

"Well, here I am. I'm glad I did run into. I wanted to apologize for what happened last night."

"Things happen. It wasn't your fault."

"Appreciate that. Thanks for being so cool. Well I better be going."

"You here to see Supreme?"

"Yes, the guy upfront accidentally sent me to the wrong studio."

"I'll walk you out."

"That's OK. I can find my way."

"But I wanted to talk to you about a mutual friend of ours."

"You must be mistaken 'cause I don't know any of your friends."

"Oh, I could've sworn you knew Nico Carter." I wanted to come up with some sort of quick denial but I couldn't. I was stunned that of all the people in the state of New York, our mutual friend had to be my worse enemy.

"As a matter of fact, I do know Nico, but from a long time ago."

"Come have a seat, Precious. We should talk."

"I don't have time. Supreme is waiting for me."

"Make time." Mike was making it clear that this wasn't a request, but more so a demand. I followed him into the lounge and sat on one of the black leather couches I had observed on my way in.

"What do you want?" I said defensively.

"Remember last night when we were talking and you told me that you rep for BK."

I nodded my head, letting him know I remembered saying it, but now wishing I hadn't.

"Then I told you I was slipping because I didn't even recognize my own. I meant that in terms of identifying the wifey of a kingpin."

"Don't worry 'bout it, 'cause I ain't nobody's wifey, especially not a kingpin's."

"Let me finish, Precious," he said sternly. "See before I got in this music game, I was a kingpin. Unlike so many fallen soldiers, I was able to get out and take my money and make it legitimate. But the streets still run through my blood.

So, I should always be able to spot another soldier, which includes a wifey. A wifey is an intricate element to a kingpin. A wifey has the eyes of death because they're always a step away from it. The only time I've ever seen that look in a woman's eyes was right before I killed my own wifey-that is until I looked in yours.

"That was so many years ago, and I'd forgotten because there aren't that many true kingpins, so there aren't many women who are truly built to be the wifey of a kingpin."

"So why did you kill your wifey?" I asked with curiosity.

"She didn't remain loyal. She caught me fucking around so to retaliate she fucked around on me. Of course, she had to die. It destroyed me to end her life, but her body was no longer sacred. Part of me died when I killed her; she was my everything. I molded her to be tough as nails on the in side, just like you, Precious. But, see, her mistake was she tried to teach the teacher a lesson."

"This makes for an interesting conversation, but what is your point in telling me all this bullshit?"

"Nico Carter is a true kingpin and you are his wifey. No matter who is supposed to be your man, you still belong to Nico until death do you part. The only reason why you're still alive, Precious, is because only Nico can end your life, and he will when he gets out. That is my message to you."

"Lucky for me, Nico will be in jail for the rest of his life.

Let me ask you a question, Mike? Did you know all this before you was pushing up on me at da club?"

"I truly admire the fire in you, Precious?"

"Answer the damn question."

"As you know, Nico garners a lot of respect on the streets, and we were all aware of his incarceration. The top heads soon learned you were the reason for his demise, but at his request everyone agreed to let him handle you per sonally. I knew your name, but I'd never seen you before. When you walked into the club I was mesmerized by you.

"My wifey was beautiful but nowhere near your caliber. When I came over and introduced myself, I thought you were in the entertainment industry. But then when you said you were from Brooklyn and you told me your name, something clicked. The first thing I did this morning was investigate. It didn't take long to put all the pieces together. You're still a baby and yet you're already a legend in Brooklyn."

"So what I'm supposed to be? Grateful for this little speech you just gave me?"

"As I tried to explain, I'm just the messenger giving you a warning."

"You mean a death sentence."

"I know Nico taught you the code of the streets. You didn't honestly believe you could walk away from him. There's always a price to pay, and it usually means death."

"Are you finished because Supreme is waiting for me?"

"We're done here."

"Good, and by the way, next time you speak to Nico, deliver a message for me. Tell him I hope he rots in jail for the rest of his life."

My heart was beating so fast. I didn't want Mike to know it, but what he said had me petrified. I reached a point in my life where I had a reason to live, and here he was, delivering the news that death was right around the corner. My hands were shaking, and I was visibly upset. I didn't want to go in Supreme's session looking so distraught. I stopped in the bathroom and splashed water on my face. I dabbed on some fresh lip gloss, trying to erase the look of defeat away. I held out my hands and the shaking wouldn't stop. "I give up. Fuck it."

"Where have you been? They called in the studio a half hour ago saying you were here."

I was surprised to see Supreme standing in the middle of the hallway.

"Baby, the guy gave me the wrong studio. I sat in the lounge for over fifteen minutes before someone told me the correct room. By that time I had to use the bathroom so bad. I'm sorry I had you waiting."

"That's cool. I just worry about you. All these vultures around here, I would hate for one of them to take you away," he said, kissing me on the forehead. "What the fuck is that nigga doing here?" I looked up and saw Mike.

"Precious, I see that you found Supreme."

Supreme eyed me suspiciously.

"Baby, studio A, the session that Mike is in, was the wrong room I accidentally went into. Mike was nice enough to point me in the right direction. Thanks again."

"No problem. Supreme I hope there are no hard feelings about what went down last night; I heard your bodyguards were in pretty bad shape."

"Nah, they recovering nicely, but I got two more here with me now, until they recover a hundred percent. Would you like to meet them?"

"No, thanks I'll take your word. But with a girl as gorgeous as Precious on your arm, you might need two more. It would be a shame for someone to come take her away."

"Nigga, stay away from her." Supreme and Mike were now standing toe to toe.

"Supreme, stop. Lets just go. He didn't mean nothing by it." I was holding onto Supreme's arm, praying he would back down. He had no idea he was butting heads with a killer.

"I think you should take your woman's advice."

I finally got Supreme to walk away, but not before Mike said, "Precious, I'll make sure to tell Nico you said hello."

"Who is Nico?"

"Nobody important. Just some dude that we both know from Brooklyn."

"Precious, I don't ever want you talking to Mike again. If you see him go in the opposite direction, 'cause that nig ga rubs me the wrong way." Supreme didn't have to say anymore, I had already come to that very same conclusion.

Holy Matrimony

For the third night in a row I woke up in a pool of sweat, suffering from the same nightmare. I'm at a funeral and my mother, Boogie, Nico, Ritchie, Butch, Azar, Boogie's nephews, Tommy, Porscha and Inga are all there dressed in black. I'm the only one in white.

I walk over to my mother, but it's like she can't see me. No one can see me. Then they all gather around the casket that is about to be lowered into the ground. I slowly move forward to get a glimpse of the person we gathered here to mourn and to my horror it's me. I blamed Mike for my de lusions, and it made me angry. In a twentyminute conver sation, he managed to turn my whole world upside down.

"Precious, telephone. It's Supreme," Rhonda yelled out, helping to shake my terror.

"Hi, baby."

"You still in the bed, sleepyhead?"

"I'm getting up now."

"What are you doing later on?"

"Hopefully I'ma see you."

"Cool 'cause I wanted to take you out to dinner tonight."

"Really, where?"

"You'll see. Wear something really nice and sexy, of course."

I was so happy Supreme planned a romantic outing for us. I could now focus on something other than death.

After speaking to Supreme, I had the energy to get out of bed and eat some breakfast. "Good morning, Rhonda."

"Good morning, Supreme called pretty early this morning."

"He wanted to tell me that he planned a romantic dinner for us tonight."

"Nice, things have gotten really serious between you guys."

"I know, so serious that I think it's time for me to sit down and let him into my life."

"What do you mean?"

"Rhonda, there are a lot of things about me that you don't know and neither does Supreme. I don't trust people and because of that, I keep most things to myself. That way no one can hurt me. But since I've fallen in love with Su preme, I want to share my world with him."

"That's so passionate, Precious. I'm impressed."

"Rhonda, this isn't funny."

"I wasn't joking, I'm serious, Precious. I think it's to tally amazing that you're going to open up to Supreme. I could always tell that you were different, but I didn't want to intrude in your life. You appear to be perfect on the out side, but you've made it clear that the inside is a lot more complex. Not to mention the way you was about to put it on Amir. I've never seen anything like that before. I'll always be grateful to you for standing up for me."

"Thanks, Rhonda. You pretty cool yourself. You did take me in as a roommate without even knowing me."

"That's called desperation, and the nine thousand dollars up-front didn't hurt."

We fell out laughing because it was the truth.

"I'm glad I was desperate, though, because you turned out to be the best roommate ever. You're unlike any friend I've ever had. Your feelings, thoughts, are all so real. In my world that quality is an endangered species. I'm keep ing my fingers crossed because I truly hope that everything works out for you and Supreme and you all have a wonder ful life together."

"Me too."

I spent the rest of the day preparing for my evening with Supreme. I went to Elaine's in Edgewater Commons for a complete spa treatment. I then took it over to my beautician to get my tresses in order. By the time I got home, it was time for me to get dressed. I put on a deep vneck plunged white dress, that had stone and bead detailing, which added a little sparkle. The length fell right above my knees and dangerously hugged every curve.

"Damn. When Supreme sees you in that dress he might ask you to marry him tonight," Rhonda said when I strutted in the living room.

"Girl, you so crazy."

"Call me crazy if you like, but you look like a goddess. No one would ever guess you can handle a gun better than a dude."

"Let that be our little secret."

"Do you know where Supreme is taking you?"

"Not yet." I was giving myself the once over in the hall way mirror when the phone rang.

"Your Prince has arrived," Rhonda announced. I grabbed my purse anxious to see Supreme. "Have fun tonight."

"I will." I couldn't get downstairs fast enough. The elevator seemed to be going so slow, but I knew it was only because I was so anxious. When I got outside, my chariot awaited me in the form of a silver Maybach. The driver was holding the back seat passenger door open for me and Supreme stepped out with the most beautiful bouquet of flowers. He had on a linen white suit, which matched perfectly with my white dress. A tear rolled down my cheek, but this time it wasn't out of pain. It was pure love.

I was so busy making out with Supreme in the backseat like we were in high school, I didn't pay attention to where we were going. So when we arrived at what looked to be an airport, I was confused. "Baby, where are we?"

"Teterboro Airport."

"What are we doing here?"

"They're fueling up the private jet. We're having dinner on the beach in Barbados."

"Are you serious? I've never been on a private jet before or dinner in Barbados. I can't believe you're doing this for me."

"I wanted this night to be special."

During the flight I kept pinching myself because this couldn't be real. My life seemed to be going too perfectly no drama with bitches, no drama with my man and nobody getting killed. It didn't seem like my life; it was like I stepped into someone else's. It was fine with me. I was ready to leave that street life behind. Who knew that a drama-free life could be so much fun?

When the jet landed a car was waiting to take us to a yacht. Then the yacht took us to a private beach where dinner was served. A path of rose pedals led to our table in the center of a glass gazebo surrounded by vandella roses and pink peony flowers. Flat dishes filled with sand displayed vanilla candles. A mini orchestra dressed in tuxedos was playing the most soothing music.

We even had a wait staff to serve us our meal and keep the champagne flowing. Coming from the bottom I never imagined what heaven was like, but this had to be it. "Supreme, I never thought I could be speechless. This is amazing."

"You're amazing. Precious, I'm in love with you. I want to spend the rest of my life with you."

"Before you say anything else, there is something I want to tell you."

"You sound so serious. What is it?"

"I don't know exactly where to start."

"The beginning would be fine."

"It's a little more complicated than that."

"Precious, just tell me, don't hold back." I took a deep breath, trying to prepare for this moment. I wasn't sure how Supreme was going to react to what I had to say, but I knew it needed to be done. It was only fitting that I purge my soul in the middle of paradise.

"As you know I'm from Brooklyn. I grew up in the projects, depending on no one but myself. Because of my mother's drug addiction, she left me no choice but to go out there and make money to support us and, in her case, support her drug habit.

So, at the age of fifteen, I started fucking around with hustlers so they could take care of me and I could bring money home to my moms. In doing that I got caught up in a lot of bullshit, and I became cold. 'Cause when you out in those streets, don't nobody give a fuck about you. I soon met a man by the name of Nico Carter."

"Nico? Is that the guy Mike mentioned when we were in the studio?"

"Yes. I lied when I told you he was nobody. He's actually my ex-boyfriend who is currently locked up doing life in prison for a murder I set up."

"What!"

"You heard me. He cheated on me and I wanted to teach him a lesson so I started having sex with his best friend Ritchie, and I made sure he found out because I knew he would flip out and kill him."

"Wait a minute, I remember that case. That happened not too long ago. It was in the paper almost every day. Nico Carter was some big time kingpin from Brooklyn. He was convicted of killing two guys. They said it was over some drug operation gone bad, but you're saying it wasn't that at all."

"No, it wasn't. It was all my doing. I wanted to make sure he spent the rest of his life in prison."

"But he was convicted of killing two guys. He killed his best friend for fucking around with you, but why the other guy?"

"He didn't kill him, I did. Nico's best friend Ritchie was trying to cross him, but Nico didn't know it. Ritchie part nered up with this guy named Butch. Butch had beef with my exboyfriend Azar and put a gun to my head, threaten ing to kill me if I didn't give him Azar's money and the room key to where he was hiding out at. I didn't have a choice but to do what he asked and he murdered Azar.

"So the night Nico came looking for me at Ritchie's house, Butch showed up unexpectedly, and I killed him. Nobody knows that but you, Supreme. Nico probably has his suspicions, but he isn't sure. He also believes I took a million dollars from him, which I did. I wanted the money so I could leave Brooklyn and start my life over again."

"So where does pretty boy Mike fit in?"

"Mike is from Brooklyn. Before he got in the music game, he was a drug kingpin like Nico. When he met me at the club and I told him my name and that I was from Brooklyn he did some checking and realized that me and Nico's Precious was one in the same. When I ran into him at the studio he was delivering me a message courteous of Nico."

"What message was that?"

"Basically, that I still belong to him and when he gets out, he is going to kill me."

"Didn't he get two consecutive life sentences?"

"Yeah, but somehow, someway, he is determined to get out and get revenge."

"Baby, he's not ever getting out," Supreme said as he wiped away the tears that were streaming down my face.

"I know, but Mike sounded so sure that death was knocking on my front door. Supreme, I know I've done some fucked up things, but I'm different now. Falling in love with you has changed my whole out-look on life.

"I never thought another world existed outside of Brooklyn that I wanted to be a part of, but I was wrong. I know I've lied to you and you have every reason to turn your back on me, but just know that you're the first man I've ever loved, and I want you to be the last."

Supreme sat in front of me quiet as hell. I knew there were so many other secrets I was leaving out, but I didn't want to overload him. I just wanted to paint a clear picture of who I used to be. Plus, no matter what, some secrets have to die with you. I mean I had changed, but the streets of Brooklyn would always be in my blood.

"Precious, I'm glad you were honest with me. It explains why it was so hard for you to let down your guards. When I look in your beautiful eyes I can't believe you've been through so much. Most people carry the weight of the world on their face, yet you look as innocent as a little girl.

"All I want to do is take care of you and save you from yourself and the people who brought you so much pain. I could never turn my back on you. What you just told me only makes me love you more because I know how much courage it took for you to do that."

Supreme stood and came towards me. I was about to stand up, too, so I could embrace him for understanding and not judging me. "No sit back down." Supreme put his hand in his pocket and pulled out a tiny black box. Before what I thought he was about to do sunk in, he got on bended knee and said, "Precious, you're the only woman for me. I want to spend eternity with you. Would you do me the honor of becoming my wife?"

Remember when I said I came from nothing but was determined to have it all? That meant designer clothes, fly ass car, some diamonds and furs. You know the material things that all project chicks want. See, that was my hood dream.

When I rep'd for Brooklyn I had all that. Niggas couldn't tell me it could get no better. Every bitch in the street wanted to be me. I was Nico Carter's girl. We were the King and Queen of the hood. All motherfuckers had to bow down. I had my Alpo, so having it all had been accomplished in my book.

But now, here I was chilling on a beach that I arrived at on a yacht and before that a private jet, and Supreme, one of the biggest Rappers in the world, who I was madly in love with asked me to be his wife. So I'll admit it. I was wrong.

There is more to life than being 'Hood Rich'.

"Of course I'll marry you, Supreme. I love you more than anything in this world." After we danced under the moonlight and everyone left, Supreme and I made love on the beach. My life was finally at peace.

When Supreme and I got back from Barbados, I started planning our wedding immediately. The manner in which he proposed to me was so romantic that I wanted our wedding to be on the beach, too. I preferred a small ceremony, but Supreme wanted something extravagant. We compromised and decided to meet someplace in the middle.

I didn't have anyone to invite but Rhonda so the guest list would be comprised of all of his family and friends.

A week after we got back from our trip, Supreme took me to meet his mother and father, who also lived in Jersey. Supreme was originally from Queens, but once he made it big he bought his parents a big house in the suburbs. They were the sweetest couple and embraced me as if I was their own daughter.

Their only reservation was that Supreme and I were both so young, but they said as long as their son is happy then that's all that mattered. And it was obvious how happy Supreme and I were together.

"I cant' believe you're moving out, Precious. I know you can't be married and living here with me, but couldn't you wait until after the wedding."

"Rhonda, I'ma miss you too, but my fiancée wants me to be with him. I love saying that."

"I bet you do. You're marrying Supreme. You're a lucky bitch."

"Who you telling? I can't wait for one of those groupie bitches to step to my man so I can flash my rock in they face and be like what?"

"You know in *Vibe Magazine*, they congratulated him on his engagement and they printed your name too."

"Word. I can' believe that."

"Yes, they also mentioned it on Miss Jones' show and Wendy Williams. So there are a lot of hurt bitches out there right now."

"Good, 'cause I ain't neva giving him up."

"Speaking of giving up, I know that wasn't Amir you were on the phone with a minute ago?"

"If I tell you 'yeah', will you hate me?"

"No, I'm not gonna hate you, but I will tell you to wise up."

"Precious, he's been trying so hard and he said he would go get counseling for his temper."

"Rhonda, listen if you not ready to settle down and be true to Amir all the counseling in the world ain't gonna help. He was dead-ass wrong for busting yo' ass, but in the same token, I knew that sneaky shit, fucking niggas behind his back, was gonna catch up to you.

"Trust me, Rhonda, I know what kind of damage cheat ing can cause. It can make the sanest motherfucker lose they mind. Niggas die behind shit like that.

"If you still want to run these streets and fuck this nigga and the third, then you need to be single and let Amir go. You shouldn't use him as a crutch, just in case it don't work out between you and one of the other dudes you messing around wit."

"I know you're right. It's difficult because before you came along and gave me a makeover, I was the corny chick that didn't nobody pay attention to. When guys started checking for me, it blew my mind. I do love Amir, but I feel like I have to make up for lost time."

"Girl, you can't neva make up for lost time. Once it's gone, it's gone. Only you can decide if you want to be with Amir or not, but if you're kicking him to the curb because you want to get your back blown out by some grimyass niggas, then you gotta check yourself. Because all them dudes want to do is smash and dash. Is that worth you losing somebody that you truly love? Don't answer that now, just think about it."

I went back in my room to pack up the rest of my belongings. I was going to miss this apartment and living with Rhonda. We really did become friends, and I had a lot of love for her. But it was time to close this chapter of my life. I was about to move on to something even better.

I picked up the only picture I had of my mother and stared into her beautiful green eyes. It was as if they were staring back at me. The picture was of her holding me when I was just a baby. Her face glowed and she appeared to be full of happiness. I can never remember a time growing up when my mother was healthy and drugfree, so I always hold on to this picture because this is the only tangible reminder I have that shows that she was. My mother still had so much to live for. Her life was stolen from her when she was only thirty-seven, and now here I was, twenty, about to walk down the aisle. It didn't seem fair.

Sometimes I stare at the picture for hours, looking for clues as to what went wrong. How did a woman that had the capabilities of having it all, live her life as though she was nothing? I wondered if she was looking down on me and knew how happy I was. Oh, how I wished she could be here to enjoy this with me. Planning my wedding, meeting my future husband and being a grandmother to the child I hoped to have in the future.

But most of all, I prayed that my mother had forgiven me. Right when she turned her life around, it was taken away because of the decisions I made. Hopefully turning my life around would be payment in full..

It seemed like overnight it was the day of my wedding. With all the planning I did to have the event take place on a beach, we ended up having an elaborate ceremony right in our own backyard. With the growing guest list and celebratory parties people threw for us, it didn't make sense to try and fly everyone out to a beach. Plus, the mansion we lived on was sit ting on six acres of land. That was more than enough space to have a lavish affair. Everyone from Michael Jordan to 50 Cent was in attendance.

It was the event of the summer. It took months to plan the wedding, but the actual ceremony lasted no more than fifteen minutes. But it was all worth it just to be at the altar with Supreme.

After we exchanged vows, took pictures and had our first dance as husband and wife, I went upstairs to change out of my wedding dress. Although it was beautiful I couldn't wait to step into the sexy Roberto Cavalli dress Supreme picked out for me. I caught every angle in the three-sided mirror and the dress clinched my body just right.

"You really are the most beautiful bride I've ever seen." I damn near tripped and fell when I turned to see who was intruding in my space.

"How did you get in here? You weren't even invited to the wedding."

"That was an oversight, I'm invited to everything." I wanted to smack the smug look off pretty boy Mike's face.

"That was no oversight. What the hell do you want any way, to deliver another message?" I said sarcastically turning my back on him.

"As a matter of fact, yes. Nico said congratulations on your marriage."

"Oh really? so you told him I got married?"

"Actually he read about it in one of those magazines and when I spoke to him he asked me was it true. You know he still loves you, Precious, but how couldn't he look at you. You're about the closest thing you can get to perfection."

"GET OUT!"

"Calm down. You shouldn't get so upset on your wedding day."

"Then leave."

"I will, but only if you allow me to kiss you goodbye, on the cheek of course."

My body was motionless as my feet remained cemented to the floor. Mike came closer and I thought to myself, *the quicker he get his rocks off by giving me some weakass kiss, the quicker I'll be rid of him for good.* I held my breath as he put his head down to kiss me on the left side of my cheek. When I exhaled, he whispered in my ear, "Till death do you part."

Mike turned and vanished as quickly as he appeared. I didn't know whether to run after him and knock him in the head with my heel or to fall on the floor and burst out crying. This was my wedding day for heaven sakes, wasn't it everyone's obligation to stick to the script.

Dead or Alive

You know they say every time a child is born someone has to die. I pondered what man would sacrifice their existence in order to breathe life into my child. A month after Supreme and I got back from our honeymoon, I discovered we were pregnant. That's how he liked to think of it. I would remind him, though, that while we were pregnant, I was the one waking up every day with morning sickness.

I'd never seen Supreme happier than on the day I told him I was with child. Sometimes life can be too perfect.

"Good morning, my little man," Supreme said as he rubbed and kissed my stomach. That was his daily routine ever since he found out I was pregnant.

"Little man? How you know it's not my little princess?"

"My gut is telling me them back shots I gave you produced my little man, that's all."

"Them back shots? How 'bout when I was riding you like a cow-girl I made my little girl?"

"Yeah, but I only bust up in you from the back or the front, never with you on top."

"You do have a point there," I admitted clobbering him over the head with the pillow.

"It don't matter, though, whether my little man or your little princess, it's nothing but love. I'm just ecstatic about my wife giving me my first seed."

"Baby, I'ma try so hard to be a good mother to our child. I wanna give this baby the type of parents I never had growing up."

"Precious, you're going to be a wonderful mother, and we will be great parents. This child's life is already starting off different than yours and mine."

"Supreme, you have great parents."

"Yeah, but I have the same hood story as mostly every other black man out here. I was blessed enough to grow up with both of my parents, but they had to break their backs to provide for us. We barely got by, and I could've easily turned my soul over to the street life, but this music game was my savior. Now I can provide for my people, and my family and kids won't ever have to struggle the way we did." Supreme sat up and put his arms around me as we lay in the bed.

"Precious, that's why when you made your confession to me, I didn't judge you or think any less of you. I know what desperation can make you do. Most people fold and either get strung out on drugs, commit suicide or lose they mind. Then they might as well be dead because they just floating through life anyway with no purpose. But your desperation gave you determination, and I admire you for that."

"With all I've seen and been through in life, I ain't nev er been one to have a lot of faith in God. But now I believe that prayers can be answered because only God could've brought someone as wonderful as you to me."

That morning Supreme and I began making love with a newfound intensity. With every thrust our bodies engulfed one another as if holding on for dear life. It was as if we were making love for the very last time.

After Supreme left to go to the studio in the city, I was looking at my day planner because his birthday was coming up and I wanted to surprise him with a party. When I stared at today's date, to my surprise I realized that it was the anni versary of my mother's murder. I had been so caught up in my new life that it slipped my mind. I got dressed and first stopped at Michael George in the city to pick up a flower arrangement to leave on her gravesite.

I dreaded going to Brooklyn, but I had to show my re spect for my mother. I purposely wore a baseball cap and a black sweat suit in an attempt to disguise myself. I didn't feel there would be no drama, but you could never be too careful. Right as I turned on the Brooklyn Bridge, I heard my cell phone ringing.

It was Rhonda. "What's up?"

"Precious, can you come by? I really need someone to talk to."

"What's wrong?"

"It's Amir."

"Please don't tell me that nigga went upside yo' head again."

"No, but I'm afraid he's about to snap again. It's all my fault."

"What the fuck did you do Rhonda?"

"Not take your advice. Amir and I got back together, but I was still seeing other guys on the side. Somehow he got a hold of my Tmobile Sidekick messages and he read all the graphic shit I said I was going to do to this guy. Girl, he just called me and he is flipping out. I don't want to be alone, Precious."

"Okay I have to make a stop, but after I'm done, I'll come over. Lock the doors and don't let nobody in. If Amir come over there wigging out, call the police on his ass. I'll be there as soon as possible."

"Thank you so much, Precious."

"No problem, that's what friends are for."

When I pulled up to the cemetery I sat in the car for a minute seeing if I observed anyone or anything suspicious. I saw a few other families visiting gravesites but nothing out of the ordinary. When the coast seemed clear, I walked to my mother's burial site.

Ms. Duncan picked out a beautiful tombstone, and she had it engraved with exactly what I wanted it to say: *A Fallen Angel Who Is Now Forever At Peace*. I laid the flower arrangement down and while praying, I felt some body walking up behind me. I was afraid to look to see who it was.

"Precious, is that you?" I heard a soft spoken woman say. I tilted my head to the side to get a glimpse of who was calling my name. I observed the familiar looking older woman.

"Ms. Duncan, how are you?" I stood up and gave her a hug.

"I thought that was you, Precious. It's so good to see you."

"It's good to see you, too."

"I was hoping I would see you here today. I've been trying to get in touch with you, but the cell number you gave me was out of service. And the only friend I knew you had was that girl Inga. But when I called, her mama told me that the poor child had been murdered."

"I heard about that. I'm sorry I never called you. I got a new phone and I never got around to giving you the number. Is everything OK, do you need some money or some thing? I'd be more than happy to help you out. Especially since you gave my mother such a beautiful funeral."

"Oh, no, honey. I don't need your money. I still have plenty left over from what you gave me the first time. This is about you, Precious."

"Me? What about me?"

"Precious, I wanted to warn you."

"Warn me about what?"

"You know I got a son, Darius, he's a few years older than you. But like so many of our young black boys, he got caught up in them streets.

"He got out of jail a few months ago, and he's been back at home, staying with me. Well, a few days ago, him and some of his friends were running their mouths like they always do, but when I heard them mention your name, I started paying close attention. They said a fellow by the name of Nico Carter was getting out of jail soon and the first person he was coming to see was you."

"You must've misunderstood. Nico is doing life in pris on. That's a mistake."

"No, Precious. They said some big time lawyer he has was able to get him out on some sort of technicality."

My whole body became weak as I stood denying over and over again that Ms. Duncan was mistaken. "Precious, baby, are you going to be alright? Why don't we go over there and have a seat on one of those benches."

"I can't. I have to go ... to go, Ms. Duncan," I said stuttering every word.

"Precious, wait," Ms. Duncan yelled out to me, but it was too late. I got in my car and drove off so fast, trying my best to run away from the truth. I took off my baseball cap and freed my hair, hoping it would stop the migraine headache I was now suffering. I was trying to think who I could call to see if Ms. Duncan's information was correct.

She said he would be getting out soon that meant he was still locked up and I had time to get to the bottom of everything. I thought about getting a hold of pretty boy Mike, but I had sworn to Supreme that I would never speak to him again. *Maybe Rhonda could speak to Mike for me and see if he had any information about Nico's release*, I thought.

I have to go see her anyway. After I help her come up with a solution regarding Amir, then I'll ask her to help me out with Mike.

When I pulled up to my old apartment building my stomach felt queasy, and it wasn't morning sickness. The moment I got to Rhonda's front door and saw it slightly open, I knew something was terribly wrong.

"Rhonda," I called out, and got no response. Everything seemed in order and, for a brief second, I thought maybe Rhonda ran out and forgot to lock the door. That thought was put to rest when I opened her bedroom door and she was spread out eagle style with her wrist and ankles tied up to each bedpost. Her naked body was bruised and beaten. There was a pillow over her face, and I removed it, only to find duct tape covering her mouth and her face was blown off. This was almost like reliving finding my mother all over again.

"That sonofabitch Amir. I can't believe he did this to you, Rhonda. I told you not to let him in," I screamed out loud as if she could really hear me. I picked up my cell phone and dialed 911. "Yes there has been a murder at 100 Crown Court, Edgewater, New Jersey. Her boyfriend Amir Jacobs is the killer."

I sat on the couch waiting for the police to show up. The wait wasn't long; within five minutes they were at the door. "Miss, are you the one who called about a murder?"

"Yes, I am."

"Where's the crime scene?"

"The bedroom on your left," I said pointing them in the direction of Rhonda's room.

"I know that you're upset but can you please answer a few questions for my partner here?"

"No problem." The police detective pulled out a notepad.

"Miss, what is your name?"

"Precious Cummings. I'm sorry, Precious Mills I re cently got married."

Congratulations."

"Thanks," I said awkwardly.

"How do you know the deceased?"

"We were roommates until I moved in with my husband."

"So if you no longer live here what made you come by?"

"We were still friends." The officer nodded his head.

I knew he wanted me to get to the point, but my mind was cluttered, thinking about Rhonda's death and Nico's impending release. "She called me today and asked me to come over. She was having problems with her boyfriend, and she was scared he was going to hurt her."

"She told you that?"

"Yes."

"Those were her words that she believed he was going to hurt her?"

"Yes. They had broken up before because he caught her cheating on him and he beat the shit out of her. I'm sorry excuse my language."

"What's her boyfriend's name?" "Amir Jacobs."

"OK, go right ahead Mrs. Mills."

"He knocked her up pretty good and only stopped because I

walked in on him and threatened to call the police. *They didn't need to know he stopped because I pulled out a 9mm on his ass* I thought to myself. "They recently got back together, and he started checking her Sidekick messages and found out that she was cheating again. She was petrified that he was going to flip out on her again, and she asked me to come be with her. If only I had gotten here sooner."

"Don't blame yourself, Mrs. Mills. When you're dealing with scum bags like this, there is nothing you can do. You're lucky you weren't here. Then I might be investigat ing two homicides. Excuse me I'm going to have a warrant issued for Mr. Jacobs' arrest."

I sat on the couch for thirty minutes, unable to move until the paramedics brought out Rhonda's body, and I stood up, reaching towards her, wanting to believe she wasn't dead.

"Mrs. Mills the New York City Police Department has Amir Jacobs in custody, and I'm on my way to the city to question him."

"They found him in New York? He wasn't hiding out?"

"Actually, Mrs. Mills he was at work when they picked him up. When we ran his name, we called the number he was listed under and a woman answered the phone. She identified herself as his wife and said her husband was at work. We called his job and they confirmed that, but they still brought him in for questioning because you can never be too sure."

"Married? Amir was married?"

"That's what the lady said. You know how men can be sometimes. They have their own secrets."

"So what are you saying, Amir didn't kill Rhonda?"

"I can't give you a definite answer on that. If his story checks out, and he was at work as his boss has confirmed, then, no, Mr. Jacobs is not the one who is responsible for your friend's death. I have your number and will call to keep you updated. But here's my card, just in case you have any questions."

I left Rhonda's apartment more confused than ever. I didn't know what was going on. If Amir didn't kill her, then who? She was seeing a few different dudes, but which one of them would want to see her dead? Whoever did that to Rhonda wanted to torture her. The person was enraged. I couldn't imagine Rhonda having any enemies like that. I had to speak to Supreme. His phone was just ringing and he finally picked it up right when I was about to hang up. "Baby, I'm so glad you answered your phone."

"Precious, what's wrong?"

"Everything. Rhonda's been murdered."

"What!"

"Baby, yes. She asked me to stop by, and when I got there, she was tied to her bed with her face blown off.

Somebody murdered her."

"Do they know who did it?"

"At first I thought it was Amir, but he might have an airtight alibi. This shit is freaking me out, Supreme."

"Precious, calm down. You're pregnant. You can't let yourself get all upset."

"Baby, please come home. There is something else I want to talk to you about, too."

"OK, I'm leaving the studio right now."

"I love you, Supreme."

"I love you, too."

Death seemed to follow me. I knew Rhonda's murder had nothing to do with me, but I felt like I was right in the center of it. I thought I had left all the bloodshed in Brooklyn but now it was here in Jersey. The gate leading up to the driveway opened, and I turned my head to look because I felt as if someone was behind me. There was nothing there. I put my head down and said, "Precious, relax. You need to stay calm for the baby."

I put my hand on my stomach, "Everything will be al right, my little angel. Your daddy will make sure of that."

Once I talked to Supreme about the conversation I had with Ms. Duncan, I wouldn't feel so stressed. Supreme was good at coming up with solutions. Maybe he could pay Nico off, or if necessary, have him killed. However it went, Supreme would work it out. Or so I thought. My whole life seemed to move in slow motion after stepping out my car. There stood the ghost from my past. Only it wasn't a ghost.

"You've done very well for yourself. I'm proud of you, Precious."

I closed my eyes because I knew this wasn't real. It was like those nightmares that made it impossible for me to sleep for days. But just like when I would wake up, that image standing before me would be gone.

"Baby, open your eyes I'm not going anywhere. I'm the real deal."

"Nico, you can't be real."

"Precious, you're just as beautiful, if not more, than the first time I saw you walking the streets of Harlem. I knew you didn't belong there. Now look at you, married to a superstar, living in a mansion.

"You made Brooklyn proud. But as much as you cleaned yourself up, you still have those dark eyes just like me. Remember I told you besides me and my father you were the only other person I ever met with the same darkness in your eyes. That right there should've been enough incentive for me to let you walk away that day, but instead I wanted you more. Because of that I had to pay the price for my decision. Now it's time for you to pay the price for yours."

"Nico, please, I was so immature back then and I made a mistake. But I'm a different person now. I've put the streets behind me and turned my life around."

"It's all good that you turned your life around, but you had to give my soul to the devil in order to get it. Not once did you think about the life you took away from me, and the money you stole. You destroyed everything we had over some pussy. A bitch I didn't even give a fuck about.

"But that didn't matter to you, because you're like me. Your pride and your ego dictate your moves. But, Precious, with every decision you make in life, there are consequences. And your consequence is death."

"Nico, don't. What can I do to stop this? I don't want to die."

"You're already dead I just came to take it in blood. But because I still have mad love for you, Precious, I won't make you suffer the way I did your friend."

"What friend?" At first I thought he was speaking of Ritchie, but he knew I did that for revenge so what friend could he be talking about?

"If I'm not mistaken her name was Rhonda," he said with that same devious chuckle I always detested.

"You killed Rhonda, but why?"

"I really didn't want to take the chance and come here to kill you. I wasn't sure what type of security you were working with, but obviously not enough," he said, glancing around the estate. You know Mike. Well he told me about your exroommate Rhonda. So I paid her an unexpected visit.

"All I asked her to do was get you over to the apartment, and I would handle the rest, but she refused. I figured if I tortured her a little bit she would give in, but she was a fighter. She was a true friend to the end unlike Inga."

I can't believe Rhonda died trying to save my life. She knew I was coming to see her anyway, all she had to do was tell Nico to wait. Rhonda sacrificed her life for me, damn.

"Nico, hasn't there been enough death in our lives? I can give you back the million dollars and more, if you like. I have a husband, Nico and I'm pregnant with his child. I'm living the life I never dreamed possible. Don't take that away from me."

"I came back for you to take what's mine, and that's your life." Nico raised his gun, and we both turned when we heard Supreme's driver pulling up. As his car got closer, Supreme could see that Nico was pointing his gun at me. He jumped out and his bodyguards followed with guns raised.

But it was too late. The loud explosion ripped through my chest. The pressure jolted me back, and I hit my car before falling down to the ground. Then I heard Nico shooting in the direction of Supreme and his bodyguards as he vanished in the darkness. Supreme ran to me cradling my limp body.

"Precious, baby, it's me, Supreme. Please stay with me. The ambulance will be here any minute. Baby, please just hold on."

"Supreme, I'm so happy I was able to see your face one last time. Baby, I love you. I never knew what love was until I found you. Please forgive me for leaving you and taking our baby too."

Supreme held me so tightly and I gathered all the strength from within, trying to keep my eyes open because the sight of Supreme's face was giving me the will to live. But as my blood continued to flow, my strength deteriorated and my body wanted to be at peace. The last words I heard before my eyelids shut was Supreme's begging God not to let me die.

A KING PRODUCTION

She's Back...and with a vengeance

Bitch

RELOADED

Part 2

JOY DEJA KING

Love for Life

The Past...
Summer 2006

They say a cat has nine lives. Although many described me as having feline characteristics, the skill of escaping death seemed to be what we shared most in common. Less than two hours ago, Nico left me for dead with a bullet to the chest. When my eyes closed, that is exactly what I believe my fate would be. As my husband, Supreme cradled my limp body, begging God to let me live, someone up above must have heard him because here I was, still holding on. My body seemed to be in another place, but my mind was perfectly coherent and I could hear the chaos that was going on around me. A male voice yelled, "Clear the area! Prepare this patient for emergency surgery!"

"Yes, Doctor," a lady replied.

The atmosphere was hectic and all I could think about was Supreme and the baby that was growing inside of me. I wondered where he was and if he believed I would survive.

"The bullet entered the right anterior chest, perforated the lung and is lodged in the right lateral chest wall. If we don't remove the bullet immediately, she will die within the next few hours," I heard the doctor explain to his staff. The nurse must have given me medicine to numb my entire body, because from the conversation, I knew they were operating, but I didn't feel any pain.

I was still in shock, not grasping that Nico tried to take me out. He didn't hesitate when he pulled the trigger. His eyes were dark and cold. I guess the same way mine looked when I was about to leave a nigga leakin' by the curb. If I survived this knock on death's door, I would have to contemplate what my next move in life would be.

After replaying in my mind Nico pulling the trigger and feeling the heat burn a hole in my chest over and over again, I heard the doctor say, "Make sure the wound is completely drained before I close the incision." *Did that mean the procedure was a success and my peoples' final visit to see me wouldn't be in black suits?* Before I could find out the answer to that question, I lost consciousness.

"Baby, can you hear me?" Supreme asked as I slowly began coming out of my daze. His face was blurry, but his signature diamondencrusted medallion was like a bright light flashing in my eyes. My vision soon became clearer.

"Supreme, is that you?" "Yeah, baby, I'm right here."

"Our baby!" I reached for my stomach, but Supreme grabbed my hands and brought them up to his face.

"Ssshhh, we'll talk about that later," he said, placing my hands on each side of his face. "You're still weak and it's touch and go. The doctor believes you should make a full recovery, but you have to relax.

"I can't believe I pulled through. I thought this was it for me," I said, straining my voice.

"We'll talk about all of this later. Just get some rest. I promise I'm going to stay right here with you day and night until you get outta here." Supreme kissed me on my forehead, and I knew that meant out baby wasn't as lucky. Nico got his wish ... well sort of. He did take my life—at least part of it. I fell back asleep because knowing that the future I wanted so desperately was no longer growing inside of me was more than I could bear.

For the next four weeks I basically slept, rested and had physical therapy twice a week to help regain my upper body strength. Just as he promised, Supreme never left my side.

"Good morning." I had just woken up, and as always, Supreme was the first thing I laid my eyes on.

"Hi, baby. How are you feeling?" he asked while holding my hand.

"A lot better, especially waking up with you beside me." "I told you I wasn't going nowhere."

"I know, but I'm ready to wake up with you beside me in our own bed, not this stinkyass hospital room."

"I see your sassy attitude is coming back. That must mean you're close to a full recovery," Supreme said with a slight laugh.

"You got that right. I'm ready to get the hell outta here. Plus, this hospital food is about to give me a crack head body. You so worried about following the doctor's orders that you won't even sneak me in no jerk chicken or rice and beans. This shit is for the birds, baby. I'm ready to go."

"I feel you. It was going to be a surprise, but the doctor is making arrangements for your release as we speak."

"What! I'm leaving today?" I screamed, ready to snatch off the rinkydink green smock and hit the front door.

"Calm down. More like tomorrow afternoon."

"Thank ma'fuckin' goodness. Another day in this place was gonna make me go postal."

"We can't have that. I don't want to take no more chances losing you."

"Especially since we lost the baby," I said, turning our light conversation serious.

"Precious, we don't have to talk about the baby." "Supreme, how long do you plan to avoid it? I know I lost the baby and I'm sick about it. This child meant everything to us." "It did, but I'm so grateful that I didn't lose you too. That's something I would never have gotten over."

"The first thing I want to do the moment the doctor gives us the green light is start creating another baby. This time we'll make sure it's protected."

"No doubt. Nico Carter will never have the chance to take another child of mine."

"Baby, what's going on with Nico? Have you heard anything?" "Besides the police, I hired three different private investigators to hunt him down. No one has seen him. They're thinking that maybe he was able to get out of the country, But don't worry, Nico is far away and won't be able to hurt you again. Wherever he is hiding, my men will find him. He's already dead and doesn't even know it."

Since being in the hospital, that night was the first night I fell asleep without Supreme by my side. He said he wanted to make sure the house was perfect for my arrival, and he was the only one that could guarantee that.

"No, no, no!" I yelled, waking up in the middle of the night. My body was drenched in sweat and my hands were shaking.

I immediately picked up the phone and called Supreme. "Hello," Supreme said in a muzzled voiced.

"Baby, wake up. It's me."

"Precious, is everything a'ight? He asked, waking up out of his sleep.

"I just had to hear your voice. I had the worst nightmare. I dreamed that Nico showed up at the house and shot you dead. It seemed so real."

"Baby, I'm fine. I've added extra security. It's like Fort Knox up in here. Nobody is getting in, especially not Nico. I'll be there tomorrow to bring you home. Now get some sleep. I love you."

"I love you, too." I closed my eyes, breathing a sigh of relief that Supreme was alive and well. It was definitely time for me to leave this hospital, because it had my imagination running wild.

The next day, Supreme greeted me with a huge bouquet of flowers and the most adorable pink baby doll dress. My perfect size six frame was down to a zero, so he went and purchased me a new wardrobe to accommodate my drastic drop in weight. I was going to enjoy stuffing my face to gain the pounds back.

"Precious, you look beautiful," Supreme said as I stepped out of the bathroom. With my hair pulled back in a long ponytail, I looked like a black Malibu Barbie.

"Thank you, baby."

"I have something else for you."

My eyes lit up as Supreme pulled out a Jacob the Jeweler box. "What is it?"

"Open the box."

"Damn, this shit is so hot," I said, gazing at the pink diamond heartshaped necklace.

"Read the back," Supreme said, turning the heart over. The engraving read: *S&P Love for Life.*

"The moment we get home, the first stop is the bedroom," I whispered in his ear, and then our lips met and our tongues explored each other as if it was the first time. My whole body tingled when Supreme embraced me.

"That's if we make it to the bedroom." Supreme smacked my ass. "Now let me put your necklace on.

"Baby, this so beautiful, I love it."

After Supreme put on my necklace, he put his hands around my waist as he sat down on the hospital bed. He pulled me between his legs and stared into my eyes. "Precious, I love you more than anything in this world. Nothing or no one will ever come between what we share. Whenever you doubt that, just hold on to this necklace and know my heart will forever belong to you."

"I don't know what I did to deserve you, but I'm just happy you're mine."

The nurse came in and brought in the wheelchair. Although I was perfectly fine on my feet, it was standard procedure for all patients to be escorted out in that manner. Supreme pushed me down the hallway, and a smile spread across my face knowing I was just a few feet closer to freedom. The automatic doors opened, and Supreme kissed my forehead as the afternoon sun welcomed us. The summer was coming to an end, but it was still slightly hot and not a single cloud was in the sky.

The Suburban was parked right out front with Supreme's bodyguards posted beside it. As my shoes touched the cement, my eyes caught a glimpse of a black van slowly approaching the entrance with its window rolled down. Before I could lock gazes with the passenger, the ringing of a machine gun spraying bullets filled the hot summer air.

"Precious, get down!" Supreme barked as he threw his body on top of mine to cover me. All I heard were the screams of innocent by-standers as the shooter tried to finish me off, not caring what other lives were lost in the process. The shots finally ceased and the van disappeared as quickly as it appeared. Supreme's bodyguards ran toward us with guns drawn, but the attackers were long gone.

"Supreme, are you Okay?" I asked, trying to move from beneath his heavy body. I didn't get an answer. My back and neck felt warm and wet, but it still wasn't registering until I heard the sobs from Supreme's bodyguards.

"Oh shit, they took my man out!" yelled Nathan, Supreme's head of security. Gently, the bodyguards and doctors, who rushed to us once the gunfire stopped, lifted Supreme off of me and laid him face up on the ground.

To my horror, his chest was riddled with bullets. My whole body began shaking as I stood over my husband, unable to speak. A doctor tried to find a pulse but it was too late. Supreme was dead and there was no saving him.

My body buckled. I fell to my knees and balled my fist to the sky. "Damn you, damn you! Why did you take him away from me!" If there was a God, I hoped he heard my cry. I knew I had done a lot of fucked up shit in my life, but I didn't deserve this. I threw myself over Supreme, wanting to feel him one last time. I wanted to breathe life back into him, but he was gone. His blood saturated my dress as I held his face and glided my fingers over his lips and whispered, "Love for Life."

Black Widow

When I arrived at the estate, I sought refuge in our bedroom. But instead of bringing any sort of solace, it brought more pain. Supreme had the whole room decorated with flowers and welcome home banners. On the wall above our bed was a painting of us on our wedding day. I had no idea Supreme was going to have that done. The painting was so beautiful that it looked as if we were real and you could reach out and touch us. Our wedding was the happiest day of my life, and today was the saddest.

Entering Supreme's closet, I started to hug and smell his clothes. His intoxicating scent briefly softened the pain eating away at me. I hurled up in the fetal position and cried until no more tears were left.

A few hours later, I was awoken by the pounding on my bedroom door. I pulled myself off the closet floor and walked to the door, still wearing the pink baby doll dress now soaked in Supreme's blood. In my mind I never wanted to take it off, because with it on I felt a part of him was still with me.

"What is it?" I yelled before opening the door.

"Precious, it's me, Nathan. The police are here to speak to you."

"Tell them to come back later."

"They need to speak to you now. Precious, you have to do this for Supreme," Nathan said, sounding choked up. He was right. I didn't like to fuck with the police, but anything to help bring down my husband's killer.

"Okay, tell them I'll be down in a few minutes." I wanted to get myself together before I spoke to the officers. I knew Supreme would want me to be strong. I grasped the diamond heart around my neck, and found strength in that. After changing my clothes and washing my face I went downstairs.

A couple police officers and a few bodyguards were in the dining area of the kitchen, surrounding the plasma television and listening to the news.

"Early this afternoon, superstar rapper, Supreme, born Xavier Mills, was gunned down in front of The Valley Hospital in Ridgewood, New Jersey as he exited the facility with his wife, Precious Mills, who was being released after suffering her own brush with death last month. Doctors pronounced the twentyfouryearold dead at the scene. Police are still looking for suspects, who witnesses say drove off in a black van with New York license plates."

"Cut that off," I said calmly. Everyone turned around and looked at me with pity in their eyes. The more pity I saw, the straighter I stood. One thing I detested more than weakness was pity, because pity was a sign of seeing weakness in someone else. I never considered myself to be weak and didn't want others to see me that way either.

"Mrs. Mills, I'm sorry for your loss," the pudgy white male detective said as he walked towards me. I just nodded my head in acknowledgement. "Can we go somewhere and talk?"

"Sure, just a moment. Anna, please bring me a Hennessy and coke; I'll be out back," I instructed the maid. "Would you officers like anything?"

"No, we're fine."

I knew I had no business drinking in front of the police, since I was not of the legal age, but I didn't give a fuck. This was my house and my husband was dead. If I wanted to pull out a vial and snort a line of coke it wouldn't be any of their business. Luckily, drugs weren't my thing.

As I sipped my second drink, I caught myself yawning as the officers did more idle talking than revealing any new facts. "So it seems you all are no closer to tracking down Nico Carter," I said, growing increasingly tired of their bullshit.

"We're not a hundred percent sure that Nico Carter is responsible for the death of your husband."

"Excuse me? The motherfucker pumped one in my chest a month

ago, leaving me for dead and he came back today to try to finish where he left off. But instead, he killed Supreme. You tryna say there is no connection? Well, I have a hole in my chest that says otherwise."

"We're just saying we need to look at all the facts. There haven't been any sightings of Mr. Carter, and your husband was a very successful rapper. We want to make sure this wasn't a hit from one of his rivals."

"You have to be fuckin' kiddin' me. I know you two rent acops ain't tryna turn this into some rap war. Y'all ain't 'bout to spin my husband's death into Tupac and Biggie Part 2. This ain't got nothin' to do wit' rap. This is about an exboyfriend stuck on revenge, period. Don't be wasting time investigating niggas that ain't got nothin' to do wit' this. Go find Nico Carter, and you'll have your killa."

Just like that, I went from victim and widow to cold blooded bitch from Brooklyn. The lady I spent the last two years trying to become took a back seat to the ride 'til I die bitch that was still in me.

"Thank you for your cooperation, Mrs. Mills." Closing their notepads and rising from their seats, the detectives didn't know how to react. "We will continue to investigate and keep you abreast of any new developments. Once again, we're sorry for your loss."

"Hum hmm, I'm sure you boys can see yourselves out," I said, sitting back in my chair, admiring the landscaping of the acres in our backyard. I looked at the pool, remembering the time Supreme and I went skinnydipping in the middle of the night. It was the first time I ever had sex under water. I stared at the basketball court where he faithfully played Sunday afternoon games with his friends.

I clasped my hands over my mouth as I went into deep thought. I had to figure out a solution to this problem. There was a trail of dead bodies left behind due to me and Nico, and it had to stop. The only way to make that happen was to finish Nico off once and for all. If only it was as easy as it sounded. I had been away from the streets for so long that I didn't know who was making what moves. But one thing that never changed in this game: Money always talks and the bullshit always walks. I had access to endless amounts of cash and I would use that to get all the information I needed.

I went upstairs and retrieved my cell. I flipped it open and went to contacts. I found my man, Smokey's number and dialed him up.

After four rings he finally answered, "What up?" "Smokey, what up? This Precious."

"The Precious?"

"Yeah, nigga, what's good?"

"Damn, from what I hear, nuttin' for you."

"I tell you what, why don't you come see me so you can tell me all about it?"

"Where you live?"

"In New Jersey. I know it's a little far for you, but under the circumstances I can't leave my house. But I promise I'll make it worth your while."

"When do you want me to come?" "Now. This can't wait."

"I'm on my way."

I gave Smokey the address and let the security know to expect him. When I lived in BK, Smoky was a smalltime dude who I used to cop weed and my heat from. He also kept his ears to the streets and knew everything that was going on in the hood, for a price, of course. Normally I didn't like to bring my street dealings to where I lay my head, but at this point in time my home was the safest and only place to conduct business.

Wanting to look as relaxed and as in control as possible, I let my hair down and put on some lip gloss and a kneelength white linen shirtdress. When I went back downstairs, Anna had finished preparing the meal I requested. The table was set outside and everyone knew not to disturb me unless they heard me screaming bloody murder. I wasn't too concerned, since Smokey would be tripledsearched before he even gained entrance through the gate, and guards would be posted at every entrance.

"Precious, your guest has arrived," Nathan said as I sat outside.

"Thank you, escort him back here. Also tell Anna she can bring dinner out."

When Nathan brought Smokey out, he still looked the same, except for having put on an extra ten pounds or so. Since he was a lil' nigga an extra ten pounds on him actually looked like twenty. His eyes were still glassy, so I knew he smoked a blunt before he came in. That's where he got the name Smokey from, because the nigga stayed lit up.

"What up, Precious? It's good to see you," he said giving me a hug.

"It's nice to see you too. Have a seat."

"Damn, Ma, you done real good for yourself. Word is bond, you living like straight royalty."

"Except I no longer have my king."

"Yeah, I'm sorry about that, Precious," Smokey said as he looked down, shaking his head. "That's why I was surprised you called me.

That shit just happened today and you already on top of yo' game. I don't know how you holding it together." "Smokey, that's why I'm in this fucked up position now, because I let shit slip. I took it for granted that other people would make sure Supreme and I would be protected instead of being on top of shit myself. Now my husband is dead and I'm a widow, make that the black widow, 'cause I fucked up.

I'll never make that mistake again."

"So how can I help?" Smokey asked.

"First, you can tell me what the streets is saying."

"Word is bond, everybody was initially hollering about Nico putting a bullet in you. They couldn't believe that nigga just got out the dusty and came knocking at your door. His lawyer got him off on that Ritchie shit, but he was definitely going down over you. We was like that nigga is slippin', leaving witnesses and shit."

"I don't know if he's slippin' or if he caught a case of bad luck. He definitely didn't expect for me to survive or for Supreme and his bodyguards to show up and ID him. So what else?"

"Everybody is wigging out over Supreme's death. That nigga was a legend. He was a young cat, but already dropped like six CD's. The whole hood ready to take Nico out. But they also saying he couldn't have done that shit alone."

"You got any names for me?"

"Nah, this shit just happened not even twelve hours ago. You got to let the dust settle. But I will tell you this, while you were in the hospital, people were saying Nico left the country, that he was in Trinidad, Jamaica, or the Dominican Republic. He was ghost out this bitch, so that's why everybody was buggin' out about Supreme's death. We're trying to figure out when Nico got back or if he ever left."

"Smokey, I want you to get word out on the streets that there's a million dollar hit out for Nico. But I want the body delivered to me, either dead or alive."

Smokey nearly fell out his chair when the words dropped out my mouth. "Did you say a million dollars?"

"That's right."

"Damn, I might have to kill that nigga myself."

"I don't care who does it, but I want it done. Or they can bring Nico to me, nice and bound and I can finish him off. How it's done is irrelevant to me, as long as Nico is dealt with." I pulled out an envelope containing twentyfive thousand dollars and handed it to Smokey.

"What's this for?" he asked, not knowing what was inside. "It's a little something for your time. I want to make sure my message reaches the streets ASAP. Also, keep me informed of any new information that comes your way. Now let's eat."

Long after Smokey left, I lay across our bed starring at the painting of me and Supreme. We were so happy and in love. Our life together was just beginning and in an instant it was over. Here I was living in a fourteen million dollar Jersey mansion, far away from the gritty streets of Brooklyn, and I still wasn't safe. The streets had followed me home—or maybe I was the streets, and there was no escaping them.

Old Friends and Fake Niggas

It took all my strength to get out of bed the next morning. I had been making Supreme's funeral arrangements and finally, was DDay. Supreme wasn't even six feet deep yet and attorneys, family members and all sorts of other motherfuckers were coming out the woodworks. See, Supreme didn't leave a will, and since I was his wife, everything was coming to me. I knew he would want to make sure his parents were financially straight, so I had no problem lacing their pockets. But then bitches were stepping to me with kids in all shades, sizes and ages saying they were Supreme's. One chick even managed to get my cell number.

When she called I said, "Listen here, if that's Supreme's seed then he'll be taken care of, no question. But see I don't do DNA tests. So get your blood work together and call my attorney. If your shit is legit then he'll make all the financial arrangements for your little one. But on the real, don't call me no more, cause, I'm not interested in knowing you or your kid."

I don't know if hood rats think that DNA test can't be done on the deceased but they were coming at me hard. But I shut all that shit down. I'm not saying Supreme was a saint but he didn't strike me as the type of dude that wouldn't claim what was his. These trickass bitches weren't stepping to me when he was alive, but now they wanted to degrade his name in death. Not on my watch.

I stood in front of the full length mirror scrutinizing myself in the black St. John suit and black crocodile Jimmy Choo pumps. That bid in the hospital really did my body in. My ass only had a slight curve unlike its normal round bump. I couldn't stress it, after a few more weeks of Anna's cooking I would be back on point.

"Precious, the car is waiting for you," Nathan said through the door.

"Okay, I'll be there shortly." I grabbed my black hat with the sheer veil. I pinned it in right above the tight bun in my hair. I held my necklace firmly and said, "Supreme, please give me the strength to get through today."

When I got downstairs, the bulletproof limo was waiting for me and two bulletproof trucks were in front and in back of me. Security was of the most importance because I didn't want another assassination on my life, especially on the same day I was burying my husband. The promise of seeing Nico die was giving me the strength I needed to get through this. In fact, that was the only reason I had to live.

"Nathan, did you make sure Supreme's parents had bodyguards with them?"

"Yes, I sent Andre and Paul to escort them."

"Good, and the security is extra tight at the church?"

"Yes, we have our own security and Atomic Records has also provided extra protection. The police are also going to be out. They want to make sure it doesn't get out of hand."

We headed towards Queens for the funeral. His parents wanted to have the service at the church Supreme was baptized in. It was only right especially since that was where he was from. When we pulled up to the church it was like reliving the chaos of Biggie's funeral. I remember how Brooklyn was shut down that day with all his fans coming out to show love. At first I wanted a private ceremony, but I knew his fans loved him almost as much as I did. The news crews swarmed me when I stepped out the car.

"Precious Mills, how do you feel about the death of your husband?" One dizzyass reporter asked me.

"Yo, Nathan, get these cameras out my face," I screamed about to punch the bitch in her mouth.

"Everybody out the way," Nathan belted using all 250 pounds of muscle to move the crowd.

When I entered the church, it looked like a hip hop industry convention. Every black rapper, actor, athlete and sprinkles of white associates filled the benches. As I walked towards the front, all eyes were on me. The glares made me hot and I held on to Nathan so I wouldn't pass out. I sat down next to his parents and his mother was already crying a river. *This is going to be a long memorial service* I thought to myself.

After the reverend spoke, Supreme's father went to speak, but had to be carried down when he fell out at the podium. I already made it clear that I wasn't standing up there and saying anything, so a few of Supreme's friends and colleagues stood up for him. One of the hardest parts for me was not being able to see his face lying in the coffin. Because of the injuries he sustained his parents and I agreed that Supreme should have a closed coffin. We wanted the world to remember him for how he looked when he was alive, not in death "I'm so sorry for your lost," I heard a familiar male voice say from behind me. When I turned around to see his face I was disgusted.

"What are you doing here?" I said, with venom in my voice. I couldn't believe that Pretty Boy Mike had the nerves to show his face at Supreme's funeral. True to form he still had the most perfect, unblemished caramel skin I had ever seen on a man and most women. With his silky jet black hair and long eye lashes you could easily forget how wicked he was.

"Precious, I came to pay my respects. Like everyone else here, I had a lot of admiration for Supreme," Mike said calmly. "How dare you!" I whispered, not trying to make a scene in the church. "Mike, because of you, Rhonda is dead, my unborn child died, and I almost died. Now, you standing here giving me your condolences when your boy Nico is the reason why Supreme is in that coffin. I don't want your respect or admiration."

"Precious, I know how upset you are, and you have every right to be. But I didn't know Nico was going to kill Rhonda or try to kill you. When he got out, he said all he wanted was to talk to you and find out why you turned on him. He said he finally forgave you and only wanted to wish you the best. Nico mislead me and when I found out about what happened to you and Rhonda I was shocked."

"You're so full of shit. But this isn't the place to discuss this," I said but before I could complete my thought, we were interrupted.

"I'm sorry to interrupt but hello, Precious." I stared at the tall reddishskinned man. His eyes told a familiar story but I couldn't place them. I didn't know how I could forget a face so handsome but I kept drawing a blank.

"Hi, do I know you?" I said still trying to place his face. "Actually you do. But first I wanted to give you my condolences."

"Thank you. Did you know Supreme well?"

"Actually I only met him a few times when I would intern at Atomic Records in the summer. But he was always humble and downtoearth when he spoke to me. He was a very talented man."

"Yes he was, but you still haven't told me your name." "Jamal."

"Jamal Crawford?" I asked in shock. I hadn't seen Jamal in five years. We grew up in the projects of Brooklyn together. But Jamal was always different. He was a bonafide genius. He was also the boy I lost my virginity to.

"Yep, that Jamal," he said with a smile.

"What are you doing here? I didn't know you interned at Atomic Records." Seeing an old friend brought a ray of light to an otherwise dim day.

"How would you? One day you just moved away." "Aren't you the new president of Atomic Records?" Mike asked, trying to squeeze in the conversation.

"That's me, and you are?" Jamal asked, extending his hand towards Mike.

"Pretty Boy Mike, the owner of Pristine Records."

"That's right. I've heard a lot of positive things about you. It's a pleasure to meet you."

"Likewise. I had no idea you were so young. How old are you, nineteen?" Mike said sizing Jamal up.

"Actually, I just celebrated my birthday my twentyfirst birthday last week," Jamal said, laughing off Mike's dis.

"Wow. You're the president of Atomic Records?" I asked. Jamal was a few months older than me. I couldn't believe that the geeky nerd I used to look at sideways was now running one of the top hip hop labels in the world. Then again, who would've thought I'd be married, better yet alive, at my age.

"Yes I am. After I graduated high school at sixteen," Jamal cut his eyes over at Mike, "I attended Harvard Business School. Each summer and winter break, I interned at Atomic Records. During my last semester the president offered me a job as his apprentice. Then, when he got a more lucrative offer from another label, Atomic's owners asked me to take over. At first everyone was a little reluctant because of my age, but my work ethics speak for itself."

"I'm not surprised. Congratulations."

"Thank you, Precious. I know you're overwhelmed right now, but in the near future I wanted to sit down and discuss some business regarding Supreme with you. Here's my card. Call me when you feel up to it."

"I will. It was so nice to see you again, Jamal, and thank you for showing your respect for Supreme."

"Of course, it was nice to see you too," Jamal said before he walked away.

"Seems you have some history with the new president of Atomic Records," Mike said, obviously fishing for information.

"You still haven't excused yourself?" I questioned, wondering what it would take to get Mike out of my space.

"Precious, don't be like that. I care a great deal about you and I want to make sure you're okay."

"You don't even know me and I don't want you to. You're a snake, Mike. Stay away from me."

The whole ride home all I thought about was Jamal. I kept reading his business card over and over again. I knew Jamal would be successful in life and have a great career making a lot of money, but the music business was the last place I thought it would be. He seemed too uptight to be around a bunch of grimy rappers.

He had changed so much. The bifocals were history and his once scrawny body was now well defined with lean muscles. I was looking forward to calling him because I needed to talk to someone from my past. Jamal would understand who Precious Cummings from the projects, not the widow of superstar Supreme, really was.

You Ain't A Killa... But I Am

The sound of my cell phone ringing woke me up at eight thirty a.m. "Hello," I answered with my eyes still closed.

"Yo, Precious I got some info for you." I recognized Smokey's voice and tried to shake myself to wake up. "What's up?"

"Can you meet me in an hour?" "Say what you gotta say?"

"I don't wanna talk on the phone. This some shit we need to discuss face to face."

"Nico business?"

"No doubt, so can you meet me?" "Where at?"

"Harlem, at the soul food spot M&G."

"A'ight, give me two hours." It had been a few weeks since I put the hit out on Nico, and I was glad Smokey finally had some information for me.

While taking a shower I debated whether I wanted to bring Nathan and one of my other bodyguards. I knew I needed the protection, but at the same time I didn't want them asking questions about my dealings with Smokey. No matter what, I was definitely carrying my heat because there was no telling what was waiting for me in New York.

"Good morning, fellas. I have to run an errand this morn ing."

"I'll pull the car around," Nathan said. "Actually, I'll be going alone."

"I don't think that's wise, Precious," he barked.

"Calm down, I got this. If there seems to be a problem you'll be the first person I'll call. But I'm good. I got my girl wit me." I jumped in the Range because all the other cars were a little too flashy.

When I crossed the George Washington Bridge and hit the Hudson Parkway, I was becoming more anxious, wondering what information Smokey had regarding Nico.

I drove around the block a couple of times before I pulled up in front of the legendary restaurant that was no bigger than my Range but served food good as hell. I saw Smokey's BMW 525 parked at the curb but he wasn't inside. I figured he was already in the spot, but I called his cell to double check. I took out my 9mm from the hidden compartment and placed the silencer on the tip of the barrel before placing it in my purse. I hoped that I wouldn't have to use it, but you can never be too careful. I slowly walked up in the spot checking in all directions who was in the place. A few couples were seated; getting they grub on and Smokey sat directly facing the door. "What's good, Smokey?"

"Hopefully everything. I think this info I got should put a smile on yo' face."

"Speak," I said, sitting down.

"One of my street informants introduced me to this cat that says he know where Nico is hiding out at."

"Word?"

"Word is bond. The nigga wouldn't give me too many details 'cause he want his bread first."

"What details did he give?"

"He said the nigga is staying at some coop downtown on the West side."

"What? That sounds crazy. You tellin' me that nigga still right here in New York?"

"That's what my man say. Besides, it's not like Nico could have gotten on a plane. Even the feds are looking for him. It makes sense, since he just killed Supreme a few weeks ago."

"How is your informant sure it's Nico?"

"The nigga still hustling. From what I understand he tryna get his paper right before he break out. My informant's cousin sold three diesels to him."

"Nico back selling heroin? Who hitting that nigga off wit' paper?"

"How the story goes, the boy's cousin is a big time hustling nigga. The kingpin nigga sent him to drop off the goods because he got backed up on some other shit. He had no idea Nico was the nigga he was delivering to. Some bitch answered the door and it took Nico a second to come out from the back. He gave him the package and he still wasn't positive it was Nico until he heard the bitch call out his name when he was walking out the door. As far as where he got the paper to buy that shit, I don't know. But I don't think that nigga's cousin be frontin' wit' his diesel so Nico got the cash from somewhere."

"So Nico hauled up wit' some bitch selling diesel? He's right under our fuckin' noses."

"Damn right."

"So what's next?"

"The nigga wanna speak to you and make sure that he'll get the bread if he delivers on the body."

"Where he at now?"

"He lives right around the corner. I didn't tell him you were coming to meet me, but I wanted us to be nearby just in case you was up to seeing him."

"So you believe he on the upanup?"

"No doubt. This nigga official. All he want is his paper and Nico is good as dead."

"A'ight, get him on the phone and hookup the meeting." I sat back and listened to Smokey make the arrangements. Something about the situation was a little suspect, but Smokey sounded so confident with his information. Plus, it was plausible for Nico to be shacking up with some bitch getting his hustle on so he could get the fuck out of New York. Your options are limited when your pockets are empty, so it did make sense. I stored my paranoia to the back of my mind and held on tightly to my purse for backup.

"He ready. I told him we'd be there in fifteen minutes so he wouldn't know we was just a step away."

"Let's do this. But for your sake this nigga betta be on the up."

Smokey and I smalltalked for a few since we had extra time. After I finished my glass of sweet tea, I followed him out the front door. We walked about three blocks until we came to a renovated apartment building in the middle of the projects. It blew my mind how these real estate motherfuckers kept putting all this money into upgrading these apartments, raising the rent so uppermiddle class white people could move in the neighborhood. It didn't matter because niggas still wasn't going anywhere; so it would always be the hood. I guess they hoped the local blacks would be wiped out from either drugs or the violence of the streets. They'd be waiting a long time. Niggas had a way to keep multiplying.

"Hold up, this his spot, but let me hit his cell so he'll know we outside," Smokey said as he dialed the number. I stood looking around feeling the area out. It was the early afternoon and the hood was slowly coming alive.

"Come on, Precious, he lives on the second floor." The guy buzzed us in and instead of us taking the elevator I told Smokey to take the stairs. In a situation like this where I wasn't feeling totally comfortable, I felt I had more room to move taking the stairs if shit was shaky. I was relieved when no niggas had they gats drawn when we reached the floor.

When we got to the door, Smokey knocked and I stood to the side clutching my purse in preparation for anything faulty. Smokey was cool, but I could tell that even though he was in the game and had his ears to the streets, he won't no official killertype nigga. I say that because he was just too relaxed. He knew I was carrying heat and he was strapped, too, but most murdertype niggas always give a quick pat to they piece just to make sure it's right there ready for them to explode on a cat if necessary. Smokey was cheesing as if he was bringing me home for dinner to meet his parents.

After standing for a few seconds, someone finally came and opened the door.

"Wass up?" he said, giving Smokey a pound.

"It's all good; this here is the young lady I was telling you about."

"How you doing, I'm BBoy?" I just politely grinned and nodded my head. Then I zoomed in on his eyes, trying to get a read on him. He looked young, but maybe that was because he had a baby face. He was tall and skinny with a Hershey bar complexion. He had an inviting smile but my gut told me he had another agenda. "Come on in," he said, completely opening the door. Smokey and I stepped inside and to my surprise the apartment was extremely neat and decorated nicely. I figured he must live with his girl because the place definitely had a woman's touch.

"Can I get ya something to drink?"

"Nah, I'm good." I never liked to eat or drink at somebody's crib unless they were my people like that.

"I'll take some soda or something," Smokey said, never being one to turn down nothing that could fill up his belly.

When the guy walked off to the kitchen, I moved closer to Smokey, "So that the nigga that knows Nico's whereabouts?" I whispered.

"That's him, he seems like good people, right?" he said nodding his head and grinning. I didn't even respond to Smokey. Instead I studied the room trying to get an indication if anyone else was here. I noticed the window was halfway open and wondered if someone sneaked out not wanting us to see them on our way up.

"Here's your drink, man," BBoy said, handing a can of Coca Cola to Smokey. "Ya wanna have a seat?"

"I'm good." I always think better on my feet. Smokey sat down on the couch next to BBoy.

"A'ight, well let's get down to it. As I told my man Smokey, I know exactly where Nico is holding court. I have no problem taking that nigga out for the right price, and from what I understand that price is a million dollars."

"Yeah, you got that price right. You get half up front, half on delivery." I paused for a minute to make BBoy comfortable like everything was sweet. "So, Nico hauled up selling coke that he bought from your cousin, that's how you found out his whereabouts?"

"Yeah, my cousin had me drop off some of that coke and I peeped your man Nico. I remembered my man Smokey telling me there was a hit out on him and I was like this is just my luck."

"You got that right," I said pulling out my nine and walking towards BBoy as I put the gun to the side of his head.

"What the fuck is you doing, Precious?" Smokey blurted and stood up from the couch. I stayed focused with my finger on the trigger as BBoy sat quietly.

"Smokey, this nigga told you he delivered three packages of heroin to Nico and now he saying coke. That ain't no small oversight, that's a major fuck up." BBoy slightly bit down on his bottom lip realizing he had messed up. It was good to know Smokey wasn't a part of this farce because by the look on his face he truly didn't see it coming.

"Damn, BBoy, this was all a set up? Word is bond. I thought you was good people."

"Do you even know where Nico is, or was that all part of the scam," I asked the snake. BBoy sat there mum. "A'ight, nigga, either you start telling me who you working for or I'm 'bout to put this bullet in you like it ain't nothin'." He was still silent, but I caught his eyes glance over by the shut bedroom door.

I put my finger over my mouth indicating to Smokey to be quiet and then signaled for him to come closer to me. Then I whispered, "Pull out your piece. There's somebody in that bedroom; you might have to blast whoever in there," I said, pointing to the closed door."

Smokey got a real shook look on his face before revealing, "Precious, I ain't neva shot nobody before. I ain't no killa."

"Smokey, either kill or be killed. That's your options. I can't be in two places at one time." As I was talking to Smokey, BBoy was fidgeting. I knew he was trying to scheme a way to get out this mess. He was also probably wondering why whoever his backup in the bedroom was hadn't come out to save his skinny ass. They were probably sleeping on the job, not knowing BBoy's cover had been blown.

"Listen here, don't even think about making a move," I said softly but sternly in his ear. "Smokey, you keep this gun to his head and I'll go check the bedroom. If the nigga flinch, lullaby his ass. Now give me your gun." Smokey had a nine like mine, so I would have no problem using it.

Smokey held the gun to BBoy's head but his nervousness was clear. I just prayed that BBoy didn't sense it and take advantage of the situation. "If you make a sound, Smokey, gonna smoke yo' ass," I said to BBoy trying to instill fear. I cautiously walked towards the door, without being in direct range. I stood on the side of the wall and put my right hand on the knob, slowly raising my left arm to firing position. As I was about to open the door, I heard BBoy scream out.

"Yo, she got a gun."

Immediately, I fell to the floor and as I crawled back behind a chair. I looked at Smokey and yelled, "Smoke that nigga!" From the quick glance I got of Smokey, the nigga was frozen. Then the bedroom door flung open and a dude stepped out with his gun raised.

"She over there," BBoy screamed out. Before the nigga could turn around in my direction, I stood up behind the chair and blasted off three shots. Two hit him in the chest and one in the neck. Both Smokey and BBoy looked with their mouths wide open as his body fell to the floor. "Bitch, you killed my brother."

With Smokey still not making no moves, BBoy used the opportunity to wrestle the gun out of his hand, but I ended all that. I was a few feet away but my aim was crazy, and my shot put a bullet in the back of BBoy's head. His head exploded and blood splattered in Smokey's face. He bent over for a minute and I thought the nigga was going to vomit. I ran in the kitchen, grabbed a towel and ran some water on it. "Smokey, wipe your face off," I said, handing him the towel.

"Precious, you just killed two niggas. III ain't neva seen no shit like that before. Where the fuck you learned ththat shit?" The nervousness in his voice had Smokey stuttering.

"The streets, but baby boy we ain't got time to talk about all that. We need to get the fuck outta here. I know somebody called the police by now. Let's go." I slowly opened the door to see if it was safe in the hallway and to my despair, I saw two dudes coming around the corner running towards the apartment. Hurriedly, I shut and locked the door.

"What's wrong?" Smokey asked, sounding like a scared bitch.

"Yo, some niggas coming, and my bet is they coming for us." Instantly, I remembered the open window. Since we were on the second floor, the jump down wouldn't be bad. I ran towards the window and kicked out the screen. When I looked down, there was a big garbage dumpster underneath.

"I know you ain't bout to jump out that window?"

"No, we are about to jump out this window. Unless you wanna wait here for them niggas to kick down the door." If Smokey knew how to handle his heat I would've waited and shut them niggas down. But I knew there were at least two dudes behind that door, maybe more. I didn't know what type of artillery they were working with, so the risk was just too great. "So what you doing you coming wit' me or staying here?" When Smokey heard the shots now being fired through the door he ran towards the window.

"Let's do this before I change my mind."

"You go first, just in case they bust through the door before I jump. I can at least fire shots to protect myself."

"You sure?" he asked knowing his scared ass wanted to be first anyway.

"Yeah, nigga, now hurry the fuck up," I barked about to push Smokey out the window. The minute he landed in the trash, the door flew open. I didn't even have time to wait until Smokey got out the dumpster. I just jumped and landed right on top of his head. We both struggled to get out as one of the dudes started busting off sparks at us.

"What have I got myself into?" Smokey questioned as we fell out the garbage.

"We ain't got time for questions, hand me my gun." I needed both weapons because if those niggas came at us I needed to blast simultaneously. Smokey handed me my nine and we sprinted towards the only way out. When we got to the corner some dude was jumping off the stairs to the front entrance of the building. By the quickness of his moves, I knew he was coming for us. I grabbed Smokey's arm.

"This way!" We began hauling ass and I couldn't believe I was running down the street in broad daylight with a gun in each hand. Luckily we were on a side street and no one was really out. When I looked back to see if the enemy was still on our tail, I saw Smokey bent over in the middle of the block trying to catch his breath. I knew the nigga was out of shape but damn, this was the wrong time for this shit. "Come on, Smokey," I screamed out.

"Precious, give me a minute. Word is bond, I'm tired than a motherfucker. I think we lost the cat anyway." The minute those words left Smokey's mouth, I saw the enemy coming up on him like the quiet storm.

"Come on, Smokey, move it, that nigga behind you," I yelled, as I ran towards him with guns aimed, ready to fire. But I was too late. The enemy discharged about five shots in Smokey's back. His body fell over on the cement. By the time he put the last bullet in Smokey, I was close enough to start blasting off and just lit the nigga up. I checked Smokey's pulse, hoping there was still a chance he was alive. But it was over for him. "I'm sorry, Smokey," I said before dashing back down the street for my escape.

Deadly Infatuation

Lying back in the marble Jacuzzi, I tried to relax after the chaotic events from earlier in the day. The French vanilla scented candles surrounding the tub and the second glass of wine I was drinking helped to unwind my body but did little to erase the memory of the bloodshed. To make matters worse, I was no closer to finding out where Nico was, and I had no answers as to who those niggas were working for. Something told me they were playing this game for somebody else and I needed to know who.

Now that Smokey was dead, I had to find another connect to get my street information from. "Damn, Smokey is dead," I mumbled out loud. I felt some kinda way about that. I was riddled with guilt for bringing Smokey in some shit that he couldn't handle. Yes, he was a willing participant but he had no idea the stakes were so high. The streets were deadlier than ever for me, because I didn't know who was who or what was what. Everybody had an agenda, including me.

When I stepped out the tub I heard knocking at my bedroom door. I grabbed my robe to see who it was. "Precious, it's me, Nathan, I have your car keys." After the shoot out in Harlem, instead of going back to get my Range, I took a taxi home. Hell I didn't know if them niggas knew what type of whip I was in. They could've been on a stake out. When I arrived home, I sent Nathan to go pick up my car.

"Thanks so much," I said, taking my keys from him.

"No problem. But, Precious what happened today? You came home looking distraught. Why was you over in Harlem anyway?"

"Damn, you asking a lot of questions."

"I'm just concerned. Supreme would want me to look out for you and my gut is telling me you involved in some heavy shit."

"I appreciate your concern, Nathan, but I'm good. If I need you I will let you know." I shut the door and sat on my bed. Supreme had a lot of love for Nathan, but I didn't trust him with my personal business. He had never done anything to me, but it was a known code of the street not to trust anyone, especially people who claimed to care about your well being.

The next day, I didn't wake up until two o'clock in the afternoon. My body needed the rest. It had been nonstop action since I was discharged from the hospital. I honestly wanted to get away from everything. Recouping on some far away island was what I craved, but Nico is what I hungered. I wouldn't be able to enjoy anything until that nigga was dead. As crazy as it might sound, I wasn't even mad at Nico for trying to kill me. I knew after I got him locked up, it would never be safe for both of us to walk the same streets. But I underestimated Nico. I thought he would be spending the rest of his life behind bars. Now that he was free, taking me out was a given, and I wouldn't expect anything less from him. But killing Supreme was unforgivable. This was between me and Nico. He took away the only man who ever truly loved me. When Supreme died, so did all my dreams.

After getting dressed, I went downstairs, starving for something to eat. "Hi Anna. I know it's the middle of the afternoon, but can you make me some breakfast?"

"Of course, Mrs. Mills." "Where are today's papers?"

"I'll get it for you. You also have a message from a Mr. Jamal Crawford." I had been meaning to call Jamal, but of course there has been nothing but drama the last few weeks. *I'm going to call him the minute I finish eating breakfast, I thought to myself.*

First thing I did when I got the New York Post in my hands was to turn to the crime section. Sure enough, the newspaper had a small article about my incident the day before. Titled, "A Bloody Massacre in Harlem." Of course the police had no witnesses; even if someone did see something, no one was talking. The streets always be watching, but rarely ever talk unless there are young children involved. No one in the hood wanted the blood of innocent little ones on their hands.

I wanted to make sure Smokey had a proper burial and that his immediate family was financially straight, but I didn't know any of his people. He mentioned he had a daughter, but that's all I knew. I didn't want to go around asking too many questions, because no one could know I was dead in the center of The "Bloody Massacre." Three of those bodies were mine. I would figure something out.

After devouring the French toast and home fries Anna cooked, I took my glass of mimosa and went outside to call Jamal.

"Jamal Crawford's office, how may I help you?" his recep tionist said. A smile crept across my face when I heard that. Ja mal had done real good for himself. I never doubted he wouldn't, but to actually see it come to fruition was amazing.

"Yes, this is, Precious Mills returning his call."

"Hi, Mrs. Mills. He was expecting your call. Let me put you through." There was a slight pause, and then Jamal picked up.

"Hi, Precious, thanks for getting back to me."

"I meant to call you a while ago, but with everything that's been going on, it has been hectic."

"I understand. I should've given you more time before I called, but there were some business matters that really couldn't wait. I spoke to Supreme's attorney and he said you're in charge of his estate, so I need your clearance for a few things."

"That's not a problem. Just let me know how I can help." "It would be great if you could squeeze me in for lunch or dinner in the next couple of days, so we can go over some paperwork."

"No problem, how about tomorrow night?"

"Great, I'll make dinner reservations at Cipriani for seven, is that good for you?"

"Actually, if you don't mind, can we have dinner here at my house? I can have Anna prepare a lovely meal. I'm just not up for going out in public yet."

"I'm so sorry. How insensitive of me. I would love to come over for dinner. Is the same time alright?"

"Of course. Is there anything in particular you want Anna to cook?"

"A good steak is always nice."

"Then steak it is. I'll see you tomorrow. Bye, Jamal."

I was looking forward to dinner with Jamal. Even when we were in high school, I always felt as if I could trust him. Something about him seemed so honorable, which was rare coming for the grimy Brooklyn projects we grew up in. I needed a confidant, and I hoped Jamal could be it. As I continued to think about Jamal, my cell rang and the call was from a 917 number that I didn't recognize. At first I wasn't going to answer it, but then I said, "Fuck it." I heard loud music in the back when I answered the phone.

"Hello," someone mumbled, but the music was so loud I couldn't hear shit.

"I can't hear you!" I screamed over the phone so whoever was calling me could either hang up and try back later, or go to a less noisy area and speak the fuck up.

"My bad, is this better now?" a familiar-sounding male voice asked.

"Yeah, who is this?"

"It's me, Mike. And please don't hang up the phone, Precious."

"Mike, what do you want and how did you get my cell number?"

"To answer your first question, I want to see you. Precious, we need to talk."

"We ain't got nothin' to talk about."

"It's about Nico. I have some information that I believe will be helpful to you."

"Now why would you want to help me? I thought Nico was your friend, or does a snake like you have no friends."

"Precious, there is no need for the venom. Like I told you at the funeral, I had no idea what Nico was up to. The streets and I are very disappointed with his actions. Supreme was a legend in this industry. He will be sorely missed."

"Oh, it was fucked up for him to take out Supreme, but it was okay for him to try and have me wiped off the face of this earth?"

"I'm not saying that, Precious, but the Supreme ordeal came from nowhere. So, can we meet somewhere and talk? I promise what I have to say is of great importance."

"Then say it now."

"I don't disclose pertinent information over the phone." "I'll tell you what, Mike. Since my first priority is to have my husband's killer brought to justice, then I'll allow you ten minutes of my time. But you'll have to come to my home alone, and of course my bodyguards will search you. So don't come armed, or you won't make it past the gate. You can come tomorrow evening at six. Don't be late." I hung up the phone dreading to see Mike. I would handle my business with him before my dinner with Jamal. Mike was a snake, but he might be the link I need to bring down Nico. Only time will tell.

I spent the rest of my day trying to decide what questions to ask Mike. I knew he had a lot of street connections, and more than likely had an idea of Nico's whereabouts. Still, I had to be careful with my approach. He might be some big time music mogul now, but just like me, the hood ran through his blood. If I played my cards right, Mike could be an endless pool of information. If I came at him wrong, I wouldn't get shit.

That evening when I went to bed, I tossed and turned the entire night. My mind was flooded with questions regarding Nico, and my body yearned to be held by Supreme. The two of them had been the most important men in my life, so it only seemed logical that at every moment of each day, one of them was on my mind.

Ring...ring...

"Hello," I said, looking at my clock. It wasn't even eight o'clock in the morning. Who could be calling me this early?

"Good morning, Precious. I was calling to confirm our meeting for this evening at six."

"You can't be serious? You're interrupting my sleep to confirm some fuckin' meeting? You're taking this music industry shit way too serious."

"It's not about the music industry; it's about handling my business. I have business with you, and I want to make sure that it's still on. My schedule is always full, and if for some reason you've chosen to cancel, I need to know so I can make room for someone else."

"That won't be necessary. Our meeting is still on. I'll see you at six." I flipped my cell phone closed, slightly frustrated. Since the first time I met Mike, I couldn't quite figure him out. There was no doubt he was extremely smart, but there was something else. Since calling and confirming meetings seemed to be the thing to do, I put a call in to Jamal.

"Hi, can I speak to Jamal Crawford?" "Who's calling?"

"This is Precious Mills."

"Hold on, Mrs. Mills." For the few seconds Jamal's assistant had me on hold, I glanced at my hands and feet and realized that a pedicure and manicure were calling my name. The next call I would be making was for an inhouse appointment.

"I hope you're not calling to cancel?" Jamal said when he picked up his phone.

"No, actually I was calling to confirm."

"Wow, that's funny. I was going to make the same call to you, but I thought you were still sleeping."

"I'll admit I'm no early bird. Someone woke me up, and you know once that happens there is no way you can go back to sleep," I said with a slight laugh.

"I understand. So we're still on for seven?" "No doubt."

"Great, so I'll see you then." Jamal was like a different person now. His voice was so confident. No one would ever believe that he used to be a certified ghetto nerd.

The day flew by. After having a conference call with my attorney for over an hour and then sitting through my pedicure and manicure, it was time to get dressed for my first meeting of the evening. My appearance had to be on point, because a woman's looks meant everything. You had a much better chance of making a man jump through hoops for a pretty face than a busted one. But just a pretty face wasn't enough for me. I liked to get a nigga's dick hard off the first glance. That way they would be so busy trying to calm down their third leg that they wouldn't be able to focus and have their guard up when I was picking their brain for information.

I decided to slip on a bangingass red number for the evening. The onepiece Chloé jersey jumpsuit hugged my body perfectly and made my now slimmeddown figure voluptuous in the right spots.

"Precious, your guest has arrived."

By the sound of Nathan's voice, I knew he detested seeing Mike come through the front door. Mike's friends were responsible for busting a champagne bottle over his head. It was a long time ago, but I guess you never get over something like that.

I looked myself over one last time before heading out.

I stood at the top of the grand staircase. Mike gazed up at me from where he stood in the marble foyer. It was like that scene from Scarface, the first time Tony Montana laid eyes on Elvira with nothing but lust in his eyes.

"I see that you're right on time," I said, slowly walking down the stairs.

"Promptness is a must in my book."

"Follow me." I led Mike into the den. Nathan and one of my other bodyguards were behind us. When I closed the door they stood post right outside. They knew he was unarmed, but hands could be just as deadly. "I have another meeting very shortly, so let's get right to it. What information do you have for me?"

"Relax for a minute. You obviously had more than business on your mind when you decided to put on that outfit."

"Excuse me?"

"You heard me. Any man would get a hardon looking at that number, but I suppose that was the objective. Well, let me applaud you," he said, clapping his hands.

"I don't find your behavior amusing."

"That's too bad, because I find yours to be. Let's get one thing out the way. I'll be the first to admit that you're probably the sexiest, most beautiful woman I've ever seen in my life. But your beauty is only going to move me but so far. It'll never blind me to the point that I lose control over the situation, like I'm sure it has with other men in your life."

"Save the bullshit. You're the one who asked to come see me, let's not forget that. So my appearance needs to be an afterthought, not your first one." I knew my voice had a tone of irritation in it and I had to calm myself down. Mike had a way of getting under my skin, but I couldn't let him know that, although he probably already did. The smug sonofa bitch had the nerve to read me. His assessment was correct, but didn't anybody ask him.

"Enough of this small talk; let's discuss what I came to see you about."

"My point exactly." I had to say that so Mike wouldn't think he was running this show.

"I don't know if you heard about this, but there was a major shoot out in Harlem the other day. From what my street informants told me, it was because of some million dollar ransom you put out on Nico."

I damn near dropped the glass of cognac I just poured myself. Luckily my back was turned away from Mike so he couldn't see the stunned look on my face. "Million dollar ransom? You need to check your socalled informants, because they digging up bad dirt. I'm letting the police handle the investigation of Supreme's murder."

"Then I guess that means you have no interest in knowing who was behind the setup. Since that's the case, then my business here is done." Mike turned to walk away and I couldn't stop myself, I wanted to know.

"Who was behind it?"

Mike stopped for a moment, with his back toward me. I imagined him grinning at me caving in, and it made my skin crawl.

"Nico. He got word about your hit and came up with a plan of his own."

"What, to have me killed?"

"I'm sure that's what he intended the end result to be, but Nico planned on walking away with the money first. From what I understand, BBoy's cousin not only has a business relationship with Nico, but a personal one. They came up hustling together. So when BBoy told his cousin about the hit that was lingering over Nico's head, he warned Nico. Nico figured BBoy could pose as the hit man for hire. Let you pay him the first half up front, and then take some fake photos with Nico dead and get part two. It wasn't a bad plan, but somehow BBoy fucked up and he ended up dead along with his brother and one of his partners. Oh, and so did your middle man," he added. "I believe his name was Smokey." Mike paused before continuing. "Answer me this, Precious, were you the one responsible for the dead bodies in Harlem?" he asked, mocking me slightly.

"You seem to have it all figured out. You should be telling me the answer to that question."

"Then I say yes, except for Smokey of course."

"Sorry, I can't take credit for ending the lives of those bitchass niggas. But whoever left them flat lining did a commendable service for the community."

"That's too bad. Word on the streets is that a woman who is not only gorgeous, but mean with the heat is responsible for the havoc up top. They speak of her as if she's some sort of female superhero. From the description, I just knew it had to be you. I was wrong. You're not the baddest bitch in New York after all."

I gave Mike a smirk of disgust. The head games he was trying to play with me had now gone beyond just being annoying. "Listen, the real question is; do you know the whereabouts of Nico? And if you did, would you tell me?"

Mike walked back and forth a few times as in deep thought. His tailored dark navy ensemble moved with each movement of his body. I always heard that real gangsters wear suits, and watching Mike draped in his was only authenticating the statement.

"You may not believe this, but I don't know where Nico is hiding out. The last time I saw him was right after he shot you."

"You saw Nico then? What did he say?" This was the first time I had spoken to anybody who had a firsthand account of not only seeing Nico, but talking to him. My whole body filled with anticipation of knowing what he discussed with Mike.

"He called me right after the shooting, and we met at the Pier. He told me what happened and that Supreme and his bodyguards witnessed what went down. That had him on edge, because he knew he would be wanted for murder. He had just beat one murder rap and was free again only to turn around and get charged with another. But of course, at that time unbeknownst to us, like the cat you are, you survived with eight lives still intact."

"What else did he say when you saw him?"

"He asked me for some money so he could get out of town. I had no time to head to the bank, so I could only come with a hundred thousand. He took it and I wished him well."

"So that's how he was able to buy that diesel from BBoy's cousin, the money you hit him off wit'. You're responsible for funding his madness."

"Precious, when I gave Nico that money, I thought you were dead. Never did I believe Nico would come back to finish you off and kill Supreme in the process. Nico told me he was leaving town. Giving him a hundred thousand was the least I could do for him. As I told you, me and Nico go way back."

"Yeah, it seems Nico goes way back wit' a lot of people." "I told you in the studio a long time ago, Nico is a true kingpin just like me. He will always have powerful people looking out for him."

"So, if Nico called you tomorrow, would you go and help him knowing that he is responsible for Supreme's death?"

"No, I wouldn't. But not because of Supreme, but because of you," Mike said, now standing right in front of me. He put his hand under my chin and tilted my face up so my eyes were locked with his. *Pretty Boy Mike*, I thought to myself. *Now I know why this nigga make me so frustrated—I'm attracted to this sonofabitch, always have been. And I hate myself for it.*

"Because of me? Why?" I questioned, trying to shake my feelings. His hand was still grasping my chin and I felt like I was being hypnotized by the penetration from his eyes. Maybe Mike was right. True kingpins are different. They got this certain darkness in their eyes. Nico had it, and so did he. That darkness always drew me in. It was like it called my name.

Just then, I heard Nathan knocking at the door. Saved by the bell. "Precious, Jamal Crawford is here to see you."

"Show him to the living room, I'll be right there." I couldn't believe that an hour had gone by already. I only planned to spend fifteen minutes with Mike, but now I wished I had an hour more.

"What is Jamal Crawford here to see you about?" he asked, taking his hand away from my face.

"We have some business to discuss regarding Supreme." The way I answered Mike's question so quickly, I knew I was in trouble. Somehow this slickass nigga managed to get next to me. I didn't want to believe it, but Mike had me infatuated.

"What type of business, if you don't mind me asking?" "Before Supreme died, he had a lot of music recorded and I own the rights, so Jamal wants to make me an offer on behalf of Atomic Records."

"How much is he offering?"

"That's what he's here to discuss."

"Before you sign anything with Atomic, make sure you let me take a look."

"They have lawyers for that, and why would you want to take a look?"

"I don't want you to get cheated and I know this business inside and out. That music is worth a fortune, especially now that Supreme is dead. I'm just looking out for your best interest."

I gave Mike a slight smile, assuming that his kind gesture was more of an attempt to score brownie points than him actually caring about what deal I struck with Atomic Records. "Thank you, I'll definitely keep that in mind before I sign on the dotted line."

"That's all I ask. Well, I won't keep you." Mike headed toward the door and I honestly didn't want him to leave.

"Wait, you never told me why?" "Why, what?"

"Because of me, you said you would no longer help Nico. Why?"

"I'll have to answer that over dinner."

Nathan was right there waiting by the door when Mike opened it. He was more than happy to show him out. I guzzled down the glass of cognac that had been waiting for me since Mike's arrival. The slight burning sensation that hit my chest as the liquor went down my throat gave me a burst of energy. I tossed my head back and sauntered out the den ready for part two with Jamal.

When I entered the living room, Jamal was sitting on the elongated couch with a bottle of wine in his hand.

"Is that for me?"

Jamal initially gave me a look as if he didn't know what I was talking about, until I motioned my eyes to the bottle. "Yes, it's for us. I thought we could drink it over dinner. I hope you like red wine."

"I'm more of a champagne or dark liquor kinda girl, but I'm up for trying something new. I'll pour us a glass." Jamal handed me the bottle and I went into the kitchen where Anna was preparing dinner.

"Anna, my guest has arrived. So whenever you're ready you can serve dinner."

"Yes, Mrs. Mills." As I poured the wine I still couldn't get Mike off my mind. His personality was a combination of Nico and Supreme. Maybe that's what I found so appealing. Nevertheless, Mike was trouble and someone I needed to stay far away from, especially since I couldn't deny my attraction to him.

When I went back into the living room, Jamal was looking through me and Supreme's wedding album. I almost dropped the wine glasses due to shock. I hadn't been in the living room since I was shot and had forgotten all about those pictures. Seeing Jamal sitting there with the book in his hands brought all these emotions to the surface.

"I didn't mean to intrude," Jamal said as he noticed I was standing before him frozen.

"No, it's fine. I just haven't seen that book in so long." "You were a beautiful bride."

"Thank you. That was the happiest day of my life. Now it's just a memory that causes me pain."

"I'm so sorry, but I know that doesn't help. I can't begin to say that I feel your pain."

"Yeah, I wouldn't wish losing the love of your life on anyone. It's kinda bizarre. Who would've ever thought that Precious Cummings from the Brooklyn projects would be talking about losing the love of her life? Not only that, but the love being the superstar rapper, Supreme. One better, is that I'm talking about it with you, my childhood neighbor and the man I lost my virginity to."

"It is a bit awkward. You never know what direction life will lead you in. But it's not surprising to me that you ended up marrying a man like Supreme. Every man that laid eyes on you fell in love, including me."

"Jamal, we were kids. What you felt for me was puppy love, nothing more."

"It didn't feel that way then. I was crushed when you stopped coming to see me."

"You knew it was only temporary. I was very honest with you," I said with a teasing smile.

"I know. You wanted to practice how to better your sex skills, so you could blow the mind of some big time hustler."

"Hearing you say that now sounds crazy." "Those were your words, not mine."

"I know. So much has changed since then."

"After you left the projects, I never saw you again. I would overhear conversations and people would say you were the wife of the infamous Nico Carter. That he treated you like a queen. You became a legend in Brooklyn. After your mother died, I went to her funeral and I hoped to see you there. I saw your mother a few times before her death, and she had changed her life around. No one could believe how beautiful she looked, just like her daughter," Jamal said solemnly. "That's why it was so tragic when she was murdered."

I nodded my head, fighting back the tears that were swelling in my eyes. "It seems that everyone that I've ever loved has been taken away from me. But you know what the worse part is?" I stated, staring directly into Jamal's eyes. "In each of their deaths, I'm somehow responsible."

"You can't blame yourself for the madness of the streets. You're just as innocent as the victims themselves."

"Jamal, there is nothing innocent about me." Jamal had no idea that he was about to break bread with a killer. He still remembered me as Precious Cummings, the girl everyone felt sorry for because her mother was a crack whore. Oh, how things had changed.

"You'll always be innocent in my eyes." I could hear the sincerity in Jamal's voice. It was rather touching.

"Enough about me, look at you. You really have changed." "You're right about that. Who would've believed I'd be the president of a hip hop label?"

"Me. Maybe not hip hop, but the president of a company— yes," I said honestly. "I knew you could rule the world if you wanted. You were just that smart."

"That means a lot coming from you," he said.

I wanted to get off the subject of me, because for some reason I felt guilty about how I treated Jamal a few years back. Yeah, we were only kids, but I was feeling like maybe I took advantage of him in some ways.

"Did you know Rhonda? She worked at Atomic," I asked. "I didn't know her well. Was she a friend of yours?"

"Yes. We were very close. She was actually my roommate before I married Supreme."

"Really? We worked in different departments, but we talked occasionally. Everyone was in shock when she was murdered."

"Yeah, so was I. Another death I'm responsible for," I mumbled under my breath.

"Mrs. Mills, your dinner is ready." "Thank you, Anna. Let's eat."

Jamal followed me to the dining room, and we devoured the delicious steak Anna prepared. Being around Jamal was so easy. I didn't feel as if I had to put my guard up as I would with everyone else. His behavior seemed genuine, without any ulterior motive.

"Dinner was delicious. We've spent so much time playing catch up, that I almost forgot the reason I scheduled this dinner in the first place."

"That's right, there was a reason. You have Supreme's business to discuss."

Jamal gave me a charming smile right before he cut to the chase. "Unlike many artists, Supreme fulfilled his record contract. He put out a CD every year, sometimes twice. Right before his death, he was in negotiations with Atomic Records to sign a new multimillion dollar deal."

"I guess that's impossible now that he is dead?" I inquired. "Actually, it's not."

"I don't understand."

"You know how much Supreme loved being in the studio. He completed enough new tracks to come out with three full CD's. Technically, he owns them. They were done on his own time and money after he fulfilled his obligations with Atomic. He let us listen to most of the tracks during negotiations, and it's his best work. That work is part of his estate, so you now own his music. Atomic Records wants to buy that from you."

"Really? For how much?"

"I'm not going to bullshit you, Precious, his music is worth a lot, especially now that he's dead. Supreme had the same type of fan following as someone like Tupac. I believe you should sit down with your attorney and discuss what type of numbers you should be asking for."

"I appreciate you being so honest with me. You could've thrown a price out and if it sounded right I probably would've taken it, no questions asked. I mean, what the hell do I know about the music business? Plus, Supreme made so many lucrative investments, I have more money than I could possibly spend in this lifetime or the next."

"Well maybe it's time you get familiar with it. Supreme has left you a very rich woman. You need to make your decisions wisely."

"Thanks for the advice. I'll definitely keep that in mind. Maybe you can come back over again soon, and we can discuss it further."

Jamal paused before saying with grin, "I don't think my fiancée would like that too much. She would take one look at you and shut it down."

"Fiancée? You're getting married?" "Yes, I am, in a few months."

"Congratulations. She's a lucky woman. Look at you. You're this handsome, successful businessman."

"Thank you, but I feel like the lucky one. Nina is a terrific woman. I think you would like her, Precious."

"I'm sure I would. Maybe one day you two can come over for dinner."

"That's an excellent idea. But let's do one better. This time you can come over to my place for dinner. I'll set that up with Nina and give you a call."

"Definitely. I'll also speak to my attorney and get back to you with a price."

"Great. I look forward to seeing you again. Have a good night."

"You too." I felt some kinda way when Jamal revealed he was engaged, almost jealous. Maybe it was because I felt he was about to embark on the life that I was supposed to share with Supreme. Whatever it was, I had to admit it made me curious. I was interested in meeting the woman who had stolen my first's heart. Besides, letting Jamal and his fiancée play host and getting Supreme's business in order would keep my mind occupied, and hopefully dissuade my potential deadly infatuation with Pretty Boy Mike.

Never Say Never

For the next few weeks, I kept going back and forth with my attorney regarding what type of money Atomic Records should be bringing to the table, and if I should shop to other places in order to start a bidding war for Supreme's music. Between that, I avoided Mike's calls because I hadn't quite figured out how to deal with our undeniable attraction. I did need him as a source of information to see if he heard about any moves Nico was making, but I wasn't sure I could trust the feedback. Mike wasn't the type of man that could be handled with kid gloves, and until I determined how to make him work for me and not against me, I decided to keep him at arms length.

Later on that day, I had a doctor's appointment in Midtown. I scheduled a meeting with a topnotch plastic surgeon to have reconstructive surgery done on the scar left on my chest from the bullet, courteous of Nico. The physician who made the original incision did an excellent job, but why not make it less noticeable if possible? After my consultation and setting up the actual date for the surgery, I decided to stop off at my favorite Dominican chicken and rice spot in Washington Heights. I doubleparked and flicked on my hazardous lights before running in the joint. After about five minutes they handed me my order, and when I walked out the door this dude smacked right into me. "Excuse me, ma, I'm so sorry," he said, picking up the bag of food he caused me to drop.

"Damn, is my food straight?"

"Yeah, luckily it's tightly sealed. Ain't nothin' come out of place." The stranger handed me back my bag and apologized again before going in the Dominican spot. I was just relieved I didn't have to go back inside and stand in that line again.

"Shit, some stupid motherfucker blocking me in. Now I gotta wait for the person to come back, so I can pull out this bitch," I vented out loud. I sat in my car, rolled down the window and listened to my Nas mixtape CD. Five minutes later the same dude that bumped me came out of the restaurant and approached the car blocking me in— he was the driver.

"Damn, ma, you must be sick of me. First the food, now I'm holding you up. My fault." *Whatever nigga*, I thought to myself, *just move yo' shit.*

"No problem," I lied. After the stranger moved his car, I pulled off, and before long I was on the George Washington Bridge heading back to Jersey. By the time I got on Route 17 North heading towards Saddle River, the normally smooth ride in my Benz was feeling rather shaky. Part of me wanted to keep going, but another part of me didn't want to take any chances. It was getting dark, and I had to go up those long winding roads to get to the estate. I reasoned it was better to get off and stop at a gas station to have my tires checked. I got off at the first exit that had a gas station. The sign indicated it was two miles away but because I was being cautious and driving slowly it seemed like twenty miles.

"What the fuck!" I screamed when out the blue, a car smashed me from behind. I was so busy looking at the signs that I hadn't noticed a car was even behind me. For the first time I was regretting that I had even allowed myself to drive today. Nathan begged me to use the driver, but being the independent bitch that I am, I wanted to drive myself. Now here I was in the middle of a darkass road with a fucked up tire and some silly fuck who just hit the back of my car.

I saw a man step out his car but because it was now dark and there were no street lights, I couldn't get a clear view of his face. I started to reach for the glove compartment to get my gun, because the situation was feeling all wrong to me. But it was too late. When our eyes locked, I realized it was the same dude that bumped into me at the Dominican restaurant. He gave me the most sinister grin as he used a hammer to bust open my window. I turned my body toward the passenger seat as the glass shattered.

"Bitch, where you think yo' ass goin'?" he said, grabbing my hair.

He held my hair in a firm grip as he pushed my entire body to the passenger side and he sat in the driver's seat. He slammed the door and tossed down the hammer and pulled out a huge sharp knife.

"What the fuck, you tryna rob me. You followed me all the way from the Heights for some money? If that's what you after, I'll get you money, but you need to put that fuckin' knife away."

"Bitch, you about to die, and still poppin' all that shit." "Die, what the fuck you wanna kill me for? I don't even know you." My mind was spinning wondering if this was some beef haunting me from the past.

"Yeah, but you knew my cousins."

"Yo' cousins, who the fuck is yo' cousins?"

"You don't remember when you shot BBoy and his brother? Them my cousins. You a trife bitch. First you try to take down Nico, and then you kill my people."

"I don't know what the fuck you talkin' 'bout, you got the wrong bitch." At this moment all I was trying to do was buy time. The nigga had a knife to my neck, but I had my girl in the glove compartment. I had been in enough jams to know that it's the one who moves the fastest that lives the longest. Right now he had the upper hand.

"Don't try that slick shit wit' me. I know who the fuck you is. But yo' death ain't gonna be quick like theirs. Nah, no guns, baby girl, I got this knife so I can slice you up real nice. Pretty soon you'll be able to join your dead husband in hell. But before that, I'm gonna enjoy torturing you. You see that road off to the side? We're going to park the car over there so people can't see us from this here street."

"Then what?" I questioned, keeping him running off at the mouth as I plotted my next move.

"I'm going to tie you up and toss yo' ass in the trunk of my car. Take you to a special place where I can fuck you up and no one can hear your screams." I knew I had to act fast. Once my hands were tied up it was a wrap. On the floor under me, I eyed my alligator purse with the steel clasp sitting on top of my bag of food. It was a long shot, but if I was going to die, I would go out fighting. The only advantage I had was that he believed I was unarmed and he was the only one with access to a weapon. Because of that he would be a little bit more lax. "That's fucked up. So your plan is to torture and then kill me. I never intended on killing your cousins. The whole situation just got out of hand. I'm sure we can work this out."

I was keeping the conversation flowing as my mind was preparing for the great escape.

"You being awfully calm for a bitch that's about to get it, but we wasting time here sitting and talking 'bout this shit." The dude was becoming animated with his hands as I got him talking more.

"Well, I guess we betta break out, so you can get this shit over wit," I said moving my head back, so the knife wouldn't be directly under my neck.

"I guess so." The nigga still had a firm grip on my hair, but for a brief moment he relaxed the hand that was holding the knife. I knew it was now or never. With quickness I bent down my head and bit as hard as I could into the flesh of his hand. The pain was so excruciating that he let go of the knife. I couldn't see where the knife fell, so with one hand I grabbed my purse with the steel side upward and bashed it over the dude's mouth. The skin above his lip opened and blood started squirting out from the gash. With the pain from his hand and now his face growing stronger, he let go of my hair to stop the blood. By this time, I reached inside the glove compartment to retrieve my gun.

"You bitch, I'ma kill you." The dude reached down to get his hammer.

"Not tonight, motherfucker," I said as I cocked my nine and sparked off two shots. One hit the side of his face the other went through his neck. Blood was everywhere. I looked around as I got out the car and walked to the driver's side. I opened the door and pushed the niggas body to the passenger side. Luckily he was an averagesized dude, so I was able to maneuver him. I then drove up to that same side street where he planned to tie me up. I had to focus. No way was I going to get the cops involved with this, but I had to get rid of this niggas body. From him scratching my face and pulling my hair, my DNA was all over his body. There was no way I could leave the dude on side of the road. Shit, I watched "CSI"— they were no joke. He had to be disposed of permanently. But I would need the help of a man for a job of this magnitude.

At first I considered calling Nathan, but that was a no go. He seemed loyal but he was also legal. He wasn't no street nigga that knew how to dump bodies and shit like that. He would no doubt want me to notify the police, which wasn't even negotiable. I only knew of one person I could call who would know how to make this problem go away. I'd owe him, but my back was against the wall. I located my purse and got my cell phone. I slowly dialed his number, hoping that another person that could help would pop in my mind, but I knew there was no one else. "I need you."

Fortyfive minutes later a silver Aston Martin pulled up behind me. I jumped out, actually relieved help had arrived.

"It must be killing you that you had to call me, huh?" "Mike, ask me questions later. Right now we have to get rid of this body and my car."

"The car I saw on the side of the road, is it the dead man's?" "Yes."

"All your paperwork and whatever else you need, take it out your car. After we leave, two of my men are coming to take the vehicles and dispose of the body."

"So what, we're leaving?"

"Of course, I have trained professionals that know how to handle this. Just go get your belongings. I'll meet you in my car." I hated turning to Mike for help, but he was the man I needed. I went through the car and trunk three times, making sure I didn't leave a thing. Before I left, I went through the dude's pockets and took his wallet. When I was alone I would go through it and find out his name and if anything led to Nico's location.

"OK, I'm ready." Hesitantly, I jumped into Mike's car. After five minutes of driving, Mike finally broke the silence. "Are you ready to tell me what happened?"

"Not really, but I guess I do owe you an explanation." "Without a doubt, especially since I'm the last person I thought you'd call to get out a jam. But then again this isn't no ordinary situation."

"No it's not. The long and the short of it, that dead nigga is BBoy cousin. He followed me from the Heights, or maybe from before that. His slick ass probably fucked wit' my tire, too. Don't mind me, I'm just thinking out loud here. But anyway, when I pulled off the highway he slammed his car into me. Next thing I know this nigga got a knife to my throat telling me how he gonna torture and slice me up. Of course he didn't know that I had my bitch wit' me, and I was able to turn the tables and light that nigga up."

"Precious, you are truly a piece of work. You're either the smartest woman I know or the luckiest."

"I think it's a combination of both. My decision to call you will be the deal breaker though."

"What do you mean by that?"

"It means, can I count on you to handle the situation without it being traced back to me?'

Mike slowed down his driving and glanced at me. "I know what I'm doing. Having people and things disappear is easier than you think, if you know what you're doing. And you know I know what I'm doing— that's why you called me."

"Can I trust you won't use this against me in the future?" "I can't promise you that."

I shook my head in disgust. "I knew I couldn't trust you."

"Of course you can't, just like I can't trust you. But you calling me to get you out of this dilemma is taking us one step closer to that. Trust is earned and through this incident we are earning each other's trust. I didn't have to help you, and you didn't have to ask for my help, but you did. So now we share something of importance."

"So why did you help me? What did you get out of it?"

"Hopefully, you. It's quite obvious that I've wanted you since the moment I saw you in that club. That hasn't changed. I've been patient, only because I know you're worth the wait."

"I can't get involved with you. It would never work."

"You say that now, but a month ago if someone said I would be helping you get rid of a body, you would've spit in their face. Now here we are driving off together, sharing a secret that could now send both of us to jail. So, never say never."

I put my head down, knowing that he was right. If I was honest with myself, I could see me and Mike in a relationship. The same way he wanted me the first time he saw me in the club, I had a strong attraction to him. But I was in love with Supreme then, and I knew he was the man for me. It didn't stop the lure of Mike. The main road block between us was that he was treacherous. Two treacherous people together were a lethal combination. Look what happened between me and Nico. I didn't want nor need that sort of drama again. But then again, never say never.

You Can't Wife A Ho

It had been a week since Mike came through and saved the day. I had only spoken to him once after that, and it was when he called letting me know not to worry because my uncle was in a peaceful place. Which meant BBoy's cousin was somewhere buried in no man's land. After going through the dead man's wallet, his New York license said his government name was Antwon O'Neal. He was from the boogie down Bronx. I knew his family would be looking for him, including Nico since that was his heroin connect. I wondered if Nico was in on Antwon's scheme to kill me, or if he planned on sharing the news with his long time buddy after dismembering my body. It was irrelevant now. Antwon was dead and gone, while I lived. In the middle of my pondering, I was interrupted by my cell phone ringing. "Hello."

"Hi, Precious, it's me Jamal." "How are you?"

"Good. I was calling to see if you were still up for that dinner I promised?"

"That's right, how could I forget about that invitation." "Yeah, because Nina is looking forward to meeting you." "Nina, your fiancée, of course. When would you like for me to come over?"

"I know it's last minute but how about tonight?" "Tonight, why not, what time?"

"Is eight okay?" "No problem." "You have a pen?"

"Hold on." I grabbed a pen and wrote down his address. I was curious about Jamal's fiancée but mentally I wasn't really up to meeting her tonight. So much other shit was on mind. Killing Antwon, figuring out Nico's whereabouts, but mostly Mike, I couldn't get him off my mind. He was cold and calculating, but I knew underneath that he had a gentle side. He had so many layers, but each one was so intriguing. I had never met anyone like Mike before. He was the first kingpin I knew that was able to really take the game to a legitimate level and make even more paper. The nigga was huge in the music business. He had mad respect in the industry but still managed to generate that same love from the streets. He had the best of both worlds. He was a hustler for real.

All that said, I still felt I needed to fall back. My heart was still aching over Supreme's death, and I reasoned that, that pain would never stop. One day I would have to move on and find a man that could hold it down for me, but I wasn't ready yet. I held on tightly to my pink diamond heart. "Love for life."

When I arrived at Jamal's condo at Trump Place on Riverside Boulevard I was in awe. "Damn that nigga really came up," I said to myself. His condo was spacious with high ceilings and a banging view of the Hudson River. All that studying and hitting them books had really paid off.

"Jamal, your place is crazy. I'm really proud of you." "That means a lot to me." I gave Jamal a quizzical look because for the first time it really dawned on me how much my approval meant to him. Realizing that also made me feel guilty about how I kicked him to the curb after I sexually turned him out. But he had moved on. So I guess everything worked out for the best.

"Where's the soontobe blushing bride?" "She's finishing up in the kitchen."

"Oh, she cooks too. How nice." I hoped my sarcasm wasn't detected.

"Here's my beautiful wife now." I almost wanted to scream. When Nina walked up, I was quite impressed. She was very pretty. With her brown skin, coal black long hair and exotic features, she put me in the mind of Beverly Johnson back in her supermodel days.

"It's nice to meet you. Jamal has told me so much about you," Nina said, shaking my hand.

"I'm sure not everything."

"Yes, he's shared it all," Miss Nina stated with much confidence in her voice. With her pleated pants and white cotton buttondown shirt, she seemed all prim and proper, but Nina had some gangsta in her. Trust, I know a gangstress when I saw one. "So, Precious, would you like something to drink?"

"Actually, this bag in my hand is a bottle of vintage Dom Perignon."

"Thank you, that's so nice."

"Can't come to someone's home emptyhanded." The real reason I bought my own liquor was because I don't trust a bitch. She might spit in my shit. We were going to open this bottle right here in my view.

"I'll take that and put it in the refrigerator, so it can get nice and cold."

"No need, it's already chilled. You can just get some glasses and we're good to go." Nina didn't flinch when she turned to go get the champagne glasses. The chick handled herself with coolness.

"I see why you're so smitten, Nina is something else," I stated, turning to Jamal.

After drinking some champagne, we sat down at the table for dinner. I was leery about eating her food, but she laid it out buffet style and I figured we were all digging from the same plate, if she fucked up my food she fucked up hers too. I doubted she would torture herself like that.

"How's everything?"

"Wonderful, baby," Jamal said, reaching over and lovingly rubbing her hand.

"Yeah, these mashed potatoes are incredible. I need to learn how to cook."

"Especially if you plan on keeping a man." Nina smiled then caught the glare coming from Jamal. "I'm so sorry, Precious, how rude of me. It slipped my mind that you recently lost your husband. Please forgive me," Nina pleaded sounding sincere.

"No apology necessary. So how did you guys meet?" After Nina's comment it had gotten way too intense, and I needed to get the spotlight off me.

"On the set of a music video," Jamal said with a big grin on his face.

"I was playing one of the leads and Jamal stopped by to see how the shoot was going, and we clicked."

Ain't this some shit? I knew that whole librarian persona she was trying to pull off was some bullshit. It was all making sense. That bitch probably performed bedroom tricks on Jamal that he had only seen in porno movies. When we fucked we were young and inexperienced. I was hardly the pro and neither was he. Between Rhonda and Supreme I knew how those chicks on the video sets were putting it down. Most rappers that had any sort of clout wouldn't even let a bitch step foot on the set unless she was coming out those thongs and getting down on her knees.

"How nice, so was that the first video you worked on?" "No, it was my fourth or fifth. It was my first for Atomic Records though." Just like I thought, a hofessional.

"I'm glad I stopped by that day, or I wouldn't have met my future wife." Nina leaned over and gave Jamal a passionate kiss on the lips. Jamal was in way over his head. He wasn't ready for the type of tricks this bitch had up her sleeves. I hoped she didn't have him too open, but my female intuitions told me she did.

I lingered around and made idle chat until the bottle of Dom P. was finished. I enjoyed talking to Jamal, but Nina was getting on my damn nerves with all that mushy shit. She was trying way too hard to come off as some loving, doting, girlfriend. It was making me nauseated. Especially since I knew she was nothing more than a paper chaser who had lucked up and found a longterm sponsor in Jamal. Now understand, I wasn't hating on the chick's hustle, because I was the queen of hustle. What bothered me most was her phony ass acting all sweet and innocent when in actuality she was a straight up ho. If she was running this game on any other man, I'd tell her to get that money, but she wasn't. She was doing this to Jamal. He was my first. Nah, I was never in love with the nigga, not even puppy love, but I always admired his intelligence and respected his drive. To see him taken for a ride by some scandalous twocent video chick was rubbing me the wrong way. But then again, who was I to judge.

"Thank you for having me over, and Nina, dinner was incredible. It's getting late, and I really need to get home."

"Are you okay to drive? You had a few glasses of cham pagne."

"No, my driver's downstairs waiting so I'm in good hands." Jamal gave me a hug goodnight, and Nina and I gave each other fake hugs and air kisses. That bitch really thought she was about to start living the glamorous life.

The next day, I was in the den reading over the documents my lawyer had drawn up to give to Atomic Records. We were seeking millions of dollars for them to buy the rights to Supreme's music, but something was telling me to hold up before signing over part of his legacy. I wasn't sure if I wanted to hand over what I considered to be the last piece of Supreme's soul. In the midst of my mulling over my decision, I heard Anna calling for me. "I'm in the den Anna."

"Mrs. Mills, there is a woman by the name of Nina on the phone for you." *Why in the fuck was Nina calling me?* I thought to myself.

"Thanks, I'll pick up the call in here." I paused and stared at the phone for a moment, wondering what the trick had up her sleeve. "What up, Nina?"

"Hi, Precious. I hope you don't mind me calling, but it was Jamal's suggestion." *Hmm, blame it on your fiancée.* "We have floor seats to the Knicks game, but something came up and Jamal can't make it. He thought I should invite you." "I think I'll pass."

"I don't want to go by myself, and I would hate to waste these tickets— they're very expensive."

"I'm sure, but you don't have no homegirls you can call?" "No, I've never had a lot of female friends. That's why Jamal suggested I call you. He speaks so highly of you Precious. He thinks we would get along great. Please, I really don't want the tickets to go to waste."

I let out a deep sigh, dreading to go anywhere with Miss Nina. My gut told me she was bad news, not for me, but for Jamal. I guess it wouldn't kill me to go with her; at least I could get a better idea what her real intentions were regarding him. "Fine, I'll go. What time should I be ready?"

"Thank you so much. You can meet me at my place around sixthirty. We can leave from here."

"Oh, I thought that was Jamal's place, moved in already?" "Pretty much, I'm basically here all the time."

"Well, I'll see you at sixthirty." I hung up the phone and realized I only had a couple of hours before it would be time to go.

Surprisingly the traffic wasn't that bad, and I arrived at Jamal's place right on time. I figured I would drive so I called Nina and told her to come downstairs. She strutted out the building with a form fitting top and skin tight pants. I guess since Jamal wasn't around she could leave her librarian outfit at home. "Damn, this shit is hot," Nina said admiring my baby blue Bentley.

"Thanks."

"Damn, you really came off marrying Supreme. I know you must be living fly. I didn't get to attend y'alls wedding but I heard it was like that. Plus I saw the pictures in *In Style* magazine."

"Yeah, it's hard to think about all that, when a few months later you're attending your husband's funeral." Nina put her head down with a look of shame for making such a shallow comment.

When we sat down courtside mad heads were in the place. I had never been to a Knicks game, but the shit was cool. It was a totally different vibe than watching it on television. With the music, amped crowd and all the celebrities it felt more like a party, but only the lights were on. With the players dribbling the ball up and down the court, it was weird having them up close in your face like that.

"You know I use to mess with one of the players on the Knicks." Nina sounded as if she was trying to brag when she made the admission.

"Good for you," I responded nonchalantly "He wasn't no star player though, just a benchwarmer. If I could've landed a superstar like Stephon Marbury, I would've hit the jackpot. But somebody beat me to him. He's married. His wife is beautiful, too, her name is Tasha. She be at the games all the time. Could you see yourself marrying a basketball player, Precious?"

"Nah, my men need a little gangsta wit' them. Like Nas say "Make sure he's a thug and intelligent too."

"I feel you. I love me a thug assnigga." I turned all the way around in my seat and gave Nina the craziest look. We both knew that Jamal was as intelligent as they come, but a thug he was not. "I mean I used to like thugs, before I fell in love with Jamal," she said, trying to do damage control. I knew I was right about Nina. She was acting like the hot box that she was now that Jamal was nowhere in sight.

The true Nina was showing her face, and all I could do was shake my head. Jamal had his head so far up in Nina's pussy; there was no way to warn him about his trifling fiancée. He would just have to find out the hard way. A ho could only hide her stripes but for so long. Hopefully Jamal would figure that out before walking down the aisle with the hussy. If not, it wouldn't be too long before they ended up in divorce court.

After the game Nina and I stopped by The Garden bar and restaurant where the courtside ticketholders kicked it. By the time I finished my second drink, I was ready to go home. As I drove Nina home she made it clear that she didn't want the night to end. "One of the players for the Knicks is having an after party at Taj. We should go."

"I'm tired, plus I'm sure Jamal is ready for you to come home."

"He had to go out of town—that was the something that came up. So I don't have to get home no time soon."

"I hear you, but I'm beat. I have to get up early in the morning, so I really need to get home."

"That's too bad, but we can always hang out another time. I think we could be good friends, Precious."

"Sweetheart, I don't have friends." "That's too bad."

"Bad for who?"

"For you. Everyone needs somebody." By this time I was pulling up to the Trump Place. "I really had a nice time with you. I hope we can go out again together."

"Maybe."

"I'll give you a call. Bye, Precious."

"Bye." I watched Nina walk up the stairs, and she wasn't that bad. She was somewhat funny, and I had to admit that I enjoyed myself. I couldn't really be mad at the chick for trying to find a longterm sponsor in Jamal. If I didn't know him, I would probably be cheering her on. Shit, living in New York is a hard knock life; you got to fit in where you can get in. Maybe a ho don't make a good wife, but they make for an excellent partying partner.

You Will Be Mine

After keeping my distance from Mike for the next couple of months, one day he decided to pay me a surprise visit. "Precious, you have a visitor," Nathan announced with an attitude.

"Who is it?" "That cat, Mike."

"What the hell is he doing here?" I knew I shouldn't have let him know where I lived.

"I don't know. I'll be more than happy to send him away." "That's okay. The guards checked him up front?"

"Yeah, he clean." I followed Nathan downstairs, upset that Mike would show up to my home unannounced. I was even more upset with myself for having butterflies in my stomach. "What are you doing here?" I asked Mike as he stood in the foyer.

"Is that anyway to greet a friend?"

"When I see a friend, I'll ask them."

"Cute, let's talk," Mike said putting his arm around my waist and escorting me towards the den. Nathan immediately stepped forward and pushed his arm away.

"Don't nobody touch Precious." Nathan snapped at Mike "Nathan it's okay."

"I apologize. I didn't mean to offend you. But in the future, just so you know, nobody touches me either," Mike said with the most endearing smile on his face while his eyes spoke a language of deadliness.

"Mike, you shouldn't have come here without calling first," I said, closing the door to the den.

"If you answered my calls, I would've." "I've been busy."

"Busy doing what?" "Just things."

"Stop dancing around my question and answer it," Mike demanded.

"I know this may come as a surprise to you, but you don't tell me what to do. Other people may have to answer to you, but I don't. Don't think because I turned to you for help, that now I have to bow down like you own me. That'll never happen. I've been busy, that's the only explanation you need." "You know what I told you about the word 'never'. But besides that, I think you're avoiding me." Mike walked over to me.

"Why would I need to avoid you?" I turned my back to him, pretending to look for something.

"Because of how I make you feel," Mike whispered in my ear. I was taking in the alluring smell of his cologne as he stood next to me. I wanted to push him away and tell him that I never wanted to see him again, but my body wouldn't let me. It had only been a few months since Supreme's death, but I was drawn to Mike, and I also missed the comfort of having affection from a man.

"I think you should go," I managed to say.

"Stop trying to fight it. Give in to your feelings." Mike's soft lips sprinkled kisses up my neck, until he came to my mouth. His hands were slowly gliding up my thighs and in that moment, I gave into the temptation. We began to passionately kiss, and he pushed me towards the mahogany desk. Mike pushed the papers out the way and sat me down and gently separated my legs. As our kisses became more intense the tingle that was once going through my entire body had moved to my pussy. Mike slid my panties to the side and massaged my warm clit with his finger. Then he took it a step further, sliding his thick, long fingers inside of me. His finger fucking had my hips rocking to rhythm of his strokes.

"Do you want to feel the real thing?"

"Yes," I said breathlessly. I couldn't wait to wrap my legs around Mike's muscular body and feel all of him inside of me. As he unzipped his pants all of a sudden he just stopped. "What's wrong?" I asked in confusion.

"We can't do this."

"If you're worried about someone coming in, the door is locked. No one can disturb us." I started kissing Mike again because my pussy was now on fire.

"It's not that." "Then what?"

"I don't want to have sex with you like this."

"I don't understand."

"I've been dying to feel the inside of you."

"Well here's your chance." I opened my legs wider and pulled him closer.

"Not like this. When I have you it won't be in some you'll be mine, and you'll enjoy every moment, before, during and after. I won't settle for anything less." Mike zipped his pants back up, and I grabbed his hand.

"Don't do this. You got me all fuckin' open and now you wanna shut me off. This is bullshit. You can't just leave me out here like this."

"Precious, you want some dick, that's all."

"No, it's not like that. I don't just want dick. I want it from you." Mike bit down on his bottom lip as if imagining us fucking. With the lust in his eyes, I thought he had changed his mind and was about to put it on me. But instead he rubbed his fingers through my hair and held it tightly. "Mike, that hurts."

"I know, but I want your full attention when I tell you this." He was looking at me so seriously, and I wondered how I let myself get caught up in Mike's games. "Get your mind right, because you will be mine. Sooner than later, and when you step in my world, Precious, the stakes are much higher." Mike gave me one last kiss and walked out leaving me completely frustrated. I had dealt with several thugs in my life, but Mike was on a whole other level. He was the first man that somewhat intimidated me. It wasn't a feeling I was comfortable with, but I also knew it was one I would have to explore.

That night as I undressed to take a shower, I stood in front of the mirror admiring my body. I was finally back to my perfect size six and the surgery the plastic surgeon performed on my scar was off the chain. It healed beautifully and the slight mark was barely noticeable. I was very impressed and knew that Mike would be, too, once he decided to stop playing mind games and we finally got naked. He was trying to make the situation so complicated. After fighting it for so long, the moment I wanted to give in to lust he makes me wait. It wasn't surprising though, Mike had to be in control of everything. He made it clear that having my body wasn't enough. He wanted my mind, and more than likely my soul.

Ring...ring... "Hello."

"Precious, I know it's early, but I need to speak to you." The voice on the other end was Jamal, and I was pissed he was waking me up so early in the morning.

"Jamal, this better be good."

"I was hoping we could meet for breakfast. We need to talk."

"About what? What is so important that it couldn't wait until at least ten?"

"It's about Nina."

"I know you're not interrupting my sleep over your fiancée?"

"Please, can I come over?" "Fine."

"I'll be there in an hour." Before I could get out another word the line was dead. I dragged myself out of bed still wondering why Jamal felt it was so urgent to speak to me regarding Nina. After getting dressed, I went downstairs where I was greeted with a room full of flowers."

"Mrs. Mills, all these came for you first thing this morning. A truck pulled up full of flowers," Anna explained.

"Was there a card?"

"Yes, I'll get it for you." As Anna went to get the card I stood admiring the beautiful flower arrangements. Everything from red rose compositions to multicolored mini calla lilies filled up the foyer. I had never seen such an array of flowers before. Anna handed me the card, which read:

Dinner tonight, be ready at eight.

Mike

That's it—no romantic poems or declaring your undying love. Mike was as cool as they came. "Somebody's very fond of you, Mrs. Mills." Anna smiled, obviously digging for dirt. "I suppose," I said walking to each bouquet taking in the aroma of the fresh flowers. "A friend of mine should be here any minute, could you please make us breakfast. We'll be eating in the den."

"Of course." Before Anna could head to the kitchen, Jamal was coming around the corner.

"Damn, did you fly over here?"

"Wow, is someone having a wedding today?" Jamal was too taken aback by the flowers to answer my question. "Look at this place. I've never seen so many flowers in someone's home before. This is crazy."

"Tell me about it." He, like Anna, was way more excited than I was.

"They're all for you?" "Yep."

"I assume it's from a man, and he obviously has it bad for you."

"We'll see. Enough about me. I want to know why you woke me up early this morning. Let's go in the den, Anna is going to bring us breakfast."

"I'm not hungry, but thanks for seeing me. You're one of the few people I feel I can confide in."

"What's wrong?" From Jamal's demeanor, it was obvious something was weighing heavily on his mind.

"It's Nina. Her behavior just doesn't seem quite right to me."

"What do you mean not quite right, like mentally?"

"No, no, no," Jamal said as he shook his head. "I think she might be seeing someone else." Nina seeing someone else wouldn't be a major surprise to me, but I figured she would be more discreet with it, never taking the chance that Jamal would find out. I mean, he was her meal ticket out of the trailers on video sets to a penthouse in the sky.

"Who?"

"That, I don't know."

"So you don't have any proof, just a hunch?"

"More than a hunch, sometimes she goes missing during the day. I'll call her at home or on her cell, and she doesn't pick up. When she finally returns my call, her excuses are either she was in an area with no reception or left her phone somewhere and just got it back. Just silly excuses, that would work once in a while, but not all the time."

"Have you confronted her about your suspicions?"

"Yeah, and of course she denies it. When I go a little deeper with the interrogation she always starts to pleasure me in the way that only she can." As Jamal continued to talk with his head down, I rolled my eyes. Nina was a girl after my own heart. She definitely had her game intact. When in trouble with your man, sex him right to make him forget all suspicions. Unfortunately for her, Jamal's forgetting only lasted momentarily.

"Hire a private investigator to follow her." "I did."

"And?"

"She takes the train, and he always loses her. Her cell phone records don't show any suspicious number."

"The train? Nina strikes me as the type of person who would've given that up once she moved in with you."

"That's the thing. When she goes shopping or is running errands, she either takes a cab or uses my car service. But at least three times a week she takes the train. I find that odd. It's as if she's purposely trying to get lost just in case someone is following her."

"That's interesting. So what are you going to do?" "Precious, I was hoping you could help me." Jamal lifted his head and turned to face me, staring at me with begging eyes. At that moment, I saw the old Jamal from the Brooklyn projects looking at me. He seemed almost fragile.

"What can I do?"

"Befriend Nina. She really enjoyed herself when you all went to the Knicks game. Nina likes you, Precious, she told me. But she said you told her you don't have any friends— I'm hoping that's not true. I'm hoping that you think of me as a friend, and will help me out."

"I don't know, Jamal. I have so much going on in my own life and wasting time with Nina doesn't fit into my schedule." "Make it fit. It wouldn't be a waste of time. I might be totally wrong about Nina, or I might not. But if I am, marrying her would be the worst thing I could ever do. I need to know.

Our wedding is less than two months away." "Okay. I'll do it."

"Thank you so much, Precious. I'll never forget this." "Don't get so excited. She might not confide anything to me. Remember she knows that we're cool." Jamal gave me a million dollar smile.

"If anybody can get to the bottom of something, it's you. I'm confident you'll find out what is going on, if anything. So how about calling Nina now and maybe have a girls night out."

"I can't tonight, I already have plans." Disappointment immediately spread across Jamal's face. "I will call her and set something up for tomorrow." The disappointment instantly changed to delight. Jamal walked over and hugged me tightly. "It's too bad we never had a chance to see if a relationship could've worked between us, because you're perfect." "Jamal, I'm not perfect, nobody is. Remember that."

"I know, but you're as close to perfect as one can get." We both smiled and I walked Jamal out. It was amazing how everybody in your life could view you differently. But then again, I seemed to show a different side of myself to each person. With Jamal, I always showed him the respectable lady in me. That's why he constantly put me on a pedestal. But then again maybe that's the side he brought out, because he was such a gentleman. Jamal would be shocked to know that with everyone else in my life I was a straight up bitch, and that was on my good days.

After eating my breakfast, I placed the call to Nina. "Hi, it's me, Precious."

"Precious, it's so nice to hear from you. I left you a few messages, but you never called me back."

"I'm sorry. I had so much going on, and I actually had to go out of town for a few weeks." That was a lie, but it sounded good. "But now I'm back and was hoping maybe we could get together tomorrow?"

"Girl, yes, there's this new restaurant I heard about. It's supposed to be hot. We should go."

"Sounds good, I'll pick you up tomorrow around seven thirty."

"Perfect. I knew we would be friends, Precious. We're two of a kind." On that note I ended the call. Nina truly believed it was all gravy with us. Under different circumstances, we might have been cool, but at the same time, her personality was always so happygolucky. Shit like that made me suspicious. I mean damn, everybody got problems, and those who don't are the ones starting them.

As it got later in the day I started preparing for my date with Mike. I was looking forward to spending some quality time with him. I never sat down and just kicked it with Mike on some relaxing shit.

Standing in front of the mirror fixing my hair, instead of my own reflection staring back at me it was Supreme's. It was probably because of the guilt I felt. "Baby, I know Mike ain't never been one of your favorite dudes, but I kinda dig him. I'm so lonely, Supreme, and it's hard for me. I wake up everyday thinking of you, and go to sleep every night wishing you were beside me. Mike can never take your place in my heart, but I think we're somewhat compatible. The streets run through his blood just like they do mine. Most people just don't understand that about me, but Mike does. I hope you understand, and you don't hold it against me, because with us, it's love for life." I spoke those words to Supreme as if he was standing before me in the flesh.

His presence was always felt, and somewhere in my mind I did believe he could hear me. Maybe it was because of the necklace he gave me that I never took off. Whatever it was, the connection was strong.

After going back and forth over how to rock my hair—up then down again—I let my golden brown waves hang loosely down my shoulders. I put on my cream fitted pantsuit and pulled out the shearling to match. It was exactly eight, and I knew Mike would be right on time. I went downstairs to have a quick drink before he arrived. Nathan was standing in the foyer as if waiting for me. "Good evening, Nathan," I said with a pleasant smile.

"You need me to escort you somewhere tonight?" he asked in a protective tone.

"No, I'm fine."

"So where are you going?"

"Out," I replied, trying to remain cool. I never liked for anyone to question me. But I knew Nathan was asking out of concern, so I didn't want to bite his head off.

"With who?" He asked one question too many, and now he was working my nerves.

"That's really none of your business, but if you must know, Mike."

"Pretty Boy Mike? Why do you deal with that arrogant nigga? You know Supreme wouldn't approve of him."

"Nathan, for one, Supreme is no longer with us. Two, I'm grown. I don't have to explain to you or anybody else who I choose to deal with. As far as approval goes, mine is the only one that counts. Now, excuse me my date is here," I said hearing the doorbell ring.

Even after the tongue lashing I just gave Nathan, he lingered behind me as I answered the door. He glared at Mike with hatred in his eyes. I tried to ignore his stares, but it was hard since Nathan wasn't exactly unnoticeable.

"Precious, you look beautiful," Mike said, ignoring the wannabe cock blocker.

"Thanks, let's get out of here." I turned to Nathan, "Have a good night, and don't wait up."

When we pulled up to 23rd Street, I wondered where Mike was taking me for dinner. The block was lined with elegant buildings more suited for private residents than restaurants. "Where are we going?" I finally asked.

"Bette. Its Amy Sacco's restaurant. She owns Bungalow 8, this exclusive nightclub I go to sometimes."

"Oh, I've never heard of either of those places."

"Well, I'm the first to show you something different."

"What type of food do they serve?"

"European grill, its delicious, trust me."

When we entered the spot, I was impressed by the elegant but yet sleek style. It had smoked glass with umber and charcoal colors. The Mobiusinspired tubular light fixture gave it an ultra modern, high tech 70s look. I let Mike do the ordering since I didn't know what was good on the menu. He got some herbgrilled black sea bass and some braised short ribs, which sounded delicious to me. We started things off with a bottle of bubbly, just the way I like.

"So I guess you want to wine and dine me before you sleep with me, huh?"

"It's not so much that. I want us to really get to know each other. I think you're special, Precious, and you're someone I want in my life on a longterm basis."

"I don't know if that's possible."

"Why not?"

"Because you knew and know two of the men who have had the biggest impact on my life. It might be too complicated."

"Listen, Supreme is no longer with us, may he rest in peace, and Nico isn't part of my life. I want to have the biggest impact on your life, in a positive way. I can see us sharing an incredible life together. I can show you things that you've never been exposed to. There is so much out there, Precious, and I want you to experience it as my wife."

"What?" I almost choked on the champagne going down my throat.

"You heard me." Mike paused as he leaned back in his chair. With his caramel complexion glowing under the light, he ran his fingers over his perfect full lips. "It's my hope that one day soon you'll become my wife."

"I just lost my husband less than a year ago. I have no plans to remarry anytime soon, if ever."

"So you have no problem having sex with me on a desk, but you don't want to consider marrying me one day?"

"Sex is totally different than being somebody's wife. We don't even really know each other."

"They say you know if you want to marry somebody within the first moments of meeting them. I never believed that to be true, until I met you. Unfortunately you're afraid of letting your guard down with me. I can't blame you, under the circumstances. It'll take time. But like any great stock, you have to invest. I'm willing to invest in you, because I believe the benefits are worthwhile."

"I'll admit that I'm extremely attracted to you. Not just physically but mentally. You seem to understand me, and at the same time not judge me. There was something about you from the moment I met you, and I think it's because I see so much of myself in you, which is a little frightening. I don't have the most endearing qualities."

"To me, Precious, you're perfect. The qualities you say are lacking in endearment are what I find most appealing. That is the reason you will be mine. I'll put money on it."

Mike and I ate our dinner as he talked to me about everything from the music business to great investments. He was truly well schooled. He told me the street life was the best form of education he ever received to prepare him for the cutthroat corporate world.

By the time we finished, we had went through two bottles of champagne and I was tipsy. As we waited for the valet to pull the car around, I caught the side profile of a woman about to go into an apartment a few buildings down. "Is that Nina?" I asked out loud.

"Who is Nina?" Mike questioned as he walked in my direction and put his hand around my waist. I shook my head because I was so drunk I could barely stand up straight.

"Just someone I know," I replied, glancing back over to where I saw her. But when I turned around she was gone.

"Where? I don't see anybody?" Mike said, peering in the direction I had my head turned to.

"Me neither, I think my eyes were just playing tricks on me. That's what happens when you have too much to drink." Mike and I got in the car, and he took me home. When he reached my house, I didn't want him to leave. "Would you like to come in?"

"No, you need to get some rest. I'll call you tomorrow." "Okay." Mike walked me to the door, and I was disappointed that our night was ending. I really enjoyed his company and looked forward to spending more time with him. "Thanks, Mike," I said before giving him a kiss goodnight. When I walked inside, Nathan was sitting in the corner pretending to be flipping through a magazine.

"Enjoy your evening?" Nathan asked with his head still buried in the magazine.

"Didn't I tell you not to wait up for me? Don't answer that, just don't do it again." I went upstairs and closed my bedroom door. Even in my drunken stupor I knew that one day soon I would need to have a serious talk with Nathan. I had to set some rules regarding him interfering in my personal life, especially since I had the feeling Mike would soon become a big part of it.

In Da Club

I woke up the next morning with a newfound anticipation. It was due to the wonderful evening I shared with Mike the night before and the many possibilities it raised. The depressing, not wanting to get out of bed feeling that I had to fight for months after Supreme died was gone. I was looking forward to my next date with Mike and what the future might hold for us.

Ring…ring…

The sound of my cell phone interrupted my daydreaming. "Hello."

"Precious, it's me Nina. I wanted to make sure we were still on tonight?" I fell back in bed, closing my eyes. It slipped my mind that I was suppose to hang with Nina tonight. But I did promise Jamal, and I couldn't let him down.

"Of course we're still on."

"Great, I already made reservations for us at this new hot spot. We're going to have so much fun. I'll see you tonight." Before I had a chance to roll my eyes about Nina's extra bubbly ass, my cell phone rang again.

"Hello."

"Good morning." Without even thinking I started grinning at the sound of Mike's voice.

"Good morning to you." I couldn't help but wonder if the tone of my voice gave away the smile on my face.

"It will be, if you say you'll see me again tonight."

"Mike, I can't. I already have plans with a girlfriend of mine."

"You have a female friend? I had no idea," he said sounding surprised.

"She's more of an associate, but nevertheless we're going out tonight."

"You can't reschedule with her? I have something for you."

"As tempting as that sounds, unfortunately these plans are unbreakable. Maybe tomorrow or another day this week?"

"We'll work something out. I'll give you a call later on. Enjoy your evening." I was furious that I had to hang out with Nina all night when I could be with Mike. But Jamal needed me, and if anyone deserved my help it was him.

With so much going on, I hadn't been focusing on finding Nico. It seemed all my leads had dried up. The police weren't making any headway and even the private investigators that Supreme had hired before his death were hitting dead ends. It was becoming frustrating. I did want to see where things could go between me and Mike, but I wouldn't truly be able to go on with my life, until I got retribution for what Nico did to Supreme. But I knew patience was what this situation required. If you keep putting your questions out there, sooner or later, the answers find their way to you. Eventually Nico and I would have our showdown, and my face would be the last he'd see when I gave him the kiss of death.

"This place is cute, Nina," I commented when we walked right in to the slick twolevel club/lounge in the Meatpacking district.

"Isn't it? The who's who always comes to this spot. Getting a table is damn near impossible, but with Jamal's connections it was smooth sailing. Now that he is the president of Atomic Records, everywhere I go, I get red carpet treatment. *Red carpet*, I thought to myself, *this chick is straight tripping. Talk about Hollywood, Nina acting like she's Halle Berry or some shit like that. Unfucking believable.*

"Yeah, it seems pretty exclusive," I said noticing Janet Jackson and Jermaine Dupri at a corner table. "What's the name of this spot again?"

"AER. Do you want to stay up here or go downstairs?" Nina inquired.

"It's up to you."

"I'll show you around then we'll come back upstairs, because this is where our table is." I followed Nina downstairs and the spot felt like an intimate private VIP room. The floor was transparent with a pulsing video projection underneath. Lining the room were plush suede couches with Lucite armrests. Nina then showed me two smaller rooms, one with nothing but a few antique throne chairs and a movie playing on the wall. The spot was definitely official.

After Nina gave me the tour we went back upstairs and Young Jeezy's new single was blasting from the speakers. The crowd was dancing on the thickly upholstered ottomans and when they would come up for air, they'd grab a drink from the metallic cocktail tables. Some other patrons were getting their party on by dancing on the banquettes and the carpeted platform that wrapped around the room. The 'it' crowd was predominately white with a sprinkle of black people, but the music was all hip hop so I was cool.

The moment we sat down, the waiter approached with two magnums. "Nina, did you order some champagne before we got here?"

"Nah," she said shaking her head.

"Sir, we didn't order no champagne, at least not yet." "These are complimentary," he replied.

"From who?"

"Who cares," Nina said with her face lighting up. "It's free, and top of the line bubbly." Nina broke out into a little celebratory dance, grinding in her chair. "Can you pour me a glass?" The waiter obliged and poured both of us a glass. In the middle of her sipping, Nina nudged my arm. I turned in the direction she was nodding her head to see what looked like some NBA players were walking through the entrance.

"I told you, Nina, I only fuck wit thug niggas."

"First of all, there are a lot of athletes that's straight gangsta with theirs."

"Name me one?" I gave Nina the screw face waiting for her answer.

"Allen Iverson." Nina paused and stared at me. "Him, and all his people carry heat." That I could believe. I didn't know who too many basketball players were, but I could see Allen Iverson being 'bout it, 'bout it.

"Whatever, he ain't in that crowd, besides he's married with enough kids to start his own NBA team."

"Girl, you so crazy, I'm engaged anyway. I was just playing with you, but it doesn't hurt to just flirt a little bit. We're just having fun."

I continued to drink my champagne, as Nina made eye contact with one of the players. To her delight they were seated at a booth across from us. Before long the dudes were offering us drinks and shit, even though we had two bigass bottles sitting on our table. But Nina didn't care— she accepted them anyway. Then they started motioning their hands for us to come join them, and I pretended that I didn't see that shit.

"Precious, they want us to join them. Let's go over there." Nina was all giddy. I really wanted to scream at Nina and tell her I didn't think Jamal would approve of her hoass antics. But I was trying to befriend her so she'd feel comfortable to do and say anything she pleased around me.

"Hell no, I'm not about to sit at a table with a bunch of niggas and ain't none of them my man."

"Stop being so uptight, it doesn't hurt to play a little bit as long as you know where to draw the line. I'm committed to Jamal, and I wouldn't do anything to jeopardize that."

"I hear you, Nina, but still. If they want to talk to us they can come over here." I don't know if the niggas read my lips or were just mind readers, but before I even completed my sentence three of the guys strolled over to our table.

"How you ladies doing?" The ring leader said as he extended his arm. Nina shook his hand and I just nodded my head and smiled. Shoot, I didn't know what he had been touching on before he came over to see us. "Can we have a seat?"

"Sure," Nina responded before I had an opportunity to shut them down. But it was a good thing they came over. Now I could see how far Nina planned on taking her socalled flirtation. "I'm Nina, and this is Precious."

"How you doing fellas?" I asked casually.

"Better after meeting you ladies. I'm Keith and these are my boys, Jalen and Mark."

"What's up?" the once mute fellas said.

I finally took a good look at the three men and they all had the same style; jeans, a buttonup shirt, fresh sneakers and enough bling between them to open up their own jewelry store. They were a variation of browns with low cut hair. Each was above average in the looks department, but nothing to make you wanna write home to your mama about.

"So, what do you ladies do?" Keith asked.

"I'm a model. I do music videos and stuff like that." Then Keith looked at me waiting for my answer.

"I don't do anything."

"What, you somebody baby mama or something, sitting back collecting checks?"

"Yes I am collecting checks as a matter of fact, but I ain't anybody's baby mama. How many do you have, while we're on the subject?"

"What you mean by that?"

"What I mean is, how many baby mamas do you have, Keith? Is that question clear enough for you?" The nerve of that nigga stepping to me asking me a question like that, and now he wanna act like he don't understand when I throw the shit back at him. Even if I was sitting back collecting checks as somebody's baby mama, it wouldn't be none of his business.

"Yeah it's clear. I actually got three." "Three kids or three baby mamas?"

"Three baby mamas." Jalen and Mark chuckled a little bit. "Seems you've been a busy bee. Are they sitting back and collecting checks from you?" I asked sarcastically.

"I'm a NBA player. I make plenty of dough, so all my kids are straight."

"Good for them. Make sure you keep making that money, 'cause you have a few mouths to feed."

"Anyway, back to you." Keith got the hint and started his conversation back up with Nina. See, that was the reason I didn't fuck with athletes. Most of them are some real soft niggas. They were pampered all through high school and then college. They expect everybody to kiss they ass. Then when they go pro and make all these millions, the ego becomes out of control. Because they was too busy practicing their hoop game they never truly had to get their hustle on in the streets. I had no time for dudes like that. A bitch like me would have to cut one of them when they crossed my path on some simple ass shit. Then my face would be spread across every paper in America. Nah, I was better off with my thug niggas.

"So you got a man or what?" One of Keith's friends asked me. I couldn't remember if he was Jalen or Mark, but I knew he might be the one with a little gangsta in him if he was still thirsty for me after I checked his friend.

"No, I'm single."

"We're playing the Knicks tomorrow, and then we fly out. Can I get your number and maybe you can come visit me, since you said you don't really do nothing but collect checks?" We both started laughing.

"Yeah, I did say that didn't I?"

"No doubt, but that's cool. I don't know if you're into basketball, but I can leave some tickets for you if you wanna see the game. It'll be a blowout 'cause that's how we do."

"Is that right?"

"That's a promise. Let me take down your number and I'll call you to set everything up."

"Okay, but I'll need two tickets. I'm bringing Nina." "No problem, I got you."

"What's your name again?" "Jalen."

"I like that. You look young. How long you been in the league?"

"This is my fourth year. I got drafted straight out of high school."

"You must be really good." "I was the league MVP."

I decided I might have to make an exception to my athlete rule, because Jalen seemed cool. He was laid back and not so boisterous with his shit. I was feeling his easygoing attitude. I was beginning to relax and get comfortable kicking it with Jalen. I still kept my eye on Nina to see just how up close and personal she was getting with Keith. I caught the occasional fake, sexy laugh she was giving him, but nothing else.

Then, in the middle of Jalen telling me one of his locker room stories, I felt the coldest hands pressing down on my shoulders. "What the fuck!" I said, turning my head to see who was testing they're life by sneaking up behind me and touching on me.

Jalen was just as surprised as me, and immediately stood up as if ready to go to blows for me. He was definitely my type of man.

"Did you enjoy the champagne I got for you?"

I instantly recognized the voice. "Mike, how did you know I was going to be here?"

"Oh, so you know this guy?" Jalen asked as he sat back down in his seat.

"Yes, she knows me very well."

"I was speaking to Precious. I don't need your input," Jalen spit.

"Young blood, I think you need to check who you speaking to. I'm not David Stern and I don't give a fuck about you being the MVP. If you want to keep dribbling that ball correctly, stay out of grown people's conversation." It was obvious Mike knew who Jalen was, but poor Jalen had no idea who he was dealing with. I'm not saying on a oneon one battle Jalen couldn't hold his own, it was the aftermath I would be worried about. Mike vicious ass might put a street hit out on Jalen just because.

"Nigga, ain't nobody tripping off of you. You can get it just like the next man. I know how to beat down grownass men too," Jalen said as he stood back up. Then the other three players that were still sitting in their booth got up and came to our table.

"Listen, this is some bullshit. Mike, let's go."

"You leaving with this nigga?" Now Jalen looked like he wanted to whip my ass.

"Yes." *Call me*, I silently mouthed. The last thing I wanted was a brawl. One thing I was sure of, Mike wasn't in here alone. Somewhere close by I'm sure he had some niggas that were strapping lingering about.

"Come on, Nina, let's go." "Do we have to?"

"Ah…yes, unless you wanna stay here. I'm out."

"Baby, you stay right here. I'll take you home." Keith stood up and put his hand around Nina's arm.

"No, I can't. If Precious is leaving, then so am I."

"Fuck her. You ain't gotta leave 'cause her punkass man is dragging her home. You can chill with me."

I just shook my head, because I knew it was about to be on.

"My man, what the fuck did you just say?" Mike asked calmly.

"You heard me, and I ain't yo' man, nigga. Nina's staying here with me."

"Understand one thing. The only interest I have at this table is Precious. Everybody else is irrelevant to me. But if you keep riffin' wit' yo' mouth like something is sweet over here, you gon' have a problem."

"Nigga, bring it on. Do you know who the fuck I am?"

It happened so fast. One minute Keith was running off at the mouth, the next he was hitting the floor. All it took was one right hand punch and Mike's fist had Keith laid out. The other players looked like they were ready to jump Mike until three niggas in all black stepped to the table with guns drawn. "Let's go, now!" I screamed. I grabbed Nina's arm and Mike followed me out the club. When we got to the car, I was mad as hell.

"Omigoodness, that was crazy in there," Nina said as if she was starstruck off of Mike.

"You always startin' some shit. When I first met yo' ass you was in the middle of that brawl with Supreme's bodyguards. That's why Nathan don't like yo' ass now!" I yelled back at Mike as I walked to my car.

"Fuck, Nathan. Besides, that nigga in there was out of line. He lucky didn't nobody put a bullet in his head." Mike ran up behind me and grabbed my arm.

"That's what I'm talkin' bout' right there. There is a time and place for everything. You can't be on no cowboys and Indians shit up in that club. How did you know I was going to be there anyway?"

"I know everything."

"Whatever. I'm taking Nina home. I'll speak to you later." I released myself from his grip and stormed off.

"Precious, wait." "What?"

"Don't be mad at me."

"It's a little too late for that."

"I'll admit, I was jealous when I saw you talking to that Jalen nigga. Before tonight, I actually dug his moves on the court. But seriously, I shouldn't have lost my cool in there. Forgive me?" Mike had opened his arms as if I would run and give him a hug.

"Honestly, I'm glad you knocked that nigga, Keith on his ass. He was a real pompous motherfucker that needed to be put in his place. But popping up on me like that and flipping out on the dude I was talking to was out of line. I'm not even your girl. You don't have rights to me like that."

"So why did you leave with me?"

"Because I was trying to keep the peace. But if you want to get technical, you followed me out."

"Oh, so it wasn't because you feeling me?"

"You already know that I dig you, but that's beside the point. Shit takes time, and running up on me like I'm rockin' your ring or some shit ain't the move."

"I apologize. I guess since I already know you're going to be my wife I conduct myself that way."

I couldn't help but laugh at Mike's comment. The arrogance that got on my nerves was the same thing that attracted me to him. He was so damn confident and that shit was sexy as hell. "Call me tomorrow so you can let me know the next time we're going out," he added.

"Hum... so you think we still going out?" I smirked.

Mike just gave me his signature devilish smile and walked away as if he knew I would be calling.

"Girl, who is that nigga? He is sexy as hell," Nina blurted out when I got in the car.

"Just a friend."

"He gotta be more than a friend coming for you like that." "Maybe a little bit more." But after Mike showed his ass in the club, I felt I needed to put the brakes on him for a second.

"He is straight gutter with his. He remind me of this other dude."

"Who?" I was curious to know. Mike was a rare breed. The only nigga that came close to him was Nico.

"Oh, just some guy I used to know a long time ago," Nina said, brushing over my question. "Precious, you gotta winner in him."

I ignored Nina's comment and jumped to something else. "Sorry, if I fucked things up for you and Keith."

"Girl, please. He had that shit coming. The whole time he was talking to me, he kept going on and on about himself. He was about to put me to sleep. Plus, that shit wasn't serious. I have a fiancée to go home to, just a little fun to pass the time."

"I feel you."

"I had a ball with you, Precious, even with all the drama. I can't wait to tell Jamal the story. He's gonna bug out," Nina said as I pulled up in front of her building "Damn sure is."

"Call me when you feel like hanging out again." Nina waved bye as she closed the car door.

"Will do." I watched her walk inside and couldn't help but laugh. Although in principle this was a favor for Jamal, Nina always tripped me out and I enjoyed her company. I really didn't have any concrete information to tell Jamal. Nina was definitely a flirt, but maybe she didn't take it any further than that. It was hard to tell, and I only wanted to speak on the facts. I would no doubt be hanging out with her in the near future, because I was determined to deliver the good or bad news to Jamal before the wedding date.

What's The 411

As I was driving to Madison Square Garden to pick up the tickets Jalen left for me, I couldn't help but think about Supreme when the melodic sounds of Usher's "You Got it Bad" played on the radio. I thought about the time he broke up with me because I went missing for a day and couldn't explain my whereabouts. He was furious, thinking I was out creeping with some other nigga, but in actuality I was out murdering my best friend, Inga, and Nico's hoochie, Porscha. "But how do you tell your man some shit like that?" I asked out loud, laughing as I thought about the answer to my own question.

It had been over six months since Supreme was ripped out of my life, but it hadn't gotten any easier to deal with. Yes, I was going out again and giving other niggas a little life, but it didn't numb the pain in my heart from losing Supreme. When my mother got killed, I just knew nothing would ever make me hurt that bad again, until I watched Supreme die right in front of my eyes.

I would never get over Supreme, but it was time to kick it with a dude that could hold me down. I wasn't sure, but my instinct was telling me that Mike could be the one. He understood what type of chick I was and had no desire to change me, but as much as I thought Mike might be the one for me, another part of me was very reluctant. Every time I was around Mike, I felt as if he was hiding a deep dark secret. I knew a man like Mike did have his skeletons, but it seemed deeper than that. But maybe it was just my paranoia.

I started pondering what life with Mike would be like when I heard my cell ringing. "Hello," I answered turning down the car radio.

"I have some information about Nico that I think will interest you."

I didn't recognize the female voice on the other end of the phone, but she no doubt had my attention. "Who is this, and how you get my number?"

"Who I am don't matter, but knowing where Nico is does." "What, you saying you know where Nico is?"

"Something like that."

"That sounds a little shaky to me. Either you know where Nico is, or your wasting my time and my phone minutes. I'm thinking you one of those silly chicks playing on the phone, but you running game wit' the wrong bitch."

"Before Nico shot you, you told him you didn't want to die, but he said you were already dead and he just came to take it in blood."

I took the phone from my ear and glared at it for a long minute. I could hear the girl repeating the word "hello", wondering what the hell happened to me. She fucked me up with that one, because I remember those words Nico spoke to me as if he said them yesterday and it still sent chills down my spine. "Yo', you made your point. Where that nigga at?"

"You know it's gonna cost you," she boasted matter of factly.

"Of course. How much you want?" I wasn't sure if the chick had heard about the million dollar ransom floating around on the streets, and I wasn't going to volunteer the information. But I had no problem paying it if guaranteed I could watch Nico take his last breath.

"How much you offering?" she asked, proving that yeah, she was holding onto some valuable information, but was definitely a rookie when it came to negotiating for that paper. "I'll let you know when we meet to discuss Nico's whereabouts."

"Who said I wanted to meet you in person?" Her voice had an underlying nervousness in it.

"Well what, you want me to FedEx your money?"

"Nah, I just need to think this through a little more. I'll be in touch."

"Wait!" I yelled but she already hung up. She called from a blocked number so I couldn't even dial her back. My insides were burning up. My gut told me she knew exactly where Nico was—if not the precise location, then enough to lead me in the right direction. I kept replaying our conversation, trying to figure out what I said that scared her off. At first she sounded so confident, but when she realized it was about to go down, she froze up. I guess it kicked in that she was rumbling with big dogs and punked out. I kept my fingers crossed that the idea of having some real cheddar in her hands would motivate the girl to call back.

After picking up the tickets for tonight's game and running some other errands, it was time for me to scoop up Nina. Her wedding to Jamal was fast approaching, and I was somewhat relieved that I didn't have any scandalous news to break to Jamal. I was ready to focus on having my own relationship, and playing "I Spy" was not my specialty, especially when it didn't have anything to do with me.

Nina was outside waiting for me when I pulled up. She was on the phone with somebody that had her grinning hard as hell. She waved at me but stayed on the phone for another couple of minutes before getting in the car.

"Who had you cheesing so hard on the phone?"

"Oh, I was talking to Jamal."

"Why didn't you get in the car instead of standing outside in the cold?"

"I needed a little privacy because Jamal wanted me to talk dirty to him. I'm sure you didn't want to hear all that."

"Nah, you did the right thing." I never pegged Jamal as the type of dude who got off on phone sex, but then again, I never thought he would be marrying an obvious hotbox like Nina either.

"I'm surprised we're going to the game. I could've sworn you said you don't date athletes," Nina said, jumping to the next subject.

"This isn't a date. I'm going to a basketball game wit' you."

"Yeah, you're going with me because dude that got you the tickets is playing in the game. If he wasn't, you know I wouldn't be here right now."

"True dat. I can't front, he got my curiosity piqued 'cause even after all that shit went down last night in the club 'cause of Mike's crazy ass, the nigga still called. I had to respect the fact that a little thing like guns blazing in front of his face didn't make him want to forget my name and number. I guess all athletes aren't soft after all," I chuckled. "But enough about Jalen. Pretty soon you'll be a married woman. How you feel 'bout that?"

"Excited. Jamal is such a wonderful man. He's so giving and he truly adores me, you know," Nina stated, making it clear it wasn't a matter to be debated. "Speaking of my impending walk down the aisle, I wanted to ask you something."

"What is it?"

"I know this may be a little awkward giving your history with Jamal, but I would love if you would be one of my bridesmaids."

I glanced at Nina for a brief moment to see if she was serious. Her facial expression gave every indication that she was. I tapped my nails on the steering wheel deliberating my response. "Nina, first let me clear something up for you. Jamal and I fucked a few times when we were teenagers. Yeah, I have a great deal of respect for him, but please spare me wit' this history shit like dude was my first love, broke my heart and now it's killing me to see him wit' you."

"I didn't mean it like that, Precious."

"Then why you throwing around words like 'awkward' and 'history'?"

"Honestly, I just didn't know how you would feel being in my wedding since you had slept with Jamal before, that's all." "Shit, fuck it being awkward for me being in your wedding 'cause of my past dealing wit' Jamal. How 'bout I barely know you?"

"Precious, I apologize. I've obviously gone about this all wrong. You're right; whatever you had with Jamal is irrelevant. Maybe the situation is awkward for me. I mean, look at you. You fly as hell, and whether Jamal wants to admit it or not, I'm sure he caught feelings for you. So maybe it's my own insecurity getting the best of me. But I have a lot of respect for you and I enjoy your company. I thought you enjoyed my company too, but I guess I was wrong."

Nina words seemed sincere, and I felt that maybe I came at her a little too harshly. Where I came from, you never gave a chick the benefit of the doubt, because they would disappoint you every time. I'd been thinking she was trying to say some slick undercut shit in regards to my past dealings with Jamal, but the truth was the shit was bothering her.

"I do enjoy hanging out wit' you, and I think you cool. And I would be honored to be one of your bridesmaids. Just don't have me in no uglyass dress." We both burst out laughing.

"Thank you, Precious. You have no idea how much this means to me. I'll have to find a way to repay you for coming through for me."

This was my second basketball game in less than a month, and I had to admit I was enjoying this shit. If you wanted to see any rapper or budding R&B princess, attending a Knicks game would for sure guarantee that. Jigga Man and Beyoncé were front and center. Right beside them was Nas and Kelis. The more I looked around, I wasn't sure if this was a basketball game or hip hop convention.

After getting an eyeful of the industry elite, I focused my attention back on the court. Jalen had the ball and he was dribbling down the court and paused as if about to pass the ball, but instead he did a slick cross over and seemed to fly in the air as he slamdunked the ball. The crowd went crazy over that shit, and so did I. As he hung on the rim, the sight of every muscle in his body rippling was making my pussy wet. I hadn't fucked in so long, and his 6'4", sexy brown ass was exactly what I needed.

After the game, Nina and I waited for Jalen to come out. Keith came out the locker room first, sporting the black eye he received courtesy of Mike. He gave me and Nina foul ass stares.

"Girl, Keith look like he 'bout to come over here and beat us down," whispered Nina.

"He can play wit' his life if he want to."

"You not scared?" Nina asked in a serious tone.

Nina had no clue as to who I am. To be scared is to have no plan, and I always had a plan. It consisted of two shots to the head, I thought to myself.

"Fuck 'im," were the only words I could muster for that cat.

While we stood trying to ignore the heat Keith was throwing in our direction, Jalen stepped out, looking finer than a motherfucker in a rich caramelcolored twopiece suit. That nigga was looking the part of an NBA superstar, and I was dying to have all of him in between my legs.

"What's up, beautiful? I'm glad you came," Jalen said, and gave me a kiss on the cheek. He nodded at Nina, and then Keith's punkass came walking over to us.

"I figured it was you that invited them to the game," were the first words out of Keith's mouth.

"Damn, we can't get a hello or nothing?" Nina asked, trying to break the tension.

"How's that eye?" I asked, looking him straight in the face. I could care less about how that nigga felt. I wasn't about to kiss his chump ass. If he had kept his mouth shut at the club, he wouldn't be walking around like he took a basketball to his face.

"So, what you ladies tryna do? Ya'll want to get somethin' to eat?" Jalen asked, ignoring the negativity Keith was bringing.

"I thought you was leaving tonight," I responded.

"Most of my teammates are, but we play in Philly tomorrow, so unless you got other plans, I can hang out with you and leave in the morning."

"That works for me," I said with a smile. I knew exactly what I had planned for the two of us.

"If it's cool, I can stay too and we can all go out to eat," Keith suggested.

We all stared at him simultaneously, and I was the first to snap out the trance and speak up. "That's cool. Is it cool wit' you, Nina?"

Nina nodded her head yes, going with the flow. I couldn't stand Keith's ass, but he could entertain Nina so she wouldn't feel like a third wheel with me and Jalen.

We headed out and decided to dine at Chin Chin on the east side. Nina recommended the spot, and none of us was disappointed. Their Chinese food was banging and tasted fresh. By the time we went through out second bottle of champagne, I was ready to break out.

"How 'bout we leave here so we can have some privacy," I suggested to Jalen.

Of course he put up no argument. "Say the word and we out."

"Nina, I'm ready to head home. Do you want me to give you a ride?"

"I'll make sure she gets home," Keith volunteered.

"Is that cool wit' you, Nina? I don't have a problem drop ping you off."

"Thanks, Precious, but I'm good. I'll call you tomorrow." I was relieved like a motherfucker that Keith had stepped up. I only had one thing on my mind, and taking Nina home wasn't it.

By the time we got to Jalen's hotel room, I had damn near taken off all of my clothes. Being backed up had sent my sexual desires into overdrive. I was dying for a nigga to twist my back out, and Jalen did not let me down. He scooped me up and gently laid me down on the bed and removed my remaining clothes. I closed my eyes as his tongue sucked my breasts and his fingers massaged my clit. At first I wanted him to start just pounding my pussy out because I hadn't had any dick in so long, but his four play felt so good it was getting me more open.

The nigga had me grinding my hips as he finger fucked me. Then he stopped sucking my tits and popped my pussy with his tongue and fingers simultaneously. He had my legs spread wide open as I arched my back about to explode. My juices flowed, and Jalen licked them up as if it were his favorite drink.

Then right when I thought it couldn't get any better, he reached for a Magnum XL condom, put it on and eased all ten inches inside of me. That shit had a bitch in pain for a second, but it quickly turned to pleasure. I wrapped my legs around his back, and he lifted my ass cheeks up so that with every thrust that niggas dick felt like it was about to come out my throat.

I came at least three times that night and it would've been more, but after twisting me out for over two hours, I finally had to put Jalen on pause. He had stamina like a stallion, but a bitch was tired. Every time I would have an orgasm, my energy would drain more and more, but it seemed to rejuvenate Jalen. When we finally chilled, I realized how much I missed falling asleep in the arms of a man.

When I woke up the next morning, Jalen was already in the shower. I knew he had to leave early to go to Philly, but I was hoping he could hit me off one more time before breaking out. I decided I would go to him, but before I was able to head to the bathroom there was a knock at the door. I assumed Jalen must have ordered some breakfast, because a dude with all that height and build must stay hungry. I grabbed his Tshirt and put it on before answering the door. "Who is it?" I asked, looking through the peephole.

"Room service," the gentleman replied. His face was looking down, but I could see he was holding a tray and so I let him in. The moment I slightly opened the door, two men kicked it open, barely giving me a chance to move back. I fell to the floor, and one of the guys rushed me. He put his hand over my mouth and I tried to bite the shit, but the way he had it positioned I couldn't latch on to any skin. The other man shut the door and pulled out his gun.

I figured these niggas somehow got word that a superstar athlete was staying in this room and decided to rob him. Both dudes were tall and big as shit. The one holding me down reached in a small bag he was carrying and pulled out some duct tape and rope. The nigga definitely knew what he was doing, because he had me tied and taped up in less than sixty seconds.

My mind was spinning, trying to figure out what to do next. I wondered if Jalen could hear any of the commotion going on, but I seriously doubted it. I finally heard the water turn off. My heart was pounding so hard. It was becoming clear that this wasn't about a robbery, because the niggas hadn't ransacked shit. After tying me up and placing me on the bed, they just stood standing by the bathroom waiting patiently for Jalen to come out.

"What the fuck!" Jalen barked when he opened the bathroom door and was greeted with the sight of me tied up on the bed. He never even had a chance to make a move, because one of the men used the butt of his gun to strike him on the side of his head. He did it with so much force that I think it gave Jalen a mini concussion, because his eyes rolled to the back of his head and he seemed to lose his balance. But if that first hit didn't take him under, the one that followed surely did.

The two men pounded on Jalen like he stole they last bag of dope. I felt so helpless as I watched them beat the shit out of him, and what made it worse was that I had no idea why. Besides feeling pity for Jalen, I feared that once the men finished him off they would then rape and beat me. Being raped by a man had to be my worst nightmare. Without access to a knife or gun, the men had all the power to have their way with me.

My mind drifted back to the asswhipping Jalen was receiving, and I realized that the moans I heard from him at first had all but disappeared. I couldn't grasp that just last night this nigga had given me one of the best fucks of my life, and now I was watching him die.

Finally, the punching and the kicking came to a cease and both men stared at me. I closed my eyes for a minute thinking that I couldn't believe this was how I was going out; being fucked and beat by some big, black grimy niggas. I decided that if the opportunity presented itself I wasn't going down without a fight. I was going to draw blood from one of those fuckers. I prepared myself to take whatever they were bringing and opened my eyes back up, but to my surprise they were gone. I was completely dumbfounded. I didn't know what this shit was about.

I tried to scoot my body over to the edge of the bed to see if Jalen was dead or alive, but I was wrapped up so tightly that I could barely move. It would take three more hours before we were found, and that's because the maid finally came to clean the room. She screamed in Spanish for damn near five minutes before someone started pounding on the door and snapped her out of her daze, and hotel security and the police were called.

When the duct tape was removed from my mouth, I explained to the officers everything that went down. I watched as the paramedics tried to resuscitate Jalen, but it wasn't looking good for him. They carried him off, and all I could do was shake my head in disbelief. I was beginning to feel like fucking with me was the kiss of death.

I was escorted to police headquarters, although I had already told the cops everything I knew, but they wanted to still drill me. When we arrived, they took me to a room that had one long table and two chairs. It was dreary and smelled of cigarettes, coffee and stale donuts.

One of the detectives pulled the chair out for me as if trying to be polite. "Mrs. Mills," the other detective who was sitting on the opposite side of the table from me addressed me. "I know you've had a rough morning, but I need you to look through some photos to see if you recognize your assailants.

I stared intently at each picture, but didn't see the two burly beasts who bumrushed the room and beat the shit out of Jalen. "Nah, I don't see them."

"Look a little closer," he persisted.

I did another look through, and still didn't recognize them. "They're not in here."

The detective then shoved the book at me, and it hit me in my chest. "Yo, what the fuck is wrong wit' you? What, you hard of hearing? I said them motherfuckers not in here. And you pushing this book at me ain't gon' make my eyes see no differently." I stood up. I was done talking to these disrespectful clowns, "Excuse me, I'm ready to go."

"You're not going anywhere until you answer my questions," the bugeyed white detective stated firmly. "I believe you know much more than what you're telling us, and you won't be leaving until I get some answers."

"I told you everything I know, and this going in circles bullshit is working my very last nerve. I'm tired and I want to go the fuck home."

"First your husband Supreme, and now Jalen Montgomery. One is dead; the other is knocking on deaths door. What do they both have in common? You. Being in your presence is costing these men their lives. Why is that?"

The detective was playing hardball, and it was working somewhat. I had been asking myself the same shit. It was as if I was cursed, but I wasn't going to give this prick the satisfaction of knowing his question was wearing hard on my mind. "Listen here, my man. That's what the NYPD get paid for, to figure out crimes. So get on your job."

Right when the detective looked as if he wanted to spit in my face, a short white man with glasses bust through the doors. Both of the detectives stared at him and then put their heads down as if disgusted.

"I hope you gentleman haven't been in here badgering my client, because I would hate to have the two of you reprimanded, or even worse, sue this department."

"On what grounds?" the detective questioned.

"I'm sure I can come up with something. Now excuse me, my client will be leaving now." The attorney walked over to me and gently took my hand and escorted me out.

"We're not done with you Mrs. Mills," the detective said in a threatening tone.

"Yes, you are. If you have any questions, please have them directed to my office, you know the number."

I followed the attorney out the door feeling a sense of relief. I had never seen him before, but I was grateful he got me out of that dark hole. "Thanks for that, but who are you?" I asked, wanting to know how he just popped up on the scene.

"Joseph Steinback, Attorney at Law. I was sent here by Mr. Owens."

"Mr. Owens?" I asked with confusion written on my face.

"Yes, Mike Owens."

"Oh, Mike. Crazy me, I'm not used to hearing him addressed by his last name."

"I understand." He smiled.

"How did Mike know I was here?" But there was no need for Joseph Steinback to answer the question. The moment we exited the police headquarters, the paparazzi and news reporters swarmed me.

"Mrs. Mills, why were you in the hotel room with Jalen Mont-gomery?" one reporter yelled.

"Do you think Jalen will pull through, or will he die like your husband, Supreme?" another barked.

"Mrs. Mills, did the men who tried to kill Jalen rape you?" I couldn't stomach another remark, and neither could Joseph. He held my hand firmly and stopped dead in his tracks, looking each individual square in the face. "That is enough. My client will not be answering any of your tasteless questions. I would appreciate if you all would step out of the way so we can get by." Joseph obviously garnered a certain level of respect, because the cameras kept flashing but they moved out of our way. The driver opened the door to the awaiting car and we drove off.

When we arrived back to the estate, I noticed Mike's Aston Martin parked in the driveway. I was in no mood to see him, but felt somewhat obligated since he retained Joseph Steinback on my behalf.

"Did you want to come in," I asked Joseph when the car came to a stop.

"No, I'm sure you're exhausted. We can talk tomorrow. But remember, don't speak to any reporters, and if the police come knocking call me immediately."

"Will do, and thanks again." I walked to the door, going over what I would say to Mike. Technically, I didn't owe him an explanation but felt that I had to give him one.

Before I even had a chance to get my thoughts together, I saw a girl that looked no more than sixteen standing at the front as if waiting to greet me. "Hi, Precious!" she chirped, sounding extremely comfortable in my space.

"Who are you, and why are you standing in my doorway?"

"Maya, girl, calm down and bring your ass inside," Mike said, reaching his hand out for me. "Precious, this is my sister, Maya. She can be a bit forward."

Seeing the two of them standing next to each other, you couldn't help but see the resemblance. Maya inherited the same gorgeous genes as her brother, except for being a shade lighter and having long hair. Aside from that, they were the spitting image of one another.

"Don't worry about it. I just wasn't expecting to see her standing in front of my door."

"Wow! So you the girl that was married to Supreme and got to lay down next to him every night. That's what's up!" Maya said, winking her eye at me.

Another grown ass girl, I thought to myself.

"We need to talk," Mike said seriously, ignoring his sister's comment.

"I'm sure, but where's Nathan?"

"They're out back. Some news media tried to sneak on the property. Nathan and the other security are keeping it under control."

I started walking towards the library so Mike and I could talk. Maya was right behind us, I guess thinking she was going to sit in on the conversation too. Of course Mike had to shut the door in her face so she'd realize it wasn't happening.

"I can't believe this shit," I said, pouring myself a drink.

"What did you expect? You got your face splashed across every station. What the fuck were you doing in Jalen's hotel room anyway?"

"I've been interrogated all morning and afternoon by the fuckin' cops. I don't need to come home and hear the same shit from you."

"If it wasn't for me you'd still be down there, so you need to be thanking me instead of poppin' shit."

"Thank you, but I got a lot on my mind right now. For one, I need to find out how Jalen is doing."

"Fuck Jalen. When are you going to comprehend that these little silly niggas ain't for you. I'm the only man that can take care of you right. Every time you get yourself caught up in some bullshit, who is the one that makes it right?"

I sipped on my drink, taking in what Mike said. From disposing of that body to helping me understand the ins and outs of this music shit now that I owned the masters to Supreme's music, and then this, yeah, Mike always seemed to be right there when I needed him the most. "I hear you. But what's up wit' your sister?" I knew my diverting from our initial conversation was going to piss him off, but my head was spinning and I needed a break from discussing that shit.

"I see what you doing, but that's cool," Mike said, rubbing his hands together as if trying to calm his nerves. "My mom's having some problems wit' Maya and asked me to step in."

"Step in how? Give her a lecture?" I asked sarcastically. "A little more than that. She wants me to keep her for a couple of weeks."

"What about school?"

"That's the thing. She got suspended for a couple of weeks."

"For what?"

"Fighting and shit."

"How are you going to watch over your sister? You going to have her go to work with you everyday?"

"That's the thing. I was hoping you could help me out."

I damn near dropped my glass when I heard the word "help" come out of his mouth. I had a funny feeling that something was up as soon as I saw his sister greeting me at the door all cheerful. "Yo, I feel for you, but there ain't nothing I can do to help with your sister. I got mad other shit going on."

"Yeah, like fuckin' wit' soft ass basketball players."

"Here we go again!" I poured myself another round, wishing I was knocked out in my bed instead of going back and forth with Mike.

"Fine, I'll put it like this: Who got rid of that body for you?"

I was glaring daggers at that nigga, mad that he even brought that shit up.

"Listen," he continued. "I'm not asking you to babysit Maya 24/7.

I'll drop her off on my way to work and pick her up when I get off. I'm asking for a favor, Precious."

Everything inside of me wanted to scream "no", but Mike had come through for me on more than one occasion. I would be dead wrong to shut him down. "How old is shorty, anyway?"

"Fifteen. She's really not a bad kid, just a little spoiled. With us growing up without our father, I tried to step in and give her everything she wanted. I might've given her too much. But besides my moms, she's all I have."

"I got you. I'll hold her down while you handle your business."

"I appreciate that, Precious. I hate to do this to you, but can you start today? I got this meeting I really need to get to."

"Is that the fuck why you had your attorney rushing down to the police station, 'cause you needed me to babysit?"

"Nah, I swear that's not why. I wanted you out," Mike said laughing. "But on the real, you need to stay away from that Jalen nigga. Didn't that beatdown he received wise you up? He ain't for you." Mike kissed me on my cheek before walking out.

Of course when he opened the door, Maya had obviously been listening to our conversation and jumped when her brother caught her. "Oh, I was about to knock on the door," Maya said, trying to play it off.

"Whatever. Listen," Mike put his hand on Maya's shoulder letting her know he was serious. "I have to head out to this meeting, and Precious was nice enough to let you stay here with her." Maya locked eyes with me as her brother continued to talk. "I don't want you giving her no problems, you understand?"

Maya nodded her head yes, and gave Mike the puppy dog eyes, looking all angelic.

"That's what's up. So I'll see you two ladies later on this evening. Thanks again, Precious."

"No problem." I walked Mike out, and as soon as I closed the door Maya wasted no time.

"So, Precious, where we going? You tryin' to hit the mall or what?"

"No, I'm hitting the shower then going to bed. You need to go sit down and watch some music videos or something. But do not bother me, I'm tired as hell. If you need anything to eat, have Anna fix it for you."

"So you just bailing on me? I thought you was cool. Guess I was wrong."

"Guess you was." I grabbed a couple of items and headed to my bedroom. I could feel Maya burning a hole in my back as I took my ass upstairs. But I was too tired to care. I did plan on spending some time with her; it just wasn't going to be today.

Rules To The Game

I was so exhausted that by the time I woke up it was the next day. The first person I thought about when I opened my eyes was Jalen, and then Maya immediately popped in my head. I didn't even say bye to her before she left, and Mike would be bringing her back over here any minute. I knew dealing with her was going to try my patience, but I already told Mike I would do it, so I had no choice but to keep my word. Before I allowed myself to lose my train of thought, I picked up the phone and called the hospital where Jalen was.

"Good morning, Mount Sinai Medical Center," the operator chirped.

"Hi, can I have Jalen Montgomery's room?" There was a slight pause, and I assumed the lady who answered the phone was checking for Jalen's information.

"I'm sorry, but this patient isn't accepting any calls," she informed me.

"Well, I'm his sister and would like to know how he's doing."

"What is your name?"

"Michelle Montgomery," I replied confidently, as if the made up name was the truth. There was another pause this time slightly longer.

"I'm sorry, but your name isn't on the patient's list, So I can't answer any of your questions."

"There must be some mistake. I just want to know how my brother is doing."

"Ma'am, I understand your concern, but I've been given strict instructions. There's nothing I can do for you."

I wanted to reach through the phone and smack the lady, but knew there was no use in arguing with her. I sat in bed for a minute contemplating who could give me an update on Jalen's condition. I thought of someone who might be able to help me.

Ring... ring... ring...

"Hello," Nina answered sounding out of breath.

"Hey, girl, what's up?"

"Precious, how are you? I called you a few times yesterday but you didn't pick up."

"Yeah, I was really out of it."

"That's understandable. So, what happened? They were talking about you and Jalen all day yesterday on the news, but nobody seemed to have their story straight."

"Nina, I promise to fill you in but I'm not in the mood right now. Have you spoken to Keith?" I asked, jumping straight to the point.

"Yeah I spoke to him yesterday."

"Did he tell you what kind of condition Jalen was in?"

"He's pretty bad, but he's going to pull through."

I let out a deep sigh, relieved that Jalen would be okay.

"Did Keith say anything else?"

"Besides that you're bad luck and he warned Jalen to stay the fuck away from you, no, nothing else."

"Thanks for the info, but I gotta go now."

"Wait, don't forget my wedding is in less than two weeks. You're the only one who hasn't gotten fitted for your dress," Nina added before I had a chance to hang up the phone.

"Well, that's because you only asked me to be in the wed ding a couple of days ago."

"I know it was last minute, but we still have to get it done."

"Fine, I'll call you later on to get the details. But I have to go now." This time I hung up the phone quickly, not letting Nina drop another word. I desperately wanted to go to the hospital to visit Jalen, because in the pit of my stomach I felt responsible for what happened. I couldn't shake that feeling.

By the time I got dressed and went downstairs, Maya was already there, sitting in the dining room eating breakfast. "Good morning," I greeted her, wanting to start the day on a good note.

"Hey," Maya replied dryly.

"I know yesterday I was in a bad mood, but I had just gone through some bullshit. I've got my rest, so we working on a brand new page. So let's try this again. Good morning!" I said extra cheerfully.

"Good morning, Precious," Maya said, putting some pep in her voice, whether it was sincere or not was irrelevant to me.

"That's better. Now, I have to run a few errands today. Are you rolling wit' me or you staying here?"

"Ooh, I wanna roll wit' you."

"Cool."

"Precious," I heard Nathan call out from the other room.

"Nathan, I'm in the dining room."

"Jamal is here for you," he said, entering the dining room.

"Thanks, tell him I'll be right there."

"Dang, who's Jamal? Is he sweet on you?" Maya inquired.

"Excuse me?"

"Just asking. You know my brother's digging you and I was wondering if Jamal was his competition. But then maybe it's the basketball dude, Jalen. That mess been all over the television and newspapers. You got a lot jumpin' off."

"I have to speak to Jamal, but mind yo' business and stay outta mine." With those departing words I went to handle things with Jamal.

"How are you feeling?" were the first words Jamal had for me as he followed me to the living room.

"I'm fine. Jalen is the one in the hospital, not me. I'm assuming that's what you were referring to."

"Yes. I had no idea the two of you were dating."

"We were in the beginning stages, but it's ended before it even had a chance to really begin."

"That's too bad, but I'm sure you'll find somebody," Jamal said sincerely.

"Enough about me, what brings you here?"

"I wanted to check up on you and ask about Nina. You know we're getting married next Saturday."

"I know, time flies. Can you believe I'm going to be one of the bridesmaids?"

"Yeah, when Nina told me you agreed to it I was shocked."

"It is your wedding, and Nina's not so bad."

"Does that mean you don't have any dirt to share with me?" he asked in a tone that seemed unsure of what the answer would be.

"Jamal, you can relax. Nina is harmless. She might flirt a little bit, but there's nobody else. She's in love with you."

A smile broadened across Jamal's face, happy with my report. "Thank you for doing this. I know you didn't want to spy on Nina, but I'm glad you put my paranoia to rest."

"Me too."

"I know you've got a lot on your mind, but I need to ask you about Supreme. Have you decided what you're going to do with his music?"

"I'm still figuring some things out. A couple of weeks ago I spoke to Mike about his thoughts since he owns Pristine Records. He's done very well for himself in this business and I wanted to get his opinion on how much I should ask for if I decided to sell."

"I can understand that. So, what did he say?"

"He told me I shouldn't sell the music, but instead put it out myself."

"What do you mean, put it out independently?"

"Yeah, or seek distribution with a major label but still hold on to the rights. What do you think?"

"Of course you know I want Supreme's music for a lot of reasons. But speaking to you on a friendship level and not business, I would advise you to really do your research before jumping into the music industry. It's extremely cutthroat, and while it's wise to seek knowledge from Mike, I would also question what his motives are. I'm going to leave you with that food for thought, but you know I'm always here if you want to talk. If nothing comes up then I'll see you at my wedding." Jamal smiled.

"Of course."

After showing him out, I got my purse and told Maya to come on so I could run my errands. I listened to JayZ's "Kingdom Come", rehashing all the bullshit that had been invading my life since Supreme's death. It was like a domino effect that wouldn't stop. I was so caught up in my thoughts that I didn't even hear my cell ring.

"Precious, here, your phone is ringing," I finally heard Maya say, snapping out of my thoughts.

"Hello," I answered, still halfway zoning out until I recognized the voice on the other end of the phone.

"You still want that Nico information or what?"

"No doubt."

"A'ight, so meet me next Saturday at twelve o'clock. I'll call you earlier that day to let you know the spot."

"Next Saturday is no good for me. What about this Saturday?"

"Do you want Nico Carter or not?" she said defiantly, making it clear it was her way or no way.

"I'll be there."

"Smart decision. I'll be in touch."

I didn't appreciate the way that bitch was carrying me, but my thirst for Nico was stronger than my anger over her behavior. I preferred not to do this shit on the same day of Jamal's wedding, but if I met the chick at twelve, then I still had a few hours to make it back in time for a three o'clock starting time. It would be tight, but I couldn't miss what sounded like a real opportunity to finish Nico off. However, if I found out this bitch on the phone was wasting my time, then the same knife I planned to use to slit Nico's throat with would find its way to hers.

"Who was that?" Maya asked after I hung up the phone.

"I coulda swore I told you to stay out my business."

"That call seemed to get under your skin. I was concerned, that's all."

"Save your concern for somebody who needs it. I'm good."

"Damn, why you gotta be so hostile? I don't understand why we can't be friends."

My neck actually snapped back due to that question. "Friends? I'm almost twentyone. How old are you?"

"Fifteen," Maya stated proudly.

"Girl, first of all, I don't have friends, and if I did it wouldn't be wit' yo' young ass. What the hell do we have in common?"

"We both used to the ghetto fabulous life. You a baller chick, and my brother got extra long paper, so I'm a baller chick too. That's a start."

"Sweetheart, let me explain something to you. Your brother has given you everything you have, ain't nobody ever gave me shit. Do you know what I was doing when I was fifteen? Busting my ass working at a detailing shop, tryna find a nigga to trick on me 'cause my moms wanted to pimp me out in the street. I lived the good life for this long," I said, snapping my finger. "Then it was all taken away from me when Supreme died. I learned to ball because I had no choice, and after getting a little taste of the streets it made me greedy. You, my dear, are trying to ball off your brother's loot. That's a big difference."

"What you mean? I got an older nigga that trick on me. He pushing keys and everything, so I ball off of more than just my brother's paper."

"Let me school you on something, youngin'. When you start fuckin' wit' them older hustlers in the streets, they not taking your young ass seriously. You just a pretty piece of pussy they want to have on they roster. They putting that real time in wit' them older bitches that got official jobs and good credit. Why? 'Cause they lacking that shit themselves. They know a lil' fifteen year old can't get no houses or apartments and cars in they name, so they hustling the older bitches that can.

"See, I always knew shit like that 'cause my man, Boogie, may he rest in peace, hipped me to that shit. Unlike you, I didn't have no richass family member hittin' me off wit' paper and whatever else I wanted. You fuckin' blessed and you wanna brag 'bout some hustler in the street breaking you off wit' chump change while you give up your most precious gift. 'Cause at the end of the day, if all else fails, your beauty and body is all you have. Don't sell yourself short, especially when you don't have to."

After I said my peace I turned the music back up. I glanced over at Maya I noticed tears streaming down her cheeks. At first I wasn't going to say anything, but then she started sniffling and I could tell she was all chokedup. I reached in the glove department and handed her some tissues.

"Thank you," she said between sobs.

"It wasn't my intention to make you cry, but I had to keep it real wit' you, Maya. Life is too short to waste it on bullshit. I turned to the streets out of survival, and it made me cold. That doesn't have to be your life. With the type of money your brother has, you have the opportunity to be anything you want to be in this world. You can be so much more than a hustler's wife. That's a hood dream, baby. You so beyond that, and that's coming from a real bitch that knows this game."

For the duration of our ride there was complete silence between us. When we arrived at the store on Fifty Second and Lexington Avenue where I was getting fitted for my bridesmaid's dress, Maya seemed to pull it together. Her eyes filled with amazement when we opened the glass double doors and entered the opulent store. The regal boutique was full of gowns, from wispy sheer dresses to mermaidstyles, and most of them adorned with delicate beading and embellished embroidery.

"Damn, I can't wait to get married," Maya beamed as we walked on the ivory marble floor following what seemed to be the yellow brick road.

"Can I help you ladies?" a well preserved tall white lady asked.

"Yes, I'm here to get fitted."

"For a wedding dress?"

"No, for a bridesmaid's dress. The actual bride is Nina."

"Oh yes, Nina. She's here now. Follow me to the back."

We could tell when we were getting close, because it sounded as if we had arrived at a block party in Brooklyn instead of an upscale bridal store. I could hear Nina's voice but couldn't see her because my view was obstructed by three women who had the type of asses and tits that would jiggle across your television screen.

"Nina, your other bride's maid is here," the sales lady said."

By the expression on their faces when they turned around, we had obviously caught them off guard. "Precious, hi! I almost forgot you were coming," Nina said, scooting by her friends.

"Sorry, I was running late, but I'm here now," I said as Nina gave me a hug.

"Nina, I'll go get Precious' dress so the tailor can get her fitted."

"Thanks," Nina said to the saleslady, then turned her attention back to her friends and me. "Everybody, this is Precious and..." Nina paused, glancing at Maya.

"This is Maya, Mike's sister."

"Nice to meet you, Maya."

"Hey, ladies," the three women said in unison.

"Wow, Nina, I had no idea we'd be having a party up in here." I glanced at the table next to the cream velvet couches, and there were two open bottles of champagne, glasses and strawberries dipped in chocolate.

"Girl, you know how I do. Why don't you let me pour you a glass?"

"No, thank you."

"I'll take some," Maya said, moving forward towards the table.

"I think not." I put my hand up, indicating to Maya not to go any further.

"Well, come sit down until they bring out your dress."

I sized up the three women as we sat down. They had hoochie written all over their faces. Each had twenty pounds of weave in an array of colors to match their various complexions, which went from butterscotch to deep chocolate. All of them had cute faces, tiny waists, and the words "thirsty for money" dripping from the sides of their mouths.

"I'm Talesha," the girl in the middle of the color spectrum said, extending her hand. Her claws were so long I thought they would sink into my skin. "This is Brittany and CoCo," she said, pointing to the other women.

"My fault. I was so caught up I forgot to introduce you to my other bridesmaids," Nina said, sipping on her champagne. "Precious, you haven't said what you think of my dress."

"What dress, the one you got on?"

"Yeah, girl, this my wedding dress. What else would I be talking about?"

"My bad. I guess I was expecting something stark white, ivory or cream, but never a pale gold."

"I didn't want to follow the traditional route. I wanted to put my own spin on this shindig. I mean, this is the new color for wedding dresses anyway."

The three musketeers gave her a highfive cosigning on her wedding gown choice.

The dress was actually very pretty, in an overthetop ballroom gown type way. It had incorporated jewels and pearls along the neck and draped down the back. Indeed, it was far from traditional and very edgy even for the most modern bride.

"You've definitely done that, but it's cool. You will no doubt stand out as the star, as you should." I started wondering what type of new of the moment dress she would have us in. I prayed it wouldn't be too far to the left. To my pleasant surprise, my dress was more traditional and very lovely. It was a pretty stardust color silk Aline dress with empire waist, chiffon halter, and back cascade. "Very lovely."

"This is hot," Maya added.

"Damn sure is. I can't wait to get married so I can pick out my wedding dress. It's going to be sick," Talesha popped.

"That's right, but you better make sure your groom's paper is right. 'Cause it costs paper to put on a flyass wedding. But Nina ain't got to worry 'bout that because she got richass Jamal footing the bill," Brittney boasted.

I watched as Nina sat back, carrying on with her girlfriends, sucking up their words of encouragement. While the tailor fitted my dress, all I thought about was poor Jamal. He was so out of his league fucking with a hofessional like Nina. There was no doubt in my mind that she would pop out one baby for insurance purposes, and the moment she got her figure back she'd be leaving the little one with a nanny as she hit the streets with her hotass friends. The next chapter would be divorce court. Oh fucking well, that's Jamal's life. It will definitely be one to grow on.

I then stared over at Maya. I was still feeling bad about trying to school her earlier, but I hoped she understood that I wasn't trying to bring her down, but instead lift her up. The streets took my soul when I was fifteen, and had a firm grip until I fell in love with Supreme. But when he died, the part of me that truly learned to love died too. The street life hadn't stole Maya's innocence yet, and I prayed it never would. By the way she was so enthralled in the hoochies' conversation, it might've already been too late. Only time would tell.

Make A Wish

I woke up on a beautiful Sunday morning with a deep sense of despair, and didn't understand why. The sun was shining bright, but instead of opening my curtains and relishing in the sunlight, I pulled the silk comforter over my head wanting to be in darkness. I tried to go back to sleep but kept tossing and turning.

Then it hit me as if getting swept away in the ocean by a strong current. It was my birthday. Today I was twenty one—finally officially legal. When Aaliyah sang in her angelic voice that "age ain't nothing but a number", she knew what was up. I had felt legal damn near all my life. Maneuvering through life's struggles and tragedies will age any person. You get to the point where no one can tell you a damn thing because you've seen too much with your own eyes and the experiences have left you bitter and cold. Here I was, supposed to be celebrating a day that many anticipate for many years and reaching an age I thought for so long was out of my reach. Being a hellraiser in the streets would certainly almost always lead to either an early death or lockdown, but I had defeated the odds. I had achieved the material gains I had aspired for, but nothing else. I was alone. I had no one; not the child I was supposed to give birth to, nor the man I should have spent the rest of my life with. It was moments like this that for a brief second I would be ready to end it all. But then my motivation for living would kick in... Nico Carter.

Every time I was ready to check out and join Supreme, I would think about Nico. He was the one who gave me so much in life and then he took it all away. I would've much rather he ended my life than take Supreme. Here I was, surrounded by wealth but deprived of what I needed the most...the love of my husband.

When I finally dragged myself out of bed, I went in the closet and pulled out the box I had put a lot of Supreme's belongings in. There were some of his prized possessions that I couldn't dare part with but couldn't stomach looking at every day. The reminder was too painful, but today I wanted to embrace that pain. In the box was a rare mix tape that he cut when he was still an underground artist, and a press kit released by Atomic Records promoting his first solo debut, including an 8x10 black and white photo and a fivepage information packet printed on stationary from Atomic Records with a little about the CD, explaining what each song is about and why he wrote it. There was also a platinum diamondencrusted "Supreme 4 Life" pendant he received from the label when his debut CD went platinum.

But, my favorite memorabilia was Supreme's notebook filled with handwritten lyrics and poetry. He would always tell me that he had memorized every rhyme he ever spit and he had no need to write them down, but chose to because one day he wanted to share his thoughts on paper for the rest of the world to read.

I spent the next few hours in the closet laughing, crying and most importantly reminiscing. In my time of deep thought, I couldn't help but ponder what would I do next after I had finally achieved retribution against Nico. What direction would my life lead me in? My mind had been so preoccupied with revenge that I hadn't looked towards the future. I guess I didn't see a future without Supreme in it, but maybe it was time for me to realize that I should. Supreme wouldn't want me to stop living because of the cards life had dealt me. He was a survivor and would want me to be a soldier.

I stepped in the shower and let the hot water baptize my body. I would handle my business with Nico, and then put the misery of my past behind me and see what the world had to offer. I knew I would never share a love greater than the one I had with Supreme, but I had to try to figure out a way to live instead of just existing.

After I got out the shower, I put on a cream Juicy Couture jogging suit and headed downstairs. Before I reached the bottom step the doorbell rang. "Who the fuck is at my door on a Sunday afternoon?" I said out loud. Annoyed, I opened the door.

"Surprise! Happy birthday!" Jamal and Nina said in chorus. They had balloons, cake, champagne and food.

"How did you guys know it was my birthday?"

"A couple of weeks ago when we went out, you left your wallet open on the table for a brief moment when you took a call on your cell phone, so I peeked at your license. I realized your birthday was coming up, and I thought it would be great to surprise you with an intimate party, especially since you agreed to be in my wedding."

My first instinct was to think back as to when I left my wallet open, since that was out of my character. I didn't want to spoil the kind gesture so I let it slide.

"Are you going to keep us standing out here? This cake is getting heavy. Come on, Precious, let us in," Nina said.

"Yeah, Precious, I don't know how much longer I can carry this stuff," Jamal added.

"Sorry. Come on in. I'm still a little surprised that you all showed up on my birthday."

"I hope you don't mind," Jamal said.

"No, it's a much needed surprise. It's either this or mope around the house all day."

"Well, we can't have you doing that. You're part of my clique now, and no girlfriend of mine is left to mope."

"Nina, that's sweet of you, but I'm not really the clique type."

"Now you are. Now let's go get this party started." Before we could get to the kitchen, the doorbell rang again.

"Did you all have somebody else with you?"

Nina and Jamal looked at each other and then shook their heads.

"Then who could it be?" I went to the door and found another surprise.

"Happy birthday, pretty girl," Mike said with a beautiful flower arrangement in one hand and a bottle of champagne in the other.

"Did someone put out a special service announcement that today's my birthday?"

"If they did, I didn't get it, but I don't need to. I know everything. By the way, where are Nathan and the rest of the security?"

"It's Sunday and I gave them the afternoon off to spend some time with their families. They'll be back this evening, and Anna will be back in the morning. Speaking of family, where is Maya?"

"I wanted us to celebrate your birthday alone, so I let her hang out with one of her girlfriends."

"I hate to burst your bubble, but we're not alone."

Mike stepped inside, only to see Jamal and Nina, who gave him a halfass smile.

"You're more than welcome to stay for the party. Two bottles of champagne is always better than one," I said, taking the bubbly and the flowers out of Mike's hands. "The flowers are gorgeous."

"Just like the birthday girl."

"You and Jamal go have a seat while Nina and I prepare the food and pour the drinks."

The fellas nodded their heads, though neither one seemed enthused about the alone time. Nina and I headed to the kitchen, and the questions kicked in immediately.

"So, are you and Mike getting serious? I mean, him showing up trying to be alone with you on your birthday. He seems smitten to me."

"Mike is cool, but we haven't gone any further than being just friends."

"Do you think if Jamal and I hadn't shown up today that maybe it would have?"

I eyed Nina. "I don't think I understand your question." "Don't be sly with me, Precious Cummings. You understand my question. If you and Mike were alone today on your birthday, do you think you guys would have taken your relationship to the next level?"

I remained silent, putting the Jamaican food on the plates and opening the champagne.

"Damn, let me say it in laymen's terms; would you and Mike be having buckwild passionate sex tonight if you were alone?"

"You over there feenin' for the inside scoop, but I have none to give. Like I said, Mike and I are cool... period. Now grab those two plates. I'm ready to eat."

"Before we go can I ask you one last question?"

Nina's tone sounded serious, but I decided to throw her a bone since they brought over some treats for my birthday. "What is it?"

"Have you ever loved anyone else besides Supreme?"

"Why would you ask me that?"

"Just curious. I'm about to be a married woman and wondered if he would be my first and final love."

"So Jamal is the only man you've ever loved?"

"Yes."

I seriously doubt that, but then again, Nina didn't really come across as the falling in love type. "Interesting. Honestly, I loved one other man."

"Who?"

"Nico Carter."

"The man Jamal said tried to kill you?"

"That's him. But hey, we can never choose who we'll fall in love with. Now enough questions. Let's go eat."

When Nina and I left the kitchen, we could hear raised voices. When we reached the dining room, Jamal and Mike were standing practically toetotoe.

"What is going on in here?" Both of the men turned to look at me.

"Oh, it's nothing. Jamal and I were just discussing busi ness."

"It must have been awfully intense, since your voices were rather loud."

"I apologize, Precious. Mike and I had a difference of opinion with what you should do about Supreme's music."

"Do we really have to discuss this on my birthday?"

"Of course not, today is about you. Everything else is irrelevant."

Mike came over and took the plates from my hands and put them on the table. I noticed Jamal giving him the look of death. I was tempted to ask Jamal to replay their conversation in its entirety, but I wanted to spend a couple of hours not focusing all my energy on Supreme. He occupied my every thought for the majority of each day and night; my brain and heart needed a break. "Cool, because if only for the duration of the afternoon I want us to enjoy each other's company."

"Whatever your heart desires," Mike said, being all extra.

We all sat down and tore up the food. Then Nina brought out the cake she ordered from Make My Cake, located in Harlem.

"Precious, you have to make a wish before you blow out the candles," Nina said. I closed my eyes and wished for Supreme's killer to burn in hell, then blew out the candles, not missing one. They all applauded.

"What did you wish for?" Mike inquired.

"If I tell you that, then it won't come true."

When it came time for me to make a toast, I was actually enjoying myself. We all lifted our glasses and I looked at the three guests who I considered the closest things I had to friends. "I want to thank each of you for making this a wonderful birthday. When I woke up this morning I wanted this day to be over before it even started, but you all made it into something special. For that I'm grateful."

When the party came to an end, I almost wasn't ready for it to end... almost. I showed all three to the door and watched as they walked to their cars. "Nina, I'll be right back. I forgot something," I heard Jamal say. He jogged back up to the front door as Nina and Mike continued walking.

"What did you forget, Jamal?"

"I just said that so it wouldn't look suspicious, me coming back up to speak to you," he whispered as soon as he reached me.

"What is it?"

"I don't mean to bring any negativity on your birthday, but I care about you, Precious, and I wouldn't be able to sleep tonight without telling you this."

"Telling me what?"

"Be careful with Mike."

"What did he say to you?"

"It's not what he said; it's how he said it. He's dangerous, that I know. So just be careful. I have to go but we'll talk later."

That night I went to bed replaying what Jamal said. There was an underlying tone of fear in his voice. The eye contact he made with me when speaking of Mike was powerful. I already knew Mike was a dangerous man, but Jamal sounded as if he had established that Mike was not only dangerous, but deadly.

One Murder At A Time

Before I knew it, Saturday rolled around, and I woke up feeling anxious. As promised, the mysterious informant kept her word and called, letting me know where to meet her, which turned out to be the city. Since the wedding was taking place at The Plaza Hotel that was convenient.

As I got dressed, I didn't know what to expect from the woman I was meeting. Hell, I wasn't sure a woman would even show up. She he could've been a decoy for a big ruthless nigga. That's why I was going prepared with two nine millimeters and a knife.

When I got downstairs, to my surprise and annoyance Maya was sitting in the living room. "Maya, what are you doing here?"

"You told Mike that I could go to the wedding with you, remember?"

"Yeah, I told him to drop you off at The Plaza at three, so why are you here and it's only ten?"

"He had to go out of town and wasn't going to be able to drop me off in the city at three, so he told me to chill at your place and ride to the wedding wit' you."

Just like a nigga, always putting they responsibilities off on the next bitch like we ain't got shit to do but babysit. How the fuck am I gonna manage this? I can't have Maya all up in the mix 'cause I don't know what might go down. I could drop her off at the hotel, but then her hot ass might start turning tricks in there. She'll be better off just sitting in the car. At least I'll know where she is and that she's safe, I thought to myself. "A'ight, get yo' shit. But don't ask me no questions and stay in the fuckin' car at all times unless I tell you otherwise. Understand?"

"Yes, I understand."

The first stop I made was to my storage spot. After all this time I still kept it. I didn't trust keeping my stash cash in my crib because too many people be coming through there. If my money came up short or missing, it could be anyone from the security to the hired help. I didn't have time for those guessing games. I knew I was the only one with a key to this spot, so if some shit was amiss, that was on me. I ran inside with a small duffel bag and got the one hundred thousand the girl asked me for. It was a far cry from the million I had floating in the street. But if the informant didn't know about it, who was I to tell?

After retrieving the money it was time for me to head to the city. Driving from my crib to the storage took me over an hour, and I didn't want to be late for my twelve o'clock appointment. The closer I got to the city, the more I started feeling nauseous. I hoped it was jitters from being in the wedding and not an omen of my fate.

Right when I pulled out of the Lincoln tunnel, I heard the chiming of my cell. "Yo!" I answered. I knew it had to be homegirl since she had been the only one calling me from a blocked number.

"You got everything?" she asked, sounding anxious. I figured she was referring to the money.

"Right here."

"Okay, meet me on 42nd and Ninth."

"The bus terminal by Time Square? It's gon' be mad motherfuckers over there."

"I know. I'll call you in ten minutes and let you know where to give me the money."

"So we're clear, I'm not giving you shit until you give up the exact facts."

"I got you."

"Long as we on the same page. I'll be waiting for your call."

Since I took the Lincoln Tunnel, I was right by 42nd and Ninth. I pulled my car on the corner block, where I had a prime view of the street but was also discreet. If possible, I wanted to figure out who the informant was before we met. With the block not being as crowded as I thought it would be, there was a good chance of seeing her. I sat there with the radio off in pure silence, scanning the area like a hawk.

"Who you looking for?" Maya asked, letting her curiosity get the best of her.

"What I tell you before we left? In case you don't remember, I'll remind you. Sit there and don't ask me no questions. Ain't nothin' changed."

Maya started fidgeting in her chair, and I knew she was dying to play Twenty Questions, but I wasn't having it. Just then my cell started ringing, and it was coming from a block number. I stared extra hard, seeing if I could peep anyone using their cell trying to call someone. In those few seconds,

I noticed five people on their cells; two middle aged white men, a young Hispanic boy, an older black man, and a black woman who looked to be in her midtwenties. I purposely didn't answer my phone to see which one would try to make the call again. My phone kept ringing as I tapped my fingernails, eyeing their moves.

"You not gonna answer your phone?" Maya asked, crossing her arms like she had an attitude.

I turned and gave her the look of death so she knew I meant business and would leave her hardheaded ass sitting right on the curb. I quickly gave my attention back to the agenda at hand. I peeped mouth movement from three out of the five people I was watching, which meant they made contact, so I scratched them off the list. The two left was the Hispanic boy and the black woman. My phone stopped ringing, and then it started again from the blocked number. I looked up to see which of the two was on their phone, and it was the black woman. This time I answered. "Yo, what's up?"

"Why didn't you answer your phone a minute ago? I was about to leave."

"I doubt that, especially since you want your money." I watched front a short distance as the black woman I scoped out yapped on the phone, talking to me. Homegirl was definitely a rookie at this, because her game wasn't tight at all. She was actually on 42nd and Ninth waiting for me like she said she would. A semipro would've held tight to see me in the spot first and watched from a distance to scan my moves before stepping on the scene, but she bypassed all that.

"Anyway, here's how it's going down. There is a telephone booth right at the corner on Ninth. Right beside it is a trashcan. Leave the bag with the money in the trashcan. Under the booth there is an envelope taped with all the information you need to get to Nico."

"Information like what?"

"The address to where Nico is staying."

"How I know this shit official?"

"You don't, but I'm telling you it is. It's up to you. So what you want to do?"

"Let's do this." I hung up the phone and noticed the girl disappear into a deli near the dropoff location.

Then I turned to Maya. Homegirl might've been telling the truth, but this shit was too important to gamble on. I needed to sit the bitch down and get to the bottom of some things. "Maya, you always wanna be so down, I got a task for you that can earn you some stripes."

Maya's eyes lit up real bright. "What is it?"

"First, twist your hair in a bun, and I want you to put on my baseball cap," I directed as I took off my hat. Luckily Maya and I were about the same complexion and fairly the same build. With the hat on, no one could tell for sure if it was me or not, assuming that the woman knew what I looked like.

Maya did what I asked and began getting excited at the thought of being down with my scheme.

"Now what, Precious?"

"Take this bag and drop it in that garbage right there," I said, pointing to the corner where the trashcan was. "But before you do so, make sure you get the envelope from underneath the phone booth. Do you understand?" I asked slowly and precisely.

"Yes. Get the envelope from under the phone booth and then leave this duffel bag in the trashcan," she repeated.

"Exactly. When you're done, I want you to wait for me in that drug store across the street. You got your cell?" Maya nodded her head yes. "Okay, I'll call you when it's time for you to come out the store. It's imperative that you follow my exact instructions."

"I promise I won't let you down."

I watched as Maya walked across the street with the duffel bag in tow. She went directly to the phone booth, patted her hand under the bottom and ripped off the envelope. She then dropped the bag in the trash and proceeded towards the drug store as instructed. With Maya in place, I slowly drove my car directly across the street where the trashcan was on my lefthand side. I eagerly waited for the woman to come out, because I was positioned much closer to where the bag was located and would retrieve it before she ever had a chance. I already had my 9mm resting underneath a jacket, and the second I noticed the woman walking towards the trashcan I swung into action. I reached the duffel bag in what seemed to be one leap.

"Excuse me miss, that's mine!" She screamed out, not realizing who I was.

We were now facetoface, and before she could say another word or run for safety I had my piece rubbed up against her ribs. "Now I can either drop you right here on 42nd Street, or you can take a ride wit' me. It's up to you.

The woman's whole body was shaking. This must have been the first time she ever felt steel that shot bullets. "Please don't shoot me!" she said with her voice trembling.

"I guess that means you'll take that ride wit' me. I'm sure you can drive, so get in the driver's seat."

"I'm not really comfortable driving a Range Rover."

"Well, bitch, get comfortable, 'cause you only working wit' two choices. Drive or die."

As the woman started up the truck, I kept the gun to her side as I called Maya.

"Hi, Precious. How did I do?" she asked with a sound of pride in her voice.

"Excellent. You still got that envelope?"

"Yes, I'm guarding it tightly."

"Cool. Can you stay there for about ten more minutes?"

"Yeah, that's no problem."

"Good. I'll call you back shortly."

"I could've sworn I saw you drop off the duffel bag and take the envelope," said the girl with tears streaming down her face. "I even waited a few minutes and watched you leave."

"Nah, your eyes were playing tricks on you, but this gun is the real deal. Now pull right over there in that abandoned parking lot."

"Are you going to kill me?"

"That's up to you. I definitely don't have a problem killing you, but it depends if you gonna answer my questions truthfully, or if you're gonna lie."

"What do you want to know?" The highyellow heifer had beads of sweat coating her forehead. She couldn't even hide her fear.

"Who the fuck gave you my number, and who the fuck sent you after me? Answer those questions and you might have a chance of seeing another day."

The girl swallowed hard. She didn't look any older than twenty three, and I wondered how she got involved in this bullshit. I could still smell the Similac on her breath.

"Listen to me. I'm about to tell you the truth," she said, twisting in her seat as she prepared to spit her story. "This girl that I'm cool with called me like a few weeks ago asking me did I want to make some easy money. And of course I was down for it 'cause I'm in school and I do little bullshit videos and stuff on the side to make a couple of dollars. So, I was like, as long as I don't end up in jail or dead I'm down for whatever."

The girl then looked down, eyeing my gun as if pleading, *Please don't kill me!*

"So the girl promised me that the job was real easy. All I had to do was call this chick up and say x, y and z, collect some money, and I'm good."

"Yo, your story sounds like some bullshit."

"I swear! Look in my purse and you'll see the notes she gave me."

I kept my gun purposely aimed at the girl and grabbed her purse that was sitting on her lap.

"There it is, right there," she gestured with her finger, pointing to a manila envelope.

I opened it and saw what appeared to be a highly specific script. It even had the comment Nico made in reference to death before he shot me. I studied every word on the script, looking for a clue. "I don't see anything on here about how much money you were supposed to ask me for in order to get the information on Nico."

"She never gave me one. That's why the first time I spoke to you I had to cut our conversation short, because I wanted to find out what amount of money to say. The girl told me to ask for whatever I wanted, because more than likely you would pay. Plus, she said your paper was like that. She did tell me to ask you for a cute amount, and give her twentyfive percent since she put me on. The deal I made with you was going to pay for my tuition, and I wouldn't have to do videos no damn more. I get tired of having to fuck bumass rappers and their boys all the time. I couldn't believe it when you agreed to the amount, but now I see why you planned on snatching me up regardless."

"So, did the girl show you a picture of me?"

"Nope."

"Did she tell you who she was working for?"

"Nope, she kept everything real simple. It's like a bunch of us that all run in the video girl circuit, and she was just putting me on to some quick dough."

"What's her name?"

"Who's name?"

"Bitch, the chick that set this shit up?"

"Oh, her name, LeeLee."

"What was the next move you were supposed to make after I picked up the envelope and you got the money?"

"She told me to call her and let her know you picked up the envelope and I got the money. That was it."

"Well then, that's what you gonna do. What's yo' name, Ma?"

"Vita."

"A'ight, here," I said, handing Vita her phone. "Call that chick, LeeLee and tell her that I must've changed my mind 'cause I never showed up. Tell her you've been waiting for over an hour, and when you tried to call me I didn't pick up my phone. You understand?"

"Yeah," Vita nodded her head.

"But yo, don't play no clue games wit' your homegirl.

'Cause sweetheart, I would hate to have your brains splattered in my Range Rover, but if that's what has to be done, then than so be it."

"No, I won't try nothing, III promise," Vita stuttered. "If I knew it was going to be all this drama I would've said forget it."

"What type of shit did you think you were being a part of when you were calling me, demanding money, and throwing faulty shit around about a nigga that tried to kill me?" I questioned.

"Honestly, I didn't want to know. Some easy money was the only thing on my mind."

"Huh, I guess nobody schooled you that all money ain't good money. Now make that call."

As Vita dialed LeeLee's number, I unzipped a bag full of goodies I brought for today's mission. I listened intently as she let her friend know the deal never went down. I could hear the frustration in the girl's voice as she asked Vita a million questions. Finally, I motioned my hand letting her know to wrap up the conversation. When she hung up I made my next move.

"Are you going to let me go now?" A naïve Vita asked.

"Do you know what information is in that envelope my partner picked up?" I asked her, ignoring the bogus question she hit me with.

"I assume the address to where the guy Nico is. I already told you that."

I hope it is the correct address, because there's nothing like the element of surprise. If Nico and whoever is helping him thinks I never picked up the envelope, then they won't be expecting me to show up. Fucked up for them, but great for me, I thought to myself. "Just checking, making sure your story is legit. Now put your hands behind your back." Vita looked down strangely at the handcuffs I was holding. "What, you ain't neva seen no handcuffs before?"

"Why, you want me to put these on?"

I chuckled for a minute, wondering why dumb broads get themselves involved in shit that's way out of their league. She is playing with her life over greed, and she wasn't even a warrior. "Vita, don't ask me no questions just make things easier on yourself and do as I say," I told her calmly.

"Are you going to kill me?" Her eyes were filled with tears and fear.

"If I wanted you dead, you would be. So just cooperate and we good."

She breathed a sigh of relief and hurriedly complied with my request. I then pulled out my rope, tied her feet up, and then put duct tape over her mouth. I pushed the seats in the back down and directed her to get in the trunk. As she lay with her feet facing me, I tied her legs up. Without saying a word, I used the butt of my gun to pound her in the back of her head, and she was out like a light. I hoped she would remain unconscious until I finished handling my business. I covered her up with blankets and pushed the seats back up.

My next stop was to scoop Maya up. I called her, and right when I pulled up to the drug store she came outside. "Is everything cool?" she asked after closing the door.

"Yeah, you did real good. Now let me have that envelope."

Maya pulled the envelope out of her pocket and I ripped it open. Nico's name was written at the top with an address underneath. I knew this had to be a setup. They were expecting me to drop the money, pick up the envelope, go to the address and then be ambushed. The shit might've worked if I hadn't snatched up Vita, but now I hoped that I had turned the tables and I would ambush they're asses.

I pulled up to the address on the paper, and I couldn't help but think the area seemed so familiar. I didn't come to Chelsea often, but I knew I had been in this area recently. I looked around trying to see a landmark, but then my cell rang, bringing me out of my thoughts. I saw that it was Jamal calling. I eyed the clock and realized it was two o'clock.

"Hi, Jamal," I said with ease.

"Precious, where are you and where is Nina?"

"Nina? She hasn't gotten to the hotel yet?"

"No. I figured she was with you. She's not picking up her phone and nobody seems to know where she is."

"No, Nina isn't with me. I got caught up in some drama with Mike's little sister, and now I'm stuck in traffic, but I should be there shortly. Nina probably left her phone someplace and is stuck in traffic too. When's the last time you spoke to her?" "Last night before she left to stay at one of her girlfriends' houses. She didn't want me to see her again until she walked down the aisle."

"Jamal, I'm sure Nina will be there any minute. There's nothing that can keep her from marrying you. Just hold tight, I'll be there shortly."

"You're right, but hurry up. I want you to be here," Jamal said, sounding much calmer.

"I will."

I glanced at Maya, and she was giving me the lips poked out look. "What?" I asked her after hanging up with Jamal.

"Some drama came up with 'Mike's sister'? How you gon' blame your tardiness on me?"

"You claim you wanna be down, so let's call you taking the blame on that earning your stripes."

"Well, if you put it like that, I'm cool," Maya said, smacking her lips like she was 'bout it 'bout it.

I refocused on my surroundings. I was parked a few buildings down from the address on the paper. I was checking to see if any familiar faces went in or came out, mainly Nico's. I wasn't expecting to see him, but then again, anything was possible. I eyed the clock again and time was definitely not on my side. If Nico was in there, then I needed to handle my business and be out.

"Maya, I want you to sit tight. I have to run up in that building, and hopefully I won't be gone too long. If an emergency comes up, call my cell, if I don't pick up, here." I handed her two hundred dollars. "Take a cab over to the hotel where the wedding is. But no matter what, don't tell anybody about what went down this afternoon. If anybody asks, just say I dropped you off at the hotel and said I'd be back shortly. You understand?"

"I understand, but you are coming back, right?" She reached over and gave me a hug. My eyes locked with hers, and I saw traces of panic and genuine concern.

"Don't worry, Maya, I'll be fine. Just follow my lead." Honestly, I wasn't sure if I would be fine because I didn't know what was waiting for me. All I knew was that I wasn't going to miss the opportunity to come facetoface with Nico Carter. I wanted to bring this chapter of my life to an end. If I didn't avenge Supreme's death, I could never move on. Nico was the holdup, and he had to go. There was no other way around it.

"Give me back the hat," I told Maya. She handed over the black baseball cap and I twisted my hair up in a bun.

"Be careful!" Maya hollered before I shut the door.

I walked briskly towards the building, and to my relief a man was about to go in. Finding someone to buzz me in was one obstacle I didn't have to encounter. On my way in, I quickly searched the buzzer for the super's name and apartment number. I peeped that there was no name listed under the apartment Nico was supposedly staying at.

I knocked on the door praying that the super would answer. "Mr. Sanchez, are you there?" I heard a television and a dog barking.

A few seconds later, a petite Hispanic lady opened the door with a little terrier right by her side. She had to be the super's wife. First she just stared at me, not saying a word. "Do you speak English?" She nodded her head yes, but still didn't say a word. "I need your help." I gave the sweetest and most sincere voice I could muster.

"Help?" Mrs. Sanchez questioned in a thick Spanish accent.

I could tell she was no pushover and I would have to give a very convincing story to get what I needed from her. "Yes, last night I got in a huge argument with my boyfriend, and before he left he stole a watch my father left me before he died. I called the police, but after speaking to my ex they said there was nothing they could do because my boyfriend denied it, and it was my word against his. I know that watch is in his apartment, and I desperately need it back. That watch is all I have left from my father. Not only did my ex break my heart by cheating on me with my best friend, but now he has my dead father's watch." I let a tear roll down my cheek for a special effect, hoping that would bring a twinge of sympathy. I studied the older lady's face, and I could see I was somewhat reaching her.

"What can I do?" She put her hands up as if confused.

"Let me in his apartment so I can get my father's watch. My ex went out of town this morning, so he's not home and he'll never know. I promise I won't be in there long."

The lady's eyes got extra big and her head switched back in forth as if stunned. "Are you crazy? I can't let you in someone else's apartment. Dat's against the law."

I lowered my hands, motioning for her to calm down. She was now talking loud and I didn't need to raise any suspicion. "Listen, no one would have to know. He's not home. All you have to do is give me the key and I'll be in and out. I promise it will be worth your while."

I finally struck a cord with the lady. She lifted her eyebrow waiting to hear what I was offering. I pulled out a knot of money, full of nothing but Benjamin Franklin's.

"What apartment is he in?" she asked in a much more co operative tone.

"SevenE."

"Oh, yes, I do see a young lady visit him often. He don't leave apartment that much, only very late at night. Must be when he come see you. He twotimer. What a shame, tsk, tsk, tsk..."

"Yes, two-timer. He was living with me and seeing my best friend."

"What a shame. You deserve your father's watch back," Mrs. Sanchez continued, now with her hand out as if every word she spoke cost me money.

I started dropping one bill after another in the palm of her hand. When I hit five I stopped.

"No key, no father watch."

I gave her five more, and she rolled up the grand and tucked it in her bra. Then she pulled a bunch of keys from her bathrobe pocket. "You get caught, I say you robbed me for key, then you go to jail." She wiped her hands, "I have nothing to do with this. I don't know what you're doing, I've never seen you before," she said with her eyes closed as if I had miraculously disappeared and she hadn't handed over the apartment key.

I said nothing. I had what I needed. I was also happy, that I had my baseball cap pulled down real low over my face so if shit hit the fan she wouldn't be able to give the police an accurate description of me. She closed the door as if nothing happened.

As I walked quietly up all seven flights of stairs, my heart was beating so fast. I didn't know if it was an adrenaline rush from being so close to ending Nico's life once and for all, or anticipation of the unexpected.

When I reached his floor, I put my ear to the door to see if I could hear anything, but there was complete silence. I discreetly pulled out my gun as I slowly opened the door with the key Mrs. Sanchez gave me. With it slightly open, I used one eye to scan the open area. No one was in view, so I took my chances and went straight in with gun raised.

I could hear what sounded like the shower running. After closing the door, I glanced around looking for clues that Nico was in fact staying here. The place was decorated decently enough, with coffeecolored leather furniture, a throw rug and a few plants, nothing spectacular but respectable. I made a beeline to the bedroom and I instantly knew that this was the place Nico was laying his head every night. He still wore the same cologne and the aroma filled the room. For a moment it brought back memories of how good he used to feel inside of me.

Hearing the water stop snapped me out of my daydreaming. I hurriedly tiptoed out of the bedroom and hid inside a hallway closet. I kept the door cracked open and watched as Nico came out the bathroom. He was butt naked, and his smooth chocolate skin was glistening, highlighting every muscle on his solid frame. He let his short, curly hair grow out and he was now sporting cornrows. Part of me wanted to fuck him one more time before I had to lullaby his ass, but that was a bad idea. I stood patiently in the closet as I saw him walking back and forth from the bedroom to the bathroom, getting dressed. When he was done, he went into the living room, turned on the television and sat down.

I waited about five more minutes so he could get comfortable and then sneaked up on him. "Long time no see," I said, sneaking up on Nico with my ninemillimeter pointing directly at his head.

His dark eyes remained fixed on mine, and he didn't flinch even with death staring him in the face. "My lovely Precious, I knew we'd meet again."

"I'm sure you did, just not under these circumstances."

"What do you mean by that?"

"Save the bullshit, Nico. I know you and some bitch named LeeLee was tryna set me up. You thought I was gonna show up here so the two of you could ambush me, but I deaded all that."

"Yo, on the real, I don't know what the fuck you're talking 'bout. I had no clue you was going to show up here. You think I would be chillin' on the couch watching TV waiting for you to put a bullet in my heard? You know me better than that."

"Actually, I don't, because not in my worst nightmare did I believe you would come back and kill my husband. I can understand you seeking revenge on me and tryna end my life because I tried to end yours first by setting you up on that murder charge. I'll take that as settling the score, even though because of your actions I also lost my unborn child. That was foul. But to then come back and blaze Supreme while we're leaving the hospital. For that you gotta die."

Nico let out a deep sigh and shook his head. He put his hands over his mouth and rubbed his chin as if thinking.

I stepped back a little bit while keeping my finger firmly on the trigger. I didn't know if the nigga would try to get slick and jump at me to try and take my weapon. He was much more powerful than I was, and I had to keep the upper hand at all times.

"We've both done some fucked up shit to one another, but I swear on everything I've ever loved, which includes you, I ain't kill Supreme. And honestly, when you said you were pregnant I didn't believe you. I thought you were trying to manipulate the situation and have me pity you so I wouldn't finish you off. I'm sorry I took the life of your unborn child, but I swear that I didn't kill Supreme. That's my word."

I felt a slight pain in my heart. Nico spoke each word so clearly and defiantly. I knew this man on many levels, and it scared me because part of me believed he was telling the truth. "You a fuckin' lie. Don't try to snake your way out this shit. You the only person that had reason, and is crazy enough to come at Supreme in broad daylight. I know it was you."

"In your heart, if you really believe I was the one, then go head and pull that trigger... go head," Nico pressed on.

I stepped forward and gripped the gun tighter wanting to blast off so badly, but something held me back.

"You know I'm speaking the truth. Whoever took out Supreme had their own agenda. It was just easy for the blame to fall on me because of what went down between us."

"Well if it wasn't you, then who?" I was more confused then ever. I was dead set on believing that Nico was the culprit, but my gut knew he was telling the truth. It wasn't him.

"Honestly, I don't know, but it wasn't me, that I can promise you."

I was so caught up in digesting what Nico was saying that I never heard the front door opening. Before I knew it, I had a gun pointing at me, and now my life was flashing before my eyes.

"Bitch, put that gun down before I waste you."

I turned to see who had me jammed up, and I couldn't believe my eyes. "Yo, I know you ain't part of this bullshit!"

I said, shaking my head.

"The two of you know each other?" Nico asked with bewilderment on his face.

"Yeah, I know Precious very well. I was gonna surprise you, baby, and deliver this bitch to you, but my girl, Talesha told me you never showed for the drop and pick up. I guess she was misinformed."

"Talesha," I repeated out loud. "Oh shit, LeeLee is short for Talesha! Ain't this some bullshit! I knew you were a scandalous trick the first time I met you, but I let my guard down, and now this." I switched my attention back to Nico. "I can't believe you got this hoe on your team. And Nina, aren't you supposed to be getting married today?"

"What the fuck is going on?" Nico seethed through clenched teeth.

"Precious, put that fuckin' gun down now and kick it towards me," Nina demanded, ignoring Nico.

I did as she said, and as I patted the back of my pants ready to grab my other gun, I realized it wasn't there. I quickly remembered that I left it on the backseat of the Range after I knocked out Vita. I was fucked up in the game right now, and didn't know how I would get out this shit. I still had my knife, but I didn't believe Nina would let me get close enough to slit her throat.

"Nina, answer my fuckin' question. How do you and Precious know each other, and what's this about you getting married?"

"Oh, so you don't know about her fiancée, Jamal?" I decided to run my mouth for as long as possible to buy some time until I figured a way out of this bullshit. "Yeah, I was supposed to be a bridesmaid and everything for this trick. So when did you decide you weren't showing up for the wedding, Nina? Before or after you planned on killing me?" Nico and I both stared at Nina waiting for a response.

"If you really want to know how this shit popped off, I'll break it down for you starting from the beginning," Nina began, taking me down memory lane after picking up my gun. "I was the one Nico called when he tried and failed to put you six feet under and had to go on the run. I'm sure he never got around to telling you this, but we used to fuck around until he got caught up in yo' silly ass. So when he needed me, I was there so I could prove to him I was a better bitch than you from day one, and he made the mistake choosing you over me. The night you came over to Jamal's house for dinner, I immediately recognized your face from a picture that Nico still carries around of you. I wanted to kill your ass right there on the spot, but instead I decided that I would befriend you and finish the job that Nico couldn't."

"But Nina, I told you I had put that shit wit' Precious behind me and was moving on."

"Oh, please! And let this bitch get away with ruining your life? She's the reason that we broke up in the first place. She's why you went to jail and you're on the run. You might've decided to let her get away with it, but not me. I had it all worked out. You was supposed to bring your slickass over here and I was gonna be waiting to empty my gun on you. Of course you had to throw salt in the game and fuck up my plan, but hell, here you are now, so it all worked out."

"Nah, Nina, you ain't takin' her out. Get that shit out yo' head."

"After everything Precious has done you're still choosing her over me? You're still in love with this poisonous bitch? I'm the one that's been holding it down for you while she's running around like she's queen bee. How can you defend her? I got a good man waiting at the altar for me, because I want to be with you."

"Yo, don't put that shit on me. I didn't even know you was engaged. You the one that said you wanted to break out of New York wit' me. I told you to stay here and not put your life on hold to be on the run wit' me."

"You left Jamal standing at the altar so you could run away with Nico? And it was you I saw that night I was coming out of that restaurant with Mike. That's why this area looks so familiar. I thought my eyes were playing tricks on me because I was tipsy, but you were sneaking in going to see your other man. It was never about Jamal. Couldn't you have broken things off wit' him instead of wasting everybody's time and his money on a damn wedding that you knew would neva happen?"

"Precious, shut the fuck up. This ain't none of your business. You're the cause of all this bullshit anyway. Nico and I would be married with children right now if he had never met you."

"Hold up, Nina. Now you're jumping into some other shit. I appreciate all you've done for me, but you can't blame Precious because she had my heart and you didn't. But even if I hadn't met Precious, I still didn't want to wife you. You were always cool people, and that's why when I was jammed up I reached out to you. Sorry shorty, but my feelings never ran deeper than that."

Nina looked crushed. If I had my piece right now it would've been the perfect opportunity to take advantage of her vulnerability. But I had nothing to surprise attack her with.

"Fuck that! Precious is a dead bitch!" Nina said coldly.

Nico walked forward. "If you shoot Precious, you have to kill me first," he stated, standing in front of me as a shield.

I couldn't believe how this episode was playing out. It touched my heart how Nico was putting his life on line for me, but I didn't think he realized just how far gone Nina was. She would fuck around and kill both of us on some "fuck the world" type shit. That hero shit had no place with Nina. She had a hardon for me, and her mind was already made up that today I was going to die.

My mind was spinning, determined to find a way out of this mess when I heard the three shots ring out in the air. I closed my eyes waiting for the sheer force of the bullets to rip through my soul. I figured the first two shots would take Nico down, and the third would be for me.

After five more seconds I still didn't feel the excruciating pain of the bullet penetrating my skin, so I opened my eyes to see what the holdup was. To my dismay and relief, Nina was dead, lying in a puddle of her own blood, and Maya had pulled the trigger.

Innocence Lost

"She's dead," were the words that rang out of Nico's mouth when he couldn't find a pulse on Nina. There were no words to describe my shock at seeing Maya holding the gun that killed Nina. But I couldn't let that put me at a standstill.

"Yo, we got to get the fuck outta here. I know somebody heard those gunshots and called the police." The first thing I did was pick up the gun Nina took from me. There was no need to wipe anything down 'cause I was a pro at this by now.

I then grabbed the gun Maya was holding and realized it was the other nine I had left in the car. She stood there still staring down at a dead Nina, not believing she was now a murderer.

Nico had disappeared to the bedroom, and I assumed he was trying to gather as much of his belongings as possible. When he came out, he was holding a few suitcases.

"You couldn't have packed that fast," I said to him.

"I was already packed. I just had to get my luggage from the bedroom closet."

I quickly remembered Nina mentioning that the reason she'd left Jamal at the altar was so she could run away with Nico.

"Oh yeah, that's right. Well, come on, you can ride with us."

"I can't, Precious," Nico said solemnly.

"What do you mean, you can't?"

"There's too much heat on me right now. You need to go. I'll be in touch."

"You promise?"

"Yes, I promise."

"But where will you go? Do you need money?"

"Precious, I'll be fine. You know how I get down. You just take care of yourself and be careful. Supreme's killer is still out there."

"I'm sorry, Nico. I'm sorry for everything."

He put his finger over my lips and kissed me on my forehead before swiftly moving out of the front door. I did a quick glance around the apartment before following his lead. On my way out I made one last stop at Nina's dead body. I lifted her finger and slid off the engagement ring Jamal gave her. Now that bitch was free to burn in hell.

I clutched Maya's hand and we jetted out. Right when I was driving off, two police cars pulled up in front of the building. I was relieved we made it out of there.

My mind then drifted to Nico. He didn't deserve living a life on the run. Yeah, it was fucked up that he tried to kill me, but if you followed the code of the streets, then I really left him no choice. That was the past. I was free and he deserved to be too. Now I had another reason besides revenge to find Supreme's killer, and it was to clear Nico's name. I could always switch up my story about who shot me.

Dwelling on guns and murder, I changed gears and shifted to Maya. "Maya, thank you for saving my life."

"You're welcome," she said meekly.

I couldn't believe the young girl sitting next to me, speaking in the low voice was the same person that committed murder less than fifteen minutes ago. "Do you want to talk about what happened?" I didn't want to push her, but I thought it was important to give her the opportunity to speak on what went down, especially since she wouldn't be able to confide in anybody else.

"I didn't plan on killing, Nina but I had no choice," Maya stated matter of factly.

"How did you know I needed you?"

"I was sitting here waiting for you to come out, and about thirty minutes after you went in I peeped the chick who was supposed to be getting married today run into the same building."

"I didn't know you had seen Nina before."

"Remember, I was with you when you went to get fitted for the bridesmaid dress. She was wearing that bustedass wedding dress."

"That's right," I said, recalling their encounter.

"The first question that popped in my head when I saw her was why she wasn't at her wedding. Then I thought maybe she was coming to get you, 'cause you were one of her bridesmaids, but that shit didn't sit right wit' me. I might be young, but I'm no dummy. Mike always told me to follow my instincts and ask questions later."

"Good ol' Mike. So that's what made you come upstairs with a gun?" At that moment, I saw the reflection of myself in Maya. I was angry at myself for allowing her to get all caught up in bullshit that had nothing to do with her. But she had been a blessing in disguise, because the little badass bitch had saved my life, and for that I will be eternally grateful.

"No, although I had a funny feeling, my mind wasn't thinking you were in no danger."

"What happened that made you realize I was?"

"Besides you taking forever to come back, I also heard noises coming from the trunk of the car."

Oh shit! I forgot all about Vita's ass being stashed in the trunk, I thought to myself.

"At first I thought I was hearing things, but the noise persisted. I checked it out and was too through when I saw a girl tied and gagged stuffed in the back."

"Damn! You didn't let her out, did you?"

"Hell no! Obviously if you had her like that it was for a very good reason. I told the bitch she better shut the fuck up before I dumped her ass in the Hudson River." We both burst out laughing. "But on the real, seeing that girl made my brain start thinking all sorts of crazy shit. As I was climbing back to the front, I peeped your gun sitting on the back seat. I figured you needed your weapon, and without it you would be in trouble.

"You got that shit right."

"Mike had taught me how to handle a gun, but never did I think I would be using what I learned today. All I wanted to do was make sure you was okay and give you your gun. But when I got to the door I could hear voices, and nobody sounded happy. When I heard the guy say something about Nina would have to kill him in order to get to you, I knew it was time to step up."

"I can't believe you held it down for me like that," I said, staring at Maya for a minute while we were stopped at a red light. "Precious, I admired you before I even met you. At first it was because you had been married to this megastar rapper, and you looked so pretty in pictures I had seen you in. You seemed to be 'that bitch'. Then when I met you and started spending time with you, I checked how thorough you are. You so smart and 'bout real talk. That day you lectured me about throwing my life away chasing after hustling nigga's was such a wakeup call, and I appreciated it. There was no way I was going to let some crazy chick take my newfound mentor away from me."

"So, I'm your mentor now? I've been called many things, but never that."

"Yeah, you are. When I grow up I want to be just like you," Maya said proudly.

I reflected on all the things I ever wanted to be in life, and mentor was nowhere on the list, but the choice was no longer mine. Maya lost whatever innocence she had left when she killed Nina. Yeah, she was protecting me, but some people don't have it in them to have another human being's blood on their hands. But those that could travel to such dark places had the potential to be a coldblooded killer if left on that path. I was one of those people, and by the look in Maya's eyes, so was she. I didn't know if I should shed a tear for the hard life she would undoubtedly face, or raise my fist for her being a soldier who would never have to take anyone's orders... except for mine.

"Maya, I'm flattered that you look up to me, but to walk in my shoes is not an easy path to follow. We can't change what happened today, but it doesn't mean you have to continue to live your life that way. How I roll, I'm constantly getting down for my crown. That mentality isn't for the soft at heart. You feel me?"

"No doubt, and I don't want it no other way. I want to learn from you, Precious. Give me the bitter and the sweet so I can be that bitch that nobody can fuck over."

"Well, the first thing you have to be clear on is not to speak on anything that happened today. I mean nothing, not even to your brother. This remains between us. You don't reply to any questions unless I already green lighted the answer. There's certain shit that you take to your grave with you, and killing Nina is one of them."

"I got you. That's our secret... and Nico's of course." "Yeah, but don't worry about Nico. He wrote the street handbook, and talking about dirt you do in the streets is off limits."

"Speaking of Nico, that dude is a cutie. He seemed like he in love wit' you."

"He used to be my man before I got with Supreme."

"Oh snap, is that the nigga that shot you?"

"Yep, but that's another Bronx Tale. I'll give you the spill on that another time. First, I need to come up with my story for Jamal."

"And don't forget about homegirl in the back. What are you going to do with her?"

Once again I almost forgot about Vita's ass. There was no doubt she had to be dealt with. "You feel like taking a ride?"

"Ma, I'm down for whatever. I got you. I hope I proved that today."

"No doubt."

I headed out of the city and got on the turnpike going south. By the time we reached the Jersey shore, the sun had gone down and the sky was lit from a full moon and stars. I parked my car near the edge of the cliff overlooking the shore in a deserted area. I had Maya stay in the front seat as I grabbed the gun she used to kill Nina, and went to open the trunk. I knew she was a soldier in training, but I didn't want her to witness me ending Vita's life. It's one thing to kill somebody from behind, but it was something totally different to face death head-on and stare in the eyes of your victim before ending her life. Maya wasn't at that place yet, and part of me hoped she never would be. But if I remained her mentor, then it was only a matter of time before she was able to drop bodies like a bad habit.

When I lifted the blanket from Vita's head, she squinted her eyes trying to adjust to the light coming from the sky. She had been in the dark for most of the day, and she started feeling relief thinking she would finally be free. Then her eyes zeroed in on my gun. The tears began gushing down, and my heart did go out to her. If there was a way I could spare her life I would have, but there wasn't. She was a weak link to everything that went down today. No matter how many times she promised never to speak a word of what she knew, I couldn't take the chance of putting my life in her hands.

I grabbed one of the pillows that I kept in the trunk from behind Vita. I took off the pillowcase and put it over her face. I lifted her head and put the pillow under her, and grabbed the other one, using it as a silencer. Vita continued to jerk her body furiously, determined not to die. But after two shots to the head, all motion instantly stopped. I then asked Maya to help me as we lifted her body out of the trunk and tossed her off the cliff. The shit had to be done. There was just no way around it.

As I drove home, I made one more stop right after we got over the George Washington Bridge, and tossed the gun that was used for Nina and Vita's murders into the Hudson River. I then listened to the dozens of messages Jamal left me. I still wasn't ready to speak to him. He obviously hadn't yet heard of Nina's death, because his last message sounded more like a jilted lover than one in mourning. After a good night's sleep I planned on speaking to him in the morning, and hoped I could get him through what would no doubt be a difficult time.

Early the next morning, I was awakened by loud voices. I was fighting to stay in my deep sleep, but the noise was persistent. I had no choice but to get out of bed and see what the commotion was about. When I came out my bedroom it was clear there were male voices having a confrontation. I recognized Nathan's voice, and shortly after, realized the second was Jamal's.

"Nathan, what's going on?" I yelled from the top of the stairs.

"Move out my way. I need to speak to Precious." Within seconds, Jamal appeared as if he rushed past Nathan.

"Jamal, what's wrong?"

"Precious, I tried to tell this man you were sleep and to come back later, but he wouldn't budge. Do you want me to throw him out?" Nathan said, foaming at the mouth.

"Nathan, it's okay. You know Jamal is a good friend of mine."

"Yeah, but he need to respect people's privacy. It's seven in the morning. What type of nonsense is that?"

"Why don't you worry about your job and not the time?" Jamal countered.

"My man, This is part of my job. Precious wasn't expecting you. You should've kept it moving until a decent hour. Now you in here disrupting someone else's household."

"Enough. Nathan, thank you, but you can go. I need to speak with Jamal." Both men frowned at one another as Nathan walked away.

Jamal caught me off guard showing up so early, but I had to focus so he wouldn't get suspicious. Then I noticed him looking up towards the wraparound banister, and I turned to follow the direction of his eyes.

Maya had also been awakened by the ruckus. "Who was down here screaming?" she asked, still not fully awake.

"It was a misunderstanding. Go back to sleep."

Maya, now more alert, saw Jamal and then glanced at me. She paused for another few seconds and then went back to her room.

"Busy morning," I said casually, trying to alleviate the tension in the air.

"What happened yesterday? Why didn't you show up for the wedding or return my calls?" Jamal's voice was full of accusatory undertones. I knew I had to use my choice of words wisely.

"Jamal, I'm so sorry. I didn't even have a chance to check my messages. I got so sidetracked with Maya and her problems that I couldn't focus on anything else. But why are you here? Shouldn't you be with your new wife?"

"What problems did Maya have?"

"An abusive boyfriend. Mike is out of town so I had to take the place of a big brother." There was no question in my mind that Jamal was now drilling me, and I didn't like it one bit but I remained cool. "So, how was the wedding? I know Nina looked absolutely stunning. Her custommade Vera Wang gown was beautiful."

"Yeah, it's too bad I never got to see it on her," Jamal said as he walked up the stairs. The closer he got to me, I could see his eyes were swollen and red like he'd been crying all night.

"I don't understand. What happened?"

"Nina never made it to the wedding. In fact, Nina is dead."

"What!" I belted. I even put my hand over my mouth for extra dramatics. "What happened? Did she get in a car accident or something?"

"No, she was murdered."

"Murdered! But who'd want to kill Nina?"

Jamal's eyes stayed locked on mine, and I knew he was searching for any sign that I was lying or knew more than what I was saying, but I refused to draw back.

"But it gets better. She was involved with Nico Carter."

"Nico Carter," I repeated, sounding confused.

"Yes, your ex and the man who tried to murder you."

"I know who Nico Carter is, but I had no idea he knew Nina. How did you find that out?"

"Shortly after they discovered Nina's body, they checked her last outgoing and incoming calls, which led them to Talesha. After hearing about Nina's death, she broke down and told the cops everything, including Nina's relationship with Nico and helping orchestrate a setup involving you."

"Nina and Talesha? That same loudmouth chicken that was up in my face at the bridal boutique? I was hanging with the enemies and didn't even know it. I can't believe they were trying to set me up; but for what?"

"Supposedly she resented your past relationship with Nico and held you responsible for him being on the run."

"This all sounds crazy and farfetched." While continuing my act of being dumbfounded, I secretly wished I had tossed Talesha over the cliff along with Vita. But luckily, I did have Vita tell her I was a noshow. Still, Talesha was so distraught over Nina's death that she developed diarrhea of the mouth. To kill her now would put unwanted heat on me, so hopefully the police and Jamal would chalk up both women as being the scandalous, grimy whores they are, and in Nina's case, was.

"At first I did too. But after cops told me they found Nico's fingerprints throughout her apartment, and the lady that runs the building identified him in a photo, and combined with Talesha's story, I knew it had to be true. But once I thought about it, it all made sense. I suspected that Nina was seeing somebody, but I could never prove it. Then when you didn't come up with any dirt, I wanted to believe my suspicions were incorrect."

"So, have police located Nico, and do they think he's responsible for Nina's death?"

"No. Once again the elusive Nico has managed to disappear, but the police aren't really saying if they believe he is the shooter. One of the detectives did tell me they believe whoever killed her sneaked up from behind. This entire ordeal is extraordinary, because never did I see all these lies coming. Nina was living a whole other life that I was completely unaware of. It's funny how you think you know someone so well, but come to find out you don't know them at all. They're a complete stranger."

"I know what you mean." I wasn't quite sure if Jamal's comment was directed at his life with Nina or me, but it was time for him to go. "Jamal, I don't mean to rush you out, but I need to take care of some things. But let's definitely talk later on." I gave him a hug and started walking back up the stairs.

"Aren't you curious to know what Nina's intentions were when she tried to set you up?" Jamal blurted out, freezing my step.

"Why don't you tell me?"

"Your death."

"It seems a lot of people want me dead."

"Indeed, but you always seem to be one step ahead."

"Is there something you want to ask me, Jamal? Because if so, then just do it." It was clear from my tone that my patience with him had run out.

"Did you kill Nina?" he asked pointblank.

"As a matter of fact, I didn't. And I resent you even making the implication."

"I have the right to know what happened to my fiancée," he said, becoming defensive.

"The so-called fiancée who not only left you at the altar, but was carrying on a fullfledged relationship with a known cold blooded killer, is that the fiancée you're harassing me about? Let me give you a little bit of advice. Stop wasting your time playing Perry Mason for a woman who obviously didn't give a damn about you."

"That's cold."

"What's cold is you cross-examining me this early in the morning in my own home. I'm beginning to regret not letting Nathan show you the front door. But I'll give you a pass this one time because Nina's death has apparently left you delusional. That can be the only explanation for your blatant disrespect. Now please leave my home before I have to call security."

"Precious, wait. I'm sorry. You not showing up at the wedding and then not returning my phone calls, then the Nico factor has my mind working overtime. This whole bizarre episode has me feeling like I'm in the Twilight Zone. I'm taking my frustrations out on you, and I apologize."

"Like I said, I'm giving you a pass this one time, but I think it's best you leave. You've already said enough." I continued walking up the stairs, dismissing his presence. Jamal needed to be well aware of my anger so he would think twice before discussing his suspicions of me with anybody else. I didn't hold too many people in a high esteem, but he was one of them. I would hate to take him out this world because of his misplaced love for a ruthless bitch. I hoped for his sake that he would let sleeping dogs lie.

It's Personal

For the next few weeks, I was constantly looking over my shoulder, waiting to get that knock at the door from the police investigating Nina's murder. The knock never came, and I hoped their investigation was taking them in a direction that had nothing to do with me. Jamal had left me a couple of messages apologizing profusely for his accusations, so I figured he bought the show I put on for him. Technically, I wasn't lying. I didn't kill Nina, but it was only because I wasn't given the chance. It would've been my pleasure to lullaby her sneaky ass.

Before I could delve any deeper, the ringing of my cell phone interrupted my thoughts. "Hello."

"Precious, please come and get me!" a frantic Maya screamed.

"What's wrong, and where are you?"

"I'm in the Bronx. I got into a fight with my boyfriend, and he straight left me stranded here with no cash, no cell, nothing. I'm using some dude's phone that I don't even know."

"Relax. Give me your exact location and I'll come get you." I typed the address in my navigation system and made a detour from going to get my nails done so I could swoop up Maya. I hadn't seen her since her suspension was up and she went back to school. I figured everything was going cool, but it was the middle of the week during school hours, and instead of being in class, Miss FastAss Maya was standing on some corner in the Bronx.

I slowed down when I got on Baychester Avenue and looked for Maya. I noticed her standing on the corner by the Barnes and Noble. I beeped my horn and she came running up to the car with a smile across her face. Besides her hair being a little disheveled, I didn't see any noticeable bruises, which was a relief.

"Precious, you're the best. I was out here 'bout to freak out," she said, getting in the car.

"What the hell happened, and who is this boyfriend you got? I hope it ain't that older dude you mentioned before."

"Nah, I don't deal wit' him no more. Clip's dumbass did this shit to me."

"Clip? How old is he and how long you been dealing wit' dude? And why did he leave you stranded in the Bronx?" I had to stop myself because the questions kept rolling off my tongue.

"He just turned eighteen. We been kicking it for a couple of months now, but keeping it on the hushhush 'cause he works for my brother. That's what we got in the fight about. I want us to step out as a couple and come clean, but he's talking 'bout 'no'."

"What does he do for your brother?"

"He push weight," Maya said, as if, *Duh, you should know that!*

"Your brother still moving diesel out here? I thought he gave all that up for this music game."

"Getting that music shit to keep poppin' off cost a lot more paper than Mike anticipated, so he uses the drug game to fund the music game. Plus, you know my brother gon' be street for life."

I nodded my head, listening to Maya becoming increasingly curious about what she was spitting to me.

"But see, Clip's tryna break into the business as a rapper. My brother was supposed sign him to his label, and today he told me it's about to happen, and that's why he ain't ready to let everybody know we're together. I'm like, shit, fuck dat! What, you care more about my brother putting you on than being wit' me?"

"What changed to make Mike want to sign him to his label now?"

Maya was halfway listening to me and partly listening to the radio. When Ludacris' "Money Maker" came on, she turned up the volume and snapped her fingers. "That's my song right there. But yeah, um, what changed was Supreme getting murdered."

I hit the brakes so suddenly on my Range that if the car behind me had been just a few feet closer, it would've rammed right into me. The person in the back of me started blowing the horn, but now the light was red so everybody was on pause. I cut that radio off with quickness and turned to Maya.

"Why you turn that off? I told you that's my song," she complained.

"Maya, what did Supreme's death have to do with that nigga, Clip?"

"Well, you know Supreme had the rap shit on lock. He was King of New York. Couldn't nobody new come out and really get no shine. My brother was actually tryna' get Supreme to sign to his label."

"You must've got your information wrong."

"No I don't. I was there and I heard the conversation," Maya said, twisting her neck.

"What conversation?" Now every car behind me was blowing their horns because the light had been turned green, but I was so entranced in what Maya was saying I hadn't noticed. After going through the light, I pulled over on the side of the street. I didn't want any further interruptions.

"Over the summer I was staying wit' Mike, and he gave me some money to go shopping, 'cause like always, he had some business to handle and wanted me gone. I didn't care, but when I was about to leave I overheard him saying that Supreme would be there in a few. Girl, you know I lost it. I wasn't positive it was 'the' Supreme," Maya said, giving quotation signs with her fingers. "But the chance that it was, was worth me sticking around for."

She continued. "Mike always had his meetings in his entertainment room, so when he stepped out I hid in one of the closets and waited, determined to see my boo. Precious, I hope you don't feel I'm being disrespectful. I know he was your husband, but I'd been in love wit' him since he did that record with Beyoncé, 'Wife You'. Me and my girls just knew he was talking about us." Maya was grinning while telling me her story, and not understanding I couldn't give a flying fuck about the crush her and every other chick on these streets had on Supreme. My interest was on Mike.

"It's cool. Finish your story."

"Yeah, yeah. So finally, Supreme did show up looking fine. He had on the white Sean John sweatsuit, all iced out. The damn rock he had in his ear was blinding me from the closet."

"Enough about what he was wearing, tell me about the conversation."

"It won't nothin' too deep. Mike basically told Supreme that he knew his deal was up with whatever label he was on, and he wanted

Supreme to sign wit' him. Mike threw out all these huge dollar amounts he'd give him. See, that's how I know my brother's so paid. That's why I don't have no problem hittin' him up all the time for paper and dare him to say no, 'cause I know all about that money he was offering Supreme. You feel me?"

I just nodded my head yes so Maya could continue spilling the information.

"Uh huh, so yeah, Mike was tryna offer Supreme more money than what Bill Gates got, and when they finished talking, both of them left. And thank goodness they did, 'cause I was loving seeing my boo, Supreme, but I had to pee."

"You haven't told me what Supreme said to Mike's offer."

"Oh, Supreme told Mike helltotheno. So I knew Supreme had extralong paper too, to turn all that money down."

"When did all this go down?" I could see Maya straining her brain trying to remember.

"Come to think of it, it was a week before Supreme got killed. I remembered I was listening to Miss Jones on Hot 97, and she made the announcement, and I was like, damn! I just saw him last week! But least I was lucky enough to see Supreme in the flesh. None of my girls can say that. But real talk, I cried when I heard he was dead. Are the police any closer to finding his killer?"

"Nope." *But I am*, I thought to myself. I didn't say a word as I drove Maya back to my house. She was so busy singing and rapping to every song on the radio that she was oblivious to the dark places my mind had gone after our conversation. I was always so positive that Nico was the triggerman in Supreme's death that I never let my mind go in another direction. Had the detectives who came to see me right after Supreme's murder been right? Was he always the intended mark? Was this about music and money, not revenge? I had to find out once and for all.

When we pulled up to the crib, Maya snapped out of her musical bliss and focused her attention back on me.

"Precious, you're not going to tell my brother about what went down today, are you?"

"You mean in regards to Clip?"

"Yeah, what else would I be talking 'bout?" she asked, not having a clue how valuable the conversation that she overheard between her brother and Supreme was to me.

"Nah, I wasn't asking, I was making a statement. Don't worry, I won't mention a word to Mike about Clip. But you do need to be careful.

That nigga left you in the Bronx, wit' no money, no purse, nothing. Do you really want a cat like that as your man?"

"I forgot to mention that I did use my purse and phone to go upside his head when he told me we still couldn't tell nobody about our relationship."

"But you said y'all got into a fight."

"Yeah, we fought wit' our mouths, and then I fought him wit' my fists, purse and phone."

"So what did he do?"

"Latched onto my arms all tight, then took my phone and purse before driving off." Maya smacked her lips and folded her arms like she was the victim.

"So he didn't hit you?"

"Hell nah. Clip ain't crazy. He knows I'd tell my brother and that nigga be dead. But he needs to give me my shit back. The only reason I didn't call Mike was 'cause I didn't want him knowing I skipped school."

"I tell you what. Everything we talked about will stay between us. There's no need for Mike to know you skipped school. But chill on the Clip situation. He'll give you back your stuff."

"So you think he's right for wanting to keep our relationship a secret?"

"It's not about right and wrong, it's about getting what you want. You have to know what battles to fight and the ones not worth stressing over. If you're meant to be with Clip, then it'll happen. Relax, Ma."

"A'ight I'll follow your advice. But how we gon' explain to Mike why I'm at your crib?"

"I'll handle Mike. I'll tell him I'ma pick you up from school so we can have a girl's day. You can spend the night and I'll drop you off at school in the morning."

"That's what's up! You're the best, Precious."

"Hum huh, but you will be going to school tomorrow. Don't fuck around with your education, Maya. It's vital to have that street knowledge, but it's just as important to hit them books. I still regret not going to college, and maybe one day I will, but having your high school diploma is a must," I said, dead serious.

"Damn, I never really thought that deeply about it before, but you're right. I promise I'll get my act together and start hittin' them books."

"I'm proud of you. Now get out the car. I got moves to make. Nathan will let you in."

"But wait. I thought you said we were having a girl's day," Maya said with a frown on her face.

"That's what I'm telling your brother. I have some things that need to be handled, but when I get back we can hit the mall and go out to eat or something."

Maya's face lit back up at my offer. "Okay, I'll see you when you get back."

I waited and made sure Maya got in the house before driving off. I did have moves to make. First thing I did was place a call to Jamal. I hadn't spoken to him since he tried to go Perry Mason on my ass, but from the messages he left me it seemed he let it go, though the reception I received on the phone would be the only way I'd know for sure.

"Hello," Jamal answered.

"Hi, Jamal. It's me, Precious."

"Wow, I can't believe it's you. I'm surprised to hear your voice."

"My number didn't come up on your phone?"

"Honestly, I was in the middle of something and didn't even check it before I picked up. But I'm really happy to hear from you. After our last conversation, I didn't think I would ever speak to you again. I was completely out of line."

I was relieved to know that he had fallen for my performance, because I needed his help. "You were in shock. You'd just found out Nina was dead. I understand you were looking for someone to blame."

"You're a bigger person than me, Precious. I appreciate your forgiveness. So, how's everything with you?"

"It's coming along. But it could be better if you could do me favor."

"Whatever you need."

"Thanks, but I rather not discuss it over the phone. Can I meet you at your office later on today?"

"Sure, what time?"

"Around four."

"That works for me."

"Great. I'll see you then." After hanging up with Jamal, I placed my next phone call, which was to Mike. After the fourth ring I thought my call would go to voice mail, but then he picked up.

"What did I do to deserve a call from you?" The suaveness in his voice almost made me forget what I was scheming on. "You're so silly.

I wanted to let you know that I'ma pick Maya up from school and let her spend the night with me. I haven't seen her since she went back to school, and I thought we could have a big sister-little sister day."

"Maya would like that. She looks up to you. Personally, I think the two of you are a lot alike."

"Yeah, she's a little MiniMe. I'm definitely gonna look out for her."

"How 'bout me? It seemed at one time I was making progress and we had a shot at being together, but then you just backed away. What's up with that?"

"I was going through a lot with Supreme's death and I wasn't ready to jump into anything serious." "I feel you, but what about now?"

"That's the other reason I called. I wanted to see if we could pick up where we left off, unless you've moved on."

"No, I'm still here. I was waiting for you to get it together and realize I'm the only nigga for you."

"Then how 'bout tomorrow? We can start off by going out to dinner."

"I have a better idea. How about I cook you dinner?"

"You can cook?"

"Can I? If I wasn't in the music game, I would've opened up a chain of restaurants and been my own chef."

"Big talk. I hope you can deliver."

"Trust, you'll be impressed."

"Then it's a date. I'll see you tomorrow night around seven?"

"That works. You and Maya have fun."

"We will. Bye."

I couldn't lie to myself. I wanted to be wrong about my suspicions regarding Mike. From the first time I laid eyes on him at the club I felt some sort of attraction. It wasn't just his jawdropping looks, he had an authoritative presence. No matter how expensive the suit or charming the smile, there was no escaping that he was a straightup thug, which is the only type of man I crave.

If I was wrong about Mike, then the possibilities were endless. But, if I was right and he was responsible for ripping Supreme out my life, then he would no doubt have to pay with his life. For my sake and Maya's, I prayed that I was wrong.

I was rattled out of my thoughts by the ringing of my cell. The call was from a block number. "Hello."

"Is anyone around you?"

"Nico, is that you?'

"Judging by the fact that you shouted out my name, I take it that you're alone."

I let out a slight chuckle by the sarcasm in his voice. "Sorry 'bout that, but I was so surprised to hear your voice. But yeah, I'm alone. How are you?"

"Just keepin' low."

"Are you still in the area?"

"Yeah, I'm tryna tie up some loose ends before I head out of here. If you don't mind, I would like to see you before I leave."

"I wanna see you too. When are you leaving?"

"Tomorrow morning. You think we can meet tonight?"

"Tonight is good." I promised Maya we would hang out, but I really needed to see Nico for my own reasons. I would make it up to her.

"Cool. I'll call you around eight to let you know where to come. Make sure you're careful. I can't afford you being tracked by anybody."

"I got you. I'll be waiting for your call."

When I got off the phone with Nico, I called Maya. She was disappointed that I had to cancel, but I bribed her by saying I would take her shopping at Short Hills Mall. That ended all the huffing and puffing. I then finished running my errands so I wouldn't be late for my meeting with Jamal.

When I arrived at Jamal's office, he was finishing up a staff meeting. It was still somewhat hard to believe that the same nerdy boy with glasses that popped my cherry was now running Atomic Records, one of the biggest urban labels in the world.

"Precious, come in. It's so nice to see you." Jamal gave me hug and an innocent kiss on the cheek. When he closed his office door, he once again started with the apologies. "I'm sorry about what happened. I feel awful for accusing you of killing Nina. To even think you are capable of murder is idiotic in it's self. Please forgive me."

"Jamal, you've said sorry more than enough, and I accept your apology. So please stop. It isn't necessary. I know how hard it is to lose a loved one. Are the police any closer to finding Nina's killer?"

"Not yet," Jamal said as he sat down in his plush leather chair that had an unbelievable view of New York City as its backdrop. "Of course they're still trying to track down Nico."

"What about the girl you said they were questioning?"

"Oh yes, Talesha. She hasn't been able to assist the police any further. She never even met Nico. Some other woman that was working with them was also found dead by the Jersey Shore."

"Do the police believe the cases are related?"

"They've been digging deeply into their lives, and each of the women was shady, including Nina. Most of the scams they pulled were lowlevel but maybe they crossed the wrong person. Who knows? But it's hard to believe that I was in love and about to marry such a deceitful woman. Do you know that Nina also used to be a drug carrier? That's how she started dealing with Nico."

"What? So when did she stop?"

"Honestly, I don't know if she did stop. Although I took care of her, she always had her own money. One of the reasons I was so impressed with her was because she seemed independent. When I would ask her how she kept so much cash, she'd say it was from her modeling gigs. I was stupid to believe that, especially since I never saw her in anything but a few music videos, and we all know how much those pay. One can truly be blinded by love, that's for sure."

I was absorbing the crazy life of Nina. Her whole groupie girl persona was an act. She was a straight street bitch, and that's why she had no problem pulling her gun out on me, ready to kill. But what was the act for? To get to Jamal or me? The more I found out, the more confused I became.

"Enough, about Nina. What can I do for you? You said something about a favor on the phone."

"Yes. This is extremely important, Jamal. I need this done right away and with discretion."

"Spill."

"I need for you to draw up a contract from Atomic Records to buy the rights to Supreme's masters. I need for it to look authentic with real dollar amounts that even the most music savvy business person would believe. I need them by tomorrow morning."

Jamal swallowed hard, and I could tell by his eye movement that his mind was spinning. "What's going on, Precious?" he asked seriously. He then stood up and walked around his desk so he was now standing next to me. Maybe he thought being closer to me would allow him to get a better read as to what was going on in my head.

"Will you do it or not?"

"It's not that simple."

"Yes, it is."

"Are you saying that the contract I'll have our lawyers draft up, you'll sign?"

"I'm saying I need the contract, and what I do with it afterwards is still up in the air."

"That means no. So, who are you trying to convince that this contract is real, and why?"

"Jamal, the less you know the better."

"If you want me to help you, then I need answers; real answers."

I debated in my mind for a second whether I wanted to go there with him. I desperately needed that contract, because without it my plan would never have the same effect. "I believe I know who had something to do with Supreme's murder, and that contract will give me the ammunition I need to provoke them."

"But you made it clear that you believe Nico killed Supreme. Nico didn't have anything to do with the music business, so what is the contract for?"

"Nico didn't kill Supreme."

"How would you know that?"

"I just do. So please don't ask me anymore questions. Are you going to help me or not?" I could tell by the intense stare he was giving me that he had a strong suspicion I had seen Nico. I knew that would lead to more questions surrounding the death of Nina. Jamal wanted answers, but now wasn't the time for me to give them.

"I'll do what you ask, but one day you will sit down and answer all of my questions. You owe me that."

"Thank you. I'll pick up the contracts tomorrow. I really have to go. But thanks again." I rushed out of Jamal's office, not giving him a chance to speak another word. I had nothing more to say to him until I was able to get the closure I was seeking. I needed to be free of all the bullshit from the past and start my life on a clean slate. After tomorrow night, I hoped it would be the end of the past and a start to a new beginning.

After leaving Jamal, I picked up a few items from Saks, and then headed to the W Hotel in Times Square. I didn't want to drive all the way back to my house in Jersey or answer a bunch of questions from Maya, so checking into a hotel was the most convenient option.

I took a long hot shower, thinking about what surprises would present themselves in the near future. I wondered if tonight would be the last time I would ever see Nico again, and if tomorrow evening I'd be putting a bullet through Mike's heart. What I did know, was after closing this chapter in my life, I wanted to fall in love again, settle down and start a family; one that was free of drama and the street life. I no longer wanted the gun to be my best friend. I was a step away from completely losing my soul, and soon it would be too late to save myself.

By the time I finished pulling my hair back in a sleek ponytail, slipping on a metalliccolored jumpsuit with a wide black belt that cinched my waist, Nico had called. He gave me an address in Staten Island to meet him. I dabbed on some lip gloss, grabbed my Jimmy Choo Mahala tote bag, and headed out the hotel room. Luckily I knew my way around Staten Island, because the address Nico gave me didn't even come up in my navigation system.

The nondescript building was somewhere in the cut on a deadend corner. The only reason I was able to find it was because I used to hit up this mom and pop soul food restaurant down the hill every once in awhile.

As directed by Nico, I drove my car down the steep hill driveway and parked in the back. From the short distance I saw someone peep through the blinds, and figured it was Nico. When I got to the door it was already ajar. At first I hesitated, but when I heard Nico telling me to come in, I felt more comfortable.

"How did you find this place?" was the first question out of my mouth.

"I still know a few people who got hideout spots."

"This is definitely one of those. Ain't nobody gonna find you here. But the inside of this place is nice," I said, observing the lush carpet, stainless steel kitchen appliances and huge open space. You would never think all this was going on from looking at the outside.

"Yeah, it's pretty official for what it is. But I'm ready to break out."

"Have you decided where you're going?"

"Yep, but don't ask me where. If you ever get yourself jammed up and they question you about my whereabouts, I really want you to be able to say you don't know. It's for your own protection."

"Am I gonna ever see you again?"

"I hope. I'll keep in touch from time to time. But if and when I get word that I'm able to show my face again, then you know I'm coming home. New York is truly all I know."

"Nico, you don't have to worry about the charges sticking for shooting me. If they do come at you, I'll tell them I made a mistake and you weren't the person who tried to kill me. I'll get on the stand and testify to that if I have to."

"I don't know what to say. Since I've been on the run, all I've done was think. Think about my life, the past, and of course you. It's still hard to believe that this how everything turned out. When I first got out of jail I was so full of rage and had nothing but contempt towards you. But there is such a thin line between love and hate. And in my heart I never stopped loving you, and even now I wish we could be together and start our life all over again someplace else. But I know that's not possible. I have to clear my name, and maybe then if you still feel the same way, we can try again."

"I can't lie, my feelings for you do still run deep. Just like I hope you've forgiven me for fucking up your life, I've forgiven you for putting a bullet in my chest. I don't know if we can ever be together again, but I do believe the police will find Supreme's killer, whether the person is dead or alive. Then you'll be able to come back and fight the charges they have against you for attempted murder."

"What do you mean, find Supreme's killer either dead or alive? Do you know who took him out?"

"Just like you don't want to tell me where you're going, this is something that I need to keep to myself. But if it all works out, after you disappear, the next time you call me I'll have good news."

"I know how you are, Precious, so I'm not going to pressure you. All I will say is be careful. Whoever took out Supreme is ruthless, and they're playing for keeps. I don't want anything to happen to you," Nico said, now standing within kissing distance. He lifted my chin and softly brushed his lips against mine. He paused, waiting for my reaction.

"Don't stop," I whispered. I didn't want him to stop. I wanted to feel what it was like for him to be inside of me again. Besides Supreme, he was the only man I ever loved. Being with Nico would numb the pain I had in my heart from losing Supreme, if only for one night.

Nico lifted me up and carried me to a bedroom in the back. We both slowly undressed one another, taking in every inch of each other's bodies.

The king-sized bed was so inviting. My warm body melted into the silk sheets. Nico's kisses trickled down from my lips to my neck, and when I felt the moistness of his mouth swallow my breast, I let out a yearning moan. Then he stopped.

I opened my eyes and saw him staring at me. With his fingers, he traced the faint scar down the middle of my chest where the doctors cut me open. I turned away. I couldn't bear for him to see what he had done to me. Pushing his hands away, I pulled him closer. "Baby, put it in. I need that dick inside of me now!" I moaned.

"Wait. Nico's fingers drifted down toward my legs, where he spread them open and buried his face in my juices. He used his mouth to fuck my pussy, and it was driving me crazy. I sank my nails deep into his smooth, milk chocolate, butter soft skin. Right when I was about to explode, he entered inside of me, gratifying my every desire.

The way he rocked in my pussy with such ease made me reflect back to when our life together was so fucking lovely. We were the king and queen of the streets. I was ready to ride it out with Nico to the fullest, but shit changed. Making love with him again brought back old feelings, and while being caught up in his rapture, the sorrow encompassing my life vanished.

When we both reached the height of pleasure, we climaxed simultaneously and fell asleep in each other's arms.

Tossing and turning in my sleep, I halfway opened my eyes and saw that it was six o'clock in the morning. Although I wanted to fall back into Nico's arms, I remembered I had to take Maya to school this morning.

I quickly threw on my clothes and sat back on the bed, staring at a still sleeping Nico. He looked so peaceful laying there. I kissed him on the forehead and softly said, "I love you," hoping this wouldn't be the last time I would be with him.

Blown Away

When I arrived home, I only had enough time to take a shower. While I was getting dressed, I heard Maya knocking at my door. "Come in."

"Dang, you up all bright and early. What time did you get in last night?"

"About midnight," I answered, straight lying.

"Oh, 'cause I tried to wait up for you but fell asleep around eleven. Where did you go?"

"I stopped through Brooklyn to see some old friends. Ended up staying much longer than I thought I would. So, what's up?"

"Yeah, I didn't bring no clothes for school. So since we 'bout the same size, I wanted to borrow something cute, 'cause you be rockin' nothing but the official gear."

"Well, I have some Juicy Couture sweatsuits that you can put on."

"I like Juicy Couture. What color you got?"

"Every color. Go pick out whichever one you want. While you're getting dressed, I'll have Anna make us something to eat."

"Thanks, Precious. I love staying here with you. You're like the big sister I never had."

"You never know, maybe it can become permanent."

"You mean that?"

"No doubt. I like having you around. But get dressed. I don't want you to be late for school." The idea of having Maya live with me was one I looked forward to. It was lonely living in this bigass house all by myself.

It was obvious from little statements Maya would make sometimes the relationship with her mother was strained, and that was putting it lightly. Maya made it clear that she didn't like her mother's boyfriend, and even made reference to him crossing the line with her on more than one occasion. I wanted to mention it to Mike, but some men were extra sensitive when it comes to discussing anything negative about their mothers, so I decided to hold off.

Regardless, I could relate to Maya living in a household under miserable conditions. I had that relationship with my mother my whole life, having to deal with watching her sell her body to fund an outofcontrol drug addiction. That is the sort of agony no child should have to endure. By the time my mother did finally get her life together and we had a chance at a real relationship, she too was ripped out of my life by the greediness of the streets.

"Precious, it's after eight. We need to go," Maya said as I sat in the kitchen, zoning out.

"Damn, you scared me. My mind was someplace else. I can't believe you're rushing me to get to school."

"I'm looking all cute in my outfit, I want to floss. Plus, I slept so good last night, I feel rested."

"I bet you do, but remember, you gotta focus and hit them books."

"I know, and I will."

"Good. Let me get my keys and we're out."

When I pulled up to Maya's school she was eager to get out. "Thanks again, Precious, for the ride, the clothes, and letting me spend the night. Don't forget, you still owe me a girl's day."

"I haven't. I'll call you later on. Make sure you stay in school all day," I emphasized.

"I will. Just make sure you don't forget about me."

I stared at Maya strangely, finding it odd she would even say that. "How can I forget about you? We're like family now. No matter what goes down, we're like this," I told her, crossing my fingers to show that meant we were tight. "Now get in there and kick some ass—not literally. I mean them books." We both laughed and Maya shut the door.

Keeping to my plans for the day, I headed to midtown to pick up the contract from Jamal. To save me the headache of having to park, Jamal left a message letting me know to call up to his office, and he would have someone bring them down for me. I did just that, and within a few minutes I had the envelope in my hand. I opened it and saw that he gave me three copies. I briefly glanced through the paperwork, and without a doubt they looked legit. When I got to the last page of the contract, it had the line that required my signature to seal the deal.

Securing the contract (the most vital part needed for my plan to work), I then stopped at a spyware shop and got the final piece for my scheme. I ordered a custommade wristwatch that could do up to nine hours of voice recording. If Mike did turn out to be Supreme's murderer, after I got him to admit it on tape I would end his life. I would have the tape edited so only Mike's confession would be heard, and then send it to the detective overseeing the investigation. I don't like fucking with cops, but I had to do something to guarantee that Nico was never charged with Supreme's murder.

Needing to relax my mind and body for my encounter with Mike later on that evening, I spent the rest of day at the spa getting pampered. I had to relax and mentally prepare myself for what might go down with Mike. He was a highly intelligent and dangerous man. I had to be on top of my game not to set off any red flags.

When I got into the passenger seat of my babyblue Bentley, I was prepared and ready for war. I had my documents neatly folded in my purse. At the right moment, all I had to do was discreetly flip a switch, and my wristwatch would begin recording. And of course, I had my bitch with me. When and if it was time, she would be ready to lullaby Mike.

I slowly pulled up to his crib, keeping my nerves intact. Killing wasn't new to me, but for some reason I was a little on edge. I rang the doorbell, and within a few seconds Mike opened the door. He was looking extra fine in a pair of russetcolored pants with a cream cashmere Vneck sweater that fit perfectly on his 6'2" frame.

"You look stunning," he said, commenting on my winter white ensemble.

"Thanks, I was thinking the same thing about you." I walked inside and was impressed with the layout of Mike's home. "This is nice. I've never been to your house before."

"That's right. It's not as luxurious as the estate you live on, but it's cool for a single bachelor."

"I bet you've had plenty of women trying to turn this bachelor pad into a family home." I couldn't blame them. The décor was off the chain. The house was roughly three thousand square feet, with floors that seemed to be marble throughout. I was tempted to take off my shoes, but since Mike didn't ask I let my heels continue to click.

"I don't bring women here."

"Last time I checked I'm a woman."

"Let me rephrase that. I don't bring just any woman here, only the special ones."

"How many times have you used that line, and does it really work?" I was trying to give him a hard time, but I believed he was telling the truth. The first rule with any nigga that hustled on the streets was keep where you lay your head a secret, especially from bitches. You never knew if one would flip out on you and set you up so the next man could rob you.

"This is the first. So you tell me. Did it work?"

"I guess you'll know by the end of the night. But I do know something smells delicious. What did you cook?"

"See for yourself." He led me to the dinning room where a beautiful candlelit dinner awaited. The table was positioned in front of a huge glass window that had a view of the swimming pool. "I made a few dishes," he said. "Some taglionlini lobster, ravioli massala, osso buco, and papardelle."

"You weren't kidding when you said you can cook. I can't even pronounce some of that stuff. But the food smells off the hook, so let's eat."

For the next hour, Mike and I kicked around conversation about different topics, but nothing major.

Then he turned serious. "Having you here, sharing this dinner with you makes me realize how much I've been missing. I've spent the last few years working so hard that I had almost forgotten the importance of companionship, especially when it's with someone you're really feeling."

"I know what you mean. Since losing Supreme there has been a void in my life. But I wasn't ready to let go. Being in so much pain actually gave me a part of him to hold on to. But I know Supreme would want me to be happy and to find love again."

"Could you see yourself being in love with me?"

"Honestly, I could."

Mike stood up and walked over to a small stand and opened the drawer. He pulled out a long silver box and came back over to the table. "Open it," he said.

My eyes widened when I saw the flawless diamond necklace sparkling at me.

"Take that necklace off and let me put this on," Mike said, taking the necklace from the box.

"Wait, I have on the necklace Supreme gave me and I never take it off."

"You can take it off this one time. Please, wear it tonight and you can put the one Supreme gave you back on tomorrow."

"Okay." He unclasped Supreme's necklace and handed it to me. I held it tightly in my hand. I was in shock that Mike had given me such a pricey piece of jewelry even though we still weren't a couple.

"It looks beautiful on you."

"It's rare, but I'm at a loss for words. I can't believe you got this for me."

"You're the type of woman I could see myself being with. Giving you this necklace was a small way of showing you that."

"You're incredible. Not only am I attracted to you physically, but you have great taste in jewelry and I respect your street and business savvy."

"Thank you. I'm actually still deciding which one is more cut-throat. The street game can be brutal, but the music business is just as lethal, if not more. You're dealing with so much money, and everybody is trying to get their share of the pot."

As I listened to Mike preach about the music industry, I realized that this was the right opportunity to strike. While he continued to talk and poured himself a glass of wine, I switched on the button to start recording. "I'm glad you brought up how vicious the music business can be, because I almost forgot about some papers I wanted you to take a look at for me. I'm taking them to my lawyers in the morning, but it never hurts to have another pair of sharp eyes to read over something this important."

"Sure, baby. What do you want me to read over?"

I unzipped my purse and pulled out the envelope with the neatly folded contract. "Here. If you don't mind, take a look at this." I handed Mike the contract, and he put his glass down giving the documents his full attention. I watched as he read intently, flipping each page. His body remained calm, but I could see the vein pulsating in his neck, revealing his anxiety.

"I know you're not going to sign this," he said, tossing the contract on the table.

"Why do you say that? I think twentyfive million is more than a fair offer. There are also bonus stipulations and other perks, including royalties."

"I thought you said that you would give me an opportunity to make an offer before selling to Atomic."

"I never said that. I had no idea you were even interested, especially since Supreme wasn't one of your favorite people."

"You don't remember me telling you to come to me before you accepted Jamal's or anyone else's offer for Supreme's masters?"

"I recall you mentioning it briefly, but I chose not to take you up on that offer. But I'm letting you look at them now." I smiled, purposely antagonizing Mike and hoping to rile him up "Yeah, after the lawyers for Atomic already drew up these bullshit papers. You can't sign this!" he belted out as he picked up the contract and tore it up.

"What are you doing?"

Mike slammed his hand down on the table. "Precious, I'm only protecting you. Jamal isn't offering you enough. You shouldn't even sell Supreme's masters. You should go into business for yourself, and I can be your partner. We can put Supreme's music out on my label—make that our label."

"So you're offering me half of your company for what, the rights to Supreme's music?"

"Yes, we can do this together, not only as business partners, but as husband and wife."

Talk about desperation, the nerve of him to give me some fakeass marriage proposal so he could control Supreme's material. I knew that once I signed over the rights, I would have been signing my death certificate as well. "Huh! You can't be serious. I don't want to be in the music business, and I'm definitely not ready to jump into a marriage with someone I don't know shit about. I mean, you have serious control issues, tearing up my contract. That's insane."

"I can't let you sign those papers."

"You think ripping up the contract is going to change my mind? I do have other copies you know."

"Don't do this, Precious."

Mike grabbed my arm with a solid hold. "Let go of my arm!" But when I tried to fling his hand off me and my arm remained still, I realized just how strong his grasp was.

"Listen to me. I never told you this, but Supreme was planning on signing with my label. While you were in the hospital, he came over here and we talked. We were this close to negotiating a final deal. So see, Supreme would want me to have his music, not Atomic records."

"You're a liar. Supreme couldn't stand you. He would have never given you his music."

Mike's jaw muscles began twitching and his patience was wearing thin. "You have no idea everything I went through to make sure that music ended up in my hands. When I found out Supreme's contract was up with Pristine, I tried every tactic to get him to come to the other side."

"You mean the dark side?"

"If you want to call it that. But every side in this here music game is dark. There is nothing innocent about it. When you decide to enter this world, you're checking your soul at the door, trust me. If you don't, you'll be eaten alive. Supreme had gotten so huge he started believing that the rules no longer applied to him. I had to show him differently."

"What do you mean by that?"

"You know what I mean. Don't stand here and tell me that it never crossed your mind that I was the one who was responsible for his death."

I felt my blood pressure rising. Mike was justifying the fear that had been bubbling inside of me. "You murdered Supreme?" I asked flatly.

"I didn't do it personally, but I hired the men that did," Mike admitted with no remorse.

"Then you might as well pulled the trigger yourself. Those men were shooting to kill anyone in sight, and that included me."

"Yes, that's true. From the moment I first saw you, I always wished you could've been mine, but with life it's all about timing. You were Supreme's wife, so if he had to go, then so did you. But when you survived, I thought maybe our time had finally come and we had a chance. You had everything I needed and wanted. Physically, you are perfect; mentally, we're one in the same, and you held the key to the power I craved. I was willing to be patient so I could have you all to myself. Of course we had our stumbling blocks when you started dating Jalen. I couldn't let some knuckle head basketball player destroy all the work I had put in."

"Wait. That was you who had me tied up as your goons almost beat Jalen to death? You're beyond a monster."

"You left me no choice. I warned you to stay away from him at the club, but being the stubborn person you are, of course you ignored my advice, and so did he. When I found out you were spending the night with him in some hotel, I had to act fast. What if you started falling in love? Then there would be no room for me in your life. That was unacceptable."

"How did you know what hotel we were at?"

"Precious, why do you underestimate me? Nina was my mole. I hired her, so I was always one step behind you and five steps ahead."

"Did you have Nina set me up?"

"No, she did that dumb shit all on her own. Falling in love can cause even the strongest woman to lose any sense of rational thinking. Nina fell hard for Nico, but he was still in love with you and she hated you for that. Nina wanted to put you six feet under on several occasions, but I made clear that no one could harm you. After Supreme died, I decided you would be my wife. But Nina let her revulsion towards you dictate her actions, and it didn't work out the way she planned."

"So, was her relationship with Jamal a part of your scheme too?"

"Good ole' Jamal. He was my backup plan. See, I have inside people everywhere, and I knew that Supreme's contract had a tricky little clause. In the event of his death, all of his music would automatically belong to Atomic Records, unless he left behind a spouse or children. In that case, they would receive royalties to his music under contract, and be sole owners of all existing music that wasn't under contract with Atomic at the time."

"Initially when I planned to kill both you and Supreme, I knew that Jamal would be the man with the power. With Nina being his wife, and the way she had that corny nigga wrapped around her finger, the power would then be hers.

"Obviously plans changed, and Jamal was no longer a key factor, so Nina focused more on Nico. She felt it wasn't necessary to keep up her charade with Jamal. She never had any intentions on marrying him. But I tried to convince her to keep it going with him because I never knew when I would need Jamal for an important business deal. But Nina was dickwhipped. She was running the streets closing heroin deals for Nico and plotting your death."

"So now what?" I asked dryly. Listening to Mike break down the madness had left me drained.

"Now I have to kill you. I mean, I've revealed too many incriminating secrets. You're a liability."

"With me dead, you'll never get the masters."

"All is not lost. It also stipulated in Supreme's clause that if his spouse or children die, then the rights will then once again belong to

Atomic, unless another agreement has been signed relinquishing the rights to Atomic and going to another party or parties. Since I know you haven't struck such a deal, then once again I'll go to my fallback plan and get Jamal in my pocket."

"You think you have it all figured out."

"That's what I do. But it's really all your fault. If you had just played your position, we would be discussing wedding plans instead of how I'm going to kill you."

"Do what you have to do. Because trust, your day will come, and we all know payback is a bitch."

"So they say. But I'm dealing with right now, and before I put you out your misery I want something that you owe me."

"I don't owe you shit."

"Yes you do. I've been waiting to get a taste of that pussy, and before you die I will." Mike jumped up from the table and lunged toward me, knocking me and my chair to the floor.

"No the hell you won't!" I mustered all my strength and crawled out of his clutches. I made a quick leap towards my purse in a bid to retrieve my gun and hopefully save my life. I wasn't fast enough.

Mike reached for my neck and latched on to the diamond necklace he had just put on. He ripped the necklace off, cutting my neck.

I lost my balance and slipped on the marble floor. "Shit!" I yelled as my back hit the floor. Even with the agonizing throbbing pain, I extended my hand out trying to reach for my purse. It was no use. Mike pinned my arms down then lifted up my skirt and was clawing my body like a deranged beast.

"This pussy belong to me!" he groaned as he forced his penis inside of me and pounded on my body with each thrust. "You see what you made me do?" he continued, breathing heavily.

I was boiling over in rage. I believe rape is the worst crime you can commit against a woman. A man is using his power to strip away a woman's right to say "no". He leaves her with no control and feeling weak because she is unable to defend herself.

Now I wanted Mike dead for multiple reasons. I would've preferred him to put a bullet in my head than to stick his dick inside of me. He was about to murder me twice. I felt his body vibrating against mine as he emptied himself inside of me. During his moment of weakness, with the metal heel of my 4inch pumps, I stabbed Mike in the calf, getting my heel about 2inches deep.

"Ahhh shit! he groaned as he pulled the heel out of his leg.

Free, I slid from under him, jumped up and got my purse. By the time he looked up, he was staring down the barrel of my gun.

"Now what, motherfucker? Killing you will be my greatest pleasure yet. First, I'ma shoot off one fucking nut at a time before I blast off your dick. Then, right when you're about to bleed to death, I'll finish you off with a bullet between your eyes." I cocked my gun ready to watch Mike's blood decorate the white marble floor.

Suddenly, something came crashing through the windows and busting through the front door.

"Police! Everybody freeze! Ma'am, put your gun down!"

My first thought was whether I could squeeze one off in Mike before I put my gun down and make it seem like a mistake. That thought quickly ended when I realized that at least a dozen SWAT team cops were aiming straight at me. Still, I weighed my options. I didn't care if they killed me, just as long as I killed Mike first. This was about more than just Supreme.

"This son-of-a-bitch raped me, and I want him to die!" I played the sympathy card. Set on murkin' Mike, I at least wanted them to know why.

"Ma'am, please put down your gun. We can't do anything to help you until you put your weapon down."

I heard what the officer was saying and I knew he was right, but Mike raping me kept replaying in my head, and each time I got angrier and angrier.

Then there was chaos amongst the officers, and I heard a familiarsounding voice fighting its way into the room.

"Sir, you need to leave. You shouldn't be here," said an officer. "Precious, please put down the gun."

My whole world stopped. "It's okay. It's over now."

Mike and I were transfixed on him, both believing our eyes were playing tricks on us. But they weren't. What we were seeing was just as real as the gun in my hand.

"Baby, please put down the gun, I'm begging you," he pleaded.

A rush of blood went to my head, and my heart was beating so loudly that I felt like the whole room could hear it. "Supreme, you're dead. How can you be standing there?"

"Just put down the gun and I'll explain everything."

My mind was moving forward, but my body was standing still. I was frozen in fear, because I didn't want to let my heart believe that Supreme was alive and standing in front of me.

"Supreme, is that really you?" I stepped forward with the gun still in my hand. The cops all followed my lead and raised their gun and stuck them out further gripping tightly.

"Yes. Now, baby, please put down your gun before they hurt you." He moved closer to me, and I could see the concern in his face.

One of the cops standing between us raised his hand, letting Supreme know not to take another step.

I lowered my gun, removed my finger from the trigger and placed it on the floor. Quickly, the police filed in, checking every corner of the house.

In the midst of the chaos, Supreme ran up and lovingly wrapped his arms around me. I was still in shock and couldn't return his embrace. I could hear the police officer reading Mike his rights as he demanded to call his attorney.

Handcuffed with his hands behind his back, Mike staggered past me and Supreme, giving us the most diabolical look. "We ain't finished, trust," he said with confidence dripping from his voice, as if he didn't know he was about to be facing mad time in jail.

"Ma'am." The officer tapped me on my shoulder."

"That's Mrs. Mills," Supreme corrected him.

"Mrs. Mills, we need to take you to the hospital and have you examined."

I nodded my head, agreeing with the officer. If the police couldn't get any other charges against Mike to stick, the rape case damn sure would. I wanted to follow all the necessary procedures to guarantee that.

Reason To Believe

Supreme remained right by my side during my visit at the hospital where a rape kit was performed and I was subjected to intensive questioning by the police. They grilled me about Nico, Nina's murder and my involvement with Mike. I was careful to give them as much detailed information as possible without selfincrimination. I did find it hard to focus because I still hadn't processed that Supreme was really alive.

"Mrs. Mills, we only have one more question for you, as I'm sure you're anxious to leave the hospital and go home," the officer said, trying to sound sympathetic.

"Yes, I am. But what's the question?"

"Do you have any idea where we can find Nico Carter?"

"No, I don't." It wasn't a lie. As far as I knew, Nico was long gone and I had no idea if and when he'd be back. "I also have a question for you." The officer looked up at me from writing something down on his notepad.

"Yes."

"How did you know I was at Mike's house?"

"You can thank your friend Jamal Crawford for that. He stopped by the precinct late this afternoon with his concerns. Jamal told us about the contract he had doctored up and that you believed you knew who killed Supreme. He had a bad feeling and for good reason. Jamal had no idea who might be involved, but we assumed from the information he gave us you knew it was Mr. Owens. We had been watching Mike for some time because of our suspicions about his involvement with the attempt on your husband's life. I wish we could've arrived sooner and prevented the rape, but I'm relieved we're not investigating another homicide. I know you have a lot more questions, but I'm sure your husband can explain the rest."

Supreme was holding my hand tightly and I stared at him. Our mouths weren't saying a word but our eyes were speaking volumes. He then opened the palm of my hand, and I saw the necklace that I had been gripping so tightly. It was the necklace Supreme had gave me, what seemed like a lifetime ago, on the day I had been released from the hospital. I had let Mike take if off, but I was holding on to it for dear life, feeling that it was giving me strength. Supreme took it out of my hand and placed it back around my neck, where it belonged. After leaving the hospital we decided to stay at a hotel because if we went home Nathan and the rest of the security would have a million questions. Neither of us was ready for that.

On the drive to the hotel I just laid my head in Supreme's lap, taking in his scent, studying his hands—he was really with me in the flesh.

When we got in our hotel room, one of the first things Supreme did was turn on the water in the Jacuzzi. He bathed me from head to toe in the hot water. It was exactly what I needed to erase the foulness Mike had set on my body. After relaxing in the water for about an hour, Supreme dried me off and carried me to the bed. My exhaustion finally took over me, and I fell into a deep sleep in his arms.

When I woke up the next morning, Supreme was sitting in the chair wide awake. "How long have you been up?" I questioned.

"Since you fell asleep last night. All this time being away from you I dreamed of just watching you sleep. These last few months have been the hardest of my life."

"Tell me what happened," I said needing to know the truth." Supreme stood up from the chair and sat down at the edge of the bed. I sat up giving him my full attention. He took a deep breath and began speaking.

"After you got shot and was in the hospital, Mike came to me offering a deal to sign with his record label. Of course I turned him down. He reached out to me a few more times afterwards, and I knew he was furious but never did I believe he would resort to murder.

When I was shot leaving the hospital with you, the doctors performed emergency surgery, and I was in critical condition, but they knew I would survive. They told you and everyone else I had died, following the orders of the police and the FBI."

"But why?"

"Because the FBI had been trying to build a case against Mike on drugs, money laundering and all sorts of other crimes for a minute. They had an informant in place that had got word that Mike was responsible for the hit on me, but the FBI needed more proof. They wanted Mike to believe that I was dead to protect me until they had all the evidence needed to get an indictment and conviction."

"But...but I saw you die."

"So you thought. But after they took me in for emergency surgery, what followed was all staged. Baby, you have no idea what the government can do. After they declared me dead and took me into hiding, the Feds transferred me to one of their hospitals, where they nursed me back to health. Having you and my parents grieving over me and watching mad people mourn my death when I was very much alive, that shit was hard. Harder than being shot seven times. Precious I was watching the whole thing on TV from my bed. Even when you were crying over my casket, you looked beautiful. I wanted to reach through the television and hold you so you would know everything would be okay because I was alive. After my ordeal, I'm starting to question whether those Tupac rumors are true."

"So where were you for all these months?"

"In a safe house somewhere in Long Island. They had me stashed under lock and key. They kept me in the dark about how the investigation was going. A few police officers were with me 24/7 for protection, but they wouldn't tell me shit. Luckily, I overheard one of them talking about the cops making their move on Mike, because they believed you were in imminent danger. I told them if they didn't take me to you I would go on my own, and the only way to stop me was to kill me. They could see I was deadass serious, so they took me to you.

"I was stressing the whole time because I didn't know what the fuck was going on. All I knew was that you were with Mike. Baby, I'm so sorry I couldn't protect you from that piece of shit. I wanted to kill that nigga with my bare hands." "I still can't believe you're alive. Since you've been gone my life has been on a downward spiral. I never thought I would touch you or hold you again. Or feel you make love to me. The only reason I wanted to live was to revenge your death."

"I know how hard it's been for you, baby. But I'm here, and starting right now we're making up for our lost time."

"Can we start by you making love to me?

"Are you sure you're ready for that? After what happened with Mike, I understand if you need time and want to wait."

"I want to forget about Mike and what he did to me. Today is a new beginning, and I want to share it with you. I need to feel you inside of me, so I'll know you'll never leave me again."

"Damn, Precious, you don't have to say no more. I've been wanting to feel what's mine for too long. I missed you, baby."

I've missed you, too."

Supreme and I made love and for that moment everything in the world seemed perfect. My husband was home, and I finally had my life back.

Life After Death

The Present...

I had beaten too many odds not to be able to battle for the life of my unborn child. Yeah, I was having a difficult childbirth, but I was determined to bring a healthy seed in this world. My baby needed me, and I needed my baby even more. With all the bullshit I had been through in my young life, I could muster the strength to push my child out, and that's what I did. I took a deep breath and put my back and everything else into it, pushing out the gem I would love more than anything in this world, including myself.

"Precious, you did it," I heard both the doctor and nurse say in unison. But I didn't need them to say shit because the thunderous cries ringing in the air were the only announcement needed.

The doctor handed me my baby, and I was at a loss for words. It seemed like yesterday death was knocking at my door, when in fact it had been months since the end of my ordeal. Now here I was holding my greatest accomplishment.

"Precious, would you like for me to bring the father back in?" the nurse asked. I kept my head down and nodded "Yes," not wanting to look away from my bundle of joy.

While in labor I demanded Supreme leave the room. His presence was just making a stressful situation worse. He was acting as if he was in more pain than me, and that shit was just physically impossible. It killed me how Supreme was so hardcore when he hit that mic, but was absolutely no help playing coach in the delivery room. It was all good though— his strengths in everything else he touched made up for it.

When Supreme walked in I glanced up and he had the most serene expression. As he got closer a smile crept across his face, and pure happiness beamed from his eyes. I knew how much the birth of our child meant to him. "Baby, meet your daughter," I said as I handed her over to the proud father. "I want to name her Aaliyah after my mother, especially since she inherited her green eyes."

"Whatever you want, baby. You've given me the most precious jewel ever. The world is yours." I knew he meant that, too. We had been through hell and back to finally be a family, but it was all worth it. Our love was stronger than ever and unbreakable. Relishing in my blessings made me reminisce about the past and how the end of one life brought about the birth of a new one.

"If you don't mind, can I have a moment alone with our daughter?" I asked, looking up.

"Of course, Mrs. Mills," the doctor said as he and the nurse left the room.

"Supreme, can you leave, too?" his eyelids got heavy, and I knew he was taken aback by my request. "Baby, I'm not pushing you away, I just need some private time with Aaliyah...a little mother and daughter bonding. Please."

"I understand. I'll go call the family and let them know we welcomed a princess into the world today." He smiled. When the door shut behind him, I released the tears that I had been holding back. There was still a part of me that I couldn't share with anyone else; including Supreme, but that had now changed. I could reveal my vulnerability to my daughter.

Aaliyah's eyes locked with mine as if she knew I needed her full attention when I purged my soul. "My beautiful baby, never did I believe, I was worthy of something as precious as you. You were the one gift in life I felt was unattainable. I know that I don't deserve you, but God has granted me a second chance in life, and I'm thankful. You will never have to experience the hell that I've gone through. I will protect you from the street life that almost destroyed me and your father.

"Holding a living creature that your blood runs through is the most potent rush in the world. My mother may have not been strong enough to fight back the powerful demons that corrupted the bond between mother and child, but my life now belongs to you. This is our first chapter, and I will turn over a new leaf, but if anyone tries to destroy what we share, I will delete them from this earth—that I promise you. I will also teach you the necessary tools to survive in this world, because if you don't know evil you can never recognize good. People think your mother is a bitch, but trust you will be the baddest bitch ever." I swear, I thought my eyes were playing tricks on me, because all I saw was gums as Aaliyah gave me a smile. "That's right, my baby, with your beauty and charm they'll never see you coming until it's too late." I kissed Aaliyah on the forehead, anointing her the future Queen Bitch.

Epilogue

After the birth of our daughter, Supreme and I moved to California to get away from the drama that still surrounded us on the East Coast. We needed a change of scenery so we could concentrate on raising Aaliyah. Supreme didn't resign with Atomic Records. Instead, he put out his CD under his own label, Supreme Records. He titled what was supposed to be his last CD, "Resurrection." It went double platinum within the first week and went on to be the biggest selling record that year. After its success Supreme had more money than he could ever spend in this lifetime or the next. He retired from being a rapper and focused on making major moves behind the scenes.

Nico still hadn't resurfaced even though the police had no intentions of charging him with the attempted murder of Supreme. He still hadn't contacted me, and I figured that once he got word Supreme was alive he would think I'd go back on my word and corporate with the police for his attempted murder against me. But I had no plans on doing so. I told Supreme how Nina was this close to ending my life, but Nico stood in front of me ready to take the bullet in my place. He understood that we had now washed our hands of the past and settled the score. I had the same cell number and prayed that one day Nico would call, and I could tell him it was all good for him to go home to Brooklyn.

When Maya found out that her brother Mike was not only responsible for the attempted murder on Supreme's life but that he also raped me, she completely turned against him. The tragic situation brought us even closer. During that time, Maya and Clip also got back together and finally let the world know they were in love. They moved to California together after Clip became the first artist signed to Supreme Records. His album is schedule to drop right before Christmas.

Jamal eventually gave up on finding Nina's killer and focused all his energy on running Atomic Records. He even found love in the workplace. He is now engaged to his trustworthy personal assistant.

Mike hired the best attorney money could buy, determined to beat his case. He even tried to bargain with prosecutors by ratting me out for the murder of Antwon O'Neal. Unfortunately for Mike he did such an excellent job of disposing the body there wasn't any evidence to corroborate his story. The police felt it was a weak attempt to blow smoke, so the prosecutors pursued their case and took Mike to trial. I sat in the front row of the courtroom when Mike was convicted and sentenced. He was giving fifteen years for raping me and twentyfive years for the attempted murder of Supreme with his time running concurrent. He gave me an icecold glare and mouthed that he would be back for my life. I knew I was being met with the face of evil, but his threats didn't faze me. I was free of Mike and had my life back.

As for me, I felt stronger than ever. I had my baby and the love and support of my husband. With Supreme's encouragement I decided to enroll in college so I could obtain my degree. I always wanted to take my education to the next level but was afraid of failure. I no longer had those fears. I realized that the only person that can stop you from obtaining your dreams in life is you.

A KING PRODUCTION

The
Bitch
is BACK
Part 3

BITCH

JOY DEJA KING

DREAMS

Many say a dream is a premonition of what the future holds but as I fought the demons in my nightmare, I prayed that not to be the truth.

"Supreme, run! He's right behind you and he 'bout to bust off!" I screamed as I watched my husband beat the pavement, dodging bullet after bullet. It seemed the dark road he traveled never stopped and no matter how far his strides took him, it wasn't far enough to escape the danger behind him. I was frozen as I witnessed the final bullet penetrate in Supreme's back. He collapsed forward in slow motion. I felt life in my legs as I ran towards my husband, desperate for him to be alive, not wanting to lose him all over again. But the deliverer of his demise was now standing over him, sucking away Supreme's last breath by putting two more bullets in his head.

I immediately knelt down and held my husband for what seemed to be the last time. It was déjà vu; back to when I thought he had been murdered right before my eyes in a bloody ambush outside of the hospital. Now it was happening all over again in my dream, and there was nothing I could do. The ski masked killer just stood there still aiming the heat at Supreme, dressed in all black and silent. As the tears continued to trickle down my cheeks, I leaped at him with blood drenched hands and ripped off his mask so I could stare into the eyes of the devil. I had to know who could be so cold as to take away my life for the second time. And my heart dropped as I faced evil... Pretty Boy Mike was back.

"Huh, huh, huh!" I jumped up in bed with my heart beating fast and gasping for air. My silk tank top and boy shorts were saturated in sweat as I awoke from my dream.

"Precious, are you okay, baby? This the fourth night in a row you've been having these nightmares," Supreme said stroking my hair.

"No, I'm not okay. I'm sick of seeing that sick fuck's face."

"Baby, Mike is upstate locked up. He's not going to hurt me or you."

"But my dreams seem so real. And that look in Mike's eyes keep haunting me. I can't shake his presence."

"You can't keep doing this to yourself. You were on the phone with me when I called the Clinton Correctional Facility. It's a maximum security prison and Mike ain't going anywhere. That man is on lockdown and will be for damn near the rest of his life."

"My ears hear you but my mind keeps telling me something else. And the thought of losing you again, Supreme, is too much."

"That's why I want you to stop..."

"Aaliyah's crying. I have to go to her," I said ripping the covers from off of my thighs and stepping on the heated marble floor as I cut off Supreme mid-sentence. Supreme continued to speak but I had blocked off his words, only wanting to hold our daughter.

When I reached the hallway, Anna was walking up the stairs clutching a bottle in her hand. Although I appreciated the fact that Anna left her family in New York to continue running the household duties for me in Beverly Hills, I resented her caring for Aaliyah. She had grown so attached to our daughter, and it was only natural since she had become like a member of our family, but it still didn't sit well with me.

"Mrs. Mills, you didn't have to get up. I'll feed Aaliyah." "Thanks, but no thanks, Anna. I can feed my daughter," I said, taking the bottle of warm milk out of her hands. "I'm sure you're tired. Go back to sleep."

"I'm fine. You go get some rest. I know you've had a long day. I can take care of the baby."

"I said I would do it." Anna knew from the tone of my voice that my decision wasn't negotiable. When I walked in Aaliyah's room and picked her up, she melted in my arms. I just held her close and rubbed her back, taking in her scent. Even though she was nine months old she still smelled like a newborn. I sat down on the rocking chair, ran my fingers through her jet black curls and watched as her tiny hands latched onto the bottle as she struggled to open her eyes, fighting the sleep. I gently caressed the side of Aaliyah's face. She greeted me with her sparkling green eyes that she inherited from my deceased mother who never had the opportunity to hold her only grandchild.

"My beautiful, Aaliyah, what did I do to deserve a daughter as precious as you?" Seeing my face and hearing my voice seemed to soothe her, because as fast as she opened her eyes she closed them and fell into a deep sleep. I removed the bottle from her mouth and laid her down in the crib. I gazed lovingly at the life I'd created before turning and walking out the door. But something made me stop and glance back at my daughter one more time.

I was overcome with this need to speak out loud as if Aaliyah could hear and understand me. "It was all worth it. Mike, the murders, the rape, it was all worth it just to have you in my life. Damn, I love you," I said.

When I returned to bed, Supreme was asleep and I laid my arm around his warm body, feeling blessed that I had so much more than what I had ever envisioned could be possible in my life.

Ring... ring... ring...!

"Supreme, get the phone," I mumbled, trying to not come out of my sleep. But the ringing wouldn't stop. I patted the space beside me and didn't feel the firm muscles of my husband's body. As the phone continued to ring I finally reached over and answered. "Hello."

"Precious, wake up, I need to speak to you." "Who is this?"

"Girl, it's me, Maya. What other female would be calling you? You ain't got no friends."

"Maya, it's too early in the morning for bullshit. What is it?"

"It ain't that early."

I looked up to see the time and it was going on eleven o'clock. I couldn't believe I slept so late. Normally my day would start by eight a.m. because I would be awoken by Aaliyah's cries. I figured Supreme or Anna had fed Aaliyah and she went back to sleep since there was complete silence in the house. "Would you say what you want before I hang up the phone?"

"Damn, it's like that? Fine, let me break it down for you, since you acting salty. I believe that nigga, Clip is fucking around on me."

"Why?" I yawned trying to wake up.

"Because the mutherfucka didn't come home last night. I was blowing up his cell and he didn't pick up. When he finally brought his tired ass up in here, he gave me some lame-ass excuse about being in the studio all night."

"Maybe he's telling the truth. Did you check it out?"

"That's why I'm calling you. I want you to speak to Supreme and see if Clip was scheduled to be in the studio last night, and if so, what time did he break out."

"Maya, I ain't 'bout to get caught up in your bullshit and I damn sure ain't about to drag Supreme in it. That's his artist, they have a business relationship. Now you want me to put him in the middle of some juvenile nonsense. You gon' have to handle this shit with your man."

"I can't believe you. You supposed to be like my sister and you throwing shade in my game like this."

"Don't try to play those mind games with me, little girl. Now if you want me to do a drive by with you and we run up on that nigga catching him in the act, that's one thing. But I can't ask Supreme to be your detective and back track that man's studio time. That's some clown shit."

"Fine, I won't ask you to get Supreme involved, but I do want you to help me investigate. Ever since his single been blowing up the airwaves and now that his CD is about to drop, he's been on some ole extra fly shit. I use to let the bullshit slide, but now I feel like he being a tad over the top wit' it."

"Maybe you need to fall back. It's the summertime, school is out and you got a lot of extra time on your hands. Why don't you get a part-time job, take up a hobby or some shit? Dude probably ain't doing nothing but putting some finishing touches on his CD and you over there tripping."

"Man, please. If Supreme didn't come home last night you'd be driving up and down Sunset Boulevard with your nine in hand ready to blast off, so don't tell me to calm down."

"That's a different situation. We married with child. Speaking of Supreme, I do want to know where the hell he's at and to see Aaliyah. I'll call you back later on. But, Maya, don't go causing havoc over nothing. Trust, if Clip out in those streets doing dirt, the trash will come knocking at your front door more than happy to reveal all."

I hung up the phone with Maya and headed straight for Aaliyah's room. When I stood over her Bon Nuit Crib in Versailles pink, to my disappointment she wasn't laying there. I held up her boudoir pillow and cream cashmere blanket with crochet trim to inhale her scent. I then went downstairs and it was ridiculously quiet. "Is anybody here?" With no response, I walked through the sunken living room that opened up to the mosaic pool and hot tub. But there wasn't a face in sight. "Where the fuck is everybody at?" I hissed under my breath. I went back inside and picked up the cordless phone as I stood in front of the steel cased windows with frame jetliner views from downtown L.A. to Pacific Palisades, dialing Supreme's number.

"Precious," I heard Supreme belt out as I was about to hit the last digit.

"Where the hell were you, and where's Aaliyah?"

"Damn, let me at least close the front door, Can I get greeted with a kiss or something when I walk in the door and see my wife?" Supreme had his arms spread open as he stood in the forty feet high limestone entry.

"Of course you can get greeted with a kiss and a lot more from your wife," I teased and let my tongue tickle his earlobe. Supreme's hands traveled down my waist to my thighs, before gripping my ass.

"That's more like it. You need to let me slide in before I have to bounce."

"Where you going, and where's Aaliyah?"

"I left the new track this producer dropped off for Clip in my office. So I had to rush back here and pick up the CD before heading to the studio. Oh, and Anna took Aaliyah to the park. They left the same time that I did."

"You know I hate when Anna goes to the park with Aaliyah by herself. You should have gone with her or at least had one of your bodyguards posted up."

"You worry too much. They're fine. We're in Beverly Hills now, not crazy ass New York. Relax, just focus on me right now." I couldn't help but smile as Supreme, rubbed the tip of his nose against mine.

"You're right. I'm going to stop worrying and focus on you. I mean, you are sexy as shit. And standing here with all your muscles surrounding me is making a bitch thirsty. I know you're in a rush, but are you still trying to slide inside or what?"

"You don't even have to ask twice. Lead the way."

Supreme followed me up the sweeping double staircase and his hands remained cemented on my tiny waist. It was like after pushing out Aaliyah my body got even sicker; tits got perkier, ass got fatter and waist got tighter. And if I believed what Supreme said, my pussy even got wetter.

I guided Supreme's arms right past the two-sided stone and glass fireplace into our Phyllis Morris Cosmopolitan masterpiece. The sculpted Lucite and sparkling crystals mixed with platinum, silver and gold leaf finishes was the sort of bed that every hood queen dreamed of getting her back twisted out in, and I was no exception. Supreme had brought me to my highest level of satisfaction on this very bed on countless occasions, but something about the ambiance of this room always made it feel like the first time.

"Oh, daddy, you feel so damn good!" I purred as Supreme did tricks with his tongue in my sugar walls.

As my body got caught up in pure pleasure, my mind drifted to how luck was truly on my side. No longer was I on the grind on the brutal streets of New York. I was lying up in a palatial estate in Beverly Hills with my husband and our daughter, without a care in the world. When Jim Jones coined the term "ballin'" in his song, he had to be rapping about me.

"My pussy feels so on point," Supreme moaned as his manhood entered me. The thickness of his dick penetrating my insides snapped me out of my thoughts. As my nails sunk into the flesh of his back and my legs wrapped around his rock-hard ass I knew my life couldn't get any sweeter. "Baby, you've made all my dreams come true. You truly are my love for life," were the last words I echoed before losing my mind in his ecstasy.

RETALIATION

After Supreme laid that pipe on me right, I was feeling like a brand new woman ready to get up into some shit. But before heading out, I wanted to soak in our blue pearl hot tub. When Supreme and I placed our order at Advent Design, we straight tripped at how the company custom carved the tub from a block of specialty marble straight from Argentina. Hell, I had never even been to that part of the world, but if it looked half as good as how my deep saucer-shaped Ravenna tub felt, then I needed to book a flight.

I tilted my head back as the hot water seduced my body. The Jo Malone orange blossom scented candle intoxicated the air as I listened to Mary J. Blige. When I closed my eyes ready to fall into a daze, my cell phone started blaring. I ignored it at first, but whoever it was kept calling. Maya's name was flashing across the screen and I let out a deep sigh before finally answering. "Yes, Maya."

"Don't yes me. Why haven't you called me back?"

"Because I was getting crazy sexed by my husband and wasn't thinking 'bout yo' ass. That's why."

"Cute, but not funny. Are you still snuggled up wit' yo' man?"

"No, he had to go to the studio."

"Well then come over."

"For what, so I can hear you complain about Clip?"

"Please, Precious. This dude got me stressing."

"A'ight' let me put some clothes on and I'm on my way." I reluctantly stepped out of the tub and wrapped the cream Egyptian cotton towel around my body. When I stood in front of the floor-length vanity mirror, my heart dropped. There was Pretty Boy Mike standing behind me with a grin on his face, wearing the same outfit he wore the night he raped me: russet-colored pants with a cashmere V-neck sweater that fit perfectly on his six foot two frame.

I turned my head swiftly around the room searching for a weapon and when I swirled my head back around, Mike was gone. I turned on the faucet and splashed water on my face. I looked behind me again making sure my eyes weren't playing tricks on me. I hadn't thought about Mike in months, but lately I couldn't shake him and I couldn't understand why. I knew he was thousands of miles away, locked up on the East Coast, but for the last couple of weeks I felt as if the enemy was sleeping right next to me in my bed. I rushed to get dressed, desperate to get the hell out of the house.

I backed out the garage of our Mediterranean-style mansion and pressed my foot down hard on the pedal of the black Bentley, a gift Supreme surprised me with last Christmas. My heart was still jumping out my chest as I drove past the tall iron security gates. I did eighty the whole drive, and by the time I reached the condo complex where Maya lived, my body was begging for a drink. I rang the doorbell and quickly became impatient when Maya didn't immediately answer. I then began banging on the door.

"Is the feds running up on you or what?" Maya joked, opening the door.

I brushed past her and hurried to the stainless steel bar in the corner space of the living room. I poured myself a double shot of Hennessey and relished in the burning sensation ripping through my throat.

"Precious, what the fuck is up with you?" Maya said, puzzled by my behavior.

"It's nothing. Can't a bitch be thirsty?" I said as I poured another shot. A chick like me didn't believe in sitting on nobody's couch and purging my soul to some therapist, but I was beginning to feel like I wouldn't have a choice if I couldn't stop shaking these Mike delusions. "So, what's going on with you and Clip?" I asked, trying to get my mind off of Mike.

Maya sat down on the couch rubbing her fingers through her asymmetrical black bob. I was still getting used to the new hair cut, but the shorter look definitely gave her a more sophisticated and mature appearance. "I believe that nigga seeing some sideline ho."

"Why, has the chick called you?"

"Not yet, but I feel it coming. He be sneaking and making calls and then hang up when I walk up on his shiesty ass. And when I check his phone, the numbers always be blocked. Then I found a bank receipt and he withdrew like thirty thousand dollars."

"I doubt Clip is hitting off some chick he fucking with that kind of paper."

"Well he damn sure didn't give it to me. I ain't seen no new pricey items coming through these doors. So who could he have given it to?"

"Did you ask him?"

"Nah, 'cause I don't want him to know I'm on to his bullshit. I'm trying to catch him out there to the point he can't deny the shit."

"Then what? You find out the nigga fucking around, are you gon' bounce or are you just gon' beef?"

"Man, I find out the muthafucka fucking around on me, talk about retaliation. This shit is gon' get brutal."

I put my glass down and sat across from Maya on the chaise. She was fidgeting with the zipper on her turquoise terrycloth jogging suit with venom in her eyes, ready for war. I knew that look because I had been there before. "Maya, I know you pissed, but sometimes the best retaliation is just walking away."

"Excuse me?"

"You heard me. The beginning of all the hell in my life started from wanting to retaliate against Nico. I found out he was fucking around on me with some hot-ass ho named Porscha and I lost my damn mind. I was relentless slew of dead bodies and brought about the murder of my mother and a very close friend, Boogie. Their blood will forever be stained on my hands. And don't forget about the death of my unborn child. So many lost lives, all for the taste of revenge. It ain't worth it, trust me."

"I hear what you saying, Precious, but what am I supposed to do, just let that nigga get away with it?"

"You don't even know if he's even doing anything. And if some foul shit is jumping off, either leave his ass or decide if he's worth fighting for. But please don't go down the path I traveled, because that shit turns serious real quick."

"Hold that thought," Maya said as she went to answer the phone. "Hello...hello? Stop calling my fucking house and not saying shit! Keep it up. I'ma put a trace on this damn phone, and when I find out who the fuck you are, I'ma beat yo' muthafuckin' ass!" Maya screamed before slamming down the phone.

"What the hell?"

"Oh, I didn't tell you about these fucking crank calls I've been getting for the last couple of weeks? This is another reason I'm mad suspicious. Like three times a day somebody calls and don't say shit. The number's private so I can't get no info. The bugged out part is that there is a block on this phone against private callers, but somehow this scandalous ho keep being able to get through."

"Maybe you should call the police."

"Bitch, what is you smoking?" Maya stared me down for a minute before continuing. "I can't believe you fuck with the police, they likely to find unregistered weapons, drugs or anything in this crib. I think living in that fairyland called Beverly Hills is starting to fuck your head up. Don't let that spectacular walled and gated Mediterranean villa you lounging in make you forget where you came from."

"Ain't nobody forgot where they came from. And who yo' young ass think you talking to all greasy like that? I can still bust yo' ass and anybody else who step in my way. Just because you getting some dick on a regular and you living with a man don't make you grown." Right when I was tempted to smack the shit out of Maya so she could remember who the fuck she was dealing with, Clip came staggering through the door, looking disheveled.

"Clip, what are you doing here? I thought you said you would be in the studio all day working," Maya inquired.

"I just came to get something," Clip said in an uneasy tone. He then turned and looked at me bug-eyed and said, "Precious, what you doing here?"

"Excuse me?" I questioned, taken aback since I came to see Maya on a regular.

"I mean, I didn't see your car outside so I just wasn't expecting for you to be here."

"I had to park on the other side of the building since there weren't any empty spaces when I pulled up."

"Why you looking all suspect, like you just robbed a bank or some shit?" Maya pried.

"Stop trippin'. I just got a lot shit on my mind," Clip responded, brushing Maya off.

"Well, that's what happens when you start trying to stash some pussy on the low."

"Here we go. I ain't fucking around with nobody else. And do you really need to put all our business on front street?"

"Precious like my sister, I tell her everything. And she already knows what time it is."

"Well then, Precious, can you please tell your sister to stop harassing me over nonsense? I'm busting my ass in the studio every night so my debut CD can go multi-platinum and I can cop one of those estates my boss, Supreme got you living in."

"As long as you got me living up in those hills right along with you we won't have no problem," Maya popped with her hands crossed firmly across her chest.

"If you keep stressing me all the time with that bullshit, you gon' be living there before you know it. Except it won't be with me off my dime, but with Precious and Supreme."

"Fuck you!" Maya snapped, throwing a pillow across the room and hitting Clip in the back of the head as he walked to their bedroom.

"Yah, is some straight up clowns. But seriously, you need to think about what I said. Squash the drama before it even starts."

"I hear you, Precious, but a lot of times it's out of your control. Sometimes the drama finds you."

As what Maya said resonated in my head, my cell phone started ringing and it was Supreme. "Hi, baby, what's up?"

"Where are you?" Supreme asked with a hint of alarm in his voice.

"At Maya's. Why, what's wrong?"

"I need for you to come home, now."

"Supreme, is everything okay?"

"I'll explain when you get here, just come home." Then the phone went dead. I grabbed my purse in a panic.

"What did Supreme say?" Maya asked with a concerned look on her face.

"He told me to come home now. But it's not what he said, it's how he said it. Even though he was trying to sound like he was in control, I could hear underlying fear in his voice. He was definitely a tad shaky."

"I'm coming with you," Maya said, grabbing her keys. "Clip, I'm leaving with Precious. I'll call you later on."

Maya and I had slammed the door behind us before even waiting to hear a response from Clip. When we got in the Bentley and I put the key in the ignition, a flood of despair came over me.

THE NIGHTMARE BEGINS

When Maya and I pulled up to the gates, they were wide open. As I drove up to the entrance, we both noticed multiple police vehicles parked in front of the circular driveway. I couldn't get out the car fast enough, and sprinted to the front door. Maya was a step behind me when we entered the foyer. I zoomed in on the two middle-aged white detectives leaning against the keystone columns. I brushed past them, wanting to find Supreme so he could tell me what the hell was going on. I found him in his two-story office having an intense conversation with another detective who was writing down notes on a pad. "Supreme, what happened? Did someone break in and rob us?"

"Officer, this is my wife, Precious."

The officer reached out his hand to shake mine but my head was spinning into too many directions to care about formalities.

"Supreme, would you please tell me what the hell is going on?"

"Why don't you come sit down?"

"I don't want to sit down. I want you to tell me what the fuck is up," I said, becoming impatient.

"Mrs. Mills, it's concerning your daughter," the detective revealed calmly, unwilling to wait around for Supreme to build up the nerve to tell me.

"What about Aaliyah?"

"Your daughter's been kidnapped."

At that moment, time completely stopped. A painful chill infested every bone in my body, and my legs buckled. But before I lost my balance and fell, I grabbed onto the mahogany desk for support. Supreme put his hand on my shoulder, but I jerked it away. I ran out the room and I heard Supreme and Maya calling my name, but I ignored them. I had to find the person who could give me real answers instead of listening to someone ask me a million questions. As the stiletto heels of my Jimmy Choo shoes clicked against the marble floor and echoed through our twelve thousand square foot domain, I found who I was looking for, sitting on a chair in the kitchen, with an ice pack on the back of her head. "What happened to Aaliyah?" I demanded to know from Anna.

"Detective, this is Mrs. Mills, Aaliyah's mother."

"Hello, I'm Detective Moore. I'm sorry about your daughter. I was going over with your nanny exactly..."

But before he could continue with his bullshit apology, I was in spitting range of Anna's face. "What did you do to my baby?"

"Mrs. Mills, I didn't do anything. I turned around for less than a second, and then someone hit me on the back of the head. I blanked out for a few minutes, and when I came to, someone had grabbed Aaliyah from her stroller. I'm so sorry, Mrs. Mills."

As if on auto pilot, my hands found there way around Anna's thick neck and I couldn't let go. My grip was secure, and the fear in Anna's almond brown eyes made them bulge. "Tell me what you did to my daughter!" I kept repeating, not caring that I was committing murder right in front of a police detective. I watched as the color drained from her olive colored skin. I knew at that moment Anna wished that she'd kept her ass in Washington Heights with her family instead of following me to California, and so did I.

"Precious, let her go!" I heard Supreme bark.

The detective's hands were latched onto my arms trying to break my grip on Anna, but my anger had given me superhero strength. It took the detective, a police officer and Supreme to pry me away from Anna. When she was finally free from my clutches, she fell to the floor gasping for air, but I didn't give a fuck. Unless she could miraculously bring my daughter home to me at that very moment, she could choke on the floor and die for all I cared.

"We're going to have to place your wife under arrest," the police officer said, holding my hands behind my back.

"Please don't. My wife's in shock," Supreme pleaded.

"Officer, I don't want to press any charges against Mrs. Mills," Anna begged, coughing between words. The detective brought her some water as she sat back down on the chair finally catching her breath.

"I understand you're upset, Mrs. Mills, but this is a tragedy and it's nobody's fault except for the person who kidnapped your daughter. Resorting to violence against the nanny isn't going to make things better. If anything, it will make it worse, especially for you. Under the circumstances, I won't place you under arrest, but you have to get a hold of yourself. The only thing we all should be focusing on is bringing your daughter home safely."

I heard what the officer was saying, but it meant nothing. I felt as if the walls were closing in on me and I was suffocating. This was worse than any dream I had the past couple of weeks. This was a nightmare that I would sacrifice my own life to get out of, if doing so would guarantee that Aaliyah would be safe and live a long and prosperous life.

"What do we do next?" I finally asked, needing to believe that some sort of plan was being put in place to bring my daughter home alive.

"We have a couple of witnesses that saw a woman running, carrying a baby in her hands, and then driving off in a black four-door sedan. One of the witnesses was able to get a partial license plate number and we are doing our best to track the car down. We're also installing a device to your home phones because we believe the kidnappers will be calling demanding a ransom. Your husband is a very high-profile celebrity, and more than likely someone is looking for a quick payday. Whoever did this has probably been watching your family for some time now. From what I understand, Anna would take your daughter to this park frequently. They probably knew she would be alone and vulnerable."

"Did anybody get a good look at the woman who was running off with Aaliyah?" I asked.

"She was wearing a dark baseball cap, and either was a Hispanic or a light-skinned medium-built Black woman. It's not much, but it gives us something to go on."

"Do you believe she was acting alone or had help?" Supreme questioned, wrapping his arms around me, doing his best to make me feel safe.

"None of the witnesses mentioned seeing anybody else in the car, but normally with kidnappings, the perpetrator is not acting alone. So I wouldn't be surprised if someone else is involved."

While Supreme continued to talk with the detective, I freed myself from his clutches, making my exit. I walked outside and sat down on a chair by the pool, gazing into the tranquil clear water. The sun was setting and a glimmer of light was hitting the sculpted water fountain in front of the gazebo. Who would ever believe that in this majestic estate of glamour and opulence a dark cloud would come over and suck all the life right out?

"Precious, I promise it will be okay," I heard Maya say, intruding on my space.

"Maya, I really want to be alone."

"I know that's what your mind is telling you, but if you listen to your heart it's saying something else."

"Yeah, it is. It's saying that when I find out who had the fucking balls to snatch my daughter, I'm going to take pleasure in slowly cutting out their heart and watching them bleed to death. But until then, I want to be alone."

"I'll let you be, for now, but if you need me, call me. I'll be back tomorrow to check on you."

As Maya turned to leave, Supreme came walking up, and I put my head down not wanting to speak with him either. "Baby, it's getting late, let's go inside."

"Supreme, just like I told Maya, I want to be alone. So just go."

"Don't shut me out. I'm your husband and Aaliyah is my daughter too. I'm hurting just like you are. We have to be there for each other."

"Then why weren't you there for Aaliyah?"

"Precious, I know you're not blaming me for this. First Anna, now me."

"You knew I couldn't fucking stand for Anna and Aaliyah to be at the park alone."

"They weren't alone, it's a fucking public park. Lots of other kids and their parents were there too."

"That's not the point. Those other people don't live our lives. Would it have been so difficult for you to have one of your bodyguards be with Anna when she would go out with Aaliyah? Fuck...shit... damn!" I repeated, holding my head down and fighting back the tears that were moistening my fingertips. "If only you had listened to me, Aaliyah would be here right now. I would be holding her, feeding her, getting her ready for bed. Instead, I'm sitting here disgusted with you."

"Don't do this. Don't let that fucking sick monster, who took our baby destroy us too. We better than that, Precious."

"I don't know. If I don't get my daughter back, I don't know what's going to happen to me, or what's going to happen to us."

"We will get her back. You have to believe that. I put that on my life," Supreme said, pounding his fist into the palm of his hand.

"I have no choice but to believe you, because honestly, that's the only thing keeping me sane right now." I left Supreme sitting by the pool and went upstairs to take a shower. Being near him was too painful. I didn't want to, but part of me did blame Supreme and the other part blamed Anna. Deep down inside I knew it wasn't either one of their faults, but I had to blame somebody in order to stop myself from going crazy.

I stripped out of my clothes ready to baptize my body in the hot water when I heard my cell ringing. I realized my phone was in my purse, and when I reached in to get it a blocked number came across the screen. "Hello."

"I missed hearing your voice."

"Who is this?"

"You know who it is. Have you missed me as much as I missed you?"

I swallowed hard, feeling as if I was about to vomit up blood. I remained silent, unable to speak.

"Precious, it's extremely impolite to ignore my question. You can't be surprised to hear from me."

I still couldn't speak.

"Well, I have to be going, but before I do, someone wants to say hello." There was a pause and then the male cries of a baby-my baby. That bastard had stolen my child.

"You sonofabitch, bring my daughter home or I swear I going to cut your fucking dick off!"

"Some things never change. You still have that lethal mouth. But that's one of the many things I find so irresistible about you. But listen, I must be going. I think it's only fair I make up for the many months I lost and start spending some quality time with my daughter. She really is a beauty. I'll be in touch."

I dropped the phone, as I stood in the middle of the room butt naked with my mouth wide open, still in shock.

"Precious, who was that on the phone?" Supreme asked, standing in the doorway.

"He has her. He has Aaliyah," I revealed in a monotone voice.

"Who?" Supreme demanded, coming towards me. He grabbed my arms and asked again, trying to shake me out of my hypnotic state. "Who has our daughter? Tell me!"

"Mike."

"Who?" he asked again, not registering what I was saying. "Pretty Boy Mike is back, and he has my baby!"

DELUSIONAL

"Mike is locked up, he's in jail. Stop with this bullshit!" Supreme yelled, while grabbing my cell phone. "Fucking blocked number," he said, scanning my call history. "I'ma see if the cops can put a trace on this."

"I know Mike's voice and I know the sound of my own child. That sick fuck has Aaliyah, and I'm getting her back. I don't give a damn what you think." I picked up the jeans and shirt I just threw off and started putting them back on.

"This is bananas. I'm going to prove to you that there is no way Mike has Aaliyah."

"And how do you plan to do that?"

"I'm going to have the detective call the prison and verify that Mike is still locked up. When that's done, I want you to stop this obsession with Mike."

"So what, you think I'm crazy and I just made up the whole conversation I had with Mike?"

"I'm saying that you're under a lot of stress right now, which is understandable. It's probably leaked out that our daughter has been kidnapped and some loco is fucking with your head."

"You can't be serious with that lame-ass excuse. Talk about reaching; the only part of your explanation that's correct is some fucking loco is playing with my head, but his name is Mike."

"If the detective can get a hundred percent verification that

Mike is still locked up at the Clinton Correctional Facility will you let it go?"

I knew I wasn't crazy, but I also knew that it was humanly impossible for someone to be two different places at the same time. If it was proven that Mike was locked down, then I had to get over it and focus my energy on finding the real culprit. "Yes, if Mike is still at Clinton, then I'll let it go." With that, I followed Supreme downstairs to speak with the lead detective on the case. The crowd had dispersed and only a few officers were still lingering around.

"We haven't gotten any new leads," Detective Moore said before we even had a chance to get out one word.

"Well, I have a lead. I know exactly who took my daughter. His name is Mike Owens."

Supreme eyeballed me with a mixture of annoyance and anger in his eyes but I could care less. I knew I was right and didn't need him to co-sign.

"Who is Mike Owens, and where can we locate him?" Detective Moore asked, and grabbed a pen out of his pocket, anxious to take down the new information.

"He's at the Clinton Correctional Facility in upstate New York," Supreme was quick to make clear.

"Excuse me, I'm confused." The detective flipped his pen on his pad waiting for clarification.

"See, Mike is a madman..."

"I got this, Precious," Supreme interrupted, putting his hand up to let me know to chill. I didn't appreciate his attitude and wanted to knock him upside the head, but decided to let him give his two cents. The sooner the detective could prove that Mike had somehow been released or escaped from prison, the faster everyone would believe he was the one who had Aaliyah kidnapped. I waited impatiently as Supreme gave the detective the spill of our past dealings with Mike up until now.

"So Mrs. Mills, you claim this Mike character called you a little while ago?"

"Yes, it was from a block number, but I'm hoping you can still have the phone company put a trace on the call."

"That shouldn't be a problem. I'll just need your phone number and the carrier. What did the caller say?"

"Mike asked if I missed him, and said someone wanted to say hello. That's when I heard Aaliyah's voice."

"That could've been any baby's voice."

"Supreme, like I told you before, I know the sound of my own child's voice." It was taking all my strength not to lash out at my husband, but Supreme was wearing down my last nerve by not believing me. I could see if I was some delusional crackhead off the corner that he didn't know from Adam, but I was his fucking wife. That should've been enough proof right there.

"Mrs. Mills, did Mike say anything else?"

"Only that he had my daughter and he would be in touch." I decided there was no point in mentioning that Mike believed he was Aaliyah's father. To me, at this point it was irrelevant and wouldn't help the police track down Mike any sooner. Plus, all it would do was cause even more tension between me and Supreme and I couldn't deal with that right now.

"Okay, well I'm going to make a few phone calls and find out if this Mike Owens guy is still locked up. I'm also going to put a trace on that call you received."

"Trust me, Detective, you'll see Mike is no longer at Clinton. He has Aaliyah and you need to get your men on it immediately. He might still be in California."

"I understand your concern and frustration. We've already issued an Amber Alert. I promise if Mike Owens is our man, we will bring that bastard down. Now let me make these calls."

I turned and walked towards the living room and sat down on the couch. I was anxious for the detective and Supreme to realize I was right. Time wasn't on our side, and the sooner everyone acknowledged Mike was buried deep in this shit, they could focus their energy on him. I buried my head in my hands replaying my conversation with Mike over and over again.

From the corner of my eye I could see Supreme walking towards me. He sat down next to me and put his hand on my shoulder. "Precious, I know you believe that Mike is the one that has Aaliyah. But when the detective comes back and tells you he's still locked up, you have to promise me you'll stop. This isn't healthy for you and it's not going to help bring back our daughter."

"I have no problem making you that promise because I know I'm right. You'll see the detective is going to find out that Mike is free. And then maybe you'll apologize for not believing me."

Supreme and I sat in silence for at least an hour waiting for Detective Moore to give us an update. I was becoming so restless that I began pacing the floor. I needed a drink but decided against it, wanting my mind to stay clear and centered.

I practically jumped across the room when I noticed the detective coming in our direction. I stepped forward in front of Supreme, wanting to be vindicated. "I was right, wasn't I? Mike is out." I rolled my eyes at Supreme, pissed at his ass for not believing me.

"Actually, Mrs. Mills, Mike Owens is still locked up at the Clinton Correctional Facility and has been there since being found guilty of attempted murder against your husband and raping you."

"There has to be a mistake. Mike called me and he had my daughter."

"It just isn't possible. The warden even went so far as to have a guard go to his jail cell to guarantee he was physically there. The phone company is still tracing the number that called you, but I believe your husband is probably right and some disturbed creep thought he'd get a kick out of playing a sick joke on you. It happens. I'm sorry, but at least we can cross Mike off our list and move on to other possible suspects."

"I appreciate you getting to the bottom of this, Detective Moore." Supreme stood up shaking the detective's hand. "Please keep us informed of any new developments. I'll also have my people working on any leads."

"I will be in touch, and again, we will do everything possible to bring your daughter home."

I watched in shock and confusion as the detective and the other officers left our house. My mouth remained open, and in my head I was screaming like a mad woman but nothing was coming out. "How could I have been so wrong?" I finally said.

"Baby, it's not your fault. You're vulnerable right now and someone is playing with your emotions. Whoever it was will be shut down, but right now we have to concentrate on finding who kidnapped our daughter. And Precious," Supreme paused and lifted up my chin so our eyes locked. "We have to remain strong and remember that we love each other. Nothing can change that. In the course of our relationship, we've been through so much bullshit and made it with chins up, and we'll do the same with this shit too. But you have to trust me and listen to me. If I have to shut down every fucking state, I will bring our daughter home." Supreme wrapped his arms around me and his embrace did make me feel secure, but it didn't shake the lump in the pit of my stomach.

That night I watched as Supreme fell into a deep sleep. Unlike him, I kept tossing and turning replaying the conversation I had with the would-be Mike imposter. The thing was, in my mind it wasn't an imposter. The tone, word selection and vibe all spelled out Pretty Boy Mike to me, and nothing or no one could convince me otherwise.

I glanced at the clock and it was two o'clock in the morning. I then looked back at Supreme and realized that I could either follow my husband's lead and live with the possibility that I would never see my daughter again, or I could follow my gut and handle it my way.

FULLY LOADED

"Please buckle your seatbelts as we prepare for landing," the pilot announced as the plane began descending into the Newark, New Jersey airport. I closed my eyes, mentally checking off everything I had to do in order to get to the truth. Following my gut had the distinct possibility of taking me on a tumultuous journey. But weighing the odds, I didn't have a choice.

After the flight landed I headed straight to the Enterprise Car Rental window. While waiting in line, I turned on my cell phone and checked my messages. There were a couple of voice messages from Maya and a ton from Supreme, not including the text messages he sent. I knew he would be furious to wake up and see that I was gone, but I had no choice. While deleting the fourth repetitive message from Supreme, my phone began ringing and it was him. I debated whether to take his call, but I didn't want him stressing, wondering if I was safe or not so I answered. "Hi," I said calmly.

"Hi is all you have to say? Where are you?"

"Handling some things."

"Things like what?"

I could tell by the tone of his voice that he wanted to explode on me but was trying to keep his cool. "It's complicated. But once I got it figured out I'll let you know what's up."

"Nah, that's not going to cut it. I wake up in the morning thinking my wife is going to be lying next to me and you're gone. Our daughter has been kidnapped, we're caught in the middle of a disaster, and you wanna break the fuck out?"

"Supreme, calm down."

"Don't fucking tell me to calm down. I've been calling you since eight o'clock this morning and your phone is going straight to voice mail. It's six or seven hours later and you want to call me back talking about you out handling some things. You 'un lost your damn mind. This shit is unacceptable. I want to know where you are right now."

"Supreme, my phone is going out. I'll call you back." I pressed the end button and turned my phone off. Having a long, going nowhere conversation with Supreme was too distracting. I was on a mission and wasn't going to allow not even my husband to sidetrack me.

After signing off on the paperwork, I got in the rented SUV and headed to the storage facility I still kept in Jersey City. When Supreme and I left the East Coast to start a new life in Cali, you would've thought I'd sever all ties to my past, but I couldn't bring myself to let go. I still kept money, a couple of weapons, clothes, pictures and other important items I took from my mother's house after she was killed. The warehouse represented my connection to my past, and for some reason I knew I would be back.

Eyeing my watch once again, time wasn't on my side. When I got to the storage spot I grabbed two stacks that totaled twenty-five thousand, pulled out the nine, made sure it was fully loaded and broke out. I then hit the FDR and made a pit stop in Harlem to purchase a burner to make all my phone calls. In no time I was driving over the Brooklyn Bridge to pay an old friend a visit. When I pulled up to the corner of a quiet working class block in the Bushwick section of Brooklyn, I turned off the truck and waited patiently.

Less than thirty minutes later, still maintaining the same schedule after all this time, my old friend came walking up the street carrying one bag of groceries, and headed into a modest brick two-story home. I waited ten minutes before getting out and knocking on the front door.

"Who is it?" the pleasant voice asked through the door.

"It's me, Precious."

"Precious, Precious who?"

"Precious Cummings." I heard the top lock being opened and the chain unclamped.

"Precious, is that really you?" Ms. Duncan greeted me with bright eyes when she saw my face. "Child, I ain't seen you in forever. Come in this house and give me a hug."

Seeing Ms. Duncan and feeling her arms around me gave me a brief moment of solace. This was the woman who would care for me sometimes when my mother was out pulling tricks. She was also the woman I trusted to make sure my mother had a decent burial when I felt it wasn't safe for me to show my face in Brooklyn. She had been one of the few people in my life that I felt I could count on without stabbing me in the back. That's what brought me to her front door, because I needed her help.

"Yes, it's been a long time but here I am."

"Look at you, still pretty as ever." Ms. Duncan gently grabbed my hand and led me into her cozy living room. Her floral couches were surrounded by a wall-length bookcase full of paperbacks and hardcover books. An elongated reddish wooden desk full of family portraits, cards that she'd gathered all through the years and desktop ornaments with passages from the Bible inscribed on them sat on the other side of the room. I knew that Ms. Duncan was a God fearing woman, but like most who came from poverty and had family members who hustled, she understood the struggle of the streets, and that's why we were always able to see eye-to-eye.

"It's so good to see you. How have you been, and how in the world did you find me?" Ms. Duncan was sitting across me, and by the gleam in her eyes I knew she had a million questions for me.

"I did some asking around and was told you no longer lived in the projects I grew up in and was now living in a house over in this area."

"Yeah, my mother passed away last year and she left me this house."

"I'm so sorry to hear that."

"Don't be. We weren't close for many years. When she got remarried, her husband didn't want nothing to do with me and my brother. Then after he died, she reached out to us. My brother was still bitter and didn't want anything to do with her, but I had forgiven her and we were able to find closure before she died."

"I'm glad to hear that." I was trying to be serene with Ms. Duncan, but under my current circumstances, hearing about her dead mother wasn't on the menu.

"Oh, child, enough about me," Ms. Duncan said, swinging her arm midair. "Last I heard you were married to some famous man and that you had a baby. Is that true, because you know I don't hardly watch any television or read the newspaper? It's always so much violence going on and I try my best to tune it out."

"It's true, but I don't want to talk about them right now." If I didn't cut to the chase, I knew Ms. Duncan would be having a catch-up-on-the-past conversation with me for hours, and again that just wasn't on the menu. This visit was about me and what I wanted.

"What can I do for you?" she asked, as if reading my mind.

"Listen, I no longer have any connections in the streets. They're either dead, in jail or missing. I need to be hooked up with a person who can get me some fraudulent documents that look official, and I need them tonight. You have to know somebody still in the game that you can trust because I don't have anybody to turn to for help but you."

"Precious, are you in some type of trouble?"

"Trouble is an understatement. This is life or death." I wanted Ms. Duncan to completely comprehend that this situation was dire. Although the way I posed the question, it seemed as if I was asking for her help. In actuality, I was demanding it, but I hoped the subtle approach would be effective because I didn't want shit to get ugly. See, not only was Ms. Duncan's son a repeat felon, her younger brother was well connected in the streets. He even somehow managed to never do any serious prison bids, only doing short stints a couple of times for minor traffic violations.

"I know if you've come to me you have no other way out. So I'll do whatever you need." Ms. Duncan rested her smooth coal-colored hand on top of mine as if trying to send a blessing through me. But the only blessing I wanted was that of a connect. "I'm going to place a call to my brother, Ricky. He can get anything done. I can also trust him to be discreet," she added.

"I appreciate this. And you know I'm going to make sure you're taken care of for looking out for me."

"You've always been good to me. Just for making the funeral arrangements for your mother, you gave me all that money to show your appreciation. Because of your generosity, I was able to keep my grandkids fed and clothed while their father was locked up and their mother was somewhere doing... hell, I don't even want to think about it. So if I can repay the favor, then it soothes my heart."

I sat back and listened as Ms. Duncan picked up the phone and called her brother. I took a deep breath, trying to calm my nerves and maintain my sanity while conducting my own investigation instead of waiting on the police to break the case was the only thing that was keeping me sane. I was never one to leave my destiny in another person's hands, and I damn sure wasn't about to do it with the most precious person in my life.

"Here." Ms. Duncan handed me a piece of paper with an address written down. "Ricky, said for you to meet him there in an hour."

"Thank you."

"Of course, you've always been special to me, Precious. Ricky is going to take real good care of you. If you need anything else, you know where to find me. I'll always be here for you—I mean that."

I nodded my head, not wanting to say too much. I could feel tears struggling to swell up in my eyes, but I refused to give in. I swallowed hard, fighting them back.

"If you want to tell me what's going on in your life that's causing you so much pain, I'll be more than happy to listen."

"Maybe another time. I really need to go." Before opening the front door this overwhelming need came over me and I turned back to face Ms. Duncan. "Would you please pray for me and my family?" I was never one to get down on my knees and beg God for anything. I got by in life with the belief that you don't wait for things to happen; you make them happen. It seemed to pretty much work for me, but at that moment something inside of my soul was moved to ask that of Ms. Duncan, because the battle I was about to fight needed more than just me. It required the blessings of a higher power.

"That's all I've been doing since you sat down on that couch." Ms. Duncan gave me a sincere smile and I walked out of her house.

When I arrived at a warehouse on a desolate stretch of Fountain Avenue, I hesitated to pull into the unpaved parking area. I took out my nine millimeter from the glove compartment, feeling uneasy. Ms. Duncan wrote down her brother's cell number on the paper so I dialed it to double check that I was at the correct location. Right then, I noticed a silver Lincoln driving up beside me flashing its high beams. I lifted up my gun ready to blast through the car's passenger window until the driver side door opened and a man who looked to be in his early forties stepped out. He had the same smooth coal complexion and big bright eyes as Ms. Duncan.

"I'm Ricky. You must be Precious."

I lowered my gun and relaxed. "That's right."

"Park your car and follow me inside."

What looked to be an abandoned warehouse on the outside was a meticulously clean, fully carpeted mini pad on the inside. There was a full stocked bar with bar stools greeting you when you first entered. On my right side there was a round table and chairs, with playing cards and stacked chips, which were obviously used for gambling. To the far left there was a complete black leather living room set with a sixty inch plasma television mounted on the wall.

"Would you like a drink?" Ricky asked as he deactivated one alarm and activated another.

"No, I'm good."

"Then let's do this."

I followed Ricky to a bedroom in the back that had a door leading to another room that looked to be an office. He then hit a button on his key chain that activated the six-drawer chest against the wall, which shifted to the side to reveal a staircase leading to the basement. The set of steps led to a criminal's paradise. Without question, he had his operation on a tight leash, which explained why he never got caught and had to do some serious time. Unless you made it down the stairs, you would think that at the most he was running an after-hour spot, nothing of this magnitude. On one table there was an array of guns, anything from AK-47s to Mac-10s. On another table was a pharmaceutical heaven, from prescription drugs, ecstasy, cocaine, heroin, and drug paraphernalia. Then there were high tech computers, tons of machinery that I assumed were used to make counterfeit money, and whatever else he needed.

"Your sister was right when she said you can get anything done. You have some serious shit popping off down here."

"Yeah, and honestly I would've preferred not to bring you down here since only a handful of people have seen all this. But my sister said you were like family to her and you needed some documentation today. With short notice like that I didn't have a choice but to bring you right here where the magic happens and get it done."

"So that's what some of these machines are for?" I asked, looking at them carefully.

"You damn right. I have the exact same equipment the big dogs use to manufacture whatever documentation is required to get clearance anywhere. My packaging is so clean that it would probably pass intense scrutiny from the Central Intelligence Agency."

"Now we talking, because I need the proper credentials to get inside a maximum security prison."

"Which one?"

"Clinton Correctional Facility."

"Over there in Dannemora?"

I nodded my head yes.

"They call that New York's Siberia due to the cold and isolation. You know everybody from Tupac Shakur, Ol' Dirty Bastard to Joel Rifkin, who is still locked up, has done time there. Their security is top of the line. I hope you're not trying to break anybody out, although for the right price it can be done." Ricky gave me a charming smile, letting me know not to underestimate his skills.

I couldn't help but laugh to myself imagining the games he probably ran around women his age and much younger. Even in his forties he was maintaining his playboy form. With a well-built six-one frame, neatly trimmed edges highlighting his waves, handsome face that still wasn't showing any signs of stressful living, and grown man clothes that consisted of tailored slacks, tucked in shirt with a belt accentuating a preserved waist and manicured hands, his appearance was as tightly put together as his illegal operations. "No I'm not trying to break anybody out. In fact, I'm going to confirm that somebody is still in and that he won't be getting out."

"I take it he isn't a friend of yours. What's his name?"

"Michael Owens. Why?"

Ricky went over to one of his computers and began typing in some information.

"What are you doing?"

He put up his finger motioning for me to wait. "The stats on here indicate that he's still locked up and has many more years to go before he'll have a chance to see the light of day."

I stood next to Ricky to see the screen he was getting his information from. "Are you accessing the prison system?"

"This is much more detailed. I've accessed the personal files of Clinton's prisoners. You see right there," he pointed to Mike's name. "I click on his name and all his information comes up. There is no reason for you to make that trip, this man is locked up."

"Everybody keeps telling me that, but I need to see it for myself. And please don't ask me to explain to you what's going on. I'll pay you whatever you want. Just give me the proper credentials I'll need to get in that prison."

Ricky didn't push any further. He started doing whatever it is he does and I went to sit down. While I waited, I checked my voicemail to see if Supreme left me a message with any updates about Aaliyah. When I came to the final message I wanted to throw my cell against the wall, because throughout all Supreme's rants, none of them gave me hope that the police were any closer to bringing my daughter home.

I put my head down, wondering if I was losing my mind. What if everyone was right and Mike was sitting pretty in his jail cell with no access to me or my daughter? Maybe I so desperately wanted to believe it was Mike so I could put a face and name to the monster who stole my child, because not knowing anything at all seemed like a worse realization to bear.

"This is crazy. I need to get my ass back on a plane and go home to my husband," I mumbled out loud. Just when I was about to tell Ricky to forget it and that I was stopping this wild goose chase before going any further, he announced he was done.

"You're finished already?" I looked down at my watch and I'd been waiting for over an hour, although it didn't feel like that long.

"Young lady, I'm a pro at this. All I need you to do is go stand over there so I can take your picture." As he snapped my picture, Ricky explained how it would work. "I've programmed all your information into the correctional facility database, so if they type your name and ID number in, your photo and job title will come up."

"US District Attorney's office? That's who you have me working for?"

"As I explained, they run a tight ship. That prison is especially prone to violence. A few guards have been killed in the last couple of years by the prisoners. The inmates are restless and ruthless. Being cautious is imperative, so it makes our options limited. His attorney of record is a man. You're not on his visitation list, and honestly, being from the District Attorney's office is about the only way you're going to get anywhere near a prisoner without raising suspicion. But to be extra careful, take this."

"What is it?"

"It's the certified letter that the prisons rarely require when you need to speak with an inmate without prior notice, depending on how anal the person working that shift wants to be. They may be in a good mood and verifying your ID information is sufficient, or they could be pissed at the fucking world and want to stick it to you. You never know, that's why it's better to be prepared. Here is your New York driver's license in case they want two forms of ID."

"This shit is no joke. You got this whole covert operation on lock. I thought only the feds were able to get all into a person's private business."

"This country doesn't have any privacy. They're always preaching about protecting yourself from identity fraud, but it's just another way for the corporate snakes to make money off of apprehension. With the right resources you can own another person's life and they'd be clueless until the walls come tumbling down. But the less you know, the better. All you need to do is prepare for your prison visit tomorrow."

"If I'm wrong and Mike is still locked up, I hope when we come face-to-face he doesn't blow my cover."

"More than likely he'll try, but remember, you have clearance, your driver's license and ID will check out as being legitimate, and he's the one locked up. They're used to prisoners showing out, so keep your cool and your only objective should be to get the hell out of there. Within thirty-six hours this identity will be completely wiped out of the system, so as long as you get out they won't be able to trace it back to you."

"So I'm straight?"

"I guarantee with what I've given you, you won't have any problem getting in. Just remember, no matter what happens, remain cool under pressure."

Remaining cool under pressure was my specialty, but I had to admit that stepping into uncharted territory had me shook. "I appreciate the advice."

"I didn't tell you anything that you don't already know. I've been in this game long enough to spot a soldier. You may be young, but your eyes carry years of wisdom. If I had to put my money on it, I would say you're a warrior."

Ricky was on point with his assessment. I was a warrior. I just carried all my battle scars on the inside. Unfortunately, the stakes were so high that I couldn't afford to be anything less than stellar with my performance tomorrow.

"How much do I owe you?"

"Five g's.

I pulled the money out of my purse and handed it to Ricky. "You going to count it?"

"Nope, I'm good at weighing money by how it feels in the palm of my hand."

"Whatever works for you." I placed the envelope with my ID, driver's license and certified letter inside of my purse. "One more thing. Can you print out a copy of all the documentation the correctional facility has on file for Mike?"

"Not a problem." After Ricky handed me the papers, I followed him back to the front and he deactivated the alarm to let me out. "It was a pleasure doing business with you."

"I feel the same, especially if it works and all goes smoothly."

"It will. You're fully loaded with all the ammunition you need. You have my number; don't falter about using it if you need me." Ricky gave me one of his charming smiles as he watched me get in my car. I gave him a slight wave as I drove off.

Something about him reminded me of Boogie. Before Boogie was murdered right in front of my eyes by his own nephew, he was the only person I looked up to as a mentor. He knew the ins and outs of the game and schooled me on it, especially when it came to gaming men. But like so many fallen soldiers, the game eventually beat him. I hoped that wouldn't happen to Ricky, because he was full of knowledge that would be priceless in the right person's hands.

That evening after checking into my hotel room, I took a long hot shower, mentally preparing myself for all of the "what ifs" that could await me during my prison visit. When I got in bed I was tempted to call Supreme, but I knew that small percentage of reluctance I had about going through with my plan could easily grow much bigger after speaking with him. With a few carefully selected words he might convince me to come home and abandon my mission. So instead, I pulled out the confidential information from Mike's personal file and read it thoroughly before falling asleep.

WELCOME TO
THE JUNGLE

The non-stop blaring sound coming from the alarm woke me up at three o'clock in the morning. I had a five-hour ride ahead of me and I wanted to be one of the first visitors there.

After washing my face and brushing my teeth, I slipped on the Dolce & Gabbana amaretto and white tweed suit I brought with me to wear for this monumental occasion. I discarded my standard designer ghetto fabulous attire and opted for a classic 3-button jacket paired with a below-the-knee flip flared hemmed skirt, and brown suede Fendi peep-toe pumps. It had the perfect combination of elite sophistication and New York City career woman flare. I brushed my below-the-shoulder wavy hair up into a tight bun. I applied one thin coat of foundation powder, black massacre and clear lip gloss to give a polished appearance. To add one last professional touch, I put on some non- prescription reading glasses, grabbed my briefcase and bounced.

I put the pedal to the metal, pushing it on the highway. My fucking nerves had me so antsy that I felt that I had been driving on Northway 1-87 for days instead of hours. My breaking point subsided when I noticed the exit I needed to take, 38N. Not long after, I was in Dannemora's main business district where the walls of the prison go right up to the streets. I inhaled deeply, counted to three, and then eased up to the first entrance to the prison.

"I need to see your driver's license." The six-three guard was enclosed in a protected armored box that had bars over the square window, and two additional armed guards were posted on either side. The whole setup was intimidating, especially for someone who was trying to bootleg their way in. The guard slid out a metal tray for me to place my license in. My heart was thumping and I tapped my nails on the steering wheel, praying my shit would clear. "I'm not going to be able to let you through. I'll need for you to turn your car around and leave the premises," he said with no further explanation.

"I'm scheduled to meet with a prisoner this morning, so what is the problem?" I kept my tone respectful but with a touch of authority as if I was confident in what I was saying and he was the one making a mistake.

"Your name is not on any list that I have, and I spoke with the guard inside the prison and you're not on their list either. So I need for you to leave now, or you'll be arrested."

I had reached that crossroad where I could put a halt to my undertaking, or push the envelope and go full steam ahead, risking having my cover blown wide open.

Knowing I wouldn't be able to have a decent night's sleep ever again until I stared at Mike's face behind bars, I chose the latter. "I'm from the US Attorney's office and I've been given clearance to see one of your prisoners this morning. So I won't be going anywhere. Do I need to have the head of my department to place a phone call to your boss?" I asked, flipping open my phone as if I was about to dial the number.

"You should've said that instead of handing me your driver's license."

"If I'm not mistaken, sir, that's what you requested from me," I answered, putting on my most proficient white girl voice.

"I need to see your ID."

I placed it in that same metal tray.

"And your paperwork," he added.

I seized the certified letter from the envelope since that was the only paperwork Ricky gave me. I watched as the hard-nosed brotha scrutinized my shit as if he wasn't another low-on-the-totem-pole worker but instead owned the prison, and would lose millions of dollars he invested if I was able to make it through those gates.

After another few minutes of waiting in silence, I was ready to snatch him out of his box and run him over several times with my rental truck. Noticing the metal tray slide back out with my ID and document, I snapped out of my illusions of torturing the watchdog. He remained on mute and I didn't know I had been cleared until the gate lifted, allowing me to drive through. I quickly snatched up my shit and put my foot on the gas before he wanted to get extra and grill me further.

I parked the SUV and sat for a second with the key in the ignition. "This is it," I said, gazing at myself in the mirror. As I adjusted my reading glasses, I noticed the mammoth wedding ring on my finger and took it off. The last thing I need is additional attention put on myself and sporting a rock of this size will for sure bring it.

It was now or never, so I grabbed my belongings, and when my Fendi pumps hit the concrete I became Angela Connor from the US District Attorney's office. I had to go through two more security checks before finally making it through the cold dreadful hall of the prison. Finally thinking I was home free, I had to deal with one last gatekeeper.

"Hello, I'm Angela Connor here to see prisoner 18699-052." It bugged me out that out on the streets hustlers had a million and one different aliases but in jail that shit didn't mean anything, because in these walls they were nothing but a fucking number.

"I need to see your identification," the hefty, light-skinned woman said tight-lipped. "I also need to check you for contraband."

"I've already been checked twice." "Now you can make that three times."

"I'm from the US Attorney's office. Do you really think I'm going to smuggle illegal goods in here for a prisoner?" I was getting so caught up in my charade that I was starting to believe I really was that bitch with the official job title.

"Miss, you have no idea how many seemingly intelligent women walk into this prison with all intent to uphold the law but fall for the bullshit one of these inmates run on them, and end up leaving as a criminal themselves."

"Point made."

After checking for contraband, she then patted me down, although I had already gone through a metal detector before getting this far. "You can go straight ahead."

I followed the direction she pointed in. Then I heard a buzzing sound and the heavy steel door opened. I jumped when it clanged shut behind me.

As I trailed behind two guards, I tried to get my thoughts in order.

We entered a closed off space and the chilly white walls reminded me of the interrogation room the cops drilled me in after Jalen Montgomery, the basketball player I briefly dated, had been beaten so badly that he ended up in intensive care. They were convinced I had something to do with it, but Mike later informed me he was responsible for the pointless bloodshed—another crime Mike was never held accountable for. That beat-down caused Jalen to miss the entire remaining season, and to this day sports critics say his once-coveted jump shot has never been the same since the incident.

I sat in the chair facing the door waiting for the guards to bring Mike down. Anger began brewing inside of me as I reminisced over all the havoc he had caused. I pulled out a folder filled with meaningless papers and a notepad so it would appear as if I was handling my business. I flipped my pen on the hard-topped table, no longer filled with the fear of being exposed. All that remained floating inside of me was hate for Mike.

I could hear movement coming from the hallway, and from the positioning of my chair I could see two guards on both sides of a man who looked exactly like Mike. *He is locked up! He couldn't have kidnapped Aaliyah. Then who did? Why didn't I listen to Supreme?* I thought. As the questions were darting around in my head, the men were getting closer. I put my head down and began writing any fucking thing on my notepad so Mike wouldn't instantly recognize me.

"The prisoner is here," the guard announced.

I kept my head down, ogling the shackles around his legs, and I slowly worked my way up his gray two-piece apparel to his shackled wrists.

"Is this really necessary?" he said, lifting up his shackled wrists. "I'm cooperating; I ain't give ya no problems on the way here."

The guards eyed me as to see if I had an objection, and my silence let them know that I didn't. Knowing they were eyeing him like a hawk with fully loaded clips, I felt safe.

When the prisoner sat down in the chair across from me, I had to admit the resemblance was uncanny, but my gut instinct was right. The man sitting in front of me wasn't Pretty Boy Mike, but a damn good imposter. He even bore a replica tattoo on the inside of his left wrist of a dagger with a teardrop on each side.

"How are you this morning?" My voice was subdued because I was digging around in my brain on what to do next. My dumb ass hadn't even prepared for this possibility, and I had to find a way to expose the truth without blowing my cover.

"Better than I been in a long time... now that you're here. Damn, you sexy as hell, even with that uptight do you got going on. You the type of woman the big boys got handling jailhouse business now? You can come visit me anytime." He licked his lips at me as if I was about to drop my panties for him. It was crystal clear why the last watchdog felt the need to school me, but I couldn't believe women would be falling for this lame game he was kicking. They had to be straight knuckleheads. I opened my folder pretending to be reading over documents.

"Your name is Michael Owens, correct?"

"That's right." He leaned back in the chair, oozing with haughtiness, and I couldn't blame him. On paper he was a dead ringer for Mike. They shared the same height, build, complexion and hair texture. With there being almost three thousand inmates, no one would think otherwise. I was dying to know how in the hell Mike orchestrated this bullshit and who helped him. "So what can I help you with..." The imposter leaned over and grabbed my lapel to read my tag, "Ms. Angela Connors?"

"Sit back. There is no touching," the guard reminded the arrogant sonofabitch.

"What's so funny?" he asked as I let out a slight chuckle.

Unbeknownst to him, the bright idea I needed in order to change the tides had disclosed itself. "Guard, I believe we have a problem," I said in my most concerned voice.

"Man, we ain't got no problem. If the flirting is making you uncomfortable I'll stop," the imposter said as if doing me a favor.

I locked eyes with the Mike wannabe and paused before speaking. "You wish that was the only problem you had."

He sat up straight in the chair as if something clicked in his head telling him he was fucked.

"What is the problem?" the guard asked, glancing over at the prisoner with a look that said he was yearning to have an excuse to bust his ass.

There has obviously been some sort of security breach, because this man is not Mike Owens."

"Bitch, shut the fuck up! You don't know what the hell you talking about," he barked, standing up from his chair. All that sugary, fake-ass charm he was delivering was gone. "I'm ready to go back to my cell. This broad crazy."

"Have a seat," the guard ordered.

He sat back down with reluctance and folded his hands on top of the table. He struggled to regain his composure, but he was breathing so hard his muscles were flexing through his jailhouse attire. The dagger from his wrist was now coming through his eyes as he fixated on my face, attempting to freeze my words out of fear. Of course, the pathetic thing had no idea he wasn't dealing with a welterweight. "This some bullshit," he mumbled, only further annoying the guard.

"This is Michael Owens. Do you have any proof to suggest otherwise?" The guard lifted his eyebrow, waiting to hear my answer.

"Nah, this troublemaker ain't got no proof. Shit, look at my wrist. That's a Mike Owens' tattoo. Don't nobody have this but me," he argued, extending out his arm for everyone to see.

"You're absolutely right, that is a Mike Owens' tattoo that you had duplicated. But just now, you had to check my badge. The real Mike Owens would have recognized me from past meetings. I'm also willing to bet that no matter how much you were compensated for this sham, you weren't willing to get the five-inch scar that decorates the upper right side of the real Mr. Owens' back," I taunted as he felt the painful squeeze I had on his balls.

I turned my attention back to the guards. "I'm sure if you check Mr. Owens' records you will see that was one of the distinguishable marks listed in his report." I cracked a smile as I witnessed the color drain from the imposter's face. There was no way for them to prove that Mike hadn't met with a US Attorney named Angela Connors, and luckily, Ricky had given me a copy of Mike's profile. If I hadn't read through the information last night, I would've never known how to back up my story.

"I'm going to need you to turn around and lift up your shirt," the guard stated.

But instead of complying, the fraudulent Michael Owens jumped over the table and clutched his hands around my throat. "You trifling cunt!" he roared, spitting the words in my face.

I gasped for air as he chocked the life out of me. I could see the guards using all their strength to wrestle the maniac off of me, but his grip was cemented around my neck. My vision began to blur as my lungs fought for air. To make matters worse, the fool started banging my head against the cement floor. *Why the fuck did I let them take those shackles of his wrists?* was all I could think. I heard a few more guards run in, and it took all of their manpower to get him off of me.

"I shoulda ripped off your head! That's what snitching- ass bitches deserve!" he continued as the guards dragged him out.

"We need to get you to the infirmary." One of the other guards lifted me up and sat me down on the chair. "No, I'm fine, just hand me that water." *That mother- fucker is as crazy as Mike,* I thought, feeling a migraine about to sneak up on me.

"Miss, you need to be checked out."

"Listen, I'm fine. When I leave here, I'll have my own doctor check me out. Your only priority right now should be alerting the police that one of your inmates has escaped."

"We're already moving on it. If you hadn't brought this to our attention, there is no telling how long they could've gotten away with it. We appreciate the tip."

"I was only doing my job, which I better get back to."

"We need for you to wait. We have to fill out a report, and the watch commander might want to speak with you."

"Of course I want to help in any way that I can, but I'm already running late and I have to be going. I will call you when I get back to my office and you can fax me over whatever paperwork I need to fill out. The commander can also call my office if they have any further questions," I said, babbling off at the mouth and gathering my belongings at the same time. Knowing every second I was in the prison I risked being discovered as an imposter made me want to hop, skip and jump out this motherfucker, but I kept telling myself to remain cool.

When I finally did exit from the confinement of gray concrete walls, I couldn't put my key in the ignition fast enough to make a getaway.

When I made it back to the hotel, before heading up to my room I had stopped at the store in the lobby and purchased some Excedrin Migraine medicine. My headache was kicking my ass the entire five-hour drive, but paranoia wouldn't allow me to stop until I reached my destination. Between my concern of someone at the prison tracking me down, and now knowing for a fact that Mike was loose on the streets, I was triple checking over my shoulder.

I checked my phone messages and Supreme was steady cursing me out on each of his messages, but the police had no leads on Aaliyah. That wasn't surprising since they had never put Mike in the mix. I prayed that soon all the news outlets would announce that he'd escaped from prison so the LAPD would get on their job.

I wanted to call Supreme and the detective to share what I learned, but then how I got the information would cause me serious repercussions. What I did was illegal, and although I had no qualms about breaking the law, getting caught was never an option. With Aaliyah being in the hands of a sociopath like Mike, I couldn't afford to be locked up not even for a day. I had to keep the faith and believe that soon the Clinton Correctional Facility would get their story straight about how they allowed that shit to go down at their prison and make the fucking information public. But all they were probably stressing was damage control, and that wasn't doing me or Aaliyah any good.

Then it came to me. Sometimes you have to force a motherfucker to crawl out from under the rock they're hiding under.

When I got in my hotel room, I opened up the phone book and found the numbers I was searching for. I picked up my burner and began making calls.

"Hi, I work at the Clinton Correctional Facility in Dannemora, New York," I paused so the person who answered could take the location in. "It's a maximum security prison," I added to someone who sounded like an older white lady on the other end of the phone. I wanted her to start imagining big black treacherous killers running free, possibly in her neighborhood, after I dropped dime on her.

"Hmm, hmm," was all I got as I assumed the perplexed woman wondered where this one-sided conversation was going.

I continued, "Well, one of our most dangerous inmates escaped a few days ago and is thought to be in the New York City area."

"What!" she gasped.

Now that I had her full attention, I continued to wheel her in. "Yes, the prison hasn't made an announcement because they're trying to spin the story, you know, for damage control."

"How dare they!"

"I know, I'm with you. I was concerned about innocent citizens, like you, being in danger, so I felt it was my duty to alert the media since the prison hasn't. But of course I have to remain anonymous because I can't lose my job—I have five kids to support with no husband."

"I totally understand. That prison should be ashamed. What is the name of the escapee?"

"Michael Owens." I could hear her writing the name down on a piece of paper. "He is a thirty-three year old Black male, about six-two and two hundred-twenty pounds."

"You've done the right thing—thank you."

"When are you going to release the information?"

"Immediately. I'll call over to the prison and give them the opportunity to comment on the story, but then I'll be sending it out to all of our affiliates."

When I hung up, I set the lines on fire, calling several other news stations and newspapers. Once I felt I had the news trickling, I rushed packing all my shit, intent on making the seven o'clock flight out of Newark.

I zipped up my last bag and was about to walk out the door when I heard my cell ringing. "It's probably Supreme," I moaned, rummaging though my purse. "Hello?"

"It must feel good to be back home. I've tried to picture it, but I can't see you being happy in Cali. You're a New York girl at heart, always have been and always will be."

A chill went through my spine that Mike knew I was in New York. I wondered if he had already got word about what went down at the prison earlier and he was trying to piece shit together by baiting me, or was it something as simple as his peeps hearing I had been in Brooklyn and they alerted him. I decided to try my own bait trick.

"How does it feel to be out of prison, Mike?"

"I wouldn't know. I'm still here counting down the days when I'll be able to finish what I started with you."

"I'm sure it'll be sooner than you think. But wait, if you're still locked up, why did you tell me you have Aaliyah? In your last phone call you did say you were spending time with my daughter... correct?"

"I lied. I don't have our daughter—yet. You know how much I enjoy playing games with you."

"Excuses, excuses. How convenient. I'll tell you what. Since my mood is in an upswing, I'm willing to give you two choices. But this offer is only good this one time."

"I'm a fair man, enlighten me."

"Your first choice is you can return my daughter unharmed on your way back to prison, or you can return my daughter unharmed and die. It's up to you. You have ten seconds to make up your mind." I began my count from ten. When I reached one, I hung up the phone. I had to muster up all my strength not to plead for Aaliyah's return, but if I was going to win this war with Mike and get my daughter back, conventional tactics wouldn't work. I couldn't let him smell not even an ounce of my horror, or he would use it to make me so crazy I would have no alternative but to check into a mental institution. Mike also believed Aaliyah could be his daughter, and that belief was her saving grace. As psycho as he was, he would never harm a child that had his blood running through her.

I closed my eyes and visualized her safe return. In the same image, Mike was dressed in an all black suit and was being lowered six feet under. We were at his funeral, and every eye was dry, including his own mother's. All the visitors who came to pay their respect showed absolutely no emotion. But once his coffin was placed securely underground, the thousands of people who showed up came alive as they threw dirt over his coffin, determined to bury him into oblivion. What a beautiful image that was, and one I vowed to make come true.

WARNING

When my flight landed at LAX, the moment I got off the plane I was swarmed by the news media. "Mrs. Mills, how are you dealing with the kidnapping of your daughter?"

"Has a ransom been demanded?" Another reporter asked, shoving her mic in my face. I kept walking as the reporters kept tossing one question after another in my face.

"Do you think your daughter is still alive?"

After one bold reporter hit me with that I stopped dead in my tracks, looked straight in the camera he had on me and said, "She better be!" They all seemed confused by my response, but I wasn't. I was sending a warning directly to Mike and whomever he had assisting him.

My comment seemed to make the reporters thirstier. They followed me to my car and trailed me as I drove home. The only thing that kept them from walking with me to my front door and having a seat in my living room was the iron gate at the end of the driveway.

By the time I got home it was after midnight, and I hoped Supreme was sleep because I wasn't in the mood for a confrontation. I opened the door quietly, ready to punch in the code so the security alarm wouldn't go off, but the entire house was lit up as if it were the middle of the afternoon. I dropped my bags and walked towards the living room. I heard intense voices that came to a halt when my presence was felt after I entered the room. Supreme, Clip and Maya all stared at me as if seeing a ghost.

"You finally decided to bring your ass home. Do you know how fuckin' worried I was? How the fuck you not gonna answer yo' fuckin' phone and not return my calls? I been stressing over my daughter and then you got me stressing over you too. You on some bullshit, Precious!" Supreme roared, throwing his glass of Hennessey across the room. When the glass shattered against the wall, all I could think about was the awful stain it would leave.

"Precious, where have you been? Supreme is amp, but we all been worried. You should've called," Maya said, trying to be the voice of reason.

"You think I'm not worried? I'm tryna bring my daughter home, so excuse me if I didn't have time to call and pacify you and my husband."

"I guess you didn't hear," Supreme said in that calm voice he used when he wanted to break your neck but was using restraint.

"Hear what? That everybody now knows that our daughter has been kidnapped?" I shot back. "I thought the detective said he would hold off on letting the media know that we're the parents so it wouldn't turn into a major freaking circus. So much for that!" I said sarcastically. "When I got off the plane damn near every media outlet was waiting for me, and they followed me home. I wish they'd put all that energy into tracking down Aaliyah."

"Off the plane..." Supreme paused as if in disbelief, then continued, "Our daughter is missing and you're taking fuckin' trips?" Supreme's solid frame stood frozen with fists clenched like he was Rubin "Hurricane" Carter ready to get his box on. "But fuck that! We have bigger problems than your disappearing act and the media. Detective Moore called earlier today to inform us that Mike had escaped. He didn't have the details, but a guard at Clinton was alerted of the prison break and now there's a manhunt for him. And, Precious, I don't want to hear it," Supreme said, raising his hand.

"Hear what? That I fuckin' told you so? See, if you'd listened to me maybe the cops could've stopped Mike before he had a chance to break out with Aaliyah. Because they wasted time, who knows where the fuck Mike is?"

"Look, the cops are now on it, but we don't know for a fact that he kidnapped Aaliyah."

"Oh, so now you want to still act like that call I received wasn't from him either? I guess the other one I got today was from a bootleg Mike too."

"Mike called you?" Supreme obviously hadn't told Maya based on the surprise in her voice.

"So wait, you spoke to Mike today but you couldn't talk to me after I left you a fuckin' trillion messages?"

"Supreme, he has our daughter. Are you seriously trying to have one up on whose phone call I accepted?"

"What did he say?" Maya wanted to know.

"In the first phone call he admitted to having Aaliyah, and I heard her crying in the background. When he called earlier he was talking bullshit, acting like he was still locked up. I knew he was lying."

"That nigga is so fucked up in the head. What type of sick fuck would steal a little baby? I can't believe we share the same blood. I'm so sorry, Precious. I hope his foul-ass actions don't come between our relationship."

"As long as you understand that your brother is a dead man, we good. What I want to know is who the fuck is helping him on the outside, because he didn't pull off this shit solo."

I zoomed in on Clip, who hadn't put his two cents in the conversation. "You been dead silent. You don't have any words of encouragement for me, Clip?"

"Umm, I mean, that's fucked up what happened and I pray Aaliyah comes home soon. I hate seeing my boss messed up like this," he said, looking over at Supreme. "I knew Mike was capable of some fucked up shit, but never did I think he'd take shit this far," he added.

"I can't believe this man is destroying my family again," Supreme said as if in his own world and talking to himself. "First, he tried to take my life, then my wife, and now my daughter. This bullshit got to stop."

I needed some alone time with husband, so Maya and Clip had to go. "You two can go home. I need to speak to Supreme."

For a second they didn't move, and then Clip went over to Supreme and patted him on the shoulder, not knowing what to say to console him.

"Precious, be strong. I know you'll get Aaliyah back."

"Thanks, Maya. I'll talk to you tomorrow." When I knew Maya and Clip were gone, I went and sat down next to Supreme. "Mike is not going to destroy our family, because we will get our daughter back. It don't matter how many casualties are left behind in the process."

I didn't realize how heavy a toll my trip to New York had on my body until I woke up and it was the afternoon. Supreme was sitting in the chair watching CNN, and when I heard a reporter mention a prison break I immediately sat up in bed to see if she was talking about Mike:

"...The details from Clinton Correctional Facility are still sketchy. Yesterday, the prison's spokesperson did confirm that one of their inmates, Michael Owens, had escaped. From what we're hearing, they are looking to question a key witness who sources say alerted prison guards of the escape, but haven't been able to do so. The only information being released on this witness is that she is a female. Unconfirmed sources are saying she was Mr. Owens' attorney, and others are saying she worked for the US District Attorneys office, but we can't substantiate what is fact at this time. We will continue to cover this story and keep you updated on any breaking news..."

They continued to show a picture of Mike for a few seconds until cutting to a commercial.

Supreme shut off the television and slammed the remote down. "Where the fuck can this nigga be?" He stood up, and all he had on was his briefs. His anger had every muscle from his neck to his chest and calves bulging as he paced the room. The imprint of his dick was protruding, and he looked sexy as fuck, but this anger I had towards him made my husband seem like the plague to me.

I took in a deep breath and wondered what I could do next, because staying in the captivity of this house with Supreme would be unbearable. "Was the detective able to trace that call from Mike?" I asked, wanting to redirect my anger.

"Nope, he used one of those anonymous prepaid joints."

"That figures. Do they have any new leads they're following?"

"No, they don't," Supreme cracked with an attitude.

"Why are you acting hostile towards me? Maybe if you spit that same fire to the white man, he would stop bullshitting and find our daughter."

"Because I'm not married to the white man. You lying up in this bed questioning me like you haven't been gone for two days, so yeah, I'm more than hostile."

"You really want to know where the fuck I was? I was out finding answers. If it wasn't for me, this investigation would be going nowhere. At least the cops know Mike has escaped and he can now be considered a prime suspect. So instead of riffing, you need to be thanking me."

"Thanking you for what? You didn't have nothing to do with that guard at the correctional facility realizing Mike was gone."

"I had everything to do with that. You know the so- called missing witness that the news reporter was talking about? That's me."

Supreme stood dumbfounded, waiting for me to connect the dots.

"I was in New York getting the necessary identification to visit Mike at the prison. When I got there, a look-alike was posing as him. It was me who alerted the guard that he was dealing with an imposter. It was also me who contacted the media letting them know that Mike escaped while Clinton Correctional facility tried to hold off on releasing the information until they could do damage control."

"Why didn't you tell me what you were up to?" Supreme asked as he sat down on the edge of the bed.

"You basically called me delusional when I told you Mike was behind this bullshit. I couldn't waste anymore time trying to convince you of what my gut was screaming out to me. Maybe next time you'll listen to me."

Supreme seemed to be digesting what I said when our silence was broken when my cell began ringing. It was Maya, and I was more than happy with the interruption.

"Hey, Maya."

"I was checking to see if you were coming by Clip's video shoot today with Supreme, because my car's in the shop and I wanted to catch a ride."

"I didn't even know Clip had a video shoot today."

"Fuck, I forgot all about that," Supreme said, hearing my response to Maya. "I got some other shit to handle."

"Sorry, Maya, Supreme's not going."

"I understand, especially with what's going on, but umm..." I could detect the begging about to come out of Maya's mouth. "But, Precious, I really don't want to go by myself. Plus, I don't have a ride."

"Then maybe you should stay home."

"I can't. I want to sneak up on him and see what he's doing. I told you I think he's creeping. He ain't expecting me to come to the video so I might catch him in some shit."

"What does any of that have to do with me?"

"You know you're my only support system. I need you with me."

"You're so fucking selfish. My daughter has been kidnapped. Do you really think I feel like running up on some damn video shoot with a bunch of niggas and video hoes? I think not!"

"You right, I'm way out of pocket right now. I'm sorry, I'll just stay home."

"Yeah, do that." Without a goodbye, I hung up the phone with Maya and got out the bed.

"Did you really have to be so cold towards Maya?" Supreme questioned as I was walking towards the bathroom.

"Excuse me? I think under the circumstances I handled her with kid gloves."

"I'm sure Maya is upset about Aaliyah too, but it doesn't mean she shouldn't go support her man on his video shoot."

"Then why don't you fuckin' take her, since you so concerned?"

"I would, but like I said I forgot. That shit was planned weeks ago and I got some other shit I have to handle here."

"Here, meaning at home?"

"Yeah," he answered, elevating his arms up and being all extra.

"Fine, I'll take her. Anything not to be stuck in this house with you!" I slammed the bathroom door and sat down on the toilet. If I was a smoker, I would've run through a pack of Newport's right now. I dug my nails in my scalp, frustrated by the sight of my own husband. *Maybe getting out the house and spending some time with Maya would take the edge off, because anything was better than here,* I thought as I stripped out of my embroidered flyaway baby-doll nightgown.

Maya was standing in front of her building when I drove up to her condo. She damn near ran to my car so I didn't even need to pull up in a parking space. "Girl, I was so shocked when you called back and said you were coming. I know it must've been hard, but thank you so much."

"Actually, it was pretty easy. I had to get the fuck out that house before me and Supreme killed each other."

"Aaliyah's kidnapping is really straining ya's relationship, huh?"

"Pretty much. I heard a traumatic incident in a marriage can either bring a couple closer or tear them apart. It seems to be doing the latter to us."

"It's making me ill inside that my brother is the cause of all this bullshit. Aaliyah being gone is hurting me too, but I'm trying to keep myself busy so I don't have to think about it every second. Because when I do, I just wanna cry and then I get angry because Mike is the one who's responsible."

"Who you telling? Between the police and the private investigators Supreme has working on it, I be hoping that any minute they'll catch a break. Then I get pissed because they were wasting time looking in every direction but the one I told them to. They say the first twenty-fours are the most essential in a kidnapping. Who knows where Mike is right now with my daughter?"

"I know this ain't gonna make you feel no better, but Aaliyah is going to come home safely, I feel it in the pit of my stomach."

"All I can keep saying is she better, because the world will come to an end if she doesn't."

"You ain't got to tell me. I've seen yo' ass in action. God willing, it won't come to that, but if it does, I'll be right by your side making the world end with you."

"That's what's up!" Maya gave me a pound and I knew she meant that shit. We had been through some battles together, and once she even saved my life, that's how we became tight. She was my soldier. "I apologize for being harsh with you earlier."

"Nah, you were right, I was being selfish. Between Aaliyah and Clip, I'm bugging out."

"Clip still giving you problems?"

"Girl, you know how that female intuition is, and mine is going berserk."

"Well, you're holding it together well. You giving off major sex appeal like you ought to be playing the leading lady on set."

"Is that a stamp of approval I'm getting from you?"

I nodded my head letting Maya know I was. The slim fitting V-neck, intense blue silk charmeuse top with black lace trim and low-rise ass-hugging black jeans were on point. The outfit highlighted her newly developing assets without screaming "I'm desperate, please stare at me," although any straight nigga would. "You'll definitely catch Clip's attention when you walk in wearing that."

"That's cool, but I'm really trying to catch the attention of whatever hoochie has her eye on my man. You know, send her a message that I'm not one of those ole frumpy chicks. If she tries to fuck with mine, there will be some stiff competition."

"I feel you," I said, pulling into the driveway of the mansion on

Marilyn Drive where they were shooting the video. "This crib is ridic-ulously hot. They giving Clip a serious budget to work with."

"Yeah, they using that director who's done videos for Kanye West, T.I., Ne-Yo, you know, a lot of major hitters."

"Supreme definitely thinks he's gonna blow, so this a good look for him."

"True, but yo, its mad cars out here. Where are you going to park?"

"I was wondering the same thing. Wait, I'ma squeeze in on the side next to that Porsche truck."

"Be careful, I don't want you fucking up your Bentley. You barely even had this shit for six months."

"You right, I ain't taking no chances. I'll back up and park on the side of the street."

"Do you think we should walk around to the back or use the front door?" Maya asked, anxious to find her man.

"I think we should walk through the front."

The door was unlocked to the European-style house and opened up to a dramatic entry with exquisite designs at every turn. With a marble fireplace and cherry wood finished wood paneled walls, the house was official.

We followed the noise to the back where they were shooting a scene around the Infinity pool. The home was extraordinary, but the view outside resembled the typical ballin' out of control rap video. You had a trickle of other entertainment celebrities stopping through for some airtime, then of course a dozen or so of Clip's so-called friends, and last but most importantly, about fifty pieces of half-naked eye candy.

Maya cut right to it and swooped in on her man and the two buxom vixens that were slithering their curves against him. I grabbed her arm as Maya moved forward. "Chill, the camera is rolling. For now all he's guilty of is playing the role of a rich player. Relax."

Since everybody was cheesing it up for the camera as if it were their starring role, it was easy for Maya and keeping a low profile, not wanting to be recognized. I was overjoyed when I left my house and only a couple of reporters were out front. They tried to follow me, but I purposely drove crazy so I could lose them. But unlike me, Maya did want to be noticed, and she stayed on the edge of her seat waiting to hear the word "cut". Instead she heard the director say:

"Tina, put your breasts closer against Clip's arm and whisper in his ear being real flirtatious."

"Those chicks are having too much fun with this, and so is Clip."

"I know how you feel, but its part of the game. I remember dating Supreme before we got married, and I hated every pretty or semi-pretty female around him. I was so jealous and I used to love to fight, so I was ready to break a bitch off, but I quickly realized it ain't worth it. Either he was going to be with me or be with them. You can't control where a man puts his dick, only what you're going to do if you ever find out he put it someplace else other than up in you."

"I'll be back," Maya huffed and then jumped up to get her man after she finally heard the word cut. I laughed as she put an extra twist in her walk, determined to make it rain on them hoes. The two females remained by Clip's side as if the camera was still rolling. The giggles and smiles vanished from all three of their faces when Maya rolled up on them. I couldn't hear the words that were being exchanged, but the two vixens did scoot off leaving Clip and Maya to handle their business. Maya seemed a bit hype, and it appeared Clip was doing his best to calm her down.

I observed the two vixens go over to a young woman who was in a chair getting her hair and makeup touched up. I assumed she was the principal. She reminded me of a classier version of Angel Lola Luv without the butt shots but with plenty of ass nevertheless. All I peeped was the vixens' mouths running nonstop as the chick eyed Clip and Maya without blinking. About fifteen minutes later, Maya and Clip ended their conversation with a kiss and she came back over to me.

"You get everything straight?"

"Yeah, we good. Like you said, it's only business. He ain't thinking about them hoochies. But I'm glad I came through and showed my face. The only reason we stopped talking was because he has to go change into a new outfit for the next scene."

"I'm glad you feel better."

"Me too. I told Clip I was going to stay longer, but I made my presence known so I'm ready to bounce."

"You sure? Because we can stay a little while longer if you like."

"I'm good, but thanks for being such a trooper. Wait right here, let me go tell Clip we about to bounce."

"Cool."

Maya was about to walk off when we both heard a cell phone ringing. "Is that you or me?" she asked.

"I think that's you."

Maya reached in her purse and snatched her phone. "Oh, shit, that's my mother. She probably heard about Mike. Precious, will you go tell Clip we leaving so I can take this call?"

"No problem, I'll meet you at the car." "Thanks," Maya said, walking off.

I turned around to tell Clip bye and he had disappeared. "Excuse me, do you know where Clip is?" I asked one of the people working the set.

"He's over in that bedroom straight ahead."

When I knocked on the bedroom door I thought the man was talking about, no one answered. I tried to open it but it was locked. I walked off thinking I had the wrong room, but stopped in my tracks when I heard the door open. The female who was eyeing Maya during her entire conversation with Clip, who I assumed had the principal role came out the room fixing her lipstick and hair.

"Is Clip in there?"

"Who wants to know?" She stood with her hand pressed against her tiny waistline.

"Trick, move out my way," I said, shoving my shoulder against the side of her body as I entered the room.

"You need to watch yourself!" I heard her scream as the door slammed in her face.

"Precious, what are you doing here?" Clip asked, seeming to be unruffled by my appearance. He continued buttoning up his shirt as if I hadn't caught some groupie coming out this bedroom.

"Maya's mother called so she wanted me to tell you we were bouncing."

"Okay, that's cool. Tell her I'll see her tonight when I get home. How are you and Supreme holding up? I wanted him to come through but I know he ain't up to seeing nobody, which is understandable. I'm keeping Aaliyah in my prayers."

"I appreciate that, Clip, but why was that chick in this room with the door locked?

"You talking about Destiny?"

"Yeah, unless another chick up in here," I said, scoping the room.

"She had to use the bathroom."

"This the only bathroom in this big-ass house? And why was the door locked?"

"The bathroom was available and I told her she could use it, and I didn't know the door was locked."

"Oh really?"

"Yes, really. I know you and Maya are close, but I promise you no shady shit was going down in here. That's my word."

"At the end of the day, that's all you got so I'm going to take it."

"It's the truth. And please don't say nothing to Maya. She's already feeling insecure I don't want you to spark it up any more."

"You said it was nothing, so I'll leave it at that. But Clip, whatever you do, be clean about your shit."

When I left the room, I caught Destiny eyeballing from a short distance away. I was tempted to go whip her ass, not because I knew for a fact she was fucking around with Maya's man, but just for making me think it. Then I thought about all the eyewitnesses and the lawsuit the trick would slap on me and decided to go the fuck home.

The sunlight that was streaming through the windows when we first arrived was now slowly setting as I walked out the front door. As I walked down the driveway and got closer to the car, I could see Maya leaning on the back of the Bentley, still on the phone. I thought nothing of the dark gray car easing down the street doing less than five miles per hour. "You're still talking to your mother?" I asked, hitting the remote to unlock the door.

"Yeah, I'm about to get off," Maya mouthed as I walked passed her.

That's when I realized the dark gray car had turned around and was deliberately coming back in our direction. I made a mental note of the California license plate number. When it coasted to a stop, I knew it was about to be on.

"Maya, get down!" I screamed, pushing her to the ground and sending her phone skyrocketing out of her hand. The rapid succession of bullets pierced my ears as they sprayed my space, busting out windows and leaving shattered glass on the concrete beneath us. I crawled behind the car and grabbed Maya's hand to follow me, as she seemed frozen from shock. For what seemed like an eternity, the sound of gunshots blaring ceased and were replaced by screeching of tires as the car drove off. Maya and I remained on the ground for a few more minutes to make sure the imminent danger had vanished.

"What the fuck was that about?" Maya asked, visibly shaken. We both swallowed hard before standing up. "That had to be the scariest shit I've ever experienced in my life. And damn, ain't nobody come outside to see what the hell was going on? Is the music so fuckin' loud that nobody heard this war zone?"

"And a fucking war is exactly what this is," I said, picking up a bullet ridden pink stuffed animal. "This is the teddy bear Aaliyah had with her when she was kidnapped."

"Are you sure?"

"Yes, you see the bracelet around the wrist? It has a tag with the letter 'A' on it. Supreme got it for Aaliyah the day we brought her home from the hospital." Staying on task, I looked in my purse for a piece of paper and pen, then jotted down the license plate number before I forgot. I sat down on the concrete with glass surrounding me, holding on tightly to Aaliyah's teddy bear. Instead of this attempt on my life leaving me with a shroud of fear, it flooded me with unimaginable strength.

A TASTE OF HOPE

By the time the police finished getting me and Maya's statements, I was exhausted. They continued to ask us the same questions over and over again as if we would change our story—to what, I had no clue. At this point I was tired of the damn po-po. With each passing day they brought no new information to the table or had any leads. I was beginning to believe they were incompetent, and that's why I held back on giving them the license plate number I wrote down. It was the only potential clue I had, and I wasn't going to let the LAPD fuck it up.

"Maya, it's cool if you want to stay at the house with me and Supreme." After mentally recovering from the ambush, I called Supreme to come pick me and Maya up. My Bentley was destroyed in the one-sided gunfight, and I wasn't about to take a stroll in a cop's car.

"I know, but I want to go home, take a bath and get in my own bed. Clip will be home soon too, so I'm good."

"I feel you. But yo, I still can't believe didn't nobody from the video shoot hear those guns popping."

"What about the neighbors? They didn't hear nothing either?" Supreme asked.

"Every rich motherfucker on that block was either out of town or just not home."

"Precious, did you see the look on Clip's face when I went back to the house and told him what happened? He thought I was gaming him until he came outside and saw how fucked up your car was—I mean is."

"That car ain't nothing but some metal that can be replaced. The most important thing is that neither one of you got hurt."

"You right, Supreme, but I know how much my girl loved that ride. Precious, remember when you called me on Christmas bragging about the new whip Supreme got you?"

"Yep, that seems like yesterday when my life was a freakin' fairytale. It's banoodles how much can change in a few months. Now I'm living in a nightmare," I said solemnly.

"We at my place already," Maya said, shaking me out of the dark place my mind had gone.

"Let me walk you to your door."

"I'm coming too," Supreme volunteered, turning off his Range.

"Dang, I feel mighty important. I get two escorts to my front door," Maya joked.

"I want you to be safe. It's my fault you got caught out there."

"Precious, you can't blame yourself for this craziness."

"The shooter was trying to kill me. If you would've taken a bullet in the process, I couldn't forgive myself."

"Then imagine how fucked up I am knowing my brother is probably responsible for all of this. So please don't blame yourself, because then I'll have to blame myself too," Maya said as we stood in front of her door.

"I get your point. We can finish this later. You go inside and get some rest."

"Maya, hold up for a minute while I go inside and make sure everything is straight." Supreme turned on the lights and did a walk-through. "The place looks intact."

"I doubt anybody's coming up in my crib, but I appreciate you looking out, Supreme."

"You my peoples."

"Yeah, so if it gets too late and Clip isn't home, call me. I'll have one of the bodyguards come over and bring you to our house," I said.

"Thanks, Precious," Maya said, giving me a hug before going inside.

"Speaking of bodyguards, from now on you're going to have one with you every time you leave the house."

"Supreme, that's somewhat drastic."

"I don't need your opinion because this isn't up for discussion," he said, slamming the car door shut.

Instead of arguing with him, I remained silent the entire ride home. I had other pressing issues, like tracking down that car. I was so pressed that when Supreme pulled the car into the garage, I couldn't even wait for him to turn off the engine before I unlocked my door and ran upstairs to our bedroom. I went straight to my walk-in closet and picked up the Louis Vuitton Sac Chasse luggage I took on my flight to New Jersey. I reached in one of the inside compartments for the burner I purchased in Harlem. I slipped it in the left pocket of my velour hoodie before exiting, only to find my entrance blocked by Supreme.

"Are you going to move out my way?" I asked casually.

"Why were you in such a rush to get upstairs, and what did you get out the closet?"

"Wow, why do I feel like you're interrogating me?"

"Because I am."

"If you must know, on our way home I realized I didn't have on the diamond tennis bracelet you bought me and panicked. I couldn't remember if I had it on before I left home today and lost it while ducking for cover trying to stay alive. But fortunately I found it," I said, pulling it out my right pocket. "I forgot I left it in the luggage I took with me on my trip."

"Why did you put it in your luggage?"

"I took all my jewelry off. Those metal detectors at the airport are so unpredictable, you never know what's going to set them off and I wasn't in the mood for any hassles. Now, are you done with the twenty questions?" I brushed past Supreme, sensing his reluctance to accept my explanation. It was the best I could come up with on a whim. Luckily I remembered putting the bracelet in my pocket after the drive-by because somehow during the commotion I broke the clasp. I ran with the story, and if Supreme didn't believe it, I could honestly care less. All I wanted to do was get out of his face and make my phone call."

"So where are you going now?"

"To the kitchen. I'm starving. I'ma get a few snacks. Would you like something too?"

"I'm straight. If you need me I'll be in my office. I have to make some calls."

"Okay." I waited for Supreme to leave before digging in my purse for the piece of paper I wrote the license plate number down on. I made a quick stop in the kitchen and grabbed some random goodies just in case Supreme came sniffing around playing eye spy again. For privacy purposes, I opted for the gazebo outside hoping it would keep

Supreme off my trail, at least for a little while.

I twisted a strand of my hair around my index finger counting each ring. I took the phone away from my ear and double-checked to make sure I dialed the right number.

"What's good?"

I breathed a sigh of relief when at last I heard a voice on the other end of the phone answer. "Hey, is this phone cool to talk on?" I asked, wanting to be cautious.

"That's why I gave you the number. What's up?"

"Ricky, I need your help. But first, thanks for the other shit. It worked perfectly."

"So I heard. I also heard about your daughter—I'm sorry. I had no idea until they showed a picture of you on television that you were married to Supreme. I knew you looked familiar, but my sister didn't tell me that much about you."

"I asked her not to. Besides, I didn't even tell her that my daughter had been kidnapped."

"So you think that Mike fella you went to see in jail is the guilty party?"

"I don't think, I know. The story is long and complicated, but I don't have the time to discuss it right now. I need to find my daughter and finally I might have a lead."

"I'll do whatever I can. What is it?"

"You have a pen?"

"Always."

"Write this license plate number down. 5JLE290."

"What state is it issued in?"

"California, but I'm sure the plate number is going to come up stolen."

"Why do you say that?"

"Because I got it from the car that was used in a drive- by shooting today, and I'm sure they were wise enough to use some bogus tags. But I'm keeping my fingers crossed that you can come up with something I can use."

"You have reason to be optimistic. Rarely are plates randomly stolen for no reason. Most of the time if it's still being used, the number can be traced back to somebody in the know. What's the model of the car?"

"I don't know the exact year, but it was an old model, four-door dark gray Acura."

"I'll be at my spot shortly and run the information. I should have something for you within the next hour."

"Good, so I'll call you back in an hour." I hung up the phone and went back inside the house to check on Supreme. His office door was closed, but I could hear him having a heated conversation with someone. I put my ear closer to door to get a better listen.

"...Fuck the cost! Just keep that nigga away from my family by any means necessary."

"Does that include making him disappear permanently?" a man asked whose voice I couldn't distinguish.

"Do I really need to define 'by any means necessary' to you?"

"No sir."

"Good, now make it happen. I don't want to discuss this again until you've gotten the job done. Now excuse me, I have some phone calls to make." Supreme dismissed the man, and I made myself ghost by hiding on the side of the wall. The medium-height, husky-framed man had on all black, including his baseball cap. I was unable to get a clear view of his face, but his skin color ran concurrent to the color of his clothes.

As I thought about the conversation I overheard, I assumed Supreme had put a hit out on Mike, which I one hundred percent co-signed on. I just wanted Aaliyah to be back in my arms safely before doing so. Understanding what page Supreme was on made me want to move even faster. His intentions were good, but until we got a break in the case, Mike was the only link to Aaliyah I had.

I eyed my watch and I only had another half hour before it was time to call Ricky back. I used it to take a shower and then mellow out by having a glass of wine in the den. I sat back in the whiskey-colored, aniline dye full-grain leather recliner, pouring my second glass of wine. When I looked up at the clock on the wall, I was fifteen minutes late with my call.

"I was starting to get worried," Ricky said when he answered the phone.

"Sorry about that."

"Don't be, the extra time was helpful."

"So you found something?"

"I did."

"What is it?" The high pitch of my voice divulged my anxiousness.

"The plates but not the car was reported stolen about a month ago. It was registered to a 2007 Yukon Denali. I then ran a check on the newly issued license plates for the Denali, and as expected, both are registered under the same name and address. I then ran every older model dark gray Acura. That took some time—there are a lot of Acura's fitting that description registered in California. I had the system run a check and flag any name or address from the Acura's list that matched the one for the Denali, and I got a hit."

"Who is it?"

"The Denali is registered to a Vernika Chavez, and the Acura was registered a couple of months ago to a Donnell Graham. Two different names, but they share the same address."

"This is good... this is really good."

"It gets better. This is what I found out during that additional fifteen minutes you gave me."

"You have more? What is it?"

"Guess where Donnell Graham just finished doing a seven year bid at?"

"Clinton Correctional Facility," I answered slowly, shaking my head from repulsion. When did he get out?"

"Three months ago. I'm sure he and Mike started coming up with their plan months before that."

"Where does the Vernika chick fit in?"

"Her record came up clean, but my guess is that her hands are as dirty as the rest."

"Wait, when Aaliyah was kidnapped, they said a light-skinned or Hispanic woman was seen leaving with a baby. I bet my life that woman was Vernika."

"What's your next step?"

"I'm about to make a house call."

"I hope you're not going alone. These people are obviously dangerous."

"Who am I going to take—the police, so what they can fuck shit up?"

"I understand if you want to leave them out of it, but at least tell your husband. He'll know how to handle it. Whatever you decide, please be careful. You're not only risking your life, but the life of your daughter."

"Let me get that address." I wrote down the information as my mind created several different scenarios for taking down Vernika and Donnell. Each one seemed risky with me as a solo act. "Thanks again, Ricky. Do you want me to wire or Western Union the money?"

"None of that. Give it to me next time I see you. Hopefully it will be soon, and you'll have your daughter with you. But until then, if you need anything, don't hesitate to call."

"I will."

After hanging up with Ricky, I had two more glasses of wine while mulling over my alternatives. The police were out of the question. I regulated them to the sidelines until the absolute very last minute. At a moment like this, I wished that Nico had never left my life. He would know exactly what move to make and when to make it. But I hadn't seen or heard from him since that time we made love before he bailed out of New York. Even with all the charges dropped against him he hadn't shown his face. It was as if he'd vanished. I promised myself that once I got Aaliyah back and this nightmare was over, my next mission would be to locate Nico.

Right now, I had to figure out a way to bring Supreme on board without him cutting me out the loop. No way would he allow me to play a part in getting Aaliyah back. He would say it was too risky and to let him take care of it. I wanted to be there when he confronted the two people who played an intricate roll in my daughter's kidnapping. I had to find a way to make Supreme comprehend that.

When I got upstairs, Supreme was stepping out of the shower. "Where were you?" he asked, drying himself off.

"I was in the den having a couple glasses of wine, trying to relax, if that's even possible during a time like this."

"No, I don't think it is possible." Supreme got into bed and turned on the television without so much as a glance in my direction.

I wanted to confide in him about what I had learned, but the wall he put up was so thick. There was only one way I knew to break it down. Although I had already taken a shower, Supreme wasn't aware of it. It would be the perfect opportunity to get naked and seduce my husband without being obvious. I dropped my bathrobe and turned on the water, waiting a few minutes before entering the shower. I knew that Supreme could see the reflection of my body through the glass wall that divided the bedroom and bathroom area. The hot water doused over my body. After ten minutes of re-cleaning my body, I turned off the water and stood in front of the floor-length bathroom mirror. I moisturized my skin with Supreme's favorite body oil, Satisfaction. With ease and precision I massaged every curve, as if pleasuring myself but in reality showcasing for my husband.

Like a snake sneaking upon its prey, I slithered past my husband as if oblivious to his presence. I let my body melt into the silk-sheeted bed, and when I felt Supreme roll over, his view was of my backside silhouette. I could feel his eyes canvassing over every inch of my body, but he refrained from touching and shifted his body away from mine. Defeat crept over me until the tip of his fingers danced through my damp hair. He latched my waves in a tight grasp, exposing the outline of my slender neck and sprinkling it with purposeful kisses.

"Don't say a word, just let me fuck you," he whispered in my ear as he put one finger over my lips.

What started off as a seduction to gain power over my husband so he would be my co-conspirator, turned into untainted lust. He gripped my firm butterscotch mounds and tweaked my hardened nipples causing shivers to ripple through my body. As his tongue traveled down my abdomen making its way to his domain, my sweet juices welcomed each scrupulous stroke. I clenched the silk sheets, wanting to scream out his name, but remembered that he told me not to say a word.

Once he inserted his rock-hard manhood, I had to bite down on his shoulder in an effort to keep my vocals in check. My walls compressed around his hardness with each thrust, sending my wide hips into overdrive. I invited the pleasurable punishment my clitoris endured as his tool propelled deeper inside of me. I buried my face in the masculine scent of Supreme's body when the orgasmic sensation ricocheted through each element, leaving me wilted in his arms. Soon after, Supreme reached the same level of pleasure and released himself in me, sending us both into a sex-induced sleep.

A few hours later I woke up to use the restroom, and to my surprise Supreme was sitting up in bed watching television. "How long have you been up?"

"Not that long. I couldn't sleep."

I went to use the bathroom and decided that maybe now was the right time to have that talk with my husband. I took my time washing my hands so I could decipher the correct approach. "Supreme, we need to talk."

"About what?" His eyes remained fixed on the mounted sixty-inch screen.

"Aaliyah."

"I don't want to talk about Aaliyah," he said with an aching in his voice that I had never heard from him before.

"I know how you feel, it's tearing you up inside, but..."

"You don't know shit, about how I feel!" Supreme yelled, cutting me off. "How am I supposed to be a man if I can't even protect my own damn family? This shit ain't tearing me apart, it's ripped out my fuckin' soul!" he howled pounding his chest with a closed fist. "I want to break down and cry so fuckin' bad, but I know if I start I won't be able to stop, so I refuse to shed a tear. This shit is worse than death, because you're alive and helpless.

So no, I don't want to discuss Aaliyah until I can figure out how to bring her the fuck home."

"Baby, I think I know how."

"What do you mean you think?" Supreme remained even-toned, not willing to show any signs of optimism.

"I took down the license plate number of the car that tried to take me under. I had a guy that I know in New York trace it, and after some thorough investigating, he came up with an address."

"Is it linked to Mike in any way?"

"Yes, the guy, Donnell Graham, just got released three months ago from Clinton Correctional before Mike escaped. And the woman's name is Vernika Chavez. Remember a witness said a light-skinned or Hispanic woman was seen leaving with a baby? Well, Chavez sounds like a Hispanic name to me."

"Why didn't you give this information to the police?"

"Because I know they'll fuck it up."

"Yeah, I'm wit' you. And we can't afford to take that chance. Alright, I'ma get my people on this, but our plan has to be bulletproof. Everything has to be lined up correctly before making a move. This might be our only chance to get Aaliyah back."

"Supreme, I want to be a part of this. Don't ask me to stay in the background. I'll let you handle it your way, but I'm going with you."

"Okay, first thing in the morning I'm getting everybody together to iron this shit out," Supreme said, reaching over to grab his cell off the nightstand.

"Who are you calling?"

"It might take a couple of days to orchestrate this plan correctly, but until then my people will have their eyes glued on that crib, starting tonight."

I told Supreme the address and listened as he gave the person on the other end strict instructions. A tranquil wave went through me, and I knew I'd done the right thing by sharing the information I got from Ricky with Supreme.

He hung up the phone and a gleam I never thought I would see in my husband's face again appeared. "They're on it. We're bringing our daughter home, I can feel it."

"Me too, baby." I wrapped my arms around Supreme, and for the first time since this shit went down my husband held me back. Hope was once again alive for us.

WRECKLESS LOVE

I woke up to the sunlight streaming through the skylights. A smile crept across my face as if a new day was upon us, and it was. I threw an ivory silk, tie-front wrap around my naked body and headed downstairs to find Supreme. I was anxious to find out what time the meeting would start to discuss bum rushing Vernika's and Donnell's house.

When I got to the bottom of the stairs, I was stunned to see a large group of men dressed in all black coming out of Supreme's office and making their way down the hall. "Supreme, what's going on?" My hand was placed on my waist with hip swung out to the side. The smile I woke up with was now gone.

"Go back upstairs. I'll be there in a moment." Supreme continued talking with the men as he escorted them to the front door. Realizing a few of the men were distracted by the sight of me in my barely-there wrap, Supreme gave me an icy stare as if I was supposed to run back upstairs like a five-year old child about to be reprimanded. But I wasn't budging. I waited for Supreme to shake the last hand and close the door before lighting his ass up.

"How the fuck are you going to have a meeting and not include me? I made it clear last night that I wanted to be a part of whatever plan you had to get Aaliyah back. I have to wake up and find the meeting is over."

"Listen, I got the ball rolling early this morning and didn't want to wake you. I was going to give you the play-by-play when you woke up."

"That's fucked up! I try to include you in what I know, but then you turn around and act as though I'm incompetent."

"Yo, you blowing this way out of proportion. I have no problem including you in anything. It was a meeting. Instead of you riffing, let me tell you what we discussed."

"Go 'head," I said, being short with him.

"Two men have been watching the house since last night. They've only seen a man, which I'm assuming is Donnell. They've taken a picture and they're going to compare it to whatever booking mug shot they get a hold of."

"Have they seen Vernika?"

"There's been no sign of Vernika, but the woman and Aaliyah could be staying someplace else. I have another set of men following Donnell wherever he goes. They are going to continue to watch the house and Donnell for the next day or so. If there is still no sign of Aaliyah, then we'll make our move and take him down... see what we can find out."

"That's it?" I asked, unimpressed with the plan.

"What you mean, that's it? Hopefully watching that nigga will lead us to our daughter, but if not, we'll just have to beat it out of him."

"But what if Donnell doesn't talk, or yanking him up gets Mike to flip and run off somewhere else with our daughter? Then what?"

"Precious, then what the fuck do you think we should do?"

"I think we should give it more than a day or so. As long as your people are following Donnell and watching the house, we should be patient. Maybe in a few days Mike will pop up and have Aaliyah. I just don't want to make a move that will trigger suspicion with Mike and he disappears with our daughter."

"I don't either. But I hate to see time go by and them niggas still on the street."

"Yeah, but at least we have an idea where they at, and that means they can always lead us to Aaliyah."

"Alright, we'll give it more than a couple of days, but on day five, whoever we see, they're bringing them in—young, old, crippled, I don't give a fuck. Somebody gon' talk." Supreme said his peace and walked back to his office and closed the door.

I sat on the bottom step, staring up at the crystal chandelier dangling from the ceiling. I remembered how scared I would be, because for some reason, Aaliyah would love to crawl across the foyer and sit right under the chandelier. She would look up as if hypnotized by the crystals. I knew it was securely fastened to the ceiling, but the idea of the chandelier crashing down would make me cringe. My mind became so preoccupied with it that I forbade Anna to allow Aaliyah to crawl in that area. Those were the types of illogical concerns I had for my daughter, never thinking there was a much more dangerous threat awaiting her outside those front doors.

I snapped out of my daydreaming when I saw Anna walk into the living room. Since I tried to choke her to death, we had only seen each other briefly. I don't know if she was purposely trying to stay the fuck out my way, or if I had been so busy we hadn't crossed paths, but now that she was in my face, it was a perfect opportunity to iron shit out. "Anna, I need to speak with you."

Anna stopped her dusting and slowly dragged her legs towards me as if apprehensive that I would try to finish what I started the other night. "Yes, Mrs. Mills."

"Listen, Anna, I want to apologize for the other night. I was understandably pissed."

"Of course. I still feel guilty about poor little Aaliyah."

"See, that's the thing. I feel you're guilty too."

Anna's face frowned up. "I didn't have anything to do with what happened to Aaliyah…I swear."

"And you know what, you probably didn't. But since my daughter was in your care when she was kidnapped, I look at you in disgust. And if you're as innocent as you claim to be, I'm sorry for my hostile attitude towards you, but until I know for sure, my feelings for you aren't going to change."

"So what are you saying, Mrs. Mills? Are you firing me?"

"Basically, I want you to pack up your shit and leave."

"But this is my home. I left my family to come live here with you."

"Actually this is *my* home, and I was letting you live here. I'm more than willing to financially compensate you for sending you back to your family, but I can't stomach seeing your face one more day."

"Mrs. Mills, I'm sorry you feel this way about me. But I forgive you for your hurtful words. I know you're saying this out of pain for losing Aaliyah. One day you'll see I'm innocent and that I love Aaliyah, and would never do anything to hurt her or your family."

Ring…ring…ring…

"Saved by the bell!" I said with contempt. "I have to answer that. So please pack up your things and I'll have the driver take you to the airport." I wanted Anna out of my house and there wasn't anything else to discuss as far as I was concerned. I went to answer the phone, putting her out of my head. "Hello."

"Why aren't you answering your cell phone?"

"It's upstairs. Maya, this must be awfully important if you tracking me down on the home phone."

"Yeah, pretty much."

"Is everything okay?"

"No. My car was supposed to be ready this morning, and I've been down here for two hours and the shit still fucked up."

"I told you not to fuck with them Jaguars. Them some bullshit cars. Something stays wrong with those motherfuckers."

"I remember your words of caution. But that candy apple red shit was looking so pretty sitting on that car lot I begged Clip to get it for me when I got my driver's license. Now I wish I would've listened to you. I be cramming my brain, dense on how a brand new car can always have something wrong with it. But any-who, Clip ain't answering his phone and I'm tired of waiting. Will you come get me?"

"Girl, you need to get a damn car service, or tell the dealership to loan you a vehicle until they get your shit fix."

"They offered me some whack shit, but I rather wait until I get my fly whip back. Come on, Precious, you need to get out the house anyway."

"Says who?"

"Says me. I know you moping around the house thinking about Aaliyah. We can go chill, get something to eat."

"Maya, let me call you back. The doorbell's ringing."

"Are you coming to get me?"

"Yes, crazy. Let me get dressed and I'll swoop you up."

"Alright, call me when you about to pull up so I can come outside."

"Cool, but I got to go. Whoever's at the door 'bout to bang it down." On my way to open the door, I glanced down the hall wondering if Supreme had heard the banging, but his office door was still shut.

"Mrs. Mills, sorry for disturbing you," Detective Moore said as if embarrassed.

I looked down and realized my wrap had come loose and I was one step from having a wardrobe malfunction. I quickly tightened the strap and folded my arms over my braless breasts. "No problem, I just woke up a little while ago and haven't had a chance to get dressed. Come in."

"Is your husband home?" he asked as I closed the front door.

"Yes."

"I wanted to share some new information. I'm sure he would want to hear it also."

"Of course. I'll go get him. Please have a seat." When I got to Supreme's office, his door was locked. I could hear him on the phone, but he was talking so low I couldn't understand what he was saying. "Supreme, Detective Moore is here," I said, knocking on the door.

"I'll be out in a minute."

"Okay." I kept my ear to the door for a few seconds hoping to overhear something but it was useless, so I went back up front to where the detective was sitting. "Supreme will be out in a minute. Do you have some new information about Aaliyah?"

"I think we should wait for you husband."

I was about to offer the detective a drink but he pissed me off with that "wait for your husband" shit, like I was the little lady of the house. I tapped my toe on the marble floor becoming restless for Supreme to bring his ass on. "Supreme!" I hollered, causing Detective Moore to jump out his seat. "I'm sorry, I didn't mean to startle you."

"That's fine. It's was just so quiet, you could hear a pin drop. I wasn't expecting..." his voice faded off.

"Expecting what, for me to holla for my husband? I mean since you're keeping your lips sealed until we're graced with his presence, I really didn't have a choice."

"Mrs. Mills, it's nothing like that."

Before the detective could finish with his lame excuse, Supreme finally popped up. "Detective Moore, Supreme's words sounded more like a matter-of-fact statement than a question.

"Not exactly news," he said with hesitancy.

"No disrespect, but why are you coming to my house if you're not bringing tangible information?"

"I wanted to keep you and your wife abreast of what's going on."

"What, your phone isn't working anymore? Because last I checked my number is good." I knew Supreme was becoming annoyed with how the investigation was going, but his abrupt attitude towards the detective had me on edge.

"I think my husband is a little concerned with how slowly things are going."

Supreme glanced at me with coldness in his eyes as if telling me to shut the fuck up because he can speak for himself. "I understand. We have all of our manpower on it. There are some potential leads pinpointing Mike Owens' location that is what I wanted to update you about. We also found a match on the gun shells left at the scene of the drive-by shooting yesterday."

"Who is it?"

"The gun was unregistered, but it did have a body on it from an unsolved murder a few years ago in New York. We're working with the officers there hoping that case can shed some light on who was responsible for the attempt on your life."

"So basically, you're no closer to finding my daughter," Supreme interjected.

"I believe we're making progress. Cases like this can take some time. But I believe your daughter is very much alive."

"What do you mean by cases like this?" I asked, fishing to see where he was going with that statement.

"A lot of times when a baby is kidnapped from someone high profile like your husband, it's for a ransom—they're looking for a big payday. Or if they have no idea who your husband is and it was random, maybe it's a disturbed woman who is obsessed with having a baby and can't conceive, so they see an opportunity and steal one. But I don't believe either of those options applies here. This seems personal and well thought out. I agree with you, Mrs. Mills, that Mike Owens is behind the kidnapping, but he has a lot of help. There has been no spotting of your daughter, although I believe she's very much alive."

"Is that all, Detective?" By the tone of Supreme's voice it was clear he was ready to show Detective Moore the exit.

"For now, but I'm optimistic that we'll have some updates soon."

"When you do, let us know."

"I will, and I also hope you'll keep me updated if you find out anything." The detective locked eyes with Supreme as if trying to read what was going on in his mind, but Supreme didn't flinch.

"Of course."

"Thanks, Detective. I appreciate you stopping by with your updates," I said, wanting to add my two cents.

Supreme slammed the door so swiftly that I couldn't catch the detective's reply.

"That motherfucker coming over here telling us shit we already know, hoping we'll lay our cards on the table. Ain't nobody stupid," Supreme murmured while pouring a glass of Remy Martin X111 cognac. "But we ain't telling them *nada*. We gon' handle this my way," he asserted before taking a shot to the head. To see Supreme drinking liquor this early in the day meant he was seriously vexed.

"I have to pick Maya up from the dealership. After I drop her off maybe we can have lunch."

"No, I have too much business to handle. Go take care of Maya. I'll see you later on." Supreme took another gulp of cognac and headed back to his office. He basically lived in his office all fucking day, and it was driving me insane. With Aaliyah gone and now sending Anna back to New York after firing her ass, this huge house felt vacant. There was security covering the grounds, but they remained on mute unless Supreme needed them to speak.

I rushed upstairs to get dressed, desperate to get out the loneliness of my surroundings. After a quick shower, I threw on a cotton-candy pink velour Juicy Couture jogging suit. I slicked my hair back in a ponytail with a baseball cap. I slipped on some shades and felt incognito.

Since word spread that Supreme's daughter was kidnapped, that's how the headlines read, the press was becoming relentless to get an interview. The one and only statement I gave when I was cornered at the airport wasn't enough. They were begging for a sit-down, but Supreme and I both agreed that we needed to keep this strictly about Aaliyah and not his celebrity. It seemed to be working as the tons of press that were initially staking out our house had dispersed, leaving only sprinkles here and there. That was a relief, but to remain guarded I continued to dress down.

When I got downstairs to retrieve my car keys, I remembered my Bentley was out of commission. I grabbed the keys to my Range but stepped back when I turned around to see one of the bodyguards blocking my path. "Excuse me, but why are you standing in my face?"

"Hello, I'm Devon. I'll be driving you around today. I already have the car out front waiting for you."

"I don't need a driver. Thanks, but no thanks."

"I'm following your husbands' orders."

"Well, now I'm telling you to follow mine. No thanks. Now excuse me."

"I can't do that, Mrs. Mills. I work for Supreme. I have to follow his instructions. If you have a problem you should go speak with him."

"Don't tell me what to do. But since I'm not up to arguing with my husband, you can drive me around today, but don't get too comfortable. This will more than likely be your first and last day transporting me around."

I sat in the back of the Maybach Supreme was normally chauf-feured around in. The blinds were down on the windows so no one could see who was in the car. The privacy was totally in affect.

"Where is the first stop?" I heard the driver ask.

"Fifteen-twenty North Wilcox Avenue." I closed my eyes during the smooth ride and had to admit it was rather relaxing. When I was behind the wheel of a car, a hint of road rage was always bubbling inside me. But being a passenger in the backseat gave me an opportunity to let my psyche travel to other places. "How far away are we?"

"About five minutes."

I flipped open my cell and called Maya.

"Where the hell are you at? I thought you would've been here an hour ago," was Maya's greeting when she answered the phone.

"I can always not come."

"Stop playing, Precious. I'm hungry that's all. How far are you?"

"Like five minutes, so come out."

"What you driving?"

"I'm not."

"What you mean."

"I have a driver. We're in a black Maybach."

"Excuse me! Sometimes I forget who you married too."

"So do I. I'll see you in a few."

Sometimes I did forget I was married to Xavier Mills, a.k.a. super-star extraordinaire, Supreme. A few years ago I was struggling, living in the projects ready to sell my body to the richest dope dealer. My biggest aspiration was going from project chick to hood queen. Now I was living on an estate in Beverly Hills, being chauffeured around in a Maybach, and my husband was unbelievably fucking rich and famous. On paper this was every hood queen's dream life, but in reality, it was a fucking nightmare. The husband I never felt worthy of having was slipping through my fingers, and our life together was crumbling more each day. In the past I was always able to concoct a scheme and have shit beating to my drum. Somehow, my mojo got missing and I had to get it back.

"Mrs. Mills, are we picking up this young lady?" he pointed to Maya who was walking towards the car.

"Are you new? Because I thought all the guards new Maya."

"Yes. I started working for your husband last week."

"Oh, well if he keeps you around you'll get used to seeing Maya's face. She's family."

"Girl, I can't wait for Clip to go triple platinum so he can cop one of these," Maya said, getting in the car.

"Where is the next stop, Mrs. Mills?"

"Mrs. Mills," Maya repeated. "Dang, Precious, he speaking to you like you Queen of Sheba," Maya joked.

"Anyway, where do you wanna eat?" I asked, ignoring Maya's foolishness.

"I don't care, any spot with good food."

"Head over to Wilshire Boulevard."

"What's over there?"

"They have this Italian restaurant that I love. The food is off the chain."

"Is that my phone or your phone?" Maya asked, reaching in her purse.

"I think that's me. Hello?"

"I've been missing you. Our last conversation ended so abruptly."

"I was wondering when you would call again. What took so long? Let me guess. Being on the run is keeping you more occupied than you originally anticipated."

"Actually, catching up on the missed time with my daughter is what's keeping me busy. I'm enjoying it though. Who knew being a father could be so rewarding?"

"You're sick."

"Speaking of sick, I thought you'd be recuperating from your brush with death yesterday. From what I was told, that Bentley your husband got you for Christmas is full of bullets. You're lucky none of them had your name on it."

"I knew that hit had your name written all over it. You're such a pussy. You couldn't even handle the job yourself."

"Who is that?" Maya mouthed.

"Your brother," I mouthed back.

"Instead of being sweet with the tongue, you should be thanking me."

"What the hell do I need to thank you for?"

"For letting you live. What, you thought that once again you beat death? No, pretty girl, I was sending you a message."

"And what message is that?"

"That your life is in my hands and I can take you out anytime I like, remember that."

"Fuck you, Mike!"

"I'm looking forward to doing that with you too. Soon, I promise. But until then, our daughter wants to say goodbye." I heard Aaliyah's babbling for less than ten seconds, and then the phone went dead. I held onto it so tightly I thought it would break in my hand.

"Precious, are you alright? What did my brother say?"

"A lot, like I figured. He was the one that ordered that drive-by."

"My own brother was trying to kill me?"

"No, you were at the wrong place at the wrong time. That was strictly for my benefit. He was sending me a message. My thing is, whoever he has working for him has to be someone in me and Supreme's inner circle."

"Why do you say that?"

"Because he mentioned that Supreme got me my Bentley for Christmas. How would he be privy to such private information?"

"Do you have any idea who it could be?"

"I'm not sure. Supreme has a shit-load of people on his payroll. Maya, I'm not up to going out to eat. Do you want to come back to my house?"

"Yeah, I can hang out over there, but can we stop by my place first? I want to get a couple of things. I need to speak to Clip too."

"Sure."

"Let me call the crib and see if he made it home yet." Maya dialed the number, then hung up and dialed another number. "He's not home and he's not answering his cell. Oh well, maybe by the time we get to the house he'll be there."

"Devon, there's been a change of plans. We're going to stop at Maya's place first and then home."

"Not a problem. What's the address?"

Maya waited for me to give Devon her address, but she saw the blank look on my face and spoke up. I remained quiet as he drove to Maya's house. I wanted to find some sort of solace, but not even hearing Aaliyah's voice on the phone brought that. I hated to admit it, but right now Mike was winning.

"Precious, are you coming up with me?"

I had drifted so far off in another world I hadn't realized the car stopped. "No, I'll wait for you in the car."

"Come in with me. It might take me a minute and you can keep me company."

"Okay, I need to go to the restroom anyway. Devon, we shouldn't be that long."

"Take your time, I'll be here waiting."

I shut the door and followed Maya upstairs to her condo.

"Precious, I'm worried about you," Maya said, opening her front door.

"That makes two of us. But we can discuss that after I use the bathroom 'cause I'm 'bout to piss in my pants."

"The one in the hallway is broke so use the one in my bedroom."

"Okay, I'll be right back." I shuffled down the hallway, almost sliding on the hardwood floor desperate to get to the toilet. As I slid up on Maya's bedroom door I heard soft music playing. I figured she must've forgotten to turn it off before she left earlier. I wrapped my hand around the doorknob to open the door and damn near pissed in my jogging suit. I gently closed the door and speed-walked back to Maya.

"Damn, that was fast," Maya said, coming out of the kitchen with a Twinkie and glass of juice.

"Yeah, I was in and out. But we need to bounce, now. I just got a 911 text from Supreme."

"Oh shit, let me grab something from the bedroom and we out."

My natural reflex kicked in and I snatched Maya's arm so she wouldn't move.

"Precious, I'll only be a second. I promise I won't take long. Let go of my arm."

"I can't do that."

"You're buggin'. What's wrong with you?"

"Maya, I don't know how to tell you this…"

"Tell me what?"

"Let's get in the car and I'll explain everything."

"Okay, the sooner you let me get what I need out my bedroom, the sooner you can tell me what has you acting so weird."

"Is what you want in the bedroom that fuckin' important?"

"What, did you leave the bathroom funky or something? You were only in there for a second it can't stink that bad." Maya freed her arm from my grip and started walking towards her bedroom. I wished that I had magical powers that could freeze her steps, but my mouth would have to suffice.

"Don't go in that bedroom, Maya." She ignored me and kept walking. "If you do, you're probably gonna catch a case!" I yelled out in a last attempt to say enough to pull her back in without revealing the real dirt. But of course with Maya being the feisty chick that she is, my pleas only made her more determined to discover what was hiding behind those doors.

"I'ma kill you!" was the threat I heard from Maya's mouth as I ran down the hall to stop her from wreaking havoc. By the time I reached her, the glass of juice she was holding had shattered on the headboard, just missing the face of Clip and the naked woman lying in bed with him. The woman was the first to get rattled out of her sleep by the crash.

"Clip, get up!" the woman said, pushing him so he could wake up. But he wasn't budging.

They had to be doing some serious fucking. That nigga must've cum so hard because he was damn near in a coma, I thought to myself.

Then Maya stormed over to the bed, and slapped that motherfucker so hard, spit flew out his mouth. Now I knew that would wake his ass up. "How dare you bring this ho up in our crib in our fuckin' bed!"

"I ain't no ho." The chick had the audacity to try and defend herself.

Maya paused for a moment, stared down at Clip then reached over and swung on the chick with a closed fist. All I heard was a loud thump as head, ass and tits hit the floor.

"What the fuck is going on?" Clip mumbled as if struggling to come out of his daze. He looked down at his naked body and seemed shocked that his dick was hanging out for all to inspect.

"Clip, how could you do this to me? You fuck this nasty trick in our bed! You could've least got a room, you disrespectful sonofabitch. I almost got killed yesterday, and all you thinking about is running up in some pussy?"

I moved closer to the bed because I wanted to make sure Maya didn't go too far. She deserved to fuck them both up, but I wanted to avoid a murder charge. As Maya continued to cuss Clip out, I peeped the other woman trying to pull herself up from that smackdown she received courtesy of Maya. She looked strangely familiar, and then it hit me. She was the female coming out of Clip's room at the video shoot yesterday. "This is that conniving heifer, Destiny, who was playing Clip's leading lady in the video yesterday," I said, blowing up his spot mad that he lied in my face when I confronted him about the trick.

"I knew you were fucking her," Maya said, pointing her finger at Destiny while she stood there with her five-foot-six framed video deluxe body on display.

Clip turned toward Destiny as if just realizing she was in the room. "What are you doing here, and why are you naked?"

Her eyes widened at his question. "Don't act like you don't know why I'm here. You wasn't saying that shit an hour ago when you had your dick all up inside me."

"Where the condom at?" Maya barked. She knocked the lamp

and papers off the nightstand, opened the drawers, and ripped off the bedspread and sheets. "You fucked this dirty bird raw? How can you be so fuckin' reckless?"

Clip said nothing. The silence made Maya fly into a rage. She jumped on top of the bed and tackled Destiny like a linebacker on the football field. She banged her head against the floor repeatedly, screaming, "You trifling ho, I'ma kill you!" After the fourth head flop, I had had enough.

"Stop, Maya. She ain't worth you going to jail over and neither is Clip."

"Fuck that!" she said, continuing her rampage.

"Girl, if I have to pull you off that trick and we come to blows, this is one fight you will not win. Now get the fuck off of her—now!" I took a deep breath, maintaining my composure. I was being patient because Destiny deserved every lick she got. She saw Maya at the video shoot yesterday and knew that Clip was her man. To bring her stank ass into another woman's bed was straight grimy. Back in the day if I had caught my nigga doing this bullshit, a bitch like me would've been plotting that ho's murder and his, but at this point in my life, this shit was trivial. I couldn't stand around and watch Maya get both of us hemmed up on some nonsense.

Clip finally got his strength together and decided to intervene. "Maya, chill. You 'bout to kill this girl," he said, grabbing Maya's arm. But she swung it off.

"Maya, get the fuck off of her right now before I bust your ass," I stood in my "don't fuck with me" stance. Maya's eyes trailed up my body until meeting my face. My facial expression said it all. She released Destiny's head and stood up.

"Are you okay?" Clip bent down next to Destiny and asked.

"Fuck if she's okay or not! You checking for this broad?"

"Maya, you almost killed homegirl. Of course I want to make sure she a'ight. But I ain't fucking with her like that. I don't know how she got in my bed naked."

"Clip, are you for real with this line you're running? I mean come on now, you insulting all three of us with that bullshit," I had to state.

"Precious, I ain't tryna insult nobody. I swear I don't know how Destiny got in my crib or my bed, and I definitely don't remember fucking her. This shit is fucking bizarre," Clip said, shaking his head.

"Maya, what you gon' do, 'cause I can't stand here and listen to this nonsense anymore."

"I'm leaving."

"Maya, don't leave like this. When you coming back?"

"I ain't, motherfucker! I'm done wit' yo' black ass!" Maya ogled a badly bruised Destiny. "He's all yours. Clip, you'll never feel the inside of my pussy again after running up in that. Fuck both of you." Maya said then spit on the floor between where both were standing.

CONFRONTATION

"I hate that motherfucker! I can't believe he played me like that," Maya belted, slamming the car door before I even had a chance to get out. She had been calling Clip every name in the book from the time we left their condo until coming back to my crib. The curse words flowed and I didn't interrupt once. I remember how heated I was when I found out Nico had cheated on me with that troll, Porscha. It was years ago, but it remained fresh in my mind. It don't matter how many relationships follow, nothing is more painful than when your first love breaks your heart. Everybody handles their pain differently. My revenge was making sure my man got put under the jail cell, so if Maya wanted to bash her man's name, that was harmless to me.

"Mrs. Mills, will you need me anymore today or this evening?" Devon asked as I was getting out.

"I doubt it. But if I do, I'm sure I'll manage without you, thanks." There was something about Devon that I wasn't feeling. He was so damn polite and professional for one, and many would call that a good thing, but it seemed contrived to me. *But maybe those were traits Supreme was looking for in his workers,* I thought to myself as I watched Maya rambling on, waiting for me in front of the double doors.

"Precious, I wanna go back to my place and fuck Clip and his hoochie up. I didn't have a chance to pounce on them long enough," Maya complained as I opened the door.

"Child, please. You did plenty of damage. You knocked Destiny on her ass and probably gave her a concussion, banging her head like that. Then slapped the shit out of Clip, and more importantly, left his ass. That's the best punishment right there."

"I guess, but what if he wife that chick and move her in the crib and shit?"

"That is highly unlikely, but if he do, that shit ain't gon' last no way. Trust, either she will fuck around on him or she'll come home just like you did and find him waxing another ho. This shit don't start nor end with you."

While Maya soaked up what I said as we stood in the foyer, all she could do was scream for the hundredth time, "I hate Clip!"

"What the hell has Clip done now?" Supreme asked as he came down the hall.

"Don't get her started," I said, shaking my head.

"No, let me start. Supreme needs to know how trifling his artist is."

"Forget I asked. That's between you and Clip."

It was too late for Supreme to back out now. Maya wanted to share her misery with everybody." I came home, and Clip was in bed with that nasty skank from his music video."

"What? Who was it?"

"That trick, Destiny, that's who."

"I can't believe that. Clip wouldn't do no disrespectful shit like that," Supreme said, trying to defend his artist.

"It's true."

"Why, because Maya said so?"

"No, because I was there."

"Supreme, I wouldn't lie about no shit like that anyway. Why would I want to lie on my man's dick?"

"I'm not saying that. You know how women can sometimes exaggerate shit and make something out of nothing. They could've been sitting down on the couch having an innocent conversation, but ya will twist that and say they fucked around and made some babies together."

"Supreme, if I hadn't seen this shit with my own eyes I might ride with you, but it's all true."

"You was a witness?" Supreme's mouth slightly opened showing his surprise

"Yep, I actually peeped it first and tried to get Maya out the apartment so she wouldn't flip out, but obviously that didn't work."

"Damn, I would never think Clip would be so careless. Why would he bring some other broad to your crib and fuck her in your bed? He outta pocket with that. I never pegged Clip with being sloppy."

"I know what you mean, because when I saw Destiny coming out of his room yesterday at the video set I was straight tripping."

"You caught him with that ho yesterday and didn't tell me?" Maya was twisting her neck and waving her hands like she was ready to slap the shit out of me, but she knew better.

"I didn't technically catch him doing shit. Destiny was coming out of his room and she was fixing herself up looking extra suspect. I confronted Clip about it but, he swore there was nothing shady going down."

"Still, why didn't you tell me?"

"He asked me not to. He said you had been feeling insecure lately and all this would do is get you extra paranoid. I was trying to give him the benefit of the doubt, but unfortunately I was wrong. He played me with a lie and I believed him. I'm sorry, Maya."

"It's not your fault. Obviously don't none of us know him as well as we thought. I feel fucked up in the game. I don't know what I'm going to do now."

"Maya, you can stay with me and Supreme as long as you like, right Supreme?" I caught the grimace on his face, but he knew how close Maya was to me and wouldn't turn her away.

"Of course, you can stay as long as you like."

"I appreciate that. With my brother out of my life and my mother making random appearances, you guys are the only family I got. Thank you both so much." Maya gave me and Supreme a hug. My heart went out to her. She always compared herself to Supreme and me and assumed she and Clip would end up married with child.

Today that dream was shattered in the worst possible way.

"It's all love. I need to speak with Supreme, so get comfortable. Pick out whichever room you want to stay in and I'll be up shortly."

"Okay, thanks again." Supreme and I watched as Maya headed upstairs.

"So, what's up?"

"Mike called me today."

"What did he say?"

"He admitted to setting up that shooting yesterday, but said he wasn't trying to kill me but sending a message."

"What kind of message?"

"That he can take me down anytime he wants. He also put Aaliyah on the phone."

"Yo, I can't wait to kill that nigga," Supreme said, pacing the floor. "Did he say anything else?"

"Yes, something that makes me believe whoever is helping him runs in our circle."

"What the fuck was that?" Supreme stopped in his tracks, raising an eyebrow.

"He knew my Bentley that was shot up was a Christmas gift from you. I didn't want to ask in front of Maya, but do you think Clip could be helping him?"

"It's one thing to be fucking around on your girl, but another to line yourself with the enemy. I know Clip, he would never do no shit like that."

"You didn't think he would be sloppy enough to fuck another female in the crib he shares with Maya, but he did."

Supreme put his hand over his mouth and started rubbing his chin as if in deep thought.

"No, Clip's my man, but beyond that he's making serious bread because of me. He wouldn't jeopardize his career, money and fame for what, to help Mike? I can't see that."

"Remember, he worked for Mike. When the world thought you were dead, Mike was molding Clip to take your spot as the king of this rap game. Maybe the loyalty is still there."

"Clip helping out Mike, that would be some foul shit!" Supreme bawled, unable to control his anger.

"Keep your voice down. You don't want Maya to hear you."

"I already did," she said, standing on top of the stairs. "What Clip did to me was fucked up, but he would never stab Supreme in the back like that. Clip idolizes Supreme."

"I don't want to believe its Clip. But some shit ain't adding up. A few weeks ago you told me that Clip was getting weird phone calls, somebody hanging up when you answered. Then thousands of dollars was being unaccounted for."

"Yeah, and I also said I thought it was because he was cheating on me, and come to find out, he is."

"That's true, but it can also be him holding down the Mike situation."

"Precious, you're making a serious accusation. Nobody can be more pissed at Clip than me, but to help my brother kidnap Aaliyah and escape from jail would make him a monster just like Mike. I can't believe that."

"Supreme, what do you think?" I wanted to know my husband's thoughts.

"I agree with Maya, but I could be wrong and I'm not taking any chances. I'll have a couple of my men watching his every move. If I find out its true—I put this on my life—I'll kill him with my own hands."

A few days had passed since the whole Clip incident went down, and the household seemed to be in a funk. Maya was moping around missing her boo, and Supreme was frustrated not knowing if Clip was a soldier or a snake. He had decided to put distance between himself and Clip until he could get the answer.

I, on the other hand, was never close to Clip, so if he turned out to be the culprit, then I say torture his ass until he came clean about Mike's whereabouts, then throw him in the ocean. The shit was real simple to me, but I understood that there were emotions running deep on both Maya and Supreme's ends. That's why after I said my peace I decided to fall back, because there was also a chance I could be wrong. The only thing I knew for sure was that Mike had somebody on the inside helping him out, and with Clip's slimy behavior towards Maya, I felt he was capable of anything.

"Maya, I have to go out and get a few things. Do you want to come with me?" Maya was sitting on the bed in one of the guest bedrooms, watching television. She had been in that same position since she got here, and I was hoping to pull her out of her darkness.

"No, I'ma stay in today. I'm tired."

"You've been tired for the last couple of days. Being depressed over Clip ain't gonna help your cause."

"Damn, Precious, I need some time," Maya countered, rolling her eyes at me.

"Time to what?"

"To get over what happened to me. I was—make that, I'm in love with Clip. You might be able to get over your man just like that," Maya snapped her fingers, "But I can't. Although I wish I was, I'm not like you. I can't be strong and pretend that my heart isn't broken. I want to move on, but I miss Clip."

"I understand, I really do. Take as much time as you need. I'll stop pushing you. But if you need me while I'm out, hit me on my cell."

"Precious!" I heard Maya call out as I was shutting her door to leave.

"Yeah?"

"Sorry for snapping at you. It isn't your fault that Clip dogged me out for some video chick. I'm hurt, and he hasn't even called me begging to take him back. It's like he don't care that I left."

"He's playing hard, hoping you'll call first. It doesn't mean he don't care."

"Yeah right. Or maybe he been seeing that Destiny girl for a minute and he's happy I'm gone so they can play house." Tears were now trickling down Maya's face and she held on tightly to her pillow. I went and sat down on the bed next to her.

"Don't do this to yourself, Maya. Clip doesn't deserve you, and trust me, its better you get rid of his sorry ass now. Imagine if you had kids with dude and you walked in on some shit like that. You're young, smart and gorgeous; you have your whole life ahead of you. Fuck Clip. After we bring Aaliyah home, I promise finding his replacement will be next on my agenda."

"You mean that?"

"Yes, I'll find you your very own Supreme."

"But there's only one Supreme."

"True, good point. I'll find you the next best thing."

"Deal," Maya said with a wide smile on her face. It was good to see her with some sort of spark. I was becoming afraid that Clip had erased that for good.

"You sure you don't want to come out with me?"

"Not today. I do need some time, but maybe tomorrow."

"Alright, I'll check up on you when I get back." When I left Maya's room, part of me did hope that Clip was responsible for helping Mike so Supreme could kill him and he'd be out of all of our lives. I hated seeing Maya in so much pain, and I wanted Clip to pay for her suffering.

As I walked down the stairs, I visualized all the different ways Supreme could murder Clip, until those visions were interrupted by seeing Supreme speaking with Devon. "You can pull the car around Precious will be out shortly."

"I'll do that now," Devon responded, heading towards the five car garage.

Supreme made his exit to his office and I was right behind him. "Supreme, I don't need Devon driving me around," I said, closing the door behind me. I sat down on the chair in front of Supreme's desk wanting his full attention.

"How can that come out your mouth with all the shit that's going on right now?" Supreme stated as he stood behind his desk, fumbling through papers.

"Yeah, that's true but..."

"But what? Are you worried Devon ain't qualified? Because I do a thorough background check on all my staff, so you in safe hands."

"It's not that."

"Then what is it?"

"I know shit is hectic, but I'm grown. I don't need a damn chaperone."

"I understand you like to be on your own program, but you not in Brooklyn no more, Precious."

"What you tryna say?"

"I said it. I know you a hood chick. I'm from the hood too, but it's time to leave that behind. We have to be more cautious with how we handle our business. You going out there following your own program can put your life and Aaliyah's in even more jeopardy. You feel me?"

"I do."

"Good. Where's Maya? She ain't going out with you."

"No, the Clip situation still got her fucked up."

"He keeps on calling me. I know he thinks I ain't fucking with him because of Maya."

"So what are you going to do?"

"Wait a few more days and see what my people come up with."

"Any luck so far?"

"Not on Clip, but they might have caught a break with Donnell."

"Really? What is it?"

"I'm waiting for my people to hit me back with the information. But the moment I hear something I'll call you."

"You promise."

"Yes, you got my word on that," Supreme said, giving me an open mouthed kiss. Affection was coming few and far between with my husband lately, but when I got a little taste I ate it up. "Now do what you gotta do and I'll see you later on." Supreme patted me on my ass as I was leaving.

When I got out front, Devon was waiting patiently in the car. Right when my hips got comfortable in the soft leather interior seat, I realized I didn't have my cell phone. Supreme said he would call me if he got any new information about Donnell, and plus, I always felt susceptible without my line of communication. "Devon, I forgot something. I'll be right back." I fidgeted with my keys, annoyed I had left my cell. I tried to remember where I had it last, and Supreme's office popped in my head.

When I entered the house it was eerily quiet. I called out Supreme's name but got no answer. I went to his office and the door was ajar. I peeped my head inside before walking in, but surprisingly he wasn't there. I noticed my cell on top of his desk right in front of the chair I was sitting in. I hurried in to retrieve it, and from the corner of my eye what looked to be a picture captured my attention. Only half of it was showing because it was under a bunch of papers that I assumed Supreme had been rummaging through earlier. I turned my head around to make sure no one was coming before going on the other side of the desk to be nosey.

The paperwork appeared to be an outline of different marketing proposals for some of his label's upcoming projects. It all seemed like unimportant bullshit until I laid eyes on the photos. There were about ten of them, and each contained a picture of the same individual. "Why in the hell does Supreme have all these pictures of Nico?" I asked myself out loud. They were obviously taken by a private investigator, and it had the date and time on each photo. "These were taken yesterday." I couldn't tell the location, but it seemed to be a major city. Some pictures had Nico coming out of a corner store, another him sitting down at a restaurant, a few more with him entering and leaving what might have been an apartment building. My heart dropped as I stared at the recent photos of Nico. His whereabouts were heavy on my mind, and here he was. Knowing this wasn't the time to start reminiscing, I put everything back where I found it, grabbed my phone and left out the house.

"Did you get what you needed?" Devon asked when I got back in the car.

"Yes, you can go."

"What's the first stop?"

"Head to Beverly Boulevard and drop me off at The Beverly Center."

I was completely puzzled as to why Supreme had photos of Nico, but I knew it added up to trouble. Supreme and I hadn't spoken about Nico in over a year, and to discover he had someone watching him sent my brain into overdrive.

I started delving deep within my memory to recall the last conversation I had with Supreme where Nico was the topic. The only thing I could recall was when I told him that I wasn't going to cooperate with the police on the attempted murder charge against Nico for shooting me. I took it too far for setting him up on a double murder charge, and his retaliation to take out my life made us even. Besides that, I explained that Nico was willing to take a bullet on my behalf when Nina tried to murder me, so now both our slates were clean. Supreme seemed to understand and even cosigned on my decision, but maybe that was a complete sham. Regardless, I had to speak with Nico and at least give him a heads up, but first I had to find him.

"We're here," Devon said, snapping me out of my thoughts as the car rested in front of the mammoth, eight-story behemoth of a building known as The Beverly Center. The shopping mall itself occupies only the upper three stories of the structure, but the lower five levels consisted of restaurants and other bullshit that tourists enjoy. I picked this spot because it was busy and nobody could really track my moves or hear my conversation. I would blend in with the other thousands of motherfuckers.

"I'll call you when I'm on my way out," I said, rushing out, not waiting for Devon to open my door or hear his reply.

I took the wavy Plexiglas tube escalators, which snake up the sides to the rooftop outdoor dining patio. When I sat down I clipped on my Bluetooth and got to dialing.

"What's good?" Ricky answered.

"What up, Ricky? It's me, Precious."

"I was waiting to hear from you. How did everything turn out with that information?"

"My husband's working on it. Hopefully we'll have some news soon, but I'm calling you about something else."

"I'm listening."

"I need you to locate someone for me. His name is Nico Carter."

"Nico... Nico Carter..." Ricky took a pregnant pause. "That's one of Brooklyn's finest."

"No doubt, and I need to find him, like yesterday."

"You don't wish him any harm, do you?" I could hear reluctance in Ricky's voice. "I mean, the way your husband, Supreme is a superstar to the world is what Nico is to Brooklyn. He hasn't walked these streets in a minute, but he's still a legend. I can't be a part of nothing to change that," he stated.

"I would never want you to. That's why I need you to find him for me. Nico and I go way back, and it's imperative that I speak with him."

"I got your word?"

"I don't even make promises, but you got my word. I promise it's nothing but love with Nico and I wish him no harm."

"Then I'm on it."

"Appreciate that, but Ricky, time is of the essence and I don't have any to spare."

"Then let me get off the phone," he said, and the line went dead.

Before I could take off my Bluetooth, my phone was popping again and I pushed the button to answer thinking it was Ricky calling right back.

"Hello?"

"Precious, where you at?"

I immediately recognized Supreme's voice. "At the Beverly Center. Why, what's up?"

"My people called and they about to make a move. I'm on my way over there."

"I'm on my way too."

"No, I want you to have Devon bring you back home and stay here until I call you."

"Supreme, I want to be there. I told you I don't want to be left out of the loop."

"You are in the loop. I called you didn't I? I could've went and not tell you shit. Now, we agreed to let me handle the situation my way. Come home and I'll call you right after the shit go down, okay?"

"You're right. I'm on my way home now. Call me as soon as you know something."

"I will. I love you."

"I love you too, baby. And Supreme, be careful."

"I will."

I yanked my purse off the table and practically did a speed leap downstairs. Between dodging and weaving through the mall crowd, I called Devon, "Be downstairs— now!" When the automatic doors opened, I couldn't get into the awaiting Bentley quick enough. "I need you to take me..."

"Home," Devon said, cutting me off mid-sentence before I could spit out the address.

"No, I'm not going home."

"That's where I'm taking you. Those are the instructions I received from Supreme."

"When did you talk to him?"

"I spoke to him right before you called telling me you were on your way downstairs."

I cringed knowing that after Supreme spoke to me he then called Devon because he didn't trust I would listen to him. Well, why not make a believer out of him?

"I don't care what my husband told you. Either take me where I want to go, or I'll find another means of transportation."

"Mrs. Mills, you're putting me in a very uncomfortable position. I work for your husband, and if I don't follow his instructions he'll fire me."

"How about this? I'm getting where I want to go whether you take me or not. If I have to get another ride and anything happens to me, you're getting fired regardless, or maybe something far worse. At least if you take me, you can always tell Supreme I threatened you and left you no choice, but you kept me safe. It's up to you, but you have five seconds to make up your mind because I have to go."

"It's your show," Devon said, making the wise decision to work with me instead of against me. With him deciding to step to my beat, I started believing having him as a driver might turn out to be an asset after all.

"Exactly! Let's go." After giving Devon the address, I felt an adrenaline rush as he headed to our destination. I wanted to get there before Supreme, but I knew that would be impossible. When he called me he was probably already en route.

The less than thirty minute ride had me twisting my hair and fidgeting with my hands until finally I unwrapped a piece of Juicy Fruit and chewed all the sweet sugar taste out. "Are we almost there?" I asked impatiently.

"Yes, but for the record, I understand why Supreme wanted you to go home. This area is not safe."

"Safe is defined by what environment you feel comfortable in. Sweetie, we in the hood and that's where I always feel the safest."

I glanced out of the shade on the back window. When the car came to a stop on Myrrhand and Willowbrook, I saw the Heritage House, an important landmark in the city of Compton. Compton was notorious for gang violence between the Bloods and the Crips.

As the Bentley continued to float down each street, the many pedestrians probably assumed one of the various hip hop stars who used to call this place home was shielded in the over quarter million dollar vehicle, taking a ride down memory lane.

As I quickly studied each passing face, it was funny how most thought Compton was predominately Black, but in actuality Latinos held the largest ethnic group in the city. This was just one of the many things I learned when I attended college for all of one semester. I did take pleasure in gaining knowledge, but I took more pleasure watching Aaliyah blossom.

Because I was trying to "better myself " by taking classes at the university, I missed out on precious mo- ments, and Anna was right there playing mommy. That's how she became so attached to Aaliyah, and when I noticed it getting out of hand I had to shut it down. I dropped out of school and decided I would go back when Aaliyah started preschool. School would always be right there, but you could never rewind the clock and make up for time lost with your child. Over the last few months since quitting school, my bond with Aaliyah had grown so strong. Now Mike had to come rip us apart. No doubt he would pay in blood.

"The house must be straight ahead, because it's off this street. What do you want me to do?" Devon said, pausing at the stop sign.

"Can you see the house from here?"

"No, I would need to drive further down."

"Cross this block and then stop at that corner before going any further." I didn't want Supreme or his people to see us, but I also needed to see what was going on.

I scanned the neighborhood watching for any suspicious activity, and couldn't help but notice the difference between Compton's supposed inner-city hood compared to where I grew up. My hood seemed as if it kept a dark gloomy cloud over it. Trash littered the streets. The building hallways reeked of piss and funk. There was no nature or greenery. Instead our feces-brown brick project buildings were reminiscent of a broken down prison. But in South Los Angeles, the yards were neatly situated on tree-lined streets. The houses looked clean and maintained, but any minute that would all change.

The sun was beginning to set and darkness was quickly upon us, and that's when hell erupted. To my surprise, the moment we crossed over the hell had already begun. "Stop!" I screamed to Devon, surprised the action was in full affect.

The light yellow house was directly facing the block in front of us, and from our spot we had a clear view of the action. It was like ten deep surrounding the house dressed in all black, with another three on the front porch. Without so much as a knock, one man kicked the red door down, and all the men swarmed in. A few moments later I saw Supreme, and he had two more men with him. I wondered where they all came from, because I didn't see one car that looked out of place parked anywhere in sight. After a few more minutes, Supreme and his men had vanished inside the house and I was itching to know what was doing down.

"What do you want to do next?" Devon asked as if the answer wasn't obvious.

"I want to sit here and see what the fuck is gonna happen. And don't say another word to me unless I ask you a question." I needed complete silence as I kept my eyes glued to the nondescript yellow house. I wondered if this was where Aaliyah had been since her kidnapping, and if finally Supreme would bring her home. "Who the fuck is that?" I asked out loud, but then quickly found an answer to my own question.

"I have no idea," Devon answered, not realizing I wasn't speaking to him but talking out loud to myself.

Instead of making him hip to it, I stayed focused on the black Denali that was being parked across the street from the house. A Hispanic lady who looked to be in her early twenties stepped out, and I knew it had to be Vernika.

"Yeah, walk up in that crib so Supreme and them can jack yo' stupid ass up too."

But then, homegirl wised up, because when she got closer to the crib she stopped dead in her tracks. Although the door was closed, either the kick-in it received made it look so fucked up it made her suspicious, or another clue was ringing the alarm in her head, something triggered a change of heart. She swiftly back stepped to her vehicle.

"Fuck that! Block that bitch."

"Excuse me?"

"Motherfucker, you heard me. Block that bitch before she can drive past the corner. Hurry up."

Devon reluctantly drove the car up the block until we came to the street that was off to the right.

"Drive a little further up and stop."

"You want me to stop in the middle of the street?" he asked, sounding surprised.

"Now you get it, Sherlock. Now put this shit in park and we gon' wait this ho out." The blinds in the back were still down so I couldn't see her truck driving forward, but I damn sure heard it when she started blowing the horn. "Is she looking at you?" I asked Devon, who had a clear angle from the front seat.

"Yes, and since I'm good at reading lips she's also cussing me out."

"Good. Put up your finger as if you're telling her to wait a minute." I watched as Devon did as told. And like I figured, she kept blowing her horn until she got so fed up she jumped out of the car, speaking fast in her native tongue. The only word I could decipher was papi. Her voice became louder and louder until she walked right up to the car. I snuck a peek out the blind, and she was twisting her neck and waving her arms being real extra with it, still speaking that damn Spanish.

Finally when it dawned on her that the shit she was spitting was getting lost in translation, she opted for English. "You need to move your fuckin' car. You can't block the street like this. Who do you think you are?"

"I'm Precious, bitch!" I said, jumping out the back seat as the door flew open. I caught her so off guard that while she continued to run off at the mouth, I was wrapping her hair around my hand and slamming that ass to the ground. "I know you the trick that kidnapped my daughter for Mike, and yo' foul ass gon' tell me where she's at."

"I ain't telling you shit!" she belted, reaching her claws up and scratching the left underside of my face. Her nails cut so deeply in my skin that she drew blood. The excruciating pain caused a reflex, and I let go of Vernika's hair to press down on the stinging from my face. She used that as an opportunity to get the upper hand and kneed me in the stomach. I hadn't had a straight- up street fight in so long, and this thickly built fool was about to whip my ass if I didn't get my game intact.

Wanting to take full advantage of my distress, she quickly got from under me and stood up and looked to be reaching in her back pocket. I forgot about the pain from my scratches, and lying flat down on the concrete I kicked my right foot straight between her legs and the pointed heel on my shoe penetrated her camel toe. She screamed so loud, I knew I would hear sirens any minute. While she bent over holding her coochie area, I ran up behind her. I put one hand around the back of her neck while firmly gripping her hair with the other, and slammed her against the car.

"Where is my daughter? You ain't nothing but a worthless piece of shit who don't even deserve to live, but if you tell me where my daughter is, I'll let you see another day." By now the tears were flowing out and she sounded like she was about to start hyperventilating. I slammed her head against the window, wanting her to understand that more pain would follow if she didn't cooperate.

"I'll tell you where Mike is and where he has your daughter stashed. Just please let go of my hair and neck before I pass out."

Vernika did seem beat down, so I eased up on my grip slowly to see how she'd react.

"I need to catch my breath."

I completely let go, and she turned to face me, inhaling and exhaling as if defeated. There was a gash on the top of her forehead from when I slammed it against the car, blood was trickling down her face, and there were also traces of blood coming from her vagina area where I kicked the shit out of it. I just knew this chick didn't have any fight left in her, until her eyes locked with mine and she charged at me like a raging bull with hands swinging. As I was backing away from her, my heel stepped on a rock and caused me to trip and fall down. I felt nothing but hips and ass tumbling, pinning me to the ground. I extended my hand out reaching for a rock to knock her on her head, but there would be no need. Her blood-drenched torso flopped on top of me.

"What the fuck happened?" I asked out loud, struggling to move her dead weight off of me. When my view cleared, I saw Devon standing in front of me with a gun that had a silencer on it in his hand. "Why in the hell did you kill her? I wanted her alive. She has information about my daughter that I need!"

"I saw her on top of you and I thought she was going to kill you. I was trying to protect you. I'm sorry."

"Fuck! Fuck! Fuck!" I said over and over again.

Trying to make the most of a bad situation, I ran to her truck, grabbed a napkin that was on the dashboard and used it while rummaging through her shit trying to find any clue about Aaliyah. There wasn't a trace, so I snatched her purse from the passenger seat, wiped down the driver side door handle and ran back to the Maybach. "Drive! We need to get the fuck outta here." I glared back at Vernika's lifeless body then her truck, hoping I didn't leave any traces of my fingerprints. I stared at the yellow house that Supreme and his men still hadn't come out of. It was as if nobody lived on the dead silent street... or maybe nobody gave a fuck.

TRUTH BE TOLD

When I got home I ran upstairs and locked my bedroom door. I stared up at the skylights trying to figure out how this shit got so fucked up. The stars seemed to be shining extra bright in the dark sky, and I was tempted to make a wish, but little girls from the hood learn early on that it is nothing but a waste of time. I wanted so much more for Aaliyah than I had for myself, but after what happened tonight, hope was leaving my body and hopelessness was taking its place.

I got off the bed and went to the bathroom. Standing in front of the mirror, I rubbed my fingers over the scratches Vernika left on my face. They were battle scars I was willing to take for Aaliyah, but I was still no closer to finding her. I wanted to believe that Supreme had better luck inside that house, but my gut told me it wasn't so. Mike was holding all the cards, and the fact that he believed that Aaliyah was his daughter was the only thing that gave me solace.

I stripped out of my clothes and took a quick shower, hoping that Supreme would be home by the time I got out. He still hadn't called me, so I had no idea what type of moves he was making. I figured Devon had reached out to him, giving the lowdown on what happened to save his own ass. Supreme would be livid that I hadn't gone home from the jump like he requested. All that and a million more things ran through my mind as I dried myself off, gathered my hair on top of my head, threw on a tank top with matching boy shorts and headed downstairs.

To my relief, Supreme was home, apparent by the yelling coming from out of his office. At first I thought someone else was with him, but the door was wide open and all I saw was him screaming on the phone. The harshness from his voice dragged my body closer until his words smacked me in my face. "Aaliyah is my daughter, and not one strand of her hair better be out of place when I get her back, or I will make sure that each time you're on the brink of death, I'll bring you back to life and kill you all over again, you sadistic fuck!" Supreme said, and slammed down the phone.

"Tell me that wasn't Mike," I said softly.

"Yeah it was that motherfucker. He had the balls to call me on my fuckin' office phone taunting me and shit. That sick bastard even said he was Aaliyah's father, and I was mourning for a child that wasn't even mine."

"Why did you have to tell him otherwise?"

"Have you bumped your fuckin' head? 'Cause you got me confused."

"Why couldn't you let him believe Aaliyah is his daughter?"

"You're officially crazy. What, you smokin' crack? You can't possibly be asking me that dumb-ass question with a straight face."

"Are you so fuckin' egotistical that you don't get it? The only reason Aaliyah is still alive is because Mike believes there's a chance she's his daughter."

"Are you telling me that you was spoon feeding this bullshit to that nigga, letting him believe that my daughter was his... is that what you're telling me?" Supreme was stomping towards me with his finger pointed towards my forehead.

"I would do anything to protect my daughter. I didn't have a choice."

"Oh, *your* daughter. I'm so sick of hearing that fuckin' shit come out of your foul ass mouth. She ain't just your daughter, she's my daughter too, right? Right? Or can't you answer that?" Before I could respond, Supreme had his entire hand spread across my neck and he had me pinned up against the mahogany bookcase that lined the wall.

"Supreme, of course Aaliyah is your daughter. I was only trying to protect her." And I was, and now I was trying to protect myself. Supreme knew I was raped by Mike, but I told him I was able to get him off of me before he got off in me. Did Supreme believe me when I said there was only brief penetration, and that it wasn't possible that he emptied his venomous seed in me? I had no idea, but I refused to consider that a baby so sacred to me could be the product of one of Satan's disciples.

But I never told Supreme about the night I shared with Nico. At the time, I thought he was dead and I felt completely alone. When Supreme came back to me, I decided that what happened between me and Nico needed to stay in the past. Never did I think I would end up pregnant so soon. I prayed that the child I was carrying belonged to my husband, although I was never a hundred percent sure. The only thing I was sure of was that after losing my first child, I wasn't going to have an abortion and kill the second. I loved Supreme with all my heart, but I loved and wanted the baby inside of me even more, so I was willing to roll the dice and take my chances.

"Don't lie to me."

"Baby, don't let Mike do this to us. You know Aaliyah is your daughter... she's our daughter."

Supreme fixated on my eyes as if the truth was buried somewhere deep within. He wrestled to see if there was any hesitation with my response. I mustered up my sincerest gaze, hoping to Jedi-mind-trick my own husband.

"What happened to your face?" he asked, rubbing the scratches, which seemed to snap him out of his outburst.

"It's a long story."

"I have time."

"How about this: If you move your hand from around my throat, I'll tell you what happened."

"I'm sorry, I didn't mean to hurt you." Supreme released me from his grip and placed a gentle kiss on my lips.

"I know, it's all Mike's fault. He has us both losing our cool. I can't believe he had the nerve to call you."

"He probably already got word that we got his man, Donnell."

"When you say 'got him', does that mean he is dead or alive?"

"He's alive. My people have him stashed up in one of my spots. But he ain't telling us shit. I want the nigga dead, but he's our only link to Mike right now. I wanted the chick, Vernika, because it would've probably been easier to break her, but when we came outside she was dead in the middle of the fuckin' street. We had to haul ass out of there because we could hear the police sirens coming."

"Did you see any indication that Aaliyah had been there?"

"Nope, and we ransacked the joint from top to bottom. But I definitely think that nigga, Donnell knows where the fuck Mike is keeping her. He's riding the shit out hard though. My men beat the shit out of him, but still nothing. I want to know who killed homegirl though. That bullshit can't be no coincidence."

"I guess you haven't spoken to Devon yet?"

"Nah, my cell went dead and I haven't had a chance to call him. Why, did something happen?"

"You know when you asked me about my scratches?"

"Oh, I know that motherfucker ain't responsible for that shit!" Supreme was getting cranked up again, and I had to calm him down before he got out of control.

"Hell no! Vernika did it."

Supreme put his head down and started shaking it from side to side.

"Yo, you so fuckin' hard headed. I told you to go home. You murdered that chick?"

"No. I had Devon take me to the house. I wanted to see what was going on. We were parked on a side street and I saw Vernika pulling up in her Denali. She must've figured out that something was wrong, because she got out the truck and then turned around and got right back inside. I couldn't let her bounce like that, so I made Devon block her car."

"I can't believe you're telling me this shit. We needed her alive."

"I know. It wasn't my intention for her to end up dead."

"So what the fuck happened?"

"She got out of her truck cursing out Devon, and when she got to the car window I got out and we started fighting. I only wanted to beat information about Aaliyah out of her, but then Devon ended up shooting her."

"Devon killed her? Why?"

"She jumped on top of me and her back was facing his. He thought she was going to use the weapon she had in her back pocket to kill me, so Devon killed her first."

"This bullshit was going on while we were sitting up in that fuckin' house? Why didn't you call me when you saw her car pull up? My men could've handled it."

"It all happened so fast, I didn't have time to think it out. All I knew was that I couldn't let her leave because she was a link to Aaliyah."

"Now that link is dead, and the other link wanna be a soldier and not tell us shit. What a fucked up operation this turned out to be. I'm grateful that Devon saved your life, but I can't believe he murdered that girl. What type of weapon was she packing?"

"I think it was a knife, but honestly I don't know. When we first started fighting she was reaching in her back pocket for something, but I didn't give her a chance to let me see what it was. Devon probably panicked and decided to shoot to kill. He probably figured you would be pissed at him for even taking me to the house, and if anything happened to me you would have him dealt with. So don't be too hard on him. Honestly, I'm glad he was there."

"He's still going to be dealt with. If he had followed my instructions and brought you home none of this would've went down."

"Supreme, it wasn't his fault. I didn't give him a choice. It was basically either you take me or I'll find another way."

"If it's that difficult for him, then he don't need to be driving you around. I'll find a more suitable duty for him to tend to. Damn, Precious, this shit is out of control." Supreme fell back on the coffee-brown leather couch and put his hands behind his neck.

My eyes darted over to a picture of me, him and Aaliyah that was placed on top of his desk. The smile on his face was in complete contrast to the conquered frown on his face right now. I walked over and sat down next to him on the couch. I put my hand on his upper leg and his body felt so tense.

"Baby, I'm sorry I didn't listen to you. I'm sorry for many things. I know things are out of control right now, but we will get our daughter back."

"I want to believe that too, but shit keeps falling apart. Every time I think we're making gain, we end up having to take a leap back."

"I know what you mean. But we have to keep the faith. You know I'm not the one to call on God and be the religious type, but times like this I think it's the only way you can cope. Ms. Duncan, the lady who used to babysit me when I was a little girl, would always say if God takes you to it, He'll take you through it. Back then those words were idle chatter, but at this moment they mean so much more."

"I hear you, Precious," Supreme said, standing up. "But when you're dealing with scum like Pretty Boy Mike, the only way to get through it is with ammunition. The way Ms. Duncan schooled you, my pops spit his knowledge to me, and he said it's better to be judged by twelve then carried by six. This right here comes down to Mike's life, or me and my family's life. I rather be facing time for ending his life than take a chance on it being the other way around."

"I feel you on that and you know I'm down for whatever, but..." I stopped mid-sentence as our conversation came to a halt by a knock on the door.

"Sorry, to interrupt boss, but Clip is here."

"Send him back."

"What is Clip doing here?"

"I told him to come over."

"You found out something? Is he involved?" I stood up ready to jump on Clip when he came swaggering through the door.

"Chill, sit back down and let me handle this."

"Supreme, what's up, my man?" Clip said giving Supreme a handshake. "Precious," he nodded his head shyly, knowing I wasn't fucking with him because of that Destiny shit. He had no clue I was also suspecting he was being a soldier boy for Mike.

"Maintaining," Supreme countered.

"I've been trying to get in touch with you. I was starting to think you had pushed my album back or was dropping me from the label." He tried to joke but you could hear the panic.

"Why would I do that?"

Clip then slanted his eyes in my direction trying to get my vibe, but I gave him no rhythm. "Well, I'm sure you heard about what went down with me and Maya a few days ago. It was a huge misunderstanding, but I know she's close to your family."

"Yeah she is, but so are you."

"I appreciate that, because you like a brother to me."

"You're like a brother to me too, that's why I wanted to include you in on what's going down right now. But of course this has to stay between us."

"No doubt. It won't leave this room."

"I think we might have made some headway with getting Aaliyah back."

"Word? That's what's up! The police got a suspect?"

"Yeah, it's Mike."

"Oh shit, he did take Aaliyah! We all heard he escaped from jail, but I was hoping he didn't go out like that. I can't believe that motherfucker would kidnap a child. Un-fuckin' believable," Clip's voice trailed off. "So, what's the cops' next move?"

"I'm not sitting around waiting on their next move. I'm making my own moves."

"I know that's right. If it was my seed I'd be doing the exact same shit. You need me to help you out in any way?"

"I know you used to do some shit for Mike in the drug game. Did he ever mention a dude by the name of Donnell Graham?"

Clip stood quiet for a few moments as if pondering hard over Supreme's question. "Nope, that name don't sound familiar. Does he go by a nickname?"

"If so, I don't know it."

"Why, what that kid got to do with anything?"

"He's the one that helped Mike break out of jail, and I also believe he assisted with the kidnapping of my daughter."

"Why you think that?"

"'Cause they were locked up together until Donnell got released a few months ago."

"That would make sense. So you got any leads on how to track this Donnell cat down? From what you saying, he seems to be that link you need."

"As a matter of fact, I got my people holding him now."

"Word? You got dude on lock?"

"Yeah, but he ain't cooperating. I was hoping that if you knew anything about him I could use the information against him. You know, like if you knew where his family or kids laid their heads at. You know something to motivate him to start singing about Mike."

"I wish I could help you, but dude's name don't sound familiar."

"You know that apartment I got over there in West Hollywood that I sometimes let artist stay at?"

"Yeah, yeah, yeah, I've been to that spot a few times."

"Well, that's where I got Donnell stashed out. I got a couple of men over there watching him. I'ma keep him on lock for a few more days hoping he'll crack. I know you still got connects in the drug game, so I would appreciate if you could make some calls and see if you can come up with anything on that nigga."

"I'm on it. Whatever you need, you my brother, and anybody that would kidnap a baby belong in a jail cell or six feet under. So if I can help bring that nigga, Mike down, then so be it."

Clip was putting on his best "I'm down for the cause" voice. Looking at that pretty motherfucker made me have a throwback Christopher Williams moment, only an updated new millennium version.

"I thought it was your voice I heard. What are you doing here?" Maya questioned, catching us all off guard as she pushed her way through the door. She stood with her arms crossed, giving Clip the head-to-toe stare down.

"Maya, I came to speak to Supreme, that's all," Clip explained, looking uncomfortable. "Speak to Supreme about what?"

"That's between me and Supreme, no disrespect."

"I already told Supreme about that foul ass shit you did with Destiny, so you late."

"That's not what I was discussing with him, and if you would pick up the phone and talk to me, you'd know that nothing happened between me and Destiny."

"First of all, you have called me once in the last, what, four or five days? And furthermore, I can't believe you still rolling with that same whack-ass story."

"Look, I'm not about to get into this with you in front of Supreme and Precious. They have real problems," Clip said emphatically. "This shit you beefing about is petty."

"Petty? Would this shit be petty to you if you had came home and found me butt-ass naked in bed with another nigga? Nah, so don't stand there and say this shit is petty. Yo' monkey ass is petty."

"Supreme, Precious, I'm sorry the two of you have to be caught in the middle of this. If I find out anything I'll let you, but, umm, I need to be going." Clip had embarrassed stamped on his face.

"Don't apologize to them, you was just telling Supreme that he was like a brother to you. Well, that's what family do, get in the middle of bullshit."

"It's not a problem, Clip," Supreme said.

"Thanks, but I'll definitely look into that for you. And of course I'm keeping Aaliyah in my prayers."

Maya continued to frown up her face as Clip brushed past her to leave. With her frustration getting the best of her, she turned around to catch up with Clip before he left.

"That was an interesting performance. Now clue me in on what it was about," I said to Supreme. I knew there had to be a reasonable explanation for all that schmoozing he did with Clip.

"I still don't believe Clip is helping Mike, but if I'm wrong, this will prove it once and for all."

"How is that?"

"Mike knows that I have Donnell and he's gonna want to cut him loose. If Clip thinks he knows where Donnell is, then he'll tell Mike, and of course they'll come looking for him."

"Do you really want to take that chance of them actually being able to get to Donnell?"

"I'm not crazy. I didn't give Clip the right location. If some people run up on that apartment in West Hollywood, they won't find Donnell and I'll know the only person responsible for leaking the information is Clip."

"That's true."

"Not only do I have a lot of money invested in Clip, I also got a lot of love for him. I'm praying that when he said I'm like a brother to him he meant that shit. But I don't have time to waste. I need to know now if he's loyal."

"Hipping him to the Donnell shit was a good look. If he is in cahoots with Mike, then this setup will let us know. But, um, dealing with all this bullshit today has made me tired. I'm calling it a night."

"Yeah, fighting in the street will do that to you."

"Funny. Are you coming up?"

"I have some calls to make. I'll be up when I'm done."

"Okay." I walked over and gave Supreme a kiss goodnight and headed upstairs. I knocked on Maya's bedroom door before going to my room, but she wasn't there. I figured she must be outside having it out with Clip. That's what your first love will have you doing—trying to fix some shit that you know is fucking broke.

When I got to my room, I checked my cell phone and saw that Ricky had called a few times. I hit him right back, anxious to hear what was up.

"You hard to reach," Ricky said, answering his phone.

"Sorry 'bout that. I had a crazy night."

"Well, it's about to get crazier."

"What you mean?"

"I took your word when you said that you didn't want to bring Nico any harm."

"It's the truth. I put that on everything."

"So that means you have no idea nor are you playing any part in what your husband is up to?" There was a long period of silence on the line before Ricky proceeded. "I need you to be straight up with me, Precious, if you want me to continue to help you out."

"Earlier today I did come across some photos of Nico in Supreme's office. It looked as if they were taken by a private investigator. It got me a little worried, like maybe Nico could be in trouble. I wanted to get in touch with him, you know, give him a warning. But then I could've been jumping the gun and making something out of nothing."

"No, your first instinct to think there was trouble is correct. It hasn't spread through the streets because Supreme is doing an excellent job of keeping the information on the low, but a reliable source told me that your husband wants Nico dead."

"What? Why?"

"I was hoping you could tell me."

"Does Nico know?"

"I doubt it. Word is, it was supposed to happen a couple of weeks ago, but when your daughter got kidnapped Supreme put on the brakes, but told his people to keep close tabs on Nico."

"Do you know where Nico is?"

"He's supposed to be in Chicago, but from what I understand he'll be in New York tomorrow."

"For how long?"

"I'm not sure. But I'm hearing that he comes to New York often. It's just that he keeps a real low profile. Only a few people know when he stops through."

"I'll be there tomorrow." The words flowed out my mouth so fast I didn't give myself time to think about how I would make it happen, but I just knew I would. "Is there anyway you can follow Nico so when I get there you can take me right to him?"

"I'm already on it."

"Good, because I'm coming in and flying right back out. Do you know what time he's arriving?"

"They say he's taking a flight from Chicago first thing in the morning, arriving at JFK."

"Alright, so I'll be there early afternoon. I'll call you when I arrive."

"I'll talk to you then."

When I hung up with Ricky, my stomach was doing somersaults. I couldn't believe Supreme was plotting Nico's murder, or why. Was it payback for him shooting me? I was so over that, but maybe Supreme wasn't. Or did Supreme find out that I slept with Nico when I thought he was dead? But I didn't tell anybody about that night. Whatever the reason was, as much as I loved Supreme, I couldn't let him kill Nico— period.

I got back on the phone and made a flight reservation for the first thing smoking in the morning. A six-forty-five a.m. flight was the earliest one available and I took it.

While I thought about the excuse I would give Supreme for having to leave so early in the morning and then not coming back home until the middle of the night, I began on my search through Vernika's purse. She had some tampons, lotion, lipstick and other random bullshit that females keep in their possession. I wasn't coming across anything worth my while. As I was about to go through her wallet, I almost fell off the bed when Supreme caught me off guard, "Hey, baby, you startled me. I thought you were going to be downstairs for a minute making phone calls."

"Me too, but some shit can't be handled on the phone."

"What's wrong?"

"I have to go to the studio. They having some major problems I have to iron out."

"You're going over there now?'

"No because the engineer has another session that he has to wrap up. I'm tired as hell, so I'ma lay down for a couple of hours and get some rest, then head over because I know we won't get done until the sun come up."

While Supreme took off his clothes, I discreetly tossed Vernika's purse under the bed. I doubted seriously that I would find any relevant information in her purse, but I didn't want to share with Supreme until I knew for sure.

"Oh, baby, I was checking my messages and I totally forgot that Ms. Duncan had told me she would be coming to LA tomorrow."

"Who?"

"Ms. Duncan. You remember, the lady I told you about who used to babysit me when I was a little girl. She's basically the only family I have. She put my mother's funeral together for me."

"Oh yeah, I think I do remember you mentioning her a few times. Why is she coming to LA?"

"They're having some huge church seminar here and she's attending. She's very religious. When I told her about Aaliyah, she suggested I join her. It slipped my mind until I listened to her message and she gave me her flight information."

"You're going to the church seminar with her?" Supreme asked, not hiding his surprise.

"I know that's not really my thing, but I think it'll be good for me, you know, with everything going on."

"That's cool. I think you should go. What time do you have to pick her up from the airport? I'll have one of the security men take you and stay with you at the seminar."

"Baby, please don't have me take security."

"What are talking about? You need security."

"I'm going to church, Supreme. I'll be safe there. Plus, Ms. Duncan is older. Having security with us might give the poor woman a heart attack. I promise I'll call you frequently so you'll know I'm safe."

"You better."

"I will, but only if you hold me until I fall asleep," I whispered in his ear.

"Oh, I was doing that anyway."

I laid my head on Supreme's chest and wrapped my legs between his legs. My body felt so safe with his muscular arms cradling me. I did love my husband, but I didn't trust him, and I had a feeling that he didn't trust me either.

FIRST LOVE

When I landed at JFK, the first call I made was to my husband. It was noon in LA, and I needed to call him before he even had an opportunity to start worrying about me. The studio situation worked out perfectly for me. When I woke up, Supreme was gone. Since I wasn't taking any luggage, all I had to do was quickly get dressed and get my ass to the airport. Now that I landed in NYC safely, making sure home was straight was first on the agenda.

"Hey, baby, I was just checking in," I said in my most innocent voice possible, which was a stretch since everyone knew there was nothing remotely innocent about me.

"How's everything?"

"Good. Her flight got in really early so I'm beat. But it's wonderful seeing Ms. Duncan. We finished eating a little while ago, and now we're heading to the seminar. How's it going with you?"

"I'm just now getting out the studio. I'm on my way home to handle a few things, get some sleep, then I have to come back. Dealing with the Aaliyah situation made me cut everybody off, and instead of them motherfuckers holding shit together it's all fucked up. Even Clip's shit ain't right, and that shit was due a minute ago. So much is fucked up, but I have to fix it and be done with it."

"Don't get too stressed."

"I'm past that."

"What time will you be home so I can wait up for you?" I asked, checking his schedule so I could know how much time I was playing with. While playing my position with Supreme on the phone, I was making my way outside to where Ricky was waiting for me. He was in a black Lincoln, and I put my finger over my mouth to let him know to be quiet when I got in the car. I didn't want to give Supreme any reason to get wary about the lines I was kicking.

"As much as I would love to hold you like I did last night, don't wait up for me. You'll be in a deep sleep by the time I get home."

"Damn, I'm missing you already. But I have to go. Ms. Duncan is waiting for me. If you see Maya when you get home, tell her I'll call her later on. I didn't have a chance to talk to her before I left this morning."

"I will. Be safe and make sure you call me later on to let me know you're good."

"Will do. I love you."

"Love you too."

I flipped my phone closed, happy I made it through round one of the check in.

"I see that you're a veteran liar," Ricky said, smiling at me through the rear view mirror.

"You call it lying, I call it survival tactics."

"Point made."

"Tell me you know exactly where Nico is, because I have no time to waste. My flight leaves at eight-fifty-five. That gives me roughly five hours to get this shit done."

"I know you're on a tight schedule and I got you," Ricky reassured me as he exited the airport, taking the left ramp onto the Van Wyck Expressway. "Nico must be awfully special for you to come all this way to speak with him for a couple of hours."

"Are you expecting me to comment on that statement?"

"I was simply making an observation."

"Like I told you, Nico and I have a long history together. He's also my first love."

"Those are pretty hard to shake. I still have a soft spot for my first love."

I couldn't help but laugh thinking about a suave older cat like Ricky pining over his first love. "You're right, but I'm in love with my husband and we're going through enough. I don't need anymore bullshit to add to the plate."

"So why are you interfering in what your husband has planned for Nico? Why not stay out of it and let the cards fall where they may?"

"I owe Nico. He risked his life for me one time."

"He also tried to take it," Ricky reminded me as if I'd forgotten.

"So you heard about that rumor."

"I did some research when you asked me to track him down. I heard originally you accused Nico, but then somewhere down the line you recanted your story and the charges were dropped against him. That right there tells me there is a lot of history, but I won't ask you to dig out none of your skeletons."

"As if I would tell. I'll leave it up to you to use your own imagination putting the pieces of that puzzle together. The only thing I will confirm is that if I can keep Nico alive, then I will, even if it means being disloyal to my husband."

For the rest of the drive there was silence between Ricky and me. I didn't know what was on his mind, but mine was on Nico. I hadn't seen him in so long, and I didn't know how much had changed in his life. The last time we saw each other he was on the run, and I was tracking Supreme's killer. Fast forward: and not only do I have a child, but my husband is very much alive and apparently wants Nico dead. The last part I'm having difficulty trying to comprehend.

I glanced out the window and noticed Ricky turning onto Avenue of the Americas. He then pulled up in front of the Tribeca Grand Hotel. I was stunned that we were stopping in Tribeca, which was located in lower Manhattan. "Why are we stopping here, Ricky? What, you dropping some drugs off for some rich white man?" I said like I was joking but was very serious.

"No, this is where Nico is staying."

"Excuse me? Why the fuck would Nico be staying between the sectors of high finance and high fashion? Although he likes money and clothes, this neighborhood don't reflect Brooklyn or the type of people he would enjoy chilling with." The moment the words left my mouth, the answer became evident. "That's the exact reason he is staying here. He doesn't have to worry about seeing nobody from BK. He can make his moves on the low without bringing attention to himself."

"Exactly. From what I understand, every time he comes to New York, this is the only hotel he stays at."

"This place costs a pretty penny. I guess business has picked back up for him."

"No doubt. You know Nico was always a major player. Once he got word that all charges had been dropped against him, the streets were his again. But from what I hear, he keeps his moves a lot more discreet now. After what went down with Ritchie, he doesn't trust anybody. No more partners, He's strictly solo."

Hearing the name Ritchie made all the foul shit that went down flash through my head. That nigga was a straight snake. He had no qualms about fucking me or fucking over Nico, and it wasn't because he had an axe to grind like I did. He was just a weak jealous cat. He couldn't stand the respect that Brooklyn and the surrounding boroughs had for Nico. If that nigga said, "Stand up," then that's what BK was doing. I felt no guilt that I was responsible for Nico snuffing Ritchie out, because if he hadn't, it would've ended up the other way around.

"That's the best way to move. I'm glad Nico is back on the comeup. The more I think about it, it ain't strange that he picked this spot to rest his head at. On our first date he took me to this joint called Butter. The place was sexy, and it was full of white model-type looking motherfuckers. Shit, this nigga the one who hipped me to Rodeo Drive." Those memories brought a smile to my face.

"Nico always moved in style. He's one of the few younger cats in the game I have respect for. He's a good dude, real diplomatic when it comes to conducting business."

"Yeah, we can trade stories about Nico all day, but the clock is ticking. So, do you know what room he's in?"

"It's the top floor, The Grand Suite. Let me write down the room number."

"Damn, he really is doing it big. Are you sure he's there?"

"I told my man to hit me if he bounced, and I haven't got a call, so yeah, he's there."

"Cool. So are you gonna wait down here for me?"

"How long do you think you'll be?"

"Maybe an hour or so."

"Take your time. Just hit me when you're done. I'll be in the neighborhood. But remember you have a flight to catch."

"No need to remind me. I can't miss that flight," I said, thinking about all the over-the-top lies I would have to come up with to appease Supreme.

When I entered the hotel, the soaring central atrium opened up to a fleet of luxurious guestrooms, a sexy lounge, and a polished cocktail bar with an adjoining restaurant. I was tempted to take a detour to the bar, but reminded myself that time wasn't on my side.

As I made my way closer to Nico's room, not knowing what his reaction would be to seeing me again had me a little nervous. When I got to the door I put my ear against it to see if he had company. I heard what sounded like a television, but that was it. I knocked and waited for a few, but got nothing. I knocked again, this time harder, and heard movement. I could hear who I assumed was Nico at the door and I figured he was looking out the peephole to get a visual, but I was standing to the side so he couldn't see me.

"Who is it?"

I instantly recognized Nico's voice. "It's me, Precious." He opened the door, and just like that the nervousness vanished and a sense of comfort took its place.

"I can't believe you're here! How did you find me?"

"Do I have to explain in the hallway, or can I come inside?"

"My fault, please come in. But first, you have to show me some love." Nico held his arms open, and I welcomed the embrace. His hold had the same spellbinding effect it did the last time I felt him, as did his intoxicating scent.

After closing the door, he took my hand and led me to the spacious, slick, minimalist-inspired haven. The soothing natural colors and rich textures were showcased the moment you stepped on the soft wool carpeting. It was fitted to be chic, but with maximum comfort. The stunning panoramic views of New York and beyond were the icing on the already delectable cake.

After sizing up the ambiance of the room, I focused my attention on the scenery before me. Nico still captured the essence of a true G. His flawless mahogany skin was no longer highlighted by the cornrows he had grown last time I saw him. It was back to a low cut, full of jet-black curls. His six-two frame was solid, and his full lips were still decorated with a set of perfect white teeth. He was as fine as the day he swooped me up on 125th Street in Harlem years ago. "It's been too long, Nico."

"It sure has, baby girl. You're the last person I thought would be knocking at my door. You haven't yet told me how you found me."

"I hired someone to track you down."

"Interesting. What is so important for me to know that you felt the need to track me down? Before you answer that, how 'bout we go to the rooftop terrace and have a drink?"

"I would love that, I really would, but I have a flight to catch."

"Leaving so soon?"

"Yeah, I have to get back to LA."

"I can't lie. I was surprised when I heard you were living in Beverly Hills. Do you remember the first time I took you to Rodeo Drive? I'll never forget the smile on your face when you realized a street like that existed. I loved how everything was new to you back then. You were like a little girl discovering a whole other world."

"It's funny you mention that, because right before I came up here I reminisced about the very same thing."

"You're no longer that little girl, but then again, you never really were. I bet you don't remember what I said to you that night on our first date when we went to the park."

"Yes I do. I've never forgotten."

"I don't believe you. Tell me."

"You said I had the same darkness in my eyes as you, and you never met a woman or a man besides your father that had that look."

"I was wrong, you do remember. But that was a lifetime ago. I know you have a flight to catch, so tell me what brings you back to NYC," he said, changing the subject.

Nico sat down on a chair and I took a seat on the couch across from him. I paused, trying to find the right words to use, but there was no easy way to say that someone wanted you dead. "There's no correct way to say this, but someone wants you dead and I came to warn you."

Nico sat quiet for a few minutes, and his demeanor remained intact. He was taking the news surprisingly well. "When you say someone wants me dead, do you mean there's a ransom on my head?"

"I wouldn't say a ransom. It's more like the person hired someone to take you out. It's was supposed to be done a few weeks ago, but some shit came up and it was postponed. I want you to be careful, watch your back because I don't know when they'll be given the green light to strike."

"Are you going to tell me who it is? 'Cause obviously you know."

"Honestly, I prefer not to. It's not like the person is going to do it themselves, so you need to watch out for anybody or anything that seems suspicious. I know it might seem like I'm not giving you enough but..."

"No, you're actually telling me a lot," he said, cutting me off. "You're telling me that you still care a great deal about me, because I know you're going through a very difficult time right now. Your daughter has been kidnapped, but you managed to squeeze in a flight to NYC to give me a heads up."

"I guess the whole world knows about Aaliyah."

"Yeah, your husband is extremely high profile. I know you must have had to go through a great deal of maneuvering to make this trip happen without him finding out. But you've always been good at maneuvering— make that scheming."

"I don't know if I should take that as a compliment or be offended."

"How about we call you resourceful, which is a good thing. I do appreciate the information and I'll do some asking around. I'm sure once that happens I'll find out who it is you're protecting."

"I'm not protecting anybody. I don't want you dead, that's all. Can't we leave it at that?"

"Out of respect for you, I'll leave it alone. I want to ask you about something much more important anyway."

"What?"

"I know you heard that Mike escaped from prison. Is he the one that kidnapped your daughter?"

"How did you know?"

"I didn't, but you have now confirmed it for me. I can't believe that nigga would do something that foul. That was never his style. Shit has really changed. But then again, I never thought it would be his style to rape you. When I read about that in the paper I wanted to show up at his trial and slice him open myself."

"I had a tough time dealing with that, but Supreme helped me through it. He was so good to me."

"I'm glad to hear that, although I wish I could've been there for you too, or better yet, been there to protect you from Mike. How did you find out it was him who kidnapped your daughter?"

"He called and bragged about it. He's a sick fuck. I guess he hasn't been in touch with you."

"Hell no! That nigga knows not to bring that bullshit my way. He would definitely be carried out in a body bag. I'd lullaby that nigga like he had snatched my own seed. The police don't have any leads?"

"Barely. You know how whack the cops can be. Supreme's working on a couple of leads, but the shit is moving so damn slow. I want my daughter home. It's killing me that she's with that fuckin' monster."

"If I find out anything that will help, you know I'll let you know."

"I know you will. We've been through some real live bullshit, but you've always been good people. That's why I'm happy to see you're still maintaining," I said, nodding my head in approval over the digs he was staying in.

"I'm making a few moves on the streets and business investments at the same time. I gotta try and hustle this game before it hustles me. I'm lucky to get a second chance, so I'm trying to make the most of it. I've learned a lot."

"What have you learned?" I was curious to know, since Nico always seemed on top of his game for the most part.

"How the drug game should be a Fortune 500 company. It's crazy how white men move way more drugs than us, but we're the ones that always get snatched up and locked down. It's set up that niggas on the bottom of the totem pole and the ones at the very top always get popped. The game is fixed so that you can only reach a certain level and your time is up. A big factor in that is the access white men have to money laundering. They have the type of relationships and connections to have their shit so clean it's damn near impossible to take them down. All a nigga can do is get a barber shop, beauty and nail salon, invest in some real estate properties, or try to open a car dealership. You can't legitimize hundreds of millions of dollars with that type of bullshit. We can't even buy paintings worth millions of dollars without every federal agency in the world knocking on our doors."

"I never thought about that before."

"You have no reason to. Supreme's making legitimate money and I commend him for that. A nigga like me wanna live the life of the rich and famous based off of street dreams. But if I want to have children and grow old watching my grandchildren come into this world, I have to minimize my street dreams. I can still be rich, just not filthy rich," he laughed.

"I feel you. I didn't put any value on preparing for a future until after having Aaliyah. That's when my priorities changed a lot. Before, I was quick to jump into some bullshit without giving a damn. Now I stop and think about the consequences. You know I'm still gonna jump in, but with more caution."

"Caution is good."

"Damn, I can't believe how much time has gone by," I said, looking down at my watch. "I hate to bring you bad news and run, but I have to go."

"Not a problem. But you know if you were able to find out I was in New York and where I was staying, then you could've easily gotten my number and called me with this information you have, instead of making a long trip."

"You're right. The truth is I wanted to see you again." Nico stood up and reached his hand out to me. I didn't hesitate to grab it. He lifted my chin and gazed into my eyes like he did so many times in the past. He used to call it his way of looking inside of my soul. Then his soft lips invaded mine, and I couldn't lie, the chemistry between us hadn't diminished and I wanted to give into the lust of the flesh.

"I'm glad you did because I've wanted to be with you again since the last time we were together," he said, breaking the momentum of our kiss for a moment before diving right back in with even more intensity.

"I can't," I said, pulling away. "This is an example of jumping in but thinking about the consequences. That kiss is the furthest this can go. You're my first love, Nico. I'll always have a soft spot for you, but I'm in love with my husband."

"Enough said. But here, take my number in case you ever need me—not for anything intimate, but as a friend."

"Thank you, and I want you to take my number too, you know, if you find out anything that can help bring Aaliyah home."

"I meant to tell you, I think it's a beautiful thing that you named your daughter after your mother. If she was alive she'd be so proud."

"Wow, I can't believe you remembered my mother's name. Most of the time I referred to her as the 'crack head' to you. I feel a great deal of shame in that now that I'm a mother. You know she had turned her life around before she got killed. I was so proud of her."

"Precious, it's okay. We've all said and done things to our parents we regret or wish we could take back. But trust me, before your mother left this earth she knew how much you loved her and only wanted the best for her. You've honored her name by passing it on to her grandchild. Let it go. It's all love."

The compassion Nico was showing for my mother made me for a brief second want to confide that Aaliyah could very well be his daughter just as easily as Supreme's, or unfortunately, Mike's. But what would be the point? Supreme was Aaliyah's father and it was best that it stayed that way. I gave Nico one last hug goodbye before leaving.

I called Ricky on my way downstairs, and thank goodness he was already waiting. "I thought you were going to miss your flight," he said when I got in the car.

"It could've easily happened, but I need to get home to my husband, speaking of him, I have to place a call. No disrespect but I need for you to be completely silent." "I'm on your clock," Ricky responded, giving one of his player smiles.

I called Supreme and waited for him to pick up, hoping he hadn't got hip to my lie.

"Hey, baby, I was about to call you," Supreme answered, sounding like he was still sweet on me, and I was relieved.

"Hi. Sorry, I'm just checking in but these seminars go on for hours and it's hard to get a moment from these people."

"Are you enjoying yourself?"

"I wouldn't say enjoy, but I'm learning a lot."

You'll have to school me in on it when I get home.

"When will that be?"

"Hopefully no later than early in the morning. When are you coming home?"

"Baby, we have to hear three more people speak, so not for a few hours."

"Okay, well call me when you get home to let me know you're safe."

"I will. Did you have a chance to speak to Maya when you stopped at home?"

"Nah, I didn't see her. I checked her room but she wasn't there. Maybe she and Clip made up."

"Maybe, but I hope not. We need to find out if he is on Team Mike or Team Supreme first. Has any suspicious moves been made at that apartment yet?"

"Not yet. So far ain't been a red flag, but my men are watching carefully. They on it."

"Do you think Maya hipped Clip that we thought he was suspect?"

"I hope not. But that's your girl. What do you think?"

I pondered briefly before answering. "Not Maya, she's a little street soldier. She understands the importance of keeping your lips locked when it comes to certain situations, even when your man or ex-man might be involved."

"Then it's all good, and hopefully Maya is right and Clip is on the up and up."

"True, but I have to get back inside. Ms. Duncan is waiting."

"Cool. Make sure you call me when you get home."

"I will. Love you."

"Love you too, baby." I hung up ready to exhale.

"You handled that like a pro. I wonder how my sister would feel being used as your alibi?"

"Is that a question? Because I know Ms. Duncan would have my back. She understands the concept of doing what- ever you have to do to survive."

"Indeed, but it makes me wonder if whether I should be pleased or disappointed that I never found a woman like you to marry."

"What you mean by that?"

"What I mean is, I admire how you're able to keep your cool under intense situations, but it's also scary that you're able to lie with such ease to the man you exchanged vows with. It's a double-edged sword, because you would be an excellent partner on the streets. I'm just not sure if the same can be said in the partnership of marriage."

"Interesting analysis, but, umm, luckily I'm not your problem so you don't have to worry. On to more important things. How are we looking on time?"

"Not to worry, you'll make the flight."

"Good. I spent much more time with Nico than I had anticipated."

"You all had a lot of catching up to do." Ricky's mono- tone voice made it hard for me to understand if what he said was a question or a general statement, so I ignored it. Catching the vibe, Ricky came at me again. "So how did it go with Nico? Were you able to resolve everything?"

"There are some people in life you'll never be able to resolve everything with. Nico is that person for me. But I was able to see him face to face and deliver the warning, so that was an accomplishment. And of course I owe that to you, Ricky. Thank you."

"That's what I do."

"Yes indeed, and you're very good at it. Before I for get, although I doubt you would let me, this is for you." I handed him an envelope full of Benjamin Franklin's. "That should be more than enough to cover all your expenses."

"Thank you, but I wasn't worried. If you didn't hit me off this time around, I knew you were good for it."

"'Preciate the confidence, but I don't like to owe people, especially the ones I'm doing business with."

"You a shrewd woman, Precious Cummings."

"Mills," I corrected him.

"My fault, how could I forget you're a married woman." It sounded as if Ricky was being sarcastic, but I had a flight to catch so I didn't have the time to give a fuck one way or the other.

"Ricky, you can drop me off right here," I directed as he pulled up beside a yellow cab that was blocking the curb.

"Are you sure?"

"Hell yeah, you see what time it is, or were you so caught up in trying to read my psyche that you stopped checking the clock? Don't answer, I have to go."

"Call me when you land!" I heard Ricky yell out the window as I entered the American Airlines terminal.

When I arrived home from the LAX airport and didn't see any cars parked along the circular driveway, the tight knot in my stomach loosened up. Supreme rarely kept his car in the garage, and if he was using a driver the Bentley would be resting out front.

I took my time going inside replaying the day's events. It was like damn! One minute I was sitting in front of Nico at a New York city hotel suite reminiscing about the past, and now I was back in Cali having to deal with my reality—my daughter was kidnapped and I didn't know when she would be back home.

It was so hush when I got in the house you would've thought the place had been abandoned. I immediately began flicking on all the lights so it would feel as if life was in the room. I walked toward the kitchen to get something to drink. My eyes instantaneously became fixated on a beautiful bouquet of flowers adorning the glazed lava stone countertop upon entering the kitchen. I was drawn to the array of Vandella roses, white hydrangeas, blue muscari and pink Peony's... it was as if they were calling my name. *Finally, something to put a smile on my face, after all the bullshit and heartache, a wonderful gesture from my husband to take away all the pain if only for one moment,* I thought as I smelled the breathtaking arrangement.

I noticed the small white envelope with "Precious" written across and I opened it to read the card inside. Before digesting the first word written, horror seized me. A jet-black curl began descending as it made its way out when I opened the card. I fell to the floor, banging my knees in an attempt to catch the locks. I preferred the hair to find a resting-place in the palm of my hand rather than on the cold marble beneath me.

"My baby! My poor baby!" was all I kept saying. I could distinguish Aaliyah's jet black curls from any head of hair. I ran my fingers through each strand on countless occasions. She was my baby, my pride and joy. To let it hit the ground was the same as me letting her die.

THE MESSAGE

"Supreme, come home right now!" I screamed in the phone. I could hear loud music in the background so I knew he was at the studio grinding, but fuck whatever he was working on. This was too much. I needed my husband home now.

"Baby, what's wrong?"

"That motherfucka's dead! He don't know it yet, but he's dead!"

"Precious, what the fuck is going on… talk to me?"

"When I got home there was a bouquet of flowers waiting for me. I thought they were from you."

"I ain't send you no flowers."

"I realized that once I opened the card."

"Who the fuck was they from…?" Supreme asked then immediately jumped to answer. "I know that nigga, Mike's punk ass didn't send you no fuckin' flowers and shit. Oh hell no, tell me I'm buggin'."

"It's worse than that."

"What, the nigga delivered that shit himself," he countered, thinking that was as bad as it could get.

"I don't know who the fuck delivered them 'cause I wasn't here, but even if he had, it's still worse."

"Tell me what the fuck it is!" Supreme barked, ready for World War 3.

"Inside the envelope was a lock of Aaliyah's hair." On that note the line went dead. I kept trying to call Supreme back, but after the sixth time with no answer I knew this wasn't a dropped call situation. He hung the fuck up. I couldn't blame him. He was probably so pissed off that his only alternative was to shut the conversation down.

Still holding on to what represented to me a small piece of my daughter, I opened up the card again to read what the sick fuck had written, but it was blank. I guess Mike figured the message he wanted to send was made loud and clear, and he was right. It didn't matter that Vernika was dead or that Supreme had Donnell prisoner somewhere, Mike was very much in control. He was running the show, and we were just hapless ticket holders sitting front row waiting to see how the movie would end.

I heard the front door opening and I knew it was too soon for Supreme to get home, but before my mind started getting the best of me, I heard a familiar voice call out, "Is anyone home?" Maya echoed.

I rushed out the kitchen, needing to see a comforting face. "Maya, I'm so glad it's you. Where have you been?"

"Girl, tryna work it out with my sorry-ass boyfriend, but that's another Bronx Tale. What's going on with you? You look even more stressed than normal, is everything okay... oh shit! Mike calling harassing you again?"

I rolled my eyes up in the air, shaking my head before giving Maya the update. "This fool's reaching out through flower deliveries now."

"Excuse me?"

"Yeah, when I got home what I thought was a sweet gesture from my husband turned out to be poison from your brother."

"Mike sent you some flowers? How you know they were from him?"

"Because the card was blank except for a lock of Aaliyah's hair. Mike is the only loco nigga that would do some fucked up shit like that."

"Yo, that nigga had some flowers delivered with Aaliyah's hair in the card—he's lost his mind. I can't believe we share the same fuckin' DNA," Maya said, looking baffled.

"Have you been with Clip since you left here yesterday?"

"Yeah. What, you thinking he had a hand in this madness? Nah, he been on lock with me the whole time, and I swear I ain't see that nigga do nothing suspect—not no discreet phone conversations or nothing. I've been all up in his grill until I left his ass a minute ago."

"I need to find out who the fuck delivered this shit. The name of the florist is on the card, but of course they closed right now. They may have some valuable information."

"That's true. Did you call Supreme?"

"Yeah, I'm hoping he'll be home any minute."

Just then the front door opened. It was my husband and he had Detective Moore with him. This shit must have had Supreme real shaken if he let the police in on what happened.

"Where are the flowers and the hair?" Supreme asked, keeping it straight and to the point.

"In the kitchen..."

Before I could say another word, both Supreme and the detective breezed past me. I decided to stay on their trail, and Maya followed behind me. They were already dissecting the goods by the time we caught up.

"I already have officers getting in touch with the owner of the shop to see if we can get any leads. Because it's so late, they may not be able to find out anything until first thing in the morning, but they're on it," I heard Detective Moore explaining to Supreme.

"One of their delivery guys definitely dropped them off because he got clearance at the front gate and left them with one of my security guards. He had the proper identification, so the guard had no reason to be suspicious."

"Do you have any other hair samples of your daughter so we can compare it to what was sent in the envelope?"

"Detective, I know that's my daughter's hair. I don't need no comparisons," I spoke up, tired of listening from the sidelines.

Detective Moore turned his attention to me as if all of the sudden my presence was felt. He rubbed his stubby fingers through his own short, spiked, flaming red hair as if at a lost for words. "I'm sure you know your daughter's hair, but for legal reasons it's always better if we can prove it without leaving the slightest doubt. Mr. Owens will be brought to justice, and proving he sent your daughter's hair using a bouquet of flowers as a disguise will not sit well with jurors in any court of law."

Detective Moore's words were fine, and I even pretended to agree to what he was saying, but he was clueless. That so-called court of law he was preaching about was meaningless. Yeah, Mike would be brought to justice, but it wouldn't be by some pompous prosecutor and some drained ready-to-go-home jurors. Street justice, which equaled a torturous death was the only appropriate sentencing for Mike, and it would be carried out by me and me alone. "That's not a problem. I'm sure I have some hair strands in one of her baby brushes."

"I appreciate the cooperation, Mrs. Mills. I know this has to be extremely difficult for you. I'm happy that you and your husband are turning to me for help. I know you might feel we're not doing enough and you can handle it on your own, but when you're dealing with lowlifes like Mr. Owens, you need the law enforcement on your side. That's what we're here for, to help and bring your daughter home."

I knew the detective was sincere with his hero speech, but it sounded like recycled bullshit to me. I briefly thought about all the parents who heard this same dialogue when their child went missing and how they latched onto every word, praying their little one would be brought home to them alive. It wasn't until they got the knock on the front door from a couple of detectives like Moore, wearing cheap suits and smelling of stale cigarettes, that reality punched them in the face. Their child wouldn't be coming home. But instead of beating the detectives' asses for not delivering on the promises made for a safe return of their child, they had to stand and listen to the bullshit condolences.

I refused to let that be the fate of my family. I was born a fighter and would die one if it came to that. "Maya, will you go upstairs and get Aaliyah's brush from her bedroom? It should be on top of the dresser right next to her crib."

"No problem, I'll be right back."

"Are you Maya Owens, Mike's sister?" Detective Moore asked, bringing Maya to a halt.

"Yes, I am."

"I've needed to speak with you, but I had some difficulty tracking you down."

"Here I am. What did you need to speak to me about?"

"Your brother. Do you have any idea where he might be hiding out? Does he have any friends or family in the area he would turn to for help?"

"I haven't had any contact with Mike since he got locked up. To me, I no longer have a brother. The brother I knew is dead."

"I understand. Well, if you can think of anything, please give me a call," he said, handing Maya his business card. Maya put the card in the back pocket of her jeans and exited the kitchen.

My eyes then darted over to Supreme, who had been on mute for a while. He was standing over the flowers with his arms folded, and seemed to be in deep thought. As if he could sense me sizing him up, his eyes met up with mine. "Detective, I believe we've handled everything here. I'll be waiting for your call in the morning about what your officers were able to find out from the florist," he said to the detective, but somehow still able to keep his eyes on me. The shit was bizarre. I couldn't fathom what the fuck was going on his head.

"I will. I can show myself out. If it's not a problem, I'll wait in the foyer for Ms. Owens to bring down your daughter's hair sample."

"Please do so."

It wasn't until the detective extended his hand out to Supreme that he finally stopped eyeballing me like he was crazy. After shaking Supreme's hand, he picked up the vase of flowers after putting on a pair of surgical gloves, and was ready to break out.

"Umm, Detective Moore, where are you going with those flowers?" I stepped forward feeling territorial.

"Mrs. Mills, I have to take these flowers with me. This is evidence for our case."

"Oh, that's a shame. I was looking forward to shredding that poisonous greenery and tossing it out with the rest of the trash, but what you need it for is much more important, so please, take it."

Detective Moore gave me an awkward grin as if perturbed by what I said. He gave Supreme and I a half- hearted goodbye and finally got the fuck out of our faces.

Once the detective was ghost, I turned my attention to Supreme. "Why were you giving me the eye like I had caught the vapors or some shit?"

Supreme sucked his teeth and rested his elbows on the counter. "Something seems off to me."

"What you mean off? I told you how everything went down with them damn flowers."

"It ain't the flowers, it's something else."

"Something else like what? You talking in riddles and shit."

"I can't put my finger on it, but shit is all off. Why did you get home so late?"

"I told you them church seminars be lasting damn near all night. Then I had to take Ms. Duncan back to her hotel, and she wanted me to stay and talk to her for a while. I mean, I didn't want to be rude, she did come here all the way from Brooklyn."

"What hotel is she staying at?" Supreme decided he wanted to get all Sherlock Holmes on me.

"Oh, mofo, I know you ain't tryna grill me like you po-po. I bring my ass home to some fucked up flowers with my daughter's hair lingering inside, and you want me to tell you where Ms. Duncan is laying her head at? If you really want to know, I stashed her in the Four Seasons in Beverly Hills. Here, since you obviously don't believe me, call the hotel," I said. grabbing the phone and shoving it in his face. praying that motherfucker didn't call my bluff. "What the fuck you waiting for? You want me to dial the number?"

Supreme put his hands up pushing the phone out his face. "I don't need to call and check your story."

"I think you do, because this trust shit is becoming more of an issue every fucking day, and I don't need the fucking stress. You tryna fault me for spending my day getting some spiritual guidance with Ms. Duncan, that's fucked up."

"Ain't nobody tryna fault you. I was picking up some vibes that was saying some shit wasn't adding up. I was wrong and I'm sorry."

I was about to keep the shit going to make him feel worse, but I knew better and backed off. I felt if I told him to call the Four Seasons one more time, he might just take me up on my offer and my lies would be exposed. "No need to be sorry, baby. We both going through heavy shit right now, and we don't need petty bullshit coming between us." I rubbed Supreme's shoulders, mitigating his hostility. He closed his eyes seeming to relax.

"Hey, is everything cool in here?" Maya asked, sneaking up on us.

"We're good. Did Detective Moore leave?" I wanted to know.

"Yeah, he bounced. I hope he finally gets a break in this case, 'cause Mike is wilding out. That nigga needs to be stopped... like yesterday."

"Who you telling? That nigga's like a bad venereal disease that keeps coming back. Can we please find a medication to zap this shit once and for all?"

"If it was only that simple," Supreme added. I could feel the tension creeping back in his shoulders.

"If only, is right. Well, I'm heading to bed. A bitch is tired."

"Did Clip wear that ass out?" I pried.

"No, I wouldn't let him stick his dick nowhere up in me—yet."

"I like how you added that yet at the end. That means he is this close" I raised up my thumb and index finger, putting a small space in between them, "To getting back inside the domain. I hope you know what you're doing."

"Honestly, Precious, I don't. What I do know is I don't want Destiny sniffing after my man, draped on his arm walking down the red carpet. If ain't gon' be me in that photo op posing with the designer getup and dripping with ice, it sho' ain't gon' be her trick ass. It won't be happening in this lifetime, and not the next if I have anything to do with it."

All I could do was shake my head at her. That was the immature young girl in her yapping. Hell, I had been there a few times in my life, and the only way you learn is going through the bullshit yourself. I mean, I didn't have no problem with Maya earning her battle scars going to war with Clip, as long as he didn't have nothing to do with helping Mike. More and more I was beginning to think that maybe I jumped the gun accusing him. He hadn't made any foul moves, and Supreme hadn't gathered any dirt on him. Maybe he was no more than a man-whore, getting his dick wet off of instant fame and nothing else. If that was the case, this was a problem Maya could handle on her own, because I had bigger issues that superseded pussy dilemmas.

"Well, handle your business, mama. But you know if you need me, I got your back."

"Thanks, Precious. I can always count on you. Goodnight you guys."

"Goodnight," Supreme and I said in unison.

"I'm tired myself. I had a long day. I'ma head to bed. Are you coming?" I asked Supreme.

"I'll be up shortly. I have to go to my office and make some phone calls. But I'm coming."

"Okay, baby." I gave him a kiss on the lips and went upstairs. I was exhausted, physically and mentally. There seemed to be no end insight to this madness. When I got to the bedroom, I fell on the bed needing to rest my drained body before taking a shower. I wanted to turn on the television and see if Aaliyah's kidnapping was still headlining news, or if was she fading into the background, being overshadowed by more current events.

I scanned the room for the remote control, but it wasn't on the dresser or the nightstand, so I got down on my hands and knees in search of the gadget. Oh shit! I forgot all about slimy-ass Vernika's purse. Last night I was so busy trying to hide shit from Supreme that it slipped my mind that I stashed the shit under the bed. I never did have a chance to finish going through her mess, although I doubt anything of importance is in there.

I tossed Vernika's purse down and noticed the remote at the foot of the bed. I clicked on the television and turned to Nancy Grace while rummaging through the purse once again. The second time around proved fruitless. I then noticed a small black wallet in what appeared to be an almost secret compartment on the side of the bag. I opened the wallet up and there was a few hundred dollars inside, a tiny bag of what looked to be cocaine, and a folded up piece of paper that had been ripped off a notepad. I opened up the paper and it had an address scribbled down. It didn't have the city or state, just the zip code, which was all the navigation system needed. I had a feeling it was located right here in the LA area. A smile crept across my face, because I believed I might've gotten a tad bit closer to discovering the vaccine to that hard to get rid of venereal disease.

ONCE AGAIN IT'S ON

I woke up ready for war. Besides the heat I would be packing, my most powerful ammunition was the address I found in Vernika's purse. How the piece of paper was all neatly tucked away in Vernika's purse, I knew it meant that shit was important. And besides doing Mike's dirty work, what else could've been that significant in her life? With the address now in my pocket for safe keeping, I laced up my Timberland boots, anxious to hit the streets.

"Baby, where you off to dressed in gear more suitable for the hoods in New York?" Supreme asked, standing in the entrance of our bedroom door.

"I have a few things to take care of, that's all." I kept it real non-chalant so he wouldn't start with the interrogation.

"This early in the morning, what you gotta do?"

I guess I wasn't nonchalant enough, because here he was with the next question.

"Ms. Duncan's leaving today so I wanted to tell her bye before she left. I need to pick up some clothes from the cleaners that's way overdue... you know, take care of shit like that. I mean is that a problem?"

"No, I was just hoping maybe I could go out and have a nice breakfast with my wife. With all the bullshit going on, we haven't had much alone time. I think we need to reconnect."

"I feel you on that, Supreme, but until we bring Aaliyah home I think we got bigger problems than reconnecting."

"That's not what I'm saying. I know having breakfast in a restaurant ain't gon' change our circumstances, but at least it will make me feel as if we still united. I've lost my daughter, but I don't want to lose my wife too."

"Supreme, don't say no shit like that. We ain't lost Aaliyah," I said, rising up from the chaise. "You talking as if all hope is lost in bringing our daughter home, and that's some bullshit." I was now within spitting range of Supreme, ready to stick my Timberland boot up his ass for even insinuating that my baby was gone forever.

"Precious, I give you my word I didn't mean it like that." Supreme held on to my hands with a firm grip as he continued. "What I said came out wrong. On everything I love, I know we bringing our baby home but I'm talking right now in the present tense and what the situation is at this moment. At this very second we have lost our daughter, and I'm only trying to hold on to you as tightly as possible, because until we bring her home, you're all I have. Believe it or not, your presence is giving me the strength to get up every morning and fight this shit without losing my mind."

Ring...ring...ring...

Supreme's cell phone went off before I had a chance to respond to what he said, but that was a good thing because I really didn't know what my comeback would be.

"Hello... What...? How the fuck that happen...? Stay right there, I'm on my way," Supreme said, and flipped his cell shut.

"Who was that? What happened?" I questioned, perplexed by Supreme's agitation after his phone call.

He ignored me and damn near sprinted to his walk-in closet to a safe that used a fingerprint scan for access. He pulled out two weapons from his arsenal of guns, and had "I'm on a mission, so move the fuck outta the way" etched on his face.

"Supreme, where are you going? And don't ignore me."

"Some shit went down at the spot where Donnell is holed up and I have to go handle it."

"Fuck that, I'm coming with you," I said, grabbing my belongings, ready to be all up in the mix.

"Let me handle this. You go do whatever you had planned this morning and I'll hit you later on."

"You can either let me come with you or I'ma find my own way. But regardless, I will be knee-deep in this shit."

From the keen expression on my face, Supreme knew I was not budging and he wouldn't win this argument. "I don't have time to debate this shit with you, so come on."

When Supreme pulled up to the small one-story brick house nestled in the cut, I wondered how he ever found this spot. During the drive, he took so many crazy-ass turns that I couldn't remember how the fuck we got here, or even what part of LA we were in. Not once during the ride did Supreme tell me what had gone down at this hideout, but from how quickly he put the Range in park and jumped out the driver's side, I knew it was some heavy shit.

"Damn, can I at least get out the passenger side before you jet off?"

"You the one who was dying to be shotgun, so keep up," Supreme cracked, not breaking his stride.

I stepped up my pace, sizing up my surroundings at the same time. Nothing in the desolate area stood out. There weren't even any houses nearby. The only neighbors on either side were dirt and grass.

"I see why you got Donnell stored in here. I mean can't nobody see or hear shit in this fucking area," I said as I finally caught up to Supreme. As we walked up the long dirt walkway, two of his watchdogs were standing outside the front door, waiting.

"Now what the fuck happened?" Supreme said, brushing past the two armed guards dressed in the prerequisite all black uniform.

"We don't know how this shit happened. We pulled up about an hour ago to relieve Chris from the night shift, and this what we found."

When we walked into the open space, my eyes im- mediately darted to the blood splatter that greeted us on the far wall directly in our line of vision. A man was tied up in a chair with his arms cuffed behind his back and ankles chained. His one-time white wife beater was now crimson red from the bullet that penetrated his chest. But wanting to guarantee that all life was ceased, the shooter put one shot through the head, spraying brain tissue on the walls.

"Let me guess. The dead man is Donnell Graham."

Three pairs of eyes leered at me with disdain, as if I had been the one who had infiltrated their secret operation.

"Where's Chris?" Supreme asked, waiting for the two men to lead the way. They guided us to a bathroom in the hallway. When one of them pushed opened the door, Chris was sitting on the toilet holding a trashy magazine with big booty chicks spreading they're shit in all sorts of creative positions. I hoped he was able to get his shit off and bust a nut before the shooter put that ass to sleep with the clear shot through the mouth.

"Fuck!" Supreme belted, damn near leaving a hole in the bathroom wall from a potent punch. "I can't believe this shit. How the fuck did someone get up in here and take out Chris and that piece of shit?"

"We trying to figure that shit out too. We talked to Chris about one in the morning and everything was cool."

"Why was he here by himself with no backup?"

"The last few nights Devon was sharing the nightshift with Chris after you took him off of driving duty. Then a couple of days ago, Chris started letting Devon leave a little after midnight, saying there was no sense in both of them staying all night."

"What?" Supreme stormed out of the bathroom agitated. The watchdogs were a step behind, trying to explain how the shit got all fucked up, leaving his top man and his potential informant deceased.

"Chris felt he could hold down the late night shift on his own. He said they didn't need two bodies to watch a chained man sleep all night. I guess he was wrong."

"Yeah, Einstein, I guess so. Has either of you spoken to Devon?" Supreme questioned, shaking his head in frustration.

"No. We've been calling him since we got here, but his phone keeps going straight to voicemail. I even called his crib, but no answer."

"That shit don't make no sense. Everybody knows they supposed to be available at all times. Send one of the men to his crib and find out what the fuck is going on. I hope whoever did this ain't got Devon tied up some fuckin' where. A crew of niggas coulda ran up in here for all we know. But how in the hell did they find this spot?"

"Yeah, that's what I want to know, 'cause ain't nobody accidentally running up on this joint. You need some serious assistance finding it. My brain damn near turned to mush trying to remember all the twists and turns you took getting here. The shooter had some help... an inside job kind," I added.

The hired goons instantly went on the defense. "Supreme, we

ain't have nothing to do with this. Chris was our boss and we followed his orders."

"No, motherfuckers, *I'm* your boss. Nobody should've been working this shift alone without clearing it with me first. I don't give a fuck what Chris told you. Now look, that nigga's dead, Devon's MIA, and we lost our only link to finding Mike. I pay ya niggas top dollar to fuckin' babysit and you can't even do that shit properly. What the fuck is this world coming to when grown-ass men with guns can't even keep a chained down nigga in a chair alive? Fuck!"

There was nothing more pathetic then watching two big-ass burly niggas sulking in the corner like scorned bitches. I wanted to tell them clowns to man-up, but it wouldn't have changed the grim circumstances.

"Listen, get this shit wrapped. Call in the cleaning crew and have these bodies disposed of. You know what else to do," Supreme stated, shooing his measly workers along with repulsion. "Then get everybody together, because we having a meeting tonight at the other spot to discuss the ramifications from this bullshit operation you niggas fucked up."

I stood in the back listening as Supreme gave his orders. For the first time I saw him in a completely different light. It was a bombshell to come to grips with the fact that Supreme was a killer just like Nico, Mike and me. He ordered his men to call in a cleaning crew with such ease that this clearly wasn't the first or even the second time he'd done so. His request was as second nature to them as pulling out their dick and taking a piss. How did I miss this about my husband? I always saw him as some dude from the hood that made good by breaking into the music industry. Never a cold-blooded killer who could dispose of bodies the way the average person tosses out trash. In my mind, Supreme was different from me. He didn't share the darkness that loomed over me. When he turned to kill-or-be-killed tactics, I assumed his survival instincts had kicked in and he was trying to save and protect his family. I didn't doubt that was the driving force behind this particular situation, but what about the ones I knew nothing about? And something told me there were many.

My mind then jumped to Nico and the hit Supreme had put out on him. Even with that, I felt there was some sort of reasonable explanation. Maybe Supreme never forgave Nico for shooting me and killing the child I was carrying, and he wanted retribution. I had to give my husband the benefit of the doubt. Although I wanted Nico alive, Supreme had to feel justified in wanting him dead.

"Let's go," I heard Supreme say, snapping me out of the distant places my mind had gone. It was then I noticed the watchdogs conducting business on their BlackBerry's, no doubt executing the orders from their boss.

When we got outside, I reached my hand out to Supreme. I wanted to feel if there was any warmth left in him. It was strange because I felt as if I no longer knew the man I was married to, but at the same time he was still my husband and I yearned to connect with him. That's why what flowed from my lips next seemed necessary.

"Baby, I think we might have one more lead that can put us back on Mike's trail," I said, sliding my fingers in the grasp of his hands. Originally, I was going to follow this probable come-up on my own, but this was the way to reconnect with Supreme. I did, however, need to pretend that I wasn't confident with the lead so he wouldn't catch on that only in the last thirty seconds I decided to bring him in on my undertaking. "I could be wrong and it might lead to nothing, but of course I wanted to share it with you."

"What lead? The two leads we had are dead and ain't no bringing them back."

"But sometimes even the dead find ways of speaking to you." I reached in my pocket and took out the piece of paper and handed it to Supreme.

"What are you giving me this for?"

"Open it."

Supreme stopped a few feet away from his Range Rover and unfolded the yellow paper. He stared down for a second and looked back up at me. "Okay, this is the address to..."

"This morning I was going through Vernika's purse and I found that paper tucked away real discreet. At first I didn't think anything of it, but maybe it's a secret location that Mike gave her." I had to switch up the time that I found the paper, because Supreme would be ready to get up in my ass for the delay in bringing it to his attention.

"This morning? But that shit went down with Vernika a few days ago. Why are you just now giving me this?"

"With Ms. Duncan and the church conference and all the other bullshit, I didn't have time to go through her purse until this morning."

"Oh, now I get it. So when you were lacing up those Timbs," he said, pointing down to my boots, "Like you was going to rumble through the jungle, tracking down this address was the real errand you were running."

"No. I was already planning on hitting the street to run some errands. While I was getting dressed I remembered that I had Vernika's purse and I searched through it. I came across the piece of paper, glanced at it for a minute and put it in my pocket. Honestly, I didn't think anything of it. I was gonna tell you about it, but at that moment it wasn't that deep to me."

"So at what point did it become deep enough that you opted to let me know about it?"

"When we were in the house and you were chewing out them silly niggas in there, I put my hands in my pockets, felt this piece of paper and remembered this fucking address. With the dude, Donnell dead and all our leads dried up, although a crap-shoot, I figured it might lead to something." I paused for a second before continuing, trying to determine if Supreme believed my half-ass story. He was biting down on his lip, which wasn't an encouraging sign, but I thought, Fuck it, and kept it going.

"Listen, don't be mad. I've had so much shit on my mind that I got caught slipping. I shoulda been more focused and got on top of this a few days ago. But, baby, you know how stressed I been and I'm doing the best I can." I put my head down and let out a tender sigh, hoping to soften Supreme up.

"All I'm saying is with all this shit going on you can't let shit slip like this. Time is of the essence right now. From now on, if you come across any information, I don't care how bogus you think it might be, you bring that shit to me, understand?"

"I got you."

"Cool. Now let's go check this shit out. I'ma have a couple of my men meet us over there just in case we might need backup. I got a nine millimeter in the center console. You know how to work that?" Supreme lifted his chin up in my direction in anticipation of my response.

"Don't play, you already know I get down for mines." I slammed the passenger door, feeling like Bonnie to my nigga's Clyde.

"Precious, that ain't for you to play with," Supreme said, pressing down on the gas and driving off. "I don't know what we about to walk up in, so I want you to have some protection since we both know you ain't gon' sit yo' ass still."

"I'm not gonna fuck this up. I'll follow your lead." I sat back in the seat and closed my eyes. I couldn't shake the feeling that I was missing something. It was as if all the answers to my questions were neatly compiled in a sealed envelope waiting for me to open. But I kept losing track of the envelope's location. I wasn't focusing my attention on the right person who had all the answers to my questions. Different faces kept flashing in my head: Supreme, Maya, Clip, Nico, Devon, Ms. Duncan, Ricky, Anna, Detective Moore, even the dead, Vernika and Donnell. With everything inside of me, I believed one or more of these people knew all the moves Mike was making. I couldn't believe I threw my husband in the batch, but this was my daughter, and at this point I was looking at everybody cross-eyed.

In my mind I revisited past conversations with each of them and tried to determine if there were any underlying messages that I was missing. The more I thought about it, the more it seemed that kidnapping Aaliyah wasn't Mike's ultimate goal. He had a much more sinister objective in mind, but what? Mike was a crazy motherfucka and there was no telling what lengths he would go to for revenge.

"Precious... Precious... Precious," I heard my name being called and then a forceful arm shaking me. I shook my head, opening my eyes. "What the fuck, did you fall asleep?" Supreme asked, turning off the ignition.

"I must've dozed off." I looked around and saw we were in an upscale apartment complex. "Where are we?"

"In Sherman Oaks, California."

"Could this be where Aaliyah has been all this time?" I wondered, sharing my thoughts out loud.

"Anything's possible, but that shit would be crazy, because she would've been right under our noses. But then again, how would we know that? I guess it's pretty easy to have a baby under wraps if you keep them indoors. But we might be getting way ahead of ourselves. This could be someplace a nigga that chick Vernika was creeping with stay at."

"True, but only one way to find out. Do you know the building number?"

"The apartment number is 6248, so I'm assuming it is building number six. Hold on a minute, let me call and see where the two men I told to meet us here are at."

While Supreme made his phone call, I scanned the place seeing if anything struck me as odd—a vehicle, person—anything. Nothing popped out, but I definitely didn't think this was a meeting spot for Vernika and some jumpoff.

"Let's go. They're going to meet us in front of the apartment building," Supreme said, getting out of the Range.

I opened the center console and grabbed the nine, making sure I was strapped for the unexpected. When we got to the lower level of building six, Supreme saw the apartment wasn't on that floor, so our legs swiftly made there way up their stairs. It wasn't until we'd gone through the entire flight of stairs and reached the very top that we found the apartment number, and standing against the wall waiting for us were Supreme's two men.

"It's about fucking time," I said, gasping for air. I knew I needed to hit the gym and start doing some cardio if I was tired from running up some damn stairs.

"Did you guys hear any activity going on in there?" Supreme asked the men leaning up against the door.

"No," one of the men answered.

I was noticing a pattern with Supreme's hired help. They all looked the fucking same: tall, black and muscular. I didn't understand how he could tell them apart, especially since their entire outfits were identical.

"Precious, you stand off to the side. I'ma knock on the door and wait a few to see if anyone answers. If don't nobody speak up or show their face, we busting the door down," Supreme directed.

I stood off to the side, hoping that no one would come out their apartment or pop up on the scene, interrupting us. It was a weekday in the middle of the afternoon, so most people were probably at work, but I didn't want any surprises. More importantly, I didn't want the police being called before we got the first crack at inspecting the apartment for clues.

Supreme knocked at the door and paused for a few seconds, then knocked again. "I don't hear shit in there." He turned to one of his men. "Yo, bust this shit open."

The man pulled out his gun with the silencer already attached and busted off two shots at the door lock, so he basically had to tap it for the shit to open.

When we stepped inside the place, it smelled of Linen & Sky Febreeze Air. The entrance opened into a living room with a butter-cream leather sofa set adorning the hardwood floor. An oval-shaped glass coffee table mounted on ivory stone rocks sat in the center, with magazines and books neatly stacked on top. Then, there it was, nestled in the far left-hand corner. A playpen. The first sign that a baby had been here—possibly mine.

Supreme's men made there way down the hallway to check the bedrooms, and I went over to the playpen, touching, looking and even trying to smell the scent of my Aaliyah.

"Supreme, I think you should come take a look at this," one of his men called out from the back.

While Supreme went to the back, I searched the kitchen and opened the cabinets to cans of Similac and baby bottles. The refrigerator had jars of baby food. "Supreme, a baby is definitely residing here," I said, walking down the hall to the bedroom Supreme was in. My mouth dropped at the pink paradise. The crib, dresser, changing table, rocking chair were all white with cotton candy colored walls and accessories. I went to the crib and rubbed my hands on the fitted sheets and picked up a cotton stuffed toy rabbit lying flat on the firm mattress. I then opened up the dresser drawers and found pull-on pants, coverall sets and socks. I held on to a floral print onesie and brushed it against my nose. It smelled of fresh baby detergent.

"Precious, no doubt a baby lives here, but we don't know if it's Aaliyah," Supreme reminded me, noticing that I was becoming lost in a world that might have not been that of my daughter.

"I know, but this can't be a coincidence. The sizes of these clothes would fit Aaliyah perfectly."

"That's not enough to convince me. We need more."

"I think we just found it," I said, staring at the rocking chair. I swallowed hard not wanting to get too excited.

"What...what did you find?" Supreme came closer to me, wanting to know what had me so transfixed.

I took a few steps closer to the rocking chair and gently grabbed the light-pink crochet trimmed cashmere blanket draped over the armrest. I turned over to the inside, and there lay the proof. Aaliyah's name was embroidered in the corner.

"This is the blanket Anna got. She always kept it with Aaliyah even when it was fucking hot outside."

Supreme grabbed the blanket from me, scrutinizing the validity of what I was saying. "I remember this blanket," he said, covering his face with it. For a moment I thought he was about to break down and cry. He stood there silent; the only thing I could hear was his heavy breathing. "Were you all able to find anything else?" he asked the men, finally coming up for air.

"There were a few clothes hanging in the closet and in the drawers... and this," the man said, handing Supreme a picture. "Maybe that's who the clothes belong to."

I instantly recognized the woman in the picture. "That's Destiny!" I squealed with repulsion.

"She do look mad familiar. Who the fuck is she and how you know her?" Supreme was dumbfounded.

"That's Destiny, the video chick that me and Maya caught Clip fucking around with."

"This is Clip's ho right here?" Supreme threw down the picture and balled up his fist. "Let me find out this nigga really got something to do with this bullshit!"

I picked the picture off the floor and stared at it again. Destiny was cheesed up, sitting on what appeared to be the same couch in the living room.

Supreme pulled out his cell.

"Who you calling?"

"That nigga, Clip. Fuck! He ain't picking up. Don't nobody want to answer they fuckin' phones today."

"Do you really think it's a good idea to confront Clip over the phone? Wouldn't it be better to see him face to face so he can't get slick and escape from us? More importantly, get ghost and not tell us where Aaliyah is? We don't need to fuck up anymore links to Mike," I contended. This was the first time since the nightmare begun that I truly felt we were close to bringing Aaliyah home, and I didn't want a hot tempered Supreme messing it up by alerting Clip over vthe phone that we were on to him.

"Let me put in a call to Maya just so we can see where Clip's at. Then we'll go to him. From there, I don't care if you hang that nigga upside down by his dick as long as he gets to telling us what we need to know. Clip's a soft nigga. He ain't gonna try to be no soldier like that cat, Donnell."

"You call Maya, and I want both of you to keep post right outside this apartment," Supreme said, pointing to his men in black. I have a feeling ain't nobody coming back to this crib, but it's best to be careful."

"Do you believe we should get Detective Moore involved? I mean he could get access from the leasing office that could be extremely helpful. Like who's name the apartment's in, who's paying the rent, bank information... just shit that they not gonna voluntarily tell us."

"You might be right, Precious. I'll give Detective Moore a call after we've gone over every nook and cranny and I feel satisfied we've obtained all the pertinent information we can get."

While Supreme and his men began rummaging through every inch of the apartment, I placed my call to Maya. She wasn't answering her phone either, and after the tenth try I decided to leave a message. "Hey Maya, this is Precious. Listen, umm, I need for you to hit me back as soon as you get this message. An emergency came up and I need your assistance, so get back to me ASAP."

After leaving the message on her cell, I called the crib and got nothing but the answering machine. I opted not to leave a message there not wanting to take any chances of raising suspicion with Clip.

"Were you able to get in touch with Maya?" Supreme asked, taking a break from his search.

"No, she's not answering her phone. It's like everybody's ghost today. This shit is crazy."

"Crazy don't begin to describe it."

"Did you find anything else?"

"Not really. Besides the clothes, there was a couple pair of shoes, toothpaste and bullshit like that."

"Where did homeboy find that picture of Destiny?"

"Inside one of the books that was in the drawer next to the bed. The broad was probably rushing so fast to break the fuck out and forgot she even left her picture there".

"Her forgetfulness is our gain. Shit, because without that picture of Destiny, there wouldn't have been anything to connect Clip. I want to get my hands on that trick so bad. I wish I had her fucking number. Besides Clip, do you know anybody else who might have an address or contact information on Destiny?"

"I'm already on it. I put in a call to my secretary to get in touch with the agent who cast the video to see if they had her shit on file. I'm waiting for her to get back to me now."

"Yeah, but we need Clip. That nigga is the one who got the answers. I doubt that simple-ass chick, Destiny knows a damn thing of real importance, like where the hell Aaliyah is at right now. Honestly, I just want an opportunity to beat her ass for being in the same crib my daughter was held captive at."

"Hold up, this my secretary now," he informed me before answering the call. "Hey Stacy, what did you find out for me?"

While Supreme was digging for feedback, I sat down on the loveseat, thinking back to that day Maya and I caught Destiny's trifling ass in bed with Clip. Damn, I wish I would've let Maya beat that ho down. Shit, I should've put my foot up her ass too. I'm trying to play nice with the trick and she was probably sitting up in this very spot sharing space with my child. Did Clip clue the silly trick in on the fact that the baby was that of Supreme's, or was she so stupid that she ran with whatever half-ass story he gave her? I guess we won't find that out until we found the tramp. "What did she say?" I asked when I saw Supreme hang up his phone.

"Not shit worthwhile. The address the casting agent has is a P.O. Box, and the number is one of those voicemail phone services."

"Fuck! It's like we keep hitting one brick wall after another."

"Who you telling? Shit, we don't even know how long ago who-ever was staying here bounced."

"Yeah, but it couldn't have been that long ago, be- cause besides the baby food jars, there was some leftover meatloaf in there, and a carton of milk that hasn't even been opened yet."

"Shit, we're just one step behind them then."

"I bet they bounced when they got word that Donnell had been jacked and Vernika was dead. Mike probably wasn't a hundred percent positive whether Donnell would roll over and start snitching or what else we would find out, so to be on the safe side he probably cleared house."

Supreme sat down next to me nodding his head. "That's logical. Not knowing exactly how much time he had on his hands, he probably decided not to fuck with the rest of the shit in the crib and just clear out where he was laying his head, not wanting to leave any direct evidence to him."

"So you think Mike was living here too? That nigga got balls."

"It would make sense. But he definitely had someone else with him, because he couldn't go outside or show his face and take a chance someone would recognize him."

"That someone else had to be Destiny. I mean, why else would there be women's clothes, shoes and shit, and that picture of her?" I reasoned.

"Destiny fucking Mike and Clip, it's plausible. They got their shared whore maintaining shit for them and carrying out baby duty."

"If she was fucking Mike in this crib, then she had to know he kidnapped Aaliyah. Damn, I wish I would've let Maya beat her ass and put in a couple of licks of my own. So what's next?"

"Besides the few items we found, the search of this place has come up empty so I think I'ma go ahead and place that call to Detective Moore. If I do it now while it's still business hours, he should be able to find out some viable information."

"Cool. While you stay here and wait for the detective, I want to take your car and drive by a couple of spots and see if I can locate Maya."

"I don't know about that. I think maybe we need to stick togeth-er."

"Supreme, there is no sense in both of us sitting here waiting for Detective Moore. We need to make the most out of all the time we have. While you're here, I might be able to find Maya and she could tell me where Clip is, but we know that's not going to happen with both of us sitting here. She's not answering her phone, and Maya is good for leaving that shit someplace, so she might not even have it with her."

Supreme kept shaking his head, not convinced that us going our separate ways was the answer.

"Listen, if I get in touch with Maya and she tells me where Clip is, I promise I'll call you before making a move."

"Precious, I don't want you to even tell Maya what we've found out until we get our hands on Clip. I know that's your girl, but she's still in love with that nigga. When I left a message for Clip, I told him it was important for him to get in touch with me over some music shit. That's the same line I want you to run on Maya."

"I can do that."

"But don't confront that nigga without me. He evidently ain't the loyal cat I pegged him to be, so ain't no telling what he's capable of."

"If I'm able to get in touch with Maya and I find out anything, you're the first call I'll make. But make sure you hit me too if you come across any new leads."

"No doubt. But Precious, please be careful and don't try to be no hero. Our main objective is to bring our daughter home. One wrong move can fuck all that up."

I digested what Supreme said as I took the car keys from him. The comment he made about the one wrong move kept ringing in my ear. We were so close to putting the pieces to this puzzle together that making the wrong move was what I wanted to avoid at all costs.

WHO SHOT YA

Keyshia Cole's new single blasted from the speakers as I headed towards Maya's apartment. I put in a call to make sure she wasn't at my crib, but security informed me he hadn't seen her since leaving early that morning. As Keyshia poured her heart out about love and pain, my heart ached about the same. But it wasn't over a man, it was about my daughter.

I didn't share it with Supreme, but I thought about how if I had searched through Vernika's purse more thoroughly the very night she was killed, I might have found the address sooner and maybe got Aaliyah back then. But instead, I rushed off to New York to see Nico and forgot about the purse until a couple of days later. Those two days might have been crucial.

What if Mike didn't find out about Vernika's death immediately and lingered at the apartment for another day or so with Aaliyah? I knew I was doing a lot of speculating, but the guilt was weighing heavy on my mind. Was it necessary for me to see Nico in person, Couldn't I have just put in a phone call? It was too late to countdown the what if's. I did make the decision to get on a plane and warn Nico, and somehow I would have to make peace with that. And the only way that would happen was to bring my baby home.

"What the fuck!" I said, feeling a vibration on top of my thigh. I looked down and realized a call was coming from my cell. I had forgotten that I put my phone on vibrate, because I knew I wouldn't be able to hear it with my loud-ass music blasting. I turned down Keyshia and took the call. "Hello?"

"Precious, it's me, Maya."

"Girl, I've been trying to get in touch with you." I glanced at the number on the phone. "Where you calling me from?"

"It's a pay phone."

"A pay phone? Did you get the messages I left you on your cell?"

"No. I forgot my cell at your house. I haven't had that shit all day. But listen, I need you to meet me somewhere."

"Okay, I need to speak with you anyway. Supreme is looking for Clip. He has some important music shit to discuss with him. It's kinda urgent. Do you know where he is?"

"Precious, I need for you to come meet me now. We can talk about Clip when you get here... just come, please."

"Okay, give me the address," I said, typing it in the navigation system.

"How long is it going to take you to get here?"

"The navi' say about twenty minutes, but you know how I drive, so maybe ten, fifteen minutes."

"Okay, I'll be waiting out front in my car."

"Cool. I'll see you in a few."

Maya's voice sounded mad shaky and it had me concerned. She seemed stressed, and I figured it had to do with Clip. She had probably caught him fucking around again and was losing her mind. But that shit was nothing compared to the bullshit the nigga had really been up to. Although Maya had caught Clip red-handed with Destiny, she still remained his biggest supporter when it came to his loyalty for Supreme. She refused to believe my suspicions that Clip was a snake who would cross Supreme at the drop of a dime. You would think after being deceived by her own brother, who turned out to be the biggest loser of all, her judgment wouldn't be so blinded by Clip. I had to remind myself that even though she played the tough girl role, she was still young and impressionable. Nobody would want to believe the man they loved was capable of playing a role in the kidnapping of an innocent child. I hated to be the one to break the news to Maya that her man had done just that.

When I exited the highway, I made a left at the first light. I drove for a couple of minutes and the further I drove, the nonresidential street appeared more and more deserted. I eyed my navigation system to make sure I hadn't made a wrong turn, but I was following the directions correctly. I then took another left turn and continued to drive for a few more minutes until I heard the computer generated voice tell me I had reached my destination.

I turned into the isolated parking lot and saw what looked to be an abandoned warehouse. I didn't see Maya's car in the front, so I drove around the back. That's when I saw Maya's candy-apple red Jaguar, Clip's baby blue Benz with the vanity plates, and a black Navigator with pitch-black tint, but I didn't know who it belonged to. I pulled the Range next to Maya's car, but I guess she was inside the warehouse.

"What the fuck is Maya doing at a warehouse? Could she have found out that Clip is involved in Aaliyah's kidnapping and confronted him, and now the nigga is in there holding her hostage? But why wouldn't she have said something to me while she had me on the phone? Maybe she wanted to sit down and tell me to my face. Then Supreme's words started ringing in my ears again; *"One wrong move can fuck that all up."* "Let me call him right now so he can know what's going down," I said to myself.

"You find Maya?" Supreme asked, answering the phone and making it clear what was on his mind.

"As a matter of fact, I did."

"Jackpot! So where is Clip at?"

"They're at a warehouse."

"A warehouse, right now?"

"Yeah, and I'm worried about Maya. She called me from a pay phone and gave me this address to meet her at. She said she would be waiting in her ride, but she's not. Clip's car is here and somebody else's car, but I don't know who it belongs to. What if he's flipped out and is holding her hostage up in there?"

"Precious, you stay in the car and wait for me to get there. Don't go inside the warehouse. Wait in your car until I get there, do you hear me?"

"Yes. But what if Maya needs my help?"

"You ain't no good to Maya if you walk in there and get yourself killed. Stay fuckin' put. Now give me that address."

After I gave Supreme my location, he hung up the phone so quickly I didn't' even have a chance to say bye. I tapped my fingers on the steering wheel, wanting him to hurry up and get here. I mean, it was killing me to keep my ass in the car instead of going inside to see what was going down. If possible, it's always my preference to dig my hands deep in the mud and get dirty. Playing the waiting game wasn't one of my strong points. I kept looking down at my watch, and what seemed like an hour would only be one minute. I ruffled my fingers through my hair, with feelings of anxiousness and fear intertwining. I then took a few deep breaths so I could relax, and when it started working, that's when it turned bad.

The explosive sounds of gun shots were echoing from inside the warehouse. Without second-guessing myself, I grabbed my heat and jumped out the car. All I could think about was saving Maya. I wouldn't be able to live with myself if I let my girl die while I was playing it safe in my ride.

I ran up on the side door, but it was locked. I took off around the front and pushed open the door. It was eerily quiet when I got inside. I aimed my gun up ready to blast any motherfucka I even thought was wishing me harm. The dark walls and empty space gave it a dreadful appearance. It reminded me of a spot that would be perfect for torturing. The soles of my shoes lightly tapped the concrete flooring. I pivoted around a corner where a flickering light was coming from a room in the back. I paused, assessing the different prospects that lay behind the closed door. I continued to proceed towards my destination, saying to myself, *Shoot first ask questions later*. There was complete silence as I put my hand on the doorknob and slowly turned it. I had my finger firmly on the trigger, ready to blaze the whole fucking room.

I opened the door and a huge wooden table greeted me. In front of the table was the back of a woman's body. When my eyes focused and got a clearer look, I realized it was Maya. She was standing as if frozen in her space. I kept my gun aimed, prepared for any surprises. As I got closer, my vision captured the puddles of blood streaming across the floor. Then Maya felt a presence and turned towards me with her gun pointed in my direction.

"Maya, put the gun down," I said calmly. The distant look on her face told me her mind wasn't all there. She appeared to be in shock. "Maya, put the gun down," I repeated, worried that she may accidentally pull that trigger and I would have to take her out on some it's-my-life-over- yours type shit. To my relief, it seemed things were clicking and she laid the gun down on top of the table.

"I didn't have a choice, Precious. She was gonna kill me," Maya said, sounding stunned by whatever just took place.

After making my way from around the table and with nothing obscuring my sight, that's when the dead bodies welcomed me. Lying face up were Clip and Destiny. I couldn't believe it, another brick wall. With both Clip and Destiny dead, we would get no answers. In my desperation, I ran and bent down beside them to check their pulses, praying for a miracle. But there would be no miracle today; they had completely flat lined.

"Maya, what happened?" She remained unemotional, not saying a word.

Then we both jumped, startled by the blaring police sirens surrounding the building.

"Did you call the police?" Maya asked as fear seemed to take her over.

"No, I called Supreme when I got here. I was worried about you. He must've told Detective Moore what was going on and they brought the whole fucking army with them."

"Oh fuck, Precious, I don't want to go to jail. It was self defense... I didn't have a choice... it was either kill or be killed. It was Clip. Precious, he's the one that's responsible for helping Mike kidnap Aaliyah," she said in bewilderment.

"Maya," I said, standing up and holding her hand, hoping to snap her out of her daze. "How did you find out about Clip? Did he tell you where Mike has Aaliyah? I need you to concentrate, Maya."

"Drop your weapons and put your hands up!" the police yelled. There were about twenty of those motherfuckas armed with enough artillery to take out a small country.

I had flashbacks to when the cops swarmed Mike's house after he raped me, then Supreme busted in and I found out that he wasn't dead after all. I had never seen so many damn cops... until now. I don't give a fuck what anybody says, having a slew of guns aimed in your face with crackers dying to pull the trigger will make even the hardest badass want to piss in their pants. That's why with the quickness I put my gun down on top of the table next to Maya's weapon and put my hands up.

"Mrs. Mills, are you okay?" Detective Moore asked, making his way through the crowd of officers. I had never been so stoked to see his irritating ass, I almost bust a smile.

"I'm cool, but I'll be better if you could get your men to lower their weapons. They're not in any threat, and ain't anybody else here." The officers still didn't budge, making it clear my words didn't mean shit.

"Is there anybody down?" Detective Moore wanted to know. I assumed he meant dead people.

"Yes, two," I answered, looking down at Clip and Destiny. Detective Moore walked towards the scene with his weapon raised and observed the dead bodies. He checked their pulses and then stood up, retrieving my gun and Maya's off the table.

"You can put your weapons down," he finally ordered the other cops.

No longer feeling like a criminal, I put my hands down and relaxed.

"Where's Supreme?"

"He's outside. This is a crime scene so they can't let him in." Detective Moore then reached inside his suit jacket and pulled out a pad and pen. "I need to take a statement. Who wants to go first?" Detective Moore instantly jumped to business as usual.

"I will," Maya said, leaning against the table.

I put my hand up. "Hold on, Maya. I think we should wait for our attorney before answering any of your questions... no offense to you, Detective Moore."

He gave me a smug stare, but I played the cops and robbers game enough times to know better.

"Precious, I have nothing to hide. I want to tell you what happened."

"I don't think that's a good idea."

"Mrs. Mills, if your friend wants to talk, then I think you should let her. All we want is to get to the truth. It might even help us with our investigation regarding the whereabouts of your daughter."

"Detective Moore, don't use my daughter as bait to get Maya to talk."

"That's not what I'm doing. I was simply..."

Maya cut him off mid-sentence. "Please, stop. Precious, I want to talk. Like I said, I have nothing to hide."

"Then go 'head," I said, tired of going back and forth with it.

Detective Moore's beady blue eyes pierced in on Maya, as he was ready to hang onto her every word.

"Earlier today I went to the apartment and met up with Clip. We were trying to patch things up after I had found out he was screwing around on me with that Destiny chick."

"And Destiny, that's the deceased who's lying next to your boyfriend?" Detective Moore double-checked before jotting it down on his pad.

"Yes. He was finally admitting what had been going on between them, and swore that it was over and he wanted a chance to work things out between us. I agreed. I was in love with him. So we engaged in some make-up sex and I fell asleep. When I woke up, I overheard him talking to someone on the phone in the living room, so I went in the bedroom and picked up the phone to eavesdrop. He was talking to Destiny. She was threatening him, saying that if he didn't meet her she would go to the cops and his life would be over."

"What did she have on him?" the detective inquired, as if he wanted to know more for his own personal pleasure than a homicide investigation.

"She didn't say, but obviously he knew what she was speaking of because he agreed to meet her. She gave him the address and I also wrote it down. A few minutes later, he came in the room and said he had to go to the studio and work on some things, and that he would be back in a couple of hours. Of course I knew he was lying, but I didn't say anything. I wanted to get to the truth, and he wasn't going to tell me so I decided to find out my own way.

"After he left, I got dressed and headed here. I stopped at a pay phone and called Precious when I got close be- cause I didn't know what to expect."

"When you say you didn't know what to expect... in terms of what?"

"I mean, Detective, I'm from the streets. I wasn't sure if I was gon' end up beating her ass for fucking around with my man or what. So I wanted to make sure I had my girl with me just in case she had brought some of her girlfriends with her. They coulda tried to tag team me. I needed backup."

I put my hands on Maya's shoulders. "Calm down, its okay," I said as she started getting extra amped up.

"I'm sorry."

"That's okay, Ms. Owens, continue."

"So, umm, after I placed the call to Precious, I came here and saw their cars parked in the back. I sneaked inside so I could try and hear their conversation because I wanted to know what Destiny had on Clip, and I..." Maya then let out a gasp, broke down and started crying.

"Maya, you'll be okay," I said, holding her up, so she wouldn't fall down.

"Would you like to sit down, Ms. Owens? Officer, bring us that chair in the corner."

"I'm fine... I'm so sorry, this is harder than I thought it would be."

The officer brought Maya a chair and she sat down and got her bearings together. I was glad she sat down because the paramedics were now carrying off Clip in a body bag, and I knew how hard it was for her to see that. "Let me know when you're ready to continue, Ms. Owens."

"I'm ready. So when I came inside, they were arguing. Destiny told Clip she had enough of the bullshitting and wanted the money he owed her. He told her the money was in his car. She said that was cool, but she wanted an extra hundred grand. He told her she was fucking crazy and that if she wanted anymore money that she would have to get it from Mike."

"Mike? Do you mean your brother, Mr. Owens?" Detective Moore stopped writing, waiting for her answer.

"Yes. Precious, I'm so sorry, you were right. Clip was helping Mike. He did help him kidnap Aaliyah. I can't believe I was so stupid."

"It's not your fault."

"Yes it is. If only I had listened to you, maybe we could've stopped him."

"Not to interrupt, but Ms. Owens, what happened next?"

"Destiny wasn't trying to hear it. She said fuck him and Mike, that she wanted her money or she would go to Supreme and tell him that he was the one who helped Mike kidnap his daughter. That's when Clip lost it and smacked the shit out of her. He then grabbed her by the neck and started choking her. But Destiny came prepared. She reached in the back of her jeans and pulled out a gun and shot Clip multiple times. He fell to the ground, and she went in his pockets to get his car keys and wallet. I walked up on her from behind and startled her. She turned the gun on me, and there was a struggle and it went off. At first I didn't even realize she had been shot. It all happened so fast."

I held Maya tightly, as I could see the anguish in her eyes. I knew she hated Clip for what he had done, but she also loved him and no matter how horrible he was. She couldn't erase those feelings just like that.

"Detective Moore, I think you should come out here," one of the officers came up and said.

"Ladies, stay here, I'll be back right back."

I nodded my head and focused my attention back on Maya. Tears were streaming down her face and I knew there was nothing I could do to make her feel better.

"Precious, I feel so responsible."

"Why? You can't blame yourself for what Clip did."

"But it's like, first my brother rapes you, and now my boyfriend helped him make you and Supreme's life a living hell by kidnapping

454

your daughter. How could I have had two monsters in my life and not know it?"

"You're not responsible for their actions."

"I wish I felt that way. And I wish I hadn't killed Destiny, because she probably knew where Aaliyah is. Now how are we going to find her?"

I didn't even try to answer that question, because I kept asking myself the same thing. For every two steps forward, it seemed we would take two steps back. I honestly didn't know how much more of this I could take.

"Mrs. Mills, Detective Moore wanted you to follow me," an officer came to inform me.

"Now?"

"Yes, he said it's important."

"Maya, do you want to stay here or come with me?"

"I'll come with you."

Maya and I followed the officer out the back door. There were dozens of police cars and news crews. I could hardly see as I was blinded by the lights coming from the cameras. The officer had to push through the hordes of people.

"What the fuck is going on? Get these people out the way!" I complained. When we finally broke through the crowd, I saw Detective Moore standing in front of what appeared to be Supreme. "Oh shit, what the fuck is he harassing Supreme about?" I said, sick of being pestered by the cops. Due to the growing crowd, it took a few more minutes for us to make our way to Supreme and the detective. But when we did, I had to grab a hold of the officer in front of me so I wouldn't bust my ass falling down. My mouth dropped and the tears flowed.

"Precious, what's wrong?" Maya called out, unable to see what I could because I was blocking what was in front of me.

"I can't believe this... this can't be real!"

I screamed out. Supreme heard my voice and turned his body towards mine. "Yes it is," he said, coming towards me. My heart wouldn't let me believe it until I locked it in. There Supreme stood, cradling our baby.

"Aaliyah, my baby!" I put my head down and couldn't stop crying. She was bundled up in blankets, and I extended my arms out so I could hold her. Her eyes were closed, but when he put her in my arms and I held her, she opened them. The beautiful eyes she inherited from her grandmother welcomed me with open arms. I put her to my chest and held her so tightly. "You're home. My baby is finally home." Supreme wrapped his arms around me, and all I could do was thank God for what I called a miracle.

"I told you we would bring your baby home," Detective Moore boasted.

I didn't know if I wanted to punch him or hug him. "Where was she?" I wanted to know.

"Buckled up in the back seat of that truck."

"She was here the whole time?" I couldn't believe it.

"Yes, we had no idea she was in there. With the dark tint on the car and how it's parked, we had no way of seeing her. The baby must've been asleep and finally woke up because one of the officers heard crying coming from the vehicle. All of us were overjoyed it turned out to be your child."

"Thank you, Detective. I mean that from the bottom of my heart."

"I appreciate that, Mrs. Mills. I know you don't want to part from you daughter, but we need to take her to the hospital and have her examined by a doctor. The paramedics did check her out... but you understand."

"Of course I understand, as long as you understand that I'll be taking that ride with her to the hospital. I won't be leaving her side anytime soon."

"Precious, Supreme, I'm so happy for both of you," Maya said, staring down at Aaliyah. "I guess things turned out okay after all."

"And we have you to thank for that, Maya," I said.

"Me? Why are you thanking me?"

"Because if you hadn't decided to follow Clip and see what the hell was going on, we would've never found this place or our daughter. You're the one who deserves the credit for bringing Aaliyah home. I'll never forget what you've done."

"She's right, Maya. Thank you. I know you lost Clip, but you helped us get back our daughter," Supreme said, giving Maya a hug.

As we stood in the parking lot and I held my precious daughter for the first time in so long, I was overcome with true happiness. I was surrounded by the only real family I had ever known. If I had learned one thing from this entire situation, it was that you have to appreciate your time with the ones you love and never take it for granted, because life is much too sacred. Once again I had been given another chance in life to make things better, and I planned on doing exactly that.

LIGHTS OUT

"Happy Birthday, Aaliyah!" we hummed in unison. I couldn't believe that Aaliyah was one year old already. It seemed like yesterday I was in the hospital, knocking on death's door pushing her out, and now she was walking and trying to talk. I felt so blessed that I was able to witness those milestones. After bringing Aaliyah home, the last three months had been such an adjustment. Supreme and I were both guilty of damn near suffocating her with our attention. We still hadn't accepted there was no making up for lost time.

"Aaliyah, Mommy loves you, baby," I said, squeezing her tightly. She looked simply delicious in her ruby-red Grace attire. The velvet dress with silk trim and bow detail made her look like a little princess.

"Supreme, you stand in the middle so I can take a picture of the three of you," Maya said, holding her digital camera. "One, two, three, say cheese."

"Che-e-e-e-se!"

Aaliyah had the biggest grin on her face as the camera snapped, loving the attention. Aaliyah snuggled in her daddy's arms, now demanding all of his adoration.

"That was perfect. You guys really are the first family of hip hop royalty. Now only if I can find me a man," Maya said as we walked towards the gazebo.

"Maya, when the time is right you will find a man. You've been through a lot. You need to focus on you, and everything else will come."

"That's easy for you to say. You have Supreme and the most beautiful little girl in the world. What do I have?"

"You have us."

"Come on, Precious. I can't live under your roof forever. Eventually I have to get out on my own.'

"Nobody is rushing you. Now that the police inves- tigation is closed and the prosecution won't be bringing any charges against you, you need some time to fall back and relax."

"It's still hard to believe that Clip is gone. I know what he did was fucked up, but I loved him and I never thought he could be capable of anything like that."

"You're not the only one. He fooled Supreme too. He won't admit it, but he's hurting over what Clip did. He had a lot love for him. That was his protégé. Clip was going to be the next big rap phenomenon, and now he refuses to release his album even though it's completed. Supreme said any profits made off that CD would be blood money. He doesn't even care that he invested millions of dollars, and all that money has now gone to waste. But I recognize where Supreme is coming from."

"So do I. Plus, it don't help matters that Mike is out there some- where."

"Who you telling? It's like he's vanished into thin air. Every lead on him comes up cold. The last time we talked to Detective Moore he said that there was a sighting of him in New Mexico, but after that, nada. I won't feel completely safe until he's captured and back behind bars."

"I know, but with all the help he had on the outside dead, I have a feeling his time on the run will be coming to an end shortly."

"That's what the detective believes too. But enough about Mike's sorry ass. Today is one of celebration and I'm not going to let that sick fuck rain on our parade. I'd rather discuss how much we love having you here with us, and how wonderful you are with Aaliyah."

"I love being here too, especially since you guys are the only family I have. I mean I could always go back to New York and live with my mother, but you know what a headache that was. But with you bringing Anna back, you're not going to need me anymore."

"First of all, I'm not even sure if Anna will agree to come back. Just because she was willing to attend Aaliyah's birthday party doesn't mean she wants to work for me again, and honestly I couldn't blame her."

"Precious, I'm sure Anna understands that you were only reacting to the fucked up events that took place. I mean, your daughter was kidnapped and she was the last person with her. It's only natural you would take your frustrations out on her."

"Regardless, whether Anna comes back or not, that doesn't have anything to do with whether you stay or go. Like I said, you're welcome to live here for as long as you want. I actually enjoy your company. You know I don't really like fucking with these uppity Beverly Hills motherfuckas. You're the only friend I got," I laughed.

As Maya and I sat down under the gazebo, I watched everyone enjoying the festivities. What started off being a few close friends and family turned into quite an event. But they were mostly all Supreme's people. His parents came and damn near all his industry friends who had kids, and even the ones who didn't. I had never seen so many baby mamas in one vicinity in all my life. This was the life of the "rich and shameless".

"Well, girl, these mofos have been at my house long enough. It's time to clear house. The party is officially over. Do you care to join me as I kick these motherfuckas out?" I joked, but was dead serious.

"Of course. Lead the way." By the time Maya and I blew the last kiss goodbye to my fellow guests, not only was it way past Aaliyah's bedtime, but I was exhausted. The only thing I wanted to do was crawl into bed with my husband and get some good loving.

"Baby, I'ma put Aaliyah to bed," Supreme said, holding our daughter in his arms.

Her eyes were closed so I gave her a soft kiss on the cheek so I wouldn't wake her up. I stood in the middle of the living room smiling, watching Supreme carry Aaliyah upstairs, feeling that my life couldn't get any better than this.

"Mrs. Mills, which room would you like for me to sleep in tonight?" Anna asked while I stood in the foyer captivated by the bond between Aaliyah and Supreme. It was a connection I never shared with my own father, a man I never even knew.

"I'm sorry, Anna what did you say?" I asked, coming out of my daydreaming.

"What room should I sleep in?"

"Your old room, but only if you agree to stay, Anna." I gave her a pleading look, hoping she would take me up on my offer.

"You really want me to come back and work for you, Mrs. Mills?" she asked with complete astonishment in her voice.

"Yes. I understand if you have reservations. I mean I treated you pretty badly. I was happy you agreed to come join us for Aaliyah's birthday party, although I figured it was because Supreme asked you."

"You know how highly I think of Mr. Mills, but I think highly of you too, Mrs. Mills and I also love baby Aaliyah very much. Nothing would make me happier than to be a part of your family again."

"Thank you, Anna," I said as we embraced. "Things are finally getting back to normal."

With everybody gone, and with both Anna and Maya tucked away in their rooms, I made a pit stop to the kitchen. I pulled out an ice cold bottle of bubbly for me and my husband. With two champagne glasses, whipped cream and strawberries in my hands I made my way to our bedroom, ready for us to toast the night away.

"What is all this?" Supreme asked as I entered our bedroom.

"I thought that since the kids played all day, it was time for the grown folks to do a little celebrating."

"What did you have in mind?"

"Some champagne, and then you rocking me to sleep. How does that sound?"

"Sounds tempting, but, umm..."

"But umm... what?"

"You want me to rock you to sleep, that means I have to do all the work. Shouldn't there be some sort of even exchange?"

"Excuse me?"

"No need to get hostile, all I'm saying is that can't you show me a little gratitude for all the work I'm about to put in?"

"A little gratitude... I think I can do that."

"I appreciate the cooperation, but first, can you take your clothes off? Gratitude is so much more fulfilling when you're naked." Neither of us could hold back our laughter.

"You're a mess, but your wish is my command." After placing our goodies on the nightstand beside the bed, I untied my midnight-blue Diane Von Furstenberg wrap dress. Then off came the laciest black La Perla bra and panty set. By the time I was done, the only thing left on me was my jewel-studded Giuseppe stilettos."

"Now that's more like it."

"Does that mean you're feeling the gratitude?" I flirted.

"You're getting there."

"Aren't you a hard one to please? I have a feeling this will do the trick, but first let's have a toast," I said, pouring champagne in our glasses. I put my hand around the necklace Supreme gave me in the hospital after surviving my brush with death. I turned over the pink diamond heart-shaped necklace, "You see that? It says 'S&P Love for Life'. That's you and me, baby. Can't nothing come between that."

"Let's toast to S&P Love for Life. You're the only woman for me, and I better be the only man for you," Supreme said, pulling me into a deep kiss. We clinked our glasses and drank up the champagne, solidifying our toast.

After tasting Supreme's lips, I continued sprinkling kisses down each crest of his chiseled chest, then stopped, using the tip of my tongue to circle his belly button. As his eyes rolled in delight, I took the whipped cream and polished his manhood, devouring each inch of him until he was ready to explode in my mouth. When he seemed as if he couldn't hold back any longer, I began to straddle him, and his dick penetrated inside of me.

"Damn, baby, my pussy feels so good!" he moaned, and pulled my breasts to his mouth.

I closed my eyes, winding my hips like I was a belly dancer. Warmth encompassed my insides as my first orgasm set upon me. "Supreme, don't ever leave me."

"I ain't going nowhere, just as long as you don't ever leave me."

"I'll never leave you. I promise you that." And as our bodies became interwoven I meant every word I said. Supreme was it for me. There was no greater love than the one we shared together.

That night, Supreme and I made love until we fell asleep in each other's arms. We had once again been through the fire, but we came out of it stronger and more bonded than ever. Our love continued to stand against every obstacle thrown our way. I guess it's true what they say: "There's no greater love than Black love."

"Good morning, baby," I said, giving Supreme a kiss on the lips.

"Good morning to you. Last night was incredible. I fell in love with you all over again."

"Damn, I need to pull out the whipped cream more often."

"Yeah, you should."

"Don't be cute," I teased, tossing a pillow over his face.

"Oh, so now you want to play. I hear a pillow fight."

"No, no, no. I don't have the time for that. I'ma have to take a rain check," I said, jumping out of bed.

"Where are you off to?"

"First the shower, then after that it's a surprise."

"A surprise for who?"

"A surprise for my husband."

A gigantic smile lit up Supreme's face.

"You have a surprise for me? What is it?"

"Supreme, if I told you what it was, then it wouldn't be a surprise, now would it?"

"So you have to leave the house to get it?"

"Ye-e-e-e-s-s-s-s!"

"Okay, okay. You got me all excited like I'm a little kid at Christmas. I don't know what I'm going to do with myself until you get back."

"I'm sure you'll think of something."

"Already have. I'll take Aaliyah in the back and play roll-the-ball. Don't ask me why, but she gets the biggest kick outta that."

"Great. And by the way, Anna has agreed to come back and work for us again."

"That's what's up!"

"I thought for sure I was going to have to send you in to beg her to return, but she didn't make me grovel."

"Anna's good people, but stop talking to me. Go get ready so you can hurry up and come back with my surprise."

"You really are acting like a big kid, but I love you so it doesn't matter. I'm off," I said, disappearing to the shower.

As the hot water splashed against my body, I decided that I would plan a family trip for me, Supreme and Aaliyah. The three of us would go to some exotic island and have quality time together away from LA and the hectic schedule that Supreme was susceptible to on a regular basis. So, the jewelry I was picking up for Supreme would only be the first part of the surprise, and our family trip would be part two.

By the time I got out of the shower, Supreme had already left the room and I assumed he was somewhere tickling Aaliyah, since that's what he loved to do first thing every morning. After getting dressed, I stopped by Maya's room to see if she wanted to take a ride with me to the jewelry store. I knocked on her door but got no answer, so I opened the door to see if she was still asleep. "Maya," I called out, thinking maybe she was in her bathroom, but I got no answer. "Maybe she's downstairs," I said and closed the door back.

When I got downstairs the house was already lively. Supreme and Aaliyah were sitting on the living room sofa, and I could smell the aroma of scrumptious food coming from the kitchen, and knew it had to be Anna in there whipping up one of her to-die-for meals. Then Aaliyah saw me and rolled off the sofa and ran towards me with her arms out. "Hi, my baby. Mommy missed you," I said, picking her up and swinging her around. Aaliyah put her head back and laughed her little heart out.

"Listen, Mommy has to go now because I have to go get a special surprise for your Daddy. But I'll be back soon, so keep Big Papa entertained until I return." I nuzzled my nose against her neck and she laughed even harder.

"Come here, little girl. Come play with Daddy until your Mommy gets back," Supreme said, taking Aaliyah out my arms and lifting her in the air. "Now you hurry back."

"I will. Oh, by the way, have you seen Maya?"

"No, I assumed she was in her room still sleep."

"No, I checked but she was gone. Maybe she had something to do early this morning. I'll call her when I get in the car."

"Do you want me to have someone drive you?"

"That's okay, I'm good. Plus, I want to take your new Lamborghini for a spin."

"Oh really now?"

"Yes, really. I know it's parked right outside. That's why I was looking for Maya. Two hot chicks in that whip, can you imagine all the men we could pick up? I'm only joking, so get that frown off your face."

"Your mother trying to make Daddy lose it up in here," Supreme said to Aaliyah as if she understood exactly what he was saying.

"Bye, you guys. I'll see you in a little bit."

Supreme and Aaliyah walked me to the door and waved goodbye as I got in the car. I put the key in the ignition and clutched my hand on the stick shift, speeding off with the morning sun shining brightly. I had Nas blazing through the speakers, and I was caught up in my own groove, oblivious to world around me. It was like that the entire time until I pulled up to the Cartier store on Rodeo Drive. Arriving first thing in the morning before the streets turned into the who's who of Hollywood, I stepped out of my car high off the notion of how fucking incredible my life was.

As I was about to exit Supreme's custom shocking- pink Genaddi Lamborghini Murcielgo Roadster, I heard answer anyway. "Hello?"

"Hi, Precious, I'm happy for you and your family. I wanted to call sooner, but I knew you and Supreme would want some time alone after bringing your daughter home."

"Nico, thank you so much. I'm glad that you called," I said, stepping out of the car. "I was wondering if I would hear from you again. I..."

"Precious, are you there?"

I heard Nico's voice but my response lingered in the air. Out of nowhere, the black tinted SUV seemed to appear like a dark cloud before the storm. I had no preparation as my body was lifted off the ground, causing me to drop my phone. I could still hear Nico screaming out my name as it hit the pavement. I was thrown into the truck, and before I could utter a word or fight back, the wet cloth with chloroform knocked me out, lickety-split.

"So we meet again. I knew we would. I've been waiting for this day for a very long time."

My eyes couldn't focus on the figure standing in front of me. I could hear a voice, but I was struggling to get out of the chloroform-induced daze.

"Wake up," the voice demanded as a hand gripped my chin. But I was finding it impossible to center my attention until a punch landed on my jaw, causing my head to rock to the side.

"Who the fuck are you and what do you want from me?" I mumbled, feeling as if my head was about to fall off my neck.

"Oh, you don't know who the fuck I am? Look real closely."

My central vision was coming back, but as soon as it did I wanted it to vanish. The image in front of me was too devastating to believe.

"Mike, you had to come back." His head was completely bald but the eyes never lie, and it was him, Pretty Boy Mike in the flesh.

"Hmm, that's the thing. I never left. I was waiting for the right time for you to put your guard down. Take a look around, because this will be your new home for a very long time," he said, spreading out his arms. He was wearing a three-piece suit and looking like a hood version of Creflo Dollar.

I scanned the room and it looked like I was in a dreary basement of a house. It was cold and had no windows. I was on the floor, with both my hands and legs tied up to a pipe. "You just don't know when to stop. I thought after Clip got killed helping out your sick ass you would've crawled under a rock and choked to death. But look at where I am now. Obviously I'm not that lucky," I spewed.

"Now, Precious, you know Clip didn't have enough balls to kidnap a puppy, let alone the baby of the great Supreme. You couldn't really believe that incompetent idiot had the brains to pull that off," another voice said from the shadows.

"Whoever said that, show your face right now!" I commanded.

"Your ears aren't playing tricks on you," the voice stated, stepping into the light.

"You! I presume you truly are your brother's keeper."

"Yes, I am," Maya boasted.

"This was all a setup."

Maya and Mike started clapping. "But wait, we can't forget about the hard work Devon put in," Maya said as Devon then stepped into the light.

"I never did like your motherfuckin' ass," I growled at Devon.

"Then we have something in common. Before I put that bullet in Vernika, it took every ounce of me not to aim at you. But I was following orders so I had to let you live."

"So you three clowns orchestrated this whole thing. Unfuckin' believable."

"Dear brother, I think I should get most of the credit. It was me who hired that dumb Destiny to make it look as if she was cheating with my man."

"What do you mean, look as if he was cheating? I caught them in..." There was no need to complete my thought, as all the pieces popped in my head and came together at once. "You conniving bitch, you set it up for me to find Clip and Destiny together. That's why he seemed so out of it when he woke up. You scandalous hoes' drugged his ass."

"Without a doubt. It started the day you came over and I put that bug in your ear about the crank phone calls I was getting at the house and the missing money that Clip couldn't account for. Then I made sure when we went to the video shoot that you caught Destiny coming out of Clip's room, you know, just to start raising doubt. Then that day I conveniently had you pick me up from the car dealership, I had already drugged Clip, and Destiny was at my place waiting for my phone call so she could put our plan in action. From the moment you caught him and Destiny in bed together, nothing could dissuade your belief that Clip was not only a cheat, but Mike's accomplice."

"Clip had absolutely nothing to do with any of this, and after using him as your fall guy you killed him?"

"Pretty much. But unfortunately I can't take credit for killing Clip. Destiny did that dirty deed for me. After you and Supreme managed to get the address to where Donnell and Vernika were staying, I knew we had to act fast. It was only a matter of time before you would find the apartment that I had Destiny staying at with Aaliyah. But of course I had to leave just enough evidence to implicate Clip without jumping overboard."

"You're feeling real proud of yourself, aren't you, Maya? You're even crazier than your fuckin' deranged brother."

"Why thank you. But let me finish." Maya smiled, showing how swollen with pride she was of her accomplishments. "It was time to cut off all loose ends. So Devon went back after his shift and finished off Chris and Donnell. Then dumbass Destiny believed she was meeting me at the warehouse to give me Aaliyah, kill I put that bullet in her, she had no idea that her services were no longer needed and her time was up. And poor Clip, he thought he was coming to the warehouse to save me. He was devastated when I laughed in his face and told him he was nothing but a pawn in my deadly game."

"I'm impressed, Maya. If it wasn't for your diligence, none of this would be possible," Mike said, patting his younger sister on the back of her shoulder.

"So, Maya, you never loved Clip. It was always your plan to use him as a cover-up to get your brother out of jail, and then what? What is your ultimate goal, to kill me? Then go ahead and do it."

"We can always count on you to be tough as nails to the bitter end, can't we, Precious?" Mike scolded.

"Let me handle this, Mike," Maya said, hushing her brother and making it clear that she was the one running the show. "I had been secretly talking to my brother for a very long time. I hated you for sending him to prison. He was the only real family I had. Nobody gave a fuck about me, including my mother. Mike was the only person who took care of me."

"How soon we forget. I took care of you, Maya. I treated you like my very own sister and this is how you repay me?"

"Get the fuck off your pedestal. You really think your shit don't stink. You took my brother away from me."

"He raped me and tried to kill Supreme. Putting him in a jail cell was a gift. He deserved to be buried alive."

"Whatever my brother did to you, you deserved it, and you were never good enough for a man like Supreme.

I'm the type of woman that can hold it down for him. I've decided I want Supreme for myself. I mean, why should I have to play second fiddle to you? Why should I have to be stuck with a wannabe like Clip?

I deserve the king."

"Oh shit, here we go!" Mike growled.

"Dear brother, you know the deal. You get your freedom and I get my life with Supreme."

"You really are crazy. You will never have Supreme. He will see right through you."

"You didn't," Maya said mockingly. "Trust me, Supreme will be so heartbroken when you never come home that he'll seek the comfort from a dear friend like myself."

"Oh please! When Supreme realizes I'm dead he'll start putting the pieces together and point the finger right to your manipulating ass."

"By the time your dead, it'll be too late and it won't matter. See, I want you to be alive and have a front row seat as I take over your life. You'll watch as I make your husband fall in love with me, and your beautiful daughter, Aaliyah will be calling me Mommy."

"You'll never pull it off."

"You better hope I do, because if not, that little precious daughter of yours is going to end up dead."

"Maya, that might be my flesh and blood you're threatening to kill, and your niece," Mike reminded her, seeming genuinely stunned that Maya would make such a threat on Aaliyah.

"Mike, shut up. You're taking this Maury Povich, I-might-be-the-father thing way too far. If it wasn't for me, you wouldn't have thought for a second that Aaliyah might be your daughter, so save it."

"Now it makes sense. Your trifling ass was the one that made Mike feel so confident he was Aaliyah's father. I guess she was the perfect bait to wave in front of your brother's face so he would be a willing participant with this bullshit plan you're trying to pull off."

"I ain't trying to do shit! My eyes see very well, and from where I'm standing, your ass is on lock and I'm the one who is free, about to go to the crib you used to share with Supreme and comfort him. So the bullshit plan you're speaking of has been pulled off as far as I'm concerned."

"Maya, you better kill me now, because if I ever get free..." my voice faded off.

"I so admire your fire. It's contagious. Here, I brought this for you to keep your heart warm at night." Maya pulled out something from her pocket and handed it to me. "I thought it was only fair you have it, since it's the last picture you will ever take with your family."

It was the photo of me, Supreme, and Aaliyah that Maya took

yesterday at her birthday party. I fought back the tear that wanted to escape my eye. This couldn't be it for me. The happiest moment of my life, ripped from me just like that. "I swear you're gonna pay for this, Maya. I put that on everything I love."

"Precious, save your threats. It's lights out for you. Bow down, I'm the new queen bitch."

A KING PRODUCTION

Queen BITCH

Part 4

JOY DEJA KING

Precious

On Everything I Love

God, protect me from my friends. I can handle my enemies. I never forgot reading that in the front pages of a novel. Those words resonated with me. At the time I read it, I didn't believe it applied to me because I had no friends, that was, until I took Maya under my wing. Now here I was, shackled up in a dreary basement, sitting on the cold cement floor with the person I considered being like my own blood staring down at me. No, she wasn't the anointed sister I never had, she was my worst enemy. I had let my guard down, and got caught slipping. Now this diabolical heifer wanted me to step out my shoes and give them to her, then hand her the keys to my cars and house so she could live in that too. To say this chick had me jammed up would be an understatement.

"Maya, you need to go 'head and slit my throat, put a bullet through my heart or however your trife ass wanna take me out, 'cause I ain't helping you take my husband. I wouldn't wish you on the worse nigga I fucked, let alone Supreme."

"Bitch, you think I'm playing wit' your stupid ass? When I said I would take your daughter out this world, I meant it!" Maya said with so much vengeance that spit sprayed out her mouth after each word. Then to make sure I got her message Maya balled up her fist and clocked me on the side of my left temple, causing my eyes to lock shut and my head to plummet down in pain. "Those are the exact type of licks your precious Aaliyah will be getting if you don't wise up and get with the plan."

This ho is truly fuckin' crazy. How in the hell did I get blindsided and not see I was dealing with a mental case? I believe this sick motherfucker might really kill my baby. I ain't taking no chances. I'll play along with her ass while I'm plotting to get the fuck up outta here and send this bitch floating in the Pacific Ocean somewhere.

"You made your point, Maya. I'll do whatever I have to do," I said, containing the rage I wanted to spew on her.

"Good, that's a smart decision. Since you can't save your own life at least you can save that of your daughters'."

"I guess that's your slick way of letting me know I'ma dead bitch once you don't need me anymore."

"But of course. I thought that was already under-stood. Once we have our fun with you, it's a wrap. Until then, I promise we'll take good care of you. On that note, I must be going." Maya looked down at her watch. "I'm sure Supreme is starting to wonder where you are and of course I must be there to begin planting my seeds."

"It's not too late for you to dead this shit, Maya. You, your brother and the third stooge, Devon, can get out of town."

"And what, let you go free? After all the hard work we've put in, to hatch this plan? That just ain't gonna happen."

Maya was determined to see this shit through and there was nothing I could do but figure out a way to break the fuck out, which under the current circumstances was damn near looking impossible. After the punch Mike landed on my jaw and the fist Maya branded on my temple, trying to concoct an escape plan had my head triple spinning in pain. I could barely keep my eyes open and wanted to succumb to my need to pass out, but when I saw Mike grab Maya's arm and pull her to the side, I willed myself to focus.

"Maya, you need to chill with all this talk about hurting the baby. That shit ain't cool. I know you want Precious to cooperate with you, but you going overboard with pretending you would hurt an innocent child, especially one that might be our blood," Mike said in a low but stern voice as if he didn't want me to hear him.

"Shit, I ain't fucking pretending," Maya boasted loudly, making it clear she didn't give a fuck who was privy to her threats. "That was some real talk," she continued.

"Maya, keep your fucking voice down!" Mike ordered, grabbing the bottom of her elbow and edging her forward.

Maya yanked her arm away, showing her displeasure of her brother's manhandling. "You getting yourself all worked up over a child that probably ain't even yours."

"Well, until we know for sure let's put a cease to all the baby threats. Is that understood?" Maya remained silent with a blank stare. "Are we clear." Mike barked loudly making more of a statement than asking a question.

"You can relax, I got you, dear brother," Maya finally said, releasing herself from Mike's clutch. "I really have to go. I don't need any suspicions falling on me."

"That's cool. So I guess I'll see you back here tomorrow?"

"Yeah, if everything's straight. Devon, you need to be leaving shortly too. I don't want Supreme to have problems tracking you down."

"I feel you. I'm 'bout to break out."

"A'ight gentlemen, I'll be in touch. Oh, and have a goodnight, Precious. I'll make sure to give Aaliyah a kiss for you." Both Mike and I gave Maya a look of disgust, but she sauntered out like she could give a fuck.

"Can I get a blanket, pillow, something? It's cold as shit down here," I asked Mike trying to vibe him out.

"What the fuck you think this is, the penthouse suite? The only thing you getting from me is bread and water," he said, coldly.

"Oh, so all that talk about taking good care of me until it was checkout time was some bullshit?"

"Letting your ass live a little bit longer is taking good care of you. Be happy you getting that."

"Like I said from jump, under these conditions you would be doing me a favor by killing me now. It's your sister that wants to keep me alive for her own twisted reasons."

"Maybe, but I like the idea of letting you suffer a bit before ending your life. Being locked up like an animal is one of the most humiliating feelings in the world, especially when you a rich nigga used to living a life of luxury. You can get a taste of how I felt being locked up at Clinton for all that time. I'ma enjoy watching your Beverly Hills ass being dead on the inside but very much alive on the outside, to see how pathetic you'll be when we're done with you."

I simply put my head down and ignored what Mike said. There was no sense riling him up any further because whatever torture plan they had in mind, I prayed it didn't include Mike raping me again.

"I'm outta here, Mike. I'll check in tomorrow," Devon said, giving Mike a pound. He had been so damn quiet, I almost forgot he was still in the room. My eyes darted around the chilly, dark basement which I would now be calling home for however long. At any moment I expected a rat to dash across the concrete floor or a poisonous spider to crawl up my leg. I was truly in hell.

"Hold up, I'll follow you up. I'm done with her for the day," Mike said, grabbing some keys off a metal chair in the center of the room. "Sleep tight, Precious. And don't bother screaming because this room is soundproof. Plus, we way the fuck out, can't nobody find you here anyway."

I watched as Mike and Devon went upstairs leaving me alone in this miserable existence as if I was nothing. I stared up at the small dim light bulb dangling from the ceiling, hoping that one day I would see the light again too. Then I heard the door slam and my body jumped, and a few seconds later it was pitch dark.

"I can't believe they turned off the little bit of light I had." My body stiffened up in fear not able to see shit. "On everything I love, all those motherfuckers gon' pay!"

Maya

Good Girl Gone Bad

As I pulled up my candy apple red Jaguar to the gates, a smile crept across my face. I knew that if I played my cards right that soon this estate and everything in it would belong to me, including Supreme.

"Hey, Maya," the security guard waved as he opened the gate for me. I simply grinned and waved back. I remembered that he was one of the only guards that Precious liked, and I made a notation to myself to fire his ass after I became the new Mrs. Mills.

As I drove up the circular entrance and parked near the waterfall, it was time for me to put my game face on. Once Supreme got wind that Precious was missing he would instantly suspect foul play. Every movement I made from the moment I stepped through the front door would then be critiqued, so from the get, I had to come correct.

I took a deep breath and headed to the door using my key for entry. Before I had a chance to close it, Aaliyah came running towards me. I assumed she had been expecting her mother the way her sparkly eyes and bubbly smile instantly disappeared when she realized it wasn't Precious.

"Hi, Aaliyah!" I gushed, bending down on my knees and giving her a hug. She reciprocated the affection but it wasn't the excitement she always had when greeting her mother.

"What up, Maya? We thought you were Precious," Supreme said, walking towards us in the forty-foot high limestone entry.

"Precious isn't here? Where did she go?"

"She left early this morning to pick up a surprise she had for me, and here it is going on five o'clock and I haven't heard from her."

"You haven't heard from her since this morning? That's strange. Did you try her cell?"

"Yeah, I been blowing that shit up but she ain't answering her cell or the car phone. You haven't heard from her either?"

"You know how I'm always forgetting my cell. I left it in my bedroom. Let me go check to see if she left me a message."

"Thanks, I appreciate that, Maya."

"No problem, but I'm sure she'll be walking through the front door any moment," I said, giving Aaliyah a kiss before heading upstairs. When I got to my bedroom I closed the door and took my cell out of my purse, tossing it on the bed. I sat down for a few minutes letting some time pass to give the impression I was checking my calls. But before I could even make it back downstairs Supreme was knocking on my door.

"Maya," I heard Supreme call out after beginning a second round of banging.

"Come in." I flipped my cell open pretending to be checking messages. I held a finger up giving Supreme a sign to wait as if listening intently. "Nothing," I sighed shutting my phone close.

"Damn, this shit is crazy. Where could she be?"

"Supreme, I'm positive she's good. Precious probably decided to get a spa treatment at the last minute and lost track of time, you know, some simple bullshit like that."

"Maybe you're right. She is good for getting side-tracked."

Ring...Ring...Ring!

"Hold on, Maya, let me get that. It might be Precious caling."

"Go head, it probably is...*not!*" I chuckled as Supreme rushed to pick up the landline. It was a shame the circles Supreme would be running around in for the next few weeks, wondering where the hell his wife was. I damn sure didn't want to see him losing his mind over Precious' useless ass, but shit had to run its course.

I decided to head in Supreme's direction to give the notion of concern for Precious whereabouts. At first I walked towards their master bedroom, but then realized the sound of his voice was coming from downstairs. By the time I reached the bottom step, Supreme's once calm voice had now raised and become animated.

"What you mean she never came to pick it up? That was hours

ago and you just now calling! Fuck that! I don't want to hear none of your fucking excuses. This is some bullshit! I'm on my way over there!" Supreme roared before slamming the phone down.

"Supreme, who was that?"

"The fucking jewelry store where Precious was supposed to be picking up something for me. They said she never showed up."

"What? She was supposed to have done that hours ago!"

"I know, and the only reason those dumb fucks called was because she was supposed to pay the remaining balance once she picked up the shit, and they worried about getting their damn money."

"So what are you going to do?"

"I'm going over there and see what the fuck is up."

"Well, I'm coming with you."

"Cool, let me go tell Anna we're heading out."

My mind began racing because I hadn't thrown in the mix the possibility of the jewelry store calling and Supreme being alerted so soon that shit was shady. *Remain calm Maya. This ain't nothing but a minor bump that isn't gonna change shit in the plan.*

"A'ight, let's go," Supreme said, shaking me out my thoughts as I followed him to the Maybach waiting out front. "Where's Devon?" Supreme asked the driver who was standing out front and opened the back door for us.

"Mr. Mills, he got held up but said he would be here shortly. He asked me to stay on until he arrived."

Oh shit! I told Devon dumb ass not to get missing. That mother-fucker better have his story airtight when Supreme grill him on why the fuck he was late for his shift.

"I'll deal with that nigga later. Head over to Cartier on Rodeo Drive," Supreme directed the driver. He then hit a button on his phone and kept redialing the same number over and over again, and I assumed it was Precious'.

"Who are you are calling?" I asked innocently.

"Who the fuck you think I'm calling? My wife!" Supreme snapped.

"I'm sorry, that was a dumb question." I opted to remain silent for the rest of the ride because Supreme was in full blaze mode right now, and one wrong word, he might have the driver pull over and tell me to get the fuck out the car.

"Don't go to the lot, pull up right in front," Supreme said and hopped out before the driver could even put the car in park.

I slid over to get out on Supreme's side, but he slammed the door in my face. I leaned back over to my side and got out trying to remain close on Supreme's tail. When I entered Cartier passing the red velvet rope, Supreme was already at the counter demanding to see the manager. It was my first time in the store, but instantly I felt at home. The over 900 square foot of retail space, two level boutique had endless decorative touches—from heavy drapes to an 800 pound Murano glass chandelier designed to make the place feel very intimate. Everything from the carpet to curtains was like what you would find in a private residence.

"Yes, Sir, I'm the manager. How may I help you?" a short cropped, dark haired gentleman asked in a funny English accent.

"I got a call from one of your salespeople about an item my wife was supposed to pick up from here earlier today."

Then a snotty, painfully thin bottled blond white chick whispered something in the manager's ear. He simply nodded his head while Supreme leaned on the glass counter as if he was about to smash his elbow through it.

"Yes, Mrs. Mills was supposed to be picking up some items we had costumed made for her. Are you here to pay the remaining balance?"

"Listen, ain't nobody tripping off your little remaining balance. I want to know what time my wife was supposed to pick up the jewelry, who spoke to her last, and what did she say."

"No need to get upset, sir. We appreciate your business and would be more than happy to assist you with your questions, but we do need to be paid for the items your wife ordered. These are specialty items and cannot be resold, that is why we were concerned about receiving the remaining balance."

"Yo, would you please stop beating me in the head about that fucking remaining balance? I heard you the first fucking time when you clowns called my crib! What, because I'ma nigga you think me and my wife can't afford to pay for the shit?"

The manager's face turned beet red.

"Supreme, calm down," I said putting my hand on his shoulder.

"Don't fucking tell me to calm down!" Supreme jerked his shoulder, blowing my hand away. A few other customers in the store and the security guard up front were all focusing their attention in our direction.

"That man looks awfully familiar. Is he some sort of actor or something?" I overheard one middle aged white woman say to her male counterpart as they browsed the accessories section.

"Sir, I'm going to need you to calm down," the manager pleaded.

"Or what, you're going to call the police? Go 'head, then you'll neva get that remaining balance."

"Then we would have to take legal action."

"Sue me, you bootleg Mr. Belvedere, 'cause I have big lawyers. So you can either answer my questions and get your fucking remaining balance, or you can keep annoying me with that damn fake ass English accent and get nothing!"

The manager let out a deep sigh. "Carol, who spoke to Mrs. Mills today?"

"I did," the painfully thin sales clerk answered.

Supreme then put his glare on her. "When?" he asked.

Carol turned her head to her manager as if waiting for his approval before she answered. He nodded his head indicating it was okay to speak and she continued. "I spoke to Mrs. Mills yesterday evening before we closed, and then this morning around ten o'clock. She said she was on her way and would be here shortly. That is why I decided to call her home because I had been waiting and she never showed up," Carol said, in that same funny English accent as her boss.

"So what took you so long to call the crib if you spoke to her around ten? It's about to be six o'clock," Supreme said, agitated.

"Sir, I had been calling her cell phone and left several messages, as that was the primary number she gave. I then realized she also left a secondary number and that is when I called."

"Damn, you shoulda seen that shit sooner. All this time has passed and I don't know what could've happened to her. Maybe some foul shit." Supreme said with distress in his voice.

"Mr. Mills, how were we supposed to know that something unfortunate could've happened to your wife?" the manager interjected before Carol could say another word.

"I understand that, but it still doesn't change the fact that I haven't heard from my wife since she left this morning to come to your store." Supreme put his head down staring as if transfixed on something he could see through the glass cases. Everyone remained frozen, not knowing what to do or say next.

"Sir, would you like to see your wife's purchases?" Carol finally asked, trying to melt the ice and, I'm sure to collect their dough. I was worried Supreme was going to choke hold the broad for once again mentioning the items, but surprisingly Supreme seemed serene about seeing them. The woman walked behind a closed door and came out with two long red velvet boxes. She placed them on top of the counter-top before opening each one up.

I stepped forward wanting to get an up close inspection of the jewels. "Precious, always had spectacular taste," I mumbled under my breath, taking in the jewelry.

"It's his and hers cuff link white diamond bracelets. The emblematic Cartier link is borrowed from the Maison's cult animal, the panther collection. As you can see the diamond paving pieces are sensually wrapped around and the fluid lines sparkle with the light of a thousand flames," Carol gave her spill extra eloquently as her boss smiled in approval. I couldn't be mad at the bitch for keeping to her sales pitch even though it was evident her would be customer was more than pissed the fuck off.

"Your wife also had the inside engraved. Here, take a look." Carol slid the bracelet closer to Supreme so he could inspect it. "It says 'Love 4 Life...Always'. That's beautiful."

I was ready to spit on Carol's toothpick ass by this particular point. She was spreading the romantic bullshit on a little too thick. All I needed was for some motherfuckers to step out playing their violins.

"Here, just bag it up for me," Supreme said, placing his American Express Centurion—also known as the Black Card—on the glass top. My mouth began salivating at the thought of Supreme using that very credit card on me as I devoured Rodeo Drive, shutting the stores down.

Carol and her manager's face lit up as she swiped Supreme's card through the machine, collecting his coins. "Here's your receipt, sir, and it was a pleasure doing business with you and your wife," Carol said.

"And Mr. Mills, I'm sure Mrs. Mills is fine," the manager added with an optimistic smile. Supreme simply grabbed the bag and receipt and said nothing.

I walked slowly behind Supreme trying to get a read on his body language. I couldn't tell if he was angry, worried, or suspect of me. Until I was sure I decided to remain mute. When we got outside the driver stepped out the Maybach and opened the door for Supreme and I to get in, but suddenly Supreme halted his stride. Without saying a word he handed the Cartier bag to his driver and sprinted off. I tried to stay within proximity to see what the fuck was going on without appearing to damn nosey.

"Oh fuck!" I said under my breath once I got a view of what had Supreme dashing off.

"Get this fucking car off the back of your tow truck!" Supreme screamed, banging on the driver side window.

The man was at a stop light about to pull off before Supreme rolled up on him, and I wished he had. "Man, what the hell is wrong with you?" the young black man said, rolling down his window. "How you going to bang on my window in the middle of the street?"

"Pull this truck over!" Supreme demanded, not caring that the light had now turned green and he was holding up traffic.

"Man, I'm on the job. I ain't pulling shit over."

"This my motherfucking car you got latched on the back of your shit and I want to know where the fuck you got it from." Now horns were blowing and people were sticking their heads out of their cars telling them to move, but Supreme didn't budge.

"Supreme, what's going on? You're holding up traffic," I said, trying to sound like the voice of reason.

"I don't give a fuck!" he said, grabbing the tow truck driver's collar and pulling him so close that their noses were an inch away from touching. "Pull this fucking truck over, now!"

Right when I believed Supreme was about to start laying blows we heard police sirens pulling up. Supreme pushed the man back, getting his composure together, but the dude began getting all extra for the cops.

As one cop began directing the traffic the other officer began interrogating Supreme and the driver. "Both of you put your hands up!" he ordered, wanting to make sure neither was armed. "What is going on here? The two of you are holding up traffic."

"Officer, this man came up to me out of nowhere banging on my window and demanding me to pull over acting crazy. Then this idiot tells me this is his car, like he can afford a half a million dollar custom made Lamborghini," he said, in a cynical voice, turning towards Supreme. He then turned back towards the officer and did a quick glance back at Supreme. "Oh shit!" The man paused as if getting a good look at the person who was ready to put an ass whooping on him a minute ago. "Oh shit!" he repeated. "You Supreme! What the fuck, music mogul Supreme just tried to jack me up! My fault, man. I didn't realize it was you," he said, with a big ass Kool-Aid smile.

Supreme stood shaking his head in frustration.

"I don't care who he is, you can't hold up traffic.

Now pull this truck over to the side so we can clear this matter up," the officer directed.

"Listen, officer. I just left the Cartier store because my wife was supposed to come by earlier and pick up some jewelry, but she never got there. When I was leaving the store I noticed the car she had been driving when she left this morning on the back of the tow truck. I wanted to know where he got the car from in hopes that it could give me a clue as to where my wife might be."

"Hold on a minute. What is your name?" the officer asked, taking out his notepad.

"Xavier Mills."

"So you believe your wife is missing?"

"I don't know, but something ain't right."

"And who are you?" the officer asked, turning his question on me.

"Maya. I'm a friend of his wife, Precious."

"And I assume a friend of her husband too?"

"Yes, we're both concerned about her whereabouts."

The officer nodded his head and jotted something down on his notepad.

"Listen, can we please go speak to the driver? I need to know where he picked up my car from."

"You stay here. I'll go speak with the tow truck driver, and when I'm done I'll then speak to both of you. Excuse me."

"Yo, these cops get on my fucking nerves. They wanna be so by the fucking *book* when it's convenient for them."

"Supreme, I know it's hard but try to relax."

"I can't fucking relax until I find out what happened to my wife!"

"We will find her. I'm sure she's okay."

"Nah, I gotta bad feeling about this," Supreme said, shaking his head as he ran his hand over his face. "God help me if Precious isn't okay, because if she's not, I'm done."

Then done is what Supreme would be, because Precious wasn't okay and never would be again, thanks to me. But who could really fault me for my actions. I mean, all is fair in love and war, and like a true friend, I would be right there to help Supreme pick up the pieces to his broken heart. Most would call my tactics ruthless or maybe just a good girl gone bad.

Work In Progress

"It's morning, now wake the fuck up!" Mike yelled in my face as I struggled to open my eyelids. I had only managed to fall asleep a couple of hours ago and now this fool was bringing me back into my misery.

"Damn, I'm finally able to get some sleep and here you come waking me up."

"I'm doing you a favor."

"How you figure that?"

"You know they say sleep is the cousin of death," Mike said, bending down to eyelevel so we were facing each other. "Now I'm sure you need to use the bathroom, so I brought this for you."

I looked at the large plastic cup and back at Mike.

"What, you expect me to piss in that?"

"This, or you can piss on yourself, It's up to you."

"Did you at least bring me some tissue?"

"But of course," he said, reaching behind him and placing the tissue next to the red plastic cup. "Now listen carefully, because if you fuck this up, I'ma have to fuck you up."

"I'm listening."

"I'm going to unlock one of the handcuffs on your wrist so you can do your thing."

"Oh, and I just assumed you were going to wipe my pussy for me after I pissed," I said, sarcastically.

"Cute, but don't get cute when I take off this handcuff, because it won't be a good look for you."

"I got you."

"Now when you're finished, place the cup to the side and put this top on there."

"I don't understand why you don't let me use the bathroom. I mean you can't expect me to shit in this cup too, now can you?" I asked mockingly.

"Ain't nobody expecting you to shit in this cup. Just do what I tell you when I tell you. I'm handling this. I know you used to being in control, but that's your past and we dealing with the present."

"Point made. But um, can you turn around and give me some privacy?"

"Oh please! I've seen everything you got, remember?"

"How can I forget? You did rape me!"

"Why don't you admit it, Precious?"

"Admit what?"

"That you wanted it. That tight pussy was hot for me."

"This cup can't hold my piss and vomit, and that's what I'm about to do if you keep on with that repulsive shit."

"Now, now, now, how soon we forget. You were practically begging for the dick when you had your legs spread open and I finger fucked you on the mahogany desk in your den."

"That was before I knew what a sick monster you are and that you were responsible for trying to have my husband killed."

"Those are all minor things and it still doesn't change the fact that you wanted me just as much as I wanted you."

"Will you please just turn around?" I waited for a few seconds and Mike finally turned his back towards me. It was some uncomfortable shit trying to squat down to piss with one wrist in a handcuff and shackles on your legs, but I managed.

As I was finishing up I eyed Mike contemplating if there was anyway I could make a move that could get me the fuck out of here. He was a few feet away from me and I could see the keys to the locks in his hand. I wondered, if I could get him closer and toss the urine in his face and then maybe use my fingers to dig in his eyes, would that give me enough time to somehow grab the keys, unchain myself and break out? Shit, under my current conditions I had nothing to lose.

I gripped the rim of the cup firmly, seriously pondering the scheme I had devised in my head. Although it seemed like a long shot, I was ready to take my chance...that was until we got company.

"Good morning, dear brother," Maya said, strolling down the

stairs. With Maya in the room I knew I would have to revisit my escape plan another time.

"What's good? I wasn't expecting you this early."

"I know, but I'm going to be a busy bee today, so I wanted to check in with you as early as possible."

"I feel you. How's it going on over there in Supreme's household? I'm sure by now he's wondering why his wife hasn't come the fuck home," Mike chuckled, smiling in my direction.

"Poor Supreme isn't taking it very well. And it didn't help that you idiots left the fucking car in the parking lot by Cartier. Why didn't you move that shit?"

"Maya, we didn't have time for all that. We were trying to get in and out without raising any sort of suspicion."

"Don't you think it looks suspicious that you left her vehicle by a store that she never went into?"

"That was the best place to grab shorty. Wasn't nobody around and we figured it would take a minute for anybody to notice the car sitting there. But shit, at least we grabbed her cell and tossed that shit. If we had left it at the scene it would've really looked like some foul play. She could've parked her car there and decided to bounce. Don't nobody know for sure."

"Damn! Could the two of you please stop talking about me like I ain't sitting right here?" I said, getting exhausted just listening to their bickering.

"As far as I'm concerned you ain't here unless I need you for some shit," Maya retorted like she was some bigwig.

"Fuck all that! How did Supreme find the car and what happened after that?" Mike butted in, wanting to get down to the facts and not dwelling on Maya's fiction.

"Cartier called wanting to know why Precious hadn't come to pick up her shit, and when Supreme and I left the store he saw a tow truck taking the car away. So that turned into a big production. He ended up filing an unofficial missing person's report with the police officer and then speaking with the driver of the tow truck."

"What you mean 'unofficial' report?" Mike questioned, and my ears were burning up extra hard hoping my husband was on the case and not falling for Maya's slick ass innocent role.

"You know, technically you're supposed to have to wait twenty-four hours before filling a missing person's report. But the officer went ahead and took it because of the whole car episode. That's why I'm pissed that you all didn't dump that shit somewhere."

"Get the fuck over it. Our priority was snatching up Precious and that's what we did. All that other shit is immaterial."

"You may not care, but I'm the one who has to keep Supreme under control. This nigga already flipping and he ain't even found a body or no shit."

"What did you expect, Maya? I'm his wife, the mother of his child. Of course he's flipping, and he gonna be doing a lot more than that when he finds out your kneedeep in this shit."

"Bitch, please! You ain't the end all be all. The same way he was getting pussy before he met you, he'll be getting it after you, so let me worry about Supreme."

"Maya, can you get off Supreme's dick for one second and tell me the move that nigga tryna make next?"

Maya gritted her teeth and rolled her eyes at Mike, obviously agitated that he wasn't a supporter over her obsession with Supreme. I figured right then that the only way I even had a slight chance of getting out of here was using Mike's hatred towards Supreme to my advantage, but how to do it was the difficult part. One thing was for sure and two for certain, Mike Owens was not to be underestimated, and he was no dummy. In fact, he was one of the smartest men I had ever encountered. That's why it was such a fucking waste that he was a complete sociopath."

"Real talk, he playing his shit close to the vest."

That's right baby, shut that trifling ho down! I smiled to myself.

"He definitely believes there has been some foul play involved, but he isn't sharing with me what or who he thinks is responsible. I don't want to pry too much and then bring suspicion on me. I'm playing it cool."

"That's the smart way to move, but still find a way to stay on top of his shit. You don't want any unexpected surprises."

"I got you."

"Is Devon coming over today?"

"I doubt it. Supreme was mad skeptical when we left to go to Cartier yesterday and Devon hadn't arrived for his shift. That's why I had told that motherfucker not to get missing."

"Was he able to smooth shit over with Supreme?"

"I think so. When we got back home Devon was there and gave him some excuse about some emergency coming up with his girl. Supreme seemed to have bought it, but I told Devon to stay within sniffing distance of Supreme until shit mellow out."

"That's cool. And how's Aaliyah?" Mike questioned, actually

sounding genuinely concerned.

"She's doing fine."

"I know she must be wondering where her mother is."

"Yeah, but kids are resilient. She'll get over it," Maya shrugged.

I tried to stay out of their conversation, but hearing Aaliyah's name made my blood start bubbling. "No she's mot gonna get over it! She ain't a puppy, Maya, she's my little girl!"

"*Was* your little girl."

"It don't matter what you do to me, Aaliyah will always be my child and ain't nothing gonna change that."

"I'm so sick of hearing your self righteous jabber. Maybe if I take this," Maya snarled as she reached towards my neck, ripping my pink diamond necklace off, "You'll shut the fuck up and acknowledge that little happy family life you were living is now over."

A shiver shook through my body and I looked down at my bare neck. That necklace was a symbol of the love and bond that I shared with Supreme. The last and only time I had been without it was when Mike took it off my neck that night he raped me. And now Maya was raping me again when she snatched it off.

"You're going to burn in hell for that, Maya!"

"You talking a lot of shit for someone who is already living there. Huh, and you stink! Mike, give this bitch a bath. I have to go and check on my man, Supreme anyway." Maya was doing her best to rub it in my face that I was without my child and my husband.

I felt a tear beating to drop out of my eye, but I refused to let it fall. I would not let that trick or her brother know they were breaking me. I took a deep breath and swallowed hard, getting pumped up.

"I ain't the only one who needs a bath!" I mocked, tossing the cup of piss I was still holding in her face. "Now who stink?"

At first Maya was so stunned by what I did she wasn't sure what I had thrown on her, but then the stench kicked in and she was incensed. "Heffa, I'ma kill you right now!" Maya howled as she lunged at me.

Mike rushed over to block Maya from unleashing her beat down as I used my one free hand to try to get some licks in. "Maya, chill!"

"Don't tell me to chill! I'ma fuck her up!" Maya continued screaming and swinging her arms.

"I'll handle Precious. You go clean yourself up."

Maya stayed eyeing me with flames sprouting from her head. I stared right back and even cracked a smile, happy to have been given a chance to fuck her day up the way she had been fucking up mine.

"I ain't done with you!" Maya warned as Mike walked her piss-soaked ass up the stairs.

My insides were dancing around and doing cart- wheels, thrilled that I had put the bitch in her place if only for a few minutes.

By the time Mike came back from walking Maya upstairs I had eliminated my joyous smile and put back on my stoic exterior.

"I was planning on giving you a decent meal today, but after that shit you pulled that's dead," Mike said, locking my free hand back in the handcuff.

"It was worth it. Maya deserved that shit and then some."

"Let's see if you feel that way when all you get is a biscuit for breakfast, lunch and dinner. But on the real," Mike said with a frown, "You are a bit funky, so I'ma take you upstairs so you can shower."

"Wow, I get a bath! Why do you even care what I look or smell like?"

"Shit, I gotta look at your ass everyday for at least the next couple of weeks. I prefer for you to be decent."

"Why are you going to keep me alive for at least the next couple of weeks?"

"Mind your business. Like I said, I'm in control."

"If you're so in control, how can you allow your sister to talk about Aaliyah that way? Especially when you know there is a possibility that she could very well be your daughter." I caught Mike off guard with that and he didn't know how to come back at me. His jaws began flinching and nostrils flaring. I wanted to get the nigga worked up and felt he had opened the door, so I decided to kick it in. "Oh, you stumped for words. Maya working you like she running the show and disrespecting your seed like you a clown nigga. I mean what's really good?"

"Yo, shut the fuck up! Maya ain't running shit."

"Then how you gonna allow her to threaten to hurt Aaliyah?"

"Maya is all talk. She would never hurt an innocent child. We brutal, but not like that. I warned her about the Aaliyah threats and you see she stopped."

"Yeah, she stopped in front of you, but you don't have any clue what Maya's doing when she get behind closed doors and is alone with her."

"Precious, I know what you're trying to do, and I'm not feeding into that bullshit. If Aaliyah is my daughter, not only will I guarantee not even so much as a hair on her head will be harmed, but she will also grow up with *me*."

"Excuse me, how in hell will you pull that off, given that you're an escaped convict."

"You always dwelling on the minor obstacles. I'm into doing major shit. Now marinate on that while I go check on Maya."

I let out a sigh of revulsion watching Mike leave. The idea of him raising Aaliyah was nauseating. Mike was a wanted man, and the only way he could raise Aaliyah was if he left the country. Without a doubt in my mind that was exactly what the motherfucker planned on doing after I was dead and out the picture. Knowing the clock was ticking with time not being on my side, I was intent on finding a way to turn brother against sister. But there was no denying that it would be over my dead body to let that scenario come to fruition. I had already begun planting the seeds and it was still a work in progress.

Maya

No Clue...Clueless

"I can't believe that bitch threw her nasty ass piss on me!" I kept belting out loud as I drove home. Luckily I always kept an extra set of clothes, shoes and other feminine products in my trunk for emergency purposes, because that shit right there was definitely an urgent situation. How would I have explained to Supreme why I smelled like some damn urine? Precious' egotistical ass was a pain even though she was on lock down. I was looking forward to the day I would lullaby that ass and have her out of all of our lives once and for all.

As I was relishing in my thoughts of ending Precious' life, my daydreaming came to a halt. I noticed one police car and what looked to be an unmarked car parked in the driveway as I drove past the gates.

"Damn, I wasn't expecting for Supreme to call in the cops so soon," I said, checking my appearance in the mirror. My once sleek jet black bob was now loaded with curls after the shower I took to kill all traces of the urine stench Precious left on me. My face was makeup free so I dabbled on some lip gloss to give a little life hoping to cover the worry lingering in my eyes.

I slowly made my way to the front door, answering in my mind every possible question that might be thrown my way. When I went to unlock the door I realized I had put my keys in my purse. I began rummaging through it and instantly noticed the pink diamond necklace I had yanked off of Precious' neck. Just then the front door opened and a familiar face was standing in front of me.

"Maya Owens, correct?" the pale white man with short spiked

flaming red hair asked. When I zoomed in on his beady blue eyes I quickly remembered who he was.

"Yes, and you're Detective Moore. How are you?"

"I've been better, and I'm sure so have you."

"What do you mean?"

"I mean with your best friend missing and all."

"Precious, yes, but has it been determined that she's actually missing?"

"Do you think it can be something else?" he questioned with a raised eyebrow.

"I have to go to the bathroom really bad. Can you excuse me for one second?"

"Sure, I have to get something out of my car. I'll be waiting in the living room for you when I get back. I have a few questions I need to run by you."

"No problem, I'll be right back." I ran upstairs with the swiftness. From the corner of my eye I noticed Supreme and another officer sitting in the living room talking. My heart was racing and I had to get away from Detective Moore. It was freaking me out that Precious' necklace was in my purse, and if he caught sight of it, the jig would be up. I ran in my room, tossed my purse on the bed, took a few deep breathes and headed back down the stairs ready for my interrogation.

"Is everything okay? You seemed to be in some sort of rush when you came in here," Supreme asked.

"Yeah, I had to go to the bathroom and didn't think I could hold it much longer. What's going on here? Did you find out anything about where Precious might be?"

"We're working on that. You suggested that maybe Precious wasn't missing. Do you have another scenario of what might've happened to her?" Detective Moore asked, walking up from behind me. I peeped a puzzled look on Supreme's face and I wanted to bitch slap Detective Moore.

"No, I don't have any other scenarios. I just didn't know that it had been decided she was missing."

"Then what could it be?" Detective Moore continued to press.

"I have no clue. Isn't that the job of a detective to figure things out? Isn't that why you're here?"

"Actually, we came to speak to Mrs. Mills about another matter, and that's when Mr. Mills informed us that he didn't know where his wife was."

I glanced at Supreme, totally confused as to what was going on. Supreme put his head down and didn't say a word.

"What something else did you come to speak to Precious about?" I inquired.

"Remember when we were investigating the kidnapping of Aaliyah and the drive by shooting both you and Mrs. Mills were involved in?"

"Yes, I remember."

"Well, we told Mr. and Mrs. Mills that ballistics matched the unregistered gun used in the drive by with an unsolved murder in New York."

"Okay, and your point?"

"It's someone that's linked to another unsolved murder in the New York area that Mrs. Mills knew." Detective Moore looked down at a piece of paper obviously trying to pretend he didn't remember the name of the murder victim. "His name was Terrell Douglas."

"I don't recognize that name," I said, lying through my teeth. I would never forget Terrell.

"He lived in New York and was the younger brother of a Nina Douglas who was engaged to Mrs. Mill's childhood friend, Jamal Crawford."

"It's still not ringing a bell, sorry."

"Mrs. Mills was one of her bridesmaids and you actually accompanied her to the dress fitting at the bridal shop in Manhattan, correct?"

"Yes, now I remember," I said, casually. "So the same gun that was used in the drive by is the murder weapon used in the unsolved killing of Nina's brother. I never knew Nina had a brother, but then again, I didn't know her that well. What a crazy coincidence."

"That's the thing. I don't believe in coincidences. What are the chances that Terrell, who was related to Nina who was friends with Mrs. Mills, would both end up dead and neither of their murders has ever been solved? Then the same gun used to kill Terrell ends up in a drive by against you and Mrs. Mills. That doesn't seem like a coincidence to me."

"Wasn't Nina working for my brother?"

"From the information I gathered from the NYPD that seems to be the case."

"Then it kinda makes sense."

"What do you mean?"

"I'm saying Mike was behind the plot to kill Supreme and the kidnapping of Aaliyah and the drive by. Maybe he was responsible for both Nina's murder and her brother's too."

"You could very well be correct. I just find it strange that right when we're starting to make some headway on the case that Mrs. Mills disappears."

"Detective Moore, get the fuck out my house!" Supreme demanded, rising up off the white sofa, pointing towards the front door.

"Mr. Mills. you need to calm down."

"No, you need to shut the fuck up! My wife is missing and you want to come over here on some bullshit fishing expedition about some unsolved murder that happened in NYC. That ain't even your motherfucking jurisdiction."

"Mr. Mills, we are following all leads, and when that weapon ended up being used in a crime that took place in Los Angeles, the investigation did become part of our jurisdiction."

"My wife ain't killed nobody and she didn't just disappear. Some foul ass shit done happened. But just like I had to do things my own way to bring my daughter home, I'll do the same to get my wife back since you dumb fucks can't never seem to be able to solve shit."

"Taking the law into your own hands is never the way to seek justice. I promised you we'd bring your daughter home, and we delivered," Detective Moore bragged.

"You didn't deliver shit! If anybody deserves credit for bringing Aaliyah home it would have to be Maya, not the LAPD."

Detective Moore and his partner both turned towards me with a look of antipathy. Shit, I didn't care because I was beaming on the inside. Maybe working my powers of persuasion on Supreme wouldn't be as difficult as I thought.

"Mr. Mills, we should be going."

"Yes, we finally can agree on something."

"If you hear from your wife, please have her contact us. But we will do our own investigating, and if we find out anything I'll let you know."

"I'm sure you will. You know your way out."

Detective Moore and his partner took their time leaving, with their eyes slithering around as if they thought Precious was going to jump out from hiding. Clueless that I had her chained up in a basement so far the fuck out that the location wouldn't even pop up on the top-of-the-line navigation system.

When the door finally slammed closed all I heard was a thunderous crash followed by a loud, "Fuck!" Supreme had thrown an antique marble vase across the room and it broke into a million pieces.

"Supreme, I know you're upset...so am I, but try to calm down."

"Maya, I don't want to hear it. Please, just go get Anna so she can clean up that shit. I don't want Aaliyah to see it."

"I understand. I'll go find Anna." After I looked in the kitchen and outside by the pool for Anna I decided to go upstairs thinking she was putting Aaliyah down for a nap.

Throughout my search, the disgusting glare Detective Moore gave me kept replaying in my head. I knew he didn't like me and that was cool, but I was more afraid of him trying to link me to a criminal act. In subtle ways he made it clear that he felt something wasn't quite right with my self defense explanation after Clip and Destiny were killed. But without evidence to back up his suspicions he couldn't prove it. He had a hard-on for me since then, and that could lead to a lot of trouble.

When I got to Aaliyah's room the door was slightly ajar and I stuck my head in, but the only person I saw was Aaliyah lying in her crib. I went closer and observed her sleeping so peacefully. "Oh, she fell asleep with the bottle in her mouth." I picked up the bottle and rubbed her cheek. "You really are a beauty. Maybe one day soon your daddy and I can give you a little brother to play with since your mommy won't be able to do so." I bent over, kissed her forehead and then headed towards Anna's room, passing mine on the way, and noticed a figure by my bed. I tiptoed closer and through the crack of the door I saw that it was Anna. At first I thought she was cleaning my room and about to make up my bed, but then I realized what she was holding in her hand.

Oh fuck, the necklace! I told that nosey bitch to stay out of my room, but she's so damn hard headed. Calm down Maya. You've come too far to start fucking up now.

"Anna, I was looking for you. Mr. Mills wanted you clean up a little mess he made downstairs," I stated calmly.

"Miss Maya, you startled me!" Anna said, grabbing her chest as her body jumped.

"I'm sorry, I didn't mean to do that. What is that you're holding in your hand?"

Anna was so caught off guard she forgot she was holding not only my purse, but the necklace in her hand. "I was about to put some clean linens on your bed and your purse fell."

I did peep some fresh sheets on the dresser so I believed she was telling the truth, but the damage was done. "I told you there was no need for you to clean my room, that I would do it myself."

"I know, but it's a habit. Mrs. Mills always likes every room to be perfectly clean."

"But Mrs. Mills isn't here, I am. I also see that you're holding a necklace."

"Yes, yes, yes, it fell out your purse. This is Mrs. Mills' necklace. May I ask what you're doing with it? I'm only asking because she never takes it off."

"How true. But Precious asked me to hold it for her before she disappeared," I said, grabbing my purse and the necklace out of Anna's hand.

"I think I should go give this to Mr. Mills," Anna said, reaching her hand out, trying to take the necklace back.

"That's okay. You go clean up that mess and I'll bring the necklace downstairs to Mr. Mills myself."

Anna was reluctant to leave and kept eyeing the necklace. But when I didn't budge she made her exit. I waited a few seconds after Anna left the room and then I threw the necklace in the bottom drawer beneath my undergarments. I sprinted out my room. Anna was halfway down the hall and I was right on her tail. After she hit that first step, I used my right foot to kick her in the lower part of her legs. She completely lost her balance which sent her free-falling down the sweeping double staircase. Her eerie screams filled the air. I then placed Aaliyah's baby bottle on one of the top stairs so it would appear to be the cause of her unfortunate accident. If only she had minded her business, none of this would've happened.

When Anna's body finally hit the bottom, landing and I heard the loud thump, I stood watching for a few moments to see if there was any movement. Once I was pretty sure she was dead, I went back to my room and closed the door. Hell, I didn't want to be the one who discovered her body. When a crime is committed, it's better to have no clue...*clueless!*

Precious

Live Till I Die

The days were beginning to run together to me. I couldn't calculate how many hours had passed, what time it was or anything. But what I did know was that a bitch was hungrier than a motherfucker. Mike hadn't given me shit to eat since I got here. He reneged on that one day he mentioned feeding me, saying it was punishment for tossing my piss on Maya...what the fuck ever! All he had given me was tap water so I wouldn't become dehydrated and die. Then that bath Maya insisted I needed was a no go too. At this point I was tired of looking and smelling myself. My once pristine white pantsuit was turning into dirty gray. My mind and body were becoming weak and there wasn't shit I could do about it.

Right when I was about to doze off the light came on and I heard the door opening. Then I heard the familiar sound of the stairs creaking as Mike came down.

"Good afternoon, Precious," Mike said as he stood over me.

I remained silent having no energy to respond. "Damn, babe, you look like a piece of shit. But I have good news. I feel that you've been punished long enough, and not only am I going to feed you but I'm going to let you bathe too."

Even with the encouraging news I was still mute.

"Precious, did you hear what I said?" Mike asked, lifting up my chin.

I nodded my head yes.

"I need for you to speak up. You need to show me some gratitude."

"Thank you," I muttered weakly.

"That's more like it. I'll be right back."

It seemed I had become numb to the pain in my stomach from not eating. But when Mike came back with a tray of food, I wanted to jump at it like a stray dog that had been eating out of trash cans for weeks. "Thank you, Mike. I mean that sincerely."

"I bet you do. It's amazing how starving an individual can bring out the best in them," he smiled. "Now do I have to feed you, or can I trust you'll behave if I take off the handcuffs?"

"I'll behave. I just want to eat." I meant that shit too. As much as I despised Mike, he was my savior at this particular moment. When those handcuffs came off I demolished the fried chicken, macaroni and cheese, greens and biscuit he prepared for me. I didn't know who cooked the meal but it was so damn good. But a can of Spam would've been good to me right about now.

"Slow down, Ma, the plate ain't going anywhere," Mike joked. But I kept on grubbing, licking fingers and all.

"I can't believe you're feeding me such good food, since you only promised me bread and water, and I had only received the latter so far."

"You got lucky. Devon brought over some lunch from this soul food restaurant and there was a lot left over. I was in a good mood and decided to share some with you."

By the time I finished eating the last chicken thigh I was completely full. Going hungry for however many days it had been made my heart ache to all the kids in the world who were truly going without. You never really have an understanding of that type of existence until you fuck around and find yourself in that predicament.

"I see you didn't leave not a crumb," Mike said, picking up my plate. "So are you ready to wash off that funk on you?"

"Been ready, but what am I going to put on? I mean there is no sense in me taking a bath if I'ma have to wear the same funky clothes."

"I got you covered."

"Oh...so why are you being so decent to me al of a sudden?"

"Real talk, you look so pathetic that I feel sorry for you," Mike laughed.

"Wel, I'm glad one of us can laugh about my circumstances."

"You're right. There is no humor in this but it is what it is. There's nothing we can do."

"Yes there is. You can let me go home to my husband and daughter."

"Precious, I feel sorry for you, but I'm not stupid. You know that's not even a possibility."

"Why, because Maya says it's not?"

"No, because too much shit has happened."

"What are you getting out of this, Mike?"

"Revenge, what else?"

"Revenge on who, me? What did you expect? You tried to have my husband murdered and you raped me. There wasn't any other option. You had to go to jail, or die one. You know how the game goes. The police were already on to you, so don't blame me because you got locked up."

"Well since you know how the game go so well, then it shouldn't be no surprise to you that you're chained up in this motherfucking basement, now should it. So do you want to keep sitting here running off at the mouth or do you want to take a fucking shower before I change my mind?"

"I wanna clean my dirty ass, so I'll shut the fuck up."

"Good choice," Mike said, unlocking the chains around my legs. "Now I don't want no shit from you, Precious. If I think you're getting out of line, I'ma break your neck."

"I know. But I won't give you any problems. I'm just grateful to be having some hot water splash against my body." When I stood up, Mike held my arms behind my back firmly. "Is that really necessary? I mean for all that you shoulda kept the handcuffs on."

"Here you go again running off at the mouth."

"Okay, I'll be quiet, but please don't walk too fast. My legs are still a bit numb from sitting down for so long."

Mike led me up the stairs slowly, and when he opened the door it was as if we entered another world—make that another planet. No longer was I in the misery of a windowless, dreary basement. I had arrived in a mini mansion that was bananas! I had been in some fly cribs, but the architectural design was downright stunning. When I turned my head to the right, I could see the spacious entry with walls of glass that led to a floating glass and stainless steel staircase. When I turned to my left there was a massive wall of glass for an incredible 180° view. The shit was truly breathtaking. I couldn't comprehend that all this was going on up here and all that was going on down there, in what I considered a dungeon.

"Mike, I ain't tryna be funny, but who in the fuck do you know that let you stay in this crib, and do they have any idea you have a hostage chained up in the basement?"

"Funny, but this my shit."

"Yeah, right."

"What, you think Supreme the only one with long paper?"

"Umm, well you have been locked up, or have you forgotten that already."

"Nah, trust I definitely ain't forgot that shit. But like I told you a long time ago, I'm one of the few real kingpins. Niggas like me still be making major moves behind bars. That shit don't stop."

"I see," I said, doing a double-take of the ridiculously fly domain.

"Come on, let me take you to the bathroom you'll be using. I left your change of clothes on the table in there. The shit you have on needs to be burned, so you can drop them in the trash bag I put in there for you."

"Fuck you! This is a thirty-five hundred dollar Chloe pantsuit that you fucked up from having me locked up like an animal."

"Maybe now you know how it feels."

"Spare me," I said entering the bathroom.

"I'll be posted right outside this door so don't try no slick shit."

"Oh please! I know when I can't win and it's time to give up," I said closing the door behind me.

Damn, it seemed that everything in this house was made of glass including the bathroom, I thought as I peeled the filthy clothes off my back. I was more than happy to toss them into the plastic bag. Besides bathing products and the change of clothes, it seemed Mike had made sure all potential weapons were banished from the bathroom. Even if I wanted to make a move I didn't see anything that I could use.

I decided to enjoy the pleasure of a hot shower and be done with it. When the water hit my skin, it felt almost as good as an orgasm. It was like the water was making love to me and I welcomed it. In the midst of being seduced in the open shower, my eye caught what looked to be the rim of a trashcan. It was behind the toilet and almost unnoticeable. At the very moment I saw it, the next second my mind began plotting. I knew it was a stretch but I had to exercise all options because I knew they would be few and far between.

After showering for a few more minutes I walked away from the still running water and dried myself off. Then I went to the sink to brush my teeth and noticed the large mirror. I stood frozen, as I hadn't seen my own reflection in what seemed like forever. I touched my face gently and my cheeks had already begun to become sunken in. I had dark circles around my eyes from not getting any decent sleep. My normal bronzed butterscotch complexion appeared dull after being deprived of sunlight for so long. Now I could see why Mike felt sorry for me. I did look pathetic.

Once I took a few moments to feel sorry for myself it was time to get dressed. I was taken aback when I saw that my change of clothes was a cotton candy pink Juicy Couture jogging suit. It was my favorite loungewear, and on a few occasions when Mike had come to visit me I would have it on. I wondered if he remembered and that's why he left it for me. But I couldn't dwell on that as I was now on a mission.

I put my ear to the door to see if I could hear any movement or if Mike was guarding the bathroom like he said. I then bent down on my knees to see if I could get a peep of his shoes under the bottom opening of the door. I didn't see anything at first, but then I saw him walking across the hallway going into the living room I assumed. I stood up and grabbed the trashcan from behind the toilet. It was solid stainless steel, exactly what I needed to cause some damage.

I bent back down to once again place Mike's movements. This time I didn't see anything. I quietly cracked the door open and it was clear. I quickly slid out of the bathroom with the trashcan in tow. I closed the bathroom door and stood behind the hallway corner out of sight. My heart was thumping so hard I felt that all of LA could hear it. I heard some classical music coming from the living room area and presumed Mike was in there chilling, although I never figured him to be up on that style of tunes. But the soothing melody was surprisingly helping me to relax and my mind to focus a tad bit better. I had no idea how I was going to get the fuck out of this damn house.

As I pondered my next move I heard footsteps and they were coming in my direction. I leaned my back up against the wall and didn't even take a breath.

"Precious, you're still taking a shower?" Mike yelled, knocking on the bathroom door. I purposely kept the water running so he could think just that. I didn't have a watch on but it felt like I had been in the bathroom for thirty or forty minutes so I was sure by now he was wondering what the hell was taking me so long. Mike stood by the door for a few more minutes and then knocked again. "Something ain't right," I heard him say as he opened the door.

Fuck, it's now or never! I leaped around the corner and his back was to me as he stepped inside the bathroom.

"Precious, what the hell are you doing in here?"

As he asked the question out loud, I swung the trashcan up high. Mike must've felt my presence from behind because instead of me getting a clear landing on the back of his head, I caught the side of his face as he turned towards me. But the power of my blow did some damage because he stumbled and fell to the floor on his back. This was my one shot at freedom and I blew wind sprinting out the bathroom and down the hall. My legs were striding as if I was competing for an Olympic Gold Medal. There was no looking back to see who I leaving in the dust as it was winner take all, and that was gonna be me...or so I hoped.

As I continued to strive to reach my destination, it seemed like I was running down a never ending hallway. I knew that shit couldn't have been as long as it felt, but the closer I got to the front exit the further away it seemed to be. My mind was playing crazy tricks on me, so I just kept running.

At last I could taste freedom. I was right there. My hand reached out for the doorknob as I unlocked the top bolt, and then swung the door open. The sun instantly shined on me like it did for Ceily in the "Color Purple" as she ran through the field towards her sister who she hadn't seen in so long. But there would be no loving embrace between families like I saw in the movie. Instead, I felt a sharp excruciating pain and my last thought before I went unconscious was that I would try to live till I die.

Maya
Foolish Fool

"I still can't believe Anna's dead," Supreme said as he poured himself a glass of Remy Martin X111 cognac. "First my wife disappears, and now Anna is deceased, all within a week's period of time. I'm beginning to believe this house is cursed."

"Supreme, don't do this to yourself. What happened to Anna was a tragic accident."

"Tragic is right...to trip on a baby bottle. How unlucky can someone be? Can you imagine if she had been carrying Aaliyah?" That thought made Supreme pour himself some more Remy. "Damn, I need my wife right now!" Supreme continued taking down his cognac in one gulp.

"I haven't given up. I believe Precious will be back soon," I said, pretending to be optimistic.

"I hope you're right."

"I am."

"Maya, I know I've been harsh with you since Precious went missing and I'm sorry. Honestly, I don't know what I would've done without your support, especially for Aaliyah. You've been wonderful with her these last few days."

"It's nothing. You know how I feel about Aaliyah. I love her as if she was my own daughter," I said, cuddling Aaliyah as she bounced on my lap.

"It's so hard for me right now because every time I look at her

I see Precious. My little angel is the only thing keeping me sane right now."

"Have you gotten any new leads on what happened to Precious?"

"Hell no! It's like she vanished into thin air. The surveillance tapes the cops confiscated showed nothing and the private investigators I hired can't come up with shit. I don't want to think it, but I have to wonder if once again Pretty Boy Mike is behind this."

"Sorry to interrupt, Mr. Mills, but the front gate called up and said that Detective Moore is here to see you."

"Thanks, Devon. You can send him in when he gets here."

"Were you expecting Detective Moore?" I asked as a feeling of anxiousness hit me.

"No, but maybe he has some news about Precious."

What the fuck is that fucking detective snooping around for this time? He ain't got no news. If anything, he's coming over here trying to dig up some news. That sonofabitch is about to work my very last nerve.

"Mr. Mills, Ms. Owens, nice to see you, although I wish it was under different circumstances. I heard about your nanny, Anna. It seems to be one tragedy after another in this family," Detective Moore commented as he took it upon himself to sit down.

"We're handling it. What brings you by here today?" Supreme put his glass down and folded his arms.

"Mr. Mills, I'm assuming still no word on your wife's where-abouts?"

"You're assuming correctly, but I hope you didn't come all the way over here to tell me something that I already know."

"Well, let's see. Did you know that your wife's cell phone records show that the last person she spoke to was Nico Carter?" I watched as the vein in Supreme's forehead pulsated and every muscle from his jaw down throbbed. "From what I understand, your wife and Nico Carter share a long history together."

"What's your point, detective?"

"I don't have a point...yet. Merely trying to connect the dots. But I have reached out to Mr. Carter. Unfortunately my office hasn't been able to get in touch with him yet."

"Are you saying you think he has something to do with my wife's disappearance?"

"Maybe, maybe not, but from what we've gathered so far he is the last person she spoke to on her cell phone. We're also looking into the possibility that Ms. Owens' brother, Mike could be behind this,"

Detective Moore said, turning his mug directly towards me. "Have you had any contact with your brother, Ms. Owens?"

"No I haven't. But with all the heat on him, I doubt he would take a chance and come back to LA."

"In my twenty years of detective work, I've learned you can never underestimate what a deranged, sick criminal is capable of, which includes your brother. He seemed to have a strong fixation on your wife." Detective Moore now turned back to Supreme. "Maybe he threw caution out the window and came back to finish the punishment on your family that he had started."

"I thought about that, but he would need resources, money, and with Clip dead I don't see how it's possible."

"Maybe he had more than just Clip and that young woman, Destiny helping him out. I mean somebody had to be behind the wheel of the car during that drive by, and I seriously doubt it was Mike. And who knows? It may also be the shooter from the unsolved murders of Terrell and Nina Douglas."

"Oh, so I guess that means you no longer suspect that Precious had any involvement with either one of those murders?" I inquired.

"I never said Mrs. Mills was a suspect."

"But you did imply that last time you came over, Detective Moore," Supreme reminded him.

"I simply wanted to ask your wife a few questions because I was made aware that at one time Mrs. Mills was friends with one of the victims."

"Precious doesn't have any friends besides me. Nina pretended to care about Precious because she was working for my brother."

"Right. Well again, this is all speculation. I'm gathering as much information as possible in hopes that it will answer all of our unanswered questions," the detective said, standing up from the couch. "I'm sure I'll be in touch soon. But of course if either one of you come across any new information, give me a call."

"Will do, detective," Supreme said as he poured himself another drink.

"By the way Maya—is it okay for me to call you Maya?" Detective Moore asked, catching me off guard because he had practically reached the front door.

"Of course. It is my name," I smiled as I continued to hold Aaliyah.

"Do you recall seeing Nina Douglas on the day she was murdered?" he asked, walking back towards my direction.

"Uh, no I don't."

"I only ask because I know you were an invited guest to the wedding but never showed up."

"And who told you that?"

"I had an opportunity to speak with Jamal Crawford, Nina's fiancée at the time. He specifically remembered that you were supposed to come to the wedding with Precious but neither of you showed up."

"That's right, but, umm, it was so long ago. If I'm not mistaken, I was planning on attending the wedding with Precious but I had some boyfriend issues. Precious stayed with me to work them out and it ended up getting too late for us to make the wedding."

"And who was your boyfriend at the time? Would that have been Clip?"

"I don't believe so. I think it was another guy. But what does any of this have to do with Nina's brother's murder?" I was about to end my statement with a four letter word but kept my tongue intact. I knew the sneaky detective was dying to get a reaction out of me but I wasn't about to give it to him.

"As I stated before, I have a hunch that the two murders are somehow connected. But I could be wrong. I would ask you for that boyfriend's name but I'm sure you've forgotten it by now," he remarked, not bothering to wait for my response. "Again, I must be going, but like I said, I will be in touch."

My blood was boiling as I watched Detective Moore finally stroll out of the door. "That man has a lot of nerve."

"Yeah, he does, but Maya, do you know anything about Nina's murder or her brother's?"

"Of course not."

"What about Precious? Did she ever mention anything to you about what happened to Nina?"

"No, but..." I cut my sentence off to give Supreme the impression I was holding something back.

"But what?"

"It doesn't matter. We need to be focusing on finding Precious not letting Detective Moore stir up trouble."

"Listen, Maya, if you know of Precious having any involvement in a murder let me know so I can do what's necessary to clean the shit up before it gets out of hand."

"I don't know anything specifically about Terrell, but after Nina was murdered Jamal came by the house to see her. He was vexed. He and Precious had a heated exchange of words. When he left, Precious said that she hoped he would let sleeping dogs lie when it came to finding Nina's killer. I did take it as if she was trying to protect her-self."

"Did she say anything else?"

"No, and I didn't ask. If she was involved in Nina's murder I didn't want to know anything about it." I reflected back on that day I put a bullet in Nina's back trying to protect Precious. After that, I won her over because I proved my loyalty. It was the exact loyalty I needed Precious to believe I had in order to take her down.

"I understand," Supreme said, shaking the ice cubes in his glass. He seemed to be drifting off into some sort of trance. But I didn't believe it was so much the possibility that Precious might've killed Nina that had him stuck. Finding out that Nico was the last call Precious received, I felt, was the real reason he was in a daze.

"Supreme, it's so beautiful outside I thought it would be nice to take Aaliyah to the park, if you don't mind." He remained completely silent. "Supreme," I called out again snapping him out of his trance.

"I apologize. What did you say?"

"I wanted to take Aaliyah to the park, is that okay?"

"Sure, let me call one of my security guys so they can escort you."

"What about Devon? He's already here."

"That works. Here, take this," Supreme said pulling out a wad of cash.

"Supreme, no, I don't want your money."

"Take it. I want you and Aaliyah to enjoy yourselves." Supreme gently rubbed Aaliyah's cheek and kissed her forehead. "Devon, just the person I wanted to see."

"What can I do for you, Mr. Mills?"

"Maya is taking Aaliyah out, so please escort her wherever she wants to go."

"Will do, sir."

"Bye baby. Daddy will see you later on. And Maya, thanks."

"I told you before; you don't have to thank me."

As I walked behind Devon while holding Aaliyah, I couldn't help but crack a smile. Supreme was vulnerable and emotionally close to the edge. All I needed to do was give him a little push so then I would be the only person he could turn to. When I got to the door, I turned around and waved goodbye to Supreme. It was crazy that a man whose presence was so strong and powerful was about to be putty in my hands.

After Devon opened the car door for me I buckled Aaliyah in her car seat and instantly got to yapping off at the mouth. "That fucking

Detective Moore is making my stomach nauseated. That white prick needs to be shut the fuck down."

"Do you really have to use that language in front of the baby?" Devon questioned as he drove off.

"Shut the hell up! It's not like Aaliyah can understand what the fuck I'm saying. You just fucking drive."

Devon shook his head as if I was doing some sort of developmental damage to the baby.

"Anyway, like I was saying, Detective Moore, is a fucking problem."

"Why do you say that?"

"He's digging awfully deep into the murders of that Nina chick and her brother. But what I'm trying to understand is how Donnell ended up using the same gun in that drive by with me and Precious. Because that link right there is what is fucking all this shit up."

"Who gave Donnell the gun?"

"It wasn't me and I know it wasn't you, so that could only leave Mike. What is that nigga up to?" I mumbled under my breath.

"But even if Mike did give Donnell the gun, why you so pressed about that Nina girl and her brother?"

"Because I have both of their blood on my hands. Ain't that many coincidences in the world, that the same gun used to kill Terrell's ass was used in that drive by. Soon Detective Moore is going to put that shit together and realize that I'm the one who is my brother's keeper."

"Yeah, that detective is going to be a problem."

"Exactly! That's why I need you to handle that."

Devon, hit the brake and turned around to stare at me.

"Nigga, you can't stop the car in the middle of the street. You gonna cause a fucking accident."

"I know you not insinuating what I think you are!" Devon wanted to clear things up as he pressed back down on the gas.

"Yes the fuck I am."

"He's a fucking police officer! Have you lost your mind?"

"I don't give a fuck who he is. That motherfucka is about to mess shit up. Keep in mind, if he puts the pieces together, not only am I going down, but so are you." Devon frowned up his face, but that was real talk. That nigga couldn't think I would be doing a bid solo if shit hit the fan.

"I don't know, Maya. Killing a police officer...that's the death penalty."

"Shit, if Supreme finds out you were behind the kidnapping of his daughter and wife, you dead anyway. Plus, the only way you gonna get the death penalty is if you get caught—but you're not."

"How can you be so sure?"

"Because we're going to make sure the shit is tight. But the sooner we get rid of Detective Moore the better off we'll be. Now, we need to head over to the stash house so I can have a conversation with my brother. But before that, take me to the mall so I can spend some of this loot my future husband hit me off with."

"You think you have Supreme all figured out, don't you, Maya?"

"For your sake you better hope I do. With the devastation of him losing his precious wife, I need for him to become a complete foolish fool."

Player's Prayer

I struggled to open my eyes, but the throbbing from my head kept me closing my eyelids shut. I tried to reach my hand over and rub the pain piercing from the back of my head, but quickly realized they were handcuffed to some shit. The energy I used to shift my arms gave me the willpower to open my eyes the fuck up to see exactly where I was. At first, shit was looking real blurry as my eyes were half opened and half closed. But although my vision was playing tricks on me, my hearing was in top form, because even though I couldn't see them, I could clearly hear the conversation going on between Maya and Mike.

"Mike, why in the fuck do you have this bitch in the bedroom? Her ass is supposed to be chained up in the basement."

"Listen, let me handle Precious. You just tend to Supreme."

"Let you handle Precious? Dear brother, this is a joint venture. If anything, we handle shit together."

"Did you come all the way over here to drill me about where I'm keeping Precious, or do you have something to say that's important?"

"As a matter of fact I do."

"Okay, then say it."

"Detective Moore has become a major problem. He's linked the gun that was used in Terrell's murder to the gun used in the drive by. And by the vacant stare on your face, you don't seem too surprised."

"I'm not."

"Then I guess you were the one who gave Donnel the gun."

"You guessed right."

"I thought you got rid of that gun a long time ago."

"It seems that I never got around to it."

"Why would you give that gun to Donnell to use in the drive by?"

"Insurance."

"Insurance on what?"

"You're a smart girl, Maya. Insurance on you. Just a minute ago you made the point that we're in this together, and you're right. With that gun being linked to both incidents, I've given Detective Moore enough ammunition to make you a suspect, but not enough to convict."

"Why would you do something so stupid?"

"Maya, you're my sister and I love you, but you can be rather impulsive. After you feel I'm no longer useful, you may get the stupid idea to hang me out to dry and claim that I was behind the kidnapping of Aaliyah, Precious and the murders of Clip, Destiny... oh yeah, and Donnell."

"I would never turn on you."

"I want to believe you and I hope you're telling me the truth, but in case you're not, like I said, I need some insurance."

"You ungrateful sonofabitch, I got you out of jail! You owe me!"

"And I've paid up. Look at you. You're living in the big house with Supreme, and I'm sure, plotting each day to go from houseguest to permanent bedmate. None of that would be possible without my help."

"We're blood, Mike? How can you treat me like your enemy?"

"If I was treating you like my enemy you would be dead. My beautiful little sister, if you play fair, you have nothing to worry about. You'll be able to live happily ever after with Supreme and I'll be able to live my life as a free man on an island somewhere. We'll both come out as winners."

"And what about Precious? When are you going to get rid of her?"

"Like I said, let me handle Precious."

"After all this time, you're still not over that bitch. Let it go, Mike, she'll never want you."

"Oh, you mean just like Supreme will never want you?" "

Speaking of Supreme, I'll be right back. I need to go to the car and check on Aaliyah."

"You left Aaliyah in the car? Are you crazy? It's hot out there!"

"Calm down! Devon is in the car and he has the A/C on. She was sleep when we got here and I want to make sure she didn't wake up."

"Let me find out your motherly instincts are kicking in."

"That little baby is the most valuable possession I'm working with. If I take excellent care of her, then Supreme will be all mine. I'm sure you've heard the saying, 'The hand that rocks the cradle rules the world.'"

"Indeed. Well I'ma go out there with you. I've missed seeing her face."

"Well don't get too attached. She's Supreme's daughter."

"Until we get that blood test, there is a very good chance she could be mines too!"

I heard the footsteps on the floor as Maya and Mike walked away. By this time my eyes were fully open and my lips were trembling from being so angry. The thought of my daughter being so close and not being able to see her, touch her, hold her, was about to make me insane. I also wanted to fucking know who this Terrell cat was and how was he connected to Maya. Being helpless was killing me.

Here I was, handcuffed to a steel framed canopy bed unable to move. The slick white, black and silver décor was much more appealing than the dreary basement I had been held captive in for weeks, but it didn't change my miserable circumstances. I then eyed the soaring ceiling and began recalling the last things I remembered before awakening to this room.

"Damn! I remember feeling *this* close to freedom, and then a sharp excruciating pain took me out cold. That must be where that throbbing on the back of my head came from. Mike hit the shit out of me with some sort of blunt object. But I wonder why he put me in this room instead of the basement?"

After going over my thoughts out loud, I then looked down at my clothes, and at first I was confused. I was expecting to see the dingy white outfit I had been wearing for what seemed to be forever, but instead I had on a fresh clean pink sweat suit and smelled of Glowing Touch body wash. "That's right, I did get to take a shower and wash my ass!"

So many things had changed since waking up from my mini coma and so many things had remained the fucking same. I could now take a sniff of my body without the odor making my stomach turn, but I was still a prisoner in this nightmare.

"I see you're awake," Mike said, entering the bedroom and startling me out of my thoughts.

"Barely. Whatever you hit me with really did a number on me. Do you mind telling me what it is you hit me with?"

"We can discuss that later. But listen. Maya's on her way back in here and don't mention that you tried to make an escape—we clear?"

"We're clear." Of course now my brain was in overdrive. Maybe what Maya said had some truth to it. Could Mike have unresolved feelings for me? If so, then I had to use that to my advantage. I detested that motherfucker, but now that I was back looking halfway decent it was time to exercise my female prowess on that nigga.

"Clear on what?" Maya said, sauntering her trifling ass pass her brother.

"I told Precious that because I now have her in the bedroom don't mean shit has changed."

"I don't understand why you put her up in here anyway.

You need to take her ass back to the basement where she belongs, but I'ma leave that shit on you. Aaliyah is waiting for me, so I have to get done what I need and be the fuck out."

"Aaliyah is waiting for you where?" I asked, not wanting Maya to know that I overheard her conversation with Mike. "She's in the car."

"Can I see her?"

"Bitch, you really have been locked up too long 'cause your ass delusional."

"It's not like she can go back and tell Supreme that she saw me."

"Precious, I'm not even entertaining your question. Here, I need for you to write something for me," Maya directed, completely brushing off my request.

"Write what?"

"A letter to your soon to be ex-husband."

"What type of letter?"

"Basically, that you've decided to leave him. You have some unresolved issues you need to work out and you don't know when or if you're coming back."

"You're fucking crazy! Supreme would never believe I would leave him, and especially my daughter."

"Look here. Detective Moore informed Supreme that the last person you spoke to on your cell was Nico. I had no idea Nico was such a sore spot for Supreme. Hell, maybe that'll be the unresolved issue you hint to in your letter."

"It'll never work."

"You better make it work. I don't give a damn what you think. Write this letter! And get it right the first time or not only will you be going back to the basement, but I'll also let my brother have his way with you," Maya said with a sinister chuckle.

"Maya, that's enough," Mike snarled, grabbing the paper and pen out of Maya's hand. "Precious, just write the letter so Maya can go."

I wanted to snatch the pen and stab both Maya and Mike in their eyeballs but thought it was time for me to start playing the game with Mike. "Fine, but can you take these handcuffs off of me so I can write it?"

Mike took the key out of his pocket and unlocked the cuffs. Maya stood smug faced, eating every second up. "Wait a minute, here's a clean piece of paper."

"What's wrong with the paper I already gave her?"

"Don't you see I'm wearing gloves? It's hot outside so it's not for weather purposes. When Supreme gets this letter, trust me, he and Detective Moore will have it tested for all fingerprint traces."

"You think you are so slick," I said.

"I learned from the best. Well, you *used* to be the best."

As I wrote the letter I knew Maya was probably damn near having an orgasm thinking she was that much closer to stealing my life. I wanted to shed a tear at the heartache I would cause Supreme when he read this bullshit, but wouldn't give Mike and Maya the pleasure of seeing my grief. When I was finished I put the pen down and Maya came over ready to run off, but read over several times what I wrote. Mike was right behind her securing my wrist with the handcuffs.

"This is perfect!" she said with a smile lighting up her face. "Oh, and I need for you to address this envelope also. Just in case you forgot, I wrote down your previous address, and at the top that's the sender address for you to use." "You didn't forget shit, did you?" I said sarcastically.

"Just write." Maya stood over me making sure I dotted every 'i' and crossed every 't'. "As always, it was a pleasure seeing you, dear brother, but of course I must be going," Maya said, taking the envelope from my hand. "I know Supreme must be ready for me to come home and I don't want Aaliyah to wait any longer. With her mother gone and poor Anna deceased, me and her father is all she has."

"Anna is dead! What happened?"

"Oh, Precious. I'm so sorry but Anna had a tragic accident. It's such a shame. Poor thing tripped over Aaliyah's baby bottle and fell down the stairs."

"Would you please stop with that ridiculous, sarcastic sugary tone of yours? That was no accident! Your demonic ass killed Anna, but why?"

"If you must know, her nosey ass came across the necklace I ripped off your neck and she started drilling me. Then the silly fool said she wanted to give the necklace to Supreme...well you know I couldn't let that happen."

"It's never gonna stop with you. You'll kill anybody that gets in your way."

"True indeed! Gotta go!" Maya breezed out of the room taking her dark cloud with her.

"Mike, I think you're scum, but I also know you're a very smart man."

"Your point?"

"The point is you know how this game works. Sooner or later you're going to be on that list of people who are in Maya's way. And the same way she had Clip taken out she'll do the same to you."

"I know how to handle my sister. She knows it won't be beneficial for her to cross me."

"Your sister is out of control. Don't you get it? She can't be handled! Soon you'll no longer be an asset to her, just a liability, and when that happens then it's lights out for you."

Mike wasn't saying shit but I knew the logic I was kicking was eating him up. From the conversation I overheard between him and Maya he had already come up with a backup plan in case Maya got outta pocket. So what I was spitting was only adding to his paranoia.

"Listen, Mike. I'm not tryna come between you and your sister. But after I'm dead I want to make sure that my daughter is safe. With Anna gone, there is no way Aaliyah will be safe with Maya. And although I never wanted to believe it, Aaliyah could very well be your daughter. Right now Maya is playing the sweet role because she needs Aaliyah to win over Supreme, but once that happens and she feels Aaliyah is in the way...need I say more? We both know what your sister is capable of."

Mike put his head down. He was trying to remain calm but I could feel his anger building up. "Look, like I said, I'll handle Maya. And don't you worry about Aaliyah, she's straight. Now I have some things to take care of. I'll check up on you later."

When Mike got to the door he turned to me one last time before leaving. "That shit wasn't cool, tryna escape today, but then I wouldn't expect anything less from you," he said, before storming out.

I hoped that I pushed Mike's buttons enough to begin my process of divide and conquer. Maya was truly twisted, and being held captive gave me limited options so it would take all of my mental savvy to bring her down—that and a player's prayer.

I Run This

"Devon, I want to move on this Detective Moore situation immediately," I said, the moment I got in the backseat of the Bentley.

"What was Mike's opinion on how we should move?"

"I didn't ask for it, nor do I care too, and neither should you."

"But this is a team effort."

"Devon, I brought you in this team, not my brother. So you follow *my* orders. I don't want you discussing our plan for Detective Moore with Mike or anyone else."

"All I'm saying..."

"Fuck what you're saying!" I screamed, cutting Devon off. Aaliyah began wailing from the loudness of my voice. "It's okay, baby," I said, stroking her hair trying to soothe her.

"I told you to stop all that cursing in front of her. Now you've made Aaliyah upset."

"Save your parental guidance lecture. There would be no need for me to curse if you would shut the fuck up and do what I say."

"You know what, Maya? I'm getting tired of you speaking to me like I'm some five dollar flunky," Devon growled, pounding his fist on the steering wheel.

I took a deep breath and changed up my approach since taking a hard line with him was defeating the cause. *What would Precious do under these circumstances?*

"Devon, I apologize for being so abrupt with you. I'm under a lot of pressure and I'm not only looking out for myself, but I'm looking out for you too."

"I can't tell."

"It's true. Do you think it was by accident that I went back to Brooklyn looking for you? That one older hustling cat I used to fuck with while I was dealing with Clip always spoke highly of you. He would preach to me that it was damn near impossible to find a loyal nigga, and that's why he made sure he always took care of you, so when I heard from one of my homegirls in BK that dude had got killed, I wanted to put you on."

"I feel you on that."

"I know how hard it is to maintain on them streets, plus you had family to take care of. I wanted to look out for you the way you looked out for him. But this the big leagues. When I recruited you I felt I made that clear. Mike is my brother and I love him. I'm grateful that you put me on to your man and we were able to get Mike out. I'm grateful for all the loyalty you've shown me and I plan on not only telling you but showing you too," I said, licking my lips seductively.

"I was under the impression you only had eyes for Supreme."

"Yeah, Supreme got all the coins and I need that to not only take care of me and my brother, but to also keep your pockets fat. But that don't mean a sexy nigga like you don't get my pussy wet. You feel me?" I was lying my ass off, but I needed this cat to do some serious dirty work for me. Supreme represented much more than an endless cash flow. I had been dying to suck his dick since I first saw him in a music video before I had even hit adolescence. Becoming his wife would give me bragging rights 'til the day I died.

"I fo' sho' feel you, Maya. You got my third leg excited over here. So when you plan on showing me how grateful you are?"

"Business first, and then pleasure."

"I guess that means we need to handle this Detective Moore problem as soon as possible."

"Now we're on the same page. But, umm, while you're mulling over when, where and how you're going to eliminate the detective, take me to the post office. I have a letter that needs to be mailed out."

When we pulled up to the post office I took out my book of stamps and peeled one off. I scanned the envelope again before placing it firmly on the upper right-hand corner. I dropped it in the mailbox, and a surge of newfound power shot through me. "Okay Devon, let's go home."

"Devon, remember, don't discuss our plans for Detective Moore with anyone. Tomorrow at twelve o'clock I'll meet you at our spot so we can graph this shit out, so don't be late. I know you're working the three o'clock shift so promptness is a must."

"I got you. I'll be there."

"Good, now open the door for me. Our relationship has to appear strictly professional. You never know who's watching," I said, looking towards the front entrance of the house from the parked car.

"Whatever you say."

"While you're at it, carry in these bags for me," I directed as I took Aaliyah out of her car seat and headed inside. When I entered, Supreme was still in the same location as before I left. But instead of standing, he was slouched down in a chair with a drink in his hand.

"Where do you want me to put your bags?" Devon asked, interrupting my stare down of Supreme. Supreme lifted his eyes in my direction as if he only then realized we had come home.

"You can leave them right there," I said, pointing to the bottom of the wraparound stairs.

Devon put the bags down and then tried to linger his tired ass at the spot to further inspect what was about to go down between me and his boss.

"Thanks, Devon, you can go now." My stiff smile screamed get to steppin'!

Devon got the hint and nodded his head. "Mr. Mills, can I be of any further assistance to you this evening?"

Supreme appeared dazed for a minute and then he silently shook his head no. But that nigga wasn't dazed, he was drunk.

I was ready to push Devon's slow dragging ass out the fucking door. He was holding up my flow. He took his time getting the fuck out and kept glaring back after each step. When he finally bounced I virtually skipped to the door and locked it, making sure he couldn't make a sudden return. I didn't say shit to Supreme. I let him continue to drown his sorrow in that thousand dollar a shot Remy Martin and grabbed my bags and headed upstairs to Aaliyah's bedroom.

"Now, I need for you to be a good little baby and play in your crib until you fall asleep," I uttered to Aaliyah as I took off her clothes and put on her nightie. "I have to go work on your daddy, and I don't need no interruptions, so I'll see you in the morning." I kissed Aaliyah on her forehead, sat her in the crib, turned on the nightlight and made my exit.

As I dashed down the hallway, I made a pit stop at a mirror hanging in the center of the wall. I scrutinized myself and my appearance was definitely not on point. I had a long day and it showed. I wanted to take a shower and freshen up but didn't want to lose any momentum toying with Supreme. I hoped that although I was in semi-form, his drunken eyes would see dime piece. I took my chances continuing my dash downstairs and opening a few buttons on my blouse, along the way.

"Is everything okay Supreme?" I asked softly, watching him pour himself another drink.

"As good as shit can get for a nigga when your wife been ghost for a couple of weeks and your daughter ain't got her mother," Supreme slurred.

"I know it's tough, but you have to be strong for Aaliyah."

"Yeah, but who gon' be strong for me?" he asked, plopping down on the couch spilling some of his drink.

"I will. I'll help you through this." I sat down beside him and rested my hand on his thigh without being too aggressive.

"Well then help me understand why my wife has been keeping in contact with the motherfucker that tried to kill her."

"You mean Nico."

"Motherfuckin' right I mean Nico!" he roared before greedily gulping down his drink in one hit.

"I think that's something you should discuss with Precious."

"I would if I could find her. Man, I shoulda had that nigga killed when I had the chance," Supreme babbled, caught up in his own world. "I ain't neva told Precious that I know this shit, but she fucked that nigga during the time she thought I was dead."

"How do you know that?" My ears perked up waiting as Supreme was revealing some new info that I knew absolutely nothing about.

"Man, towards the end of their investigation on Mike, the feds had a wiretap on Precious' cell. They wanted to see if he would make any incriminating statements to her over the phone so their case could be even stronger. I didn't find out until months later after they reviewed all the recordings what had went down between her and Nico."

"Who told you?"

"One of the agents I had got extra cool with when they had me in protective custody felt I had the right to know. He heard a few of the conversations between Precious and Nico and it was evident them motherfuckers shared a goodbye fuck. I promised I would never say shit because he could lose his job behind that bullshit."

"And you never confronted Precious about it?"

"When I found out I wanted to beat the shit out of her, but she was pregnant and of course I couldn't hurt our baby..." the word "baby" faded out from Supreme's mouth. "To this day Precious is clueless about that shit, and you need to stop frontin' like you didn't know what had went down."

"I swear I didn't, Supreme."

"That's supposed to be yo' girl and she ain't neva told you about it...but then again Precious is the secretive type. She don't trust nobody."

"I guess you're right because I damn sure didn't know. I feel bad that you've been carrying this around for so long. It's gotta be painful."

"It was. The only thing that made it a little easier to cope with was that when it happened, she did believe I was dead. Sometimes people turn to a familiar face for comfort when they hurtin'. Fuck, I don't know, because how can you go back and fuck a man that put a bullet through your chest? It makes me wonder if their connection is that strong," Supreme said, trying to stand up but quickly losing his balance and having to sit right back down.

"Supreme, I think you've had too much to drink." I leaned over brushing my breast against his chest as I took the glass from his hand.

"I'm straight. But I do need to go to bed. Dealing with that detective telling me that the last person my missing wife spoke to was a nigga I detest just as much as Pretty Boy Mike completely exhausted me."

"Let me take care of you. I'll put you to bed," I said, gently stroking the side of Supreme's face and rubbed my fingers through his low haircut. I got up and walked over to the bar and put down the glass and came back to the couch feinding to finish my seduction on Supreme, but his eyelids were closed shut and he was knocked out.

"Supreme, wake up...wake up!" I started shaking him but Supreme was out cold. Damn, my fuckin' luck! I was this close to riding that nigga's dick like a stallion and he want to pass out in a drunken stupor. I was so pissed I didn't even get him a blanket. I left his ass right there on the couch and I went upstairs to bed.

I was awakened early the next morning by the wet Pamper and I'm hungry screams of Aaliyah. I put the pillow over my head determined to kill the sounds echoing through the mansion. "Damn, babies are loud as hell," was all I could keep saying. That shit remained persistent for the next ten minutes.

"Anna, go get Aaliyah!" I screamed out, but then became conscious of the fact that Anna had died like a week ago. That was the first time I slightly regretted taking her nosey ass out. "Fuck!" I belted. I was used to Supreme caring after Aaliyah in the morning but he was probably still laid out on the couch from drinking himself to sleep.

I finally found the strength to drag myself out of bed, madder than a motherfucker. When I got to Aaliyah's room her nose was running, snot coming out from crying so damn hard. and babbling "Daddy" and "baba" for a bottle.

She was pulling at her nightie, and when I got closer I saw it was soaking wet. Her urine-drenched Pamper was halfway off and it had saturated her nightgown.

This shit is for the fuckin' birds! This is what you have to go through as a mother. Getting no damn sleep, changing dirty Pampers, feeding a motherfucker and having to jump every time they start wailing. I don't know how much more of this shit I can take, especially since I ain't getting no dick!

I kept praying that at any moment Supreme would stride up in here and tell me he would handle this and I could go back to bed. But as the time slowly passed he was still a no show. It took almost thirty minutes for me to get Aaliyah cleaned up, take off the dirty sheets and tidy shit up.

With Aaliyah locked on my hip we took it downstairs so I could feed her. By this point I was tired of her sucking on her pacifier as if breast milk was spilling out. When we passed the living room Supreme was exactly like I left him and all I could do was roll my eyes, while Aaliyah started reaching out and once again calling out for her daddy. Not once did she call for her mommy so that let me know that she didn't have me confused with her mother. I didn't know whether to be mad or happy.

By the time we reached the kitchen, Aaliyah threw her pacifier on the floor and pointed towards the HDTV Sub-Zero refrigerator freezer. "Can't nobody ever say that you ain't got your mother's temper," I commented, grabbing a bottle from the fridge.

Aaliyah seemed to be ignoring me as she clapped her hands at the LCD TV DVD hookup with radio. I couldn't believe how far technology had come and what money could buy you. Who would've guessed that a piece of appliance that at one time was strictly to keep your food cold now included a top-of-the-line entertainment center.

"Yeah, I could most def' get used to this style of living." While I warmed up the bottle and began daydreaming of my life as the rich and fabulous, I heard the doorbell ringing. I glanced at the clock on the microwave and it was barely after nine o'clock.

"Who the fuck could this be?" I said, picking up the bottle with Aaliyah in tow. She yanked that bottle out my hand and latched onto the nibble as if starving. "What in the hell is he doing here?" I huffed, looking out the peephole.

"Good morning, Maya," Detective Moore greeted me as if we were friends. "What an adorable little girl," he said, doing some silly ass shit with his fingers towards Aaliyah. "I see you're making yourself right at home, Maya. I wonder what you'll do when the Mrs. comes back."

"What do you want, Detective Moore?" I ignored his slick under-handed comment because again I knew he was trying to get a rise out of me.

"I came to speak with Mr. Mills. I have some new developments that I wanted to share with him."

"Supreme is sleep."

"I thought a successful businessman like himself would be up by now."

"He had a rough night. But you're more than welcome to tell me what your new developments are and I'll be happy to pass it along when he wakes up."

"No, I rather talk to Mr. Mills personally. I'll stop by later on ei-ther this afternoon or evening."

"Which one is it, afternoon or evening?"

"I don't know," he said, in a self-satisfied tone. I was now a hun-dred percent sure that this pompous sonofabitch was fucking with me. "I guess you'll know the answer to that when I pop back up."

"Suit yourself," I said, shutting the door in his face. I stood in the entry and then leaned my back against the wall. I had to bring an end to whatever the pesky detective was conjuring up once and for all.

"You're late!" were the first words that left Devon's lips when I sat down at the table in the quaint restaurant on Robertson Boulevard.

"I know this, but it took forever for Supreme to wake up and I wasn't about to bring Aaliyah with me."

"Wake up...what had him in such a deep sleep...did you and him?"

"No. Your boss was too drunk to do anything or anybody. He passed out on the couch and didn't wake up until after eleven. It was torture trying to take a shower and get dressed with a baby up under me. Now I understand why every rich bitch has a fuckin' nanny. Boy, chicks in the 'hood would appreciate that shit. I think it's time for Supreme to start taking applications to fill Anna's position."

"Do you think that's wise with all the shit we have jumping off right now? I mean I would hate for another nanny to end up at the bottom of the stairs because they started asking one too many questions."

"You have a valid point, but damn, I don't know how much longer I can play this mother role."

"If you plan on being Mrs. Supreme Mills you better get used to it fast. That baby comes with the package."

"You don't have to remind me. I'm well aware of that fact. But enough about babies and shit. We need to address what this meeting is really about. Man, I've had enough of our little friend. Do you know he showed up at the crib this morning?"

"For what?"

"My take, he's fuckin' wit' me. But he claims he has some new information to share with Supreme and that still spells fuckin' wit' me."

"Did he say what the new information was?"

"I asked, but of course his answer was that he wanted to personally speak with Supreme. Thank goodness Supreme was sleep because in a perfect world the detective will never get the opportunity to say another word to him."

"I take it you want to move on this immediately?"

"Is 'like yesterday' soon enough?"

"I came up with a scenario that should work." Devon moved in closer and put his elbows on the center of the square wooden table. "I did some research with a few of my sources."

"Oh fuck! I told your stupid ass not to tell anybody what we were up to."

"Yo, calm down," Devon whispered, pulling my upper body towards him. "I didn't tell nobody shit. I have ways of getting information without arousing suspicion."

"You better," I warned.

"Listen, I'm putting my livelihood on the line. Do you really think I'ma do or say something to put me in jeopardy?"

"I feel you...go head, finish what you were saying."

"Well, I got our little friend's address, and I'm thinking a home invasion gone wrong would be the best look. Anything else will make it appear as if he was a target. But attempted robbery...shit, with the economy being so fucked up they running up in cribs first and taking names later."

I sat back taking in what Devon said. An attempted home invasion might be the strategy to run with. That would lead the investigation towards robbery instead of who might have a grudge against the relentless detective. Anything else probably would have officers prying into his open cases and leading them in my face for a million and one questions. "I think it could work. So are you going to actually go in his crib or what?"

Devon pulled me back in and I wanted to puke because dude's breath smelled real tart. I wanted to give him a Tic Tac, Big Red or something but figured we had to take one thing at a time, and wiping out the detective was top priority.

"I'm looking to get him right outside his front door. On the low, I scoped out his house. He lives off a main street so that's a good thing because mad cars be coming through. He also has a lot of high bushes surrounding the entrance. I figure I can sneak up behind him and put a bullet through the back of his head and be out."

"I like the sound of that, Devon. So when is all this going down?"

"I'm leaning towards tonight. Detectives normally work late shifts so I was gonna head over there after I got off of work, but if I'm too late then tomorrow night. I'm off tomorrow so I'll have time to chill in the cut and wait him out."

"Damn, that means he'l have time to speak with Supreme today."

"Maya, you can't expect for me to do him in broad daylight. It's gotta be at night. Keep Supreme busy. Get him out the house so the detective can't talk to him. You're resourceful. I'm sure you can come up with something to keep Supreme occupied."

"Yeah, I'll suggest we take Aaliyah out for some ice cream or some child friendly bullshit. Try your hardest to make it happen tonight though. I don't think I can keep him away from Supreme for two days in a row. He's pretty fuckin' persistent, which is why he has to go."

"Then tonight it is. When you wake up tomorrow the detective will no longer be our problem, and then of course we'll have some celebrating to do."

"No doubt. I'm looking forward to it."

"Me too. A conniving bitch like you got to have some good pussy and I can't wait to be all up in it."

I simply grinned at Devon's remark. If his desire to take a dip in my juices would speed this murder up then I was willing to give him a taste right now. At this stage in the game anything was doable as long as Devon understood that this is my show and I run this.

Precious

Role Play

Being locked the fuck up will definitely humble a bitch. That's all I could think about when I woke up the next morning with my stomach growling. It was hitting me harder and harder each day that I went from chilling in a luxurious estate to being someone's prisoner, unable to have control over my next move.

After my slick antics with Mike yesterday he didn't show his face for the rest of the night. I yelled out a few times because not only was I starving, but had to piss. After wearing out my pipes for over an hour off and on, I finally accepted the fact the nigga wasn't fucking with me. I eventually fell asleep, pissy, hungry and now waking up to the same shit. As my eyes darted around the room trying to entertain myself I glanced down at my feet and got fixated on my chipped French pedicure, "Damn, I fell off!" was all I kept repeating until I heard the bedroom door being unlocked.

"I see your up," Mike said as if he didn't have a care in the fucking world. But why shouldn't he? It was obvious this nigga hadn't missed a meal or a grooming.

"I know you heard me last night screaming my ass off in here. Even prisoners get a bathroom break," I said, sucking my teeth.

"In this prison, using the bathroom is a privilege which you lost after trying to make your great escape."

"Oh, so what, you gon' have me pissing on myself for the duration of my stay?"

"Hopefully you've learned your lesson and it won't come to

that, but we shall see." Mike came towards me and began unlocking my handcuffs.

"What are you about to do to me?"

"You wanna take yo' ass to the bathroom don't you?" That was one question that didn't even need a response. "Now come on, but I'm telling you now, I ain't in the mood for no bullshit this morning."

"I won't give you any."

"Aight, let's go."

It wasn't until I was in an upright position that Mike took a gun from his back pocket and held it to my spine.

"Is the gun really necessary?" I smacked.

"I learned my lesson dealing wit' yo' crazy ass, and for your sake I hope you did too."

When we entered the hallway the smell of breakfast food smacked me in the face. My stomach immediately started grumbling and I was tempted to start begging Mike for some food, but thought I needed to take one objective at a time. When we got to the bathroom I stepped in the entrance and started closing the door so I could handle my business on the toilet.

"Nah, you leaving the door open, shorty," Mike said, pushing the door back open.

"What the fuck, you got a gun patrolling my every move. Can't I at least do what I got to do in private?"

"No, you lost all rights to privacy. Now hurry up."

"I shouldn't have to share this wit' you but I need to shit."

"Go head, just make sure you spray that Oust afterwards and turn on the fan."

"That's how this is going down? I have to shit with the door open and you posted at the door?"

"Exactly. Now hurry the fuck up before I start making yo' ass wear diapers for now on."

"Fine, but could you at least turn around so I can maintain a little bit of my dignity?" Mike obliged my request but I still felt like less that zero grunting and shitting in front of this motherfucker. I knew I had done some foul shit in my life but this punishment right here was almost too much to endure. By the time I finished and wiped my ass all my pride had damn near diminished. I went to the sink and washed my hands, feeling defeated.

"Come on, it don't take that long to wash your hands, and don't forget to spray 'cause you stunk up the joint for real."

Once again as we began what I call the prison walk back to the bedroom, the smell of the food lingering in the air had my stomach sounding like a disgruntled tiger.

"What the fuck you stopping for?" Mike pushed the gun firmly in my back as I suddenly stopped a few feet away from our destination.

"Mike, I'm so damn hungry! Can I please have something to eat?"

This nigga didn't say shit. He stayed quiet and I imagined his trifling ass laughing behind my back.

"Don't make me beg, but I will," I said, not giving a fuck. What in the hell did I have left to lose? This nigga already had me shitting in front of him. We had come to the point where anything goes.

"I don't know. Last time I demonstrated some kindness and fed you, the favor was returned by you getting all this strength up to clobber me with a fuckin' trashcan and tryna break out. Food seems to be to you what spinach was to Popeye."

"Mike, I'm being serious right now."

"Shit, I'm serious too. Ain't nobody playing. The reason I didn't fuck wit' you none last night was because I was zoned out on medicine tryna get rid of the migraine you left me with. I ain't up with playing those types of games with you today."

"If you feed me I promise I'll be on my A game. I won't try no bullshit. I give you my word on that."

Mike came from behind and stood in front of me staring into my eyes intensely. I wanted to spit in his face and rip my claws through his skin, but instead I conjured up some big crocodile tears, enough to water up my eyes real good but not let a single one trickle down my cheeks. This would give a more convincing performance. Because everybody knows I don't shed a tear over shit, so this would give the appearance of me being on the verge of breaking down but trying to remain strong. Honestly, that wasn't far from the truth, but I'm a soldier. I don't lay down, I gets down, and slowly I was implementing my plan.

"Yo, are you about to cry?" Mike had a perplexed look on his face, stunned by my crushed expression.

I tilted my head down as if trying to hide my embarrassment of admitting defeat. "No, I'm good. Everything's cool," I said, clearing my throat.

Mike lifted my chin gazing in my eyes like this was some fucking love story. Negro please! was all I could think to myself. "No, you're not cool. I see this situation is finally taking its toll on you. I wondered how long you could remain tough, but even you have your breaking point, Precious."

"I said I was good, Mike. You can stop pretending like you give a fuck if I'm okay or not. I know you don't give a damn how I feel."

"That's not true. I do care about how you feel."

"I can't tell. You've tried to humiliate me every chance you got."

"I only wanted to humble you. Since the first time I met you, you've always had this mentality that the sun rises and sets on Precious' ass. I needed for you to understand that it doesn't."

"Your point has been made," I said, clapping my hands as if giving a mock standing ovation.

"Precious, stop! I'm kicking real shit right. From me kidnapping you and having you hauled up in here has always been about teaching you a lesson. You've always farted around like you was Miss Untouchable. I needed to show you that you're not. At this moment was the very first time that I've seen that you know that you aren't."

I wanted to burst out laughing that this slimy motherfucker who raped me had the audacity to stand in my face and give me a sermon on teaching someone a fucking lesson on humility. But, hell I was willing to play this bullshit out for this self righteous snake.

"I can't front. I don't like to admit I'm wrong about shit, but what you're saying is valid, I'll admit that."

"Wow, progress has finally been made." This nigga stood grinning real proud, as if he was being honored at some prestigious award ceremony. This clown was carrying on like I was some charity case that he reformed.

"Who would've thought that you, Mike could be the one to make me admit to my flaws. Once again, I've underestimated how much influence you have over me when I let my guard down."

Mike didn't respond verbally to what I said. Instead he grabbed my arms and led me into the bedroom and handcuffed me back to the bed. He left the room, still silent, closing the door behind him.

Oh fuck! Did I take that kissing ass shit too far? I thought I really had my performance tight and he was licking that shit up like a lollipop. Damn, right when I finally felt I was making a breakthrough with that sociopath I play my cards all wrong.

I kept shaking my head trying to figure out at what point did the conversation go wrong. I was dissecting each word that was exchanged between us so hard that at first I didn't hear Mike come back in.

"Sorry I took so long but the food was getting cold so I had to warm it back up," he said, as he placed a tray of food on the dresser.

I was grinning so damn hard inside. I'm still that bitch!

"That's okay, I'm just so thankful you decided to bring me some food. You have no idea what you've just shown me." *That fucking a nigga will let you have him for one night, but stroking a nigga's ego will let you have his mind for a lifetime.*

"Yes, I do. That I'm genuinely concerned about what happens to you," Mike said, un-cuffing my hands.

"Exactly," I said, reaching for the tray of food. This dude had prepared a bacon and cheese omelet with grits and buttered crescent rolls. Then he had me washing my meal down with freshly squeezed orange juice.

"Precious, if you continue to cooperate with me your stay here can be a pleasant one." Mike was now eyeing me the same way I did my plate of food before quickly devouring it down.

"I don't see how any stay can be pleasant when you know eventually you're going to die."

"Plans can change. This doesn't have to end with you dying."

"So you say, but I don't think Maya is going for that."

"I told you before, let me handle Maya. All you need to focus on is being loyal."

"Loyal to you?"

"Of course."

"What I was trying to say was I'm surprised you want my loyalty because it's not like you need it," I said, trying to smooth over how appalling his request sounded to me.

"I do need it."

"Why?"

"Because if I let you stay alive I would need to know you would never cross me."

Boy oh boy, Mike surely had game with him. It took me a second, but I now understood what was going on in dude's head. He definitely was scheming to maneuver some pussy out of me, but see, the thing was he didn't want to have to take it like he did last time. This demonic fuck wanted me to spread my legs willingly!

"I understand the whole loyalty thing, but I can't lie and say that I don't have trust issues. A lot of foul shit has happened between us and it's hard to be loyal to someone that you don't know will be loyal back to you."

"That's real, Precious. That's why I'm making an effort to show you. I know I only have a little bit of time to prove that, but if you let me, I will."

"Why do you say that you only have a little bit of time?"

"Because within the next week I'll have my money and will be able to get out of LA and start a new life, hopefully with you."

I almost choked on my orange juice when Mike used the words "new life" and "with you" in the same sentence. "You want me to come with you?"

"You and Aaliyah. For the short period of time I spent with her it was as if we bonded. I can't help but believe she really is my daughter. Of course this is all contingent on you proving your loyalty," Mike quickly added.

"I woke up this morning ready to die and now you've given me a reason to live. How ironic is that shit?"

"It's a lot to swallow but I think it could work. From the moment I laid eyes on you in the club a few years ago, I knew you had all the makings to be my wife. That shit ain't changed."

"The thought of being with Aaliyah again, this all sounds so promising, but I can't see Maya going for it. I don't think you understand how ruthless she is. You look at her as your baby sister, but trust me, Maya is no longer a little girl."

"You think I don't know that? I hardly recognize her anymore. But I try to be patient with Maya because I know a lot of it is my fault."

"Why do you feel like that?"

"Maya never knew her father and it affected her emotionally," Mike revealed with regret in his voice.

"I can relate to that. I still don't know who my father is."

"Neither does Maya. Even though my dad disappeared from our lives before Maya was born, she always believed we had the same mother and father, but we don't. I don't know who Maya's father is. My mother never told me and I didn't bother or care to ask. I figured he was another low life, like the rest of the men that came in and out of our lives. So Maya turned to me to be that father figure and I let her down."

"How?"

"I didn't protect her from the sorry ass men my mother would have up in her crib. I mean I don't believe none of them messed with Maya physically, but psychologically she always felt unwanted, as if our moms was choosing being with the men over her."

"Damn, I feel like I'm reliving my childhood all over again."

"The difference is Maya had me and I should've stepped up to the plate and been there for her, but I was too busy doing me. I was in those streets building a drug empire not understanding or caring that I was simply throwing money her way so she could stay out my face and let me do what the fuck I wanted to do. Now look at her. She's a killer just like her brother."

"Mike, you didn't make her into a killer."

"You don't have to spare no punches wit' me, Precious. Maya has no soul. The only reason you got yours back is because you fell in love and had a baby. The same would have to happen to Maya if she has any chance at redemption."

I swallowed hard, agonizing over what Mike said. This nigga was treacherous but he knew his shit. That is what saved me, and it was killing me inside that Maya was turning to Supreme to do the same for her. The difference was the love Supreme and I share is as real as it comes. It was no manufactured concocted bullshit. I was praying that he would remain loyal to our vows and commitment and not fall for the poison Maya was feeding him. But once he read the fake ass letter Maya had me write, I knew there was a strong chance all that dedication was history.

"Mike, I'm going to ask you a question and I want you to be honest with me."

"Go head."

"You're hoping that Maya will be able to make Supreme fall in love with her, aren't you?"

"Yes, but it isn't because I want to hurt you," he answered, taking my hand as if to appease me. I wanted to commence to whooping Mike's ass right there on the spot but kept telling myself to play the game or I would never see my family again. "But because when I leave I know she won't have anybody else. Maya needs Supreme, and with you gone he's going to need her too."

"Supreme deserves better than Maya, and so does my daughter."

"I feel you, and that's why Aaliyah will come with us. As for Supreme, you know I ain't checkin' for that cat, but if he can make Maya feel love and bring her some happiness then I'll let him be. Maybe this can right the wrong from her childhood and take away my guilt. Because no matter what, she's my blood and I love her."

"Mike, this is too much for me to deal with all at once. You're willing to strip away my life and hand it over to your conniving sister. She's got you feeling so guilty about the past that you ain't grasping how vicious she is. This ain't no Little Bo Peep has lost her sheep nursery rhyme shit. Your sister has some serious issues."

"There are some magazines in the drawer. Sit back, read them and relax," Mike said, standing up from the bed, obviously not wanting to face the harsh reality of who his sister truly is.

"What about the handcuffs?"

"I told you I was working on gaining your trust. This is a start. I will be locking the door but having the freedom to walk around the room will hopefully make you feel less like a prisoner and more of a welcomed guest."

"Wow, the surprises keep on coming! I certainly wasn't expecting this, but again, thank you."

"I'm making an effort so I need you to do the same thing."

"Meaning?"

"Give what I requested of you a chance."

"You're talking about the loyalty thing."

"Yes. Or have you already made your mind up that it ain't gon' happen?"

"If it could mean being reunited with my daughter, then I'm willing to try."

"I always knew you were a smart woman, and the love you have for your daughter makes you even that more appealing. I'll be back later on to bring you lunch. Bye."

I stood up and then sat right back down wondering what the fuck had just happened. Could this nigga be serious or was this another sick game he was playing to further torture me? The vibe was clear that the attraction he had for me was very much intact, but wanting to fuck me and having us run off together with Aaliyah was two totally different things. Mike was a slickster in every sense of the word, but until I figured out what he was truly up to I would continue my role play.

Maya
From Nothin' to Somethin'

I rose up from my queen-sized bed feeling exactly like that...a queen. Today felt like a new beginning because if all had gone as planned, Detective Moore should be somewhere in the coroners office. I was tempted to call Devon to get the full report but opted against it, especially after that disclosure from Supreme about the feds putting a wiretap on Precious' cell phone. There was too much at stake to blow it all on a fucking phone call. Today was Devon's day off so I would have to wait for him to make contact.

I flipped on the television switch and turned to the news to see if there was any coverage about Detective Moore's murder. I twiddled my thumbs for over fifteen minutes watching everything from the weather report, entertainment news covering Paris Hilton's latest sexual exploit, and local to international news, but nothing on a shooting death of a cop. I stared at the bottom of the screen for a breaking news alert but still nothing.

"Fuck it! Maybe his body is still sprawled out on the front of his doorstep and hasn't been discovered yet. Or better yet, maybe the police department is keeping his murder under wraps not wanting to alert the media yet until they have a suspect. The last thing the city of LA needs is another unsolved murder of a cop," I said, switching off the television.

Anxious to celebrate the demise of the once potentially toxic detective, I took a quick shower and planned a day of pampering. Yesterday, after keeping Supreme and Aaliyah out all afternoon and evening in an attempt to block the detective from speaking with him, Supreme surprised me with some cash and it was much more than what he hit me off with the first go round. He said it was to show his gratitude for taking such wonderful care of Aaliyah during these hard times and being such a good friend to him. He even made me promise that I wouldn't spend the money on anyone else but myself because I deserved it. Shiiiit, Supreme didn't have to ask me twice! I wrapped my hands around that cash with all my pearly whites showing like it was Christmas. I always knew that Supreme was generous by the way he splurged on Precious, but I had no idea that just being nice to his prized little girl would entitle me with so many perks. Aaliyah was truly an asset that I hadn't counted on.

After confirming my appointment at the beauty salon, I sashayed my ass downstairs ready to head out for my transformation. I damn near had an "Anna" moment and fel down the fucking stairs, when to my shock Detective Moore was standing in the foyer with Supreme.

That fool is supposed to be dead with a bullet to the back of his head. What the fuck happened? Devon, you have some explaining to do!

"Good morning...well I should say afternoon, Maya," Detective Moore said with a pleasant smile.

"Hi," I replied dryly. "Back so soon? I see you couldn't stay away."

"I did come back yesterday to speak to Mr. Mills. I understand you, him and the baby were out all day."

I slightly nodded my head, giving no verbal feedback.

"But today's visit is courtesy of Mr. Mills. You see he gave me a call today and I rushed right over."

"I'm sure you did. Supreme, is everything okay?" I asked, trying to disguise my annoyance with the detective.

"No, nothing is okay anymore."

"What's wrong?"

"I got a letter from Precious," he revealed with pure depression in his voice.

Yes! I cheered inside. "A letter? What did it say...is Precious alright?" I sounded so damn concerned for a second I forgot that I was the one that had the bitch on lockdown.

Supreme didn't respond, as if in a state of shock, so Detective Moore decided to be his spokesperson.

"Apparently, Mrs. Mills feels she needs some space and isn't sure if she's coming back to her family."

"What! That doesn't sound like Precious."

"You know, Maya, I have to agree with you," Detective Moore

said in an eerie way. "I met with Mrs. Mills numerous times during the kidnapping ordeal of their daughter and she didn't strike me as the type of woman who would walk away from her family. If for some reason she did want to leave she would tell you to your face not in a letter."

I felt my cheeks burning up and hoped they hadn't turned the color red. "What do you think, Supreme? Do you believe it...did Precious really write the letter?"

"It's definitely her handwriting," he acknowledged.

"But I'm going to have it submitted to our crime lab and have the validity authenticated," Detective Moore added. I expected that would happen anyway, that's why I was so fucking careful with the handling of the letter.

"I think that's a good idea. Maybe Precious didn't write it, Supreme."

"Or maybe somebody forced her to," Detective Moore said out the blue, damn near knocking the wind out of me.

"Forced her! What do you mean by that?"

"Maya, you seem like an intelligent young lady. I think you know what the word 'force' means."

"Of course I know what it means. I'm simply asking who would force Precious to write that letter and why would you think somebody did."

"Because I'm a detective and that's what we do, think of every scenario when investigating a case...especially one that is as complex as this."

If I'd been packing, more than likely I would've pulled out my heat right then and started blasting on that loose lip fool.

"Mr. Mills, I'm personally delivering this letter to the crime lab today and I'll get back to you when I find out anything."

"Thank you, I'll be waiting to hear from you."

Supreme walked Detective Moore to the door and I waited in the living room. The detective had me so worked up I had to sit down and relax. I was supposed to be acting as Supreme's rock and couldn't let him see the chips falling off my exterior. I stood up when Supreme came in the living room ready to lend my support.

"Supreme, I'm sure after the crime lab runs tests it'll reveal that Precious didn't write the letter," I said, knowing it would reveal the opposite.

"It damn sure looked like her handwriting to me. I tore this house up looking for every piece of paper Precious wrote—anything on to compare to the letter, and I know in my heart it was her hand-writing."

"But what about the detective's theory that somebody forced Precious to write it?" I had to know if Supreme believed that because if he did, he would never let go and I wouldn't have a chance in the world to win his love."

"I want to believe she was forced because the thought of her turning her back on me and Aaliyah...I don't know if I could deal with that. Precious is the love of my life. What could I have done to make her stop loving me and to leave our daughter? And the only person I keep going back to is Nico."

"You think Precious could've left you for Nico?"

"I don't know, but he was the last person she spoke to on the phone and they do share some sort of sick connection."

"I know what you mean," I said as if reluctant.

"Why do you say that? Did Precious say something to you?"

"One day when we were having girl talk and discussing the men in our lives. I was saying how Clip had been my first love and I couldn't believe I fell so hard for such an evil man. She then said her first love had his own streak of evil in him. Of course that threw me off because there isn't anything remotely evil about you, Supreme."

"So what did Precious say?"

"Her comment threw me off, so I said, 'Precious, what are you talking about? Supreme is the sweetest man I've ever met. Why would you say he had a streak of evil in him?' That's when she told me she wasn't speaking about you, but of Nico."

Supreme put his head down as if he wanted to cry like a baby.

"I'm sorry, Supreme. I didn't want to hurt you. You asked me a question and you seem so torn. I only wanted to help."

"I know, Maya but I wasn't expecting to hear that. But honestly, I'm not totally surprised. If you'll excuse me, I need some time alone."

"I understand. Where's Aaliyah?"

"She's upstairs taking a nap."

"I was going to run some errands but I can stay here so when Aaliyah wakes up I can take care of her."

"That's sweet of you, Maya, but my parents are flying in today. They should be getting on my private jet any minute now."

"Oh how nice. How long are they going to be visiting?"

"Just for the day. They're taking Aaliyah back to Jersey with them. I'm going to have her stay at their house for a couple of weeks so I can handle things on my end."

"Just know that I have your back and I'll be more than willing to help you take care of Aaliyah for however long you need."

"Thank you. I might have to take you up on that when Aaliyah returns in a couple of weeks. But they miss their granddaughter and right now I have to get down to the bottom of this bullshit with Precious. With Aaliyah here I wouldn't be able to focus on this the way that I need to."

"I understand. Does that mean you want me to leave too?"

"Maya, no," Supreme said, reaching out taking my hand.

"I don't know what I would've done without you. You've been a source of sanity for me these last few weeks. You can stay as long as you like. I actually welcome the company. I mean look around. This place is pretty fuckin' huge."

"Thank you, Supreme. I thought with Precious gone you might be ready for me to leave since we are best friends—or at least I thought we were. Part of me wants to believe that something bad has happened to Precious so I can understand her leaving and not telling me where she went. I too would feel betrayed if she ran off with Nico without at least telling me bye and explaining why she did it."

"I've been so caught up in how this bullshit got me fucked up that I haven't even considered your feelings. I apologize, Maya. I know Precious is like a sister to you so I know you're hurting too. You've been so strong through all this shit that I took it for granted."

"Don't apologize. We have to continue to be strong for one another and hopefully Precious will be coming back home soon." Supreme hadn't yet let go of my hand so I took it one step further and gave him a slight hug, and to my delight he reciprocated with a firm squeeze.

Damn this nigga feel good...and smell good too! I know Precious going through withdrawals missing the dick downs this fine chocolate motherfucker was stroking her with.

"Since you don't need me, I'ma head out and run my errands."

"Okay, I'll see you later on."

"Yeah, and make sure you give Aaliyah a goodbye kiss for me. Tell her Auntie Maya is going to miss her."

"I will. I know under the circumstances it will be difficult, but try and enjoy yourself today, you deserve it."

"You keep telling me that, Supreme as if you don't deserve to enjoy yourself too."

"One thing at a time," Supreme smiled before heading to his office.

When I got in my car the first thing I did was dial Devon's number. I started the ignition, anxious for dude to pick up.

"Yo!" he said, like he had been waiting for my call. "Meet me at our spot...now!" I said and hung up. I kept the call short and to the point, because although I doubted it, you never knew who was listening in.

I slipped in my Year of the Gentleman CD needing to listen to some smooth R&B with all the drama unfolding, which seemed crazy since I was the one behind most of it. As I drove towards the restaurant on Robertson Boulevard, all the reasons that had brought me to this place in my life right now streamlined through my head. It all started and ended with Precious. I had these love/hate feelings towards her. She was everything I wanted to be and had everything I wanted which made me hate her, but those very same things made me love her too. The reasoning behind this shit was so twisted that it was difficult for me to grasp sometimes. But one thing was for certain; I intended on keeping my eyes on the prize... Supreme.

When I pulled up in the parking lot I noticed Devon's car was already there. "Shit, he must've been already circling the area when I called," I said, rushing to get out of the car because I was determined to make my hair appointment.

"I can explain," Devon stood up and said as soon as he saw me coming up to the table.

I sat down, motioning him to do the same. I didn't want to draw any attention to us and his big black ass standing up as if he got busted fucking around, and trying to apologize wasn't helping.

"What, was you around the corner when I called?"

"Not exactly around the corner but close to it. I had a feeling I'd be hearing from you. But listen," Devon lowered his voice before continuing. "The reason I couldn't hit old boy off was because he came home with some honey. I guess even cops have late night booty calls. I didn't want to take no chances and have to kill both of them. Tonight though, I'm on it. He's going down, and if he got somebody with him, they going down too."

"Delete that."

"What? You don't want me to kill whoever with him too? I mean we can't leave no witnesses."

"No, I mean delete killing Moore...at least for the moment." "Why?"

"Supreme got that letter from Precious I had her write. He took it upon himself to call in the detective. Let's just say the detective is suspicious about this so-called letter and is having it checked out at the crime lab. Of course Precious did write it and I want the detective to get the information and bring it back to Supreme. If we kill him before that it would do us more harm than good."

"But you know he's a problem. How long do you really want to keep him around?"

"Until I set a few more things in motion. You never know. The detective might become useful."

"If you say so, but I don't see how."

"You sure are singing a whole other tune. At first you didn't want any parts of taking the cat out, now you mad that I want you to cease fire."

"You made a strong argument as to why he had to go and I felt you on that. But if you want to keep him around a little longer, I'm game."

"Wonderful. But of course I'll let you know when to make your move."

"I got you. But I guess that means I won't be getting my gratitude treat anytime soon?"

"You never know, so keep your finger on the trigger. Now, I have an appointment to get to. I'll be in touch." I grabbed my purse and I was off to my next stop.

I had fifteen minutes to get to the salon, but luckily it was on North Canon Drive, which wasn't too far from where I was. The traffic was light so I breezed to the spot, and what a spot it was. This was the type of high-end establishment that you were on time for, because unless you were one of their many celebrity clients, coming late meant your name was crossed off the appointment book. The valet was waiting with a smile on his face when I stepped out of my Jag. The much younger knockoff looking Brad Pitt attendee even offered to give my car a detailed washing while I was getting my hair did, and of course I agreed.

I strolled into the sexy bungalow-style salon feeling like a star myself. I thought the place would have a typical, overrated Hollywood that thinks they are somebody aura, but it was the opposite. The staff of bleach blondes, red heads and brunettes were too friendly and almost overly accommodating, offering me everything from champagne to a personal stylist to pick out a new wardrobe to go with my new hairstyle. The life of the rich and privileged had my name written all over it.

"Miss, you can come this way," the stylist who I assumed was doing my hair said. When I sat down I fell in love with the garden terrace that was complete with fountains and rose bushes. I had a clear view because of the floor-to-ceiling windows.

"This is the life for me," I mumbled out loud.

"I'm sorry, Miss, what did you say?"

"Oh nothing, just thinking out loud."

"So what are you having done today?"

"I want some coloring, highlights and hair extensions."

"Great! Did you have a color and style in mind?"

"Yes, I even brought a picture to make your job a little easier."

"Perfect! Let me have a look," she said as I dug in my purse. I then handed her the photo and she eyed the picture and then stared at me.

"Wow, you resemble the woman in this picture an awful lot."

"Everybody says that. But it should be expected. We used to be sisters."

"Used to be?"

"Yes, her name was Precious, but she died not too long ago."

"I'm sorry for your loss."

"Thank you. I've always admired her style, but now that she's gone I think she would appreciate me carrying it on."

"That's a nice way of looking at it. They say imitation is the greatest form of flattery. So let me work my magic. First, I'll start with a scalp treatment. It's a massage of special oils and steamer."

"Sounds divine."

"It is, so sit back and relax."

It was effortless to do precisely that. I closed my eyes and let my mind travel to where I wanted to be...my life as a queen bitch. I visualized diamonds in all colors, shapes and sizes, a walk-in closet full of designer clothes, shoes and bags that even Kimora Lee Simmons would have to respect, and pushing whips that I can't even pronounce let alone spell. Each day I was getting closer to living my dream and going from nothin' to somethin'.

Precious

Walk In My Shoes

I woke up for the first time in I didn't know how many weeks without being handcuffed to a fucking bed. This new chapter in my life had now taken another bizarre turn. After Mike had fed me that delicious breakfast he kept his word and came back for lunch and dinner. Then he took another chance at letting me bathe, and this time I pulled no shenanigans. He was so impressed with all my cooperating he filled my drawers with undergarments, a few loungewear outfits and beauty products. I was almost starting to feel a sense of normalcy, if that was possible under the circumstances.

If Mike was trying to prove that what he said he was willing to do for me was true, then he was doing a damn good job. If he really wanted me to leave the country with him and I could bring Aaliyah, then I would do it. Once I got to wherever the fuck he took us, I would scheme up a plan to break the fuck out and go back to Supreme the first chance I got. But right now the most important thing was finding a way to stay alive. Playing up to Mike seemed to be the best and damn near only way to make it happen. As the idea of being reunited with Aaliyah played in my head I heard a knock at the door.

"Precious, are you up?" I heard Mike ask. What the hell, this nigga knocking now, tryna respect my privacy? Shit really has changed.

"Yeah, I'm up. Come on in, Mike." He came in carrying a tray with food and one long stem rose in a slender glass vase.

"You're feeding me another fabulous meal. You're not poisoning me on the low are you?"

"I suppose I deserve that question," Mike laughed. "But no poison. I want you alive not dead."

"Wow, pretty soon you'll let me out this bedroom and I'll be able to walk around," I joked.

"Funny you should say that. I was going to ask you if you wanted to come in the living room and watch TV or a movie."

"Mike, now you're officially buggin' me out. You have done a complete 180 in less than forty-eight hours. I get you're tryna show me a different side, but this is what one would define as drastic. Marinate on that while I eat my breakfast."

Mike sat down on the bed and got comfortable as I poured syrup on my buttermilk pancakes. I was tripping how all of sudden I went from being on the verge of starvation to being plentiful with food.

"These are bangin' and I ain't even big on pan-cakes," I said, savoring each bite.

"Precious, I'm sorry."

"You don't have to apologize. Like I said, they bangin'."

"I'm not talking about the pancakes."

"Then what are you apologizing for?"

"I'm sorry for raping you."

I stopped with my fork in midair. "Are you sure you want to take the conversation there, because I don't think I do."

"I understand if you don't want to say anything and simply listen."

"Do I really have a choice?"

"If you don't want to hear what I have to say then I'll end it right here."

I couldn't front, I was somewhat curious to how this clown planned on coming at me. "Go 'head."

"I never wanted to admit this, because if I did, I would have to own up to being a rapist. I've murdered, stolen, cheated, committed numerous crimes, but never did I believe I would find rapist on that list."

"Well it is."

"I know, and I'm ashamed. For so long after it happened I kept telling myself that I didn't rape you, that you wanted to have sex with me."

I put my head down because Mike and I both knew that at a point before I believed he killed Supreme, I did want to have sex with him. On one occasion I practically begged for the dick, but none of that changed what happened the night he did rape me.

"But you didn't. You gave every indication that the last thing you wanted was for me to touch you, but instead I took it. I'll never forgive myself for that."

"Where did this big epiphany come from?"

"In my heart I knew the truth, but my mind wouldn't allow me to recognize it. I was angry for being locked up like an animal. I wanted to blame somebody and it was easy to make you the target. If I came clean and said you did nothing wrong then the only person I could blame for my demise would be me. I wasn't man enough to do that."

"But you man enough now. Forgive me if I'm not..." Mike turned around to see what had caused me to stop mid sentence.

"Isn't this cozy! My dear brother with my worse enemy!" Maya spit. "Maybe I should just kill you both right now." There was a long pregnant pause before Maya smirked. "I'm joking," she teased, placing what appeared to be a brand new designer bag on the dresser.

"What the fuck did you do to yourself?" Mike walked over to Maya with his mouth opened in confusion.

"Mike, I told you she was crazy. Maya sweetie, I hate to fracture your frame but you'll never be me. I don't care what color the hair or how long the extensions. There is only one Precious Cummings AKA Mills."

"Let's let Supreme be the judge of that."

"Maya, what are you doing? The hair, these clothes you're wearing, this ain't you."

"It's the me I've always wanted to be."

"Trick, please! Admit you want to be me. Your brother and I were just having a conversation about admitting shit, maybe you need to be a part of this."

"Damn, Mike, Precious must toss one hell of a salad because I'm assuming that's how she got you to lose your fuckin' mind. First, you move her upstairs from the basement, and now this bitch handcuff free, eating pancakes like she staying at a five star hotel instead of being a prisoner."

"I see you tryna ignore what I said, but that's cool," I commented, taking the last bite of my pancakes.

"Maya, I'm concerned about you. I know you want to win Supreme over, but turning into his missing wife might not be the move."

"Mike, fuck being concerned about me! I think you need to be concerned about yourself. Precious is playing you like she's done every other man in her life. Do you know that when she thought Supreme was dead she slept with Nico? Can't you see what type of skank she is?

Her supposedly dead husband wasn't even cold in the ground and this ho was spreading her legs for the man who tried to take her out this world. And you call me the crazy one," Maya said, pointing her finger directly at me. "Maya, that's on her. You may not agree with the choices Precious made, and I'm sure she doesn't agree with yours."

"I can't believe you're defending this tramp. She's responsible for putting you in jail, Mike."

"No, I'm responsible for that all on my own."

I watched as the color drained from Maya's face.

"What the fuck is going on? The next thing you're gonna tell me is that you want to free this bitch and let her go home to her family." Mike remained silent which aggravated Maya further. "Fuckin' say something! Don't stand there on mute!" she screamed, raising up her hands and pushing her brother in the chest.

"Calm down," Mike said, holding Maya's arms still.

"Mike, I can't believe you're letting her do this to us. We're family! First, you set me up with that gun bullshit and now you're siding with the woman who has ruined both of our lives. What happened to us being a team?"

"Maya, how did I ruin your life? I treated you like we were blood," I interjected.

"Shut up! I don't want to hear a word out of you. This is between me and my brother."

"Maya, let's go out there and talk."

"Fuck that! Don't try that blah, blah, blah shit with me. You say what the fuck is going on right here, right now."

"Fine. In a few days I'll have that money I've been waiting for and you already know after that I'm leaving. But the thing is, I'm bringing Precious with me."

"I never thought I would think this about you, but you're a fuckin' fool. But with you holding that bullshit gun situation over my head, there isn't too much I can do about the decisions you make. Remember, when Precious leaves your dumb ass high and dry on whatever island you chillin' on to come back for her husband and daughter, don't be mad at me when I put a bullet straight through her eyes."

"She won't be coming back."

"And you're so sure because what, she's confessed her undying love for you?" Maya said sarcastically.

"Not her undying love for me, but for Aaliyah. We're bringing her with us."

"Mike, didn't you hear what I said? Precious slept with Nico too.

That means he also could be the father. More than likely Aaliyah isn't even your child."

"All that is true, but what we do know is that she's Precious' child and they deserve to be together."

"I have to give it to you, Precious, you must have some unbelievable pussy. It's been how long now since my brother raped you, and he is jumping through hoops to get back between your legs, or has it already happened?"

"That's enough, Maya!"

"No, Mike, this is enough. Not only do you want to take Precious with you, but you're trying to take Aaliyah too. It doesn't matter anyway, Aaliyah's not even here."

"Where is she? Maya, so help me if you did anything to hurt my daughter…"

"Save it, Precious. Aaliyah went back to New Jersey with Supreme's parents for a couple of weeks."

"Then we'll wait for her to come back before we leave," I said, making it clear to Mike that I wasn't bouncing without my daughter.

"We can wait, that's not a problem."

"Mike, I never knew you could be so accommodating. But it doesn't matter, Aaliyah still can't leave with you."

"What's the excuse now, Maya?" Mike asked, becoming impatient.

"Aaliyah is my lifeline to Supreme. I need her here in order to win him over."

"You're never going to win him over anyway."

"Shut up, Precious. That's the last warning you'll get. You may have my brother's nose wide open but I have no problem taking you out."

"Maya, leave Precious out of this. I want Aaliyah to leave with us and that's not negotiable. You're going to have to find another way to win Supreme over."

"Here we go…once again you're deserting me like you did when I was a little girl, never protecting me, always choosing everyone and everything else over me. Neither you nor our trifling mother ever wanted to be bothered with me. For mother, she picked her pathetic boyfriends who were always itching to get a taste of my virgin pussy, and you picked your work. Always in those streets hustling not giving a damn what my life was like in that hell hole. Now I'm nineteen years old and you still don't give a damn about me. All you care about is what's best for you."

Mike and I both stayed quiet. It seemed crazy that yesterday the two of us was discussing this very topic, and here Maya was shoving it back down our throats, trying to gain sympathy votes from her brother.

"My dear brother can't be speechless. You always have some shit to pop."

"Growing up I did let you down and I carry a lot of guilt around over that. I also know that you believe I'm letting you down now, but I'm not. A mother and her daughter deserve to be together. This has to be a give and take situation. I'm giving you the opportunity to have a life with Supreme, so I have to take the one thing that means the most to Precious. The same way I have to right a wrong with you, I'm trying to right my wrong with her."

"Okay, Mike. I'll do what you've asked, but like I said, Aaliyah won't be back for a couple of weeks. That will at least give us some time to figure out how I'll give Aaliyah to you without it leading back to me."

"True. I'll brainstorm on it. Maya, thank you for doing the right thing."

"You're not giving me a choice, Mike. This is your show, so I'll play my part. You two enjoy your evening," Maya said before leaving.

Mike laid his back flat across the bed and put his hands over his face. "What the fuck happened to us?"

"Are you asking me?"

"No, I'm asking myself."

"Yeah, 'cause yah some fucked up motherfuckers. I thought I was damaged, but the Owens family got me beat."

"You don't have to rub it in, Precious."

"I mean am I really telling you something that you don't already know? The scary part is, as fucked up as your thinking is, I believe you're trying to make the best out of the horrible situation you created. Maya, on the other hand still ain't comprehending that this is some bullshit. She doesn't think she's doing anything wrong."

"I'm hoping that she'll get there."

"Nah, she ain't got no conscious. Even when I was out in them streets causing havoc I felt remorse for a few motherfuckers I had to take out. But at that moment I felt I didn't have a choice. It was like my life or theirs, so of course I chose mine. Maya don't even seem to have the capability to have remorse and that's frightening. And Mike, not too many things frighten me. Thank God Aaliyah is going to be with Supreme's parents. That will help me sleep a little bit better at night."

"I was glad to hear that too. Maya's obsession with winning Supreme over has her being erratic."

"Damn sure do, so you better be careful. Maya is determined not to let anything or anyone stop this fantasy life she's created in her mind with Supreme."

"True, but that's why I had to utilize my gun leverage."

"Would that have something to do with the cat named Terrell?"

Mike lifted his upper body off the bed and turned towards me.

"How did you know about Terrell?"

"I heard you and Maya arguing about him the other day. Who is he?" I could tell Mike didn't want to tell me which made me want to know even more. "Mike, you might as well tell me. I'm a prisoner for goodness sakes! Who am I gonna tell?"

He let out a deep sigh like fuck it. "Terrell was Nina's younger brother."

"Nina...the Nina that was engaged to Jamal and working for you?"

"Yep, that Nina."

"What is Maya's connection to him?"

"That was supposed to be her quote man unquote. Maya's young hot ass was in way over her head with that dude."

"What happened?"

"He was a lil' young hustling nigga from Queens makin' paper. He wasn't a major nigga in the drug game, but he fo' sho' was on a come-up makin' moves. Somehow him and Maya started dating. Again, me being so caught up in my own shit I had no idea she was dealing wit' cat, not until I got a phone call one night."

"From who?"

"Maya. She was crying being all hysterical. She told me to come get her from this townhouse in Jersey. When I got there she let me in and I see Terrell on the floor laying in a puddle of his own blood."

"What, did somebody run up in the crib and kill him?"

"Yeah, Maya's crazy ass."

"Wait a minute, Maya killed him?"

"I didn't stutter. She killed that nigga over some young girl bullshit. He was supposed to be her man and he was fuckin' around on her. The kid was only eighteen. What the fuck do you think an eighteen year old nigga, makin' money in the streets is gonna to be doing? But she was fifteen and out of her league."

"So she killed him?"

"She claimed it was an accident. That she was only tryna threaten him with the gun but it went off. I knew she was lying. I was looking in the eyes of a killer. I knew those eyes. I had them too."

"Wow, and I thought when she killed Nina it was her first time. No wonder it seemed so effortless."

"Maya killed Nina too?"

"You didn't know that? I thought for sure Maya would've told you."

"No. I always assumed you killed Nina."

"It was your sister. That was the incident that brought us so close together, because Nina was about to kill me and Maya shot her first. I had no idea that Maya even knew Nina before I introduced them."

"They didn't."

"But Maya was dating her brother."

"She was fuckin' her brother and she was just one of many. But when I saw him lying on the floor I recognized his face immediately. He used to get drugs from me and I knew he had an older sister that he was holding it down for."

"You're talking about Nina."

"Yeah, that's when I decided to recruit her. She could work for me and I would put money in her pocket now that her brother was dead because of my silly ass sister. So at the funeral I approached her and took it from there."

"Why did you hold onto the gun?"

"I know it's crazy, but I swear every time I was about to ditch that shit something kept holding me back and I'm glad I did. Trust me, if I didn't have that gun situation lingering over Maya's head there's no telling what she might do."

"So why do you fuck wit' her?"

"Unless you have your own brother or sister it's hard to explain the bond. You can be at each other's throats but you rise and fall together."

"I understand, but if you don't mind me asking, what did you do with the gun?"

Mike gave a slight laugh. "I feel like I shouldn't tell you."

"Why? It's not like I'll ever have a chance to get it. After we leave LA we're off to another country. It doesn't really matter if you tell me. I'm just curious."

"You're right, what's the harm? After Donnell did that drive by shooting for me I had him take it back to New York."

"You had that nigga take that shit all the way back to New York? How?"

"All those details aren't necessary. The point is he got it there and back to its proper resting place."

"Its proper resting place...I'm lost. Where would that be?"

"The apartment Nina lived in and Terrell paid the rent on until he was murdered. Call it twisted, but it was like my gift to Nina. When her brother died she was crushed. Me stashing it at the spot Terrell would hold down for her was like me putting the shit to rest."

"If you say so."

"But now it's even more ironic. I mean they both died at the hands of Maya. And the gun she used that could put her away for the rest of her life is stashed at a spot that both of them called home at one time."

"Who lives there now? Nina's been dead for a minute."

"I have somebody that checks up on it every now and then, but nobody. Nina always maintained that spot even after she moved in with Jamal, but it was mostly for me. The apartment was in a low key neighborhood in Queens so I would use it for some business purposes occasionally."

"So what, you keep paying the rent every month to maintain it?"

"Right before she died, Nina resigned the lease. I paid that shit up for the whole year in advance. To this day that landlord ain't neva asked no questions and don't even know that Nina is dead. When it's time to renew the lease, he puts it under the door and I get my people to pay that shit up front for the year. And you know how motherfuckers are. All they want is the loot and no tenants complaining about the noise. I'm two for two on that."

"Interesting. You better hope Maya doesn't ever find that spot."

"Nope, like I said it's a real low-key spot. She doesn't know anything about it. That's exactly the way it needs to be. Having some collateral is good because you can never be too careful. But like I said, Maya and I share a bond. It won't ever come down to that."

I heard what Mike was saying, but that so called bond he shared with Maya appeared to be one-sided to me. I wanted to be wrong because with his help I would get my daughter back. But see, I was always taught that when a man was sleeping, a woman was thinking, and in this particular case I think that applied to brother and sister too. Maya wasn't going to let anybody—including Mike—get in the way of her being able to walk in my shoes.

Maya

Prelude to a Kiss

"Ah-h-h-h-h-h-h-h!" was all I screamed for twenty minutes straight when I left from seeing my brother and Precious at the stash house. Those two motherfuckers were trying to ruin everything that I had worked so hard for. I couldn't fathom how Precious was able to turn my brother against me. The power of pussy, kept flashing through my brain. It had to be that because what other reason would Mike develop a conscious? I thought back to when I first started seeing glimpses of it. It all came around to Aaliyah. He had a soft spot for that little girl and for her mother. I preferred for Precious to be dead, but I was willing to let Mike ride into the night with that manipulative tramp, but not with Aaliyah too. Supreme would be devastated and would spend the rest of his life searching for her and leaving no time for me and him to become a family. I had to figure out a way to work this shit out, and it started tonight.

When I got back to the house Supreme wasn't home and Aaliyah was gone. His parents must have been in and out. I wondered what Supreme was working on that had his full attention. I knew Precious was at the center of it but I wanted the specifics. I couldn't focus on any of that right now. I didn't know how much time I was working with before Supreme would be home and I had to try and work my magic. I ran upstairs and headed straight for the shower.

It was now or never so I had to go hard. I stepped out the shower and began the completion of my transformation. It would be the tiny details that would make all the difference and I wasn't missing one.

Every ten minutes I would check out the security camera to see if Supreme was pulling up, and on the fourth look I peeped his Lamborghini zooming up the driveway. My hands were shaking because I was so nervous, but there was no backing out.

I hurried down the stairs, dimming the lights and positioned myself right in front of the steel case windows. With the moonlight beaming through, the views from downtown LA to Pacific Palisades were even more spectacular.

When Supreme opened the front door, my back was facing him. I heard the door shut and his footsteps on the marble floor. His pace was quick when he first entered but became slower with each step. I knew by that, he had noticed my presence. I remained motionless as if a well sculpted wax figure. The steps got closer and closer and I was ready to jump out my skin from nervousness, but I wanted this shit to work out so damn bad I wasn't about to fuck it up.

Then I felt the strong arms I had been dying to feel, wrap around my waist. Supreme took in his favorite Dolce & Gabbana light blue scent I had purposely taken from Precious' room and sprayed on my body. He buried his face on my slender neck immersing in the seductive aroma.

"Baby, I knew you wouldn't be able to stay away. I've missed you so much. I'm so happy you're back home," Supreme whispered, gliding his hands up the silk negligee to my breasts and massaging his fingers against my hardened nipples. "Don't ever leave me again." He pressed his lips against my skin, sprinkling kisses up and down my neck. With forcefulness he turned my body around now pressing his lips on mine with eyes closed. I let our tongues intertwine and then closed my eyes too, letting my body melt in his arms. I never knew that a kiss could feel almost as good as the actual act of sex. Then it happened...all motion stopped.

"Maya, what the fuck are you doing? I thought you were Precious!" Supreme said, pushing me away. Although his voice was raised, I didn't see anger in his eyes.

"I'm sorry, Supreme. When you walked up and put your arms around me, I got caught up in the moment. Please forgive me."

"But look at you, your hair...you have on Precious' nightgown and that perfume. That's the only kind Precious wears because she knows it's my favorite." Supreme backed away from me and sat down on the couch. "I can't believe I did what I just did."

"Supreme, it isn't your fault. I can understand how you mistook me for Precious, that's the only reason why you were attracted to me.

I should've stopped you, but I didn't. I'm so wrong for that."

Supreme sat with his head down, still baffled by what happened. "Why do you look like that—like Precious?" he asked. I knew he was trying to make sense of a situation I carefully calculated.

"Well you told me to go treat myself and I decided to get a makeover. The stylist suggested the hair color and extensions. It didn't really register with me that it was so similar to how Precious wears her hair until I got home and saw all the pictures around the house. As for the negligee and perfume, Precious actually gave it to me a long time ago when I was with Clip and we were having problems. She told me this was a guaranteed way to seduce him and make him forget any other woman he may have been creeping with."

"I hear you, but this is too much."

"I know. I can't say I'm sorry enough. I haven't felt pretty in so long, and after getting pampered today I came home and wanted to feel sexy. You weren't home and I never expected for you to see me dressed in this. I only came downstairs to have a drink before going to bed, but it was like this view," I said pointing towards the window, "Was calling my name. I was daydreaming, off in another world. I didn't even hear you come in. Then when you put your arms around me and kissed my neck..." my voice trailed off. "I had no idea I was so lonely until you held me."

"You don't have to apologize, mistakes happen."

"Supreme, if for now on you're going to be feeling uncomfortable around me, I'll leave."

"What do you mean leave?"

"I'll pack up my stuff and move out. School will be starting back soon and I can get housing there in one of the dorms. Until then, I can go back to New York and visit with my mom."

"That might be for the best."

"I think so too, but is it okay if I leave tomorrow?"

"Of course. If you need for me to get you a plane ticket or anything let me know."

"I'm fine, but thanks for offering. I should head up to bed. Goodnight."

"Goodnight."

Supreme sat in the dark as I went upstairs to my room. I got in my bed feeling fucked up. That was a bold move I made, but with the walls closing in on me what was I supposed to do? Precious is somewhere on lockdown but was still winning. I fell asleep with depression and defeat engulfing my body.

Knock! Knock! Knock!

I thought that sound was coming from a dream I was having in my sleep but as it continued and became louder, I realized it wasn't the case. I slowly opened my eyes and looked at the clock on the nightstand to see what time it was. "Nine-fifteen in the morning," I said out loud, rising up in the bed. "Come in."

"Sorry to wake you up," Supreme said, standing in the doorway in a navy blue track suite.

"Supreme, I'm catching the red-eye tonight, so can I please sleep for a couple more hours before you toss me out?"

"That's the thing. You don't have to leave."

"Excuse me, but last night you told me you thought it was a good idea for me to go back to New York until school started."

"I mean you can leave if you want, but I don't want you to feel that I'm kicking you out."

"I know you're not kicking me out, but I need to leave. I was wrong, and you shouldn't feel uncomfortable in your own house to be around me."

"I don't feel that way at all."

"You don't have to ask me not to leave because you feel guilty. I'll be fine."

"It's not that," Supreme exhaled. "I don't want you to leave."

"Huh?" I sat up extra straight in the bed as if that would help me hear better.

"I want you to stay...if you want to stay."

"Honestly, I don't think I want to stay. I'll miss Aaliyah and I'm going to miss you too, but it's best if I leave." As bad as I wanted to jump up and down, I never forgot what Precious told me. First, you latch your hook into a man. Then once you got him you pull away, because all men want what they perceive they can't have.

"Why?"

"Because I crossed the line yesterday and it's best if I go."

"No you didn't."

"Yes, I did. I let you kiss me knowing you thought I was Precious."

"That's not exactly true."

"What isn't true?"

"When I first came in the house and saw you standing by the window, I did believe you were Precious. When I started kissing you though, I knew something was different, but fuck it, I'm a man and it felt good. I pushed you away because no matter how good it felt, it was wrong so I stopped myself."

Bingo! I knew I didn't see anger in Supreme's eyes when he pushed me away. "I know where you're coming from, Supreme. Precious is gone and you're lonely. It's natural that you reach out to somebody for comfort. That somebody happened to be me last night."

"Hold that thought, Maya. I'll be back in a little while. That must be Detective Moore at the door. He called a minute ago saying he would be here in a few."

"Okay, I'll be right here." Supreme rushed downstairs and I rushed out my bed so I could eavesdrop on their conversation. I knelt down at the top of the staircase and Supreme had just let Detective Moore inside.

"Can I get you something to drink?" Supreme offered, being surprisingly polite to the detective.

"No, I can't stay that long. But I wanted to come over and discuss this with you in person."

"Sure, what did you find out?"

"The lab did analyze the letter and indeed it was Mrs. Mills' handwriting."

All I could do was smile.

"I knew it!" Supreme yelled, punching the air with his fist. "How could she leave me and our daughter?" Supreme said out loud a few times before Detective Moore decided to interrupt.

"Mr. Mills, I know this is tough, but I'm still not convinced this is as black and white as it appears."

"What are you talking about? You said the handwriting is Precious'. What else could there be? My wife is probably off with Nico Carter somewhere, not giving a fuck about me or our family. Have you been able to get in touch with Nico yet?"

"No, I haven't. But because he was the last person your wife talked to on her cell, doesn't mean that she is with him."

"Why are you defending Precious so much? You don't even like her."

"I never said I didn't like Mrs. Mills, I actually somewhat admire that fiery personality of hers, but that's beside the point. As a detective, my gut tells me that there is a lot more going on here."

"What do you mean?"

"That's the thing. I can't figure it out. But I think that houseguest of yours may know a lot more than what she's saying."

My smile had now turned to a frown.

"You talking about Maya? What does she have to do with this?"

"I can't put my finger on that either, but again, my gut never lies."

"If Maya knew anything that could help us find Precious she would tell me. Precious is like a sister to her. She's just as worried about her whereabouts as I am."

"That might be the case."

"It is. Now that we know Precious is alive and well, I suppose you can close that missing person case."

"That's standard procedure, but I'll still be continuing my own private investigation, and let me know if you discover any new leads."

"I will. I appreciate your assistance, Detective, and I'm sure we'll be in touch," Supreme said, shaking Detective Moore's hand.

I scooted back to my bedroom as Supreme let Detective Moore out. I rushed into the bathroom and turned on the shower. I jumped in and let the water drench my body, then hopped back out and went to my bedroom door, peeping out of the slightly opened crack to see if Supreme was on his way up. I figured he would want to share with me his discussion with Detective Moore, and I had to do something to divert the suspicion the detective was casting in my direction. As I suspected, Supreme was coming up the stairs to see me, no doubt.

I ran back to the shower, hopped in one more time so my body would be freshly wet, and then stepped out, patiently waiting for Supreme's arrival. When I heard him knocking at my door, I ignored him, not saying a word, but willing him to come inside. He continued to knock and then called out my name. When I heard his hand on the doorknob, I ran back to the shower and turned off the water.

"Maya, are you in here?" Supreme asked, walking in my bedroom, and right on cue I made my entrance.

"Supreme, what are you doing in here!" I screamed as if embarrassed that he caught me coming out the shower butt ass naked. There is nothing like a wet glistening body to get a man's dick extra hard.

"Maya, forgive me. I knocked and called out your name but got no answer."

"Yeah, because I was in the shower and obviously didn't hear you. You need to get out, right now!" I continued my tirade.

"Of course. I'm sorry."

"You should be, now please leave. I need to get dressed."

"Sure. When you're done, please come downstairs because I need to talk to you about some things."

"Fine, now get out!" I was popping all that shit in my birthday suit without a towel in sight to cover up my tits and ass. When Supreme walked out with his head hanging down looking pitiful, I slammed the door and locked it as if I was done with him. How proud and pissed

Precious would be. I was using every trick she ever taught me to score her own husband.

I took my time getting dressed, purposely making Supreme wait. I hoped this new drama I conjured up would scoot out that bullshit Detective Moore had left on his brain. To be on the safe side, I added an extra prop. I walked slowly down the stairs carrying my suitcase. The way Supreme's eye bulged, I knew he was thrown for a loop.

"Why do you have your suitcase? I thought we decided you were going to stay."

"No, you said I could stay and I've decided not to."

"Why?"

"What did you want to talk to me about?" I asked, intentionally switching the subject.

"Oh yeah, umm…the letter."

"What letter?"

"The one I got from Precious."

"You mean the fraudulent letter that someone must've forged?"

"No, it wasn't forged. She wrote it."

"What!" I dropped my suitcase to the floor for a dramatic affect.

"I know. In my heart I wanted to believe she didn't write it, but my head kept telling me she did."

"I can't believe it! Why would Precious leave you and Aaliyah? You seemed like the perfect family. I admired your relationship so much. I hoped that I would share that type of love with someone, someday."

"I thought we were the perfect family too. I don't know where I went wrong."

"What else did the detective say?" I inquired to see if he would mention the suspicions the detective had about me.

"Nothin greally. They're going to close out the missing person case, but he's still going to do his own investigating."

"Why?"

"You know detectives. They never give up until they have all the answers."

"What are you gonna do?"

"Honestly, I don't know. My first priority is to make sure Aaliyah is happy. It's good that she's with my parents right now."

"I hope everything works out for you and Aaliyah, but I need to be going."

"I thought your flight didn't leave until tonight."

"It doesn't, but I have to take care of a few things."

"Maya, I really am sorry about what happened earlier. I hope that isn't why you're leaving."

"I was angry at first, but when I thought about it, I know you didn't mean to walk in on me naked. I'm leaving because with Precious gone and now that I know she may not come back, there's really nothing left for me here. I was thinking of even enrolling in a college in New York instead of coming back to LA."

"Is that what you want?"

"I only came to LA to be with Clip and because Precious was here, but now that they're both gone, why should I stay? For all I know, Precious could be back in New York. You know she will always be a Brooklyn girl at heart."

"You think Precious could really be in Brooklyn?"

"Hell, I don't know, but ain't Nico from Brooklyn also?"

"So you think she ran off with Nico too?"

"I'm sorry, Supreme, that was insensitive of me to even mention Nico. I was voicing my thoughts out loud. I'm trying to understand what or who would make Precious abandon her life here in LA with you."

"I was contemplating the same shit and I keep coming back to Nico. The fucked up part is that nigga seems to have fallen off the face of the earth too."

"I'm confused. What are you talking about?"

"I've had my own team of topnotch private investigators hunting that nigga down and it's like he's ghost. The last lead was him setting up shop in Chicago. Now they can't locate that motherfucker nowhere. I'm wondering if him and Precious done ran off to some island somewhere. But best believe, I don't know when, but one day both of them will have to answer for this shit, I guarantee that."

"I feel you, Supreme, and I wish you the best of luck."

"I appreciate that. I hate to see you go but you have to do what's best for you. Call me when you get to New York. Let me know you got there safely."

"I will. I'll talk to you later. Bye, Supreme."

"Bye, Maya."

Bye, my motherfuckin' ass! My sweet, innocent persona was working beautifully on Supreme. I walked out the front door to the estate more confident than ever with my position in his life. This nigga was a wounded dog. He was convinced that his ride and die bitch, Precious had tossed him to the side to ride off with the next dude. There was no one more vulnerable than a heartbroken, lonely man. Last night's prelude to a kiss was only the beginning.

Precious

Boss Man

I eyed the clock, and I knew Mike would make his appearance at any moment. We were on some sort of set schedule now. I already had breakfast and he would give me a snack an hour or so before lunch. With this new arrangement, Mike was becoming more lax with each passing day. He wasn't allowing me to walk the house freely—yet, but I had a feeling it would be happening soon.

"Come in," I said when I heard Mike knocking at the door, looking forward to the treat of the day. That was something I never thought would happen. But being dead in the center of this shit I see now how hostages become brainwashed by their captors. You seriously start appreciating whatever kind gesture they show you. Technically you know it's some bullshit, but your head be so fucked up, you'll take the shit anyway you can get it.

"Where's my snack?" I asked, feeling an instant letdown when Mike came in the room with nothing in his hand, not even a glass of water.

"I thought maybe today you would like to come in the kitchen and eat your snack."

"Seriously, or are you gonna change your mind again? Yesterday you invited me to come watch a movie then backtracked when I took you up on the offer. Is this round-two of the teasing?"

"No teasing, come with me and see for yourself."

I let my leg dangle from the bed for a few seconds giving Mike a chance to say "Sorry, the jokes on you, you ain't going anywhere", but when he didn't, I got the fuck up ready to bolt. Any chance I got to step away from the depression of being stuck in a room, I jumped at.

"So this is where you whip up all my meals," I said, looking around the hi-tech kitchen.

"This is it. Now have a seat." Mike went to the stainless steel refrigerator and pulled out a fruit platter. "Do you like Jamaican fruit punch?" he asked getting a couple of glasses out of the cabinet.

"I never had any."

"Today will be your first time then. I think you'll enjoy."

I didn't care to drink or eat anybody's shit, but hell, the worst thing that could happen was Mike would poison me and I'd die. And the odds were stacked against me in that favor anyway.

I nibbled on the sweet melon and sipped on my punch, sizing up Mike's every move. "Mike, you seem to be in an awfully good mood today. What's up?"

"Maybe knowing that soon I'll be out of LA a free man and a lot richer is making these last few months being on the run worthwhile."

"You know, I've been meaning to ask you how you pulled that off."

"Pulled what off?"

"Breaking out of Clinton Correctional Facility. That ain't no low-level prison. They pretty tight with security, so how in the fuck did you pull it off?"

Mike stopped in the middle of spreading Miracle Whip on a sandwich he was making and glanced up at me with a devilish smirk. "I don't know if I really need to be discussing that with you."

"Back to that again. Like I said before, who the fuck can I tell?" I said, discreetly scanning the room to see if I could spot a phone anyplace, but no luck. Besides the knife Mike was holding to spread his dressing, I didn't see any useable objects that could stand in as a weapon.

"True, but some things are best left not being discussed."

"Come on, Mike, stop being so secretive and share the inside scoop," I smiled, trying to soften him up.

"Real talk, it wasn't that complicated."

"Okay, so spill."

"When Maya was setting this shit in motion she brought Devon on board. She showed him a picture of me, and Devon said this dude he used to run with could damn near pass for my twin. Of course I didn't believe that shit and neither did Maya."

"I bet yah did when you got a look at that nigga. Because when I laid eyes on the dude, I was a believer."

"Fo real! Yo, when Maya showed me his pic all I could do was say 'Damn!'. Luckily he was down for the switch too for the right price."

"He was willing to do the whole bid for you? I can't imagine no price being right for that."

"Nah, he wasn't supposed to be in there that long. Just enough time for me to get the fuck out the country, but of course you fucked that shit up when you came to the prison and busted him."

"Don't even go there. Let's get back to your story. You say dude wasn't supposed to be there that long. How was yah gonna get him out?"

"Now you know I had inside help. How else do you think I was able to pull the shit off in the first place? Big time dealer I used to do business with had a brother that was a security guard at the prison. When the imposter came to see me for a visit he was dressed incognito. The guard let him go to the bathroom first and I went in after. He tossed me his street clothes in exchange for my prison attire. After that, there was no looking back."

"That shit sound simple as hell."

"Shit is simple when you got money and know motherfuckers in the right places. It's too bad that you busted dude, because when the security guard got word, he was supposed to get homeboy the fuck outta there. Now that nigga stuck doing his own bid behind the shit."

"Why you looking at me like I'm the cause of that shit? Didn't nobody tell yah to orchestrate a prison break. I was tryna get my daughter back, that's all."

"I know, but still..."

"Still nothing. Shit, when you got the fuck out of that prison, I doubt you was bit more thinking about when and if that imposter was going to get caught or when he would be freed."

"You right. When I tasted freedom, I said they would have to kill me before I ever got caged up like an animal again."

"I bet you did." Right when I was about to throw some more questions Mike's way I heard the doorbell.

"He can't be here this early," Mike said, looking down at his watch.

"Who can't be here?"

"The money man I'm closing out my dealings with. Listen, I need you to go back to the bedroom. You can come back out when I'm done."

"I can stay in here. You don't have to worry about me blowing up your spot."

"I ain't worried about that. This is my man. We've made a lot of paper together. He wouldn't turn on me no matter what you said to him."

"So then why can't I stay right where I'm at?"

"Because I'm handling business and don't need no interruptions. So would you go back to your room, please?"

The doorbell started ringing again and Mike was rushing me off. I headed to the bedroom knowing damn well that I would be listening my ass off.

I closed the door shut extra loud so Mike would think I was safely stashed in the bedroom. I tried to peep around the hallway corner to get a look at the man as he walked towards the living room with Mike, but all I could see was his shoes—a slick pair of smoke gray Gucci loafers.

"Quentin, my man! I appreciate you coming all the way from New York to bring me this paper."

"Not a problem. I needed a change of scenery anyway. All work and no play is never any good, especially for a player."

"And no doubt you are definitely a player." The two men both gave a slight laugh. "Can I get you a drink or anything?" Mike offered.

"Just a glass of water for me. I have some more business to handle with a new connect named Genesis when I leave here, so I want to keep a clear mind."

"Always on your job, Quentin."

"Got to. How else do you think I continue to be the boss of these streets for over twenty years?"

"I feel you, man. When I grow up I want to be just like Quentin Jacobs."

"You on your way."

"Nah, this is it for me. I'm officially out the game. I got the cash I need, and now it's time for me to get the hell outta LA—shit, make that the US."

"I hate shit got to end like this for you. Not able to show your face, on the run, that ain't no kinda life."

"It's better than being locked up in a prison wit' some punk ass guards telling me what the fuck to do twenty- four-seven. It may not be the freedom I want, but it's damn sure the freedom I need to get by day after day. Now with all this loot, I'm good."

"What is Maya going to do now? Who is going to look after her?"

"Maya is a survivor, she'll be fine."

"She's a young girl. I know she needs help."

"You always concerned about Maya and you ain't neva met her but what, twice? Let me find out you gotta thing for my sister. You know I have much respect for you, Quentin, but you a little too old to be sniffing after Maya." Both men laughed in unison again.

"It's nothing like that. I remember you mentioning that she wasn't close to her mother and you were the only family she had. Now that you'll be gone, I know things might be somewhat difficult for her. I was offering my help if she needs it."

"That's good lookin' out, and it means a lot to me."

This Quentin character had me curious. I wanted to get a close-up on this man who seemed to be a crooked nigga with a heart of gold. I mean why else would he give a fuck about Maya's reckless ass. I knew Mike would be pissed the fuck off, but I had to match a face with the deep baritone smooth voice. I tip-toed closer to the male voices coming from the living room and not making my presence felt until I walked right up on them.

"Mike, sorry to bother you but I need to use the restroom." Mike and Quentin both stared in my direction.

"Then go. You know where the bathroom is," Mike said, with annoyance in his voice.

"I just wanted you to know that's where I would be in case you came looking for me."

"Thanks," Mike replied, turning his face back towards Quentin.

"Do I know you?" Quentin asked, brushing past Mike and coming towards me. He reached out his arm and we shook hands. He was ridiculously handsome, especially for a man with some age on him. He appeared to be a well preserved, in the upper 40ish age range. If you went by his wheat brown chiseled face and tall lean body, he could've easily passed for mid-thirties, but he maintained an old school aura with a sophisticated flare that only age and living could bring you.

"No, you don't."

"You look awfully familiar. What's your name?"

"Precious Mills."

"Mills...I don't know any Mills."

"Like I said, you don't know me. Well, I need to go to the bathroom. Excuse me," I said, breaking free from the strong grasp he had on my hand.

"She reminds me of a woman I used to know a long time ago," I heard Quentin say as I walked down the hallway towards the bathroom.

When I got to the bathroom, I closed the door and turned on the sink faucet. I sat down on a chair pushed against the wall, getting my aggravation under control. I had so many emotions running around inside. I didn't know if it was Mike or Quentin that had me infuriated, or maybe both. But it had to be Quentin. I had already been through the I Hate Mike phase twenty million times. What about Quentin had gotten so under my skin? He hadn't been rude to me, in fact he was no doubt a charismatic cat. But when he shook my hand, the vibe was off. Maybe I was pissed that he was concerned about Maya, but then it wasn't like he knew that trifling heifer was doing her best to steal my life, the life I busted my ass to get. It was something else, but I couldn't put my finger on it.

Knock! Knock! Knock!

"Precious, you can come out the bathroom now," Mike said through the door.

"I'll be out in a minute."

"No, come out now, and I hope you ain't up to nothing stupid."

"Oh please! Ain't nobody hatching shit up," I said, turning off the water. Shit, I learned my lesson from my first attempt at freedom. Unless I had a gun or a big fuckin' knife, my odds of overpowering Mike were nil. I opened the door and there was Mike standing in front with his own gun in hand.

"We back to that again?" I questioned, looking down at his weapon and then rolling my eyes.

"I couldn't take any chances."

"Mike, please. You can put the gun away. You promised that you would get my daughter for me, so I'm not gonna do nothing to fuck that up."

"Then why did you come out the room and interrupt my business meeting?"

"It didn't sound like no meeting to me. Ya sounded more like old friends."

"That's not the point. I told you to stay in the bedroom until I was done."

"I had to use the bathroom. What was I supposed to do, wet my pants?"

"Whatever! Your mother must've never taught you that a hard head make for a soft ass."

"Nah, I didn't have those types of conversations with my moms. But seriously, Mike, you can put that gun away. It ain't called for."

"Cool, but stop being difficult. You had been playing your position with ease, then the minute company show up you wanna show your ass."

"Speaking of company, how you know that Quentin dude? He seem a bit old to be a lil' nigga you was kicking it with on the playground."

"Funny, but he was the man that put me on."

"Put you on in the drug game?"

"Yeah."

"How did that happen?" I questioned, following Mike back into the kitchen.

"Damn, that was so many years ago, I couldn't have been no more than fourteen or fifteen years old. My moms had just had Maya and we were struggling. With no man around I had to step up to the plate and put some food on the table."

"What about Maya's father? Where was he at?"

"I told you, my moms never told me who Maya's father was. But I knew it wasn't my dad because he had been out the picture long before Maya was even conceived."

"True. So how did you meet Quentin?"

"Everybody on the streets of New York had heard of Quentin Jacobs. This was the first man we knew of that was not only moving major drugs, but pimping women too. We all worshipped that nigga. So one day when I was standing on the corner in front of the bodega with my dudes, Quentin pulled up in a spankin' new Benz. He rolled down his window and signaled for me to come over. For a minute I didn't move because I couldn't believe he was asking for me. Then he called out my name and I leaped to the car. You didn't keep a nigga like Quentin Jacobs waiting."

"How did he know your name?"

"I wanted to know the same shit but felt it best not to question him. Me and my nigga was always in some bullshit around the way and I figured he heard about us being on some menace to society type shit."

"I can see that."

"But, umm, like he had heard my prayers. When I got to his car, Quentin offered me a chance to work for him. He started me off on some low level gofer type shit, but I followed his directions meticulously without ever fucking up, and soon my pockets stayed thick. After that my mother and Maya never had to worry about food, clothes or shelter again. I became the man of the house and shit was straight all thanks to Quentin Jacobs."

"That's some story. Quentin was the family savior."

"No doubt, and he still the savior now. Even when I got locked up he was helping me make moves from behind bars. He made arrangements for me to be able to stay in this house. Now he came through with this money I need and I'm straight."

"Shit, everybody needs a friend like Quentin."

"We more than friends. Quentin said I was always like a son to him and he definitely became like the father that was never there for me."

"He don't have no kids of his own?"

"He is married and he does have kids with his wife, but he don't really talk about them. He keeps them shielded, out the life. As long as I've known Quentin, I've never been to his house or met his family."

"Wow, talk about keeping shit on the low."

"Yeah, that's probably why he's been able to stay on top of the game for all these years. Can't nobody fuck wit' you if they don't know how to get to you. But enough talk about Quentin. Let's eat."

I watched as Mike put some plates and silverware on the table, and although I was hungry my mind remained fixated on Quentin. Something about him was intriguing and it just wasn't because he was a boss man.

Maya

Up In Smoke

"What are you doing here? I thought you were on a plane to New York."

"I missed the flight," I lied as I stood in Supreme's bedroom doorway.

"What time is it?" Supreme eyed the clock and I noticed the half empty bottle of liquor on his nightstand.

"I hope you don't mind that I came back here, but I had nowhere else to go," I said, moving slowly towards his bed.

"Why are your clothes wet?"

"It's pouring down rain outside."

Supreme stared up at the skylights and saw the rain splashing against the glass. "You're right, I'ma little out of it."

"That's okay, you've had a rough day."

"You mean a few rough days."

"Yeah, but it'll get better," I said, stroking my fingers on the back of his head.

"You should go change and get out of those wet clothes before you get sick."

"Supreme, you're always so concerned about everybody else. I don't know how Precious could've ever left you. But you're right, I do need to get out of these clothes. I peeled out of my ultra teal, off-the-shoulder jersey dress, and let it drop to the floor. I stood in front of Supreme with only my cream lace thong and three-inch jeweled thong sandals.

"Maya, what are you doing?"

"I think it's pretty obvious," I said slipping, off my panties. "It's okay to want me because I want you too." I lifted the blanket from Supreme and his fine ass was already naked. That nigga had sculpted muscles from his shoulders down, but the most important muscle was sticking straight up hard as hell, ready to fill up my wet pussy.

"Maya, we can't do this! It ain't right!"

"You let me worry about what is right," I said, wrapping my other lips around his solid long, thick tool. I stroked my tongue up, down and around his dick before focusing my tongue action on the tip of the head.

"Damn, Maya!" Supreme moaned, leaning his head back.

"I know you want this pussy," I purred, knowing he hadn't fucked since Precious disappeared. I knew he was horny as hell and I was taking full advantage. Like a vampire needing a blood fix, Supreme reached for me and devoured my neck with passionate kisses until finding his way to my breasts.

He was sucking on them so hard it almost felt like bites, but the roughness of the shit was turning me on. Supreme cupped my ass with his hands and jammed his humongous dick inside of me. I screamed so fucking loud I thought the glass would shatter.

"Maya, do you want me to stop?"

"No, please don't stop! This dick feels so good! I can take it!" And I could. Shit, if I had my way I would be taking this dick on a regular. Now all I had to do was get rid of Precious once and for all.

"I got your message. What's so urgent?" Devon asked as he sat across from me in our regular meeting spot.

"There's been a change of plans and I need your help to execute it."

"Does that mean we're back to taking out the detective?"

"Not yet. That might not be necessary."

"You sure?"

"I ain't never sure about shit until after it happens, but we need to handle Precious first."

"Precious? Mike told me he had that situation under control."

"When did you talk to Mike?"

"The other day I went by to see him."

"And what did he tell you?"

"That Precious and the baby were leaving the country with him.

They were waiting for Aaliyah to come back and they were out. He said he already discussed it with you."

"Yeah, he did but I never agreed to it, and I'm not agreeing to it now. Precious has to go."

"Hell, I don't give a fuck either way. I don't even like that chick, so I'm down for however you want to move forward."

"Good, that's what I wanted to hear. Let's head over to the stash house and we can discuss it further in the car."

After discussing the plan with Devon on our drive over to the house, I then thought about how relieved I would be to get rid of Precious and no longer feel I was living in her shadow. That wasn't possible as long as she was alive. Her death was my only solution. Even after Supreme and I had that incredible night of sex I knew Precious was heavy on his mind. Even though he believed his wife left him for the next nigga, he was still mourning her ass. The shit was about to drive me crazy. I was going to take great pleasure putting us both out of our misery.

"Maya," Devon huffed.

"*What!*" I said with an attitude because I didn't like how he called my name.

"I've been trying to get your attention for the last few minutes. We're here."

"Oh," I said, seeing the house out of the backseat window. "You remember the plan, right?"

"Of course. Shit, I'm ready."

"Well get what you need from the trunk."

"Already did that while you was spacing out."

"Funny! Let's go then."

When we walked in the house Mike and Precious were lounging in the living room watching television like they was a fucking married couple.

"Isn't this cute, love in the afternoon," I mocked at my simple ass brother.

"What yah doing here? We ain't got no meetings on the calendar," Mike said, getting up from the couch.

"Oh, now that you're playing house with Precious, I need a reason to come visit my big brother?"

"Maya, don't start with the bul shit today. I'm not in the mood."

"I hope you're in the mood for something else."

"Something else like what?"

"Excuse me, Mike, do you mind if I get something to drink from the kitchen?" Devon asked, reciting his line perfectly.

"Go head, man, help yourself."

"Thanks. Maya, do you want something?"

"No, I'm good. I have some things to discuss with my dear brother, that's all." I watched as Precious was eyeing the situation and Devon's movements. That bitch wasn't stupid. She knew some shit was up.

"Spill it, Maya. What's so fuckin' important that you had to stop by on a sunny Saturday afternoon?"

"That's no sort of greeting for your sweet younger sister."

"Maya, we both know there is nothing sweet about you."

"I think Supreme would disagree with that." I saw Precious balling her fist as she sat on the couch, no doubt ready for an all out beat down, but she would have to hold tight—I would get to her in a minute.

"If you came over here to fuck with Precious about Supreme, you can leave with that bullshit. We already discussed this shit, and she knows Supreme is all yours. We don't need you coming over here rubbing that shit in her face."

"Aren't you the superhero. But sorry, your kryptonite has run out."

"What the fuck are you babbling about? I don't like word play."

"We're sticking to the original plan. Precious has to go...today."

"I told you she was gonna try this shit, Mike. Maya won't feel content until she knows I'm dead."

"Precious, nobody ever said you weren't a smart girl. You know we both can't be walking this earth, one of us has to go, and unfortunately that's you."

"You lowdown, pathetic piece of shit!" Precious spat, now standing next to Mike.

"Both of ya calm down. Ain't nobody doing nothing. Maya, Precious is leaving with me and you're leaving this house. The only time I want you to come back is when you're bringing Aaliyah so we can get the fuck outta here."

"You're not getting it, Mike. I'm not bringing Aaliyah, and Precious is going to die, today."

"I ain't letting that happen, Maya."

"I had a feeling you were going to say that."

"Mike, watch out!" Precious screamed, but her warning was too late. Devon had already used his stun gun to knock Mike out. Precious then kicked Devon in the crotch area in an attempt to get the stun gun out of his hand.

"Back the fuck up!" I said, pulling out the .44 magnum I was packing. "Devon, you handle my brother and I'll tend to Precious. Get to walking, G.I. Jane, before I bust a cap in your ass," I directed.

"Maya, somehow, someway you gon' pay for this shit."

"One things for sure, the payback won't be from you because soon you'll be on your way to hell. Now get the fuck in that room." I shoved Precious in the bedroom and locked the door.

"You *will* get yours!" Precious yelled out through the door. She could scream all she wanted because all that was coming to an end.

"First thing first," I said, going back to the scene of the crime. Devon had already carried Mike downstairs to the basement. Mike was a solid nigga, but Devon was a humongous gorilla dude, so lifting him was lightweight work.

"Hand me the cuffs," Devon said, as he chained up Mike's feet. "He already starting to come too." I tossed Devon the handcuffs, not wanting no fuckups.

"Yo, what the fuck happened?" Mike said, shaking off his few minutes of a blackout.

"Dear brother, I'm so sorry it had to come to this."

"Maya, why the fuck do you have me chained up?" he asked, realizing the tables had turned and he was now the prisoner. "No, you can't be doing this. And Devon, you in on this bullshit too?"

"Of course he is. He works for me, I hired him, remember?"

"So what, you wanna lock me up so I can stay out the way while you kill Precious? And then what?"

"Actually, you got it backwards. We're going to kill you first and then Precious."

Mike's entire face dropped, and for a brief second my heart ached for him. "Maya, I'm your brother. We're blood."

"I know, and it does pain me that I have to kill you too, but you've made all these demands that I can't accommodate."

"What demands?"

"For one, letting that bitch live. I always knew in some way that Precious would be your downfall. I remember the first time I saw you two together, and I had never seen you look at a woman like that before. It was as if you were completely infatuated with her, almost obsessed. Now you see where your obsession has gotten you...a death sentence."

"No, it's your obsession that has led to this, and it's what will be the end of you. It's a damn shame how bad you want to be Precious. Having her husband isn't enough for you, you want her daughter and her life. Precious warned me that you'd turn on me too, but I didn't believe her. I refused to see how far gone you really were. Maya, don't do this. There is no turning back if you kill me."

"You stupid fuck, I don't want to turn back! I'm about to have the life I've dreamed of. Too bad you won't be around to see it. But you can give me a going away present."

"And what would that be?"

"Where's the gun, Mike?"

"Wouldn't you like to know?"

"You're going to die anyway, you might as well tell me. I'll make you a deal. If you tell me where the gun is, I won't torture Precious before I kill her."

"What happened to you? I know I'm a fucked up individual, but you're on a whole other level."

"I guess I'm the worse case scenario of what happens when a little girl grows up without her father's love, or her mother's for that matter. Or maybe no love at all, because I didn't have yours either."

"Yes, you did. I was a kid myself. I did the best I could."

"No you didn't. I was never your first priority. You chose the streets over me and now a woman like Precious. Fuck both of you!" I said, blasting off putting the lights out for my brother. When his brains splattered on the concrete wall I didn't even shed a tear.

"That was quick," Devon said, seemingly in shock at how I had no qualms about killing my own brother.

"Yeah, now come on. The next round is what I'm really looking forward to."

When we got upstairs to the bedroom where Precious was stashed, she was banging on the door as if help was going to come for her ass.

"Devon, kick that motherfucker door down," I whispered so Precious wouldn't have time to get out the way. Devon's big ass put all his might in that kick and the door flew open, knocking Precious' ass across the room. "We're back!" I hummed.

"Where's Mike?" Precious wanted to know as she tried to pick herself off the floor.

"Mike is no longer with us. He sends his love."

"You killed him, didn't you?"

"You already know the answer to that."

"Killing your own brother is low even for you, Maya."

"Devon, grab a hold of this bitch for me."

"Don't fuckin' touch me!" Precious yelled and screamed, swinging her arms and kicking up her legs trying to put up a decent fight, but she was no match for Devon's monstrous ass.

"Give it up, Precious."

"Yeah, before I break your neck," Devon warned, getting tired of the little but painful jabs she was putting in. Devon now had Precious all wrapped up with her arms behind her back and legs held between his.

"Perfect!" I said, slipping on some old school brass knuckles and commenced to beating the shit out of her. "Take that, ho!" I said with a left hook then right hook, sending blood gushing from her mouth with each swing of her jaw. I then further punished her with body shots.

"Fuck you!" Precious managed to say even while I was beating her ass. It incensed me even more that she wouldn't bow down, even under all this duress.

"So you know that's what me and Supreme was doing the other night. He fucked me so good, I'm still on a high. I'll keep sucking his dick just right, and soon he'll be like 'Precious who?'"

"You can whistle on his balls and I'll still be in that nigga's heart. For Supreme and me it's love for life..." were the last words Precious spoke as my final blow sent her to her deathbed.

"Drop her ass!" I ordered Devon. Precious fell to the floor and blood was coming out of her mouth and nose and it even looked to be seeping out of her ears. I fucked up her face so bad she was unrecognizable. "Come on, let's burn this motherfucker down and get the fuck outta here.

As we poured gasoline around the crib, I searched for the gun I wanted from Mike but came up empty. "You ready?" I asked Devon, giving up on my search and ready to get the fuck out.

"Yeah, let's light it up and get the fuck out."

"Hold on a minute, let me check out something real quick." I noticed a black leather suitcase on the kitchen table. When I clicked open the locks my eyes lit up like a Christmas tree.

"What you see?"

"Oh nothing, just some paperwork, but I better take it just in case some important documents are inside."

"Cool, but we need to go. Our business is done here."

Before Devon and I made our exit, I stood in the entrance and lit a match, and it was up in smoke for that motherfucker.

Precious

Hello Brooklyn

"Is anybody in here?" I heard somebody screaming out. "If somebody's in here, make some noise so I can find you." The voice was clear, but it was as if mine was on mute. In my head I was yelling out for help, but my entire face was in so much pain I couldn't even move it. I literally had no strength left in me, but I had to find some. I had to fight to live so I could get back home to my family and to destroy Maya. With all my force I crawled to the door. It felt like I was moving as slow as a snail, but I was making progress.

"Help me!" I cried out, being barely audible. I could feel the burning heat from the floor, and that's when I realized the house was on fire. My face was so fucked up that my nostrils couldn't even smell shit. I picked up my pace determined to live. I gave one final push into the hallway and then I blacked out again.

"Where am I?" I moved my arm, and a pain shot through my body that sent me into a fetal position. I slowly lifted my shirt to see what the cause of all my pain was, and my entire torso was covered in bandages.

"Precious, you woke up," I heard a familiar voice say. But my eyes were swollen shut and my vision was blurry. The harder I focused to see the image, the more my head would start throbbing.

"Who are you? What happened to me? Where am I?" the questions kept rolling of my tongue. "It's okay, baby. I'ma take care of you."

"Nico, is that you?" I asked, wanting to break down and cry. I felt as if I didn't know myself anymore.

"Yes, baby, it's me. You're safe now."

"What happened? Where am I?" "You're in Brooklyn."

"How did I end up back in New York? I have to get back to LA and be with my family." Flashes of Devon holding me down as Maya beat the shit out of me had my voice sounding hysterical. That deranged bitch whipped my ass so bad she had me about to go crazy.

"Precious, you have to calm down. You are in no condition to go anywhere. We have to get you well first, and then you can go back to your family. But first I want you to tell me who did this to you. Was it Mike?"

"Oh God, Mike! Mike is dead."

"What? So if Mike didn't do this, then who?"

"His sister."

"Maya? Wasn't she the girl that killed Nina?"

"Yes, that crazy fuckin' Maya. She killed Mike too."

"Her brother?" he questioned as if he believed I was delusional.

"Yes, her brother. If I told you the nightmare I've been stuck in for the past few weeks, it would blow your mind, and Maya's sick ass was behind the whole thing." It was evident by the silence in the air that Nico still wasn't getting it.

"Precious, it's clear you've been through hell, ain't no disputing that. But you're telling me that Maya—Mike's little sister—is the cause of your predicament?"

"Yes, that's exactly what I'm fuckin' saying."

"I know how you get down, and ain't no way Maya got you looking fucked up like this."

"Of course she had help, but she's behind all this bullshit. Man, she been plotting this shit against me for I don't know how long. All I know is she got Mike out of jail, helped orchestrate the kidnapping of Aaliyah, and this crazy bitch is determined to not only see me dead, but take my fuckin' life, literally, which includes my husband. That's why I got to get the fuck outta here," I said, trying to get out of bed. "Oh shit!" I grabbed my side, bending over in pain.

"Yo, you need to rest," Nico said, laying me back down on the bed.

"How can I rest knowing that psycho is playing house with my family?"

"We can deal with Maya after we nurse you back to health."

"Nico, I haven't even thanked you for saving my life."

"Don't thank me, thank the man upstairs," Nico said, pointing his index finger towards the ceiling. When I saw that house burning down I had no idea you were in there."

"What brought you to that house?"

"When we were on the phone that day and you went silent, I kept calling you back but got no answer. My gut told me something was wrong, but I wasn't sure what. I thought maybe Supreme had walked up on you and maybe you didn't want him to know you were speaking to me. The shit was buggin' me out. Then I called you a few days later and your phone kept going straight to voice mail. But when some detective dude..."

"You mean Detective Moore?"

"Yep, that's his name. When he left me a couple of messages saying he wanted to ask me a few questions regarding your whereabouts, I knew some serious shit was up. I mean dude wasn't going to be calling me unless some shit popped off. And for him to even have been able to get my number, I knew he must've traced it back from my cell phone call to you."

"Right, so did you ever call him?"

"Hell no! You know I don't fuck wit' no police. But what I did do was make some calls to find out if anybody knew what the fuck was going on. Didn't nobody really have no answers. All they kept on saying was Mike was still on the run and last they heard he was in LA. Then finally I got a break. There's this nigga named Quentin Jacobs that has been in the game forever. Motherfuckers call him like the Godfather."

"It's a small world. I met that cat."

"When?"

"He came to see Mike."

"Well that's the break I got. His right hand man is my people. He told me Quentin had been in touch with Mike and went to LA to close out some business and give him some loot because Mike was breaking out for good. He gave me the location and I'm hauling ass cause I'm thinking this my last chance to ever find out what the fuck happened to you, so I chartered a plane. I was prepared to go LA and kill that nigga."

"Nico, thank you for caring."

"Fuck, is you crazy? Baby girl, you gon' always be my heart."

When I thought about how fucked up I must look and for Nico to say something like that, it made me realize that shit could be a lot worse right now. "Thank you."

"I have nothing but love for you, baby, don't ever forget that."

"I won't."

"But back to how I found you. So my man gave me the location, and when I pulled up, the crib was up in smoke and I swear I thought I had the wrong address. I was about to break the fuck out."

"Why didn't you?"

"That's why I told you to thank the man upstairs, because something kept pulling me back to that house. I couldn't bring myself to leave. Precious, when I saw you I was afraid I had lost you for good."

"I can imagine how fucked up I looked when you found me. Shit, for a minute I thought I was dead too."

"Luckily I have some dealings with these Dominican cats in LA. They told me to take you to this private doctor they all fuck with if one of their crew members get fucked up during some criminal shit and they don't want to take them to the hospital. "

"So that's who bandaged me up."

"Yeah, he pretty much saved your life."

"No, you did that, Nico."

"Okay, well he followed my lead. He also prescribed you some medicine for the pain, which you're going to take after I feed you this soup. Precious, I know you're a fighter, but you won't be able to win the war if you don't let me take care of you."

"I know. I can't go back to LA looking like this anyway. I would scare the shit out of Aaliyah and Supreme wouldn't recognize me. I need to get strong."

"I'm glad you get that."

"Shit, I don't have a choice. I can barely get out of bed... forget about walking."

"What in the fuck did Maya do to you?"

"She had her flunky, Devon hold me while she hammered my face and body with her fists. To make it even more painful, she wore brass knuckles on both hands."

"Damn, that's brutal," Nico said, shaking his head.

"Maya will get hers though."

"I'm sure. If I was a betting man, I would no doubt put my money on you."

"Good choice. Right now all I want to do is get better and look halfway normal again."

"You will. The doctor said there was no permanent damage and you would make a full recovery in a few weeks. He also gave me this topical cream called Arnica to treat the bruising. I heard this shit really works too."

"Well, give it here," I said with a slight chuckle. I couldn't laugh too hard or it would feel like a knife was poking me in the ribs.

"I got you. I put some on last night when we got here."

"How long did I stay at the doctor's?"

"For a few hours. He didn't feel you needed to stay overnight. I was glad I had chartered that plane because it was waiting for us and I didn't have to go through no bullshit. You were medicated up so you didn't know what the fuck was going on. This the first time you woke up since all this shit went down. I can finally relax a bit."

"Nico, I'll never forget what you've done for me."

"You better not. Now be still so I can put this cream on your face."

"Fine. I'll use the time to give you the play by play on how Maya's wicked ass orchestrated all this shit. Take your time with the cream 'cause this gon' take a minute."

As Nico began the process of nursing me back to health, I sat back to tell him the drama of how I went from LA to now saying "Hello, Brooklyn."

Maya

Prove You Wrong

"Cheers!" Devon and I said in unison as we clicked our champagne glasses in a hotel suite at the Peninsula Beverly Hills. When we left the burning house I knew I needed to shower and change clothes, and what better place to do so than a five star hotel, especially with my newfound riches. I hit the jackpot three times in one day.

"I can't believe I'm finally rid of Precious fuckin' Cummings. This has to be the best day of my life."

"Dang, ma, that chick really got under your skin. I ain't like her neither, but you hate her ass."

"*Hated.* She's past tense now. The bitch is dead, remember."

"I was there. I can't forget about her or Mike."

"Mike," I repeated out loud as if it was now hitting me that my brother was dead. He wasn't only dead but that I had killed him. "It's a shame what happened to Mike but he left me no choice."

"Right," Devon said, nodding his head and sipping on his champagne from the thousand-dollar bottle I purchased. "So what's next?"

"Next?" I asked, not knowing what next he meant.

"We got rid of Precious and Mike. Is the detective next? What are we doing?"

"We're not doing nothing. I don't think the detective will be a problem."

"Don't you think it wil be best to get rid of al the loose ends?"

"Devon, let me do the thinking."

"I'm only considering your best interest. They will find the bodies in the house and eventually identify them as Mike and Precious. You know when that happens, Detective Moore will come sniffing around you."

"He can sniff all he wants, but making a case against me is something entirely different."

"It's on you, but hey, I'm more than willing to put the nail in his coffin."

"I'll keep that in mind," I said, standing up. "Enjoy the suite and I'll be in touch."

"Where are you going? You not staying to enjoy the suite with me?"

"Not tonight. I have to go."

"But I thought this was our celebratory evening together," Devon said, grabbing my wrist.

"And we did celebrate," I shot back, pulling my wrist from his grasp. "And now I'm leaving."

"That wasn't our agreement. You told me I would be fully compensated for my services."

I reached in my purse and pulled out one of the thick roll of bills I had got from the briefcase. "This should be more than enough compensation," I said, tossing the cash in his lap.

Devon flipped his thumb through the hundred dollar bills. "Where did you get all this cash from? I'm sure you got some good pussy but not good enough for Supreme to hit you off with this kind of cash."

"Watch your mouth, Devon. And don't worry about where I got the cash, you've been compensated and that should be your only concern."

"The money is good, but I want a taste of that right there." Devon stuck out his thick pink tongue, pointing his finger towards my coochie. "I want what I was promised."

"So you rather get some pussy than all that cash?"

"Oh no, I'm keeping my money," he said, gripping the loot tightly. "But I'm getting both."

"You sound real confident in that."

"I am. We share a lot of secrets. I know you'll do the right thing. Come on, it won't be so bad. When I lay this pipe on you, trust you won't never want a piece of Supreme again."

"Is that right?"

"I promise you. Come over here and get a feel." Devon rubbed his hands over his crotch area as if I was going to come crawling over begging for the dick.

"I tell you what. Hold that thought. Supreme is expecting me and I don't want to raise any suspicions with all the shit that has gone down. But how about we meet back here tomorrow around the same time? You can show me what you holding down there." I walked right up on him and brushed my ass against him.

This fool had the audacity to grab my hand and press it against his dick. "Feel how hard you got my shit. You getting all this tomorrow night," Devon boasted.

I wanted to scream, "All what, you little dick nigga", but I needed him, so I kept my mouth shut. "That's right, baby, I can't wait. I'll see you tomorrow."

"Okay, and don't give Supreme none of my pussy until after I tap that ass. I want that shit nice and tight. Oh, and so you know, first thing tomorrow morning I'll be giving my boss a call to tell him I quit!" Devon hollered as I was walking out of the room. That comment stopped me dead in my tracks.

"Why in the hell are you quitting your job?"

"I'm tired of kissing that nigga's ass and talking all proper and shit around him like a corporate professional."

"Devon, you need your job."

"Not anymore. Shit, why I need to be on that nigga's payroll when I can be on yours?" he said, holding up the wad of cash I dropped in his hands. "Plus your benefits package is much better suited for my needs."

"That's a mistake," I warned.

"It's a mistake I'm willing to make."

"What are you going to tell Supreme?"

"The truth; that I got a better job offer and I'm moving on. I'm sure he won't have a problem replacing me. I mean he is Supreme."

"Have it your way."

"I plan to. We can work out my payroll schedule after I get done twisting your back out tomorrow."

All I did was smile at the dumb fuck before closing the door. If I had to stay in the room with Devon's nasty ass for one more minute, my head was going to explode. Getting thousands of dollars wasn't enough for the greedy fuck. He had to get between my legs too and quit his job. Now he looking at me to be his full source of income like I'm an ATM. It seemed that after I got rid of one problem there would always be another lurking around the corner, and the shit had me stressed.

When I got to my car I popped open the trunk and pulled out the briefcase. When I opened it up and saw the stacks of endless amounts of hundred dollar bills it was the only thing that brought me solace. "I'm a rich bitch!" I beamed.

I shut the briefcase back up and closed the trunk. And to think, if I hadn't been the curious chick I am, all that money would've burned up in flames with Mike and his beloved Precious. There were so many things I wanted to do with the money; for one, I wanted a fresh ride. I was tired of driving around in this same ol' Jaguar. I wanted some new hot shit. But before I went out splurging like a fool, I had to be extra careful. I didn't need anymore unnecessary heat.

After pulling up to the estate, I was disappointed because I didn't spot Supreme's car or his driver out front, and I was looking forward to seeing him. Ever since we had sex the other night, he was distant, as if he was purposely trying to avoid me. I knew it was out of guilt, but Supreme had to get over that shit.

The house was ghostly quiet and empty. When I turned on the lights the first thing that slapped me in the face was the life-size painted portrait of Precious and Supreme from their wedding day. It was as if Precious was haunting me in death. I wanted to take a knife and slash that shit in shreds. "I killed you! Would you die already and go away for good?" I screamed at the portrait as if Precious could hear me. As I was about to continue my hysterics I heard the door open. I quickly turned my head and saw Supreme coming in.

"Is everything alright? I heard yelling. Who were you screaming at?"

"That picture of Precious."

"Huh?" Supreme gave me a quizzical look like I was wilding out.

"I'm frustrated and hurt that Precious is gone. I want to yell at her, but since I can't I yelled at her picture. I know it sounds crazy, but all this anger has built up and I exploded. I feel betrayed that my best friend left and hasn't even reached out to me."

"I know what you mean," Supreme said, tossing his keys down on the table. "I can barely stand being in this house anymore. Everywhere I turn there is a reminder of her. So I know what you mean about exploding. Every second of each day I'm one second away from doing just that. I can't even stand being around people at this point."

"Is that why you've being avoiding me?" I asked, Supreme as he poured himself a drink.

"No, I've been avoiding you for a slew of other reasons."

"Like..."

"Like, I had no business having sex with you in the first place."

"Why?"

"Why? Do you really need to ask that question?"

"Because of Precious. At this point, what do we owe her? She left us both. How long are we supposed to mourn over her?"

"You mourn over people who are dead. My wife is very much alive which makes this shit that much more difficult to deal with."

"Do you want to deal with the fact that Precious left you, or do you want to hang on hoping she'll come back?"

"I don't know what the fuck I want." Supreme's face was riddled with emotions, from agitation, pain and confusion.

"You need to man up and figure it out."

"Excuse me?"

"You heard what the fuck I said. Your wife left you, accept it. You ain't the first man that had their wife leave them. Besides, you knew what type of woman Precious was before you married her."

"Now you saying I brought this bullshit on myself." Supreme stood up pounding on his chest.

"What I'm saying is there is truth to that adage, 'When you play with fire you might get burned'. Precious burned you, so get over it."

"Yo, fuck you, Maya!" I had Supreme raging and I was loving it.

"Fuck you too!" I said, pointing my finger in his face. I felt I needed to change up my approach and go hard core with Supreme. That sweet shit wasn't getting quick enough results with him.

"Get your fuckin' finger out my face."

"I'll do more than that. I'll get out your face for good. I don't need some confused nigga crying over a bitch that don't even want him and left for the next man. You can sit here and whine by yourself. Fuck you!" I stormed away and I felt Supreme grab my arm.

"Where the fuck you think you going?"

"Away from you and this dark cloud you got hanging over your head."

"No the fuck you ain't. You staying right here." Supreme clutched my face and stuck his tongue down my throat. He then lifted me up and sat me down on the white grand piano and ripped my panties off.

"You sure you want this pussy?" I murmured in his ear softly but clearly.

"You know I do," Supreme growled as he tore off my blouse and ravaged my neck. I smiled behind his back as he hands dug into my scalp, pulling on my hair. There was nothing more passionate than an angry fuck.

"Who the fuck is blowing my phone up?" I moaned, still half asleep. I put the pillow over my head hoping it would silence the noise but the ringing continued. "Supreme, turn my phone off, please." Within thirty seconds my cell was right back to the same shit and I got no response from Supreme. I tossed the pillow off the bed and sat up looking around. Supreme was nowhere in sight and my phone was steady going off.

"I knew I shoulda left this shit downstairs last night," I said, getting out of bed to see who the stalker was on my line. "What the fuck is wrong with you?" I answered.

"What took you so long to answer the damn phone? You bet not be laid up with Supreme."

I took the phone away from my ear and stared at it, and then made sure the digits were correct across my screen before I responded. The nigga was still popping off at the mouth, and I walked over to the door to make sure Supreme wasn't lurking around anywhere. "Devon, why in the hell would you be blowing up my phone? You know Supreme could've easily looked at this shit and saw your number."

"Fuck that nigga! I don't work for him no more. Why would I care."

"You need to care. If he finds out we got dealings, our whole cover will be blown, you fuckin' idiot."

"Chill with the name calling. What time are you meeting me at the hotel?" Devon questioned, jumping to the next subject. "I already told my baby moms that I was working the all night shift and wouldn't be home, so we can spend the whole night together."

"Is that why you're blowing up my phone, not for no emergency shit but to see what time I'll be at the hotel?"

"Running up in some new, prime pussy is an emergency in my book. So what time should I be expecting you?"

"Listen Devon..."

"Un un, I don't want to hear none of that shit. Save the excuses. We have an understanding, one that I warned you not to back out of."

"Ain't nobody giving you excuses or backing out of shit."

"Then what were you about to say?"

"I was going to ask if you can get a room at another hotel."

"What's wrong with the place we have?"

"Supreme made a comment, and to be on the safe side, I think we should get a room somewhere else."

"What type of comment?"

"Devon, can you stop drilling me? Do you want to hook up to-night or not?"

"Of course. So what, I'll get the room and you'll reimburse me when I see you?"

"Yeah, I'll reimburse you." I couldn't believe this cheap mother-fucker wanted some ass and wanted me to pay for him to get it.

"Cool. I'l cal you later on with the hotel and room number."

"Can't wait." I shut my cell and tossed it on the bed. The thought of fuckin' that nigga had me ready to puke. How could I go from get-ting twisted out by super sexy Supreme to getting squashed by Dev-on?

"What has you in such deep thought?" Supreme asked, walking into the bedroom catching me off guard.

"Waking up seeing you were gone and wondering where you went."

"I got up early and went in my office to catch up on some work."

"I thought maybe we were back to square one and you were avoiding me again."

"No, I understand your position on the situation. Precious left me, not the other way around. It's time for me to stop stressing over shit I have no control over."

"What does that mean for us?"

"I do have feelings for you, but I can't make you any promises."

"Can you at least promise to give us a chance?"

"A chance to what, be in a serious relationship?"

"What, is that so hard to imagine happening?"

"I don't want to take advantage of you, Maya. You're young and vulnerable. You went through all that bullshit with Clip, then you and Precious were close and I know her leaving has fucked you up, not to mention having someone like Mike for a brother. I don't want you to depend on me emotionally and I let you down too."

"I'm not worried about that."

"You should be. With Precious leaving, besides my love for Aali-yah, I don't think I have anything left to give."

"You say that now, but time heals all wounds. After Clip broke my heart I thought I was done with love until I fell for you, so it is possible."

"With youth brings optimism, but unlike you, I'm not a teenager anymore. It seems the more time passes the more enraged I become.

You have too much ahead of you to become seriously wrapped up with me."

"Supreme, stop speaking for what I want and need. All I ask is that you give us a chance, nothing more nothing less. I'm not putting any guidelines or stipulations on our relationship. I just want to give us a try. Will you do that?"

"Yeah, we can do that."

"I'm going to make you so happy, you'll forget about all the pain in the past. I promise you," I said, wrapping my arms around Supreme's neck and embracing his lips with a wet kiss. Months ago I made up my mind that Supreme would be mine and there was no denying me. Only obstacle left was to take care of one last bump in the road, and its name was Devon.

After sealing the deal with Supreme I left out the house to get all the materials I needed for my evening with Devon. I spent all afternoon meticulously planning my shit out to go off without a hitch. As I was going over the operation in my head I heard my cell phone ringing. I eyed the caller ID and it was my nemesis.

"Hey, Devon, what's going on?"

"I was calling to give you the hotel information. I got us an official bungalow at The Beverly Hills Hotel."

"I bet that cost a pretty penny."

"Yeah, but since you footing the bill and money don't seem to be nothing but a thang to you, I went all out."

"How considerate, but I have to admit I'm getting very excited about being with you tonight."

'I bet. After you got a feel on how my dick hanging down there, you dying to throw that pussy on me. That shit better be tight too. You better not have given Supreme none. I'll be able to tell if you did."

"I got you, baby. This will be one night you'll never forget."

"Cool. I'll see you soon."

I parked my car across the street, clutching my purse tightly as I sprinted towards the hotel. I spotted Devon's car in the parking lot and knew he was probably in the room rubbing his thumb-sized penis, imagining all the different positions he would fuck me in. When I knocked on the door Devon answered so quickly you would've thought he had been posted right beside the doorknob.

"What took you so long? I was about to start blowing up your cell."

"No need, I'm here now," I said, scooting past the wannabe cock blocker.

"What's all that you got in your hands?" Devon questioned at the Sephora bag I was carrying.

"Bath and body products. I wanted to spoil you with a hot bath, washing you from head to toe before we did the nasty."

"That sounds sexy."

"It is. I even have scented candles so you can be completely re-laxed." I began taking out the candles and placing them on the table. "Did you order some champagne?" I asked not seeing any.

"It should be here any minute," Devon stated right as someone knocked at the door.

"You get the door, Devon, and I'll be in the bathroom setting up the candles." Devon didn't move and I wondered what he was waiting for. "What's the problem?"

"I need some money," he said, putting his hand out.

"Oh, stupid me. Here, this should cover it." I whipped out several hundred dollar bills and slapped them in his sweaty palms. While Devon was grinning, I hurried my ass in the bathroom not wanting to be seen by the waiter.

After I set up the candles I turned on the faucet in the Jacuzzi tub and poured in some L'Occitane foaming bath and oil. I heard the door shut and came out to the room and saw Devon holding two glasses.

"Here you go, baby. The waiter already poured it for us," Devon said, handing me my glass.

"Thank you, but go and check on the bath and make sure the water temperature is just right for you."

"Let me do that. Can't take any chances of that water burning my pretty skin," he said, rubbing his ashy arm. "Hold this for me." Devon handed me his glass.

"Of course. I'll be right here waiting for you." The second Devon was out of view, I opened my purse and poured the strong sedative in his glass of champagne. I added extra since Devon was a big mother-fucker. I used my finger to stir it in quickly. "How's that bath coming?" I yelled, making sure Devon didn't pop out of the bathroom surprising me.

"I'm good. Come on in and bring the champagne." When I got

in the bathroom, Devon had already stripped out of his clothes and squeezed his big ass in the Jacuzzi.

"You looking mighty comfortable," I commented in a flirty tone.

"I am. But, umm, I don't think there is enough room for you to get in too."

"Don't worry, this is simply for your enjoyment. I'll get my pleasure by making you feel good."

"Maya, you my kind of woman. You pay for everything, wanna nigga to feel good, and you sexy as shit. I see our relationship lasting for a very long time."

"Me too. Now here, drink up." I handed Devon his glass. "But first a toast to the beginning of both of our futures."

"That's right." Devon gulped down his drink in one gulp. "Pour me some more, baby."

"Would love to, but before I do that, let me turn on some music."

"You making this real romantic."

"Oh fuck, I forgot the bottle in the bedroom. I'll be right back."

"Hurry up. I don't want your fine ass out of my sight."

I grabbed Devon's glass and happily refilled it and added some more of the sedative. I needed for him to be as relaxed as possible. Halfway asleep would be the easiest for me. "Here you go, baby. I hope I didn't keep you waiting too long."

"I'm good, but I want you to stand over there and strip for me. Grind to this music, get a nigga extra hard."

I damn sure didn't want Devon to have the pleasure of seeing me in the flesh, but I did need to stall so the sedatives could kick in. "You got it, you sexy black motherfucker." I stood a few feet from Devon and slowly began taking off one article of clothing at a time.

"Move them hips like Beyonce be doing when she grinding on stage," he directed, as if he was paying me Beyonce type money when this nigga wasn't kicking out loot for nada.

It had taken me over fifteen minutes to unbutton my silk blouse and the sedatives hadn't made a dent in Devon. I moved on to my crisp white pants, unzipping them just as slowly. Soon I found myself standing in my white lace bra and panties, slithering my body. Right when I was about to unclip my bra, I finally got some much needed indication that the shit was hitting home.

"What's wrong, Devon?" He was rubbing his eyes and bubbles were sliding down his face.

"I'm okay," he said, trying to shake off the drowsiness."

"Let me rub your shoulders, give you a little massage so you can feel real good."

"No need, I'm straight."

"Stop it. I want to make my man feel good." I went behind Devon and cemented my hands on his shoulders before he could protest any further. I felt his muscles getting weaker and his body wanting to collapse. "How does that feel?"

"That feels good," he mumbled, barely able to use his mouth to speak.

That's when I went in for the kill. I pulled out my syringe and filled it to the very top from the bottle of Potassium Chloride I had gotten earlier in the day. "Baby, it will all be over soon," I giggled as I plunged the needle in Devon's upper left shoulder. His body flinched but his muscles were too relaxed to react.

"What the fuck..." he stuttered.

I sat on the ledge of the Jacuzzi watching the anguish in Devon's eyes. "Devon, sweetie, you're having a heart attack. I know it's painful but soon you'll be in a more peaceful place. Better than that, after your dead and the coroner performs an autopsy they'll think your big ass died of natural causes."

Devon tried to lift up his arm and reach for my neck but it was a no go. He was entirely too weak at this point.

"Gotta go, and I won't be missing you or that little dick of yours." With the swiftness I gathered all my shit but made sure not to leave a clue that would lead to me.

"You brought this on yourself," I revealed, giving Devon a kiss goodbye on the forehead, leaving him for dead. "You thought this was your show to run. You left me no choice but to prove you wrong."

Precious

All Eyes On Me

"You're starting to look like your old self again," Nico said, standing in the doorway.

"Maybe on the outside but not on the inside." I stood in front of the mirror over the dresser able to truly see all my features and recognize my face for the first time in weeks. "Who knew that it took so long for bruises to heal after getting your ass beat?"

"But they're healed, that's the important thing. How is your rib?"

"Much better. Still some slight pain when I move, but at least I can walk without feeling as if I'm about to pass out. Thank you for nursing me back to health."

"Remember that, in case I ever need for you to do the same for me."

"Nico, I can promise you that if you ever need me, I'll be there no matter what."

"I believe you."

"It's the truth. I put that on everything."

"Precious, you don't have to convince me, I know your heart. Most people are fooled by that tough exterior but I know you."

"Then you also know I want to go home. I was too weak before but I need to be with my family."

"Are you sure you're ready?"

"Yes. I have to take care of a few things here, but after that I have to go straighten shit out with Supreme and see my daughter."

"Do you want to call him?"

"I thought about it so many times, but I have to handle this face to face. Then that letter Maya had me write..."

"What letter?"

"I was so busy telling you about the torture Maya put me through that I forgot to mention that bullshit letter the heifer had me pen."

"What did the letter say?"

"Basically she had me tell Supreme that I left him and I didn't want to be with him anymore."

"Word? I know he's fucked up behind that."

"Yeah, I'm sure Maya has taken full advantage, filling his head with all sorts of ridiculous shit."

"You mean shit about us?"

"Huh?"

"You don't have to 'huh' me, Precious. I know it was Supreme that put that hit out on me. You know, the one you came to New York to warn me about."

I let out a deep sigh and walked over to the bed to sit down. I was torn, but felt Nico deserved for me to be honest with him about a few things. "I guess I shouldn't ask how you found out."

"The same way I found Mike. I can find out pretty much anything if I ask the right questions to the right people."

"How long have you known?"

"It's been awhile now. When you gave me the warning, I put my sources on it and a few weeks later I got the info."

"You have to understand why I couldn't tell you who it was."

"He's your husband, I get that, which is the only reason I didn't try to retaliate against him. That, and I learned he pressed the pause button on the hit. But my question to you is, why did he want me killed?"

"Originally, I figured he harbored a lot of animosity for you trying to take my life which caused me to lose our baby. But I learned the real answer a few weeks ago."

"But you were on lock down a few weeks ago."

"Yeah, Maya was more than thrilled to inform me what Supreme had confided to her."

"Which was?"

"That he found out we had sex during the time I thought he was dead. I assumed it was our secret. Never did I think he would ever find out, but he did. That's what happens when the feds start recording your phone conversations."

"Leave it up to them motherfuckers to expose some bullshit that has nothing to do with them. Now I see where the Maya thing fits in. You figure she's telling him you ran off with me."

"Exactly. And with me being MIA and our history, I can't blame him. I have to look him in his eyes so he knows I'm telling the truth. I also don't want him to give Maya any type of warning so she can plot and scheme her way out this bullshit she created."

"You think Supreme would get caught up in her lies?"

"One thing I've learned the hard way is to never underestimate that bitch."

"I feel you. So when are we breaking out?"

"We?"

"Yeah, we. I know you don't think I'm letting you go back to Cali by yourself."

"Nico, I can't bring you back to Cali with me. That would only further feed into the paranoia Supreme has about our relationship."

"Look, it ain't safe there for you. I ain't gonna let you walk into a danger zone by yourself."

"I won't be walking into a danger zone. Maya thinks I'm dead. She's probably dancing on top of a makeshift grave she created in my honor. When I make my presence known she will be caught totally off guard."

"Sorry, baby girl, I'm not willing to take that chance. Either we go together or you'll have to call Supreme and have him come meet you here. You need protection by someone you can trust, and that's me."

"I get it. But if you're going back to Cali with me, we have to do it my way."

"Don't we always have to do it your way?" Nico grinned.

"Whatever! But before we break out, I have to pay an old friend a visit, then we outta here."

"Who is that?"

"Nobody you know."

"Hi, welcome to Atomic Records. May I help you?" the middle aged, attractive receptionist asked.

"Yes, I'm here to see Jamal Crawford."

"Is he expecting you? Because he's in a meeting right now."

"No, he's not expecting me, but let him know that Precious Mills is here...*now!*" I gave the lady a half-ass smile and sat down on the typical black leather couch that all record companies seemed to have.

When I sat down, I noticed the receptionist staring at me but not picking up the phone. I was confused and annoyed by her hold up. "Excuse me, but is there a reason why you're not getting Jamal on the phone?"

"Well, Miss..."

"It's Mrs.," I interrupted.

"Mrs.," the lady sighed. "As I said, Mr. Crawford is in a meeting and I've been directed not to interrupt."

"I'm directing you to interrupt, and quite honestly it's not negotiable. Now call Jamal."

"I simply can't do that. I work for Atomic Records and Mr. Crawford. I have to follow his rules, not yours."

I chuckled out loud not in the mood to deal with the bullshit. Although my face had pretty much healed and with makeup on you couldn't see a flaw, my mind, spirit and body were still fucked up. This chick sitting behind the desk was blocking on some 'this is my multi-million dollar company', when in all actuality she was just another employee. I had no time for this shit and was done playing with her.

"Listen," I began as I walked up on her. "This right here," I motioned my hands with the back and forth movement. "It's stopping right now. I don't have time to be playing paddy-cake with you. Get Jamal on the phone now, before I bust it over your head!"

The lady's mouth dropped, stunned by my threat, but I wasn't sure if she understood it was more than that. It was about to become her reality if she didn't speed up the tempo with her actions. I stood with my arms folded, staring the chick down, not flinching once. I counted to three in my head, and when she continued to act as if she was deaf, dumb and blind I bent over and seized her phone. "Now, are you going to call Jamal or are you going to be carried out this motherfucker in a stretcher?"

"I'm calling security right now!"

"You do that, but by the time they get here I would've busted your ass, spoke to Jamal and broke the fuck out. So like I said, what we doing?"

The lady picked up the phone slowly, and I wasn't sure what option she chose until she said, "Mr. Crawford, a Precious Mills is here to see you." She waited a few seconds and then hung up the phone. "Mr. Crawford said he would be right out."

"Now, was that so hard?" I grinned, flashing all thirty-two's.

I didn't even bother to sit back down. I began to walk back and forth waiting for Jamal, and by the time I got to my second turn back, Jamal had appeared. I instantly recognized the tall, reddish-skinned handsome man in the tailored coal gray suit. But no matter how distinguished Jamal grew up to be, in my mind he was still the bona fide hood genius from the projects I grew up in who popped my cherry.

"Precious, I'm surprised to see you," Jamal said, dryly. For some reason I was expecting a different greeting. There didn't have to be firecrackers and explosions, but at least a warm smile.

"Surprised or disappointed? I mean by the look on your face it definitely ain't happiness."

"Follow me. Let's go somewhere in private where we can talk."

I turned my head around and noticed the receptionist damn near falling out her chair trying to hear the words being exchanged between us. I rolled my eyes and picked up my pace so I could get down to it with Jamal. He led me to a conference room and we sat down across from each other at a table that could seat at least forty people.

"How have you been doing?" I asked, with a pleasant smile. I cared, but then I didn't care about the answer to that question. I had so much shit on my plate, but truth was I needed Jamal's help. And though I was itching to get right to it, I tried to play nice first.

"I doubt you care," he said, not trying to hide his true feelings. But this is how you play your game right?"

Okay, clearly Jamal was putting me on Front Street, airing my tactics out on the table. I was relieved, because again I was in no mood to dance around the topic. "You're right, Jamal, I don't care. From the looks of you, you're doing just fine. Maybe if my life wasn't so fucked up I would care, but that's not my circumstances."

"Yeah, last I heard you were missing. No one had spoken to you, not even your husband, Supreme."

"Jamal, I know who my husband is. You don't have to tell me his name," I said, becoming defensive. For the first time I looked down at Jamal's hand and saw that he was wearing a wedding ring. "Congratulations. I see you took the plunge."

He eyed down at the platinum band. "Yep, I'm a married man, and this time my fiancée didn't leave me at the altar, but then my first one technically didn't either. She was being murdered."

"Is that what the chip on your shoulder is about, Nina?"

"Of course! I know that you murdered her, Precious, and when the cops make their case, you're going to jail."

"Oh really? You're so sure about that?"

"Damn straight! I spoke to Detective Moore."

"Jamal, I'm not gonna even lie to you. I've done a lot of fucked up things in my life and I'm sure I'll do a lot more. But on everything I love, I didn't kill Nina. But let's be clear, she did deserve to die."

"Why should I believe you?"

"Because I know who did kill her. At the time, I thought she saved my life and I wanted to protect her. Now I know that she's just a manipulator."

"Kinda like yourself?"

"No...worse."

"When I came to your house that morning after learning Nina was dead, you looked me in my eyes and lied to me with a straight face. I believed you and you were lying to me."

"I told you I didn't kill Nina and that was the truth. I meant every word I said that morning. Nina was a loser. She didn't love you. What the fuck! You're married now. You're still hung up on that trick?"

"That's not the point. I trusted you as a friend and you deceived me."

"Oh please, Jamal, save the theatrics. We're talking about my life. You think I was willing to go to jail for a loser like Nina, who I didn't even have the pleasure of killing? Your so-called fiancée set me up. She wanted to kill *me*, and for what—so she could live out some fantasy, made up life with Nico. She was delusional and crazy. Those are two very dangerous components."

"How do you justify the way you live your life?"

"The same way you justify yours. Don't judge me, Jamal. That's not your right. You're a sinner just like me, and don't forget it."

The room went quiet, as if Jamal was soaking in all the words that we battled with. I knew I had blood on my hands, but I never killed anybody that I didn't feel deserved it. Was that my right to do? Well that was something I would have to settle with God.

"What do you need from me, Precious?" Jamal finally asked, breaking the silence. "I know you didn't come to see me because you missed me," he said sarcastically.

"You're right. I know it doesn't matter to you, but you are one of the very few people I respect, believe that." Jamal put his head down and didn't say a word. "Back to what I need from you: Have you ever been to an apartment that Nina had in Queens?"

"Queens? Nina didn't have an apartment in Queens."

"Yes, she did. Obviously you didn't know about it, like you didn't know about the apartment she kept on the West Side."

"You mean the one she kept your ex-fugitive boyfriend, Nico stashed in."

"Yeah, that one. Let's pause and backtrack for a moment because the petty hostility isn't giving me what I need."

"Why should I help you get what you need anyway?"

"Don't you want the person who is responsible for killing Nina to be brought to justice?"

"I find it hard to believe that you're doing all this to get justice for Nina, especially since you've made it very clear you're happy she's dead."

"You're right, it's not about Nina. Having her killer rot behind bars is an added bonus for you and the ultimate payback for me."

"I would like to see that happen, but again, I don't know about any apartment in Queens that Nina lived at. Did you run a search on her to check all previous addresses?"

"Yep, but no listings came up in Queens. Maybe the apartment wasn't actually in her name. I don't know, but I need that address," I said, tapping my fingernails on the mahogany conference table.

"Precious, where have you been? Are you back with Nico?"

"Where the hell did that come from?"

"Last I heard, Detective Moore said you were missing. You have a family, a daughter that was recently kidnapped, but instead of being in LA, you're here in New York searching for an address on Nina. Does this have something to do with Nico? I know you and him go way back. The two of you have some sort of twisted relationship that keeps you connected. I hope you're not throwing your life away to be with him."

"Are you done with the multiple questions, because Jamal, you don't have a clue to what you're talking about. Me coming here to see you and this search on Nina's address I'm doing, is all being done so I can be with my family again.

Yeah, you right, Nico and I do share a deep connection. Some people may describe it as twisted, but it ain't nobody's fuckin' business. But best believe my family comes first."

"I think I might know."

"You don't know shit about me and Nico, Jamal."

"You're right, and I don't want to know. This is about Nina."

"Oh," I exhaled noisily, trying to calm down. "What do you know?"

"I have a box of Nina's belongings that I never got rid of." I gave Jamal a peculiar stare. "The same way I don't understand your love for Nico, you don't understand my love for Nina, and let's leave it at that,"

Jamal stated as if reading my mind, and I couldn't argue with what he said.

"I get it. Now continue."

"Nina had an address book that she would always keep with her. When she died, I went through it trying to find her relatives to let them know what had happened to her. She always told me she was estranged from her family, but of course I felt they needed to know that she had died."

"Did you get in contact with any of them?"

"No. There were a lot of names in there but none of them knew anything about Nina's family. A couple of people mentioned a person by the name of Terrell. They said it was her brother, who was dead. It was mind- boggling to me because Nina never even told me she had a brother who died. I apologize. I'm losing focus on the point I was trying to make."

"That's okay, take your time." It seemed like for the first time, at that moment I realized just how much pain Jamal was in over Nina's death and all the lies she told him. I never cared to understand or sympathize with his loss. Nina was less than zero in my eyes, but when I looked in Jamal's eyes, she was so much more.

"The point is, if I'm not mistaken I never threw that address book away. I believe it's in that box with some of her other belongings. It could be a stretch but maybe the Queens address is in there."

"Maybe so," I said, not wanting to get my hopes up too high. "I don't have any other options so it can't hurt."

"When I get off work, I'll go home and get the address book."

I leaned back in my chair and gave Jamal this look. It was this look I would get in my eyes ever since I was a little girl. It meant, *Don't fuck wit' me!*

"I know that look."

"I know you do. We did grow up together."

"How about I go get the address book now?"

"How about I think that's a plan?"

"I'm sure you do." Jamal smiled for the first time since I got here. "If you like you can come with me. Maybe meet me my wife."

"I'm sure she's lovely, but I'm not in the mood to pretend like I'm happy to meet someone. No offense."

"None taken. I hope you find everything you're looking for, Precious. It seems that in all the years that I've known you, I've never seen you happy."

"In my world, happy is a baby word, Jamal. All I want is for me and my family to stay alive. On that note, I need to go and so do you."

"Here, meet me at this address in an hour and I'll give you the book." Jamal jotted down the address on a piece of paper and handed it to me.

"Thanks again."

"Don't thank me yet. I don't even know if you're going to find what you're looking for."

"Even if the address isn't in there, thank you for trying to help. You really didn't have to."

"Yes, I did. I want you to bring Nina's murderer down."

"You haven't even asked me who it is."

"I don't need for you to tell me. I have faith that you will handle it."

"I always knew you were a genius, baby. See you soon," I said, walking towards the door.

"Precious."

"Yeah?" I stopped and turned around before exiting.

"So you know, it does matter to me."

"I'm glad."

I left out of Atomic Records even more driven than when I went in. I wanted to find the apartment location in Nina's address book, but I wasn't going to give up even if I didn't. I needed my life back, the one that always seemed to be a few feet out of reach for me. I thought about what Jamal said, how he had never seen me happy. Long-term happiness did seem to elude me to the point I had accepted that it wasn't supposed to be a part of my life. I exploded into the world in the center of destruction, and I had been fighting for my rightful place ever since. Maybe the word 'happy' could find a place in my world. If I didn't feel I deserved it, my daughter damn sure did. And Maya or nobody else would deprive her of that. That meant I would have to do whatever needed to be done... even if all eyes are on me.

Maya

After All

"Supreme, I'm so happy Aaliyah is back home. This place wasn't the same without her," I said, bouncing her on my lap.

"I know, she lights up the whole house."

I watched as Supreme stared adoringly at his daughter. I knew he was thinking of Precious. He couldn't help it since it looked like Precious spit Aaliyah out. "Why don't the three of us go to the zoo today? It'll be fun." I didn't want to go to no damn zoo but I had to break up all that reminiscing Supreme was in the middle of.

"Sure, that would be fun. I know Aaliyah would love seeing all those animals."

"Great! I'll go get her dressed and we can get ready to go." I picked up Aaliyah and headed upstairs. When I reached the mid point I heard the doorbell ringing. "Supreme, are you going to get that?"

"Yeah, but I wonder who it could be and why the front gate security didn't let me know somebody was here," Supreme said, walking to the door.

I continued upstairs until the familiar voice made me stop and head back down.

"Detective Moore. I should've known it was you. You come to visit so often the security no longer feels the need to announce your presence."

"I'm flattered. Can I..."

"Of course, come in."

"Thank you." I heard Supreme close the door as I reached the bottom step. "Well look it here, it's Maya Owens. I see you're stepping into that mother role with ease. That baby gets cuter every time I see her."

"Hello, Detective Moore. As always, it's a pleasure to see you," I mocked.

"Same here."

"Detective, we were on our way out, so what brings you here today?" Supreme asked.

"I have some news that I wanted to share with both of you."

"Did you find out where Precious is?" Supreme couldn't even control himself from wanting to know the whereabouts of his beloved Precious. Even with the bitch dead, she was still living in our house.

"No, but I know one place she is not."

"Where?" I wanted to stay out of the conversation but my anxiousness got the best of me.

"With your brother, Mike Owens," Detective Moore turned to me and said.

Supreme grabbed his arm and turned him back around.

"What makes you so sure?"

"Because Mr. Owens perished in a fire a few weeks ago."

"What? What happened?" Supreme questioned, becoming animated.

"It seems he had been staying at a house in Calabasas and a horrific fire started, and not by accident," he added, cutting his eyes in my direction. I kept swinging Aaliyah on my hip as I didn't peep his shade.

"It was arson?"

"Yes, it was. The whole house was pretty much destroyed."

"Then how are you sure it was Mike that died in the fire?"

"It took a long time, but the medical examiner was able to get a partial fingerprint, and of course they ran it threw the system. With Mike having a criminal record his name came up. His body was found in the basement. Whoever set the fire shot him first."

"That motherfucker finally got his!" Supreme said, slapping his hands together.

"Maya, you don't seem surprised by what happened to your brother."

"Should I be? I'm sure with the life he lived he made a lot of enemies."

"I can't believe that motherfucker was living right here in California. What the fuck was he sticking around for?"

"Mr. Mills, that's interesting because I was trying to figure out the same thing. I was hoping Maya here could help me."

"How can I help? Like I told you, I haven't had any contact with my brother."

"You did tell me that. Mr. Mills, you can rest a bit easier knowing that the man who brought so much tragedy to your family is now dead."

"Damn, straight! But there goes another dead lead when it comes to finding Precious. I'm glad he doesn't have her, but I do want to know where she is."

"Was Mike staying in the house by himself?" I asked.

"I'm sorry, Maya, what did you say?" Detective Moore put his finger behind his ear and leaned forward.

"I said, was anybody else in the house with Mike?"

"Not that we know of. Again, the house was burned pretty bad, but they didn't find any other bodies."

That can't be! Precious died in that fire too! Maybe her body was burned so bad that there wasn't any sort of trace. But there would have to be something left. Or maybe Detective Moore is playing games with me trying to get me to tell on myself. Only the person who set the fire would know that another body shoulda been found. Yeah, Detective Moore is definitely trying to set me up. He's been suspicious of me from day one but can't get anything to stick. He is counting on me to slip up and put the nail in my own coffin. Nah, you gon' have to come better than that. If you sticking to the story that only Mike died in the fire, than so am I.

"Detective, I appreciate you coming over here and informing us about Mike."

"Of course. I'm sorry we haven't been able to find any leads on your wife. I hope you haven't given up finding her."

"Of course not, but I also can't stop living my life. It seems that there hasn't been any foul play and her life isn't in jeopardy, so I have to assume she left on her own free will."

"It would seem that way, but again, I'll keep my eyes open. With the way the pieces to this puzzle are coming together, anything is possible."

"Maya... Maya..."

"Huh?" I finally answered Detective Moore, snapping out of my deep thoughts.

"I guess you got something heavy on your mind," the detective pried on the sly. "Are you going to be okay?"

"I appreciate your concern, but I'll be fine."

"Good, I'm sure you will. What I wanted to tell you was that we tried to get in contact with your mother so she could claim your brother's remains, but we haven't had any luck."

"I'll take care of it."

"Here's my card, if your mother has any questions."

"Thanks," I said, snatching it out his hand.

"I'll be going now. I don't want to overstay my welcome but I'm sure I'll be back. Like you said, Mr. Mills, I'm a frequent visitor."

I stood on the side watching Supreme escort Detective Moore to the front door. That man truly made my skin crawl and I regretted not letting Devon kill him before I took him out. Now with Devon dead I had nobody to finish off the job. But as long as I played it cool I was untouchable. I had gotten rid of all the loose ends. Everybody who had any dirt on me was dead. I had to remain focused and calm. I was this close to having everything I wanted. Supreme was still in love with Precious, but slowly he was accepting the fact that she left him and their baby. As much as he loved her, Supreme would never be able to forgive such betrayal. And now with Precious dead, he would go to his grave never knowing otherwise.

I strolled down Rodeo Drive on a beautiful afternoon, ready to shop away all the memories of yesterday's visit from Detective Moore. Before I got started, I decided to make a pit stop at the Peninsula Spa. I needed a top-of- the-line manicure so my hands would be stunning as I handed over Supreme's credit card to the cashier. Then my pedicure had to be flawless so when I tried on pricey stilettos my feet would be the perfect decoration.

When I arrived at the spa, it was completely quiet. Since it was a one-person nail salon it cut out any hoopla. I sat down to get my Pacific Coast Manicure and watched the standard California bleach blond with over enhanced silicon tits sip champagne while getting a signature pedicure. It was a Reflexology, an herbal foot bath, and jasmine oil massage. It was a cool $155, but it was worth it for seventy-five minutes of foot heaven.

"I love your purse," the bleached blonde babbled between sips of her bubbly. The Chanel, metallic calfskin bowling bag I was carrying was official. I couldn't even front on that.

"Thank you. It was a gift from my boyfriend."

"Your boyfriend has great taste. He seems like a keeper."

"I would have to agree, on both."

"Well you better hurry up and try to marry him while you can. We're in Beverly Hills, young lady. These women are treacherous. I'm in real estate, and although business is booming for me, with this economy being such a mess some of my competitors are willing to do anything, and I mean, *anything!*" she stressed, "To close the deal, if you know what I mean," she said, and winked her eye.

"I know what you mean. It's pretty competitive in my business too. Women are willing to kill to get what they want," I laughed as if joking, and the lady laughed back, having no idea how serious I was.

"Well, if you ever do get that man down the aisle, and when you're ready to start a family, call me. I sell the most luxurious homes money can buy. Whatever the request, I guarantee I can fulfill it." She reached in her purse and pulled out one of her business cards.

"No, thanks. I appreciate the offer, but we already live in a beautiful gated estate in Beverly Hills."

"Work it out! Kudos to you for learning at a young age to use what the good Lord above gave you to get what you want."

"I'm trying."

"With the bag you're carrying and an estate in Beverly Hills, darling, you're more than trying, you've seemed to have figured it all out."

I was really enjoying the fake white girl bullshit with this lady and chuckled, then found myself imitating her phony hand gestures and the whole nine. I could see how chicks like Lil' Kim and them ended up 100% plastic after getting caught up in the allure of Hollyweird.

"Hold on a moment, I have a call," I said, sounding all extra valley girl like the realtor did. "Hello," I said, speaking into my Blue Tooth."

"Bitch, you shoulda stayed in that hotel room until you knew my black ass was dead!" I thought my heart had jumped out my chest when I heard Devon's voice on the other end of the phone.

"Devon, is that you? You fell asleep the last time I saw you and I haven't been able to get in touch with you. I was worried," I said, trying my best to play this shit off with him.

"Is that him on the phone?" I caught the realtor chick mouthing as I turned my head in her direction. She was cheesing from ear-to-ear while pointing her finger at my Blue Tooth. I smiled back and nodded my head 'yes', wanting to quickly shut her down. My five minutes of pretending to be a Hollywood socialite were over. This phone call kicked me back into hood life reality quickly.

"Shut the fuck up with that lying, Maya! You know fuckin' well I wasn't sleep. You drugged me and then tried to poison me, you triflin' bitch! Luckily, I'ma big nigga, and I had the strength before that shit kicked all the way in to pick up the phone and get some help."

"Devon, I don't know what you're talking about, but I'm glad you're okay."

"No you're not. You wanted me dead, just like your brother and Precious. I can't wait to tell Supreme how you murdered his wife."

"Devon, calm down. There is no need for threats." The palms of my hands were sweaty and my fingers were shaking. The lady gently pressed down on them to stop it, but it wasn't helping.

"Ho, this ain't no threat. I'ma fuck your schemin' ass up!"

"Wait, I can get access to a lot of money—it's yours." The phone went silent and I knew Devon's greedy ass was considering what I had said. "I'll give you a million dollars," I added, although there was much more in the suitcase I took from Mike, but he didn't need to know that."

"How do I know you ain't playing games, Maya?"

"Because you're holding all the cards," I spoke softly, not wanting anybody to hear what I was saying. "All I ask is you give me a week to get the money."

"Fuck that! You got three days or I'm going to Supreme."

"Devon, a million dollars is a lot of money. I need some more time. I'm good for it. If you blow up my spot with Supreme then you'll have nothing. We will both end up in jail and you'll be broke," I whispered.

"Five days. That's all your evil ass gets. I swear if you don't have my million dollars by then, I guess we'll both be serving life sentences." Then the phone went dead.

"Is everything okay?" the realtor asked a few minutes after she noticed my mouth was no longer yapping.

"I'm fine. I just got some unexpected news."

"Good, I hope."

"What's your name again?"

"It's Kitty."

"Kitty, let me get your card. I think I will need your services after all."

$\mathscr{P}recious$

Last Bitch Standing

From the moment Jamal placed Nina's address book in my hands I had been consumed with it for the last four days. She had so many names and numbers you would've thought it was the yellow pages. There were several addresses in Queens listed, and I had spent two days visiting those places and none of them were the spot. I got tired of knocking on doors and coming up with bullshit excuses as to why I was at their front entry. Based on the description Mike had given me, I knew most of the spots I rolled up on couldn't have been the correct place, but I was so desperate I would try regardless. Mike said the place was in a low-key neighborhood, but I would pull up on a block with a gang of dealers kicking it on every corner rolling dice knowing, shit wasn't going to be in my favor.

Besides the address book, Jamal also gave me a pair of keys he found inside a jewelry box Nina had. Again, he wasn't sure but he thought that maybe they were the keys to the apartment I was looking for. When I would go to certain spots that seemed to fit the bill and I knocked on the door and no one would answer, I would try the keys but zilch was opening up so far.

After staying up day and night, I was finally down to the last five pages of the book. There were four addresses listed for Queens. If none of these worked, then I would have to come up with another plan because nothing was going to stop me from bringing Maya all the way down.

Knock! Knock! Knock!

"Come in, Nico."

"Have you found what you're looking for yet? I'm getting concerned."

"So am I. I only have four addresses to go. If this don't work, I don't know what I'm going to do."

"We'll stick to the plan, go to LA and tell Supreme what the hell that crazy ass Maya did to you."

"Of course I'm going to do that, but I want Maya in jail forever. I really want her dead, but I'm a mother and Aaliyah needs me in her life not locked up behind bars."

"That's smart thinking, Precious."

"Yeah, but I have to get the evidence I need to seal her fate."

"But you can tell the police she was the mastermind behind all that bullshit and that she kidnapped you."

"True, but you know she's going to place all the blame on Mike, and with him dead, it's a gamble and she might get off. I'm sure she'll get some slimy attorney who will insinuate that I'm making the whole story up out of jealousy because of her relationship with Supreme. Trust me, with this shit being more bizarre than a daytime soap opera, combined with my shady past, I need the smoking gun to make sure Maya is officially done, case fuckin' closed."

"I understand all that and you know I love having you around. But you need to get home to your daughter and your husband. The longer you have Maya around your family, the worse it's going to be."

"True. Well then, we need to check out these last four addresses, and even if we come up short, tomorrow I'll be going home."

"Now you're talking, so let's go."

It felt as if Nico and I had been driving around in circles all day, or better yet, at a standstill in afternoon traffic, and it had all been in vain. We had three strikes in a row, and I was drained but undeterred. I wasn't expecting to hit gold in my search, but I did want to be able to say that I tried every option given to me. I laid my head back on the reclined seat gazing out the window, finding one positive thing in this entire situation. This time tomorrow, I would be holding my baby girl. Knowing that put a smile on my face.

As Nico turned the corner onto the block of a quaint street in the Astoria, Queens neighborhood, the longing feeling of holding my child again was put on pause. "This is it," I said, as a calmness came over me.

"Huh?" Nico turned to me like he didn't understand or hear what I said.

"This is it. This is where the apartment is." I sat straight up in the seat looking for the address that was written on the second to last page in the book. It simply had 'Mildred' as the name with the address underneath, but I knew this was the spot. No matter how hard I had tried to make myself get that feeling of hope when I had pulled up to a minimum of twenty-five apartments in the last few days, none of them gave me that, until now.

"What makes you sure?"

"I'll put it like this: Remember when we were together and my gut told me you were fuckin' around on me? My gut instinct is doing the same shit right now about this apartment."

"I can't knock that shit."

"No you can't, now pull over. There's the building," I said, pointing straight ahead."

When we got out of the car I practically ran to the entrance of the brownstone building. The door was locked and I reached in the back pocket of my jeans and pulled out the set of keys. I knew this was do or die time. I put the first key in the lock but it wouldn't open the door. I could hear Nico letting out a disappointing sigh. He knew how desperately I wanted this shit to work out in my favor and he didn't want me to hit another dead end—and he wouldn't have to. When I put the second key in, that shit turned and the lock popped as if I had been opening this very same door all my life.

"Motherfuckin' right!" Nico pumped his fist in the air sharing in my enthusiasm.

"It's apartment Number 2. There seems to be one apartment on each floor so it must be one flight up." We skipped up the stairs, and when I got to the apartment that had #2. I put my ear to the door to make sure no one was there. Nico did the same thing and neither of us heard anything suspicious. I put the first key in, and again that shit opened right the fuck up.

Surprisingly, the joint was in great condition. It was apparent that whoever Mike had checking up on the spot was on top of their job. The two bedroom apartment was sparsely furnished but very clean. The place wasn't huge but it was spacious enough that the gun could've been stashed in numerous places.

"Where do you want to start?" Nico asked, reading my thoughts.

"I'll take the first bedroom, you take the one in the back and we'll work our way out front."

"Sounds like a plan. Let's get to it."

When I went into the bedroom, the first thing that caught my eye was a picture on the nightstand. It was Nina standing next to a young man that I assumed was her brother, Terrell. The resemblance was undeniable— the thick black eyebrows, rich brown complexion, full lips and high cheekbones, gave both model-type features. Now I understood what Mike meant about all the women this cute, young nigga had. Maya didn't stand a chance. He had 'heartbreaker' stamped on his forehead.

I put the photo down and got down to business. I looked under the bed, mattress, drawers, closets, behind the television, anyplace that could remotely conceal a gun. I thought finding the correct apartment would be the hardest part, but finding the gun was already proving to be an exhausting chore.

"Any luck?" I heard Nico ask after I had been up down, and around, back on my hands and knees for over an hour, not missing a crack.

"No, you neither."

"I searched the bedroom and the bathroom, now I'ma search the living room and kitchen."

"I'll help because it's definitely not in here."

Nico started in on a hardwood floor check, making sure there weren't any secret compartments underneath us. I began with the couches, and again coming up empty. After what seemed like an eternity we took it to the kitchen with no such luck. After over three hours of nothing, I was running on empty.

"Maybe Mike was lying and he didn't hide the gun here."

"I didn't get that vibe from him, plus I can feel that gun. It's here, I'm telling you. It's crazy, but I think after you have kids, if you listen carefully, your female intuition triples."

"I'm really scared of you now. Women don't need no more extra power over us."

"Nico, I'm being serious."

"Shit, me too."

We both fell back on the couch, tired as hell. "Never did I expect this to turn into a real life treasure hunt game. I figured it wouldn't take us no more than fifteen minutes to find this damn gun—thirty at the most. The way it's looking it's turning to an all day and night affair," I said, looking at the bookshelf against the wall.

"You got that shit right. Baby girl, you know I would stay and search this place for as long as you like, but I'm becoming skeptical about the information Mike gave you."

I got up while Nico was talking, halfway listening and halfway remembering things Mike had said to me: "*...It's proper resting place... My gift to Nina...Me stashing it at the spot Terrell would hold down for her was like me putting the shit to rest...*"

I looked intently at the cream-colored photo album with the gold script words engraved on the front that read "Nina and Terrell Douglas". I smiled and picked it up. It was so heavy I almost dropped it.

"Precious, what are you doing? We don't have time for you to be looking at some photos, we have to find the gun, and looking at that clock on the wall, we're running out of time."

"Our work here is done. We can go now."

"You're giving up? We haven't found the gun, unless you believe I'm right and Mike didn't stash it here."

"It's here. Look inside," I said, opening the bootleg photo album. The first two pages had photos, then the third page was blank, and when you turned it, there was a deep opening, and sitting pretty was that smoking gun.

"How did you know? I would've turned everything in this place upside down and still not touched that fuckin' album."

"One, getting into Mike's twisted mind, and two, that female intuition I keep stressing."

"Your odds are on point. Now let's break the fuck outta here. We have a flight to catch in the morning."

When our flight landed at LAX on Saturday afternoon, I was thrilled to be coming home. I replayed the million questions Supreme would have for me when I walked through the door and what my response would be. Then I wondered if Maya would be there and visualized the stunned look on her face when she saw the person she left for dead was not only alive, but had the weapon that would send her away doing football numbers. Then, most importantly, my baby.

"How are you feeling?" Nico asked, squeezing my hand as we sat in the back seat of the chauffeur driven car.

"I'm fine."

"No you're not. There's nothing wrong with being nervous, Precious."

"I didn't say there was."

"You didn't have to."

"You know me too well, Nico."

"You're right, I do. I want you to know that being with you these last few weeks have been wonderful. It was like old times you know, besides the fact we weren't sharing a bed," he joked.

"Yeah, that does a make a difference. But seriously, I enjoyed spending time with you too. I'll never forget that not only did you save my life, but you nursed me back to health. Our bond is thick, baby."

"It is and it always will be. But I have to let go. You don't belong to me anymore. You're another man's wife and you have to go home and claim your family.

"The way you know me so well, I know you too.

This is difficult for you but you're being such a man about it, and it makes me love you that much more."

Nico lifted my chin and placed the most endearing kiss on my lips. "My beautiful, Precious. No longer are you just radiant on the outside, but you're finally just as radiant on the inside. I always knew you had it in you."

I kept my composure refusing to shed a tear. This was no time to soften up and be weak. I was about to enter a territorial war zone with Maya and my shit had to be solid as steel. There would be time for me to rejoice in my newfound inner peace after I brought Maya the fuck down. When the car started driving up to the estate, I couldn't wait.

"I wonder why the gates are open and there is no security out front. That's strange," I commented.

"It could be the middle of a shift change or something like that."

"True." When we drove up to the driveway the only car I noticed was a silver big body Benz parked in front. "I wonder whose car that is."

"You'll find out shortly."

"Are you sure you don't mind waiting in the car? I feel bad."

"Don't. You didn't want me coming at all."

"It's not that, it's Supreme's paranoia about us."

"Precious, you don't have to explain. We've been through this. All I want to do is make sure that you get home safely to your family. I'll wait here for a little while until I know you have things under control. Then I'll leave."

"Thank you, Nico."

"Stop with all that. Make me proud. Go in that house and let everybody know the queen is back!"

I got to the entrance and rang the doorbell. I could hear heels clicking on the marble floors and my heart was racing. This was my moment and I planned on embracing every second of it.

"Hello there, you must be my three o'clock appointment." The extra bubbly blonde greeted me after opening the door. "Are you alone, or is your husband coming in?" she said, looking over my shoulders at the car Nico was in the backseat of.

"Who are you and what appointment are you talking about?"

"I'm Kitty, the realtor. It's a pleasure to meet you," she said, extending her hand. I brushed her hand away because I was afraid I would break each bony finger if I got a hold of them.

"Well what do we have here? Is there a problem, Mrs. Hughs?"

"My name ain't Mrs. Hughs. It's Precious Mills and I own this house with my husband, so get the fuck out!"

"There is no need to take that tone with me. I was hired by Mr. Mills' attorney to sell this house. This is its first day on the market..."

"And its last," I cut in.

"I don't even know you. The only woman I know Mr. Mills to be involved with is his girlfriend, Maya Owens. She was the sweet young lady that introduced me to Mr. Mills."

"And where might they be? Are they inside right now?" I asked, mowing my way past the silly broad.

"Excuse you!" she snarled, patting her tweed suit.

"Where is Supreme?"

"Who?" she asked, revealing a heavy southern accent that she had been covering up thus far.

"Mr. Mills, where is he?"

"I have no idea. All I know is that they wanted to start fresh in a new place and moved."

"Where, to a new house in Beverly Hills?"

"No, out of state."

"Out of state? Are you sure?"

"Yeeeessss," she said, singing the word. "I'm very sure."

"But you don't know which state?"

"No I don't, because the only place I sell houses is here in Beverly Hills. I have no idea where they went, but I'm sure they're going to be just fine."

"Lady, get the fuck out my house!"

"This isn't your house."

"Take a good long look at that portrait on the wall right there," I pointed my finger firmly in case the dizzy chick had vision problems.

"Well, I'll be damned! That is you! What a beautiful picture. Are you some sort of model?"

"Listen, I'm in a very bad mood right now. So get your skinny, plastic ass out of my face before I break it."

"Precious, what's going on?"

"Are you Mr. Hughes? I think you need to calm your wife down."

"Did you just not see the picture on the wall? I'm not Mrs. Hughes. My name is Precious Mills and my husband is Supreme AKA Xavier Mills. Now remember that as you're walking out the door and don't ever come back!"

"But I have a three o'clock appointment. My clients are my first priority."

"Even before saving your own life?" I balled up my fists so she completely comprehended my question.

"I'll be going now. But I will be calling Mr. Mills' attorney and informing him of what took place today."

"Do that...after you get the fuck out."

"Goodbye. Oh, and here is my card in case you change your mind," she said, handing it to Nico. "Again, my name is Kitty and I sell the most luxurious houses in Beverly Hills," were her parting words as she closed the door.

"What the hell was that about?"

"Supreme has vanished with my daughter and Maya is with them."

"What?"

"Yes. That was some realtor that Maya introduced Supreme to, and he hired her to sell our house before they left town, to start fresh, as Kitty put it. But that's cool. I will turn this motherfucker upside down and find my husband and child. Maya can play if she wants to, but I will be the last bitch standing!"

A KING PRODUCTION

Last Bitch Standing

Part 5

JOY DEJA KING

Precious

I've always been told that life's a bitch and then you die. If that's true, then I should've been dead a long time ago. But yet, here I was, still standing. And why? Because I was on a mission—driven by my need to demolish the one person who thought she was bad enough to outsmart me. I'll admit, the tables had been turned and it wasn't in my favor. But see, I had been left for dead on more than one occasion. My husband had died in my arms—or so I thought—and my daughter had been ripped out of my life. So this shit right here was nothing to me. Because like my man, Jay-Z says, "Difficult takes a day, impossible takes a week". Yeah, what I had to accomplish might take a little longer than that, but one thing was for sure: Maya was going the fuck down! I put that on everything.

"Are you ready to go?" Nico questioned, taking me out of the journey my mind was on of destroying Maya. It took me a few moments to answer, because I wasn't sure if I was ready to go. We had been doing time in Atlanta, based on a tip that led us nowhere so far. There was a so-called "Maya sighting" from one of the numerous private investigators we had hired to track the heffa down. I thought this one could actually be the real deal, but we'd hit yet another brick wall. Over the last few months every potential lead would come up empty. This chick had literally vanished, and took my husband and child with her. The shit had me perplexed an agitated like a motherfucker. I needed answers, but all I kept getting were more questions.

"I guess we're done here," I said, looking around my hotel room. I had been living out of my suitcase like a rapper on the road doing shows, and trying to make a come-up, and at the rate we were going, it wasn't going to stop anytime soon.

"Precious, don't get discouraged," Nico commented, as if reading my mind.

"I can't front, all this searching like we're in the dark with no flashlight is irritating the fuck outta me. I really thought this time, that scandalous trick was mine."

"And she will be...please believe that."

"I ain't got no choice, because if I didn't, I really wouldn't have a reason to live."

"You don't mean that."

"Yes the fuck I do! That deranged broad has my child. I still love Supreme and I want my husband back, but hell, he's grown. He can protect himself. But Aaliyah, she can't, she needs me."

"I understand, and I promise there ain't a mountain I won't move to make that possible. I just don't want you to give up."

"Never that!"

As Nico drove to the airport, I looked out the passenger window, wondering if Maya really was out there somewhere in the ATL and we just simply missed her. Or worse, Maya had seen us and was now someplace gloating that she had once again won the game of hide and seek. I prayed that wasn't the case. It would be much easier for me to stomach that we had simply been directed to the wrong city, than to find out that Maya was still here, carrying on with a life she'd stolen from me.

"Nico, I can't put my finger on it, but something keeps tugging at me as if there is some sort of clue or answer that we are leaving behind."

"You mean here in Atlanta?"

"Yeah, I can't shake it."

"Precious, we've been here for weeks and come up with nothing."

"I know, but my gut keeps telling me something is here for us. I don't know what it is, but the feeling is so strong."

"So, what do you want to do, stay? I mean, supposedly from what another investigator told us, there are some very good leads in Philadelphia. This tip seems reliable."

"And so did all the other ones, but we ain't got shit!"

"I know you're frustrated. So the fuck am I, but we can't stop looking!"

"I know that. Shit, I don't want to stop looking! I can fuckin' taste that bitch's blood like I'm a damn vampire. We ain't gon' never stop looking, but it's just this feeling I got. But it could be my agitation fuckin' with me."

"I think that's exactly what it is."

"Yeah," I sighed, falling back in my seat. "Let's take this flight to Philly. It could turn out to be beneficial... at least I hope so."

"Me too."

"Delta flight 1018 to Philadelphia will begin boarding in fifteen minutes," I heard the lady announce as Nico and I walked up.

The waiting area was jam packed, so clearly the flight was full. Although I had lived in New York for the majority of my life, I had never been to Philly even though it was damn near just down the street. I wouldn't know how to maneuver my way around even with a GPS, so luckily I had Nico with me. With hustling drugs for many years, Philadelphia had become like his own personal neighborhood playground, which was exactly what I needed.

"I'ma stop over there and get something to drink before we get on the flight. Do you want anything?" Nico asked, as I was about to sit down.

"No, I'm straight."

"Cool. I'll be right back."

As Nico was walking towards his destination, I heard a female voice call out his name. I glanced over to see who the fuck was screaming for dude all the way in Atlanta. With Nico's baller status in the drug business, there was no question that he was nationally known in the street game. But hearing his name echoing through the airport threw me off for a second.

I watched intently as an extremely pretty chick greeted Nico with a too lengthy hug, as if he was her long lost love. I could damn near count every tooth in her mouth with how hard she was cheesing. But even with all that smiling and laughing the woman was doing, she had mad swagger. She definitely wasn't a sack chaser bum bitch who had nothing going on upstairs. She was a bitch that knew how to handle her business. That was clear from just observing her style game. The perfectly cropped jet black haircut, to the simple yet sexy sleeveless blouse, five pocket jeans with stud embroidery on the pockets, a leather belt with a prism shaped buckle and a large shoulder bag with what looked like hand braided chains and interlocking 'G' detail, topped off with some velvet high heel cuffed booties. Her entire outfit was jet black like her hair. The chick was on point and that was being peeped from one gangster to another.

As if Nico could feel me sizing their interaction up, he pointed at me, then said something to the chick, and they started walking towards my direction. I played it cool as if I wasn't thinking about homegirl, and honestly, I wouldn't have been if it wasn't for the fact she seemed a little too comfortable for my taste around Nico. No doubt he wasn't my man any longer, but he was my first love, and a part of me would always be ready to snatch- a-bitch-up over him. I was territorial that way I suppose.

"Precious, I want to introduce you to a very good friend of mine," Nico said charmingly, as if giving me my respect. "This is CoCo Armstrong."

CoCo grinned at me and started to reach out her hand, but saw that mine were still folded in my lap, and quickly rescinded her gesture.

"Nice to meet you," I remarked coldly.

"Precious, I used to do a lot of business with CoCo before we lost touch," Nico said, trying to thaw the ice.

"Yeah, you mean before I had to sit down and take that vacation for a few months," CoCo countered, causing them to both chuckle.

I knew "vacation" was a code word for a bid in jail, which actually made me feel a little less icy towards the woman. I mean, don't nobody want to see the inside of a cell, but from one female to another, if you're able to do it and come out looking as good as she did, then I had to give her props off of that alone. Clearly she did the time, and didn't let the time do her.

"CoCo is actually on the same flight as us," Nico informed me.

"Oh, you from Philly?"

"No, I'm actually from Atlanta, but I live in Philly now." I nodded my head as I continued to feel the chick out.

"We have to hang out while you're visiting Philly," CoCo suggested, turning her attention back to Nico.

"This trip is more business than pleasure. I doubt we'll have time to hang out." CoCo stared at Nico suspiciously, and then tried to eye me on the sly but I caught that shit. She was trying to figure the situation out without coming right out and asking.

"I understand, but if shit changes, you have my numbers now.

Give me a call. If we can't kick it on some fun shit while you're in Philly, definitely hit me up about business. I got a new partner now, and we making major moves."

"Cool...that's what's up. I'll be in touch for sure."

CoCo gave Nico a goodbye hug and then said, "It was nice meeting you, Precious," before walking off. But I couldn't help but feel this wouldn't be the last time my path crossed with CoCo Armstrong.

Maya

I stared out at the open water of the bay, with the unobstructed view to the dockage, as Supreme lounged on the yacht with Aaliyah. The calmness of the ocean had almost tricked my mind into believing there wasn't a storm brewing, that with each day, I was constantly fighting to divert.

The Georgian-style mansion that I had been living in with Supreme was nothing more than a high-priced, exquisite prison. From the flowing hardwood espresso floors, indoor waterfall, magnificent glass double staircases and soaring ceilings with arches and pillars, it was the sort of layout that MTV's *Cribs* was built on back in their heyday. But for me, it represented fear—fear that it would all be taken away from me if even one of my skeletons stepped out of the closet.

Not only was Devon out there lurking in the shadows waiting to seek revenge, but there was also Precious, my one-time mentor that I had meticulously plotted on to steal her life. My plan had seemed to come together so beautifully...until my brother replaced his brain with his dick. Then, Devon's nasty ass got greedy. And finally thinking I left Precious for dead, I now know she is very much alive.

I remember like it was yesterday, when Supreme got the phone call about the estate in Beverly Hills. Kitty, the airhead realtor I convinced Supreme to hire, had called his attorney in an uproar because she told him that some woman showed up claiming to be Supreme's wife and threw her out the house. I could see the glimmer in Supreme's eyes when he thought Precious had finally come back to him. But that glimmer instantly turned to hatred and rage when his attorney added that Kitty also said Precious showed up with some man, and from the description given, it sounded exactly like Nico. When his attorney asked him what he wanted to do, I'll never forget what Supreme said:

"Let her have the house, but do not tell her my whereabouts. As far as you know, I've vanished and don't want to be found." He calmly hung up the phone, but less than two seconds later, he trashed the place. If I hadn't seen it with my own eyes, I would've sworn up and down that a tornado had hit.

Hours later when Supreme had finally half-way calmed down, he admitted to me that he believed Precious had shown up to tell him it was over, that she was leaving him for Nico, and not only did she want a divorce, but she also wanted their daughter. I could see that Supreme was letting his paranoia get the best of him. "I won't let that happen," he stated firmly. "I can't make Precious leave Nico, but I will fuckin' make sure she never takes Aaliyah away from me."

With that idea cemented in Supreme's head, it actually helped my need to stay in hiding, because in a way, he was hiding too, but for totally different reasons. He felt he was protecting Aaliyah, but I was trying to protect my secrets. I knew all it took was one conversation between him and Precious and my cover would be completely blown. All my lies would explode in my face, and Supreme wouldn't want anything to do with me. And the one plan I was trying to orchestrate to salvage our relationship, if and when he found out, wasn't coming together. Why? Because I needed Supreme to be a willing participant, which I couldn't make happen.

Even with all the anger he had against Precious after that phone call from his attorney, Supreme refused to even touch me. It was as if believing Precious had truly moved on and chose Nico had castrated him. His sexual desires were zilch. The shit had me straight tripping, and also making it impossible for me to get pregnant. I figured if shit did hit the fan, Supreme would never hurt me or abandon me if I was carrying his child, but if I couldn't get no dick, then we couldn't make no baby.

So, here I was, in a sexless relationship with a man who devoted all his time to his daughter as he secretly yearned for his wife. But some of that shit needed to change rather quickly—mainly the sexless part— because the clock was ticking. No matter how low-key we remained, knowing how relentless Precious was, she would eventually find us. The more I thought about it, the more I realized how limited my options were. It was either wait to be gotten, or go do the getting.

Whichever way I chose to move, there were great risks, but I needed to make a decision soon, because time wasn't on my side.

"I'ma take Aaliyah for a ride. We'll be back," Supreme said on his way out the front door. I was so preoccupied in my scheming that I hadn't even noticed or heard them come inside.

"Wait a minute, I'll come with you."

"That's okay. I want to spend some alone time with Aaliyah."

"What do you mean? You were just alone with her for over an hour sitting on the yacht. I'm sure Aaliyah won't mind sharing you with me for a car ride."

"Fine...come on," he responded with no enthusiasm. But I didn't fuckin' care. I had to try and break down the walls that Supreme had built up, and I had a much better chance of doing it by spending *some* time with him than none at all. With each passing day, that shade was getting thicker and thicker with him. If I didn't make some serious progress soon, we would go from sharing the same bed with no sex, to sleeping in separate bedrooms altogether. If that happened, it would be a done deal and my time would officially be up.

As Supreme drove down the coastline seeming to be in deep thought, I stared back at Aaliyah, who was falling asleep. There was no denying that with each day, she resembled her mother more and more. There was also no disputing that as she was getting older and her personality was making more of a breakthrough, she had also inherited Precious' fire. Armed with her mother's looks and personality, and her father's money, I knew for a fact that once Aaliyah reached a certain age, she would be a force to be reckoned with. I wasn't sure I wanted to be around to witness that, unless of course I could deliver her that little brother.

"Supreme, we need to talk," I said, more determined than ever to bring my thoughts to fruition.

"What do we need to talk about?"

"Us."

"Us," he repeated, slightly laughing.

"That sounded funny to you?" I was unable to hide my annoyance. Supreme looked over at me, and then turned his head back around, looking straight ahead.

"Is this conversation you're trying to have with me really necessary?"

"I think so."

"I think not," he replied matter-of-factly.

"So what, you want to be roommates now, Supreme? Is that it?"

"Where are you going with this?"

"No, the question is where are *you* going? We go from leaving Beverly Hills to start fresh in Miami, to now you treating me like we're strangers."

"It was your idea to move to Miami."

"True, but you weren't exactly fighting me on the suggestion! As a matter of fact, you said you were ready to leave the bullshit behind and try and regain your sanity. You don't remember that?"

"Of course I remember, but shit changed," he mumbled.

"Shit like what?" I demanded to know, raising my voice.

"Keep your voice down! Aaliyah is sleep!" he demanded, in a loud whisper.

I wanted to yell out that I didn't give a flying fuck whether his golden child was sleep or not, this was about me, but restrained myself. "Listen, I don't want to argue with you. I care about you and I love Aaliyah. If you don't want us to have that type of relationship no more, then I'm cool with that. I'll stay in one of the guest bedrooms and help you with Aaliyah until you find a full time nanny."

"Where will you go?"

"Does it really matter? Isn't the point finally being able to get rid of me?"

"Maya, you know I care about what happens to you."

"I understand that, but you clearly have a lot of unresolved issues to work out, and I think the only way you'll be able to do that is if I give you your space." I was rambling on, saying some shit I figured would be in a self-help book, knowing I didn't mean not one fucking word. There was no way I was exiting that palatial crib I was luxuriating in, no matter if I felt like a prisoner or not. This was all game, and at the moment I had no clue whether it was working in my favor or not. But fuck, desperate times call for desperate measures. You have to keep tossing shit out there until something sticks. And with the curve balls I was throwing, trust me, no matter how skilled Supreme was, he wouldn't be able to dodge them all.

Precious

During our flight to Philly, I basically slept the entire time. Getting rest had become an afterthought for me these last few months, and my body was now using any opportunity it could get to reenergize. And the sleep did do me some good, because instead going to the hotel, I was ready to handle business.

"How much longer until we get to the spot?" I asked Nico as he drove down what seemed to be back roads.

After our flight landed, he swooped up the rental car and we were off and running. Actually, we did have one interruption. Nico stopped and chatted with the chick, CoCo for a few, promising he would make time to see her, if only briefly before he left town. I could hear her swearing it was about business, like she needed to clarify that for my benefit.

"For the first stop, in a few more minutes."

"First stop?" I asked confused, since I only knew about one."

"Yeah, I gotta go get us some artillery. We can't be running up in places wit' no sort of backup. Baby girl, you of all people know how niggas be gettin' down in the streets. We can't take no chances."

"You know, I feel you on that. It's just that you didn't mention nothing, so I figured you didn't think we needed it. Are you skeptical about the dude we're supposed to meet with? I hope this tip is legitimate."

"Anytime a motherfucker is giving up info, I'm skeptical, so that's why we need to be prepared for anything. The shit is supposed to be legit, but it's hard to call it at this point. Supposedly this cat got information on Devon's whereabouts. And since he was the nigga working with Maya, I'm sure he's been in touch with her."

"No doubt, and I can't wait to take Devon's sheisty ass out. I gotta special bullet for him."

"Hold up! We need Devon to lead us to Maya, then we can talk about that bullet you got with his name on it."

"No worries, I'ma make sure we got no more use for him before I lullaby that ass."

"Stay right here, I'll be back in two seconds," Nico said, pulling up to some store. "I'ma run in real quick and get our shit. These my people around here, so you'll be straight. But if anything seems suspicious, blow the horn. There's always that one knucklehead that might try you," Nico grinned.

"I'm good."

As Nico ran up in the small corner store, I began thinking about the great pleasure I would take in shutting Devon the fuck down. When I first laid eyes on him, I knew he wasn't shit, but I slipped up and didn't follow my initial gut instincts. And what a costly mistake that was. The whole time he had partnered up with Maya to take me down. Every time I reflected back on what went down, I got more pissed with myself for not paying attention to key signs.

The biggest one was when Devon killed Vernika during my fight with her. He claimed he was trying to protect me, but in reality, he was protecting himself. She could have blown his cover, and he wasn't taking any chances. I remember how angry I was when she died, because it literally led to a dead end, but it was also what made me soften up to Devon because my dumb ass thought he had my back. Yeah, Devon definitely had to catch hell for tricking me up.

Just like Nico said, within a few seconds he was back. "A'ight, we good now, let's go," he said, closing the driver's door.

"Damn, they must've had that shit already bagged up for you."

"Pretty much. I hit 'em up at the airport, letting him know I was on the way. Here, this yours," he said, handing me my weapon of choice—a nine millimeter with a silencer already attached.

"Cool! I feel better already."

About ten minutes later, Nico pulled up to a brick building on an eerily quiet street. "We're here."

"Damn, ain't nobody out today," I commented.

"Mostly elderly people live on this block. They're probably all inside." I followed Nico as we walked up the stairs, and he rang the doorbell. After several seconds passed, he rang the doorbell again and knocked on the door.

"Is the dude expecting you?"

"So I thought."

"Have you spoken to him?"

"Nope, he ain't got no phone."

"Not even a cell? How old is this dude?"

"I don't know, but he was told we were coming. Oh, that might be him right there," Nico said, looking over my shoulder. I turned around and noticed a man getting out of a dollar cab. He gave the driver some money and started walking in our direction.

"What up? You must be Nico."

"Yeah, and you must be Curtis."

"Yep. I hope you ain't been waiting long. I got held up over at my job. I'm on parole, and I can't fuck around and miss work or they'll toss me back in jail. I'm sure you understand."

"No doubt."

"Cool. Well, let's go inside." The dude nodded his head at me as he brushed past me to open the door.

When we got inside, he led us down some stairs. He lived in a basement apartment. The building brought back memories of the projects I grew up in while living in Brooklyn. No matter how huge the mansions or fly the whips I pushed and the diamonds I rocked, the Brooklyn projects ran through my blood.

"So, I understand you got some information about Devon," I said, as soon as we got inside of dude's apartment and the door closed behind us. I wanted to get straight to the point, tired of constantly coming up empty.

"Yeah... umm... I ain't got nothing but some water and beer. Would you all like some?"

"No, we good," Nico let it be known, because he saw me slit my eyes, ready to cut up. "So, you got information for us?"

"I do," Curtis replied casually while popping open his beer before sitting down on a dingy vomit-brown colored sofa.

"Cool, so spill," Nico countered.

"Well, Devon used to do some work for my cousin who was from New York, before he got a fancy job working for some big time nigga in Beverly Hills." I knew dude had to be talking about Supreme.

"Has he still been in contact with him?" Nico further pried. I could tell that like me, he was ready for the nigga to get to the point.

"That's the thing. For months he didn't hear a peep outta dude. He figured shit was going real good for Devon, and my cousin was happy for him. Not me though. I always thought that nigga was a snake. He seemed real sneaky. Then, he used to make smart ass comments that my cousin got all the smarts and I was the dummy of the family, shit like that. I could tell he thought he was better than me, so I figured he got around all those fake ass Hollywood people and forgot where fuck he came from—you know, his homies back in the 'hood."

"Right," Nico nodded as if in agreement.

"But then, one day a few months ago, out of the blue, here comes Devon, calling my cousin saying he had got jammed up and needed some financial help. Because, you know, my cousin be making that major paper out in the streets. I used to make a little money myself before I got locked up. I used to be the..."

"Listen, we ain't got time to reminisce with you. Tell us what the fuck you know so we can bounce!" I spit, agitated with the nigga already.

"You have to excuse her. We had a long flight and she's a little restless."

I was vexed that Nico was making excuses for me, but I also understood why. But I can spot a full of shit clown, and this nigga sitting on the couch was one, with his crusty mouth, unkempt clothes and the long overdue haircut that was crying his name.

"I feel you. So, like I was saying, I used to be the man. Making money, living good, with countless women checking for me. You get locked up, come home with no bread, shit changes real quick."

I didn't know how much longer I could stand to listen to this broke man's sob story.

"But I'm sure your cousin is looking out for you," Nico said, playing into this nigga's foolishness.

"Look around this joint. Do it seem like he's looking out for me? Naw, he say that wit' me just gettin' out the joint and being on parole, I'm too hot to fuck wit'. He gives me a few bucks every once in a while, but he one of those niggas that's funny wit' his money. Always saying you got to earn your way in life. You know, like they can actually take it wit' 'em once they die."

"I feel you. Then the money I agreed to pay you should come in handy."

"Most definitely."

"Cool. I'm sure the dude that linked us up already told you that once you've fully cooperated and I make sure the information is legit, we good."

"Oh, it's legit. I promise you that."

"So, let's hear it."

"But... umm... the thing is, I think I'ma need a little bit more money than we originally agreed to."

"Here the fuck we go with this bullshit!" I huffed, knowing this clown was gon' be a problem.

"How much more money you talking about?" Nico asked him.

I wanted my hands on Devon more than anything, but I felt Nico was being way too soft with this clown. What if he was popping a bunch of lies? Maybe at one time his cousin knew where Devon was, but maybe he didn't know shit now, and dude was taking us for a ride.

"You tell me. For you to come all this way, the information must be pretty important to you."

"How about I double the money?"

"That number is sounding better," Curtis nodded, but from the expression on his face that still wasn't enough.

"How 'bout I triple it," Nico added.

"Fuck that!" I barked, jumping over the raggedy table in front of the couch Curtis was sitting on, while pulling out my heat at the same time. Before he had time to blink, my nine millimeter was pressed against his temple.

"Precious, calm the fuck down!" Nico yelled out.

"Nah, this nigga play too much! See, Nico is the patient one, I'm not. I will take you out this fuckin' world and not think nothin' of it." I really didn't want to blast this nigga just in case the information he had was on the up-and-up, but I couldn't let him know that. He had to believe that I would not think twice about laying his ass out unless he got to running his mouth.

"Man, you need to calm your girl down! She trippin!"

"I run this show! And if I say you gotta fuckin' go, then that's what it is!" I roared. The dude stared over at Nico with pleading eyes, but Nico just shrugged his shoulders and followed my program.

"You trippin, ma! I ain't mean no harm. I was gonna give you the information."

"Then stop running yo' mouth about bullshit and tell us what the fuck you know...now!"

Curtis swallowed hard before speaking. His body was trembling, so I knew he was shook and really believed I didn't give fuck about blowing his brains out.

"You gon' still give me the money though, right?" he finally said.

"Yeah, the fuckin' money you originally agreed to, you greedy motherfucker!" I said jamming the gun harder to his head.

"Devon is in Philly. He came back to do some work for my cousin.

'Cause like I told you, my cousin believes you got to earn your money. He ain't giving you shit."

"You got an address on him?" Nico asked.

"Yeah, it's written down on a piece of paper in my pocket."

"Stand up!" I ordered. "Which pocket?"

"The back one on the left hand side." I reached inside his pocket and pulled out the paper and handed it to Nico.

"Now can I get my money?"

"How do we know we can find him here?" Nico asked, looking up.

"I promise you it's good. But if I was you, I would catch him alone. My cousin surrounds himself with a lot of men that are paid to shoot first and ask questions later, Devon being one of them."

"Who is your cousin?"

"His name is Delondo, and right now he got most of Philly on lock. Just be careful, especially running around with this firecracker you got right here," he said, nudging his head in my direction.

"Nico, give this nigga his money so we can get the fuck outta here."

"Listen, if this shit turns out to be garbage, we will come back for you, and this time I'll let my girl have it her way," Nico stated before handing Curtis his dough.

"It's good, believe me."

"And don't go running your mouth letting anybody know what went down here," I added.

"Are you crazy? My cousin would have my ass! But I don't like Devon... never have, so I don't give a fuck what happens to him. His punk ass always thought he was better than me, but he had to come back begging my cousin for a job. That's what the nigga gets. He deserves whatever he got coming his way!"

I could have not agreed with that statement more. Devon was sitting almost right next to Maya on the loser totem pole.

"Devon here we come," I smiled, finally feeling we were making some real headway in our quest to find and destroy Maya.

Maya

Determined not to let Supreme call my bluff, I did exactly what I said I would—moved into one of the guest bedrooms. I really didn't have a choice. After our initial conversation in the car, I thought Supreme would make an effort to get closer to me, but he didn't change up shit. I was sleeping on one side of the bed, and him on the other. If I stayed, then he would believe I was just running off at the mouth and had no backbone to stick with what I threatened to do. So, a couple of days ago while he was out, I got my belongings together and moved to one of the bedrooms down the hall. When Supreme came home and realized what I did, even though he didn't say shit, I could tell he was surprised. I peeped him checking the closets to see if I had really taken everything, and motherfuckin' right, I did. I took it all, even down to the soap I liked to use.

He could act hardcore if he wanted to, but he would eventually miss me, if only because he no longer had a warm body next to him in bed. Hell, I missed him already, but this had to be done. *You gotta fuckin' do what you gotta do to get what you want.* I mean, isn't that what Precious would say? As much as I couldn't stand that bitch, I still found myself using her play book with every scam I tried to run, especially on a man—her man in particular.

As I started thinking about what my next move should be, the ringing of my cell phone distracted me. I looked to see who it was, and immediately recognized the number. "Hey, I've been waiting to hear from you. Any news?"

"Nothing on Precious, but I do have a lead on Devon."

"Where is he?"

"On the East Coast."

"Steve, can you be a little bit more specific?"

"I last tracked him in the Bronx, but I don't believe that's where he's residing. I think he was only visiting. By the time I found out where he was in the Bronx, he had already left, so I lost track of him."

"Yeah, he got family in the Bronx. He was probably visiting them. But fuck, he can be anywhere now!"

"I'm working on some leads. I've been asking some questions to the neighborhood people, but you know I don't want to scare them off because they think I'm the police or something."

"Whatever to that! With the money I'm paying you, I just want you to get an exact location on him, and let me know the minute you do."

"I will."

"And what's the hold up on Precious?"

"She must be staying on the move, because I can't get a lead on her for nothing."

Yeah, she's probably too busy looking for my ass to stay still, I thought to myself. "A'ight, just keep me posted," I said before ending the call.

I was putting the money I took from my brother after I killed him and burned the house down to good use. Once I was certain Precious was alive, I paid a pretty penny to have Steve track both Devon and Precious. I wanted to find them before they found me. The only downside was that Steve wasn't an assassin that I would have to handle personally. Although someone who could execute both was ideal, I didn't want to take a chance and get swindled by an undercover cop and end up in jail behind a murder plot. At this point in the game, I had to be very careful with every move I made, or all eyes would be on me.

Knock...knock...knock

"Come in."

"Hey, I have to run out for a couple of hours. Aaliyah is sleep, but can you watch her in case she wakes up?"

"No problem." *Now this motherfucker wants me to be his personal babysitter with no benefits! This some straight bullshit!*

"I appreciate that."

"I know you do. So go 'head, take your time, do what you need to do. I'll be here when Aaliyah wakes up," I smiled, trying to sound sincere. This was all about who could outwait who without snapping. But those who are patient usually win it all, and that's what I was counting on when it came to Supreme. He figured that since I wasn't getting no dick and moved to the guest bedroom, I would turn on him and not want to watch his prized daughter anymore. But no, I planned on doing the exact opposite. I mean, being a nurturing mother figure to Aaliyah after I had Precious chained up in a basement, was how I suckered Supreme in the first place. Shit, I was willing to take it back to the basics and start over again.

"Thanks, Maya," Supreme said, sounding surprised by my gracious behavior. Clearly my act worked. He left my bedroom, and I went over to the window and watched him make a call before he got into his car.

"I wonder who Supreme is calling. It's probably nothing," I thought out loud, but the curiosity was heavy on my mind.

I left my bedroom and decided to take advantage of being alone with only a sleeping baby to worry about. I went downstairs to Supreme's office, and of course it was locked. But unbeknownst to him, one afternoon while he was taking a long nap, I took the key and had a duplicate made. I even let Aaliyah tag along on my adventure to make sure she didn't disturb her daddy and wake him up before I finished doing what I needed to get done.

This would only be my second opportunity to use it, as I was hardly ever in the house alone. Supreme rarely went anywhere, and if he did, it was never long enough where I would feel comfortable doing some serious snooping.

When I opened the door, I headed straight for his mahogany desk. There were a lot of folders and a ton of paperwork, but it was mostly business contracts, legal correspondence—nothing I gave a fuck about. I continued to go through his drawers, being very careful to leave everything in place. Luckily, Supreme wasn't one of those anal types that had all his shit in perfect order.

Finally, something caught my eye, the reason being because it was bank documentation, but it wasn't in Supreme's name. It was some company called Direct Express Enterprises. There were a ton of large deposits being made, but the bizarre part was that they were all going to the same account, to a person by the name of Arnez Douglass. It was as if a dummy account was set up just to transfer money to this one individual. *Hmmm, who in the world is Arnez Douglass, and why is Supreme giving him all this fuckin' money?* I wrote the dude's name down and the address associated with his account on a post-it, because he was clearly somebody of importance if Supreme was hitting him off with this sort of cash. I checked around one last time to make sure everything was in place before leaving. After locking the door, I went back upstairs to my bedroom to make a call.

"Hey, Steve."

"You can't possibly think I have some new information for you already. I just got off the phone with you less than an hour ago."

"No, of course not. I need you to do something else for me."

"Is it pertaining to the case I'm already on?"

"No, it's something different."

"Different case, different money."

"Have you had any problems getting paid from me so far?"

"No, and I want to keep it that way."

"You worry about doing what I've hired you to do, and let me worry about the money. Are we clear?"

"We're clear. So, what do you need?"

"You have a pen?"

"Yep."

"Okay, write this name and address down," I said, speaking slowly and clearly so he wrote the shit down accurately.

"So, who is Arnez Douglass?'"

"That's what I'm going to pay you to find out."

"So, you know nothing about him?"

"Nope. How long is it going to take you?"

"Not sure, but give me at least a couple of days."

"I can do that. I'll be waiting."

When I got off the phone, I laid back on the bed and stared up at the soaring ceiling. I was now consumed with knowing everything I could about this Arnez guy. I had a feeling that whoever he was, Supreme would've preferred it if he remained a secret. But secrets are never safe with me, and I was determined to get to the bottom of it.

Precious

We had been by the spot Curtis gave us for a few days straight, and there was no sign of Devon. After the second day, I was ready to go back to Curtis' crib and stomp his ass, but Nico convinced me to make sure we had been conned before lashing out. So, by us staking out the location each day all day, we pretty much knew the routine of mail delivery.

On the fourth day, since we knew the mail person was a middle-aged woman, we decided to use Nico as bait. I hid in the car while he pretended to be going into the building where Devon supposedly lived. He turned on his charm and flirted with the mail lady. She ate that shit up. Nico convinced her that he was a family member who was now staying at the apartment, and he would be more than happy to take the mail. From what I could see, he didn't have to do too much convincing. She practically stuffed the mail down his shirt, along with her phone number. And to my surprise, Curtis had told the truth, because the mail was addressed to Devon. We figured Devon was out of town, either for business or personal, and we would have to wait it out.

"Yo, I was considering doing something, but I wanted to see how you felt about it first," Nico said, as we sat in the rental car across the street, watching Devon's crib.

"Ask me."

"I wanted to call CoCo and see if she knew any information on this Delondo cat, since Devon work for him. I mean, if he's supposed to be a major nigga in the drug game for Philly, and she's in the same business, maybe she can be helpful."

"Like instead of us sitting here every damn day twiddling our thumbs waiting for the fuck to show up, she may actually be able to tell us an exact day...helpful like that?"

"I don't know if she could tell us the day, but something. Maybe Devon got another spot he rests at that Curtis don't know nothing about. But what I do know is this Philly drug game is very cliquish, and everybody be watching how each clique moves."

"But you know mad people here. Ain't nobody else you can call besides CoCo that might have some useful info?"

"Yeah, I do know a lot of people here, but with CoCo I can trust she won't run off at the mouth, making announcements that I'm inquiring about homeboy."

"So, you trust her?"

"Are you jealous? Because you don't have any reason to be."

"Don't flatter yourself. I just want to have as few people in our shit as possible. But if you trust her, then make the call." And that's what he did. I could hear her through the phone, acting all extra ex-cited to hear from Nico. I had to admit that it *was* jealousy making me catch an attitude, because the chick hadn't did shit to me, and I couldn't stand her ass.

"That was a quick conversation. I guess she didn't know shit."

"It's not that. She wants us to talk in person. With her getting caught up in that fed shit and being locked up, she don't like to discuss nobody who is affiliated with the drug game on the phone."

"That's understandable. So, are we about to meet up with her now?"

"No, she's in the middle of some business at the moment. She said tonight would be better for her. But I know you're probably tired and could use the rest, so you don't have to come with me. I can handle it on my own."

"I'm good. We can go together. This a team effort, remember?"

"Of course, and you know I always enjoy your company. So, do you want to head back to the hotel, rest a little bit before we head out tonight?"

"That works for me."

When we got back to the hotel, I went in my room and took a long hot shower. I needed the time alone to try and clear my mind, if only for a few minutes. But instead of thinking about absolutely nothing, I wondered what Aaliyah was doing at the very moment, and if Supreme was holding her. I missed the two of them to the point that pain had almost become numb. It was as if my heart had built a shield around it, because if I actually continued to feel how much it ached, I would die from heartbreak.

What made it worse was that I knew Supreme had fucked Maya. I remember vividly how she rubbed it in my face. Devon held my body firmly while Maya beat the shit outta me with those brass knuckles, and taunted me about her getting dicked down by my husband. I could tell by the look in her eyes and the venom in her voice that it was true. I also knew that she didn't have his heart—which belonged to me and always would. But it didn't make it any easier to accept. But Supreme and I had been through so much, and this was another hurdle we would overcome together...or so I hoped.

But I wasn't naïve to the fact that a lot of damage had been done on both parts. He knew about my indiscretion with Nico, and with all the poison Maya had drenched on him, Supreme was probably convinced I was somewhere laid up with Nico right now, getting my fuck on. It would take all my strength and his to salvage our marriage, and with the more time that passed with us apart, the more worried I was becoming.

When I stepped out of the shower, the hot water hadn't washed away any of the burdens placed upon me. If anything, it made them worse. I stared at my reflection in the mirror and thought back to being held captive in that house, and the first time Mike let me take a shower. When I first saw my face again after all that time, it almost startled me. I barely recognized myself. Here I was again, feeling the same way, but this time for a different reason. No longer were my cheeks sunken, or dark circles around my eyes, or my complexion dull from being deprived of sunlight. In fact, many would say I was glowing and looked radiant due to my deep tan, courtesy of the hot summer weather. But I knew better. The fire in my eyes was slowly simmering out, and it was because everything I loved seemed to be slipping further out of my grasp.

Ring...ring...ring
"Hello."
"How long will it take you to get ready?"

"I thought you said we weren't meeting up with homegirl for at least a couple of hours."

"CoCo just called and said she wrapped up shit sooner than she anticipated and we could meet now."

"Give me thirty minutes," I said, ending the call. I wondered if CoCo was rushing Nico, thinking he was coming solo, or if she knew I would also be in attendance. Just in case she didn't, I decided to put on the only one cute dress I brought with me. All my other clothes were street gear, since none of my recent trips had been for pleasure. But I figured for emergency purposes, a woman should always come prepared with at least one sexy item, and this one was mine.

Exactly thirty minutes later, Nico came knocking on my door, and lucky for him, I was dressed and ready to go.

"Wow, you look incredible," were the first words out of his mouth when I opened the door. "For the last couple of months all I've seen you in is sweats and sneakers. I almost forgot how hot you are."

"Funny!"

"I'm joking. You know I love your casual around-the-way-girl look. But this is nice too. I hope you dressed up for my benefit."

"Let's go. We don't want to keep your friend, CoCo waiting."

When we pulled up to a restaurant in Center City, I was actually hungry, which was surprising to me since my appetite had been pretty much void lately. "This spot is cute, like they may have some good food in here."

"You're hungry?" I could understand why Nico sounded astounded.

"Yep! And trust me, you can't be more surprised than I am. So instead of dwelling on it, I'ma try to enjoy a fuckin' great ass meal. Hopefully they have a big juicy steak."

"Damn, you really are hungry. Good for you!" Nico laughed, playfully nudging me on our way into the restaurant.

When we got inside, there was a hostess greeting us with huge smile. "Welcome. Are there only two in your party?"

"Actually..."

"Nico, over here!" CoCo stood up, waving her hand before he finished his sentence, but now there was no need to. The hostess trailed behind us with two menus, and put them down on the table once we sat down.

After hugging up on Nico, CoCo turned her attention to me. "Precious, what a cute dress you're wearing."

"Thank you," I said, dryly.

"Nico, I'm glad you were able to meet up with me. I know this is supposed to be strictly about what's going on with you, but I couldn't help but try and take advantage of this time and discuss a little business."

"I wouldn't expect anything less from you, CoCo. If you didn't do that, I would say you were slipping."

"And you know that ain't happening. I'm always about my business. Speaking of business, here comes my partner now."

My back was towards the door so I couldn't see who her partner was, and honestly, I didn't fucking give a shit.

Nico might've not cared that she managed to turn this dinner into her own personal business meeting, but I wanted to reach across the table and slap the chick so hard it would knock out the two carat clear rocks adorning her ears."

"Nico, Precious, this is Genesis, my business partner.

The very first thought that popped into my head when my eyes landed on Genesis was God had truly been good to that man. He was unbelievably gorgeous. And trust me, I knew gorgeous men, because both Nico and Supreme were running strong in the race for the looks department. But the dude standing before me had something special that I had never witnessed in another man. I don't know if it was called swagger, the X-factor... but whatever it was, Genesis was winning the race with it hands down.

"It's a pleasure to meet you both. CoCo has spoken very highly of you, Nico," Genesis continued, as he shook Nico's hand. "I hope we'll be able to do business together."

"Same here."

"I apologize for running late, but I had to put my son to sleep. He's so stubborn," Genesis said, affectionately.

"No problem, we just got here ourselves," Nico let him know.

"How is my baby?" CoCo smiled, gazing lovingly into Genesis' eyes.

"You all have a child together?" That shit slipped out so quickly that I hoped it didn't come off as if I sounded surprised.

"No, but I always refer to Amir as my baby."

"Truth is, you have become like a mother to him since the day he was born," Genesis stated as he gently touched CoCo's hand.

There were so many questions running through my head, mainly like; where was the child's birth mother? Because there was no way in the world any sane woman would leave a man like him. But that was none of my motherfuckin' business, so I opted to keep my mouth shut.

"Thank you. You know I love him like he was my own." I was trying to get a read on their relationship but it was tricky. I couldn't tell if they were fucking or if the closest CoCo had gotten was only making love to Genesis in her mind.

"That's a beautiful thing, CoCo. It's nice hearing about this motherly side of you. Normally with you, it's straight business, but I see you got a sensitive side for the babies," Nico teased.

"Enough of this. Let's get back to business," CoCo slightly giggled. "So, before we discuss the proposal we have about our shit, let's discuss what you need to know."

"Ms. Armstrong, will you be having your customary bottle of champagne for the table?" the waiter asked, interrupting my curiosity of needing to know if CoCo and Genesis relationship was platonic or not.

"Yes, unless the two of you would like something else instead."

"Champagne is fine with me. How about you, Precious?"

"It's fine with me too."

"Wonderful. I'll be back shortly with your champagne and to take your orders."

"Thank you, Roberto."

"My pleasure, Ms. Armstrong."

"Now, back to you," CoCo said, directing her attention back to Nico. "You wanted to get some information on Delondo."

"I really needed some information on someone who works for Delondo. His name is Devon."

"I can easily find out that information for you. Delondo is a major player out here. One of his lieutenants is actually very cool with one of our top workers. We're considering merging on some business together, but details haven't been worked out."

"Well, I'ma be straight up with you. I have no beef with the dude Delondo, but the nigga, Devon is a problem that needs to be taken care of. I'm letting you know in case that will jeopardize whatever you're trying to make happen over there."

"No, I can't see that being a problem. The nigga, Devon can't be an important member of his team, because I haven't heard of him. Have you, Genesis?"

"No, I haven't."

"If you don't mind me asking, why is finding this Devon person so important?" CoCo inquired.

"Because we're looking for a young lady named Maya Owens, and Devon might be able to help us locate her."

"Maya Owens," Genesis said, with a hint of interest in his voice.

"Yes, do you know her?" I directed my question right at Genesis, locking eyes with him.

"No, I don't."

Without skipping a beat, Nico continued on, and CoCo was giving him her full attention, but Genesis, not so much. He had now become lost in his own thoughts, and I knew it was because he was lying. He did know a Maya, and I had a strong feeling it was the same Maya we were looking for.

"Excuse me for one second, I have to make a phone call," I heard Genesis whisper to CoCo before excusing himself from the table. The two of them were so enthralled in their conversation that when I told Nico that I had to use the restroom, he smiled at me, nodded his head, and kept talking.

I couldn't get out my seat fast enough. I made a direct beeline to Genesis, who was in the corner of the hallway trying to have a discreet conversation. His back was facing away from me, so I tried to sneak and see if I could hear anything he was saying, but dude was talking too low. He kept the call short, and when he was done, I made my move.

"Genesis, how do you know Maya?" I kept my tone even and firm.

"I told you, I don't know a Maya. Now, if you'll excuse me..."

I shifted my body, positioning it so that I almost had him boxed in. "I know you don't give a damn about me."

"I don't even know you."

"Exactly. That's why I know you don't give a damn... and it's cool. But what's not cool is if you don't tell me what you know about Maya. Her treacherous ass is with my husband and my daughter, and I need to find them before it's too late."

"I don't understand."

"What the fuck don't you understand? Your little son that you were just gushing over a few minutes ago, well that's how the fuck I feel about my own daughter! And Maya has schemed to the lowest level to keep me away from her and Supreme. Now, if you have some information that can get me back to my family, then you need to tell me."

"So you're Supreme's wife."

"That's right, I am."

"Precious Cummings—excuse me—I mean Precious Mills. It's nice to finally place the name with the face."

Maya

As I lounged by the pool in my taupe suede string bikini, which was clearly made to prance around in and not for swimming purposes, I wondered how long it would take to catch Supreme's attention. I had lathered my body in baby oil so my skin was glistening. At first, I was even going to put on some open-toe stilettos, but felt that would make this entire setup too obvious. But trying to seduce him in this scorching heat was starting to get the best of me. But I had no other way to pull this shit off. I couldn't walk around the house butt-ass-naked. That would surely send the "desperate" bells ringing. Lounging by the pool on a hot summer afternoon was very conceivable, even if I didn't know how to swim.

As the time kept ticking away, Supreme was nowhere to be seen. Luckily I had brought out plenty bottles of water to make this situation not so unbearable. But the more the heat beat down on me, the rawer my nerves became. *Where the fuck is this nigga at? I know he took Aaliyah out for breakfast, but that was hours ago. He play too much. Don't he know I got a seduction going on today?*

As I became more and more frustrated, I got jarred out my thoughts by the sound of my cell phone ringing.

"Hello," I answered without even checking to see who was calling. I knew that only a handful of people had my new number after getting rid of the old one, which of course was done mainly to dodge Devon's ass.

"I have good news and great news. Which one would you like first?"

"Good news."

"The good news is that I found out some interesting information about Arnez Douglass. Not to get into your personal business, but if he's someone you're interested in dating, stay the hell away from him."

"Why?"

"He's a drug lord and a dangerous one at that; although I've never heard of a harmless drug lord."

My P.I. was borderline corny. So I gave him a pass. He didn't understand that words like 'drug lord' and 'dangerous' equaled intriguing to a bitch like me. "Continue."

"His operations used to be based in Atlanta, but for the past year he's been operating out of Philadelphia, which leads me to the great news."

"I'm waiting."

"That is where Devon is now living...in Philadelphia."

"Really?"

"Yes *and*," he stressed. "I have an address on him."

"Steve, I'm very pleased with you today," I admitted in almost a singing tone.

"I knew you would be. It might take me some time, but I'm very thorough and I always come through."

"Yes, you do."

"So what's my next move?"

"You stay there and keep an eye on Devon until I'm able to come."

"So, you're coming to Philadelphia?"

"Exactly. I'm on the first flight out tomorrow. I'll let you know where to meet me so I can get the address from you and pay you your money."

"Sounds like a worthwhile trip to me."

"I figured you'd say that. I'll be in touch." Right when I was about to rejoice on the good news from Steve, Supreme finally decided to bring his ass home.

"I see you're doing some sunbathing."

"Yep, you know they say the sun energizes you."

"Oh, I thought it just made you sweat." I sensed some sarcasm in his voice, but chose to ignore it.

"So, where's Aaliyah? I missed her today," I lied, but it sounded good.

"Sleep. After we went to eat, I took her to the park and she's exhausted."

"I'm sure she loved spending time with her daddy. She always does."

"Yeah, being with her makes everything feel right."

For a brief moment, I almost felt guilty for being so jealous of Supreme's relationship with his daughter. It was obvious the nigga truly adored her, but instead of feeling happy for him, it made me disgusted. I mean damn, why couldn't I have grown up with a daddy that gave a fuck about me? Shit, growing up, my daddy wasn't even around. I had to count on Mike to fill them shoes, and he did a poor motherfucking job at it. He was too busy hustling in the streets to give a damn about me. All he would toss my way is some cash. *Life is so fuckin' unfair,* I thought.

"I'm sure children do that for you. Hopefully, one day I'll have some of my own and I can experience it for myself."

"It'll happen for you."

Yeah, motherfucker, if you would just get with the program and give me some dick! You're the hold up with the process, not me!

"I think so too, but not right now. I have so much more I need to accomplish." I threw that at the nigga to put him at ease. If I told him I was looking to become "sperminated" immediately, he probably wouldn't even breathe in my direction again.

"That's a good idea. You're young, and you should experience a lot more before settling down with a child."

"My sentiments exactly." I smiled and turned over on my stomach so my plump ass was smacking dude in his face.

"So, what's up with you tonight?"

I could see Supreme trying his damnedest to look in every direction but the flesh of my oil downed glistening butt. "Packing."

"You're going on a trip." He raised one of his eyebrows. I wasn't sure if it was out of surprise, or from disappointment.

"I wouldn't call it a trip. My mom called me. She didn't sound too good. I think maybe she's lonely, so I told her I would come visit."

"How long are you gonna be gone?"

"A few days, unless you want me to stay longer?"

"No, I was just curious. I think it's good you're going to spend some time with your mother. I know your relationship with her has never been good. It's never too late to change that."

"True. I guess this trip will let me see if that's possible."

"So, when are you leaving?"

"Tomorrow morning."

"That soon?"

"If I didn't know better, I would think you were going to miss me." I was a tad flirty with my delivery to give Supreme and easy opening to reciprocate if he so desired.

"It's nice having you around...I mean, you really help me out a lot with Aaliyah."

Oh, so now this motherfucker mad because his live in babysitter is going out of town. Listen to this bullshit right here! Niggas!

"I'ma miss her. Aaliyah is a wonderful little girl. I'll have to keep my trip brief if only because I'll miss her so much." Right when Supreme was parting his lips to respond, I glided my body in an awkward way so one of my nipples slipped out my bikini top. "Is something wrong?" I asked innocently, pretending I hadn't even noticed I was giving Supreme a mouthful view of by right tit.

"No, I'm good. I have business to attend, so I'ma leave you to your sunbathing."

"Okay, I'll talk to you later on." *That's right, baby, hurry away so you don't give into temptation and tap this ass. But run all you want. Eventually I'll catch you out there slipping, and when that happens, you'll at least have to put up with me for a minimum of eighteen years.* The very idea of that put the biggest smile on my face.

When I arrived in Philadelphia, I had two missions: kill Devon, and meet Arnez Douglass. I wanted to know why Supreme was filtering all that cash to a drug dealer. *Were they in business together? If so, was it drug related? And why would Supreme feel the need to do that, because he's making a shit load of money in the music industry...or at least I assumed but then again with some people they can never make enough paper*, I thought to myself as I tried to figure all the shit out.

I was becoming impatient waiting for Steve at some raggedy ass diner. I was ready to find Devon, kill him, and then spend the rest of my trip finding out what the connection was between Supreme and Arnez.

"Can I get you anything else?" the waitress asked, smacking way too hard on her gum.

I really wanted to say, 'Just you staying the fuck out my face,' but instead I said, "Another Coke." I didn't need to bring any unnecessary attention to myself, and cussing out the waitress would do exactly that. A few seconds later, Steve walked in, and I was damn happy to see him because I was ready to go.

"Sorry I'm late, but I got lost looking for this place," he explained as soon as he sat down.

"That's why I picked it because it's hard to find."

"I get it."

"I figured you would, since trying to locate people is supposed to be your specialty."

"And it is," he said, sliding a piece a paper across the table.

"I take it this is the address I need."

"Indeed."

"Did you also dig a little deeper on that other information I asked you for?"

"I don't know why you're interested in this man. I told you he is a ruthless criminal. If anything, you should be trying to stay away, not get closer. I don't understand the logic behind that."

"That's not your concern. I have my reasons. Now, what did you find out?"

"From my understanding, when he's in town he dines every day at a restaurant called Lacroix at the Rittenhouse Hotel. So much so, that he even has a certain table he always sits at."

"Interesting. What else?"

"He has a condo at the Murano in Center City."

"Is he in town now?"

"As of yesterday he was, because he had lunch at the Lacroix."

"And you know this because?"

"I paid one of the waiters that works there a nice piece of change that you're going to reimburse me for, to inform me when he came."

"He could've been lying."

"No, because once he called, I went to the location to confirm."

"What sort of confirmation?"

"See for yourself." Steve handed me a 9x12 envelope.

"So, this is what Arnez Douglass looks like. Not bad...not bad at all," I said, staring at the photos of him leaving the restaurant. "Who is that man with him?"

"His bodyguard. The waiter said he never leaves his side. From what I understand, a few months ago his other bodyguard was killed."

"Do you know what happened?"

"The car blew up, actually near this restaurant. The food must be awfully good for him to still go back," Steve remarked sarcastically.

"This is getting more interesting by the minute. So, I'm assuming this is the best place to run into Mr. Douglass?"

"After what I just told you, you still want to make contact with this man?"

"I'm sorry, maybe I need to check my birth certificate, but I don't remember you being my father. So, moving on, answer my question."

"The waiter said he's supposed to be there tomorrow for lunch at noon. I told him to call me the moment he arrives."

"Perfect! So then you call and give me the heads up. Now, what about Precious?"

"No luck," he confessed, shrugging his shoulders. Why is it so important for you to find Devon and Precious?"

"Do you always ask your clients this many questions?"

"Only the ones that pique my interest."

"And why do I interest you so much?"

"For one, you have to be the youngest client I've ever had, and I don't even understand how you can afford me."

I'm so happy I gave this nosey motherfucker a bunch of fake information, because he would probably investigate me too, if he hasn't already. He can try to pull up some shit on that fake name I gave him if he wants to, but he'll come up empty.

"So, are you going to answer my question or not?"

"You mean about why I'm looking for those two people?" Steve nodded his head. "They were very close friends of my brother, but somehow they lost touch. Before he died, he asked me to find them because he left them both something that was very meaningful to him."

"I see."

"The least I can do is fulfill his dying request. Especially since it's his money that's paying for it."

"What do you mean?"

"Our parents died years ago, and he had no other family, so I was the sole beneficiary of his insurance policy."

"I think it's admirable that you're carrying out your brother's wishes, but with whatever money you have left, I hope you're being careful and not letting it go to waste."

"I promise you, I'm putting his money to very good use. He would be proud."

Precious

"I don't give a damn what that motherfucker says, Genesis has some information on Maya!"

"Precious, ever since we left that restaurant the other night, you've been saying this same shit. And my questions to you are the same; how would Genesis know Maya? And if he did, why would he try to hide it?"

"If I knew the answers to those questions, we wouldn't be having this conversation right now!" I barked, sick of Nico not siding with me on this.

"Why is it so hard for you to believe that I'm right, and this nigga, Genesis is full of shit?"

"Because I don't get that impression of dude. He seems legit, like he's cool people."

"Cool people my ass! Don't let all that swagger fool you, he's hiding some shit."

"So, you think he got swagger?" Nico glanced over at me and asked as he turned the corner headed towards Devon's crib. He got word from CoCo that Devon was due back in town any day now, so we decided to do some drive-bys until his ass popped up.

"I'm not even going there with you," I said, slitting my eyes.

"Going where? You made the comment."

"It ain't even worth expanding on. All I know is the nigga is lying, and I want to know why."

"Well, baby girl, if he is lying, which I personally don't believe, we have no way of finding out the truth. We have to keep our money on Devon knowing where Maya is."

"That's another thing."

"What?"

"Don't you think it's strange that Devon is in Philly working for this nigga, Delondo?"

"Maybe he and Maya thought they should keep some distance between them until shit cooled down. I mean, they killed Mike, and I know by now they know you didn't die in that fire. They're probably nervous. I know if it was me, that's what I would do."

"True."

As we sat across the street from Devon's apartment, I thought about all the players in this game. And I didn't give a fuck what Nico said, in my book, Genesis was now officially one of them. But what drove me crazy about him was that I couldn't figure out how he fit in. I wondered if he had been cool with Mike, but I never heard him mentioned, and Genesis wasn't a name you would forget. The not knowing was making my brain itch.

"I hope you ain't still thinking about that Genesis shit," Nico commented, knowing me all too well.

"No, I'm not."

"Stop lying. Precious. This is Nico you're talking to."

"I know who the fuck you are."

"Then admit I'm right...come on now."

"I'm not admitting shit, and stop harassing me and answer your phone," I said, punching his arm.

"I ain't done wit' you," he huffed before taking the call.

While Nico was on the phone, I continued playfully punching his arm and making faces, until I realized the shift in his tone. It suddenly turned serious. "What's wrong?" I immediately asked when he got off.

"That was Ricky."

"Is he okay?"

"He's fine. It's Ms. Duncan...she died a few days ago."

"What! What happened?"

"She had cancer."

"I didn't even know she was sick."

"Neither did her brother. He said supposedly she got diagnosed about a month ago, and by the time she found out, it had already spread."

"I can't believe Ms. Duncan is dead."

"Ricky tried to call you, but of course the number he had ain't good no more. That's why he called me, so I could let you know. They're going to put her to rest this Friday."

"I wanna go to her funeral. That woman did so much for me. I have to pay my respects and tell her goodbye."

"Say no more. We'll go. By the time we get back, Devon will fo' sure be in Philly, and we'll handle him then."

As I stood at the same cemetery where my mother was buried, watching Ms. Duncan's coffin being lowered into the ground, I couldn't help but think of how unfair life could be. Ms. Duncan was one of the kindest people I had ever met, yet she was dead, and a lowdown trick like Maya was running around, free as a bird, wrecking peoples' lives. There was no rationale in that.

"Precious, I'm so glad you came," Ricky said, giving me a hug.

"Of course I came. You know how much your sister meant to me."

"And you meant a great deal to her too. She loved you, and she was so proud of you."

"I don't know why. I haven't lived my life in the most Godly way."

"Let he who is without sin cast the first stone. And that's nobody. My sister knew and understood that, and lived her life accordingly. I'll tell you again. She was so proud of you, Precious."

"Thank you, Ricky."

"You have nothing to thank me for. But I would like for you to do something for me."

"What is it?"

"Before you leave New York, stop by her house. She left something for you."

"Okay, I will."

"Good."

"Did you see where Nico went?"

"Yes, he's right over there," Ricky said, pointing towards a tree behind me a few feet away.

"Thanks, but I'll definitely see you before we leave," I said, giving Ricky a hug goodbye.

Being at the cemetery where both my mother and Ms. Duncan were buried flooded me with sadness. I wanted to leave and escape the pain, because all I kept thinking about was Aaliyah and her losing me like I had lost the two most important women in my life.

"Nico, I'm ready to go." I could see he was in the middle of a conversation with someone, but I didn't care.

"Can you give me a few minutes?"

"No, I want to leave now."

"Babe, I know this is hard for you. Just give me a couple minutes." Nico lifted up my chin gently, and it was hard to deny his request. In his eyes, I could see he felt my pain.

"You must've been very close to her," I heard the man say who had been talking to Nico. His back was facing me when I walked up, so I hadn't paid him any attention... until now.

"Excuse me?" The attitude and annoyance was obvious in my voice because I didn't try to hide it. For the life of me, I couldn't understand why this nobody was inviting himself into my personal space. Just because he had been speaking with Nico didn't give him the right to talk to me.

"There's no need to get upset," Nico said, placing his hands on my shoulders as if to massage my frustrations away and diffuse the hostility.

"It's understandable you would be upset. She was a wonderful woman," the man continued, trying to force me into some dialogue. I turned to face the man for the first time, that's when he extended his hand and said, "I apologize. I should introduce myself. I'm Quentin Jacobs."

I shook his hand, and I instantly remembered meeting him at the house where Mike had held me hostage, and I couldn't help but wonder if he remembered me too.

"Growing up, we all looked up to Quentin, and we still do," Nico grinned. "That was rude of me. I should've introduced you. Quentin, this is Precious Mills."

I quickly freed my hand from the man's grasp, but he wasn't deterred. "Precious, how did you know Ms. Duncan?"

"She used to take care of me when I was a little girl."

"Really, I knew all the little girls Ms. Duncan used to take care of, and I don't remember a Precious Mills."

"What about Precious Cummings? That was her name before she got married," Nico informed Quentin, clearly in awe of him.

"No, that name doesn't sound familiar either."

"Then I guess you didn't know all the kids Ms. Duncan took care of after all. Now if you'll excuse me... Nico, I'll be waiting for you in the car."

For some reason, I had a strong urge to rush off and get away from that man from the very first time I met him. And even now he had this way of getting under my skin. I didn't know if it was due to the arrogance he exuded, or because it disgusted me how Mike, who had been at the top of his game at one time before he died, and Nico, who many considered to be a legend in the streets, was dick riding this nigga so hard. Whatever it was, I didn't want any parts of it.

"Did you have to be so cold to him?" Nico questioned when he got in the car.

"Cold to who?" I asked, pretending not to have a clue as to what he was talking about.

"Stop with the games, Precious. Why did you have to be so disrespectful to Quentin? That cat is a straight up Godfather in this game. The respect he garners extends from the East to West Coast, trust me on that."

"I don't give a damn. Remember I told you that he came to visit Mike when I was being held hostage?"

Nico was quiet for a minute, as if thinking back to the conversation. "I do remember you mentioning something about that."

"Yeah, he didn't even acknowledge that shit."

"That was months ago, and it was only briefly. He probably doesn't remember that shit."

"You mean the same way Genesis doesn't know who Maya is."

"There you go on that Genesis shit again. I'm convinced this Maya situation has made you paranoid. Everybody you meet is either lying or trying to manipulate you now. Pretty soon, you gon' be saying I'm the enemy."

"Just forget it. I'm the crazy paranoid bitch...fine." I shrugged my shoulders, not even wanting to discuss the shit any further.

"Who the fuck is this?" Nico mumbled before answering his cell. "Hello...damn...thanks for letting me know."

"What happened?"

"Another headache. We need to get back to Philly...now!"

Maya

When I checked into my Chairman Suite at the Rittenhouse Hotel, I walked into the marble bathroom, and wondered whether I should take a long bubble bath in the oversized Jacuzzi, or drench myself in the separate shower with massage head. I chose a hot bath, mainly because I wanted to rest my feet. I had been hammering the downtown Philly boutiques all day in my quest to find the perfect outfit to lure Arnez with. I knew the shit wouldn't be easy. The nigga was clearly a seasoned hustler and probably was apprehensive about what chicks he fucked with, so I had to be careful with my attire and approach.

After soaking in the tub for what seemed like at least an hour, I slipped on the plush bathrobe and slippers that the hotel provided, then stood in front of the huge window with a city view. It was amazing how hot Philly looked at night with all the lights shining brightly. I continued to take in the scene and thought how relieved I was to have additional time to plan my shit out.

Originally, Arnez was supposed to have lunch at the Lacroix, but then at the last minute the waiter called Steve to let him know that Arnez's bodyguard had cancelled, and wanted to make sure that his regular table would be available for dinner instead. With that happening, it allowed me preparation time I desperately needed, because I always heard that the first impression was the lasting one.

That's why I felt I could make no real headway with Supreme, because he didn't see me as a bona fide woman. He remembered me as Precious' little play sister and Clip's girlfriend. No matter how good I sucked and rode his dick, I wasn't grown and sexy; just a little girl trying to play dress-up. But I refused to give up on my quest to have Supreme as my man, and maybe forging a relationship with Arnez could smooth the progress of that.

I pulled out the Fiesta Red one-shoulder dress I had purchased earlier today. After hours of coming up short, I was ready to give up my search until I hit gold. It was dangling smack in the middle of the high-end Italian boutique's store window. I instantly thought about Precious and the time she said, "If you want to fuck a nigga without giving him no pussy, strut around in his face with a bad ass red dress and he'll do anything to get a taste." I need that shit to work for me tonight.

As I slipped on the dress and the four-inch heels that further accentuated every curve in my body, I thought about how proud Precious would be of me. It was the exact sort of attire she would approve of: giving you the goods without exploiting the goods. As I turned around in the mirror admiring the excellent choice I made, I heard my cell ringing. "What's up, Steve?"

"I hope you're not too far away, because Arnez just got to the restaurant."

"I'm very close. I'm staying at the hotel where the restaurant is at."

"Aren't you a smart girl!"

"I like to think so. So, the waiter is expecting me and will make sure I get a seat near Arnez, correct?"

"Indeed. He is expecting you. He wanted me to ask you what you'll be wearing and how long before you show up."

"He won't be able to miss me. I'll be in a red dress. Tell him I'll be there in fifteen minutes."

"Will do...and be careful."

"Don't worry about me, I'll be perfectly fine. Now, call the waiter and let him know to be looking out for me shortly."

After touching up my makeup and scrutinizing my entire look a few more times to the point that I knew it out. I strolled down the hallway towards the elevator and noticed a room door slightly open, but nobody came out so I kept on my way, not thinking too much of it. When I turned the corner, I heard a door slam shut. The sound of keys dangling let me know how much closer the person was getting. I hit the down button on the elevator again, because for some reason I was getting an uneasy feeling.

When the elevator door opened, I damn near leaped inside. There was a middle aged Asian couple looking at me bizarrely, and they practically jumped to the other side trying to get as far away from me as possible. I couldn't front, my entire vibe was giving off a cra-zy-chick-up-to-no-good, especially when I diligently kept pushing the button to close the door.

Right when I moved back to the corner to breathe a sigh of relief because the elevator was almost completely shut, a huge hand with long thick fingers latched on to the steel which caused the doors to open right back up. I swallowed hard, about to break out in a sweat. I didn't understand why I was tripping so hard, but the pouncing in my stomach indicating to me that shit was off wouldn't stop.

Oh shit! Maybe Devon's worthless ass got hip to me being in Philly and 'bout to take my ass out right here on this elevator with these Asian motherfuckers watching. Damn, it's gon' be a massacre, 'cause he gon' get ya' too. I started feeling inside my purse. *Oh shit, I ain't even got no heat on me! I'm fucked! Damn, maybe I can grab one of they asses and use them for a shield. Fuck that! I ain't going out like this. This nigga gon' have to come harder than this.*

All this shit was running around in my head, and I was about to snatch the Asian lady since she was the closest to me, but then I caught his face and the fear vanished. The nigga was clean; I mean I'm talking custom designer shit that I wouldn't even know the brand of. It seemed to be tailored to fit his physique, and *his* only. He was in all black, but the richness of the fabric even had the Asian folks sizing him up, like who the fuck is this Negro? Then I caught the blinged out pinky ring. The shit was flashy but classy, and you wouldn't think a ring that big with so many diamonds could be described that way.

When the elevator door opened, I was strongly considering di-verting my original plan to seduce Arnez, to get at dude instead. The nigga was so on point that I started thinking about any celebrities I had seen that he might be, but I couldn't think of any, and his hotness superseded theirs anyway. He exuded confidence, which took his sex-iness even higher up on the radar. What also intrigued me was that even in my red dress, dude wasn't paying me no mind. It was like he had an agenda, and sniffing after some pussy wasn't on it. I knew I had business to tend to, but was drawn to this man. It was as if I had to know what the fuck he was up to. As I tried to stay out of view but watched his movements, there was something dangerous about his aura too. That also had me open.

I diverted towards the front desk area to make it look as if I was off his trail, and once he went outside to the front, I quickly went to the glass opening to be nosey. There were three black Yukon's parked behind each other. The mystery man first stopped at the last truck, and the passenger window rolled down. A few words were exchanged, and then the window rolled back up. Then he went to the next truck, and the same exact thing occurred. He finally went to the truck parked in front. A big burly dude stepped out and opened the back door for the mystery man. He got in, and then all three trucks drove off.

I wasn't a psychic, but some shit seemed terribly off to me. That pouncing in the pit of my stomach hadn't left, but I decided there wasn't shit I could do about it, so I continued on to what brought me out to this motherfucker in the first place.

When I entered the restaurant, like I knew it would and should be all eyes were on me. Even the old undercover KKK type mother-fuckers were drooling at the mouth, causing their knifed up elderly wives to curl up their lips in disgust.

Right when the hostess was making her way over to greet me, the waiter, who I assumed Steve had put on the payroll, cut in. "Amanda, she'll be dining in my section. I'll seat her," he said, taking the menu from her hand. She gave him a confused stare, but didn't put up a fuss. I gave her a pleasant smile and followed him. "You were supposed to be here fifteen minutes ago," he said, in a lecturing whisper.

"I got a little held up."

"You're lucky we're not swamped tonight or I wouldn't have been able to hold your table." He had somewhat of a diva attitude with him, but I let it slide since his services were needed.

"Sorry, but I'll make sure to leave you a good tip. How 'bout that?" He gave me a gracious smile, so I guess all was good now.

"One table over to your left." He winked, then followed with a, "What can I get you to drink?"

"Bottled water will be fine." I wanted liquor, but I needed to feel the situation out first. It didn't take much to give me a buzz, and I wasn't sure how much work I had to put in to get Arnez's attention.

I looked over at the table the waiter informed me about, and saw Arnez sitting there, having an intense conversation with another gentle-man. I then noticed a man standing behind him who I recognized from the pictures Steve showed me as being his bodyguard. I wasn't quite sure how I was going to pull this shit off. He came across just like the man on the elevator; too much business on his mind to think about sniffing after some pussy. The red dress I was rockin' wasn't going to be a powerful enough tool. I needed to be butt-ass naked to pull this shit off.

I ordered some food that I knew I wasn't going to be able to eat, not because I wasn't starving, but figuring out how to maneuver this shit was consuming too much of my energy to devour any food. As the time ran away, I was coming up short.

I went to the bathroom twice, switching my ass slowly hoping to get a glimmer of his attention, but got nothing. The bodyguard was so in tuned to watching over his boss that he didn't even glance in my direction. A bitch was stuck.

Once my dinner came, I used the fork to play with my food, wishing for a miracle to fall in my lap, but death seemed to land instead. As my mind was wandering about, my eyes fell upon a familiar face. Devon had just entered the restaurant, dressed in all black, and I knew he had come gunning for me. *How did this motherfucker know I was here? Maybe the dude on the elevator really was after me, but was playing it cool so I wouldn't get suspicious. Oh shit, I can't believe it! I have to get the hell out this place, now! There has to be a back way out!*

I turned my face away, hoping that Devon had not yet noticed where I was sitting. At the same time, I was searching for my waiter so he could tell me how to get the fuck outta here. My hands and legs were shaking so badly that my knees were knocking up against the bottom of the table. I didn't see my waiter anywhere, and I didn't know what the fuck to do. I didn't have a weapon on me, so I grabbed at the knife on the table but quickly dropped it, knowing it wouldn't do shit for my cause. My brain was spinning, determined to come up with a plan, and I decided precisely what my next move would be.

I grabbed my purse and slid from my chair, and walked directly up to Arnez's table. His bodyguard moved forward, and Arnez put his hand up as if telling him it was okay. "Yes?" Was the only word he spoke in a calm but firm voice. The man sitting across from him looked up at me, and then back at Arnez.

"Don't make it obvious, but the man standing near the entrance dressed in all black is here to kill you."

"How do you know?"

"Because when I went to the bathroom, I overheard a gentleman on the phone giving a description of a man that needed to be taken out. I didn't realize he was talking about you until I sat down and looked over at your table. You've been warned."

Arnez immediately tapped his bodyguard and nodded his head as if directing him to look forward. From where he was sitting, his view was somewhat obscured, and I guess he needed someone he trusted to legitimize what I said. I slightly turned my head to see if Devon was still standing in the same spot, but to my horror he was coming in my direction, and right beside him was the big burly man who opened the car door for the mystery man I saw on the elevator. *Damn! That nigga brought backup so just in case he missed, somebody else would finish the job. Were the rest of those motherfuckers in them trucks here for me too? Oh shit, I'm fucked!*

As I saw them getting closer, I turned back around to Arnez, and that's when I caught his bodyguard pulling out his metal. At that moment I hit the floor, because I knew in only a matter of seconds it would be on and poppin'.

Less than two seconds after I hit the floor, the man that was dining with Arnez followed my lead, but he was one second late. The bullets I was sure were meant for me caught him instead. His hand was grabbing onto the back of my ankle, and I had to kick my leg to get free as I hauled ass, trying to make an escape. The entire restaurant was in an uproar, as they couldn't believe 'hood violence had made its way to their elite establishment.

The chaos persisted as all the patrons and staff were bolting towards the same exit while trying to dodge bullets. I refused to stand up, preferring to crawl fast and try to stay unnoticed, which I knew would be difficult in a bright ass red dress. I observed a bunch of staff rushing towards the kitchen, so I knew there had to be an exit that way, so I crawled as quickly as I could in that direction. When I made it out, I could hear the mayhem continuing, but my life was still intact and that was all that mattered. So what if innocent people had to die so I could live? It was them or me, and I chose them.

Unsure whether Devon and his people knew what room I was in, I decided not to take a chance and go back inside the hotel. Instead, I ran to the parking garage where my rental car was. I drove slowly around the corner, wanting to see if the cops had made their way to shut shit down, or whether the shootout was still in effect. As I drove closer, I could see that they were already beginning to lock the street down.

While in the process of making a U-turn, from my rearview mirror I could see what looked to be Arnez running down a back street. I figured that the nigga was dead, but since he was still alive, I decided to use it to my advantage. I sped down the street to catch up with him, and the car screeched loudly as I pressed down on the brakes pulling up beside him. He was visibly shaken until I rolled down the window and showed my face. "Get in!" I said, unlocking the door.

At first Arnez hesitated, but then looked back and saw all the police going down the street. I figured after weighing his options, he decided to ride with me.

Precious

The entire ride back to Philly, I kept wondering what the fuck could've happened that we had to leave Brooklyn ASAP. All I knew was that CoCo had placed a call to Nico, but because she was so paranoid about saying certain shit on the phone, she wouldn't give him any details. The most he got out of her was that there had been some major drama, and we needed to come back now.

Before even going back to our hotel, Nico went to a warehouse CoCo told him to meet her at. When we pulled up, I only saw a white Range Rover, which I assumed belonged to her.

Once inside, the huge warehouse had millions of dollars worth of weapons and drugs. *This chick must really trust Nico to bring him here.*

"I hope you didn't have any trouble finding the spot," CoCo said, when she came walking out from a back room.

"No, your directions were on point. So, what the fuck is going on?"

"I know that shit must've been irking the fuck outta you. Driving all the way from New York to here, not knowing what the rush was."

"Pretty much. So, what is it?"

"Last night there was a shootout at this restaurant over there in Center City."

"What!"

"Yeah, that spot at the Rittenhouse Hotel."

"Somebody shot up a restaurant at that joint! Yo, I know them crackers was going crazy up in that motherfucker."

"Damn right!"

"Who were they gunning for?"

"This nigga, Arnez Douglass."

"Why does that name sound so familiar?"

"That's the dude I used to do business with in Atlanta for a while."

"Yeah, that's right! Arnez was a major player."

"Still is, but when shit got hot in ATL, he came to Philly tryna take over."

"Okay, but why is him getting shot at an emergency to me? I don't know that nigga like that."

"Here's the thing. The person responsible is Delondo."

"Delondo! As in the cat Devon works for?"

"That's the one. Devon and one of Delondo's other workers were the two men that went in the spot busting bullets like they were out there in the Wild Wild West. Arnez's bodyguard got killed, and another nigga he was with and one of Delondo's men got killed. The other one is at the hospital in critical condition. I don't know which one is still alive, but if it's Devon, I figured you'd want to try and speak with him about that girl you're looking for in case he don't make it."

Upon hearing this information, all I could do was put my head down. The first time a real lead panned out, this bullshit had to happen.

"Fuck!" Nico yelled out. "Even if he was the one alive, I know there has got to be a cop keeping watch at his door."

"Maybe, but I'm sure that can be handled. I already put in some calls trying to verify who it is at the hospital anyway. But since the shit happened last night and didn't nobody have ID on them, and it ain't like motherfuckers coming forward claiming folks, it's taking a minute to get names and shit."

"So, what the fuck is going on between this nigga, Delondo and Arnez that they bringing gunfire to the Rittenhouse?"

"That nigga, Arnez is a foul motherfucker, do you hear me! He's the one responsible for turning my sister against me. He's also responsible for having Genesis' best friend killed, and we believe his wife also!"

I can't believe Genesis was married and his wife got killed. She must be the mother of his son. Wow, that's some sad shit right there. I ain't feeling that nigga because of that Maya shit, but my heart goes out to him for having to experience that kinda loss.

"Besides the beef we have with him, there is a major turf war going on between Arnez and Delondo, and of course Arnez is the one who started the shit. After Arnez had Delondo's original crew wiped out, Delondo has been determined to finish him off. But Arnez's ass managed to escape death again. I can't wait for that nigga to get his!"

"Damn! Shit is serious out in these streets. I've been on the low for the last couple of months, so I haven't been dealing with the madness, but it's interesting to see what is waiting for me."

"Trust me, I can't wait to break free from this shit. When I got locked up, damn near every dime I had made after all these years of grinding dried up. And the Feds practically wiped Genesis out. If it wasn't for Quentin putting us back on, we would've been fucked up out here. That's why I'm buggin' over how Arnez is maintaining."

"But I remember dude was making serious paper, right?"

"Yeah, but then shit dried up in Atlanta because it got hot there, and then he was doing it big in Philly for a minute. But when Delondo came down from New York, he dominated and froze Arnez up. But somehow, Arnez kept coming up with the cash to stay afloat even in these hard times. If I didn't know better, I would think that he had some sort of connect funneling him paper, but I know all the players that got it like that, and don't none of them fuck wit' Arnez. So, I don't know what the deal is. Maybe in his heyday he was doing way more saving than I gave him credit for."

I couldn't believe how small the motherfuckin' world was. First, there was Mike, then Nico, now I had to add CoCo and Genesis to the ever-expanding list of Quentin Jacobs' dick riders. He had more fans than a pop star. The shit was utterly annoying. Refusing to think about that motherfucker any longer, I had to get back to what was important.

"CoCo!" When I said her name her face look startled, as if she forgot I was in the building or maybe it was because I was loud with it. Plus I had been on mute while she was running off at the mouth. "When can you get that information on Devon? If the nigga is dead, then it doesn't make sense for us to waste any more time in Philly," I said, turning towards Nico. "We need to start coming up with new leads. If he is in the hospital, we need to get to him and not waste any time."

"Let me call one of my street informants now. Maybe some new news came in."

While CoCo was making her call, Nico stepped to me with disillusionment in his eyes. "I can't help but think that maybe if we would've stayed and not gone to New York, we could've got to Devon before all this shit went down."

"I can't front, that very thought went through my mind, but we don't know if he even came back to the address we had on him. For all we know, he could've been stashed some place with Delondo and the rest of his crew, waiting and plotting to take that nigga, Arnez out. Regardless, we did the right thing going to Ms. Duncan's funeral. I would've felt some-kind-of-way if I didn't go and pay my respects. When I was growing up, there were days I woulda went hungry if it wasn't for her. My mother was so busy pulling tricks and smoking that pipe that she didn't give a damn if I was fed or not. You know I want to find Maya's scandalous ass, but that was one stop I would've never forgiven myself for if I hadn't made it."

"I feel you. No matter which way the shit falls, we stay on our hunt. Maya can't hide forever. Eventually, we'll catch her ass."

"Nothing yet. Supposedly the police are keeping information closely guarded. But of course, the minute I find out anything, I'll hit you up," CoCo let us know.

"Do that. We're going back to our hotel. But I'll be waiting to hear from you."

"Cool."

When I woke up, I didn't realize it was the next day until I looked outside and saw it was daylight. When Nico and I got back to the hotel it was early evening, and I only planned on taking a nap, but I guess my body had other ideas. I had to admit, the rest did me some good and I probably needed a lot more of it, but there simply wasn't time.

I looked at my cell to see if I had any missed calls from Nico, but I didn't. I knew that meant he hadn't gotten any new information regarding Devon. If it wasn't for the fact that I hoped he could lead us to Maya, I would've felt justice was served if Devon was deceased, even if it was not by me, but we were placing a lot of stock in him getting us off of our dead end trail.

As I was about to call Nico, to see what he felt should be our next move, my cell started ringing. It was marked private, which I never liked to answer, but very few people had my new number so curiosity got the best of me.

"Hello."

"Good morning, Precious. I hope you slept well."

"Who is this?" The voice had a familiarity to it, but I couldn't place it.

"This is Genesis."

"How did you get this number?"

"I have my ways."

"What do you want?" I asked, not amused by him, or his word usage to play games.

"Can you meet me for breakfast in say...an hour?"

"For what? Last time I saw you, you didn't have too much conversation for me. Has anything changed?"

"I guess there's only one way to find out. Are you going to meet me or not?"

My head wanted to tell the motherfucker hell no, but my mouth said, "Name the spot. I'll be there."

I decided not to tell Nico that I was meeting with Genesis. I hung the Do Not Disturb sign on the doorknob and headed out. I was meeting Genesis at a restaurant that was only a block from the hotel we were staying in, so I figured he somehow knew that information too. He could've easily gotten it from CoCo, as I was sure that Nico had shared it with her.

When I arrived at the cute but tiny location, Genesis was already sitting at a table in the back. He glanced up from what looked to be a newspaper he was reading, and then right back down, not giving me any sort of facial expression. I took a seat, and several seconds passed before he even acknowledged my presence.

"Are you hungry? Because I ordered you something to eat," he said.

"You don't even know what I like."

"I decided to take a chance. Maybe I got it right. But they have the best pancakes in all of Philly, so you'll enjoy them."

"If you say so. But honestly, food isn't on my mind. I want to know why you called me, and what do you want?"

"I wanted to apologize for what happened a few nights ago. I should've been more considerate of your dilemma."

"You could've told me that bullshit on the phone."

He let out a slight chuckle, and then said, "If you don't mind me asking, how did you meet Supreme, and then get him to marry you? Because you seem like the sort of woman that puts a man through a lot of changes."

"If you don't mind me asking, how did you get your wife to marry you? I mean, because you seem like the kind of man that would put your woman through a lot of deadly changes...if you know what I mean."

Dude gave me this ice-cold look, like it was taking all of his strength not to reach over the table and take me out of this world. But that's what the motherfucker got for wasting my time and then talking slick to me about how I got my husband.

"It doesn't feel good, does it? Fuckin' wit' somebody and then they come back and fuck wit' you harder, especially when it gets extremely personal. So, my advice to you is don't play those type of games with me, Genesis. And the reason why is because I know no boundaries."

"No wonder your husband left you and ran off with another woman, because you are a straight up bitch. Right on time! Here's our food. I promise you, you're going to love the pancakes."

This nigga had fuckin' pissed me off, and it wasn't even because of the "bitch" comment. Hell, I was a bitch...the Queen Bitch at that. I wore that title with pride, because it meant don't fuck with me, and don't underestimate me, I run this! It was the part about my husband running off with another woman that had me ready to stab him with my fork. But I knew the fuckin' reason he said that shit was to get under my skin, and I refused to give him the pleasure of seeing it on my face.

Yeah, I was human, so he knew in my heart I was hurt behind his statement. But trust, that wasn't enough gratification for a confident nigga like him. He wanted to see me squirm...not! So as my insides burned up in anger, I spread the butter on my hot pancakes, watching as it melted in before pouring the warm syrup over them. Instead of using my fork as a weapon to kill Genesis, I killed my pancakes, slashing through the stack of three, consuming every bite until they were all gone. I then washed it down with a tall glass of orange juice. "You were right. These were the best pancakes I've ever had." I smiled, savoring the fact that I had kept my cool even though inside my rage was boiling over.

"I knew you would enjoy them," Genesis said, returning the smile. "Yes, she's finished with her food. Can you clear her area? Thank you," he instructed the waitress, acting as if he was the consummate gentleman.

"So, now that we've cleared the air and finished eating, why don't you tell me why you really invited me here?"

"I already did. As I stated, I should've been more considerate of your dilemma. I won't make that mistake again. As much as I would love to stay and keep you company further, I have a lot of business to handle today. But I'll be in touch."

Then without any further explanation, Genesis made his exit, and for the first time since I could remember, a man had actually left me in a state of confusion.

Maya

I observed as Arnez was having a telephone conversation with somebody that was causing him to act extra animated. He was pointing his finger midair as if the person was standing in front of him and he was up in their face. Then he pulled the phone away from his ear and looked at it as if he was saying, 'No the fuck you didn't just say that bullshit to me' but whoever he was speaking to, really did, which caused his over-the-top hand gestures to continue.

While I sat on the couch, I tried to pretend that I was all into the Young and the Restless and normally I would be glued. But at this moment, I was straining my ear trying to listen to every word Arnez was spitting out of his mouth. After forty minutes of a heated exchange, he finally ended the call and pounded his fist on the table. I didn't say shit. I kept pretending that the showdown between Victor and his son Adam had my full attention.

"Describe the man you saw when you went to the bathroom."

"Huh?"

"The man you saw on the phone, describe him." I can't front, it took me a minute to process what the fuck Arnez was saying. For one, he hadn't really said more than a couple of words to me since we got to this rundown motel in some backwards ass town in Pennsylvania. Then, I almost forgot my own lie because his question was so fuckin' out the blue it threw me off.

"Oh, you talking about at the restaurant," I said, buying myself some time to conjure up a bullshit description of some fictitious nigga that I didn't see on my way to the restroom. But instead I did what came easier. I described the nigga I was lusting after in the elevator.

"Of course, where else would I be talking about?"

"Don't mind me, I was so caught up in my soap, I wasn't really paying attention to what you said."

"Ok..." he nodded his head but at the same time letting me know to get to it.

"He was medium height and build, maybe a shade darker than you with a low haircut but had waves. He sported a thin mustache and was very well dressed."

"That sound like that nigga Delondo!"

"Who?"

"Delondo...this nigga I'm having some serious beef wit'. I can't believe that motherfucker had his men come up in the Lacroix blasting like that. But then again it would be the perfect spot to catch me off guard. It would've worked if it hadn't been for you."

I sat silent and baffled for a few. Is he saying what I think he's saying...that the hit was for him? That Devon wasn't even in that spot looking for me he was coming for Arnez. Wow, that is some crazy shit right there. So the dude on the elevator was a nigga named Delondo that Devon was working for? If this is true then shit did work out in my favor because Arnez looking at me like I saved his life and technically I did although initially I was tryna' save my own.

"I'm glad I saved your life but it wasn't my intention to get in the middle of some beef between you and some man."

"Why were you there anyway? I don't remember seeing you with anybody."

"I was visiting from out of town and was supposed to be meeting a friend but at the last minute he couldn't make it. Since I was already at the restaurant and hungry, plus my hotel room was at the Rittenhouse, I figured I should stay and have dinner."

"I'm glad you did, luck was on my side. But I promise you, Delondo won't be so lucky. This the second bodyguard I've lost behind that nigga."

At first I couldn't believe dude was speaking so freely in front of me but then I thought about the circumstances. He almost got killed. He does believe I saved his life. Then when he was on the street running for cover I gave him a ride. Now we're hauled up in this motel because he's hiding out. He probably needs someone to express his frustrations to and I'm the only outlet he got.

"Listen, I'm happy I was able to help you out but I need to be going. I have a flight to catch and I need to get back to my hotel." What I was saying was a bunch of bullshit but the nigga could never know that I had actually tracked him down and I was exactly where I wanted to be. As long as I played the role of wanting to get away from his ass I shouldn't raise any suspicion.

"You can't leave."

"Excuse me?"

"I need you to stay here, you have a car."

"I'll drop you off wherever you want to go. I'm sure you have friends in Philly."

"In the business I'm in, I don't have friends only business associates and people that work for me. But after last night, I don't know who is looking out for me or who might hand me over to Delondo. Until I figure it out, I need to keep a low profile. That's why I had you bring me to this motel."

"What business are you in?" I asked, playing naïve.

"Put it this way...a very dangerous one."

"I figured that much after what happened but I didn't want to jump to any conclusions."

"I like to say I'm in the import and export business."

"Of drugs I suppose?"

"Listen, I'll make your time worthwhile. You'll be well compensated. I just need you to stay put for a minute until I figure out my next move." *Nigga please...I ain't going nowhere. Trust me on that.*

"How long are you talking about? I don't want my family to worry."

"Give me a couple of days," he said shaking his head. "Damn, I need Chanel right now."

"Who is Chanel...is she your girlfriend?"

"She was my everything but she was taken out my life too." I wasn't sure what he meant by that. I mean did she leave him or was the bitch dead? But I decided not to pry. I had the feeling that if I played it cool, the longer I stayed around the nigga, the more information he would voluntarily share.

Ring...ring...ring

"Yo, did you get my message?" I heard Arnez say to whoever was on the other end of the phone. But I was pissed because I couldn't hear what the other person was saying.

"He had his people come at me."

The person on the other end must've said Delondo's name because then Arnez answered, "Yep."

Arnez then stood up from the bed and walked to the bathroom and shut the door. That was one conversation he didn't want me hearing and I was vexed! I was tempted to press my ear against the door to listen but if I got caught then whatever little trust he had for me at the moment would go right out the window. I paced the small area hoping to come up with an idea to get information I wanted on Supreme from Arnez. I also needed to find out what was going on with Devon. Even if he didn't come up in the restaurant to kill me, our eyes locked briefly last night so I know he saw me. If he wasn't looking for me before he would definitely be on the prowl for me now. While considering my options Arnez came busting out the bathroom door interrupting my thoughts.

"Come on, I need for you to take me somewhere," he stated in a rushed tone.

"Where are we going?"

"I'll tell you when we get in the car." I grabbed my purse and headed out. His purposeful strides to the car let me know that wherever we were going he wanted to get there quickly.

"Do you know how to get back to Philly?"

"Yes."

"Good, once you get there I'll tell you where to go."

When I pulled out the parking lot, Arnez's cell phone started ringing.

"Yo' I'm on my way. I should be there in about an hour," he said, then ended the call.

"Where am I taking you?"

"Just drive." *What the fuck have I got myself into? Excitement is good but only when I know what the hell is going on. But right now even though I was driving, Arnez was in complete control and that shit had me antsy.*

As I continued to drive, making my way towards Philly, Arnez's phone kept blowing up. That shit had to ring at least every couple minutes. Some calls he took, others he ignored. But every time the phone would ring I couldn't help but wonder if Supreme was on the other end of the call.

"Get over to your right. We're getting off at the next exit," he informed me a few minutes after entering Philly. "And when you get off, veer to your left." I followed his directions anxious to see where the final destination would be. "Turn right at the next light...keep going straight... okay slow down. You're about to make this left."

"Into the hospital?"

"Yes, and park right over there." Arnez pointed towards a somewhat discreet area.

"What are we doing at the hospital?"

"Remember I said you would be well compensated for your help."

"Yeah, but what help do you need from me at the hospital?" Arnez pulled out a small piece of paper from his pants pocket and unfolded it.

"I want you to go inside and ask what room," he glanced back down at the paper, "that Devon McNeil is in. Tell them you're his sister and he was shot last night." I couldn't believe that Arnez had led me right to my enemy. If he only knew I would gladly try to find out this information for free.

"I can do that. Hopefully whoever is at the front desk won't put me through a bunch of changes to get the information."

"Just go in there and be convincing. If you get it, it'll be some of the easiest money you've ever made."

"Who is this Devon guy to you...is he a friend of yours?" I already knew the answer to that was hell no but I wanted to see what Arnez would reveal.

"No, he's one of Delondo's men, the one that survived the shooting. I need to know his condition." *So do I*, I said to myself.

"Okay, I'll try to find out everything I can. I'll be back."

As I walked towards the hospital entrance I peeped a few people ogling me strangely and I was trying to figure out what the fuck was wrong with them. Then I looked down and I don't know how I could forget that I had on my fuckem' dress. This bright red shit was hot for a night of seduction but for a daylight hospital visit, it was a tad inappropriate. I could either feel like a fool coming up in the hospital looking like a high priced hooker or I could use the outfit to my advantage.

When I walked in, I stood to the side for a minute and observed the staff. I sized everybody up and saw a younger woman who seemed to be about to start her shift. I waited a couple more minutes for her to get a little situated and for some of the other staff who had probably been there for awhile to get out her face. Once the traffic seemed to be dispersing I made my move.

"Excuse me Miss."

"Yes, can I help you," she said trying not to noticeably stare me up in my outfit.

"I hope so. I've been here all night. I haven't even had a chance to go home. My brother was brought in here last night because he got shot. I was trying to find out if his condition had improved. The woman who I spoke to earlier told me to come back and she would see if there were any updates."

"He came in last night...you said he is your brother?" I nodded my head yes, trying to give off a real gloomy mood. "What's his name?"

"Devon McNeil."'

"And what's your name?"

"Tawana McNeil."

"He's still in critical condition."

"Have they moved him to another room?"

"I don't know, I just got here but he's in room 302. Is that the same room?"

"Yes, I was checking because they said they might have to move him."

"That was probably if his condition had changed."

"Yeah, that makes sense. Well, thank you for your help."

"No problem."

I turned around and a huge grin crossed my face. Critical condition was good but I needed Devon to be dead and I had a feeling Arnez wanted the same thing. I left the hospital anxious to share the inside scoop with him. I knew he would be pleased and I couldn't wait to find out how he planned on utilizing the information.

As I got closer to the car, I realized Arnez wasn't inside. I looked around but didn't see him. "Where did he go?" I asked out loud. I kept walking towards the car and halfway there shit seemed to come to a halt and then transition to a movie scene clip.

"Get dooooooown!" I heard what sounded like Arnez's voice yell out. I turned around towards the sound of his voice and that's when I locked eyes with my worst nightmare. She was a few hundred feet away but even from the long distance, it was no doubt the image of Precious Cummings speeding towards me with her gun already raised. I was in complete shock, to the point that I couldn't move. My feet were cemented to the ground. I could hear the *pop...pop...pop* and if it wasn't for Arnez throwing me down to the ground. At least one of those bullets would've ripped through me.

"Come on...come on...come on..." he screamed in my ear, trying to snap me out my daze. He damned near dragged me to the car and threw me in. Precious was getting closer and closer and I couldn't tell if the sound of her gun blasting off was louder, or my heart thumping. One thing I did know though was Arnez was a pro. We were in broad daylight being shot at but the nigga was completely focused. After tossing me in the car his hands didn't shake once as he put the keys in the ignition. The closer Precious got the calmer he seemed to get. Once he started the engine he put it in drive and slammed down on the gas, making a beeline straight towards Precious. She busted off a couple more shots before jumping out the way to avoid being ran over by Arnez. Before the car was out of view, I turned to face her and our eyes met one final time. Precious' fierce glare said it alL The bitch was back and out for my blood.

Precious

"Yo, are you fuckin' crazy! Get in the car!" Nico, yelled out as he pulled up beside me. I jumped inside and slammed the door. "I can't believe your crazy ass is busting bullets in the fuckin' parking lot of a hospital! You better be lucky there weren't any cops around or we would both be in jail," Nico barked, speeding off and checking in his mirror making sure no cops were on his back.

"I was this close to getting that heffa," I said, pounding my fist in the palm of my hand. That low-life ho is in Philly...ain't that some shit. I bet you she was coming to the hospital to see Devon. But how the fuck she know he was here?" I was running off at the mouth extra amped up. Seeing Maya for the first time in so long had my adrenaline pumping.

"We can't even go inside the hospital and try to speak with Devon now! Them motherfuckers probably got that shit on camera."

"What the fuck was I supposed to do, let her get away?"

"I understand you pumped and seeing Maya got you all riled up but you can't do sloppy shit like that. You got a child to think about. We got the evidence we need to make sure she spends the rest of her life in jail. If we can take her out and get away wit' it cool...otherwise we do it the legal way and make sure she get locked up. But running 'round here playing vigilante in broad daylight is not the move."

I knew Nico was right but I let my emotions get the best of me. When CoCo gave us the information on Devon I couldn't get to the hospital fast enough. Learning he wasn't dead and there was a chance that he could deliver some much needed 411 on Maya had me excited. Nico and I decided I should go in first and try to maneuver my way in Devon's room. So when I got out the car and noticed a woman in a bright red dress coming out the hospital, even from the far distance I knew it was Maya. All reasonable thinking escaped me within seconds.

"I wonder who that dude was with her. I guess one good thing, it damn sure wasn't Supreme. Do you think Maya is up here with Devon?"

"I don't know. All this shit is getting more and more confusing. The only person that can probably give us some answers is Devon. Maybe I can go back to the hospital by myself and try to speak with him."

"That probably would be best. Because you're right, we don't know if anybody saw me turning that parking lot out and we def' don't need the drama."

"Okay, so I'ma drop you back off at the hotel and then head back to the hospital. But Precious I want you to stay in your hotel room and wait for me. Please don't just start lurking the streets in search of Maya."

"I'm not, plus her scared ass probably someplace hiding right now. I can't believe how close I was to ending her life."

"You need to be thanking God that you didn't because if you had, on everything, you would be in handcuffs right now facing murder charges."

As much as I wanted Maya dead spending the rest of my life behind bars wasn't worth it. Aaliyah would grow up without her mother so my revenge would be in vain. I had to be smart about this shit. If I could murder her ass on the low and get away with it then that was mos def' option number one. But anything short of that meant all I could do was give her a good old fashion ass whooping before I let the authorities toss her in jail.

"You're right and I'ma act accordingly. Getting Maya off the streets and out of my life is what's most important."

"I hope you mean that, Precious, because we talking about not only your life but that of your daughter. This shit..." Right when Nico sounded as if he was about to go into a full fledge lecture I heard his cell phone ringing. I was ecstatic because I respected that he was kicking real shit but I didn't want to hear it. The hatred I had for Maya ran so deep that it was almost blinding. If I didn't have my daughter to live for there was a very good chance I would be willing to spend the rest of my life in jail just for the pleasure of killing her myself and watching as she begged to live.

"We're on our way right now," I caught Nico say before getting off the phone.

"You're not about to drop me off at the hotel so you can go to the hospital?"

"No, that was CoCo and she told us to meet her at the warehouse now."

"I wonder what the fuck done happened now. This shit need to be quick because you need to go speak with Devon."

"CoCo said it's important. And she understands the magnitude of shit that's going down right now, so if she's telling us to come, it's must be some serious shit."

When Nico pulled up to the warehouse I saw the white Range Rover, which I knew belonged to CoCo but there was also a cream Bentley but I had no idea who owned that. When we got inside the first person we saw was Genesis so I assumed that Bentley was his shit. I didn't tell Nico about the breakfast I had with Genesis earlier this morning and I still had no desire to. Mainly because I felt he was purposely trying to play me out and I until I figured out why I was going to keep my feelings to myself, especially since it seemed Nico actually liked the nigga.

"What's up man," Nico said, shaking Genesis' hand. "Good to see you again."

"Likewise, and how are you, Precious?" he asked in an almost condescending tone but I was sure that shit went right over Nico's head.

"The same."

"Where's CoCo, she called and told me it was important we get right over here."

"She's in the back on the phone. I actually just got here myself."

"I don't mean to rush her, but I'm trying to get over to the hospital and see if I can get any information from Devon about Maya. We actually ran into her at the hospital."

"You ran into Maya?" Genesis questioned.

"Yeah, but I'm sure you would have no interest in that since you don't even know who Maya is," I cut in and said, taking a jab at Genesis, letting him know I knew he was full of shit. But he didn't flinch instead he carried on with his conversation with Nico until CoCo came out.

"Sorry I kept you waiting but I was trying to get all the details together before you got here."

"What details?" Nico wanted to know and so did I.

"Devon is dead."

"What!" I swung passed Genesis' wanting to knock him out my way. "We just left the hospital less than an hour ago."

"Well whoever killed him must've done it around that time or close to it because he's dead."

"What do you mean whoever killed him?" Nico took the words right out of my mouth, because I was perplexed by that statement.

"There was supposed to be a guard in front of Devon's room door but somebody got to him. They came in, put a pillow over his head and popped one bullet through his face. By the time the nurses came in the perpetrator was long gone. My sources are telling me Arnez is behind the hit. You know, sending a message to Delondo that you took my man now I've taken both of yours."

"This is too fuckin' much! Devon was supposed to tell us where Maya might be or where she had been so I could find my husband and daughter! Now that motherfucker is dead and I had that hussy within my reach and lost her ass. This shit is beyond fucked up!"

"Your husband...I had no idea you were married," CoCo made known. I glanced at Nico and then at Genesis because for some reason I assumed that at least one of them had told her, but apparently I was wrong.

"Yes, my husband is Supreme, and Maya has damn near single-handedly destroyed my marriage."

"Supreme...is that like a street name or are you talking about 'The Supreme'", CoCo stressed wanting clarification.

"She's talking about 'The Supreme'", Genesis said, taking it upon himself to answer for me.

"Rapper turned music mogul Supreme," she continued as if she needed further confirmation.

"What, you know the nigga...yes that Supreme!" I was already in a foul fuckin' mood and this chick triple asking me the same question wasn't helping my cause.

"No, I don't know him," she snapped. "I'm surprised that's all. I mean it seems somebody would've told me that you were his wife."

"Well now you know but it don't change shit. Devon is still dead and Maya is still missing. We back at the starting point but I don't even know where the finish line is anymore."

"Precious, I know shit seems a bit bleak right now, but I promised you I would get you home to your daughter and I will." Nico's words were so sincere but I needed more than that to get back to my family.

I saw him pull CoCo to the side and I figured he was picking her brain trying to get all the details on what went down with Devon, hoping it could help locate Maya. But I was stuck on the fact that Maya was almost mine but I let her get away. I know I didn't technically let her get away but no matter which way I flipped it she was gone and I was no closer to finding Supreme and Aaliyah.

"Precious, can I speak with you?" I heard Genesis but wasn't in the mood to lift my head up and acknowledge his request. I wasn't mentally up to partake in the game I was for sure he wanted to play. But being the relentless nigga that he is, he chose to ignore my stay-the-fuck-away-from-me body language. "I think you'll want to hear what I have to say."

"I doubt it, but umm, you're not giving me much of a choice are you?"

"Your husband and daughter are in Miami. I have their last known address and I believe it's still good." My mouth dropped when I heard those words come out of Genesis' mouth. This man continued to shock me and now I was speechless which was a rarity for me. I almost wanted to believe he was playing a sick joke on me because to find out Genesis was telling the truth would bring me happiness, a feeling that I had been deprived of for so long.

"Is this real? I mean is what you're saying to me true?" I knew Genesis could see the pleading in my eyes of putting all my hope in what he said.

"It is true. I'ma give you the address to where they are living in Miami and I hope you can work things out with your husband."

"Why...why are you giving me this information now?"

"My wife was taken out of my life and my son will grow up without ever knowing what an incredible woman his mother was. There's nothing I can do to change that but I can change this. Go get your daughter, love her and be the best mother you can possibly be."

"I'll never forget that you did this for me...thank you." As Genesis wrote down the address instead of rejoicing my mind speculated on what this man's agenda was. I didn't doubt he genuinely wanted me to reconnect with my daughter but I was absolutely positive he was hiding a huge piece of the puzzle from me and I needed answers. But for now it would have to wait. I was booking a one-way flight to Miami determined to be reunited with my family.

Maya

"Who was that woman and why was she trying to kill you?" When Arnez asked me that question we had reached a fork in the road. My choice was to either come clean or lie. So I decided to do what I do best.

"I made the mistake of getting involved with this man and he lied to me. He never told me he was married. I only found out recently and that's why I came to Philly so I could end it once and for all. He was the friend that I told you I was supposed to meet at the restaurant. But somehow his wife got my cell number and she called threatening me, it got crazy. We decided it was best he didn't come."

"So how do you think she knew you were going to be at the hospital?"

"That's what I'm tryna figure out, unless it was just crazy coincidence."

"It's a possibility but she came prepared."

"You ain't lying. If you hadn't been there I would be dead right now."

"Saving your life was the least I could do because you did save mine."

"Now we're even. You don't owe me anything."

"If it wasn't for me making you go to the hospital and get that information for me then that man's wife would've never had the opportunity to try and kill you."

"You didn't make me do anything. I wanted to help you."

"And you did, more than you know."

"Where are we going?" We had been driving for awhile but playing out the episode that had went down with Precious over and over again in my head had made me oblivious that I didn't know where the fuck we were going.

"Why, are you ready to go back home?"

"No, I really don't have anything to go back home to. But if you don't need me anymore, you can take me back to my hotel."

"What if I told you that I wanted you to stay?"

"I would ask you why?"

"Because I think you have a lot of heart. When you heard that conversation about what was about to happen you didn't have to warn me, you could've walked out and went about your life. Then I asked you to go in the hospital and get that information for me. You did it with no problem. Most females would be too scared to do what you did but like I said you showed a lot of heart. I appreciate that quality in a woman."

"I'm surprised a man like you doesn't already have a woman like that."

"I did and she was a true soldier."

"Was it that woman you mentioned earlier?"

"Yes, Chanel."

"What happened?"

"Life...life happened. As you know by now danger surrounds me and it seems to surround you too," he remarked, glancing over at me. "It's different circumstances but danger is danger. Unfortunately the danger finally caught up to Chanel."

"You see soldier potential in me?"

"I see something...what, only time will tell. That's why I want you to stay so I can observe you, watch how you move."

"What if I don't have any interest in being your soldier?"

"If that was the case, you wouldn't have stuck around but you're still here."

"I'll tell you what, I'll stay but only if you promise we don't have to go back to that awful motel."

"You don't have to worry about that. Trust me, it was harder on me than it could ever be on you. Living extremely comfortable is all I know." *Shit motherfucker, me too.* But Arnez didn't need to know all that. If a hustler knows a woman is accustomed to the good life the first thing they want to know is how and who got you like that. I never forgot Mike taught me that. He said it was their way of knowing how many times you'd been around the block or if you were fresh meat.

Most top-notch hustlers preferred fresh meat and if you had been broken in, anything more than twice was considered damaged goods. They could still fuck around with you but wife you was a no go.

"That's good to hear but I still need to get my stuff from the hotel."

"When are you due to check out?"

"Monday."

"That gives us two more days."

"What about clothes? I'm ready to burn this red dress."

"Don't do that, it looks good on you."

"Really, I didn't' think you noticed."

"I'm a man aren't I, of course I noticed."

"Well, thank you but I'm ready to take this shit off."

"I understand. I'm ready to take these clothes off too. Wearing the same thing two days in a row isn't cool. We're almost in Jersey. When we get there we'll stop at the mall, get a couple of things and then find a hotel. Does that sound like a plan?"

"Yep, sounds like a very good plan to me."

It was amazing what some shopping could do for a bitch. After hitting up The Mall at Short Hills, I felt like I was gettin' my sexy back. I went from feeling like the broke-down ho Julia Roberts in Pretty Woman, when she was strolling Rodeo Drive trying to spend up all of Richard Gere's money but nobody would give her play. To the new and improved hooker after Mr. Gere personally accompanied Julia on a shopping spree and everybody kissed her ass. Yep, this was exactly what I needed particularly since Supreme had been treating me like some washed up pussy he was done fucking with for the last couple months. Although Arnez hadn't made any sort of sexual advances towards me, being treated to an afternoon of shopping instead of the on-call babysitter had me feeling like a young, desirable woman again.

So when we went to check in to our hotel and Arnez was going to get us separate rooms, I shut that shit down.

"Two suites please."

"Arnez, you don't have to get me a suite."

"I know, but I want to. If I'm gonna be staying in a suite then you should too. I told you, I like only the best."

"I understand that and I appreciate it but what I mean is that, I don't want my own suite. I want to stay with you."

"You know you don't have to do this. Because I took you shopping doesn't mean I expect sex from you. Trust me, it's not that serious."

"I don't do anything I don't want to do."

Arnez gave me the most alluring smile and then said to the lady working behind the front desk, "That'll be one suite."

When Arnez closed the door to our hotel room, my tongue was down his throat before he could even put down the key. I was craving for a touch of a man and some dick. I thought Arnez was the perfect fit. His strong arms cupped my ass and lifted me up off the floor, carrying me over to the king sized bed. I tugged at his shirt and pants simultaneously feeling like a dog in heat. I kissed, licked and bit on his neck and chest. The faint scents of his cologne still lingering in his skin making me crave him that much more.

"Damn baby, you want the dick like that," Arnez whispered in my ear.

"Yes, yes baby, I do," I purred back. So when Arnez finally entered me, I welcomed the warmth as my walls surrounded his thickness. He rocked inside of me taking it deep and then pulling back to the very tip so I could beg for the dick to be back inside. Arnez was no doubt skilled in the technique of fucking because although I knew he had absolutely no love for me, that nigga worked his tool like I was the only woman in the world for him, so at that moment I did feel like we were in love.

Precious

"Precious, I don't want you to worry. I already got the private investigator on it to follow up on some other leads and CoCo is..."

"Nico, stop."

"Stop, I know you don't want to give up because we can't!"

"It's not that."

"Then what?"

"I know where Supreme and Maya are." Nico slammed down on his brakes so hard it caused my body to jerk forward then back. Luckily we were on an isolated back street and no other vehicles were behind us or shit would've been ugly.

"What the fuck are you talking 'bout and when did you get that information and why are you just now telling me?"

"If you would slow down with all the questions I'll tell you!"

"I'm listening." Nico parked the car on the corner block and stared at me still gripping the steering wheel.

"When you were in the warehouse talking to CoCo, Genesis told me."

"What! Come the fuck again!"

"I told you he knew much more than what he was letting on but right now that's not important. What is important is that he gave me the address to where Supreme and Aaliyah are living. They're actually in Miami."

"Miami, wow...Miami," Nico repeated as if digesting what I told him.

"I can't believe after all this time we've found them...I mean Genesis found them."

"Nico, you deserve a lot of credit too. I didn't even want to come to fuckin' Philly! I wanted to stay in Atlanta, so if we hadn't come here we would've never had met Genesis to get the information. Everything happens for a reason."

"Precious, you don't have to try and stroke my ego. I'm happy you finally found your family. I don't care who gave you the information."

"It's not about stroking your ego. I want you to know how appreciative I am for riding this shit out with me. I know I've been a real pain but you stuck it out and I know you would've went to the end of the world with me if need be and I love you for that."

"So when are you going to Miami?"

"I'm taking the first flight out in the morning."

"Do you need me to come with you?"

"Under the circumstances, I don't think that would be a good idea."

"You're right. I guess after being with you every day for the last few months has made it hard for me to want to let you go. But then again, why lie to myself. I'll never be able to let you go."

"But how selfish am I because I don't want you to be able to let me go." In my heart I didn't. I was married to another man and I loved Supreme more than anything but I loved Nico too. And although I had found happiness with another man I didn't want Nico to find that same happiness with another woman. He had been my crutch for so long that to accept anything differently wasn't an option for me. But I had to let go, because Nico was my past and Supreme was my future.

"Thank you for taking me to the airport."

"I had to make sure you got on the airplane safely. I wouldn't be able to ease my mind if I didn't."

"So what are you gonna do now?"

"I'ma stay in Philly a few more days. I have a lot of business to discuss with CoCo and Genesis. We're going to try and collaborate on some shit."

"I think that's a good idea. Even though I was right about Genesis knowing more than what he was telling me, I think you was right about him too. He's a decent dude. I have no doubt the three of you can make a shit load of money together." Nico and I both smiled at the same time. "I really do love you." I knew I shouldn't have said that but I couldn't help myself.

"I know and I love you too. But you're right, you belong with Supreme." I nodded my head in agreement.

"But listen, you need to catch your flight. We've come too far for you to miss it. And listen, no worries I'll still find Maya. The evidence we have against her is safely put away and I promise she'll never be able to hurt you and your family again."

"Okay. I'll call you when I get to Miami. Wish me luck!"

"You don't need it," Nico grinned before kissing me on my forehead and walking off. To watch him leave brought a deep sadness in my heart. Part of me hated that I loved him so much but the other part wouldn't want to change that for nothing in the world. I took a deep breath ready for the next chapter in my life...going home to my family.

When my flight landed at the Miami International Airport my emotions were mixed. I would be able to hold my daughter after being away from her for so long but I was scared about the reception I would receive from Supreme. I wasn't expecting him to welcome me with open arms but I hoped that he would at least hear me out, I deserved that—we deserved that. During my taxi ride, I continued to think of different scenarios of how it would all play out and I had to admit, my nerves were getting the best of me.

"Are we almost there?" I asked realizing we had now entered a residential area with elegant mansions and riverfront estates situated on high bluffs overlooking pools and terraced grounds.

"Yes only a few more minutes," the taxi driver informed me. He continued to drive and when he started to slow down and look around I knew we were getting near. "We're here," he said, making a right into a driveway with open gates. I saw a fuchsia Ferrari parked in the circular entrance and I hoped that meant Supreme was home.

"Beautiful home...here take my card. Call if you ever need a ride." I reluctantly took his card but hoping never to need his services again. I grabbed the one bag I had and stepped out the taxi. It took me a couple of seconds to close the door as I stood staring at the entrance until finally slamming it shut ready to face my fears.

It felt like I was moving in slow motion as I made my way to the front door. I swallowed hard before ringing the doorbell. It was like déjà vu from when I rang the doorbell at our home in Beverly Hills and my world was shattered when I realized I had returned to nothing. That couldn't happen to me again. I wouldn't be able to handle it. Not getting an answer, I rang the doorbell again and pounded on the door no longer afraid but determined. As the door opened I stepped forward and when my eyes met with Supreme's a natural reflex kicked in. I dropped my bag on the front step and wrapped my arms around his neck pulling his mouth to mine. His lips and tongue gave into mine and for a few minutes the passion the connection was strong. Our love was intact as if we had never been apart. Then the fantasy vanished and reality was ready to kick my ass.

"It would be nothing for me to kill you right now!" Supreme roared, wrapping his hands around my neck and slamming me against the wall in the foyer. I was trying to speak but he was choking me and I wasn't even able to gasp for air. He was doing all this with the front door still wide open, not giving a fuck who witnessed it. I quickly began feeling light headed as his grip became tighter. It was like Supreme was trying to break my neck off. The bulging of my eyes must've made him realize the severity of his actions because right when I thought it was about to be lights out, he released me from his clutch as my body hit the cold marble floor.

As if an afterthought, Supreme slammed the door shut and walked right over me leaving me right where I was. I was gasping for air trying to figure out how I went to passionately kissing my husband to laying on the floor grateful to be alive. I watched as Supreme disappeared into what appeared from where I was positioned to be the living room. While getting my bearings together I thought about how quiet the house was and wondered where Aaliyah was and would she remember me.

I got my strength together and headed in the direction I saw Supreme go. He was sitting on the couch having a drink. He had to know it was too early in the morning for that shit but clearly he didn't give a fuck. But after almost killing your wife, I supposed he would need to drink something powerful. I too needed a drink, I went over to the bar and poured myself a glass of water.

"Where's Aaliyah?"

"Did you really think you could come here and I would just fuckin' greet you wit' open arms," he barked ignoring my question. "Do you even know how much I hate you!" he screamed throwing his half filled glass of liquor as it shattered against the fireplace.

"Please hear me out. If you would listen to me, you'll realize we've both been taken on a fuckin' rollercoaster ride." I was trying to remain calm because one of us had to if we were going to make any progress. If both of our tempers were flaring the dark place we were already in would only go deeper.

"What…listen to your lies and try to dig yourself out the hole you dug! Get the fuck outta here! I would rather you tell me the truth so I can fuckin' hate you for the rest of my life!"

"Oh you want to hate me…how 'bout I want to hate you too for not believing in our love and that I would never abandon you and Aaliyah! Or how 'bout I want to hate you for fuckin' Maya! But as much as I want to hate you I can't because I fuckin' love you too much!"

"How do you know about me and Maya?" that was the first question Supreme asked me in a normal tone instead screaming and yelling.

"She told me."

"When did you talk to Maya?"

"When she had me chained up, held hostage in the house with Mike."

"What?" Supreme stood up pacing back and forth for a moment and raising his arms in confusion. "I don't understand," he continued pressing his fingers against his temples.

"Let me help clear it up for you. Maya played me for months, hell it might've been years…I don't know. What I do know is after Mike got locked up for rapping me she plotted with him to break him out of jail, have it appear like Clip was the one behind everything so she could get rid of me and have you and my life for herself."

"This don't even sound plausible. It sounds like some outlandish made-for-TV movie. Is this the best lie you could come up with to excuse you leaving your family to run off with Nico!"

"Look at me!" Now screaming running up on Supreme. "Look at me!" I screamed louder, grabbing his arm turning him to face me. "Look at me!" I bolted again, now at the top of my lungs pointing my fingers towards my eyes, emphasizing my face. "I would never leave you or Aaliyah for Nico or any other man! You look at me and tell me you don't believe me because I know in your heart you do. That day I thought you died in my arms I didn't want to live anymore."

"It didn't stop you from fuckin' Nico when you thought my body was still cold."

I put my head down in shame for a moment because I did regret Supreme ever found out about that. "I thought you were dead. I know that doesn't change the pain you feel for finding that out but I was completely lost without you and I needed to feel connected to somebody."

"So the man who left you for dead and killed our unborn child was the person who was able to do that for you."

"Supreme, don't do this. There is nothing I could ever say that would make my relationship with Nico sound sane."

"Because it isn't sane! The shit is sick!"

"That could very well be true but it doesn't change the fact that I chose you. Nico was never an option, it was always you."

"What about the letter. You wrote that."

"Maya forced me to. She threatened to harm Aaliyah if I didn't. If you only knew the torture I went through behind that conniving bitch!"

"How was Maya able to pull all this shit off by herself?"

"She had help. For one, Devon."

"Devon McNeil the bodyguard that worked for me?"

"Yes that Devon."

"What! This is getting more bizarre by the minute."

"Well get ready for this…it was Maya who killed Mike."

"Her brother…Maya killed her own brother?"

"Yes, Mike wanted to let me live and help me get Aaliyah and of course Maya couldn't let that happen. She was using our daughter to get close to you. I forgive you, Supreme. I need for you to know that. I forgive you for unwillingly being a part of her manipulation and ultimately giving into temptation by having sex with her." He turned towards me and then looked away. "Devon held me as Maya beat me unmercifully, leaving me for dead before she burned the house down."

As if Supreme couldn't stand to hear anymore he collapsed on the couch and buried his face in his hands. But I refused to let up. If I wanted my husband back, which I did, he needed to believe every word I was saying. I couldn't leave a doubt in his mind that my story was nothing short of a hundred percent truth.

"When I was being held captive, Maya ripped off the pink diamond necklace you gave me. I guarantee you somewhere in this house with her belongings she has it. That necklace represented a symbol to her that she ripped us apart and that she won." Supreme lifted his head up and stared at me and for the first time I could see regret as his eyes watered up.

"How can you ever forgive me? I want to say sorry but it sounds like such a baby word right now. I was sleeping with the enemy all that time. I let her take care of our daughter." Misery flooded Supreme's face and my heart broke for him. I knew I could forgive him but the real question was would Supreme be able to forgive himself.

685

Maya

Being with Arnez for the last few days gave me a different view on my relationship with Supreme or lack thereof. When Arnez was inside of me I could feel how much he wanted me and desired my body. With Supreme it always felt as if there was someplace he'd rather be or better yet someone else he would rather be with. I wasn't ignorant to the fact his preference was Precious but I had convinced myself if I put it on him just right his wife would eventually become an afterthought. With all the time and energy I put into making Supreme mine I wasn't ready to abandon my plan just yet. While Arnez was out, I decided to call him and see if my absence had made him miss me at all.

I rocked my leg back and forth sitting on the edge of the bed waiting for Supreme to answer the phone. "Hello." When a female voice answered his phone I instantly hit the end key. I waited a few seconds and called right back thinking maybe I dialed the wrong number but the same voice answered and I didn't want to believe it was who it sounded like.

"Who is this?"

"Precious Mills. Who is this?" I was silent not knowing what to say. "Is this Maya?" Precious asked without hesitation. "Why don't you speak the fuck up? I know that's yo' sorry ass on the other end of this phone. Yeah, heffa I'm back and Supreme know everything!"

"You'll pay for this, Precious."

"Ho, I've already paid. The fact that I know you was fucking my husband is payment enough. But we good now. And trust, I got something for yo' sneaky ass. Wherever you at, whatever you doing, enjoy this little bit of freedom while you can, because baby girl your days are up. Now get the fuck off my husbands' phone!"

The line went dead but I was still holding the phone in an attempt to convince myself the conversation that took place hadn't.

"The other day Precious was in the parking lot in Philadelphia unloading her weapon on me and now she was answering Supreme's phone, how the hell did that happen? I laid up in the bed with Arnez for a few days and my entire life has changed," I stated out loud in bewilderment. I fell back on the bed, stunned by the turn of events. What really had me confused was how Precious was able to find Supreme. He had done everything to make sure Precious couldn't track him down but there she was back on her throne. All I could do was scream at the top of my lungs and punch the pillow on the bed as if I was beating the shit out of Precious.

Knock...knock...knock

"Is everything alright in there?" I heard the cleaning lady ask through the door.

"Sorry 'bout that. Everything's fine. I accidentally ripped a dress I was putting on and got upset," I lied. Precious had my mind in another world that I forgot I was in a hotel. This wasn't the time for me to lose my mind if anything I needed to come up with a new game plan and fast. My cover was officially now blown and I wasn't sure what Precious' next move would be. Would she turn me into the police for kidnapping and the murder of my brother, Clip and a few other folks? If she did, would they even believe her story. With Devon dead who could corroborate the shit.

On the other hand, Precious wasn't exactly the fuck with the police type. There was an excellent chance she would decide to get that street justice, which meant I would be looking over my shoulder for the rest of my life. Either way the dice weren't rolling in my favor and I was fucked. I had to come up with a way to get back in the driver's seat. My brain was going in deep scheme mode when I heard Arnez using his key to open the door. Normally I would welcome his company but I couldn't think about dick right now. This was about life, death, freedom or jail.

"I thought you would be dressed by the time I got back," were the first words out of Arnez's mouth when he saw me.

"I slept late."

"We need to be heading out, we have a busy day."

"When you say heading out are you talking about leaving for good?"

"Yep. We have to stop in New York for a day then head back to Philly. Things have gotten somewhat calmer so it's time for business as usual."

"What are we going to New York for?"

"Business and pleasure."

"What sort of pleasure?"

"There's a party going on tonight that I need to attend."

"I'm not in the mood for a party tonight. Would you mind if I didn't go?"

"Of course I would mind. This wasn't a request. You will be attending this party with me. I've already picked out what I want you to wear."

"Arnez, I don't feel like going. You can go to the party. I'll wait in the hotel room for you."

If it wasn't for the severe stinging on my cheek I would've completely missed the smack that Arnez landed on my face. That's how sudden and unexpected it was to me.

"Don't you ever tell me what you won't do. Do you not know who I am? But don't worry, you'll learn. As I said, you have soldier potential. Nobody has taken the time to teach you but I will."

"You hit me...I can't believe you hit me." I really couldn't. Too many things didn't fuck me up in terms of disbelief but this had. I didn't think Arnez was a softie but woman beater went right over my head. He was passionate but gentle as a lover. The few times we went out he was a complete gentleman. He was not the man I would pick out of a line up to be the type who would snatch-a-ho-up on some bullshit but he was that man. After he slapped me, I stared in his eyes and saw that he was crazier than me and that was scary.

"Believe it. It's part of training camp. If you're a fast learner I'll only have to do it a few more times. But you're very young so you might be hard headed which means I'll have to knock you around several times before I break you in."

That fool said that shit like he was about to train me and put me through something simple like a cooking course. I could tolerate a bunch of bullshit from a nigga I was feeling. I even got off on some excitement in a relationship but a motherfucker beating my ass never turned me on. Because a nigga that would beat your ass is a nigga that would kill you and the bottom line was I didn't want to die. Now instead of focusing my energy on how to one-up Precious, I had to figure how to get the fuck away from Arnez's crazy ass.

"I'm a fast learner. You won't have any more problems from me. If you want me to go to the party then I will."

"That's my girl. Now go shower and get dressed. Like I said, we need to leave."

On the ride to New York, I was plotting on how I would break free of Arnez. Luckily I was born and raised there so I knew how to maneuver my way around with no problem. But I had to be careful. I already had Precious aiming at me, I didn't need to add a psycho like Arnez to the list.

"Turn the music down, this is an important call." I was about to ask him what was wrong with his hands but quickly remembered who I was dealing with and a remark like that might land me a blackened eye.

"You've been hard to catch up with the last couple of days."

"My wife got back home so I've been extremely busy." *Oh shit, that sounds like Supreme!* Now I was happy as hell I turned the volume down because their conversation was clear as shit.

"I understand, family always comes first." I had to roll my eyes hearing that come out of Arnez's mouth. He seemed like the type that would have his entire family petrified that if everything wasn't precisely the way he wanted everybody was getting fucked up.

"Yeah, but what's up with you. I thought for sure you would have that Nico situation resolved by now."

"Me too but for the last few months he hasn't been making any moves...no business. Something had him occupied."

"Or someone."

"Excuse me?"

"Nothing, so what's up with him now?'

"Word came to me today that he might be partnering up with a woman named CoCo and this dude Genesis."

"Who the fuck are they?"

"Some people I'm not on good terms with. So if he's dealing with them, I would need to come up with a different approach in getting him to do some business with me."

"I advise you to come up with that approach at rapid speed because I've funneled way too much money in your business for you to bring me nothing."

"You know that I appreciate all that you've done."

"I don't need your appreciation or want it. If you can't get done what I need you to do then I'll have to take my money someplace else."

"Come on, we've worked together way too long for you to say something like that. I've made you millions of dollars."

"Yeah whatever."

"I got you. When you asked me to resolve that issue I didn't think it would be that complicated. But you know the problems I've had recently and like I said he's just starting to get back to handling business. There's a delay, that's all. But not the sort of problem that you would need to sever our business relationship."

"I hear you. I have to come that way tomorrow to stop by my parents' place to pick up my daughter, so before I leave I wanna see you. And our conversation needs to go differently. You know what you need to get done...so make it happen. I want Nico Carter out of commission...'nough said."

I had been dissecting each sentence from that discussion and I couldn't figure all the shit out but one thing seemed evident, Arnez worked for Supreme and Arnez was a drug dealer. So added to Supreme's list of business ventures was running a drug empire. I didn't think Xavier Mills had it in him. Now I had another reason why it was imperative I get the fuck away from Arnez. Because Supreme was coming to town and if he found out Arnez was dealing with me, I would be added to that out of commission list Nico Carter was on.

"I have to get rid of Genesis and CoCo once and for all. They're going to fuck everything up." I heard Arnez mumbling under his breath. I hoped if I remained mute he would continue on oblivious I was interested in every word he was saying.

"If I could just find Genevieve because having someone make prank calls pretending to be his sister isn't enough. I need her for bait."

Damn this nigga off the chain, getting fake motherfuckers to call pretending to be that man's sister. If he wasn't a woman beater, we could put our minds together and come up with some fabulous scams. He's more calculating than me.

"We're going to the Greenhouse in Soho. 150 Varick Street between Vandam & Spring," Arnez told the taxi driver. After letting him know our destination he turned his attention to me. "Did I tell you how sexy you look in that dress?"

"No, but you have great taste in clothes, so it's all you."

"True, but you've pulled if off perfectly," he said, admiring the black Alexander Wang sheer sleeved mini- dress. It was a cute dress, I'll admit. But Arnez had me feeling like I was his personal dress up doll which wasn't cute.

"So who is this party for?"

"The spokes model for Akil Walker's new women's clothing line."

"Oh, I've seen a couple of ads for that, his shit is hot. So he's giving the party for the person who's modeling his clothes?"

"She's the exclusive model for his women's line. And this is like her introduction to the heavyweights in the industry."

"Sounds exciting for her."

"I'm sure it will be." Arnez didn't strike me as the type who would give a fuck about some models' party to celebrate her introduction to the scene. I knew there was a lot more to this but I would have to sit back and observe to find out.

When the taxi pulled in front of the club it had that red velvet rope, I wanna be a star feel. Two cut the fuck up security men were keeping post at the entrance and some chick with a clipboard and headpiece was working the guest list. Arnez said a couple of words to the girl and slid on through. The spacious bi-level club was cute in a unique sort of way. I noticed a little sign that read 'first eco-friendly nightlife destination' I assumed that was important to the folks running the establishment because me as a guest could care less.

I followed behind Arnez taking in the interesting design of the place. The transparent ceiling fixture had a bunch of crystals, which seemed to be designed to emulate a rolling landscape. Then the bars were clear glass, that displayed lush natural scenes and I assumed it was all recycled since this was supposed to be an eco- friendly spot. None of it was my style but when I noticed the interior projection screens mounted on three separate walls playing what seemed to be the photo shoots the spokes model did for the clothing line. Then the name 'Nichelle' kept flashing on the screen and I assumed that was the model's name.

"Come on, we're going to sit in the VIP section on the upper level." I nodded my head and kept following Arnez, curious as to what he was up to.

"Maya," I heard someone call out my name but Soho wasn't my neck of the woods so I glanced around to see who it might be. "Maya..." I heard the same female voice again. But this time I saw who it was.

"Tashawn, girl what are you doing here?" We gave each other a quick hug.

"You remember Dionne."

"Yeah, you talking 'bout Dionne from Queens?"

"Exactly, she dragged me to this bullshit. She heard Akil Walker would be here and thought if she showed up, she'd get discovered and be his next spokes model." We both burst out laughing because that sounded like some dreamer shit Dionne would come up with.

"Has she found him?"

"Hell no! And if she did, his head is probably so far up the ass of his new model up there," Tashawn pointed toward the projection screen, "so he wouldn't give Dionne a second thought. Plus she know the PR chick that put this shit together and supposedly Akil nor is that model Nichelle showing up. Akil's publicity people just threw that out there to get a bigger turn out and I see it worked...but moving on, what are you doing here. We ain't seen you in none of the boroughs for a minute. Where you been?"

"I've been in Miami for a minute."

"So what brought you here?"

"Him," I said pointing at Arnez who was making gestures for me to bring my ass on.

"Girl, he don't look cool wit' you being over here talking to me."

"That nigga a nut. Don't nothing make him happy but himself. You driving?"

"Yeah, why?"

"How much longer you gon' be here?"

"Dionne in the bathroom. When she come out we probably leaving in a few. This not my type of party. And Dionne only came to meet that Akil dude, now that she know he ain't showing up, she ready to go."

"I hear that so can you do me a favor?"

"Sure, what is it?"

"Let me get a ride wit' ya'."

"Girl, that ain't nothing. It'll be like old times when we used to skip school together and ride the trains going no fuckin' where."

"Yeah, but we ain't getting on the train...not tonight," we laughed thinking about old times.

"So do you want me to just come get you when we're ready?"

"I'ma ditch homeboy so I don't want him to have a clue I'm bouncing. Here put my number in your phone. I'll meet you on the corner of Spring within ten minutes. But if I don't show up, you got my number, send me a text."

"Cool, we'll be in a black Explorer."

"Thanks, Tashawn. Girl, I owe you big time." I was so happy I ran into Tashawn, I was tempted to break into a two-step in the middle of the dance floor. But I remained cool and smiled when I reached Arnez. He appeared as if he was ready to choke a bitch up.

"Who were you talking to?"

"This girl I went to school with. I hadn't seen her in a minute so we were playing catch up. So what's up, are you enjoying the party?" I asked wanting to switch the dialogue off of me.

"It's cool, I just wish the guest of honor would hurry up, show her face."

"You talking about her, that model Nichelle?" I pointed at the screen.

"Yes, but her name is Genevieve," he huffed like I didn't know who I was talking about.

"Huh? That model up there, her name is Nichelle."

"Yes her..."he shrugged, seeming annoyed.

"Oh baby, that's the closest you gon' get to seeing her face."

"What are you talking about?'

"She's a no-show and so is the dude Akil."

"Who told you that?" he practically screamed the question in my ear.

"There's no need to get upset. I'm sure you'll be able to see them at some other party."

"Just answer the question," he pulled on my arm.

"Listen, I'm getting tired of you manhandling me!"

I was ready to take off my shoe and go upside dude's head but since I knew I was about to make a getaway I calmed it down. "I apologize baby, what was the question again?"

"How do you know Genevieve isn't showing up?"

"Who is this Genevieve chick you keep talking about?"

"Excuse me, I meant to say Nichelle."

"The girl I was speaking with, her girlfriend is cool with the PR chick that did this event and she told her neither one of them was showing up."

"Are you sure?"

"I mean I wasn't there taking part in the discussion but I'm sure you can go ask the girl yourself. My friend told me she was upstairs. Ask for the PR chick and she's wearing one of those headsets."

"You stay right here." Arnez pointed his finger in my face like I was five years old. "I'll be right back."

"No problem baby, take your time I'll be right here...Not!" When I saw Arnez motherfuckin' ass make that turn to go upstairs I grabbed my purse and hit it. Whatever shit he had bought me at the mall he could keep it. I had all the essential goods right here in my purse. I bolted out that club so fast and never looked back.

Precious

I stood in Aaliyah's bedroom thinking about all I had missed out on from being away from her these past few months. Looking at her pictures, she had grown so much. Although she looked a lot like me, it was amazing how much she resembled my mother. When I came across one particular picture on her dresser, it took every ounce of strength I had not to completely lose it.

"Yo' ass will be mine! I don't give a fuck what I have to do!" I spit, holding a picture that Maya and Aaliyah took together. The anger that had come over me wanted to rip the picture into tiny shreds, but then I was torn, because my sweet Aaliyah was also in the picture, and for some strange reason I would feel guilty tearing up her image too. So, I did the only other thing I felt comfortable with. I tossed the shit in the trash.

"We're gonna take a flight out in the morning."

I jolted slightly, not expecting to hear Supreme's voice.

"I didn't mean to startle you."

"That's okay. What time does our flight leave?"

"We're taking the jet, so whenever we get there."

"Well, I'll be ready first thing in the morning, because I can't wait to see my baby."

"I know she'll be happy to see you too."

"Do you really think so? I mean it's been so long that I'm afraid she won't remember me."

"Of course Aaliyah remembers you. I always showed her your picture and told her that this was her mommy."

"You did?" The shock in my voice was evident.

"Yeah, I did. I know, as angry as I was with you, it surprised me too, but something just made me do it. And I'm glad I did."

"So am I. I know with everything you believed, the last person you wanted to talk to Aaliyah about was me."

"For the last couple of days I've been tearing this house up, searching for that necklace."

"I was wondering what you were looking for."

"In my heart I knew what you told me was true, but..."

"You weren't totally convinced," I said, completing Supreme's thought. "I knew that. That's why you still haven't touched me, because part of you believes that all this time I've been having this fling with Nico, that I left you and Aaliyah to be with him. I do pray that you find that necklace so you can put your mind at ease and have some sort of proof that I'm telling you the truth."

"I know that you are," Supreme disclosed as he moved his arm from behind his back and lifted up the necklace. "It was in a satin pouch in the pocket of a coat hanging in a closet I never knew existed. That's what happens when you live in a house that's way too big."

"Baby, I'm so happy you found it," I sighed, feeling for the first time that there was a chance Supreme and I could get back what we once had.

"If you want, I can put it back on for you."

"Of course I want you to." I walked to the hallway where Supreme was standing and turned around. He lifted my hair and latched the necklace around my neck, putting it back in its rightful place. I then felt the softness of his lips on my shoulder, and he began sprinkling kisses up to my neck. A warm shiver shot through my body as it yearned for the touch of my husband.

"Damn, I missed you!" Supreme whispered in my ear before the tip of his tongue stroked my earlobe. He turned me around and pressed my back against the wall, sliding his hand up the loose fitting dress I was wearing. The firm pressure from his hand caressed the flesh of my thigh.

"Baby, I missed you more," I said breathlessly.

My arms were pinned up and my eyes were closed as I gave in to the pleasure I'd been longing for. Supreme's tongue made love to every inch of my body before he even entered inside me. When he lifted his shirt off, the flexing of each muscle reminded me of how secure I felt in his arms. I needed him so badly that it scared me. He clasped his hands around my waist and lifted me up, and then laid me down in the middle of the hallway. I didn't mind, because I couldn't wait any longer and the bedroom seemed too far away. I wrapped my legs around his back and pulled him in closer as our kisses became more intense and our tongues went deeper. Then, when he let his long thick dick massage my clit, I had an orgasm based on the anticipation alone. And once he dipped inside of me, if possible, I fell in love with him all over again. It was clear that emotionally, physically and mentally, we were both trying to make up for all the months of being apart, which made our lovemaking that much more passionate, and let me know that I was finally home.

When the private jet landed at Teterboro Airport, I was anxious to go to Supreme's parents' house and get Aaliyah. I missed my baby so much that it hurt.

"Listen, I have some business I need to handle. The car will take you to my parents' house, and I'll be there later on when I'm done."

"I don't want to be away from you. Can we go get Aaliyah and then we come with you?"

"Precious, this is business, not pleasure. I'll be back as soon as I can," Supreme promised, kissing my hand.

"Okay, baby." I watched as he got into the other awaiting limousine. I speculated about what business was so important that he had to go directly from the jet to handle. But I also understood that the lifestyle we lived required more money than I ever thought was possible to even make. Maintaining this standard of living required a lot of work from Supreme. So, if he had to go and handle business, then I had no choice but to understand no matter how much I wanted to spend time with him.

After Supreme's limo drove off, I got into the other one. Before I could even get comfortable, my cell started ringing and saw it was Nico calling. "Hey you!"

"Hey you back. I hadn't heard from you since your flight landed and wanted to make sure you were straight."

"Everything's good. I actually just got to New Jersey."

"Jersey, what you doing there?"

"Supreme and I came to pick up Aaliyah. She was here visiting his parents."

"Well, let me let you go, 'cause I know he doesn't want you talking to me."

"I'm alone. He had to go handle some business, so he's gonna meet up with us later."

"Cool. I know you can't wait to see your daughter."

"Nico, with all the bullshit I've been through these last few months, holding Aaliyah again will make it all worthwhile. But I'm still gonna stick it to Maya's ass. Speaking of Maya, have you gotten any new leads?"

"I was gonna wait until I got more facts before telling you, but since you brought her name up—"

"Tell me!" I insisted, cutting Nico off.

"Maya might be in New York. One of the investigators on the case said they believe she was spotted in her old neighborhood. He's had someone watching her mother's house for some time, but hadn't seen any activity. But supposedly yesterday she was seen in the area. This hasn't been verified yet, so I don't want you getting amped just yet."

"So, when do you think you'll know for sure?"

"I can't say; maybe in the next few hours, maybe not until tomorrow. But of course I'll call you the moment I get the facts."

"Are you still in Philly?"

"Yeah, but me and Genesis are heading that way now."

"You and Genesis?'

"Yeah. I told him I wanted to already be in New York in case what the investigator told me turned out to be accurate. He said he had some business to handle that way, so he would take the ride with me."

"I really do appreciate you staying on top of this for me. With everything I got going on, I don't want Maya to slip through the cracks."

"And she won't! You need time to reconnect with your family, so I'ma hold this shit down for you...no worries."

"I gotta feeling Maya might really be in New York. She knows I'm with Supreme, so she can't go back to Miami, and—"

"Hold up! Maya knows you're back with Supreme?"

"I've been so occupied tryna' get shit right with my husband that I forgot to tell you. I spoke to her."

"When?"

"The other day. She called Supreme and I answered. At first she was on some juvenile bullshit, playing on the phone. You know, hanging up then calling back. Finally, I called her ass out and she spoke up."

"What did she say?"

"Nothing much. She basically listened. I told her ass to enjoy her little freedom, because I was gon' tap that ass when I saw her.

She tried to act like she wasn't shook, but I could tell I had the hussy nervous."

"I bet."

"That's why I believe she probably is in New York. She knows she can't come back to Supreme. With Devon dead, there's no need for her to stay in Philly, so why not go back to her comfort zone in New York to come up with a master plan?"

"True...but before you even told me about your conversation with Maya, I felt the same way. That's why I decided to head to New York. But now, with what you just told me, basically confirms it."

"Well, we're pulling up to Supreme's parents' house. Call me when you get to New York or find out anything else...whichever comes first."

"Got you. And I know she's never met me, but please give Aaliyah a hug and kiss for me."

"That's so sweet, and I will. Bye."

I couldn't get out of the limo fast enough. By the time the driver got out to open my door, I was about to ring the bell. Mr. Mills must've heard the limo pull up, because he came out with open arms before I reached the entrance.

"It's wonderful to see you, Precious!" He said, giving me a hug.

"It's great to see you too. Where's Aaliyah?"

"With Grandma," Mr. Mills said affectionately. "They went to the park earlier, and they're on their way back now. I know how excited you must be."

"I am. I miss her like crazy."

"She misses you too. We told her yesterday that Mommy was coming to get her, and she's been smiling ever since."

I followed Mr. Mills inside the house, anxious for my baby to come home. "I see Aaliyah has her toys everywhere," I commented, looking around.

"Yeah, that's one of the beautiful things about having grandchildren. They're so full of life. With their toys and curiosity, they can't help but keep us old folks full of life too."

"I know you all were planning on having Aaliyah much longer, and I apologize for cutting her visit so short, but..."

"You don't have to apologize for wanting your child to go home with you. I know that you, Supreme and the baby have been through hell. I'm just pleased you all have come back together and are trying to work things out."

"I am too."

"We've been married for over thirty-five years, and it hasn't been easy. I know it's hard work, but my son loves you, and I can look into your eyes and see that you love him a hell of a lot too."

"I do...I really, really do. I just hope our marriage can last as long as you and Mrs. Mills' has."

"Stay faithful and in prayer, and it will...hold on, let me answer the phone. Have a seat and get comfortable. They'll be home soon," Mr. Mills continued before leaving the room.

A big smile crossed my face, and I sat down on the couch with an enormous amount of happiness consuming every part of me. For months, I didn't think I would ever feel this sort of contentment again. But here I was, sitting in the living room of my husband's parents' house, waiting for the arrival of my daughter. Growing up, I never experienced this sort of normalcy, and I had to admit, it was one of the most gratifying feelings in the world. My daydreaming of feeling on top of the world was interrupted when Mr. Mills came back into the living room.

"Mr. Mills, what's wrong?" His once jovial face now appeared to be cracked and broken.

"We have to go to the hospital."

"What happened?" I jumped up. "Say something!"

"My wife has a minor concussion, and Aaliyah's gone." Mr. Mills' voice was calm, but his hands were shaking and fear consumed his face.

"What do you mean Aaliyah is gone?"

"I don't know what happened yet. The police officer didn't know all the details."

"The police! Oh Dear God, this can't be happening to me, not again! Let's go, now!" I screamed, rushing out of the house.

When we got to Mrs. Mills' hospital room, she was sitting up in the bed and incoherent. Tears welled up in her eyes when she saw my face.

"Precious, I'm so sorry! I'll never forgive myself if anything happens to Aaliyah!" Tears were now streaming down her face, and I swear to you, I honestly didn't care. Her tears meant nothing to me.

"It's okay," Mr. Mills said, trying to console his wife.

"No, it's not okay! What happened to my daughter?"

"After we were finished playing at the park, we walked to the car, and when I was buckling her in the car seat, somebody snuck up behind me and knocked me on the back of my head. I must've loss consciousness, because when I woke up I was in the hospital bed."

"Thank God you're alright!" Mr. Mills said, rubbing his wife's shoulders. "It wasn't your fault," he continued, and then he turned to look at me, wanting confirmation that I didn't blame Mrs. Mills. He was right, it wasn't her fault, but it didn't change how fucked up I felt at this very moment.

"Are you the missing little girl's mother?" a police officer entered the room and asked.

"Yes I am, but can you wait one moment? I need to take this call." I sprinted out the room, wanting some privacy.

"Nico, somebody took Aaliyah, and I put it on everything that Maya's motherfuckin' ass had something to do with it!"

"Get the fuck outta here! When did this happen?"

"It couldn't have been no more than an hour or so ago. She was at the park with Supreme's mother, and somebody rolled up on her from behind and knocked her out. Then, they took Aaliyah. That sounds like a Maya move."

"Fuckin' right! She's desperate. She knows you're holding all the cards, so what can she do but revert back to the only thing that gives her leverage...Aaliyah! I might have to kill that bitch myself !" Nico roared. "Wait, hold on one second, that's the P.I. beeping in on the other line."

I wanted to leap out of my skin as I paced the hospital floor. Fuckin' around with Maya's demented ass was gon' have me with a head full of gray hair before I even knocked on thirty.

"He got something!" Were the first words Nico said when he clicked back over.

"What did he say?"

"Early this morning, Maya rented a car over at Enterprise."

"Which one?"

"The one in Englewood."

"She must've stopped there before she took Aaliyah, because Supreme's parents live in Teaneck which isn't far from Englewood at all."

"Yeah, because the dude that helped her said she didn't have a baby with her. But she did ask him if he could recommend a hotel in the area, and he suggested the Crown Plaza on South Van Brunt Street. She even asked him for directions and he wrote them down for her."

"I'm on my way over there."

"Precious, why don't you wait for me? We just passed Exit 13 on the turnpike."

"I'll see you there. I gotta go get my daughter!" I rushed back to Mrs. Mills' hospital room on a mission.

"Mr. Mills, I need your car keys."

"Why, you're leaving? You should stay here. Supreme is on his way."

"I'll call Supreme when I get in the car, but I need your car keys, now!" Mr. Mills just stood there staring at me like he didn't hear what the fuck I said. "Am I speaking a foreign language? I need your car keys, now!"

"Give her the keys." Mrs. Mills smacked her husband's arm, and he reluctantly handed over the keys to me.

"Thanks!" I said, snatching them out of his hand and rushing out. I heard the officer calling out, trying to get my attention, but I ignored him, because for what I was about to do, the police would only be in the way. I know I had agreed with Nico that our first option was to let the legal system work and let Maya rot in jail, but that option was now off the table. Maya was now officially a dead bitch!

 Maya

"This baby is so cute! Whose little girl is this?" Tashawn asked me while she looked at a sleeping Aaliyah.

"She's my niece."

"I didn't know Mike had a baby."

"Yeah, he found out about her while he was locked up. And before he got killed, he always told me that if anything happened to him to make sure I took care of her."

"She is such a cutie. She do kinda look like him."

"I think so too."

"So, where's the little girl's mom at?"

"She fell on hard times and she ain't really got no family. She called me yesterday asking if I could keep her for awhile, you know, until she got back on her feet.

That's my niece so I couldn't say no."

"True. That's real big of you though, Maya. Kids ain't no joke. They're a big responsibility. My sister got one, and she stays struggling."

"Exactly. I'm just glad I was in New York, which made it easy for me to go pick Aaliyah up from her."

"Yeah, that worked out good. So, how long are you staying? I mean, a hotel ain't exactly the best place for a baby."

"I know, and I need to get her so much stuff. I mean homegirl didn't even give me no clothes or nothing."

"Damn, she must've fell on real hard times. But I guess she was doing the best she could, because the baby looks like she was well cared for."

"Yeah, but I need to get her some stuff before we hit the road. That's why I asked you to meet me here. I was hoping you could watch Aaliyah while I went to the store and got some stuff for her."

"Oh, you need me to baby-sit? Girl, that ain't no problem, and she's asleep."

"Tashawn, you my girl. This is the second time you've come through for me. Here, take this," I said, going in my wallet and pulling out some money.

"This is five hundred dollars! What you want, for me to babysit her for the month!"

"Tashawn, you so silly!"

"You don't have to give me all this money."

"What, you don't want it?" I said, reaching out my hand.

"I ain't say all that," she laughed, tightly gripping the money and pulling her hand back. "I ain't crazy. If you want me to have it, I won't turn it down. I was just sayin' it wasn't necessary to give me this much."

"Girl, don't worry about it. I appreciate you helping me out at the last minute like this. I shouldn't be gone that long, because I really want to hit the road tonight."

"Where you going?'

"We have to stop through Philly for a minute before we go to our new home."

"You bought a house?"

"Yep, it's in Miami, and it's beautiful."

"Damn girl, you doing good for yourself. Your money must be right—or should I say *his* money!"

"No, it's all mine. Mike had a huge insurance policy, and when he died all the money came to me."

"He didn't leave none for his daughter?"

"Well, he wasn't sure how stable her mother was, and he didn't want her to splurge all the money on herself and then his baby end up with nothing anyway. He knew I would make sure that if need be, my niece would be taken care of."

"You proved him right. Well, girl, when ya' get situated, you need to let me come visit you in Miami. I ain't never been there before, and I heard it's the shit!"

"Yeah, you'll love it. I'll definitely send for you so we can ball out and pop some bottles and shit."

"That's what's up!"

"Girl, let me head out and handle my shit before Aaliyah wakes up."

"Take your time. I know how to care for a baby. I baby-sit my nephew all the time. I got this."

"Thanks, girl. Hit me on my cell if you need anything."

"Will do."

As I rode the elevator down, I thought about how perfectly shit was coming together for me. Overhearing the conversation between Supreme and Arnez while we were in the car made the bullshit I had to deal with from that maniac Arnez worth it. I would've never known Aaliyah was with Supreme's parents, and my window of opportunity to snatch her up was a small one. I had to move swiftly if I wanted to get the job done.

From the months of living with Supreme and Aaliyah visiting his parents during that time, I knew their address, which was a serious plus point. After I had a cab drop me off at the rental car place not far from their house, and once I got the vehicle, all I had to do was park in an inconspicuous place and wait for the right opening to make my move. When I saw Supreme's mother come out of the house with Aaliyah, I knew the opportunity had come knocking. Once I followed them to the park and let grandma wear her little granddaughter's ass out, it was too easy to knock the defenseless old lady to the ground and take Aaliyah.

Now that I had the best bargaining tool possible, when the time was right, I would contact Supreme and see exactly what he was willing to give up to get his daughter back, or *who* he was willing to give up, because I refused to allow Precious to be happy. She thought she could come back and reclaim her old life as if shit hadn't changed. The nerve of her answering Supreme's phone as if she owned him. But once again, I showed her who the real queen bitch is, and it's me. I'm always one step ahead of her.

I would've given anything to see the look on her face when she got the news that the reunion with her daughter she'd been wishing for was not gonna happen. I couldn't help but laugh to myself. Precious had come up short once again. For a second time, I was the hand rocking the cradle, so that means I rule the world.

Skipping to the car, smiles and giggles continued as I thought about all the misery I was bringing Precious. *That bitch is somewhere crying right now, and Supreme probably so sick of all the drama that comes with dealing with her ass that he ain't thinking about wiping away the tears. Yep, Precious, when I'm done torturing you, you will have lost it all; your daughter, husband and mind.*

"Oh shi-i-i-i-t!" I bawled as my moment of celebrating was instantly brought to a halt. Right as I put the key in the ignition, I saw Precious in some sort of old school Cadillac, cruising slowly as she looked around the parking lot. There was no doubt in my mind she was looking for me. When the car started, the sound of the engine must've caught her attention, and the evil glare she hurled in my direction made me put the car quickly of the parking lot. Of course her nerve-wrecking ass was on my shit as I hit South Van Brunt going towards Nordhoff Place. I then suddenly veered to the right on Route-4W hoping to lose the bitch, but when I looked in the rearview mirror, there she was, keeping the fuck up. I then made another abrupt right, which put me on Decatur, and that insistent broad did too.

"Bitch, get off my back!" I screamed out, determined to lose her once and for all. When I tried to make a hasty left on Alfred Avenue, I lost control of the car and smashed into a parked car. The impact was so hard that it caused the airbag to discharge.

"Fu-u-u-u-uck!" I shouted as I tried to start the car back up, but got absolutely nothing. "Fuck it...fuck it... fuck it!" I repeated as I grabbed my purse and soared out of the car, concluding that I would have to lose this bitch on foot.

I glanced behind me briefly and didn't see Precious, which brought a small sense of relief. I cut through some houses trying to maneuver through the back streets.

"Damn, I'm tired," I groaned, almost out of breath. I knew I couldn't run forever, so I decided to call Tashawn. It was either call her, or a taxi, and I was too tired, frustrated and pissed the fuck off to try and get some local taxi information.

"Hello."

"Hey Tashawn," I said, still breathing extremely hard.

"Maya, are you okay? You sound out of breath."

"Girl, somebody just tried to rob me."

"What!"

"Yes, I was able to keep my purse, but they took the car."

"Are you serious? Did you call the police?"

"Yes, I'm waiting for them now so I can file a report. But can you pick me up? I could ask the police officer when he gets here, but I need to go back to the rental car place, and I know that they're not gonna want to do all that for me."

"Don't even trip. I'm sure you don't wanna ride in no police car anyway. Tell me where you at and I'll come get you."

"What about my niece?"

"Girl, I have a car seat. I always keep one in the car because I never know when I might have to go get my nephew."

"Great, I owe you again."

"You gave me five-hundred dollars, so we good. Now where you at?"

"There's this gas station right beside this store on the corner of Hancock Avenue. You know, like if you were going towards Route-4 E."

"I think I know where you talking about, but I got navigation on my phone so I'll be straight."

"Girl, you really are a life saver."

"Don't worry about it. I'll call you when I get near there."

"Cool, I'll be there." I stood behind a house for a few more minutes. I could see a main street, and a gas station right next to a store, from where I was. After making sure there was no sign of Precious, I felt confident enough to walk across the street and wait for Tashawn near the gas station. When I went to the store, I was thirsty and I had to piss, so I figured I'd empty my bladder first, then get a drink.

I dashed inside the stall, almost ripping off my jeans. I didn't even have time to lock the door because I was afraid I was about to urinate on myself. When I bent down over the toilet, I shut my eyes in relief as the pee seemed to flow forever. When I finished, I felt much more relaxed. My mind was now clear enough to figure out my next move. "At least I got rid of Precious' dumb ass," I said, after flushing the toilet.

"Think again, bitch!"

My heart dropped when I realized Precious was standing in front of the bathroom stall with her fists balled up, each resting solidly on her waist. Before I could say a word, her spiked stiletto heel was puncturing my stomach, thrusting me back against the mechanical flush valve.

"Ahhhhhhh!" I screeched out in pain. I thought I heard my back crack, but before I had time to know for sure, Precious was digging her nails in my scalp as she slammed my head inside the toilet bowl.

"You just had to keep fuckin' wit' me and my family!" she yelled, yanking my head out of the toilet bowl water. "You gon' regret the day you ever decided to go up against me!" she continued, then jammed my face back in the water. This heffa had me thinking I was gonna drown in the toilet bowl. I was trying to clench my hands on the floor to get some balance and maybe get Precious off of me, but she was not letting up.

Precious yanked my head out of the toilet again, and I tried to catch my breath thinking she was gonna baptize me once more, but instead, as she maintained the grip on my hair, she opened the stall door and slammed me against the wall.

"I want you to see my face as I beat yo' ass! Oh, and check out the pink diamond heart. Yeah, bitch this shit is where it belongs." Precious barked before taking her knee and shoving it up my pussy, not once, not twice, not even three fuckin' times, but over and over again. I felt like the bitch was giving me a botched abortion, and I wasn't even pregnant.

"I can't take no more...please, stop!" I begged.

"Stop! Bitch, we ain't even started!" she boasted, smashing the back of my head repeatedly against the wall.

"You ain't so bad when you ain't got Devon holding me while you beat me wit' some brass knuckles, huh? Don't go silent on me. The fun just about to start."

My body was halfway numb from pain by the time Precious hauled me over to the sink. When she swung my face like it was a baseball bat against the bathroom faucets, I just knew I was dead. Blood splattered everywhere as my nose and mouth ripped open. The collision with the sink also caused my two front teeth to come out. Although I wasn't dead, I no longer wanted to be alive.

"Precious, you win...please stop!" I pleaded as blood gushed out of my mouth.

"I'ma be honest with you. I am gonna kill you. But if you take me to my daughter and not a strand of her hair is out of place, instead of mutilating you while you're still alive, I'll simply slit your throat and let you watch yourself bleed to death. You can decide while I'm taking you to the car."

Precious pushed me down on the floor, wrapped my hair around her hand and dragged me out of the bathroom as if I was a bloody ragdoll. I could see the horror and disbelief on some of the customers' faces who were in the store, but she didn't give a fuck about any of them. She kept pulling me down the aisle like this was her world. When she opened the door and I hit the pavement, it felt as if the concrete was ripping the skin from my face.

"Help me!" I called out barely audible because of the excruciating pain I was in, but it was as if nobody cared, or maybe they were too damn scared, because only a crazy motherfucker like Precious could be this bold. When we got to her car and she was opening the passenger side door, I heard a car zoom up and stop right in front of us. The way Precious had me positioned on the ground I couldn't see shit though.

"Yo, Precious! What the fuck are you doing!" I heard a male voice yell out.

"Before I murder this bitch, Maya is gonna take me to my daughter...ain't that right, Maya?" Precious smiled down at me, knowing I didn't have the strength to reply even if I wanted to.

"I know you're pissed, but this shit right here is crazy. You're dragging a badly beaten woman out in public. I know how angry you are; fuck, I'm angry too, but this ain't the way to get shit done."

As I listened to some man trying to reason with Precious, I heard a car door open and then shut.

"Genesis, can you please try and reason with her?"

I felt Precious shift forward in one swift movement as if reaching for something, because of course, with the hold she had on my hair, when she moved, I moved too.

"Nico, get the fuck away from me! When I spotted Maya's sneaky ass crossing the street, I shoulda' never called you and told you where I was, 'cause I don't' want to hear this shit!"

"Yo, I can't believe you took my gun like that! Give me that shit back!"Precious stepped forward, evidently steadily holding the heat.

"Don't make me use this on you, because I will."

"Precious, what are you doing? you're smarter than this."

"Genesis, you need to stay the fuck outta this! You have no idea the hell this bitch has put me and my family through. And when I finally made it back to them, she kidnaps my daughter...again! This sick bitch deserves to die. Now, both of ya' get the fuck out of my way. I'm sure somebody is gon' call the police soon, if they haven't already. So I need to go!"

"Precious, Nico explained to me everything that Maya has done to you and your family, and she deserves to be punished. But I can't let you kill her."

"Excuse me? I didn't know I asked for your permission."

"Listen. I was trying to wait for Quentin to get here, but—"

"Quentin! What the fuck did you call Quentin for? Quentin ain't got nothing to do wit' this shit! Yo, get the fuck out of my way, both of you, before I just start blasting!"

"Precious, that's your sister you're about to kill, and Quentin Jacobs is both of ya's father. I swear it's true. When he saw you at that funeral and you told him your last name—not Mills but Cummings, unlike the first time when he met you with Mike—he had a feeling, but to be positive, when I had you meet me for breakfast that morning, it was to get your DNA so Quentin could have it compared to his."

"So what? You're a forensic scientist now? I can catch you on an episode of *CSI!* Nigga, get the fuck outta here with that bullshit!"

"It ain't bullshit, Precious. Maya is your sister."

"Let's say for argument sake you are telling the truth...so fuckin' what! I wouldn't give a damn if she came out my own mother's pussy and we were full blood sisters! This ho gotta go!"

"I'm not gonna let you spend the rest of your life in jail because of Maya. You have a fuckin' daughter to live for! You've always been so hard headed and stubborn. Is this piece of shit really worth your life without your daughter in it? Especially since we got the proof we need to send her to jail. I've already been in contact with Detective Moore. He's hungry to lock her ass up, and I told him I have the evidence he needs to do it," Nico continued to try and plead his case.

I wasn't sure what distressed me more; learning that I had a father I knew nothing about, or a sister I despised. Either way, my life was completely fucked, or over. Because, if Precious spared my life, I would still spend the majority of it locked up in a cage, or she could kill me, and honestly at this point, that sounded like a better alternative.

"Precious, Nico is right. You have everything to live for and nothing to gain if you kill Maya. Give Nico the gun so we can go find your daughter. Isn't that what it's really about, being reunited with your daughter? Don't let your emotions cause you to make a bad decision that you'll have to pay the consequences for, for the rest of your life."

Whoever the nigga, Genesis was, he had a profound effect on Precious, because she did hand the gun over to Nico, and right then, I heard what sounded like an explosion.

"What the fuck!" Precious walked a few feet forward, still dragging my ass. I guess when she put the gun down, that didn't include putting me down too.

"Some truck and a car just crashed into each other.

I can't see how anybody could have survived that shit!" Genesis said, as I assumed he had the best view of the accident. "I'ma go check and see if anybody is alive and needs some help."

"Precious, can I trust you won't go do no crazy shit to Maya if I go see if I can be of any help to Genesis?"

"Nico, go head. I'm not gonna do nothing. You and Genesis made your point. I'm positive Maya is gonna tell me where my daughter is," she said, yanking my head. "And then once we know Aaliyah's safe, we can toss Maya's ass over to the police."

"A'ight, don't fuck around and do nothing stupid."

"I won't. Plus, Supreme should be here any minute too. I had left him a message letting him know I spotted Maya, and where I was at. See, I think that's him pulling up now."

"Cool. I'ma check to see what's going on with the accident, and I'll be back."

With the fucked up luck I had today, I would deal with it all if it meant that Supreme wouldn't see me like this. The idea that the last image of me inscribed in Supreme's mind was of my cut up mouth and face, missing teeth, and covered in blood, made me want to get a hold of Nico's gun and end it all.

"What is Supreme doing? What is taking him so long to come over here?" I heard Precious mumble to herself out loud. "Genesis, did you see Supreme?"

"Yes."

"Where is he?"

"He's over there by the where the accident was."

"Oh, he's trying to help. That must mean there were some survivors."

"Precious, come with me for a minute."

"Hellooooo...Genesis...I have to stay here and watch Maya, remember."

"Here comes Nico. He'll make sure Maya doesn't go anywhere until the cops come arrest her. Nico, I was just telling Precious that you'll guard Maya while she comes with me."

"That's right. Go with Genesis. I got Maya."

"Ya' worry too much. I told you I wasn't gonna kill Maya. She still has to tell us where Aaliyah is. But if ya' feel better letting Nico play watchdog, then so be it. I wanna go talk to Supreme anyway."

When Precious unleashed my hair from her grasp, my head hit the pavement so hard that my once fading headache was back. I managed to lift my head up and caught a glimpse of lights flashing and sirens roaring from the ambulances that were on the scene. Precious was completely out of my view, and it was Nico who was now beside me.

"Thank you for not letting Precious kill me."

"Don't thank me yet," he said, pulling out his gun and sticking the barrel to my head. "Do you know who was in one of those cars that crashed? Aaliyah! And so help me, if she dies, I promise you, I will kill you myself."

After Nico's warning, a piercing scream filled the air, and I knew it was the cries from my sister...Precious.

Precious

"My baby can't die! Supreme, do something!" I screamed, becoming hysterical as we entered the emergency room.

"We're going to need you to wait here," the paramedics ordered as they rushed Aaliyah in.

"Precious, she'll pull through," Supreme said, trying to sound encouraging, but it wasn't working.

"This can't be happening. When will this hell we're living in end?" I wanted to know as my hands were shaking and my voice cracked.

"Your daughter doesn't have any medical conditions or allergies, correct?" the ER nurse asked.

"No, I already told the paramedics that on the ride over in the ambulance."

"I understand, sir. I was just checking, taking every precaution."

"How is she?" Nico asked frantically, walking in with Genesis.

"What the fuck is he doing here?" Supreme barked, making it clear that Nico's presence was not wanted.

"Supreme, please! Nico is concerned, just like Genesis.

"Mr. and Mrs. Mills," we heard the doctor call out.

"Yes! How is our daughter? Is she going to be okay?"

"I'm Dr. Katz. We're going to do everything we can to save your daughter. She's being prepped for surgery as we speak."

"Are you saying she might die? Oh God, no!" My knees buckled underneath me, and I would've hit the floor if Supreme hadn't been there to hold me up.

"Excuse me, I have to go to your daughter," Dr. Katz told us, rushing off and leaving me in a state of shock.

"Precious, what did the doctor say?" Nico asked, coming near Supreme and I.

"She's about to go into surgery. My baby can't die... she just can't!" My voice sounded almost tranquil. I let go of Supreme's hand and went to sit down. I refused to believe that my daughter would die. If she did, then somebody should walk up to me right now and kill me too.

This was all too much. Nothing made any sense. Right when I was about to kill Maya, I learned that she be our father. Then some chick who was on her way to pick Maya up gets in a horrible accident that kills her and leaves my daughter barely holding on to her life. Everything that could go wrong had, and now it seemed to be getting worse. This wasn't the happy ending I had envisioned. It was actually more horrible than anything I could've imagined.

"I know that feeling you have right now, but you have to fight against giving into it," I heard Genesis say as he placed his hand on my shoulder.

"How do you do that? Tell me, please, because it hurts more than anything I could've ever imagined."

"When Talisa died, I knew my son's chances of surviving were slim to none, but I stayed in prayer and kept the faith," Genesis divulged as he bent down in front of me and placed my hands in his. "You have to do the same. Aaliyah needs you to be strong, and so does your husband. Because trust me when I tell you, he may not admit it, but the pain he's in has him ready to take out this entire hospital if they don't save his daughter's life."

"Genesis, I've been strong all my life. I didn't have a choice, if only to avoid becoming a statistic. The life I was born into was one where being nothing was expected. When I married Supreme and had Aaliyah, she was supposed to have everything I was denied growing up: a loving father, beautiful home, and a mother who protected her. I got the first two right, but I've failed miserably with the last one."

"Precious, this isn't your fault. You had no control over what Maya did, or that girl who was driving the car Aaliyah was in."

"Then why do I feel responsible?"

"Because you're a mother, and that's your child. It's called 'love' and it's the most powerful tool we have as parents. So, hold onto that love and use it to fight for Aaliyah. It's easy to give into the pain and feel defeated, but for the sake of your daughter and husband, don't do it."

As I soaked in Genesis' words of wisdom. We both jumped in shock due to the loud interruption, courtesy of Supreme and Nico.

They were having a heated exchange, which had escalated to a shoving match, and then Supreme threw a punch that landed on Nico's upper right jaw, and Nico returned the favor.

"Would the two of you stop!" I belted, pissed the fuck off that they would behave like immature little boys on the playground in the middle of such a major crisis.

Before shit got any further out of hand, Genesis was able to break them apart. "Nico, chill. This ain't the time or place for this bullshit." Genesis pulled Nico away, taking him to the other side of the waiting area.

"Supreme, our daughter is in there fighting for her life, and you want to fight with Nico! What the hell is wrong with you?"

"He shouldn't be here! I'm sick and tired that every time I turn around this motherfucker wants to be up in your face."

"That's not what's going on right now. He was there when the accident happened. Of course he's gonna want to make sure that Aaliyah is okay, just like Genesis. I understand the two of you don't like each other, but I don't need this shit right now, and neither does Aaliyah. She needs all of our prayers while she's in surgery fighting for her life."

"I know, baby. I'm sorry," Supreme said, embracing me tightly as I closed my eyes, giving in to the calmness of the moment. I felt so safe in his arms, as if he could protect me from anything.

That moment of calmness didn't last long, because when I opened my eyes I saw Quentin Jacobs walk in. I broke free from Supreme to confront him. "What the hell are you doing here? You need to leave, now!"

"Precious!" Genesis stated in a hardened tone as if he knew he was my voice of reason.

"I wanted to see how my daughter and granddaughter were doing."

When those words came out of Quentin's mouth, it made me want to vomit. "Why don't you go check on Maya? She's the only daughter that needs you!"

"You're also my daughter. You both need me."

"I can't take anymore of this *Maury Povich* bullshit! This is public property. If you want to stay in this hospital, so be it. But stay the hell away from me and my family."

"I'll respect your wishes, but here, please take this." Quentin extended an envelope to me.

"I don't want nothing from you."

"It's not from me. It's a letter Ms. Duncan left for you. Ricky said you never came by to pick it up, and he wanted to give it to you."

I snatched the envelope from Quentin and stormed off with Supreme, refusing to bring any added stress on myself. I had to stay strong and focused for Aaliyah. I would figure out how to deal with Quentin Jacobs after Supreme and I got over this hurdle with our daughter.

When I sat down, I thought back to the funeral and Ricky telling me that Ms. Duncan had left something for me. Nico and I had to rush back to Philly, so I never had a chance to stop by her house and pick it up. With so much drama going on, I had honestly forgotten. I opened the envelope to what were the last words Ms. Duncan wanted me to hear from her.

Dear Precious:

As you read this letter, please know that I'm now at peace and in a better place. When I found out I had cancer, I cried every day and night for over a week. The doctor told me it was too late to get any treatment, and that I was going to die. Those words cut me like a knife. I didn't want to die. I felt like only in the last couple of years I had truly began to live and appreciate life, and to now have it taken from me was a heartbreaking reality. But once I prayed about it, had several conversations with God and accepted it, I then began a new journey in my life. I wanted to free myself of secrets that had been so heavy in my heart. And that's why I'm writing this letter to you.

Precious, you know you were always special to me. As feisty as you was, I could always see that sparkle in your eyes, a sweetness and gentleness that you rarely revealed. I knew a lot of that had to do with all the struggles you had to endure at such a young age. But you've grown to be such a beautiful woman, and I'm so proud of you. Please believe that.

And now you have your own family, and you know how important it is for a child to have both their mother and father in their lives. I truly believe that a great deal of your pain came from never knowing who your father was. And that's why I've decided to tell you. I know you're grown now, but I have to believe that the saying, "Better late than never" applies here.

Your mother knew he was your daddy, but for her own personal reasons, she never wanted him or you to know. Unfortunately, she's no longer here to answer any of those questions, but your father is very much alive. After reading this letter, if you decide you want him to be a part of your life, my brother, Ricky knows how to contact him. Your father is a man named Quentin Jacobs. If you ever want to understand who you are, talk to that man, because he is truly one of a kind, just like you.

Love Always,

Ms. Duncan

Before I could even let myself go through the emotions of what I was feeling after reading Ms. Duncan's letter, I saw Dr. Katz approaching.

"Mr. and Mrs. Mills," Dr. Katz said, keeping his voiced composed.

"How is she?" both me and Supreme asked at the same time.

"We were able to stabilize your daughter, but she's still in critical condition. Aaliyah has lost a massive amount of blood and is going to need a blood transfusion."

I swallowed hard as my heart sank, realizing that even though the surgery went fine, Aaliyah wasn't in the clear yet. I saw Nico, Genesis and Quentin walk near us so they could hear what Dr. Katz was saying. Having Genesis and Nico by my side did seem to give me more strength, and I totally needed it.

"So what's next, Doctor?" Supreme questioned.

"I'm going to be very straight with you. African American Blacks in the United States have a disproportionately large number of individuals with rare blood types unique to race. Those who need a blood transfusion require an exact match of certain blood traits with their own, statistically, because these traits are inherited. A patient's most likely match is another family member. Unfortunately, over seventy-percent of African American Blacks can not find a blood type within their own family. The reason I gave you the long-winded background information on this is because not only does your daughter have those odds working against her, but she also has a rare blood type of AB-negative. Do either one of you know your blood type?"

"I don't," I stated.

"Neither do I," Supreme admitted too.

"We can perform a test and get that information very quickly. But just in case neither one of you are a match, we've already begun searching our database, but I would recommend you contact any family members who might be a match. Your daughter's life depends on it."

"Take the blood test, do whatever you have to do because my daughter will survive. I put that on everything I love," I promised...

The Future

Aaliyah

"Hi!" I waved at the security guard as I entered the palatial estate. I then blew him a kiss and a flirtatious wink. I couldn't help myself, he was outrageously sexy. I knew the shit made him uncomfortable, because he knew my dad would have his ass even though he wasn't doing anything wrong. It was all me. But my dad wouldn't care. In his eyes, his precious Aaliyah could do no wrong.

I parked the new sports car my dad got me for my birthday behind one of his fleet of vehicles. He had the silver drop top specially designed to my liking, and I adored him for it. "Where is my daddy?" I asked one of the maids when I walked in.

"He's in his office, Ms. Aaliayah."

"Thanks, Maria. And would you prepare my lunch? I'll be eating outside by the pool."

"Of course, Ms. Aaliayah."

I gave her a gracious smile and hurried off to see my dad.

"Daddy!" I started calling out before even making it down the hallway. I always did that. It was my way of preparing him for my arrival. When I got to his office, the door was open and he was sitting behind his desk, wrapping up a phone conversation.

"There's my princess!" he said, coming from behind his desk to give me a hug. "How's your day been going?"

"I went to the spa and got a manicure and pedicure. You know, the typical stuff I do during the summer when school is out. But I better enjoy it while I can, since school starts back in a couple of weeks. This summer flew by. Hold up, let me get that. It's Mom calling," I said, answering my cell. "Hey, Mother, what's going on?"

"Just checking up on you. What are you doing?"

"Standing here talking to Daddy."

"Put your father on the phone. I need to ask him something."

"Mom wants to speak to you," I said, handing him my cell.

"Precious, how are you?"

"Good, and you?"

"Everything is going very well."

"That's good to hear, but I wouldn't expect anything different."

"So, what can I do for you?"

"We're having a huge back to school party for Aaliyah and all her classmates, since it's her senior year. I wanted to see if you would be able to attend. You know how much she would enjoy that."

"How would your husband feel?"

"Nico, don't start. You know Supreme would want Aaliyah to be happy, and you being there would do that, so he's fine with it."

"Just asking. Didn't want to ruin Aaliyah's party because Supreme would have a problem with me being there."

"Must we have this conversation every time I speak with you? Supreme accepted years ago that you're Aaliyah's biological dad, but he is also a father to her too. So, I'll see you next month."

"Precious, how are you really?"

"Nico, I have to go."

"You haven't answered my question."

"We agreed not to do this anymore. And you wonder why Supreme has a problem with you. It has nothing to do with your relationship with Aaliyah, it's because he feels *we're* still in a relationship."

"We are. It is called 'co-parenting.'"

"Goodbye, Nico. Enjoy the rest of the summer with your daughter."

"Mother didn't have anything else to say to me?" I questioned, taking my phone from my dad.

"No, she had to take another call, but she said she'll call you back later on." Before I could find out why my mother ended her call so abruptly I got a pleasant surprise.

"How's my favorite niece?"

"Uncle Genesis, I didn't even know you were here!" I smiled, giving him a hug. "Did Amir come with you?"

"Yes, he's out by the pool."

"I have so much to talk to him about. I'll see you both later. Bye, Daddy. Bye, Uncle Genesis." I gave them my signature rich-girl-next-door smile, and rushed off to find Amir.

Uncle Genesis was like an uncle to me, but Amir definitely wasn't like a cousin. He was way too stunning for me to ever put him in that category. He was the spitting image of his daddy, and every time I laid eyes on him, I was thankful we weren't related by blood, only by association. Unfortunately, Amir didn't see it that way. But I considered that to be a small obstacle, nothing to stress over too much. I mean, with every passing month I was blossoming more and more into a certified banger. There was only so much self-control any young, hormone crazy, boy could have. Eventually, I would catch Amir at a weak moment, and whisper the right thing in hs ear. Then, all that "we're cousins" shit would be out the window.

"Amir, baby, what is up?" I greeted him, extra bubbly and interrupting him in the middle of some text message he was typing.

"What's good with you?"

"A whole lot. I have a proposition for you. Are you down for making a lot of money?"

"Aaliyah, what are you talking about? We have money and a lot of it."

"No, our fathers' have a lot of money. I think it's time we start making our own. Are you in or what?"

"Like my father always says, when people come to him with a business proposition, speak...make me want to open my wallet."

"Well, baby, I'm not asking you to open your wallet. You follow my rules, I guarantee you, I'ma put money in it."

Once I gave Amir my signature rich-girl-next-door smile, I knew I would close the deal.

Read The Entire Bitch Series in This Order

A KING PRODUCTION

Bad Bitches Only

ASSASSINS...

EPISODE 1
(Be Careful With Me)

JOY DEJA KING

Chapter One

HE LOVES ME

Bailey strutted out the Hartsfield-Jackson Atlanta International Airport, in her strappy, four inch snakeskin shoes, wearing matte black wire frame square sunglas ses and a designer suit tailored to fit her size six frame perfectly. The brown beauty looked like she was a partner at a powerful law firm, when actually she was barely a second year law student. But school was the least of her worries. Bailey had other things on her mind, like the promise ring she was wearing. It cost more than some people's home. Don't get it confused, this wasn't a promise of sexual abstinence. This was a promise of marriage, from her boyfriend of five years, Dino Jacobs.

"Keera," I was just about to call you girl," Bailey said, getting in her car.

"I was shocked as shit when you answered. I was expecting to leave a voicemail. You said you was gonna be in some conferences all day," Keera replied.

"Girl, I was but I checked out early. I'm back in the A."

"You back in Atlanta?!" Keera questioned, sounding surprised.

"Yep. That's why I was calling you. So we could do drinks later on tonight at that spot we like." Baily was getting hyped, as she was dropping the top on her Lunar Blue Metallic E 400 Benz.

"Most definitely...so where you headed now."

"Where you think...home to my man! Stop playin'," Bailey laughed, getting on interstate 75.

"I know yo' boo, will be happy to see you."

"Yep and his ass gon' be surprised too. He thinks I'm coming back tomorrow night. But I missed my baby. Plus that conference was boring as hell. All them snobby ass lawyers was workin' my nerves."

"Get used to it, cause you about to be one," Keera reminded her.

"Yeah but only cause Dino insisted. You know

I wanted to attend beauty school. I love all things hair and makeup. I have zero interest in law. But that nigga the one paying for it, so it's whatever," Bailey smacked.

"Girl, don't be wasting that man money. You better get yo' law degree and handle them cases!" Keera giggled.

"Okaaaay!! I believe Dino just want me to be able to represent his ass, in case anything go down," Bailey snickered.

"Well, let me get off the phone so you can get home."

"Keera, I know how to talk and drive at the same damn time," she popped.

"I didn't say you didn't but umm I have a nail appointment. You know they be swamped on a Friday," Keera explained.

"True. Okay, go get yo' raggedy nails done," Bailey joked. "Call me later, so we can decide what time we meeting for drinks."

"Will do! Talk to you later on."

When Bailey got off the phone with Keera, she immediately started blasting some Cardi B. The music, mixed with the nice summer breeze blowing through her hair, had her feeling sexy. She began imagining the dick down she'd get from Dino, soon as she got home.

"Here I come baby," Bailey smiled, pulling in the driveway. She was practically skipping inside the house and up the stairs, giddy like a silly schoolgirl. You'd think hearing Silk's old school Freak Me, echoing down the hallway, in the middle of the afternoon, would've sent the alarm ringing in Bailey's head. Instead, it made her try to reach her man faster.

It wasn't until she got a few steps from the slightly ajar bedroom door, did her heart start racing. Next came the rapid breathing and finally came dread. You know the type of dread, that seems like it's worse than death but you don't know for sure because you've never actually died. It was all too much for Bailey. Her eyes were bleeding blood. She wanted to erase everything she just witnessed and rewind time.

I shoulda kept my ass in DC, she screamed to herself, heading back downstairs and leaving the house. Once outside, Bailey started to vomit in the bushes, until there was nothing left in her stomach.

ORDER FORM

Name:

Address:

City/State:

Zip:

QUANTITY	TITLES	PRICE	TOTAL
	Bitch	$15.00	
	Bitch Reloaded	$15.00	
	The Bitch Is Back	$15.00	
	Queen Bitch	$15.00	
	Last Bitch Standing	$15.00	
	Superstar	$15.00	
	Ride Wit' Me	$12.00	
	Ride Wit' Me Part 2	$15.00	
	Stackin' Paper	$15.00	
	Trife Life To Lavish	$15.00	
	Trife Life To Lavish II	$15.00	
	Stackin' Paper II	$15.00	
	Rich or Famous	$15.00	
	Rich or Famous Part 2	$15.00	
	Rich or Famous Part 3	$15.00	
	Bitch A New Beginning	$15.00	
	Mafia Princess Part 1	$15.00	
	Mafia Princess Part 2	$15.00	
	Mafia Princess Part 3	$15.00	
	Mafia Princess Part 4	$15.00	
	Mafia Princess Part 5	$15.00	
	Boss Bitch	$15.00	
	Baller Bitches Vol. 1	$15.00	
	Baller Bitches Vol. 2	$15.00	
	Baller Bitches Vol. 3	$15.00	
	Bad Bitch	$15.00	
	Still The Baddest Bitch	$15.00	
	Power	$15.00	
	Power Part 2	$15.00	
	Drake	$15.00	
	Drake Part 2	$15.00	
	Female Hustler	$15.00	
	Female Hustler Part 2	$15.00	
	Female Hustler Part 3	$15.00	
	Female Hustler Part 4	$15.00	
	Female Hustler Part 5	$15.00	
	Female Hustler Part 6	$15.00	
	Princess Fever "Birthday Bash"	$6.00	
	Nico Carter The Men Of The Bitch Series	$15.00	
	Bitch The Beginning Of The End	$15.00	
	Supreme...Men Of The Bitch Series	$15.00	
	Bitch The Final Chapter	$15.00	
	Stackin' Paper III	$15.00	
	Men Of The Bitch Series And The Women Who Love Them	$15.00	
	Coke Like The 80s	$15.00	
	Baller Bitches The Reunion Vol. 4	$15.00	
	Stackin' Paper IV	$15.00	
	The Legacy	$15.00	
	Lovin' Thy Enemy	$15.00	
	Stackin' Paper V	$15.00	
	The Legacy Part 2	$15.00	
	Assassins	$11.00	

Shipping/Handling (Via Priority Mail) $7.50 1-2 Books, $15.00 3-4 Books add $1.95 for ea. Additional book.
Total: $_____FORMS OF ACCEPTED PAYMENTS: Certified or government issued checks and money Orders, all mail in orders take 5-7 Business days to be delivered

9 781942 217350